Jean Vautrin was born in 1933. ~~~~~~~~~~~ a long
and varied career, including a spell teaching French
Literature at the University of Bombay in India,
working as a reporter and cartoonist on the *Illustrated Weekly*, and working in films alongside direc-
tors Roberto Rossellini and Vincente Minnelli. His
novels include *Un grand pas vers le Bon Dieu* which
won the Prix Goncourt, France's highest literary
accolade, in 1989, and *Symphonie Grabuge*, which
won the Prix Populiste in 1994.

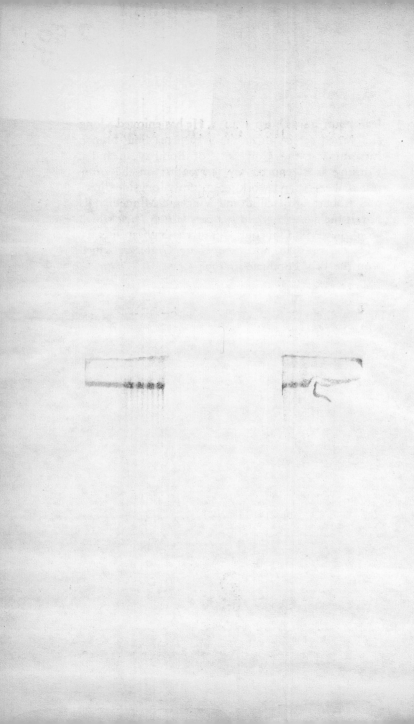

The Voice of the People

JEAN VAUTRIN
Translated by John Howe

PHOENIX

A PHOENIX PAPERBACK

First published in Great Britain in 2002
by Weidenfeld & Nicolson
A Phoenix House Book
This paperback edition published in 2003
by Phoenix,
an imprint of Orion Books Ltd,
Orion House, 5 Upper St Martin's Lane,
London WC2H 9EA

First published in France in 1999
by Éditions Grasset & Fasquelle as
Le cri du peuple

Copyright © Éditions Grasset & Fasquelle 1999
This English translation copyright © John Howe 2002

The right of Jean Vautrin to be identified as the
author of this work has been asserted by him in accordance
with the Copyright, Designs and Patents Act of 1988.

The right of John Howe to be identified as the
translator of this work has been asserted by him in accordance
with the Copyright, Designs and Patents Act of 1988.

A CIP catalogue record for this book
is available from the British Library.

ISBN 0 75381 683 0

Typeset by Deltatype Ltd, Birkenhead, Merseyside

Printed and bound in Great Britain by
Clays Ltd, St Ives plc

For Dan Franck

CONTENTS

PART 3 TIME OF THE ASSASSINS

PART 4 CRAZY DAWN

TARPAGNON

GRONDIN

LA PUCCI

Dessins de Tardi.

The corpse is on the ground and the idea is still standing . . .

VICTOR HUGO

They killed it with shots from Chassepots
With shots from machine guns
And rolled it with its flag
In the clayey earth.
And the rabble of fat hangmen
Thought they'd got the best of it.
But all that notwithstanding
Nicolas
The Commune isn't dead!

EUGÈNE POTTIER, COMMUNARD

Boldness is the splendour of faith. It is because they dared that the people of 1789 stand at the pinnacle of history, and it is because they did not flinch that history will find a place for the people of 1870–71 who had a faith they were willing to die for.

PROSPER OLIVIER LISSAGARAY
(*Histoire de la Commune de 1871*)

PART I

THE GUNS OF 18TH MARCH

I

Trollop under the
pont de l'Alma

On the evening of 17th March 1871 a woman's corpse was spotted in the Seine, drifting at low tide near the third pier of the pont de l'Alma. The body was naked, its breast disfigured by a great powder-burn.

News of this grim discovery, made at dusk by a waterman called Clémens van Cooksfeld, from Liège, soon reached the fire brigade at the Malar barracks, who alerted the river brigade. They in turn called in the Commissaire of Gros-Caillou district, Isidore Mespluchet, a zealous and scrupulous man whose attention was soon to be distracted by other, more pressing matters.

The body had been brought ashore at la Bourdonnais landing. As the investigators made their first observations they were interrupted by the clattering arrival of a messenger from the new Prefect of Police, General Valentin. He dismounted, came to attention in front of the Commissaire and saluted. Two gold stripes gleamed on his sleeve.

'Lieutenant Arnaud Desétoiles!'

The messenger's red kepi identified him as an officer of the 107th Light Cavalry, quartered at the Babylon barracks and on secondment to the Luxembourg palace. The note he carried contained news of grave developments on the right bank.

Ignoring the thickening downpour of freezing rain and sleet, Mespluchet tore open the envelope and stuck his pince-nez on his nose. The note bore the heading of the Quai d'Orsay, where the Council of Ministers had been sitting.

'In it again up to our necks . . . an utter dog's dinner . . .'

The Commissaire's spontaneous groan ended in a sudden sneeze. He produced an enormous snuff-cloth, blew his nose furiously, swabbed his moustache and directed a sidelong scowl at this workers' Paris from which mess and disorder were threatening to erupt once again.

'Saint-Ouen! Rochechouart!' the policeman recited incredulously. 'The rue des Trois-Frères, the Horse Pond, Saint-Vincent, Mont-Cenis and – needless to say! – the place de Puebla in that . . . that Aventine Hill, Belleville!'

He sank his head between his shoulders, thrust his fists deep in his pockets and turned away, giving the young cavalry officer a view of a neck as red and inscrutable as a brick wall.

'The military must be mentally defective to want to go stirring up the red districts,' he muttered to himself. 'If those socialist vermin ever wake up, we're not going to get out of it without a bit of blood and clamour.'

He swept a rancorous eye across the great arch of the bridge. His gaze wandered through it and along the stone faces of the buildings on the far bank, his mind fully alert as it deserted, for a time, his motionless form. Soaring free, far across the dark city, the most disobedient part of him bore the Commissaire willy-nilly towards inadmissible thoughts of arson demolishing the smart new districts built by Haussmann, throwing down the arrogant bank-like façades and reducing them to a landscape of ruins, giving a clear view of sunlit, verdant workers' hills beyond.

Mespluchet gave an involuntary shiver.

'How does the situation look?' he asked abruptly, turning back to the despatch rider.

'Six thousand men of the Faron Division have been detailed to seize the guns in the 19th and 20th *arrondissements*,' the Prefect's envoy said curtly. 'That's what I've heard. And General Susbielle is already moving on Montmartre.'

'Won't the rain and snow hamper troop movements?'

'The difficult thing is finding teams and tackle to control the guns in the steep streets.'

'How are the soldiers feeling ... about these murmurings of civil war?'

'I wouldn't want us to start playing the macaroni,'.[1] Arnaud Desétoiles muttered, shrinking slightly under the policeman's inquisitorial stare. He stepped back a pace, clamped his mouth shut and sank his chin into the collar of his tunic, clearly in a hurry to get away. Mespluchet detained him with a suave smile.

'On the score of intelligence practice, Lieutenant,' he murmured amiably, 'I don't mind forgiving you for your discretion. But let's not beat about the bush. All the reports I get are saying the same thing ... morale among the troops is about as low as it could be.'

The officer lowered his eyes.

'I don't know anything. There's nothing I want to say.'

'Enough of this garbage! You can't give away an open secret!'

'I have my orders.'

'And I have a mind to tell you not to teach your grandmother to suck eggs! Ah! Listen!' the neighbourhood detective went on, so carried away that he came close, breathing a pestilential odour of snuff into the other's face, 'I have it from an impeccable source that troop morale is at rock bottom! Your comrades of the 67th Foot are encamped without groundsheets or straw in the mud of the Luxembourg gardens ...'

'Field conditions ...' the young officer mumbled evasively. 'The quartermasters will soon have things to rights.'

'I'm not your shill, Lieutenant Desétoiles. You can't take me in with this claptrap. It's public knowledge: troops of the service corps are wandering about the town mixing with the population. In Belleville, the men billeted on the inhabitants are turning revolutionary. Fraternising! *Garibaldising!*'

'That's very wrong of them.'

'It's very *hungry* of them! Damnation! With this level of understanding it won't be long before bullets are messing up people's linen again,' the Commissaire predicted gloomily.

Eyes staring straight ahead, he remained immobile for a long

---

[1] *Translator's note*: An ungrateful reference to the long and chaotic struggle for Italian unification, waged by (among others) the patriot Giuseppe Garibaldi, who was still active and had supported France in its recent painful war with Prussia.

moment sampling the sounds of the night, listening for untoward noises, the squibbing of firearms that would announce street fighting. So far so good. Cold air flapped the skirts of his overcoat.

A wind from the northern plains buffeted the sky, shredding the smoke and vapours of the city. A sudden squall enveloped Mespluchet in a flurry of snowflakes, lifted the bowler hat from his head and rolled it briskly across the mud and jetsam towards the water's edge.

'Hell and damnation! My capsule hat!' exploded the Commissaire, lumbering after the headgear. 'If the Seine gets it it'll sail down to Chatou!'

Mespluchet was a short man who could move at considerable speed on his short thick legs. He galloped down the shingle and scooped up the wayward tile just as it launched itself on the current.

This exploit was applauded by the thirty or so idlers who had gathered at a slight distance, kept back by constables; a piece of cheek that got them banished to the edge of the quay above. One or two of the noisier individuals, leaning comfortably on the parapet, made the mistake of complaining audibly.

'God damn it, Barthélemy!' the Commissaire barked to one of his men, 'move all these loudmouths on for me, will you? They're cluttering up the view.'

He mopped his furrowed brow and walked past General Valentin's messenger, who turned stiffly, head rigid on shoulders, and marched after him.

'I knew it,' Mespluchet was muttering to himself. 'I saw it coming.'

'What seems to be happening, sir, exactly?' Barthélemy ventured. Thirty-six years old, a townsman born and bred, he was a long pallid beanpole of a man, dressed in dark blue and at present giving a fair imitation of a heron being mobbed by rooks. He was sticking his head out from behind the timber piling.

He was rather in Mespluchet's good books at the moment.

'What's happening, Hippolyte,' the Commissaire grumbled, 'is that Monsieur Thiers wants to seize the Parisians' weapons before the Assembly takes place. So what's *really* happening in the first instance is that with this guns business we're heading straight for an insurrection.'

'That's real big trouble, sir. None of them's going to lie down and take it, not the mob, nor the Central Committee, nor the National Guard. None of them.'

'Thiers is being egged on by his clique ... Favre, Ferry and Picard in the corridors ... D'Aurelle can't control his command. We're rushing headlong towards live musketry, between Frenchmen!'

Mespluchet was so incensed by the absurdity of what was happening that he had wholly forgotten the emissary from the new Prefect of Police. Hands behind his back, shoulders straight, he mulled over the directives he had just been given as he climbed the ramp to the quay, grumbling quietly into his coat collar. A diffuse weight seemed to press down on his entire being, telling him to drag his feet in this business with the guns.

What saint could he pray to? To what durable authority was he to turn? First Kératry and Edmond Adam, and now Ernest Cresson had resigned, 11th February, and been hurriedly replaced with this character Valentin, of all people. How could he not resist, from the depths of his being, the edicts of a new hierarchic superior whom he did not know: a gendarmerie colonel – a mere brigand-hunter! – promoted brigadier-general for the occasion and propelled into the Préfecture. In very good time too, no later than the 16th: yesterday. While the excellent Choppin, who had held the job down for a month, had been rewarded with instant banishment to pen-pushing and filing, fatigue duty taking statements, subsidiary tasks.

Devil take it! The longer he chewed on the gristle of his rancour, the more convinced Commissaire Mespluchet became that every detail of the Council of Ministers' latest policy was a calculated insult to common sense. Every declaration, every ruling, every conviction uttered by these gentlemen exuded a lordly and condescending contempt, an ignorance of the terrain they were supposed to be governing so profound that it took your breath away. Even when they meant well, they paid no heed to the discontent of the Parisians, the misery of the people, the moral exhaustion of troops bruised by successive defeats, the run-down state of the police service, whose officers hardly dared show their faces in some districts for fear of attack by armed mobs. No. There was nothing, nothing at all, to incline the police chief of Gros-Caillou district to play the zealous lackey, the bleating accompanist, of decisions so clearly against the public interest.

'By Christ,' he growled quietly to the young lieutenant, 'it's broad across the arse, this Republic of Monsieur Thiers's! It might not fit through the barricades.'

Rebuttoning his overcoat against the cold wind, the Commissaire strode off towards the hunched outline of the police doctor, bent close over the cadaver of the drowned girl, and asked in a roguish tone:

'Well, Morel! Got the hussy to talk yet?'

2

A number 13 glass eye

'She's not very talkative, Commissaire.'

Mespluchet scowled down at the body.

'Playing dumb, is she?'

'She's not telling the whole truth,' the doctor answered.

Nudging Morel's leather instrument case aside with a heavy boot, the Commissaire bent his right knee and leaned over the young woman's cadaver in his turn.

He turned back the cloth the surgeon had thrown over the body and stared down into the dead girl's face, taking in every detail: its beauty even in the waxen pallor of death, the straight nose bruised and swollen, the wide, clear brow, the loose hair ... gaze fixed on the vacant turned-up irises, he gently followed with the ball of his thumb the contours of the girl's high cheekbones, absently stroked the cold flesh as if to memorise its pretty lines.

'Clear enough,' he murmured after a long moment. The cloth fell back into place. '*Crime passionel*. A jealous husband's been here. Some back-street Othello caught his missus leaving an assignation and gave her a charge of shot, point-blank ...'

'The gunshot wasn't the cause of death, 'the surgeon interrupted. 'It's true that a large portion of the right breast was mutilated and carried away by the charge, but the injury, although serious, was far from mortal.'

'Hang it, Morel! What are you trying to insinuate?'

'That your murder victim was snuffed by other means. That the little lady died more than once ...'

The Commissaire thought for a second.

'Yes, of course! I'm with you! Her great bullock of a husband drowned her as well, if that's what you're getting at. I already knew that.'

'There's a problem there too, my dear fellow,' Morel said, getting to his feet. 'Your lovely client has virtually no water in her lungs ... so she hadn't been in the Seine very long. I'd say long enough to get here from the île Saint-Louis ... half an hour at most, with the flood-tide.'

'She'll have died from loss of blood, don't you think? Or she could just as well have died of pneumonia ... shock ...'

'Not a bit of it, my friend. The poor girl was dead before she was thrown in the water. Before that, someone had tanned her hide all over, as if to punish her. Slaps, punches. A real going-over, all down both sides. Temporal bone fractured. Her head collided with something hard.'

'All right, but it's still straightforward. The cuckold catches her *in flagrante*. He beats her up, she escapes, she's backing away from him. He pulls his weapon, shoots her, she's only wounded. She falls bleeding and hits her head against a fireplace or some corner. She passes out. She's had it now! The murderer panics. He thinks he's killed her. He waits until dusk and gets rid of the poor woman in the river ...'

'She's been knifed too. A pigsticker with a locking ring. Two nasty wounds in the abdomen.'

'So the woman's a neighbourhood slut! A doe! A bodkin, a nobody!' the Commissaire exploded irritably. 'A streetwalker perhaps. Several pimps fighting over her.'

He had just noticed Lieutenant Desétoiles, standing nearby with the reproachful look of one who has been cast aside like a worn-out glove.

'I'm thinking about your guns,' the policeman assured him. He turned back to the surgeon.

'Get anything else out of her?'

'She had this clenched in her fist.' With thumb and forefinger the doctor took an object about the size of a marble from his waiscoat pocket, and placed it on Mespluchet's outstretched palm.

'What's this, then?' the Commissaire asked, rolling the thing about.

'It's a glass eye with a blue iris,' the medic said. 'There's a number 13 on it.'

'Means nothing to me,' the Commissaire admitted.

'Nor me,' Barthélemy echoed.

'Well, *I'm* certainly not a specialist in the one-eyed and dubious,' the pathologist teased them.

'Look,' the cavalryman interrupted, managing to sound both dry and plaintive, 'I have to take an answer to Mr Prefect Valentin.'

Mespluchet turned towards him. The policeman seemed confused by the combination of different circumstances.

'Let's see, er . . .' he began vaguely. But the officer had had enough and stepped forward, cutting him off. His face hard, he demanded in a firm voice:

'Will you, sir, yes or no, undertake to have the esplanade of the Invalides cleared and the surroundings of the Ecole militaire secured, so that the Bocher brigade can keep the seized guns and ammunition there?'

The official of Gros-Caillou blinked rapidly several times. Snowflakes had settled on his bushy eyebrows.

'Lieutenant Desétoiles,' he ground out at last. 'Tell General Valentin that I'll do what I can.'

The soldier's words were polite, but his voice rang hard.

'Forgive my insistence, but I need a less dilatory sort of undertaking from you.'

'Tell him I'll act in accordance with his directives, but that we have to expect deficiencies of personnel.'

The Commissaire felt himself increasingly cornered, and his rage mounted. He was annoyed with himself for allowing it to happen, and turned the resulting evil humour on his interrogator.

The cavalryman bore the smouldering ferocity of his gaze without flinching.

'You can see for yourself that I can't be in two places at once!' Mespluschet bawled suddenly at the end of a long silence.

In a puff of wind he had become once more the son of the long-dead baker in the rue du Rendez-Vous. The former child of the 12th *arrondissement* had just discerned, behind the soldierly stiffness, the arrogance of a man of family. And having been reminded of his origins, Commissaire Mespluchet felt a pure and impassioned desire to lay waste to that young lieutenant's glacial composure.

'The streets are full of villains!' he yelled. 'My men are swamped with looters, unemployed, vagabond riff-raff! Crime is everywhere! Most of the time it goes unpunished! Why, on top of all that, must I be entangled in an operation that ought to be strictly military?'

'Because these are entangled times, monsieur! Because France is in danger! Because public order is under threat! Because the police are auxiliary to the army and the government needs your cooperation to ensure the element of surprise on the terrain . . .'

'Nice oratory! And all you want to do is take from the people guns that the people have paid for! Artillery pieces cast to order after a nationwide public subscription! You might as well dance the fandango,' jeered the policeman, running out of arguments.

'The government can't allow part of the nation's weaponry to fall into the hands of a faction,' the officer persisted. His set face, blind to reason, reawakened Mespluchet's vehemence.

'I can promise you some kind of performance at least, when the Parisians tumble to what's happened. All these big schemes are stirring up revolutionary feeling. You're going to bring the people of Paris out on the streets!'

'We're going to restore order.'

'You're going to remember a famous disaster. Brothers bayoneting brothers! Think about it!'

The Commissaire's face had grown scarlet with fury. Rumbling incoherently, he took a couple of paces in one direction, then another, panting as if he had been running. His gaze darted savagely about. The soldier looked at him impassively.

'Christ Almighty!' Mespluchet snarled at last, banging the ferrule of his stick down on the cobbles. 'You may think they're ready for anything, but they won't want to fight Frenchmen.'

'I'm sure we can depend on you to perform your civic duty,' Lieutenant Desétoiles stated formally. He clicked his heels, gave a cold regulation salute and turned away. Hooves sounded on stone as he untethered his mount from a nearby tree.

3

A man called
Horace Grondin

'Right! Here's how it is! Smartly now, lads!' cried Commissaire
Mespluchet to the constables holding back the crowd. Exuding
the naïve enthusiasm of a curate teaching Sunday school, he
clapped his hands together to draw their attention.

'Dupart! Rouqueyre! Houillé! All of you!' he barked to his
sergeants. 'Back to the shop! I want the day-shift back in.
Meeting round the pillar of the Grenelle artesian well in one
hour. And I do mean all of them. Got that, Houillé? Everyone!'

'Right, guvnor! But, er ... what about the tart, sir? Any
orders?'

'The *tart*, sergeant?' Mespluchet had already forgotten the
dead girl. Houillé was grinning from ear to ear.

'Her we been calling the pont de l'Alma trollop.'

'Good question, sergeant,' the police surgeon agreed as he
closed the jaws of his instrument bag. 'D'you want an autopsy
on her,' he added to the Commissaire, 'or shall I put her back in
the river?'

'Finish your job, Dr Morel,' Mespluchet answered with all the
human warmth of a slamming door. 'I'll expect your report.'

He was already pulling on his gloves and striding towards his
carriage. 'Barthélemy!' he barked into the air, certain that his
whey-faced minion would be close behind, 'put on your seven-
league boots and go and look out Mr Horace Grondin for me. I
need his abilities. He's a dab hand at unravelling this sort of
underworld business.'

Barthélemy, racing away on the instant, came to a sudden stop.

'Er ... I don't know where to find him, sir,' the stork-like inspector stammered. 'Or how to make him come in, if I do find him.'

'Oh, do stop wittering, dolt!' grumbled Mespluchet as he climbed into the swaying coach. 'Ask around! Run and look for him! Tell him I need him!'

Barthélemy shifted from foot to foot in embarrassment. 'Grondin isn't one of us any more,' he muttered. 'He's been promoted elsewhere.'

The carriage door swung open again and the Commissaire looked out.

'Advancement? Just like that, over people's heads? The scoundrel has ability, then.'

'Horace Grondin is a person out of the common run, sir,' Barthélemy said, his undertaker's pallor accentuating the gravity of his tone. 'He's got the protection of big players ...'

'Who's taken him off me?'

'The Secretary-general of the Préfecture himself. On the express recommendation of Monsieur Ernest Cresson, the Prefect who resigned on 11th February.'

'Balderdash, Hippolyte! You're trying to save my feelings!' exploded Isidore Mespluchet. 'Cresson's just a turnip. Try to get it into your head that I can recognise the hand of the honest Monsieur Claude when it shows itself in my own backyard!'

Barthélemy's downcast eyes were an admission. Mespluchet swallowed.

Secret police wars were raging. Several of his best men had already been poached by other services. He had no doubt that Monsieur Claude, head of the Sûreté and a masterly director of occult corridor manoeuvres, was behind this new blow, aimed at curbing a neighbourhood commissaire thought too susceptible to the libertarian ideas of popular insurrection.

Hands resting on the pommel of his stick, the stocky policeman chewed this latest bitter pill for a moment and decided that face-saving would be best.

'I smelt it coming, everything that's happening,' he improvised. 'Although we got Grondin from the provinces – Mont-de-Marsan or Auch, somewhere like that, a good bit of yokel there –

I soon noticed a whiff about him of some special destiny ... I'd scented, how should I put it? His stature ... His implacable sense of duty ... Hatred of lies and corruption ... His ... his almost religious ability to track down criminals, and at the same time – it's strange! – a sort of intimacy with the underworld ... a curious gaze too, humble and haughty at the same time ... a mingling of shadow and light ...'

Mespluchet's cascade of words ended abruptly. He was mildly astonished to realise that the things he had just said seemed to him to be true. Stroking his moustache, he muttered to himself: 'Yes, it's like that ... The man is out of the ordinary ... A mixture of sulphur and crystal ...'

He looked up to seek his subordinate's agreement, and saw with some relief that Barthélemy was nodding sagely, happy to acknowledge his chief's foresight. The two men shared a silent moment of confused realisation. Sleet whirled around them. Barthélemy, too, had been ruminating freely.

'Horace Grondin seems to me like someone with a terrible secret,' he said suddenly.

'What do you mean exactly, Hippolyte my lad?'

Mespluchet leaned out of the coach door. He wanted to hear this all right.

'Well? Talk!' the Commissaire repeated, watching from the corner of his eye an interested stirring among the idlers along the parapet.

'Look, sir, I'm only repeating what they're saying in the alleys,' the Commissaire's lackey began cautiously. He bestowed a yellow leer on his chief and took a short, prancing pace to one side. Hail lashed down on the quay in volleys and his conspirator's figure was enveloped in a flurry of sleet, while the wind whipped open his greatcoat to the first button and blew the tails out horizontally behind him, exposing improbably long legs encased in deplorable kersey trousers. He leaned forward, his black-nailed fingers writhing together in an instinctive praying gesture. The smile vanished.

'Nobody knows who the honourable Horace Grondin really is,' he said.

'Ah, you ugly brute, you've pricked my curiosity there.' The

Commissaire clapped a hand to his hat in the nick of time. 'Have you heard something I ought to know?'

'Nothing sir, no ... nothing reliable. Just a feeling ... a whisper here, a trace there. The way people react ... bit of a murky pond, Grondin's past.'

The frozen informer stopped abruptly and seemed to shrivel. He raised his round, worried eyes and, meeting the gaze of his superior, managed to distil his bile.

'Worrying, sir, don't you think, the underhand way the Administration made our man an underchief in the Sûreté? Occult ... but not official. And just as puzzling, it seems to me, are these orders from who knows what kind of bed-canopy being painted wall-colour to pass it off among the common people ...'

'What pap are you trying to feed me now, wretch? If I follow you all the way, our man is now a spy infiltrated into Monsieur Thiers's police?'

'Did I ever say that? Be damned to that, guvnor! Go back a bit instead. Get your information from nearer the source. Not so long ago Grondin might not have been who he is now.'

'Grondin's got two faces?'

'Uh-uh!'

'An agent of the Emperor?'

The starved-looking inspector straightened his shoulders and pulled the owlish enigmatic face of one whose lips are reliably sealed.

'Christ, are you ever going to talk, you blockhead?' exclaimed the Commissaire, controlling with difficulty a shiver to the depths of his being. 'What role does he have in your toy-box? *Agent provocateur*? Regime repairman? Troublemaker? Back-street archangel?'

'That's it! You put your finger on it! He's a man of the lower depths, that's for sure,' exclaimed the slanderer. Aware of the interest he had aroused, he drew closer to Mespluchet and, venturing on a new level of familiarity, placed a spidery mittened hand on his forearm. He leaned even closer.

'Grondin, in the past, was the boss of a work gang in Marseille jail ... and before that ...'

'What gipsy melody are you singing me now?'

There was nothing Mespluchet could do but wait.

'Before that . . . ,' Barthélemy resumed, his manner that of a nervous dog ready to nip an ankle, his mouth so close to the Commissaire's ear that only he could hear the whispered words, 'before that . . . there's every reason to think that Monsieur Claude's new protégé had been a jailbird himself . . .'

These thunderous revelations left the Commissaire poleaxed.

Barthélemy had stepped back. His sombre eyes drifted towards a white form that two porters were carrying off to the morgue.

'Poor little thing!' he murmured, his voice breaking. 'So young, to be sent on her way.' A blast of freezing wind brought tears to his jaundiced eyes.

Horace Grondin, he mused, Horace Grondin. Right now, he's got to be in some hot spot. Where history's going to be made . . . he's lurking on a street corner somewhere, watching. Unyielding, like the bar of a door . . . Teasing out the truth . . . He's sampling the mood of the mob. I can feel him . . . see him . . . he's on the edge of the fringe. With the Communers,[1] the poor . . . with ragpickers, stay-makers, fishwives and ruffians . . . on the prowl, he calls it. The inspector withdrew his blank gaze from the shadowy far bank and turned to Mespluchet.

'Have you ever noticed how his look scares people, sir? He's got eyes that . . . fillet you.'

But the Commissaire had withdrawn into the depths of his carriage to escape the north wind and placed his hat on the seat beside him. Head back, chin stuck out, hands resting on the ivory knob of his stick, mind busy, he ruminated for a moment.

'Hell's bells, Barthélemy,' he murmured suddenly, opening his eyes, 'you're not really telling me Grondin's an old lag? You may have really got hold of something there!'

[1] Translator's note: Supporters and members of the Commune are nearly always referred to by the popular name 'communeux', evidently the term most widely used at the time, which I have rendered as 'communer' or 'communers'. The more formal and respectful term 'communard' appears a few times later in the book. Some people think 'communeux' is a play on the word 'gueux' (=destitute person) and therefore disparaging, but it is used here by commune sympathisers as well as opponents.

The Commissaire had inadvertently addressed his subordinate using the formal *vous*. In the blink of an eye, Barthélemy had been restored to a dignity and stature that ten years as a uniformed constable had gradually worn away.

'I'll find out more before long,' he bragged. 'When he was first in Paris, it was me who guided Grondin through the maze of streets ... He was happy to have my company ... talked about us being a team ... I'll see him again. Even if he isn't where we expect him to be these days, I'll see him sooner or later ...'

The Commissaire did not seem to be listening. Head back in the shadows, he seemed once again lost in supplementary calculation. Hippolyte stood in the freezing gale, his head bent modestly forward over the scraggy neck and stiff collar, waiting for the scales to fall from his patron's eyes.

When was Mespluchet going to realise that he had under his orders a magnificent, seasoned sleuth, devoured by ambition and eager to serve?

'Inspector Barthélemy!' the Commissaire said abruptly, as if in answer to this thought. 'You're to sort out the matter of the drowned girl at the pont de l'Alma. That's the way I want it. I'm giving you the job.'

(That *vous* again!) The inspector made a poor job of suppressing a greasy, incredulous grin. He took off his hat.

'Thank you very much indeed, sir!'

Mespluchet's red-rimmed, exhausted eyes scrutinised him for a moment.

'And while you're about it, remember to keep me informed of anything you pick up. That Grondin ... I want to know more.'

'Your wish is my command, guvnor.'

'I value your ear, my boy. You know how to keep it to the ground. Flap it round corners. And I like that. I need it!'

The Commissaire rapped on the glass with the end of his stick as a signal to the waiting driver.

4

Monsieur Thiers's troops

Paris awoke with a start.

Uniforms of the Faron Division were flowing like living water along the ramps of Belleville. Troops fresh from the barracks, summoned by alert without bugles, were climbing the slopes of the Buttes-Chaumont, saturating the hillsides of Montmartre. Light infantry came first, moving at the double, led by a colonel, the whacking of their hobnailed boots on the cobbles like a sudden shower of very heavy rain.

Shutters opened as they passed. Faces showed in the windows, their eyelids swollen from sleep.

Another column, running. Fifty men, leather gaiters and chinstraps.

The invaders were coming in hard, like men making an opposed landing. Rolled groundsheets danced on their shoulders.

Running men. Death charged in their rifles: a river of death to make you dizzy.

Why at night? *God*, it was cold. What was the National Guard up to?

As the serried horde of shakos jogged past their windows, the river of weapons, the torrent of running red trousers, the *pantruchois*[1] discussed the invasion from house to house. How many men were there? Where were they from? Everyone could see the streets were full of purposeful-looking soldiers. Their fixed bayonets had a nasty glitter. There was so much all happening at once! This tide of men. This spreading red stain. How should people react?

Some distance from all the excitement, in an ill-lit back alley,

[1] *Translator's note*: Parisians, as e.g. 'cockneys' are Londoners.

Horace Grondin was standing invisible in the shadow at the entrance to a draughty passage. He stood very erect, his collar turned up against the cold. A dark cavern under the hat-brim, massive shoulders in an iron-grey Inverness cape, one big fist grasping a heavy stick of wild medlar-wood, silver-mounted and armed with a forged steel spur.

His policeman's gaze brushed without interest over a couple of passing drunks, a tanned youth in a hooligan's cap and a little pale old man with a halo of white hair and pince-nez askew on his nose.

The unsteady pair had just spotted the tall shadowy form under the arch with a simultaneous start of ill-coordinated alarm. They took him for a late-operating housebreaker or local bully relieving himself against a wall, and lurched out into the roadway to give his intimidating mug the widest possible berth. But Grondin was waiting for other meat.

As their footsteps died away he listened, still as a statue, to the distant sounds of troop movements. He sniffed in the freshness of the wind, registered with a comprehensive sweep of his eye the stir of life in the buildings opposite, and stepped from the shadows of the archway.

Ignoring the cry of surprise that arose from a woman in a chemise at the first-floor window of a laundry, he walked heavily away across the uneven cobbles, his *makhila* – a traditional Basque cudgel – wedged in a gloved fist behind his back.

'Hey! Citizen!' the laundress called after him. 'What's it all in aid of, this 'ere pageant? Where'd he fetch all them redpants from? What's the National Guard supposed to be for? D'you think them troopers are going to have a go at us?'

He did not answer or look round. He knew where he was going. His solid back moved steadily away towards the rue du Poirier.

The washerwoman stared after him, leaning on the sill and craning out of the window to see better in the dim gaslight. The movement exposed a large white breast decorated with a cheerfully prominent nipple.

She was not a woman to take a public slight quietly, even at such an early hour. A magpie-like squawking filled the narrow street for a moment.

'What are yer, a Chinaman? Go on then, Bonaparter, sling your hook! Bleedin' grease-spot!'

Grondin stopped at the corner of rue Berthe. He stood immobile for a moment against the buttress of the wooden staircases leading to the rue Bénédict. A few seconds later he was no longer there. He did not seem to move, but rather to dematerialise.

More soldiers were passing. Water-bottles, cartridge belts, bullet pouches at their waists. Field order. A bugle called from a distant assembly point. Another sharp shower of running hobnails. A serrefile sergeant's urgent voice:

'Come on, lads, shape up for Christ's sake. Step out! Get a fucking move on!'

The Vinoy battalions were securing all the main road junctions.

General Faron had occupied the Belleville town hall. Push had come to shove in the place de Puebla, where four companies of the 42nd Foot had seized sixteen artillery pieces and seven machine-cannon. Their long bayonets glittered in the darkness.

People were pouring out into the streets. Waiters and waitresses, café-owners, mattress-makers, labourers, typographers, schoolteachers, unemployed; militant workmen, laundresses, thieves, neighbourhood loafers; people of all the working classes. All shared a strong presentiment of misfortune.

Groups of citizens gathered everywhere to consult and exchange information. The inhabitants of the 18th *arrondissement* had plenty to discuss. Plenty to say, and not quietly. Their eyes stared as the soldiers invested one quarter after another.

'D'you see that lot?'

'Who are they?'

'Bastards!'

'They're pouring in! The streets are full of them!'

'It seems they're the monarchists.'

'Nah. Ballocks to that. It's d'Aurelle de Paladine's lot.'

'God! A right blister, that one! I'm sure I had his epaulettes off him after Coulmiers!'

Shouts on all sides, interjections.

The streets leading to the Butte were filling up with shivering crowds of people. Here and there an armed national guardsman would emerge into the street, wander about briefly like a headless goose and then head for Château-Rouge. These men were looking for someone to lead them.

A rising tumult of shouts. The units of General Lecomte and General Paturel were climbing the rue du Télégraphe.

'It's an invasion!'

'They'll be skittled by the guards!'

'They're putting up posters.'

'What's the time?'

'Half-past four. Bakehouse oven time.'

'Didn't anyone try to stop them?'

'It seems not.'

'They can't have heard them coming at Belleville.'

'They moved very quick.'

'No knapsacks or equipment.'

'To be lighter on their feet, by God! Like thieves!'

In Montmartre, the Paturel brigade had just reached la Galette mill unopposed. A message from Lecomte announced the imminent capture of the Solférino tower.

Clamour everywhere: the rue de Tholoxé, the rue de l'Empereur, the rue du Premier-Chemin.

People dragged out of bed by the tumult. Loud voices calling vociferously to one another, answering in kind.

The outline of a brave dog scratching its belly under a gaslight. Running clogs clattering on cobbles. A window banging open, a mob-cap in the opening, a woman's voice seeking news from elsewhere ... In the distance the wailing of a bugle dying into silence.

Angry laughter. Curses. The echo of distant street sounds.

A rumble of artillery wheels. The first of the guns, being dragged about by hand.

5

A hundred forms
of courage

The children were roused by the adults moving about. They clambered sleepily out of bed to see what was going on, hopping on their heels – toes turned up to avoid contact with the cold tiles – and blundered about in the dark looking for the washbasin. Now they were going to twist Badinguet's conk, they boasted (using the common nickname for Napoleon III). Their reward as often as not was a tap on the snout or a light clip across the ear.

'Go and wash your feet! You can't make revolution with jammy toes.'

'Is this the revolution?'

'Looks very like it.'

'Who are we fighting?'

'Dunno yet, dear.'

'But, Mum! Who *are* we fighting against?'

'How do I know? Against fourpence a day wages! Against butter at four francs! Against years of hunger and injustice!'

A clean-shaven, craggy-faced officer placed himself before the front rank of troops, raised his sword and cried: 'Forward!'

'Left! Right!' the company sergeant-major barked behind him. 'Left, right, left. Elbows in, dammit! Heads up! Shoulders back!'

Shutters opened on the tumult. The river of marching red trousers flowed on and on, hundreds of greased boots hammering the cobbles in unison. The unsynchronised running feet of an hour before had been assembled into something much more formidable.

People could feel it. The ground was shaking.

Outrage at the effrontery of these actions aroused a spirit of rebellion in the tenements. The people bristled with righteous anger. And it was the will of the poorest classes, only recently recovered from the grinding misery of the siege, that revived the spirit of the Commune.

Blanqui's heirs had awoken. They rushed into the street. The first to emerge was a youth in a nightshirt. Avalanches of men thundered down the tenement staircases and gathered in the courtyards. Some carried weapons.

Guillaume Tironneau, fifteen years old, a packer, the son of a stay-maker, opened the postern gate of number 7, rue Lévisse, and slipped out into the street. He darted across the place du Phare between the leafless chestnut trees.

Since the age of eight Tironneau had worked fifteen hours a day in a factory making glazed tiles, nailing crates until noon before stopping to eat a bit of bread sitting on a kerb. Sometimes he treated himself to a three-sou Harlequin – a plate of broken meat sold on by the better restaurants to the sort of eating-house he could afford – washed down with a one-sou pot of beer or two.

Now he came running back across the square, slipped on some mud and fell clumsily, spraining his wrist. He came into the courtyard holding up in his good hand a poster still wet with paste. It called on the inhabitants and national guardsmen of Paris to support the action taken by the government authorities.

'This is a move by Monsieur Thiers,' a woman's clear voice said. 'He's trying to disarm the people.'

This lucid person was a dressmaker called Jeanne Couerbe. 'We have to warn Louise!' she added immediately, untying her apron.

Pale, intelligent blue eyes dominated her thin, energetic face. Her whole body, exhausted by repeated pregnancies, was frighteningly thin, but the eager tremor of the lip promised enough force to move mountains.

'I've got to warn Louise,' she said again. 'She's on duty at the Vigilance Committee. She'll know what to do!'

'Who says we need some woman to tell us what to do?'

A gravelly man's voice: Abel Rochon. They all knew him. Jeanne looked him in the eye. People pressed close to listen.

Rochon was a braggart and loudmouth. A big man, toothless, a house painter. When he had the money he drank four litres a day of strong rotgut, a poisonous second wine sold under the counter at a low dive in the rue des Poissonniers.

He lived in an insalubrious hovel at the back of the courtyard with a frail and gentle creature prematurely aged by privation, Adelaïde Fontieu by name: an 'unmarried woman known to the police' or prostitute. A public woman whose bully lived on her earnings: Rochon was nothing but a ponce, it was murmured all the way up rue Girardon to the Abbesses, where the Johns of the neighbourhood came to jingle their small change in the vicinity of Adelaïde's patient crotch.

'Louise Michel?' the decorator jeered, 'What do we want a badly fucked old crow like that on our necks for?'

'Keep that talk to yourself, Whitewash!' Jeanne retorted briskly. 'You'd do better to exercise your lungs feeding your family.'

'What d'you mean? Rochon's right!' interrupted a dwarfish, hunchbacked cobbler, weighing in on the pimp's side. 'In rue Lévisse we're big enough to go to bed by ourselves. No need for her to tuck us in, I mean the red virgin!'

'Who told you to go back to bed?' Jeanne Couerbe asked coldly, turning her back on the ugly little mischief-maker. Forgetting him instantly, she raised her voice to the people around her.

'Anyone who's up to it, bring your weapons and let's go into the street.'

Some of the men applauded. There were a good thirty of them by now, clustered at the foot of the tall building. Energised by their support, cheeks slightly flushed, Jeanne seemed to have grown taller. She called to some women who were still standing a little apart:

'You're a grateful lot! Who taught all your kids to read in her school? Who supported you when you were on strike at the glove factory? Who gave your kids food in the bad months? Who organised workshops in the town halls with women sharing the profits? You know very well it was Louise Michel! And you, Léonce,' she said to a widow, 'it didn't take you long to forget that your Marion owes her job to Louise.'

She stared them down, mother and daughter, hiding behind each other, holding hands. Picked them off with pale blue eyes that seemed to pin them down and scrub them clean.

The cobbler, known locally as Velvet-Eye, had insinuated his misshapen outline into the middle of the circle. He caressed the audience with beautiful brown irises under heavy lids, leered comically sideways through long lashes at the nearest woman, and reached over his shoulder to pat the hump sitting there like a polished hill.

'No need for schoolmistresses round here,' he said, twitching suggestively. 'The girls break their seals at thirteen. They get enough exercise on my ... desk ... to be able to write their pages at home.'

Jeanne ignored this salacious interruption. Her eyes were fixed on Léonce. On Marion. She stared at them. Exposed them.

'If you aren't coming, get out of my way,' she told the two women. She stepped forward. 'Get out of the way, Léonce. When this is all over, I'm going to look at you every day, and you're going to feel ashamed of yourself.'

'Why's it always got to be us what's got to go and get done in and chopped into cutlets? Why's it got to be us poor people, workmen and artisans?' the cobbler persisted. 'The politics'll go on just the same without us.'

'Look, stop yapping, you fucked-up apology for a man.' The new voice was quiet, breathless, but compelling. Jeanne's supporter was a locksmith called Emile Roussel. 'If the red-pants want to touch the guns in Montmartre, they'll have to haul them over us first!' He climbed onto the unstable perch of a coal-barrow to distract people's attention from the grotesque cobbler.

Emile was as thin as a rail. He had not breath enough in his body to sing 'Mon petit riquiqui' or 'Fatma la danseuse', or to be a speaker in the Central Committee, having caught a nasty cough working in the gypsum quarries as a boy, but he had the gift of the gab. The locals liked and valued the muted, salty chatter of this sparrow of the Butte.

His nickname was Wire. Eyes shining under the hood he wore against the wind, he cut through the clamour by straining his squeaky breathless voice to the utmost.

'There's too much going on for you to go back to kip, comrades. Those guns are ours! Stand up to the soldiers. And if it comes to fightin', bare your chests. Dare 'em to shoot you! Everyone's equal in the face of canister! There's no stopping the battalions of the poor!'

He waved an arm at the group of sceptics. 'To hell with cowards and milksops!' he cried. 'Revolution is for people who get up early. Forward!'

Shouts of assent. Fists went up, some holding weapons.

Jeanne Couerbe was forging through the crowd, effortlessly brushing aside Velvet-Eye who tried to get in her way, banishing him back to the shadows where he belonged with his hump and his girl's gaze.

'To work, everyone!' she cried. 'And stay angry!'

Intent faces hedged her passsage. She recognised neighbours from her landing: Marceau, Ferrier, Voutard. And Blanche, a dressmaker who worked with her.

'Come on, all of you!' she said. 'Find billhooks. Chisels from workbenches. Get hold of a weapon!'

She was gone, cutting diagonally across the square. Marion followed, dragging her mother by the hand. Other women streamed after them. Already they were an army of a hundred forms of courage.

'How I love you all!' Jeanne told them without turning her head. Her voice stopped abruptly.

Small-arms fire had broken out not far off, somewhere east of the Butte.

6

Drums in Montmartre

The firing stopped almost at once.

Alerted by a shout followed by another shot, closer at hand, Guardsman Turpin of the 61st battalion, National Guard, on sentry duty at the main artillery depot at the 'Polish field', put down his pipe and advanced to the edge of the sandbag emplacement, puffing smoke into the night air. Peering into the darkness, he thought he could discern moving shadows over by the rue Müller. They seemed to be getting closer.

A moment later he could plainly make out paramilitary constables advancing towards him ahead of Lecomte's units. He recognised the dark uniforms of the Empire's town sergeants, deeply loathed by the Parisians. Swearing under his breath, he unslung his weapon, assumed the regulation stance with bayonet to the fore, and issued the regulation challenge.

They were coming right at him, dozens of them it looked like. 'Halt!' bawled the sentry again. He cocked his weapon and assumed firing position.

On the order of a Major Vassal the gendarmes opened fire immediately, and the unfortunate Turpin fell without firing a shot, mortally wounded. The newcomers, many of whom seemed to be Corsicans, were deployed rapidly and efficiently. Vassal seemed to know what he was doing.

So when men from the National Guard headquarters at 6, rue des Rosiers ran hastily up to deal with the situation ten minutes later, they were pinned down by fire so heavy and so cunningly angled that the miserable fellows surrendered immediately. Only a few stragglers were able to escape by diving down nearby alleys. Some panted up the snowy slopes of the rue des Moulins and the rue Traînée, and spread out to alert other districts. Others tumbled down the wooden staircases to get back to the town hall.

As they raced away, they passed without seeing it the shadow of a man standing motionless among the branches of an old pear tree near the foot of the staircase, indistinguishable from the blotchy dark greys of the great wall rising into the darkness close behind.

Their frantic footsteps receded. Smoothly, the arresting mask of Horace Grondin emerged from the curtain of night and glided for a moment into a patch of gaslight: an iron-grey ghost swathed in an eddy of freezing wind. He looked at his watch. In less than half an hour, at seven o'clock on this murky morning of 18th March, under the six-branched ogival vaulting of the apse of St Peter's church, just behind the choir, he was due to meet Mr Edmond Trocard, alias 'The Goldsmith': a player, a big fish, a murderer and racketeer from the banks of the Ourcq, and one of Grondin's established contacts.

The new assistant to the director of the Sûreté looked past the flame of the street lamp into a sooty sky from which a little light rain stil fell. Huge filthy speeding clouds parted raggedly for a few seconds on a faint glow of moon.

Stick grasped in a knotty fist, Monsieur Claude's policeman listened for a moment to the music of the wind in the dripping trees, of the water babbling along gutters. His eye swept gently over the jigsaw of houses, the façades bathed in gaslight, the shadowy little gardens.

Quite suddenly a sound arose in the middle distance: a staccato grumbling that built quickly to a deep, angry crescendo. The sound of the drums of Montmartre, dozens of them, traps and kettledrums rattling out overlapping waves of rolls and flams, signalling that enough was enough, that all agreements were suspended, that the sky was going to fall.

His face set, one hand wedged in the small of his back, his pace steady, his breathing deep and regular, Horace Grondin ascended the stairs, his leaded stick tapping the tread of every other step. His eyes, tarnished by solitude, held a strange fixed light. He moved like a sleepwalker oblivious to his surroundings.

No one would ever have divined that the injuries left by a time of horror suppurated unseen in a locked dungeon of his soul. No one would have imagined that the compelling stare, the lithe body, the powerful muscles and energetic face of that inflexible man masked a daily familiarity with irreparable hurt.

As his massive figure steadily climbed the steps leading to the place du Tertre it was overwhelmed by distance, woven into the background by the drizzle, faded into unreality and weightlessness.

On the heights above a church bell broke into a shrill, belated alert.

7

Monsieur Claude's policeman

The bells of Montmartre were ringing wildly, and at Clignancourt the drums were sounding a general call to arms. People crowded the streets leading to the Butte. They walked with a heavy tread, anxious but determined.

As he stepped onto the terrace in front of St Peter's church, Horace Grondin could hear clattering in the middle distance: the heavy rumbling of gun carriages on cobbles. A shadowy footpath alongside the ancient Calvary cemetery led to a locked gate through railings under a gnarled, dripping elder tree. Producing a key from the depths of his greatcoat, he opened a well-oiled lock with the facility of long practice.

He was in the garden of the Royal Abbey of Montmartre, on a path that followed the old Way of the Cross put there by Richelieu. Reaching the last Station, at a crossroads of four paths in an overgrown thicket of acacia trees festooned with ivy and brambles, Grondin plunged unhesitatingly into the dense undergrowth and disappeared among the strong-smelling foliage.

Emerging from the copse at the corner of a stagnant pool ringed with reeds, he paused for a moment to ensure that no one was near. A tiny gleam from the rising sun glowed for a moment like a vivid red dress in the depths of a wardrobe, drawing a fine gold line along the horizon and holding out the promise of more clement weather to come.

Now Grondin's path meandered across a patch of wasteland cut across with channels and fissures: a jumble of old graves and sarcophagi dating back to Merovingian times, all overgrown with brambles and fallen trees. A place devastated by an indifferent but relentless history, damp and mournful, once animated by tumult, laughter, humiliations and anathemas, inhabited now only by the pestilential vermin that swarmed in every cranny. But the sombre landscape of tumbled gravestones and gaping vaults, the gnarled black bulk of old yew trees, did not seem to affect the policeman's mood.

He strode along with an unlit pipe clamped between his teeth, the blood surging in his veins, but his face impassive. Grondin was in his element. His instinctive preference for neglected or forgotten places like the Abbey of St-Martin-in-the-Fields, his familiarity with submerged and outcast worlds, his intimacy with the dead, were not apparent in official police reports. But they were what made him the exceptional hunter he was, inflecting his certainties as a law officer and giving him an uncanny ability to track down murderers without alerting them.

He broke cover in a muddy lane, skirted a property with barred doors and windows and was once again among habitations. It was still very dark, the end of a stormy night of snow and hail, but the new day had begun imperceptibly to illuminate the rooftops. He sidled along a bench at the corner of a building used as a powder magazine until he had a clear view of the Polish field.

Major Vassal's men were attempting to move by hand a dozen or so of the smaller-looking artillery pieces. Groups of gendarmes, grunting in unison, were heaving fat, stubby masses of metal mounted on gun carriages towards the place du Tertre. These were 'machine-cannon', multi-barrelled devices designed by Captain Reffye, inspired by the rapid-fire weapons developed during the American Civil War: their many barrels were fired in succession by turning a crank. Their rate of fire was up to 150 rounds a minute, but they weighed 800 kilograms without ammunition or limber and were almost as unwieldy as much bigger field pieces.

A battalion of the 88th Foot had taken up position at the foot of the Solférino tower. Grondin reached into the recesses of his Elbeuf-tweed coat, swapped his Zouave's-head pipe for a linen-bound notebook and started meticulously to note on the red-and-black-ruled pages the number and type of the weapons being seized. He noted, too, that they represented an insignificant proportion of the hundreds of heavy pieces ranged nearby in impeccable military order. Consulting his watch, he noted further that at 6.37 a number of the inhabitants of the 18th *arrondissement* were seen converging on the artillery park.

Frowning in concentration, Grondin wrote carefully that the crowd of Parisians appeared agitated and was shouting at the gendarmes in a hostile manner. He also noted that the name of Louise Michel was being bandied about by one angry group after another. And that her imminent arrival was rumoured in the street.

Indeed, a lot of women were approaching now. Grondin stepped down from his vantage point and stood back to watch them pass.

More than a hundred of them came pouring down the Cottin passage. At their head tumbled a sort of jester, a narrow-chested cockerel of a man with a voice like a rusty hinge, waving a three-decker hooligan's cap draped in a piece of blue silk.

'Make way for the ladies! Make way, mind your backs there! Here come the people!'

Horace Grondin wrote his name in the notebook. He knew the skinny and voluble agitator well, having had many times to assess his skill as a locksmith, or rather as a virtuoso maker of skeleton keys for burglaries and safe-breakings. A cunning dabbler in burglary called Emile Roussel, alias Wire: a native of Auxerre, who claimed to be the last living descendant of a popular song hero endowed with three of everything, the Usher Cadet-Rousselle.

Roussel was a lot richer than he looked. He owned at least three or four houses in different parts of Paris, which he used to hide political friends in trouble with the authorities and stash his ill-gotten gains. There was even talk of a hotel in the Marais for his retirement, and of a manor house in Touraine; but gossip could be malicious.

The truth of the matter – so far, anyway – was that the trail leading the police to the whys and wherefores of his vertiginous ascent had petered out for lack of evidence, and the cunning lock-picker continued to hoodwink the common herd by cutting a modest figure in his busy, thriving shop at 7 rue Lévisse, Montmartre.

The strangely intimate relations between underworld high-ups and senior policemen, the convoluted forms of collusion that can result, have often been described. To the uninitiated they suggest vice and corruption; in reality they are the product of daily contact in a common, closed world, in which the leading lights cannot help comparing reputations and end up, if not exactly fond of each other, as it were stuck together by the arse like cockchafer beetles.

That is how things were between Wire and the underchief of the Sûreté. Grondin admitted to some esteem for a clever cracksman who had never been caught on the job by his men. The other affected a noisy, jovial contempt, trusting in his lucky star and the continuing exercise of his difficult profession, sure that unless he was nabbed in the act of stealing something the policeman would keep his word not to search his properties.

Grondin stepped forward as Roussel approached and murmured at him as he passed: 'I'm going to skewer you, Wire! I'll have you. Won't be long now.'

The other, with a broad smile, replied in the same teasing, affectionate tone: 'Could well be, my old rozzer! Not just now, though. I'm a bit busy today.'

'Burgling again, are you?'

'Leave off, Mr Executioner sir! You tell me how I can be making keys or locks when I've just got married to the Commune!'

'A bad match, Wire.'

'Not for sure, Monsieur Grondin. The troops may be on our side. The whole shooting match could go up like a human tornado!'

The burglar had already darted away through the crowd like an eel, loosing a thunderous fart in his wake. To show the rozzers what was what. He always passed wind at the Law.

His strained voice bawled over the tumult: 'Make way for the ladies there! Mind your backs! Cowards and milksops stand aside! Here's Louise! Louise has arrived!'

8

Louise Michel

She appeared suddenly, striding at the head of a large group. A carbine was visible under her coat.

Her hair was drawn back severely, the pale oval of her face hardened by a thin pinched mouth. At first glance the lover of Victor Hugo and Henri de Rochefort did not seem to possess much in the way of feminine allure.

Everything about her – the plain white-collared dress, the simple cameo brooch for ornament, the brusque manner – seemed designed to accentuate an austere presence. But when she spoke to one of the women who accompanied her – to Marie Laverdure, to Jeanne Couerbe or to Henriette Garoste – her wide brow radiated intelligence and the sombre intensity of her gaze carried the unmistakable authority of a leader.

Her voice was crisp, the words brief and unadorned.

'What's happened here?'

She listened patiently to the confused babble of replies.

'Where is he?'

The other women followed her in among the soldiers. General Lecomte ignored them. He was pacing up and down in the background, worrying about the teams that had still not arrived, the unease of his men, the growing clamour from the streets nearby.

Louise handed her carbine to Jeanne Couerbe and ran forward, scattering soldiers, to where the unlucky Turpin lay stretched on the bare ground. A young doctor was giving first aid to the wounded man. She recognised him by the sash across his chest as Clemenceau, the Mayor of the *arrondissement*.

'This man's going to die,' he explained shortly. 'He must go to hospital.'

As they were passing through the forward line of his troops, Lecomte appeared, as if by magic, and stopped them. He did not want the wounded man to be taken away. Jaw set, stony-faced, he stared into the young aedile's glittering black eyes set deep between high Slavic cheekbones and thick bushy eyebrows.

'Let us move this man,' Clemenceau cried. 'In the name of humanity!'

Lecomte wasn't having it. He had his own priorities.

'I know what you people get up to in riots, parading corpses around on stretchers,' the officer snapped back. 'This is no place for you, Mr Mayor. We've got our own medic.'

Dr Clemenceau's mouth twisted into a rictus of rage which his Frankish moustache failed to hide. The mayor was thirty years old and still taking his first tottering steps in the political arena. The blood surged in his veins. His deputy, Dereure, was staring at him accusingly, as at a person on easy terms with generals. Damned imbecile! Clemenceau's temper boiled over. He managed not to say anything, turned his back abruptly and left for the town hall.

Louise Michel knelt quietly beside the dying man and did what she could to comfort him. A canteen waitress helped her.

Not far off, Horace Grondin snapped his precious notebook shut, fastened it with its loop of elastic string and stowed it away in the special wide pouch sewn into the armpit of his coat, a sort of poacher's pocket known as a *valade* in local underworld argot. He moved off.

Soon he was overtaken by Louise Michel and her comet's tail of women. He scanned their faces until his eye fell on the Communard. For as long as she was in sight it was on her that his gaze rested: discreet, practised and intent.

Louise. In his own fashion, the Sûreté officer knew her inside out. He had read a large number of reports about her. He knew about her humble background. He knew she was illegitimate, a bastard, albeit a cultivated one. He knew that she was poor and overworked. That her thirst for knowledge had led her to read physics, to study chemistry and algebra. He admired her resolute will, her enthusiasms.

He knew, too, that she had been given firearms training outside the country.

She rushed down the Butte, carbine under her greatcoat, crying: 'Treason! Treason!'

Watching that intrepid woman until she was out of sight – for such is the mystery of human character – the security man felt admiration for her commitment, her high-mindedness, her modernity. He understood her impatience to have done with the old world.

Grondin – that timeworn slave of his own obsessions – came to a halt at the edge of the pavement and for a moment stood perfectly still. He watched silently, doing nothing.

Leaning on his weighted skullcracker, he listened to the enraged cries of the populace: 'Kill them! Death to the carpetbaggers!'

A moment later, shrinking from the unforgivable words, the hate-filled stares that slapped at his face, reducing him to the rank of a mere government informer, he stepped back, hesitated, turned away. He faded into the shadows in the direction of the cemetery.

9

At St Peter's church

The underchief of the Sûreté hurried unseeing past the ancient gravestone of Adelaïde of Savoy, founder of the royal Abbey of Montmartre, and the more recent one of Louise-Marie de Montmorency, guillotined in 1794.

The gravity of the situation filled his head with gloomy thoughts. He was brooding on the recent fate of one of his men, agent Vincenzini, lynched by a crowd while noting the unit numbers of soldiers taking part in demonstrations. He had been savagely beaten, dragged to the river bank and thrown in the Seine, where he had drowned.

Grondin's mask bore an unconscious scowl. What was going to become of the secret police services if legions of workmen, tired of being used as lubricant to grease the cogs of the bosses' machines, managed to overthrow Monsieur Thiers's tottering Republic and seize power?

As he approached the place of his meeting with the famous Goldsmith, Horace Grondin slipped in a muddy puddle, almost losing his footing, and as he recovered his balance collided violently with someone rushing headlong in the other direction. The other man, slighter than the policeman and off balance in his haste, landed on the gravel in a sitting position.

'Sorry, townsman!' the projectile said breathlessly. 'Piling on the coal. Never seen you coming.' He peered into the gloom to discern the features of the man who had just sent him sprawling. Irritated by the answering silence, he sat up and growled in a much less conciliatory tone: 'I seen you before, my large friend.' He was rubbing his forehead and scalp which had hit something hard.

Strands of wavy, carrot-coloured hair fell across a greyish face. He looked about fifty. A great ugly scar turned up the left corner of his upper lip and curved across the cheek into the side-whiskers, giving the impression of a perpetual smile. A red scarf was knotted about his long neck. He wore a work shirt and trousers flared at the bottom in the style favoured by cut-throats. He looked in truth much more like a burglar making a getaway than an honest toiler hurrying to work. He climbed to his feet.

'A right bang on the nut,' he said. 'I seen mauve angels!' He was inspecting his clothing, turning this way and that. 'Will you just look at all this! Jesus Christ, a hole in the arse of me trousers! Just what I need!' He stared nastily at the motionless grey shadow.

'Got the necessary, have you? Bit of brass by way of compensation? Gold watch? Little drink, like?'

The geezer was just standing there, not a word. The redhead took a cautious pace forward.

'It's, like, there's a little problem,' he explained. 'You haven't paid the cabaret. Wages for the tumbler.' He was poised for action, but hesitant. The other looked quite a big geezer, athletic. Not backing off. Silent, face like a stone. Like a town sergeant in plain clothes. On this thought, the ruffian leapt suddenly backwards out of truncheon range and blustered: 'Stay where you are!'

'Not moving an eyelash, my dear fellow.'

'Keep your hands off me, comrade, all right? If you try anything with me you won't like what happens.'

'I'm much too frightened of you scratching my parchment with your pipe cleaner.' A trace of amusement was apparent in the calm, controlled voice. The Spectre was leaning quietly on his *makhila* like one contemplating a view.

'Well, cough up then,' the red-haired man said, clearly irritated to find himself at a disadvantage. 'Trying to make a fool of me, are you? Perhaps you take me for a booby?'

Horace Grondin's wolfish smile pierced the gloom.

'Nothing like that. I'm just listening to you playing your harp. And trying to advise you to be careful.'

'All right, I can see you're big. But listen, who are you, really?

You look like a man that's seen a bit of the world. Like you sleep leaning on that skullcracker of yours. You're rattling country talk like mum and dad, the real thing. I'd say you'd been on the road a good while.'

'You're right there, by God! Just remember that where I've come from, you have to be quick on your feet and never blink.'

The cornered ruffian stood up straight, advancing into a patch of light, a long horse's face with a nervous eye and a knowing expression.

'But there's something else,' he rasped. 'I think I know the sound of your pipes ... Yeah, that's what it is. When you talk, it reminds me of something.'

Curiosity smouldered in the depths of his eyes. He had begun cautiously to circle the man-mountain with the iron chest, the mystery in the Inverness cape, who continued to face him calmly without seeming to move. 'Mouth rusted up, is it? Cat got your tongue? P'r'aps you want me to lose control of meself. Is that it?'

The roughneck's voice had acquired a slight tremor, frightened and angry, which he tried to cover with aggressive sarcasm. 'I'm well scared now, ain't I? You got a funny looking toothpick there, my friend. Sure as two codfish smell the same, you're a real bruiser ... bloody great teeth when you bite ...'

The spectre's hand rested gently on the *makhila*, almost hiding the dull gleam of its steel spur. 'I mean you no harm. Keep your distance and you won't be stung.'

'Or was you spying?' the cut-throat persisted. 'You wouldn't be a flycatcher, would you?' The words echoed strangely: flat, solitary, peppered with the accent of the Paris streets, strangled with apprehension. Still the other man did not move, almost invisible among the stonework. Following his new train of thought, the bully went on: 'You might be an enemy of the people. Eh? Bit of a shit-stirrer? A stone-faced joker from the Big Shop?'

Grondin moved slightly. A Lefaucheux pepperbox revolver appeared instantly from the front of the roughneck's blue shirt, and six large bores were aimed at the stranger's stomach. The hand holding this formidable weapon shook slightly. Its palm would be starting to sweat already. Frankly, Grondin thought, what with the man's tense appearance and shaking hand, the thing could go off any time, two or three barrels at once, likely as not. A slip of the trigger finger could give the long stone slabs a new customer.

'Don't go taking me for a simpleton!' the red-haired man yelped. Yes, he was definitely frightened enough to be dangerous. 'Say what yer up to or you'll find out how much it hurts to . . .'

His voice trailed away. He stared open-mouthed at the receding back of the man he had just threatened to shoot in the guts, who had civilly touched the brim of his hat before turning away as if the revolver did not exist, and was now walking off with the measured tread of one out for a Sunday afternoon stroll. His voice, slightly mocking, drifted back through the gloom.

'Forgive me, my good fellow, for leading the bear away, but I have business to attend to and I don't want to be late.'

'Oi! Hang on a minute! Where you off to like that, comrade?'

'Where I have to be at seven.'

'Oh, right then. I got a rendezvous at seven too.'

The broad-shouldered grey figure paused for a moment, almost out of sight among the gravestones. The deep mocking quiet voice carried with absolute clarity.

'In that case, Caracole, you'd better come too, or you won't get there in time.'

'You know my monnicker then?'

In his amazement he had put the question politely, but there was no reply. The pistol went back inside the blue shirt, and the red-haired thug took a hesitant step or two in the other's wake. His mind was in turmoil. Recognition had dawned on him at last.

That bass rumble, that offhand and mocking attitude to danger, that steely personality had unearthed a cluster of long-buried memories. Echoes of forgotten voices clamoured in his ears and his heart pounded as if from strong emotion.

Could it really be him?

10

A taste of the past

Buttonholed by an importunate past, the man called Caracole looked as if he had been turned into a pillar of salt. A passer-by could have taken him for an unusual monumental sculpture, carved on the spot and rooted for ever in its plinth of mud. He stood in the middle of a large puddle, listening openmouthed to the steady, diminishing click of a steel ferrule on the path.

'Well, blow me down!' he muttered at last. 'I knew there was something about him. Soon as I 'eard that voice I knew it. From inside. Inside! You don't forget twelve years' hard, not in a hurry. And unless I'm very much mistaken, we've got some unfinished business, that man and me . . .'

The former convict suddenly started to move, hunting in the undergrowth for the hat lost in falling. A moment later, brushing mud from the headgear, he rushed excitedly after the other man. Light on his feet, nimble in every movement, he managed without slowing down to tighten the red flannel sash about his waist and run a comb through his unruly red hair and meagre whiskers, at the same time whistling through his teeth to repair his image as a fine devil-may-care fellow. The stranger's firm tread sounded ahead of him. It seemed to encourage him.

Oppressively stylish once again, with his hat over his right ear, double-flapped trousers and bravo's demeanour, Caracole was about to call out when he realised that the dark shadow had evaporated before him as if by magic, and the tapping of his progress had given way to a thick silence. He had arrived at the small square, enclosed by railings, in front of St Peter's church. Cursing a bit over this new surprise, the blackguard noticed that the gate had been left ajar, as if in invitation. That devil had entered the house of God! Say what you like, that's pretty rich, he chuckled to himself. That's a good one, that is.

He reached the church porch, guarded by a squad of decapitated saints, and turned a farewell smile on the sky. As if in response, the cloud parted in the east, white and lacy like a maiden's little hanky. Day was dawning slowly on the scattered houses of Montmartre village, the shredding cloud throwing light on the belfry and pinnacles of St Peter's church, then on the stripped flank of the Butte, the grey marks of the gypsum quarries, the forked branches of chestnut trees crisscrossed on the pale horizon.

Caracole pushed open the heavy church door and went inside.

11

Souls and torment

Horace Grondin walked slowly down the nave in the pearly half-light. From early habit (or perhaps moved by obscure forces inhabiting the place) he had taken his tall hat off and was carrying it in his hand. His demeanour suggested a measure of reverence for the place, although St Peter's was no longer consecrated and its holy water stoops had been dry for years.

The essence of the original architecture, on the foundations of a Gallo-Roman temple, had been preserved, but the building – which during the Revolution had been rebaptised the Temple of Reason – was leprous with patches of damp, its stonework scarred by violence and its glass sadly vandalised. The cornices in the nave and the vaulting in the transept were crumbling; the spiral stair to the pulpit dating from Peter the Venerable was riddled with woodworm; deathwatch beetles clicked in the confessionals; colonies of mice and insects had given the tapestries the appearance of battle-standards ripped by grape-shot.

The policeman stopped behind the choir in front of an empty altar, now strewn with the remains of a passing tramp's meal, which had once witnessed the devotions of Thomas à Becket and St Ignatius Loyola. Pigeon droppings caked the floors of the side chapels, one of which was still dominated by a large crucifix.

As he took a pace towards it, a ray of morning light fell on his tormented face, the abnormally white scalp, the faint red mark of the hatband dividing the high narrow forehead, the thinning salt-and-pepper hair.

Grondin looked up into the face of Christ, his untamed gaze searching the reproachful, upward-looking eyes painted in the style of Francisco de Zurbarán. He examined the lengthened proportions of the dislocated body, the intense suffering gaze fixed on the clouds in a painted sky where, between two patches of damp, the blessing hand of the Eternal Father could still be seen.

God, he was thinking, you aren't from my neighbourhood! And you know it, God: it's sixteen years now, since the fiery serpent entered my mouth, sixteen years! Without being aware of it he was voicing these words in an angry undertone. He put his hat back on his head. His pronounced features, spare frame and pallid complexion were those of a man who had survived ordeals and reaped harvests of experience.

With a mixture of attraction and repulsion, he examined the rictus of suffering and compassion carved into the features of that young, pale, demanding God of thirty-three, who had offered men the truth of his wounds and his suffering and dedicated his last breath to saving the world. Horace Grondin shrugged his shoulders, and the angry unconscious murmur resumed:

'No use trying with me, Old Man! You've *forsaken* me. I was made for punishment, for chastisement. My heart is a wasteland. My fists are hard. You know my spirit accepts only hail and drought . . .'

He was suddenly alert. The scrape of a foot on stone told him that Caracole had arrived and was approaching with cautious steps. Swiftly and silently he withdrew into the hollow of the side chapel and found refuge behind the mouldings of an old tomb.

12

Ironfist and Caracole

'It's me,' a nervous voice said. 'It's me, Caracole.'

Grondin had already heard the rustle of clothing nearby. 'I know it's you, Léon Chauvelot,' he rumbled quietly. Startled, the ruffian retreated to the other side of the chapel. 'Looking like a greenhorn as usual, although you may not feel properly dressed up ... you can't help it, Caracole, can you? ... Well? I'm listening.'

'Er ... the *individual* has got held up. He can't come. I've come instead.'

'The *individual* is in breach of our arrangement. He was supposed to deal with the job I gave him personally.'

'I represent Edmond Trocard. I'm his second-in-command. Better get used to the idea.'

'No names, dunderhead, or you're for it,' Grondin hissed furiously. The horse-faced redhead gulped, but went on stubbornly:

'I represent my ... boss and I belong to the Ourcq gang. We don't tolerate milksops or blabbermouths. Them we cure with the steel treatment.' His eyes stared towards the invisible Grondin. 'You put in an order for a certain item of information, Monsieur de la Sûreté, and we've all been working very hard to make you happy.' He paused.

'Anything new?' Grondin's voice was impatient.

'I hope so,' Edmond Trocard's representative answered with boastful casualness, 'because we've found your man for you.'

This unexpected news reduced Grondin to total silence. He withdrew into the darkness, his brain in turmoil. Could it really be that the underworld had tracked down the man he had pursued for so long? That his search was over and the murderer of his beloved ward was at last within reach of his justice?

'Bit open-mouthed, eh? Flabbergasted like?'

Caracole could not help sniggering with pride over his revenge on the old crocodile. The sound of Grondin's panting breath gave him a sudden feeling of true well-being. All right! The great tight-lipped bastard was on his knees now! Mister Bruiser! He was longing for the moment when the copper's hardwood face would turn towards him, full of curiosity.

He did not have long to wait. Grondin emerged from his hiding place and walked blindly forward with an air of mingled fear and curiosity. Léon Chauvelot was transfixed by the hypnotic force of the slate-grey eyes, the visionary stare of that heavy-boned man with butcher's hands, that traveller of a solitary road; the look of a man apart, forged out of the collision of two furies: one rooted in a soul twisted by suffering; the other tightly imprisoned in a mind obsessed with the thirst for vengeance.

Plague and pox, Caracole was thinking, I knew it! My nose told me you was a wolf in sheep's clothing! But his emotion was not caused by the sight of so much concentrated savagery in a human face. His own mind was filled suddenly with the howling of distant winds, the humid misery of interminable nights, the memory of a pallet shared with rats, lice and cockroaches, of the thunder of surf covering the passage of years. Léon Chauvelot had just realised that the man facing him had once been shackled to him by a chain for three very long years.

'It's you, ain't it?' he burst out, completely carried away with excitement. 'Is it really you, 2017? It is! Ironfist! Charles Bassicoussé in person! It is you, ain't it, my old hitching post? My one-time chain-mate?'

The ex-convict was staring into the eyes of his old cellmate and companion in misfortune.

'It's me all right,' Grondin said in a muffled voice.

'And just look at you now – in the rozzers!'

The two men embraced, pounding each other roughly on the shoulder to show how they felt. Both had been deeply shaken by the backwash of painful memories, and the shoulder-thumping expressed a sort of mutual joy.

After a minute they stood apart. Caracole was curious about something. He assumed an amiably foolish, buck-toothed expression and said in meticulously accented English: '*Stupendous, isn't it, my friend? Stupendous!*' He was showing off the limited vocabulary he had acquired during an unscheduled stay in Brighton prison, part of a short and disastrous trip to England. Dropping the joke face and accent, he continued: 'When I left Cayenne in '60, you'd still got another twenty years to do. How come you're here so soon?'

'It's a long story,' Grondin evaded. 'Don't ask questions Caracole. Just tell me where my quarry's hiding. How do I spot him.'

'Patience, 2017! Patience, my old ball and chain! I've got a few questions too. Big ones. *Important* ones. And the first one is, what magic did you use to … you know … get out?'

'What's it to you?'

'I want to understand who I'm dealing with, Bassicoussé. I left a convict and now I find a rozzer. What happened in between? How'd you turn it round?'

'No one escapes from Devil's Island,' the ex-convict said.

'So how did you manage to slip your halter?'

Number 2017's pitiless gaze rested on Léon Chauvelot's ginger-stubbled, lead-coloured face with its ugly, leering scar. 'Bassicoussé is dead, comrade,' he said quietly. 'All of that's in the past. It's slippery business, it can't be talked about. Best not try to find out. It's my business, Caracole. My past. Mine. No one has a right to look in it. And it's very dangerous to try.' Two furrows had been gouged in Grondin's cheeks by the weight of unspeakable years, the stigmata of an earlier life so harsh that only the instinct for violence had enabled him to endure it.

'It's true people were always a bit scared of you,' Chauvelot murmured at last. 'You knew how to get respect.'

'With my fists. My own strength. But I never throttled anyone. Let alone knifed them.'

'Well that's a new one! D'you think I've forgotten what you was sent down for? Sixty knife wounds! Unforgettable! The double murder at le Houga-d'Armagnac, the woman and child. Big killing that was!'

'I was innocent!' Grondin cried, loudly despite himself. The other man was staring into his face. The ugly ginger brute was smiling. His scar was smiling.

'Innocent, Professor? You used to sing that song to us all year round, Bassicoussé. But you're an educated man. You could always prove anything to anyone. You was known for it.'

'I'd done nothing, I swear it.'

'There was more than a whiff of crime about you, Mr Notary.'

'I paid someone else's penalty.'

'The one you're looking for?'

Grondin gave a savage grunt of assent. The claim he was making was not unusual among men convicted of atrocious crimes. Caracole had heard it more than once. It was an obvious lie that he might have used himself. But he also knew that justice could be twisted or simply mistaken.

'No wonder you want his hide, then,' he said neutrally.

'He snuffed out all that was most precious to me in this world! . . .'

Grondin suddenly fell silent, gulped several times and looked down at the floor. He had become aware of the sincerity, the heartfelt emotion, in his words and voice, the weakening of his image that they represented. As he strove to master himself he stared fixedly at a shimmering patch of blue and mauve thrown on the flagstones by a surviving fragment of stained glass at the top of a window. After a long moment he stepped forward and laid a heavy hand on Chauvelot's shoulder. The stony mask was back in place.

'Well?'

'Well . . . ' Caracole raised a hand, rubbed the thumb and forefinger together and produced another English word. '*Money* first. If you want to know, you pay. That's what Trocard the Goldsmith said.'

'How much?'

Caracole named an exorbitant sum.

'I'd pay willingly. But I'm not well off.'

'Sell something.'

'I lost everything during the trial. I'm ruined.'

'You've still got a bit of land down in the sun. That's what Trocard says.'

'Gascony? The Gers farms? He's been misinformed ... it's arid soil. Nothing grows there but a bad, scraggy vine and a few ears of parched maize ... '

Caracole sighed theatrically. 'That won't get you far, old miscreant. Think it over. To get your revenge you have to pass the turnstile. Either you find the money to recompense us for our work, or Trocard wants you to hand over Mormès and Perchède. Perhaps les Arousettes as well.'

'No.' They were houses where she had lived during the golden years. Before. 'I can't.'

'Fair breaks your heart, don't it, letting a family property go,' the underworld ambassador opined. 'They tell me that Mormès is a nice little place, too. Welcoming, like. Smiling landscape. Thick walls, hectares of roofs, Louis XIII furniture ... the sort of place where Parisians soon get used to *foie gras* and armagnac ... Makes it simple, though. Trocard reckons he'll send his girls down to your farms when they need a rest. That's what he told me. And he seemed serious.'

'Damnation!' Evil rage smouldered in the eyes of the under-chief of the Sûreté. 'Don't imagine that just because you've found a name for me you've got me on a plate! You have no hold on me. I can crush you all, Léon Chauvelot, starting with you, you little villain. I can put you back behind bars where you belong, number 2015.'

'You wouldn't do that, Charles,' Caracole replied soberly. 'Put your life in danger. An accident ... an accusation against you ... anything could happen. You know as well as I do that these are precarious times ... '

'Enough of your bluster,' the policeman said coldly. 'I'll pay in gold. My word on it. The price you ask.'

'Done! I don't see any reason for you to welsh, so I'll take your word for it. Here! See how your old pal trusts you? Read this and be saved! The man's name, where he's stationed, his address, his barracks, his landlady's address ... All good stuff, all yours.'

Feverishly, Grondin's knotty hands opened the tightly folded scrap of paper the scoundrel had given him. '88th Foot ... Babylon barracks ... you mean my quarry's a soldier?'

'He's an *officer*, no less. A fine fellow, looks the part, but the real thing too! Campaigns, wounds, exploits in Mexico ... got his lieutenant's bars after the assault on Puebla. He served under Bazaine ... I seen him just now, just before I met you, dragooning away, sabre in hand.'

'What do you mean?'

'He's with Lecomte's troops down there. At this very moment, most likely somewhere between the Polish Field and Solférino tower. Chance has decided to put him under your hand, so to say. Neat, ain't it? You've got him!'

The clock of the world, Horace Grondin murmured to himself. His wide-open eyes stared through the grey and rusty stains on the walls as if to discern the face of the man he had tracked for so long. His stillness was total, his breathing deep and regular. Hazards of the great wheel of life, he thought. After a moment the blank slaty gaze shifted and focused on Caracole.

'Thank you,' he said simply. From the pockets of his overcoat he withdrew two purses of copper coins and extended them to his old cellmate.

'Here. I'll take the principal to Mister Trocard myself. I want to see him get it. I'll come to the Glass Eye in person.'

Léon Chauvelot stared at the two purses lying on his palms. He could not have looked more bewildered if they had burst into song. 'Er ... comrade, is this instalment meant to be for me by any chance?' He looked down again. They were still there.

'So that you forget who I am and where I'm from.'

'Where's that, then? Friendship's not just a word with me,' Chauvelot said in a tone of vibrant sincerity. The yellow-fanged robber hefted the two purses and swept a deep music-hall bow. '*Good luck, sir!*'

As he turned to leave, Caracole remembered something and turned back with a wide grin. 'Ah, I almost forgot. If you ever find yourself on the banks of the Ourcq, 2017, take this passport with you. It'll take you all the way into the Goldsmith's holy of holies without your throat getting slit . . .' Between thumb and forefinger, he held out an agate-coloured marble.

'What's this?' Grondin's piercing eyes held a mixture of curiosity and repugnance.

'A glass eye. The sign of fraternity. All members of the gang have got three of them. In the fist of a corpse, it's a signature. On the open palm of a live person, a guarantee of friendship.' Something flickered in the policeman's gaze. 'This one, number 13, is mine,' Caracole explained. 'It'll show you've come from me.'

Grondin nodded his acceptance and slipped the precious safe-conduct into his pocket. 'Go on. I've got things to do,' he rumbled.

'*Yessir*! *At your service, sir*!' The sarcastic flunkey's English accompanied a final obeisance. The red-haired man whirled on his heel and was gone, darting like a rat close along the wall. His shadow flickered briefly in the open doorway against the morning light outside.

13

The land of
dreadful images

A single thought pulsed in Horace Grondin's brain, filled his consciousness to overflowing, thundered in his ears like the unending surf on the shores of Cayenne: He's here! The target, the object, the quarry of years, here, in easy reach, under your hand, just ahead in the road, unsuspecting ... ah! The wretch doesn't know it but he's in your grasp! You've caught him, and now you're going to savour his death, sweet as mother's milk!

It was time to leave, to act, to complete this stage of his destiny, but Grondin's legs felt unaccountably heavy. His gaze drifted up to the great crucifix, involuntarily, as if drawn there by some outside force. A weight seemed to press down on his shoulders, dissolving the proud rigidity of his habitual demeanour.

He felt his knee come into contact with the cold tiles. A moment later he became aware that he had crossed himself. A violent shiver passed through his body, the shock of emotions long buried convulsing in the depths of his being. Eyes closed, he struggled to master the mounting tumult of his soul, head bowed before the image of that God who had carried the burden of human suffering, but had never bothered to comfort his own. Fist clenched in an attitude of unconscious defiance, Grondin scratched ruthlessly at his sore, his wound, giving free rein to a procession of ever more obscene and shameful images, memories of despicable deeds and acts of mad savagery, the repeated spectacle of his own harshness and intolerance, his anger, his vices, stating and restating the mean dimensions of human unreason.

Amid the procession, in an unusually vivid flash, came the image he did not need to remember, the one he could never forget, the one that was with him all the time imperfectly hidden by raw scar tissue: the livid bruised face and big beseeching eyes, the head sticky with the same blood that was sprayed on the wall, the network of little black veins he had never seen before on her temple. The fly walking across the staring eyeball of Jeanne Roumazeille, nineteen, who had had a queenly bearing. The splayed thighs, the soiled belly, the matter seeping from the open exposed sex. The white lolling tongue. The disarranged linen.

Dear God!

He could never stop seeing the black blood on the wallpaper, on the unmade bed, the legs splattered with afterbirth. He could never forget that consciousness, that intelligence, shut out of the world for ever. Her blameless fingers reaching out in frozen supplication.

Grondin's guts churned in a spasm of nausea. An odd feeling of intense cold gripped the small of his back.

September 15th, 1855. The stench in the room. The still air. Sixteen years! He had yet to tear his gaze from the dreadful hole between the dead girl's thighs. In all that time there had not been a day – not an hour – of respite from the nightmare. The fount of life . . . that little bag of meat, the baby, expelled with God knew what superhuman effort as the beast knelt astride the girl the better to strike. To tear her with the knife again and again. To let out the black blood. Until the bright flood of perfect warmth had drained from her poor body. To sit back panting from the effort, the vile emotion. To finish the job by taking a hammer to the baby – perhaps the murderer's own child – and snuffing out the seed of life at the moment of its entry to the light. Turning the germ of new consciousness into crushed bone and sap, small broken limbs. The unbearable pathos of blood-caked whites in eyes that would never learn to see.

Some things are too ugly to bear. Sometimes, he thought, the words stick in your gullet and you run out of tears. Perhaps new souls, too, have to pay their dues to the Lord. But it's impossible to look without horror on the murder of a child.

Grondin was thirsty and stiff. He became aware that he was kneeling, head down and shoulders bowed with affliction, one fist still raised. His breathing was uneven, the sort of panting that precedes tears. He was afraid.

'Lord, I told you,' he murmured softly, 'there's no point in trying with me. I'm the one who won't sleep, who won't let a single chance go by, until justice is done. No peace, no rest, until the monster has paid.'

Time passed. His breathing eased, deepened. An unfamiliar silence pervaded his troubled soul. His mind was empty, his internal monologue stilled. Something intolerably mystical seemed to have occurred in his dialogue with the unknown. Horace Grondin had agreed to look himself in the face.

Fragments of forgotten text came unbidden, one by one, stuttering, repetitive, to his mind's eye. He recognised them as the words of a prayer. A needle of pale sun glittering from a high shard of coloured glass – or some such trick of the light – had given an improbable look of mildness to the secret policeman's eye and sketched on his hard mouth the momentary semblance of a faint smile.

Church bells were ringing, a lot of them, near and far, calling the people of Paris to arms.

14

Captain Antoine
Joseph Tarpagnan

Grondin's avid eyes rested on his prey. So there was the man! It really was Tarpagnan!

The energetic face and fine head of black hair had not changed. Nor the dark laughing eyes of the Gascon *gouyat* who had wheedled and coaxed the girls on dance nights, and left them crying if they were so weak as to lie down with him on a carpet of dry pine needles. The same vivacity, the same hot blood and ready fists that he had shown on *gnasque* nights, when *drolles* drunk on *madiran* would fight each other outside the arena. The same open athlete's gaze, the same wild strength, the same twinkling eye and musketeer's moustache.

Although nearly forty, Antoine Tarpagnan had retained the confident bearing, elastic gait and spirited demeanour of a hearty companion intended by nature for happy days. His presence was accentuated by military uniform worn with panache, the dress uniform of an officer of the line with epaulettes, kepi, sword and revolver.

A gaggle of women was following him about, trying noisily to persuade him to disobey orders. From time to time he would stop to reason with one or other of the agitators, his white teeth sometimes showing in a laugh. He was busy trying to keep his restive, dispersed men in their formation, scolding them to keep their positions amid an increasingly invasive and familiar crowd.

There was an ominous feeling about the Polish field on that morning of 18th March. A feeling of something badly awry. Like the presence of a great reservoir of unreason, a torrent that once started might be difficult to stop.

The artillerymen had finished counting the heavy pieces. A hundred and sixty-one guns, their inventory said.

The army was drawn up in battle order. But discipline was lax. The troops were fidgeting and gazing about. Wiping their weapons. Most of them had come from Le Havre, sixteen gruelling days rattling about in trains, lugging their gear between stations, camping in the snow. They were yawning. They were not afraid, not even interested: they didn't give a damn. They were hungry.

They had been chivvied out of barracks as soon as they arrived and brought here at the double, without food or haversacks to move faster. Now they were waiting. The cavalry was supposed to take the guns away, but there was no cavalry to be seen. The horses had been left behind by mistake.

The crowd was growing by the minute, telescoping into a dense jam at the front.

The red sun swimming in a freezing, glorious dawn had brought Montmartre gradually into view between its four windmills. Le Radet, or the Moulin de la galette (the Pancake Mill); the Pepper Mill; the Blute fin and the Moulin rouge stretched their motionless sails over the slate-roofed houses and gardens, the jumble of charming or dangerous streets in a borough where pleasure jostled slums, where vines were culti- vated alongside loose women, where there were pleasure-gardens and thieves' dens, ruffians and singers.

Here on the Butte, freedom-loving hearts pounded at the prospect of struggle. Beyond, the vast unheeding life of Paris had reached daytime speed. From time to time you could hear its distant roar.

The troops of the line were surrounded by women. Jeanne Couerbe was among them, and Marie Laverdure, and Henriette Garoste. Léonce from the rue Lévisse with her daughter Marion. Blanche the dressmaker. All the girls from the glove factory. Others were still arriving, pale in the early morning, fat tears of cold trembling on eyelids dark with sleep. They swarmed out of alleys and passages, attics and garrets: girls paid three francs seventy-five for making a jacket or two-fifty for a pair of trousers – tasks worth six francs or more. Girls who knew they might have to yield their honour to some low counter-jumper just to get that work. They had no warm dresses or overcoats. Their skirts were crumpled and muddy at the hem, their shoes broken. They wanted to know how to be useful. They were ready for anything.

Others were there too, prostitutes and catamites who lived bad lives. The decorator Rochon's acquiescent meal-ticket Adelaïde Fontieu was there, still warm from her bed, backed by her gaudy friends from the Abbesses and the rue Girardon. Many had not slept. Their eyes were wild and bloodshot and their language made the gunners blush. They shrieked and grimaced, flashed their underwear, sugared their tart discourse by eyeing the officers invitingly and goosing the sniggering troops.

Among them in the thickening crowd came the metalworkers, basketmakers, typesetters, joiners, bookbinders, railwaymen, eating-house owners, porters, concierges, solicitors' clerks, bakers' boys, milkmen, schoolteachers, dyers and journalists.

But especially women. Women who worked under skylights in overheated sheds; women from rope-factories; women who ironed and sewed for fifteen hours a day in garrets; women who peddled bread for thirty-seven centimes a kilo; women who begged and starved themselves to feed their children; women who would never share the culinary ecstasies of Monselet or Auguste Luchet, who would never eat at Voisin's or the café Anglais, or taste Dugléré's 'poularde Albuféra' or sauce Choron, or Bellanger's much-vaunted claret at twenty francs the bottle.

For these women, so prettily named Palmyre, Louise, Constance, Emma, Marie, Juliette, Leonie, Victorine, there was no swooning, no vapours, no smelling salts. No touches of migraine. No coming over all queer just for a little miscarriage. That stuff was for madames.

They were making it clear that they intended to share the risk with the men.

15

Tin Pan Alley

The narrow rue des Rosiers was choked with people. The patriots had been joined in the street by local residents, the curious, the frivolous and indifferent. Velvet-Eye and Abel Rochon had noted the change of wind-direction and were swaggering about trying to get the riot going, banging on tavern shutters and bawling that it was high time they opened.

The people's gullet was dry and fancied a bit of breakfast. It was immense. It laughed. It grumbled irritably. It needed a drink. All this standing about was making the crowd restive. Ill-tempered curses filled the air.

Emile Roussel, alias Wire, struck a match on the seat of his trousers and lit with enjoyment a nasty little cigar. Unlike many, he was in a jovial mood. With him were Marceau, Ferrier and Voutard, friends and neighbours from 7, rue Lévisse. They trooped into a wine-shop, wrung the necks of a couple of bottles and analysed the character of Adolphe Thiers: his ill-fitting wig, his dwarfish stature, his ugly mug – like a rodent with a bad liver – and his frantic rabbit-like sexuality, lavished indiscriminately on Madame Thiers and his sister-in-law Mademoiselle Dosne.

Velvet-Eye and Abel Rochon were at the next table. They were trying to rehabilitate themselves by standing drinks for an *arrondissement* delegate, who had some news. It seemed that on first arriving at Belleville, the line troops had refused to point the machine guns at the town hall. Glasses clinked. Here's health, gents! Let the wine flow free, but no freer than the talk! For a good half hour, they glugged down tumblers of heavyweight red to mark the major points of a comprehensive political review.

They emerged from the tavern with copiously lubricated

gullets and a warming quantity of the grape under their belts. They walked up and down the ranks of the noisier idlers, bawling that Paris wasn't about to surrender its standing as capital city because of 'an old tart in glasses and a handful of capitulationists'.

Louise Michel had come back with her followers. The whole Vigilance Committee was there: Louise's worshipper Théophile Ferré, old Moreau, Avronsard, le Moussu the curate-eater, Bourdeille, all their friends from the International. Cries went up:

'The people of Paris will not surrender their guns!'

Like other imbibers, Wire was gesticulating. Saying people needed to be well-watered to make revolution properly. He bored through the crowd, shoving people aside, ferreting about listening to what people were saying. At the corner of the street he ran into a group of skirts and scarves, tarts engaging a group of soldiers with the non-lethal armoury of the bordello in a scene of utter bedlam.

Jostled by the crowd, Captain Antoine Joseph Tarpagnan had just shown his teeth in a scowl. He was losing control of his men. Half a dozen of them looked ready to put up their weapons. People were giving them wine and food.

An emancipated woman approached the officer and touched his arm. Looking into the brunette's face, the officer was greeted by a fresh smile showing pretty teeth.

'You'll come with us too, won't you?' the woman said. 'Help fight those murderers at Versailles?'

He smiled back. How could he take against such a nicely filled bodice? A clever woman who used her charms so well? She was leaning forward.

The woman was Léonce, Jeanne Couerbé's Léonce from the rue Lévisse, who had hesitated to follow Louise Michel's example. A woman so poor that in winter she would think twice before spending five centimes on charcoal for her foot-warmer. She was holding her daughter Marion by the hand.

Marion had eyes of honey and milky skin. She earned less than two francs fifty a day. 'You're not from round here, Handsome,' she said.

'No. I'm from Gascony.'

'You're in Montmartre now!' the girl cried. 'In the land of windmills and marriageable girls!'

She spun round in front of the good-looking officer, brushing against him, deliberately provocative. She had a rounded figure. The fringe of her shawl whipped softly across his face. Nice slender pins under the flying skirt.

A bullet-headed infantry NCO caught her by the shoulders and held her still for a moment. He set his midnight-blue, jonquil-trimmed kepi slightly askew over her pretty little face.

Tarpagnan took a pace forward.

16

Camisoles and overalls

From under the wall skirting the wide space of the Polish field,
Horace Grondin observed for a while the guns mounted on their
carriages in orderly rows. Then, helped by a swirling movement
of the crowd, he left his vantage point and drew closer to his
prey.

From time to time he caught a glimpse of Tarpagnan's kepi
over the heads of the crowd. Noisy, quick-witted women
swarmed everywhere, offering the nice soldiers four-pound
loaves of bread, pickled pork, mugs of coffee. Through momentary gaps in the sea of heads and waving arms Grondin watched
the Captain's strained smile, his growing irritation amid the
clamour that surrounded him and his men.

Women's white headdresses were working their way in among
the swords and epaulettes, the indigo tunics with coloured braid,
the greatcoats and caps. Everywhere you looked there they were,
elbowing impatiently, never in one place for long, talking,
talking, talking. Their remarks were filled with rancour against
the bourgeois Republic which, they hissed again and again, had
sold France out to the Boches.

Foremost among the vipers was Blanche the dressmaker, who
had come close enough to Captain Tarpagnan to touch him. Her
skin was warm. With the distracted, competent air of a busy
housewife, she asked: 'When did your troopers last get a bite to
eat, fine Captain?'

'Before we left . . .'

'But that's dreadful! Here, let's see . . . I bet this young lad's
feeling a bit peckish.' She raised the flap of her double-lidded
basket and held out a piece of bread and jam to the corporal.

Looking at his officer out of the corner of his eye, the little two-striper accepted it and took a large bite. From the other side of the basket she produced a half-bottle.

'Drink up, son. It's genuine Montmartre plonk!'

Antoine pushed the woman back as politely as he could. 'Back off, missus, please. Try to understand ... we're soldiers. We do as we're told ...'

But Adelaïde Fontieu and the sweeties from the rue Girardon had already ambushed him from behind. Two tugged at his arms as if to lead him upstairs, while others posed, giggled, fluttered their eyelashes and generally gave him the treatment:

'Come with us, Colonel! Bet you'd fancy a taste of our rabbit sauté ...'

In this way disenchantment, frivolity and insurrection rubbed along comfortably together. The troops had been definitively and irreparably infiltrated by the crowd of mothers and wives. They talked sweetly. They teased the soldiers. They surrounded the machine guns. They scolded the young recruits from Le Havre with affectionate reproaches and patriotic objurgations.

Feeling was running high. All over the parade ground, hundreds of armed Montmartreans were getting in the way of the NCOs, dishevelling their moustaches. Seasoned street-urchins like the early-rising Guillaume Tironneau, young women in lemon-yellow or baize-green camisoles, zigzagged in among the Line troops. Nippers hardly out of the cradle swarmed underfoot everywhere.

Messing with the troops' rifles. Climbing about on the guns.

17

There goes the Gen'ral!

General Lecomte had just emerged from his HQ in the rue des Rosiers. He was weighing up the situation as he crossed the agreeable little garden in front of the house.

The mocking, curious spectators of an hour ago had become a huge crowd, intrusive, threatening and still growing denser by the minute. People were scolding the troops, taking them to task. The groundswell of brandy bottles, femininity and political blather was getting nasty, taking an overtly Social tone, speaking ill of that pallid fellow Thiers and showing scant respect for Fabre, Vinoy of the heavy fist and the rest of the bourgeois republicans.

The crowd was a sort of human barricade which had flowed in among the men and guns and immobilised everything. Disconcerted, the General turned to his subordinates.

'By hand!' he ordered. 'I said: move the guns by hand.'

'General, the ground . . .' The blast of Lecomte's glare shrivelled the engineer officer who had dared to reason with him. He knew that the ways down off the Butte were more like muletracks, tumbling down the hill into Paris, than proper streets. He could see their slippery mud surfaces, still snowy in places.

In a wet hollow in the ground, covered by a groundsheet, the sentry Turpin lay groaning and forgotten.

A few men, each carrying a regulation Chassepot rifle, waterbottle and field knapsack with rolled coverlet, wearing gloves, leather gaiters, belt with pouches, sheathed long bayonet and double bandoliers, attempted to obey orders by unsticking some of the guns, carriages and limber.

To move all the *matériel* in favourable conditions would have taken eight hundred horses, so the results achieved were not just unimpressive, they were barely perceptible. Clay clung to the gun carriage wheels and the soldiers' feet, doubling the weight of everything.

Flat-chested but loud-mouthed, Wire and his friends watched the efforts of the increasingly muddy red-pants. Cat-calls and raspberries rang out. The locksmith's strained creaking voice: 'Sling your weapons, troopers! You're stuck in the shit!'

But he didn't leave it at that. He put himself about. He was everywhere. He swapped a bit of tobacco with an old villain of a sergeant directing operations. A wine bottle appeared from his shirt-front.

'Little belt of heavy red, comrade? Warms the cockles, that does!'

A little further on, there he was again. Where had he found a step-ladder? In three hops he was perched on it. The sparrow of the Butte harangued the bogged-down riflemen in his rusty-hinge voice.

'Don't go untidying them guns, mates! Our Montmartre nippers have got 'em lined up so nice!' This sally earned snorts of laughter from some of those within earshot. An NCO consulted a watch the size of a turnip. A young soldier lost his footing and sprawled in the mud.

At the cost of great, coordinated, draining effort by many men it was in fact possible to move the guns, one at a time, very inefficiently and dangerously. But where was the need? It was a hopeless idea. The gun carriage wheels bogged down in the slush. The men stopped pretending to try. The officers and NCOs stopped pretending to urge them on.

'Where are you young fellers from then?'

'Hey! don't touch that, sonny!'

The crowd closed in. Women scolded. Children teased. Drunken civilian men started to lurch about among the Line troops.

18

Charles Bassicoussé's
mad plans

Horace Grondin took his eyes from his prey, unattainable for the moment amid all these people. He sampled the mood of the surging crowd.

Very cautiously, like a bather lowering himself by slow degrees into freezing water, the policeman eased himself into the edge of the barracking crowd, among people whose attention was fixed on the event itself, or on the sound of their own voices. How was he to to penetrate to the middle of that sea of heads? He felt uneasy in his overcoat and tall hat, both garments calculated to make him conspicuous amid the shirt-clad people.

Cautious as a tenderfoot, he sidled gently into the edge of the throng, a little at a time. Soon his tall form was visible among the waving fists – billhooks and carbines too – above people's heads. He slipped firmly, unaggressively, as quickly as possible, between people's shoulders and backs. He felt eyes on him, the blind force of the crowd. He heard their shouts, their calls, their yelled slogans.

As he passed, a concierge was pressed up against a baker in a floury shirt tied at the waist with a scarlet sash.

'*Name* of a . . . !' she cried. 'Bleedin' chimp! 'Oo's that geezer?'

'What geezer?'

'The wardrobe there . . . huge! Feet you could sleep standing up on, he trod on me with 'em and all!'

'I still can't see him . . .'

'*There*, ninny! Straight in front of you: topper, cloak, see him?'

'Never seen him before.'

'A nark ... a executioner in civvies, could be!'

'Pr'aps we should have a word and ask him.'

'I wouldn't advise it. 'E's got a mug must have put the fear of God into his mum when she seen it.'

Grondin turned and levelled a slaty, shotgun-like stare at them over his shoulder. They fell silent. He sidled forward another metre or so. The human sea closed around him. Now two tarts were peering curiously up into his face. He looked right through them. His aspect struck fear into many. Even a bad-tempered, gravel-voiced bawler with a mouth like a dungheap went quiet at the sight of his steely eye and strangler's hands: the loudmouth snarled to himself, but lay low until the tall spectre had passed.

Gradually he worked his way into the depths of that turbulent human lava, its unpredictable movements sometimes sweeping him helplessly to and fro. At such moments he had difficulty in keeping his footing and felt as fragile as a gnat. With frequent cautious pauses, moving this way and that, often obstructed, he drew closer to his objective. To make himself less visible he had taken off his tall hat and was carrying the Inverness cape over his arm. Despite the cold and his baldness he was now only thirty paces from his quarry.

His intention was to arrest him on the spot. Ready to hand under the folded overcoat lay his terrible weighted cudgel and a large-calibre revolver. He had resolved on a straightforward plan. He would go up to him. He would stare into his eyes. He would say: 'Remember Jeanne? Remember what we had engraved on the handles of our *makhilas*? *Hitzá Hitz* ... my word is my bond, something like that, wasn't it? Remember that? Remember 15th September 1855 at all, by any chance?'

And he would clap on the bracelets while the villain was still casting his mind back, putting a name to this alarming face from the past. He would let the muzzle of his revolver show from under the folded coat. He would say: 'One false move and this is what you get.' He was going to kidnap him amid the confusion. He would hold him in his own house. A tumbledown dwelling, a miserable hovel between Temple and Château-d'Eau, a sweating, dripping den prepared long ago. Two bad rooms off a spiral stair winding down into the entrails of a deep cellar, walls metres thick, the silence of the tomb, a well-like dungeon fitted out for its guest.

Grondin would get a confession. He was certain of his ground. He knew from his own experience that solitude, fatigue, captivity, perpetual night, damp and uncertainty in the end always got the better of even the hardest nuts. Grondin would secure justice. There would be no mercy for Jeanne's murderer! Once the case was made he would be shot through the head. The grave had already been dug in the next cellar. No delays. No agonising. No remorse.

After that, perhaps, Grondin would be able to sleep again. He could go back to his native Gers. Sixteen years nearly of knocking about! There could begin at last that gentle, motionless progress, that exploration of the smallest byways of the soul, the internal inventorising of omissions, the catalogue of gentle regrets; that migration of the spirit that, step by step, breath by breath, leads the individual to the ultimate slopes of memory, to the extreme point of youth, the first memory of the self, the mysterious contact with air, the first babbling, the same moist, almost astonished gurgle that reappears at the hour of death; a shock through the body, pain before the ending of a mystery. While over there, nowhere, in infinity, unrolls the blindingly bright illuminated carpet that takes us back to the gateway to earth, to the wellspring of amniotic fluid, and deposits us – guileless, washed, new, devoid of all pride – in the frozen hands of the great Officer of Heaven.

It was all planned. A simple, fulfilled old age awaited Charles Bassicoussé, the life of a country gentleman taking a well-earned rest from the cares of the world. His last years were going to be a time of serenity woven from gold, from silk and prayer. Unless, of course, the malicious fate mentioned by Caracole decided to take a hand.

19

The corporal and
the beauty

Human destiny is often blocked. Men who fancy themselves avengers, politicians, generals, are in truth but toads beneath the harrow. And nothing in this vale of tears ever turns out quite as we expect.

Grondin's plans were sabotaged by a raucous bark from a colonel. In response, Captain Tarpagnan had obediently marched his troops to a position at the other end of the artillery park. He had placed his men in two ranks, and the front rank at his order had dropped to one knee.

The Captain's closed fist rested on the hilt of his sword. He was calm. He watched the excited seething of the crowd, the women moving purposefully from group to group, the children who were present everywhere, urging the soldiers to put up their weapons and come over to the people. He was frowning a little, his eyes narrowed. He had recognised that insurrection was in the air.

He was looking at a brand new red flag that a pretty girl had just stuck in the ground in front of a corporal. She had pinned a scarlet flower to the hollow of her bosom. The NCO, a tall dishevelled boy run rather to seed, leaned smiling on his rifle.

A fugitive gleam passed through the officer's sombre eyes as he watched them together. It was as if a trapdoor had opened willy-nilly onto the subsoil of his being, casting there a very strange light. He envied the language of these unconventional young, their talk of sharing and fraternity. A strange shiver of agreement climbed up his spine, giving his body a feeling of weightlessness.

He struggled for a moment against a strange impulse to admit his agreement with the new ideas, to change sides and help the insurgents destroy all that symbolised judicial or military violence, that belittled and ignored poor people and workers. Vaguely, Antoine Joseph Tarpagnan tried to express what he was feeling. He opened his mouth two or three times, but not a sound would come out.

Soon the trapdoor closed again and darkness returned to the crypt of his consciousness. His muscles, a particularly strapping set, began to respond once more to his commands. He stood up straight and stuck his chest out. Rolled his shoulders a few times. Loosened his sword in its scabbard. Thought of his duty as an officer.

He strove to assume a look of cold hauteur, and in a loud metallic voice ordered his men: 'Ready your weapons!'

The rifle-bolts clicked in a loud rustling of metal.

20

A pale red sun

The mood was changing for the worse. Gradually, imperceptibly, the early-morning feeling of an improvised fair or market, a
spontaneous party, was turning sour. The rising tide of discontent was almost palpable, and the throbbing of the people's
drums had recommenced. *That's the general call to arms ... hear
it?*

Troops led by reluctant NCOs were still struggling ineffectu-
ally to move some of the heavy artillery pieces. A young soldier
slipped in the mud and fell on all fours. A gun carriage wheel ran
over his hand, and he let out an agonised scream. Gendarmes
moved in to lend a hand. People started shouting 'Death to the
traitors!'

Nasty remarks were being exchanged, and dirty looks. Both
sides were ready for trouble on the slightest excuse. A number of
other officers – Captains Beugnot, Dailly and Franck among
them – had managed to regroup their men, following Tarpagnan's example. A company of the 88th Light Infantry found
itself facing men from the 79th National Guard battalion.

Between the massed weapons of these groups, the wandering
civilians suddenly began to look very vulnerable indeed. Not
everyone was aware of this, but some people were. 'Women get
out of it!' growled a scarred old private. 'This ain't pat-a-cake no
more.'

General Lecomte raised his arm, a distant expression in his
eye. He gave the order to open fire. Women immediately started
shouting at the soldiers.

'Are you going to shoot at our dresses? Murderers, are you?'

'Hey, laddie, you there, with the fuzz on your chin! Would you fire on your own mother?'

'They're going to kill the daughters of the people!'

'Ever so heroic, I'm sure!'

'Oi! It's our husbands, brothers and children what you're goin' to be shootin' at!'

Only a few paces now separated Grondin from the man he believed to be his ward's killer. The crowd undulated like an ocean swell, surged back in a sort of undertow. Suddenly it splintered and broke into violent jostling flight, rolling over the policeman and carrying him helplessly backwards, barely able to keep his footing, his body pressed between walls of chests, shoulders, bellies and waving arms. He allowed himself to be swept along, he tried to regain control, but could not. He bobbed like a cork in a torrent, breathing odours of armpits, stale sweat, onion and wine breath. He tried to stand firm and get his bearings, but try as he might he was swept on by the people.

The expected volley did not come. The crowd's headlong retreat slowed, stopped. People peered back, turned round again. Now they were talking, asking each other what they thought. Still a bit subdued. Shocked. Resentful. Grumpy.

The future incendiaries recovered almost at once, recovered their colour and courage, retraced their steps carrying their red flags, mingled with the troops once again, talked back to the officers, looked the General up and down where he sat apart on his fine horse. They wormed between the reformed ranks of riflemen, shoving bayonets out of the way with white hands.

'Bunch of no-goods! Ain't you ashamed of yourselves?'

Breath against breath, eye to eye: hips, bellies and breasts against the muzzles of weapons. The women enveloped the dejected line troops and physically touched them – men already light-headed with fatigue, thirst, hunger and humiliation.

Wire, by now soused to the gills, was scorching the air with fiery insults. His throat warmed by wine, he was exposing his skinny chest to the rifles opposite and decking his language in bizarre boasts: 'Them biffins are strictly for the birds! I'll take four, sliced on a platter!'

'If you're men, fire! Go on, fire on the people!' added one of his friends.

'Go to it, you poxy bunch!' bawled another. 'Make the poor people bleedin' suffer! Go on then, shoot!'

'Yus! Don't be scared if people look at yer!' yapped the fifteen-year-old dressmaker's son, Guillaume Tironneau. 'Go on! Shoot yer brothers and sisters!'

Opposite them, in the line, holding weapons ready to spit hot lead, in the aim, fingers on triggers, the little soldiers were not at all proud of the situation in which they found themselves. They did not like what they were being asked to do. They were immobile, their NCOs uncharacteristically quiet, eyes down, glancing sidelong from one officer to another. Stomachs knotted. Bilious. Dumb.

At one end of the ranks, a choleric old cavalry sergeant had finally had enough of these squalling civilians. 'Shut yer yap, sonny! I'm not one to starve yer of lead if that's what yer want!' He hauled out his heavy service revolver and fired it in the air. In the momentary silence that followed, a pigeon clattered out of a nearby tree and a café waiter, using his profession's standard interjection to indicate that a customer's order had been understood, echoed: '*Boum!*'

'*Boum! Boum!*' answered voices here and there in the crowd. Everyone burst out laughing. It was as good as the Café Madrid on the Boulevards. There is something so childish about riots.

Something so blind about them too. Fifty yards away, the crowd's tension was about to be released in a different fashion. Wire was the cause. Swept up himself in a whirling human eddy, the little locksmith recognised Grondin, also being swept helplessly hither and thither by the crowd. The two men found themselves side by side for a moment.

'Pressed together like a pack of cards, eh, my old partridge?'

Grondin simply showed his teeth. He had no wish to resume their dialogue. He was trying to move against the current. The human flood lifted them along, hovered for a moment, and set them down at the foot of the Solférino tower.

Back there, where they had just come from, an enormous tumult arose sending ripples through the crowd. What looked like a hundred or so blue-shirted workers were raising a fist in sign of victory. Children shouted. Women wept in an explosion of joy.

Looking over people's heads, the policeman saw soldiers of the 88th waving their rifles butt upward and muzzle down. Others were handing their Chassepots over to the federals. Rifles with their butts in the air, rifles threatening only to earthworms, rifles reinvented so as not to hurt a fly.

No one was going to die today. A wild murmur of triumph and relief ran through the crowd, zigzagged through the ranks too, the victims of an unjust conscription system, the old sweats, barrack-room lawyers and troublemakers, and brusquely informed the brass hats that there would be no butchery today. The people opposite spoke the troops' language, had the same hungry bellies and were invoking fraternity. The troops were not going to look into their eyes and kill them. Not today. That was that. The cry went up:

'Long live the Commune!'

Wire was still close to Grondin. Now he lit another of his two-sou *infectados* cigars with a thoughtful air. 'Actually, copper,' he said in a musing voice, 'what *are* you doing here, in our hair like? Gone Communer, have you, or are you just spying on us?'

'I'm witnessing yet another spectacle of defeat.'

'Speak for your own side!' The locksmith's hackles rose instantly. 'The people's winning this battle! Writing History without mistakes!'

The two men eyed each other, unyielding. 'These are great moments!' Wire added.

'A red interlude,' the policeman said dismissively. 'The dregs of the proletariat and the scum of the women making common cause with deserters. Rabble and murderers.'

The two men fell silent, but remained side by side. Horace Grondin towered over the other man like a dead tree. Wire, reeking of wine, was convulsed by a sudden fit of coughing. 'That's my "quintal of gypsum" catching up with me,' he explained, wiping his streaming eyes. 'All that dust I swallowed down the quarry when I was young.'

His unsteady gaze wandered across the policeman's *makhila*, the hat in his hand, the greatcoat folded over his arm. 'It was me who recommended you to unfrock yourself, wasn't it?' he rasped suddenly. A malevolent glint had appeared in Emile Roussel's red-rimmed eye.

'Here for the Big Shop, eh? You've took off your bleedin' copper's cassock, but you're spying, ain't yer? I think what you need is a little spanking as a souvenir of the 18th of March!'

The safecracker was so drunk that he had forgotten or discounted their pact of mutual restraint, and started pointing out the policeman to those around them, many of whom were in a worse state than he was, and more eager for action.

'Look here, mates!' he bawled, 'at what I've found among us! An officer of the law! A running dog of Monsieur Thiers! A nark for Foutriquet! A flycatcher for old man Transnonain!'[1]

Hostile excited looks converged on them suddenly from the surrounding crowd. It was not difficult to identify the man who was out of place.

'An enemy of the people!' the locksmith was yelling. 'Get hold of him!'

'To the Town Hall with him! Take the copper to the Town Hall!'

'Shoot him!'

'Up against the wall!'

'Give his mug a proper going-over!'

A tidal wave of fists, cudgels, rifle-butts and elbows bore down on him, everyone jostling furiously to deliver the first blow. Grondin took a firm stance, brought up his left forearm, with the Inverness cape wrapped round it, to use as a shield, and with a violent shove catapulted his nearest assailant backwards into the others. Spur end outward, wielded like a mace, the *makhila* cleared a space around him. His face was terrifying. He exposed the muzzle of his revolver.

---

[1] *Translator's note*: Two of the many popular nicknames that the very unpopular Monsieur Thiers had acquired during a long political career. Foutriquet is dismissive but without a specific meaning; Transnonain is more pointed, a reference to the murderous repression, in a Paris street of that name, of a number of '*canuts*' – activist artisanal weavers roughly equivalent to the earlier English Luddites – that Thiers had ordered in 1834 when Minister of the Interior.

Without a word a foundry-worker in front of him, thinking his last moment had come, launched a desperate blow at his head. A billhook wielded at the same moment by someone else gashed the pugilist's wrist, cutting the veins, and struck Grondin in the forehead drawing a bloody streak between his eyebrows.

The sudden splash of vermilion released an explosion of violence, a disordered hail of wild blows aimed at Grondin. A collective crime was being committed. The mob hacked and gouged. The wounds were ugly. Grondin's hand went up to protect his bloodied face, to cover his bared head. His *makhila* had gone and was already in the possession of a wine-seller's son from the rue Lepic.

Wire had escaped by scuttling on all fours through the trampling legs of the crowd. He fled, horrified by what he had done.

What a terrible sight is that drowning of a man in a human surf! The mob swirls, tramples and strikes, bits of words alternating with furious truncated gestures, voices uttering chopped-up, yapping cries.

The children watched their first lynching in amazement. They were going to see plenty more. Soon they would know the taste of their own blood.

The victim's contorted face disappeared, reappeared, bobbed back and forth. One eye was closed, hugely clotted with blood, but Grondin fought on. Through his remaining eye he could see the pale red sun that was now clear of the horizon. A fist holding a camp-stool rose and fell, battering again and again at the shoulders and body of the giant who wouldn't fall.

A rifle-butt caught him heavily across the temple and he finally lost command of his limbs, but was pressed so closely among his assailants that he could not fall. He was borne up by the human tide, floating inert and limp on the tumult like a drowned man, his one-eyed gaze still fixed blindly on the sky.

Raising his battered and wobbling head, he spotted at last a very small opening in the crowd and fell, curled up like a gun-dog, on the clog-trampled earth. At this point the mob suddenly lost interest in him, stopped flailing at his bruised and tattered body and drifted away.

It had other fish to fry.

21

They soon shall hear the bullets flying. 'We'll shoot the generals on our own side!'

General Lecomte sat stonily on his horse, white with rage. Line troops, more and more of them, were waving the butts of their Chassepot rifles in the air. To the officer, who came from Lorraine, it was a sacrilegious act, the absolute sign of revolution. The drums had stopped.

For the third time, the General ordered the infantry to fire on the crowd.

'Ready your weapons!'

Bolts clicked, locking cartridges into the chambers of the weapons.

'Aim!'

Stocks were pulled into the hollows of shoulders. The men looked miserably down the barrels of their rifles at the crowd.

'Fire!'

One by one, the muzzles sank towards the ground. The troopers of the 88th, nearly all of them, lowered their weapons. From the mouth of the General issued the strange plea:

'Fire once, at least, for the sake of honour!'

But the men remained frozen like statues.

'So you want to give in to this rabble?'

'That's all we ask,' a trooper's innocent voice answered simply from the ranks. The man's head drooped with unfeigned sadness. The eyes of the other troops, those of the whole crowd, stared strained and unfocused for long agonising seconds. General

Lecomte looked down from his horse and in a harsh voice poured curses on the heads of his troops.

A tall, dark young woman advanced from the crowd, loosening her hair and baring her chest as she did so. She moved like a queen. Two gendarmes stepped forward and crossed their rifles in front of her. Unflustered, she began to sing.

The song was 'The Rabble', sung before her by Rosalie Bordas after the murder of Victor Noir. The young woman's name was Gabrielle Pucci, but everyone on the Butte knew her as Caf'conc'. A cabaret singer whose realism, combined with a taste for comfortable sofas upholstered in salmon-pink velvet, had led her to turn courtesan, she was the trophy, the kept woman, of an underworld boss called Edmond Trocard.

Her voice was strong and true. Her plebeian beauty, the carnal truth of her body, her childbearing hips, sensual mouth and decided character made the lovely nightclub shouter a symbol of female boldness. She stood directly in front of Lecomte, his tunic buttoned to the neck behind an unbreachable rampart of lordly pride.

The crowd listened to la Pucci with a shiver of enthusiasm, and joined in the chorus:

In the old French city
There lives an iron race
Whose soul, hot as a furnace,
Has bronzed its limbs and face.
Its sons are born on beds of straw,
Its palace is a sty,
They call it the rabble
And part of it am I!

The die was cast. Nothing could stop it now. The people were advancing. One of the federals unfurled a second flag, the French tricolour. The man carrying it, dressed only in a shirt, seemed astonishingly impervious to the cold. As he walked the flag came alive, licked at his energetic profile. Strong neck on knotty shoulders, broad chest, solid and muscular forearms, gaze locked with that of Captain Tarpagnan whose troops were holding their fire, the bareheaded, unarmed man steadily walked the thirty paces between the crowd and the troops.

The crowd held its breath as he walked up to the levelled rifles. His demeanour was peaceable. Locks of blond hair blew back from his temples. As he approached, the officer discerned steady eyes, a sensitive face, a brow sculpted by intelligence. As the federal stopped in front of him he was assailed by a strong yet unidentifiable emotion. The two men sized each other up. Would it be peace or war?

Tarpagnan stared intently at the man facing him, who was young and whom he did not know. He judged him an equal and a brother.

The federal smiled faintly and extended his open right hand towards the officer. Tarpagnan gripped it warmly, as if it were that of an established friend.

'Théophile Mirecourt, photographer.'

'Antoine Tarpagnan, Captain of the Line.'

'Let's banish hatreds. Let's embrace!'

They did so.

Matters of the heart are as simple as that. Their expression is so unfettered and spontaneous, so commonplace and at the same time so solemn, that when two men clasp hands and fraternise the pen-pusher recording the event might as well just shut up.

On 18th March 1871, in damnable cold in a situation of mutual mistrust, a friendship had been born. Following their example, the Line troops and National Guards also started to fraternise. Senior officers were swamped by a mutiny that passed instantly out of range of their indignation. Infantrymen tossed their rifles into waiting hands. A thousand chests vibrated to the same cheer.

Théophile took a step backward and started to sing the 'Marseillaise.' Antoine stuck the point of his sword into the muddy ground and placed a hand on the other's shoulder. Like a rising tide the words of the song – a hymn to the same people, a call to the same humanity – came unbidden to his lips: Antoine Tarpagnan found himself singing the 'Marseillaise.'

He had just gone over to the Commune.

PART 2

FREEDOM UNBOUNDED

22

A rude awakening

When Antoine Tarpagnan's eyes opened on his new territory, he became aware of a confused feeling that he no longer belonged anywhere; that his name was inscribed on no lists, no registers or timetables. He did not know the time, the date, the room in which he lay or to whom it belonged.

None of this caused him any moral anxiety, hardly even a prickling of apprehension. He felt happy, protected by the mountainous feather eiderdown that wrapped his body in agreeable warmth. Still entangled in the shadows of sleep, his mind slowly scanned a landscape of marshes, whose frontiers were so foggy and whose outlines were so obscure that he deliberately prolonged the period of half-sleep, wallowing in the woolly comfort of the dream-state and trying to ignore the burgeoning insistence of worldly reality. He yawned luxuriously.

He withdrew his gaze regretfully from a wispy length of muslin decorated with fantastic birds that undulated gently above his head in the draught from an open window, in which two heavy curtains of patterned velvet kept a cheerful sun at bay. Where was he? Why was he naked in the soft warmth of an unknown bed? Whose room was it? Why did his tongue feel like the sole of a boot?

Very carefully, moving his pounding head gently about on the pillow, he tracked down the peaceful ticking of a black marble Louis-Philippe clock. The roman numerals on its face told him that it was two o'clock. In the afternoon, he reasoned sluggishly. For sure.

Antoine stretched his limbs luxuriously, and discovered that they ached as if he had been on a gruelling route march. He sat up and placed a cautious foot on the floor. The floor tilted and the room lurched sickeningly with it. He became aware of a raging thirst.

These infallible signs told him that he had been drinking with unwise abandon the night before, so deeply indeed that – apart from his meeting with Théophile Mirecourt – the bulk of what he had said and done on 18th March escaped him for the moment.

He stood up carefully. His military tunic and red-striped trousers had been thrown carelessly across the back of a sofa. His mud-spattered boots lay on the floor nearby, and civilian clothes – a clean shirt and a suit with waistcoat – were laid out for him on the back of a chair.

He walked unsteadily to the washstand and immersed his face for some time in the basin of freezing water. He cleaned his teeth with Dr Bonn's powdered dentifrice, and improved his buccal hygiene still further by gargling with Botot water. He went on attacking the traces of the previous evening's libations with the whole range of toilet products available to him: sluicing, rubbing and massaging every inch of his body with lettuce-juice soap. He completed these ablutions with a splash of toilet-vinegar and slapped on a little milk of iris to tighten his facial skin. With his hair brushed into some sort of order, the resurrection of the handsome Captain was complete. He eyed himself in the glass. His face bore an expression of disdain. He had just remembered something.

'Jesus Christ, Antoine,' he burst out suddenly, 'you're nothing but a deserter! A renegade. Meat for the firing squad. Eleven bullets and a blank: that's the fate in store for you. And you damn well deserve it!'

Memories of the previous day were now surfacing in a flurry of clamorous images. The Polish field! The people and the guns! General Lecomte! Antoine saw himself amid the end square of his men. The federal walking up to him. That fine open gaze that had touched something similar in himself. The crazy idea of surrendering. 'Better, comrade, to become your friend and brother!' 'The awfulness of spilled blood, Théo!' How could he ever forget 18th March, that unforgettable day of exuberant brotherhood and noble unreason?

The sounds of the rue des Rosiers flooded his ears, shouts, drums, fanfares; clenched fists waved, and a thousand faces – round ones, hook-nosed ones, fresh ones, spotty ones, snaggle-toothed ones – paraded past his eyes. He remembered women's delicious smiles and voluptuous bosoms.

He heard the 'Marseillaise' sung as he had never heard it before, the bass growl of a people in tumult, of a general uprising. Of thousands of voices roughened by a quarter of a century of anger. The deep anger of poor folk marginalised by the selfishness of the rich.

Comic episodes came back, too: Wire giving a thumbs-up sign to his friends, the locksmith pointing out the captain and the photographer with the air of a gipsy horse-trader. 'They're ours, those two, my hand on it! They're the people's property!'

Human destinies are sometimes played out on the level of bucolic farce. Obediently, the locksmith's cronies Marceau, Ferrier and Voutard, with others, had lifted Tarpagnan and Mirecourt onto their shoulders and borne them away in triumph. That was the moment when everything had started to go hazy . . .

Antoine's gaze had met that of Gabriella Pucci. Never had he seen such welcoming eyes, so intimate a smile. The Italian's resolute bearing, her loose hair, her fine bosom under a simple blouse of Irish linen, her lacy straw-coloured skirt, seemed to him a blinding vision of beauty. He could not tear his eyes from the delicate sheen of her skin, the perfect line of her bare round shoulders. Caf'conc' for her part seemed to have eyes only for the Captain. One would have thought she burned with longing for him.

Of course what had occurred was no more than a spell woven in the air, the spark of real lightning in a flirtatious glance, a shared half-second of enchantment. But to the handsome Captain that meeting of looks meant a fusion of souls for all time. It carried the weight of a promise. Gabriella was the one he had been waiting for. She would be his companion, his lover. She was made for him.

Antoine blushed scarlet. Caf'conc' threw her head back in a laugh that showed all her teeth, rendering her more seductively animal than ever. But before they could speak, Tarpagnan felt himself seized by a dozen hands and his feet were snatched from the ground.

He see-sawed about on the elbowing tumult of humanity, and eventually found himself perched on Voutard's solid shoulders. Velvet-Eye, Whitewash and others had hoisted Mirecourt onto their porters' necks at the same time.

'Three cheers for the Line!'

'*Vive la République!*'

'Long live the Commune!'

The crowd cheered them too. Antoine blew kisses in all directions. Caf'conc's supple, long-legged figure strode, graceful and erect, between the two beasts of burden Voutard and Ferrier. The magnificent young woman was laughing up at the Captain. During a pause in the procession she had caught hold of Tarpagnan's hand and forearm, causing him to bend towards her. Hooking him by the back of the neck, she tried laughingly to plant a kiss on his lips.

Their faces grew in close-up as she hopped on tiptoe to reach him. She laughed and walked backwards, still trying to kiss him. He caught the peppery scent of her breath, swam in the light of her dark irises. Antoine began to slip off the shoulders of those carrying him. Voutard, staggering, growled at the troublemaker to drive her away and jerked his burden back into position like a slipping sack. The crowd kept advancing, pushing forward with blind force. Antoine sat up straight, gasping like a drowned fish. The lovely Italian had captured his gold-laced kepi and perched it playfully on the cascade of her brown curls. Théo was laughing uproariously a few feet away. He had abandoned his flag to the crowd and was trying to shout above the clamour:

'My photo apparatus! My photo apparatus! I left it with some kid!'

'It's coming, it's coming!' called a squawking voice. A few ranks behind them the youth Tironneau, with his bandaged wrist, waved the tripod and precious hardwood box over his head, forty-five pounds' weight held at arm's length. Théo was humped along from shoulder to shoulder. The crowd filtered slowly through jammed alleyways. He was looking backwards to keep an eye on his camera.

'Would you teach me how long a pose is?' the youth asked. 'Show us how to look through the plate?' His dirty fingers pointed to the camera's big bellows, the brass-ringed dark blue eye of its lens. 'I want to be a reporter.'

'It's a promise! In a minute we'll take everyone's photo. You can be my assistant.'

Guillaume beamed with happiness. Théophile leaned forward and tapped his porter on the head. Velvet-Eye peered up at him in sooty-lashed reproach.

'Don't you like travelling on my hump?'

'Very much! I just wanted to know where you were taking us.'

'Round by us: rue Lévisse! That's where everything's happening now, by God! We're going to drink some famous old wine, Château bleedin' 'undred per cent . . . me mum's own plonk . . .'

Rochon, alias Whitewash, added:

'Stoke the old furnace up a bit, eh?'

Wire pranced along in front, yelling: '*Mind* yer backs! *Stand* aside! Make way for the people's heroes!'

'Rue Lévisse!' the women called to one another. 'We're making officer pâté! Dancing the waltz! About time somebody give us one!'

Léonce, Marion, Adelaïde Fontieu, the tarts and good-time girls, added their joyous accompaniment of scarves and tippets, of doll-like bosoms decked in green, in red, in blue . . . troopers of the 88th trailing in their wake. For each girl, a soldier.

The youngsters walked along as if skewered together. Guard, girl, infantryman; skirt, camisole, two caps . . . the joy of it! Everyone in love, in a sudden promise of warm sensuality.

23

Miss Pucci goes
home early

The neighbouring streets were filled with the same joyous clamour. A vast seething mass of waving flags, bayonets and kepis came and went, undulating, trampling, scattering and coming together. The news cascaded down from the heights of the Butte: the people had won! General Lecomte had surrendered! He had been taken prisoner! The Susbielle brigade had fled the slopes under a shower of leeks taken from costermongers' barrows!

Spontaneous processions formed on every street corner. Line troops and National Guardsmen, cheering, arm in arm.

'Three cheers for the Line!'

'Long live the Guard!'

What chaos! Like a disturbed anthill.

Paris, so gloomy the day before, so hangdog, so defeated, was raising her head. The inspiration of women had rendered the city triumphant. Thiers's army was in rout.

Demoralised troops, a lot of them, dreamed of returning to civilian life. Some had even changed out of their uniforms in shadowy courtyards, reappearing in civilian garb acquired secondhand for five or ten francs, sometimes as much as a louis. Many a town sergeant had tossed his kepi into the undergrowth. Gardens and backyards were strewn with black leather equipment, gaiters, cross-belts, pouches.

But at the end of the day in rue Lévisse, after they had danced a boisterous *chaloupe*, eaten, photographed a few barricades, met people, sworn to see them again and forgotten them, Gabriella

Pucci's smile had faded on her face. She had consulted her watch, more than once. She had shown signs of nervousness.

'Antoine,' she had said, 'forgive me. Whatever happens, forgive me. Today has been like a wonderful breath of fresh air. I swear it!'

For a while longer they had whirled round, enlaced, welded together like a single person. Her head turned to look back over her shoulder, *one* two three, the waltz; she passed one way, then the other, lips moist and eyes half-closed against a spinning background of fairy lights, heartbreaking little hollows in her cheeks. Then she had gone suddenly rigid in her partner's arms, prised the Captain's uncooperative hands from her waist, fled among the dancers and vanished. At ten minutes to six Caf'conc' had simply evaporated, between one measure and the next.

The first thing Antoine noticed when she had gone was that he was thoroughly drunk on Velvet-Eye's Château bleedin' 'undred per cent: a modest wine from the left bank of the Sioule that shrivelled the mouth and went up the nose sideways but did no immediate harm even when consumed in quantity. It might have tasted a bit sour, but as bottle succeeded bottle the illusion grew that pain and anxiety had been miraculously stifled.

Boozily, Tarpagnan had beckoned to Wire and tried to find out the reason for his partner's flight. The safe-specialist had stiffened slightly, brought his hand up to the peak of his cap and muttered out of the side of his mouth:

'Forget it, my son ... Gabriella's *property*. Married, like ... listen to what I say. There's her nursemaid, look, back on the job.'

With a small jerk of the chin he pointed out a skinny figure in full-fall trousers and a modish three-button jacket who was just taking up position in an alcove: horse-faced, red-haired, with a scarred cheek. Conscious of Tarpagnan's stare, the man pretended to be absorbed in contemplation of the dancing couples.

'Caf'conc' is one of those shrimps that hide from the light,' the key-carver whispered. 'You can't try to see her in daylight. She's a slippery little beast, closely watched.'

Antoine had been trying to catch the bully's shifty eye, and was becoming enraged. 'You don't think I'm going to be intimidated by a comic-opera pimp like that, do you?' he growled in Wire's ear. He stroked his moustache and groped mechanically for his sword, only to remember that he had abandoned the cabbage-chopper on the field. 'If I can't pierce his ears, I can give him a bloody nose!' he exclaimed, his Gascon accent thickening by the second as he reverted to cock-of-the-village type. 'Poke his eye out, by God!'

Emile stepped hastily in front of him and firmly blocked his path.

'You've had too much Château Hundred, Captain. The man you want to thrash is called Caracole ... real name Léon Chauvelot. He's a snake. An escaped convict. A very nasty killer. Do anyone in, he would.'

'Ye gods! After charging Juárez's Mexicans at Puebla, I think I can cope with a gutter Paganini in the 18th *arrondissement*.'

'You don't get it, do you? Caracole's more the sort that sneaks up behind and cuts yer leg tendons.'

'Whassat to me? I didn't get the "Cordova fly" either, that laid its eggs in the French army's nostrils ...' The Gascon was drunk beyond reason. Dancers scattered as he lurched across the floor towards Edmond Trocard's lieutenant. Taken unawares, the ginger-haired man had only time to assume a surprised expression before a bludgeon-like fist smashed his nose like an overripe tomato. He staggered back several paces, swayed for a moment, shook a threatening finger towards his aggressor and collapsed across the corner of a loaded table.

Careless of his rear, the hero of Puebla was back beside Wire in a moment. 'Well?' he asked eagerly. 'Where does she live? Where does Gabriella live?'

'Whassername street! In a cage of chatterboxes!'

This was not good enough for the Captain. He wanted more. He lifted the locksmith by the collar and began squeezing him by the throat. He was beside himself with drink, hardly knew what he was doing. After a couple of seconds Wire started to utter cracked, guttural sounds. His eyes watered and rolled back in his head, and he turned an alarming shade of purple.

Antoine slackened his grip. No sooner had he taken a breath than the little lunger was seized by a violent fit of his famous 'gypsum cough'. His head in his hands, he uttered a series of deep, cavernous barks almost as alarming as the earlier symptoms of suffocation.

'Jesus!' he gasped, 'I'm going to cough me lights up.'

'All right, all right, that's enough,' muttered Tarpagnan impatiently. 'Tell me where she lives.'

'In her own nest, done up special.'

'Give me the address.'

'Abs'lutely not, my son. If I sent you to her place, first of all you'd get your noggin took off. And I'd be for it too, straight away. Cold steel between me shoulder blades, ooh, ta very much!'

Wire turned his back on his persecutor to signal that the interview was over, that he was going to cough his lungs up somewhere else. He set off with a measured tread for his shop. Never had his chest sounded so hollow, his cough so sombre, so bloodcurdling.

24

No turning back

If the ex-officer of Lecomte's army had had the sense to follow Emile Roussel outside, he would have been amazed by the burglar's swift recovery on exposure to the fresh air. He stopped wheezing and spluttering, his voice returned to normal, his cavernous lungs breathed freely. Spotting Léon Chauvelot in a corridor, he slipped up behind him and tapped him on the shoulder.

'What cheer, Léon!'

The other man jumped like a grasshopper and spun round with a ferocious scowl, ready to defend himself.

'Oh, it's you, Roussel,' he said, relaxing slightly. He was swabbing his nose with a large bloodstained handkerchief.

'I think so,' Emile said, registering the red-haired man's pallor. 'Fancy a little nip of something hard? That'll set you up.'

Without waiting for a reply he led the way to his workshop, rummaged in a worm-eaten dresser and produced a bottle of plum brandy.

'Here, try this, neat. Guaranteed! Distilled fog-clearer.'

A furious nasal mumbling came from behind Caracole's wadded handkerchief: 'I *still* can't believe it! Your three-stripe Captain won't have long to wait for his turn. D'you know what he called me? *"Knight of the Bidet"*! Caracole's honour, I'm not going to forget that one! It's going to be payment with interest!'

He unbuttoned his bloodied waistcoat and waved it about like the standard of an avenging army. 'Tell your soldier-boy he'd better sleep with his eyes open from now on,' he said through gritted teeth. A new thought struck him. 'That's the second time today I've got took short by a geezer in a hurry. So far it's cost me a ruined weskit and ripped breeches. That's *two times*,' he added with a swerve into his wobbly English, 'me clothes been ruined.'

'You can't do nothing about it, Léon. That's life. You get these bad days.'

'Give me his name anyway. He hit me without saying a word. Where's his etiquette?'

'He's called Antoine, Antoine Tarpagnan. He's a hero of the war in Mexico. But more to the point, he's an infantry officer who's ready to fight like a lion for the Commune.'

'That's a point in his favour, I suppose.' Chauvelot moodily drank his glass of *gnôle*. 'But you tell him to keep his hands off of Caf'conc'. Edmond Trocard's not in the best of humours these days. He don't like people rolling about in his flowerbeds.'

'I'll pass it on for him.' The locksmith refilled his guest's glass, went and peered through the shutters to see if anyone was listening, and returned to his place. After a short pause he added:

'I don't suppose you've jus' come to keep an eye on Edmond's woman . . .'

'Correct.' Caracole emptied his second shot of plum. He looked visibly restored. His nose had almost stopped bleeding. 'The *boss* said to tell you that the job's set for tomorrow. You'll need your precision gear. We meet at midnight.'

'At the Glass Eye?'

'As usual, number 7.'

'I'll be there, number 13. But remind the Goldsmith I don't want no blood.'

Hand on heart, the former convict replied: 'Promise. Should go calm as a millpond.'

'I seen you at work last time, Caracole . . .'

'Look, it just went wrong, *last time* . . . because little Baroness de Runuzan came home from the Folies-Dramatiques before the end of *The Duck with Three Beaks*! You got to admit no one would have expected the first night of a Moineau operetta to quack like that among the *gentry*!'

'All right, the baroness come home early, granted. But that wasn't no reason for her to end up in the Seine.'

'You're like a kid, you are. What else was we to do? While the

coachman's unharnessing, her ladyship nips up the back stairs to
save time. Instead of coming in the front door at midnight like
she ought, she rushes into the bedroom at ten o'clock and finds
Gaston de Runuzan flat on his back and stark naked, having his
flute played by Amélie la Gale what we put in his bed special.
Right off, the baroness starts screaming the place down. She
wants a pistol to get justice, like on the front cover of the
Illustrated Journal. You should have seen her! Yapping and
running about ... Right! She thinks there's a shooter in her
husband's desk drawer. Next thing, she's bursting into the room
where you're working peaceful on the peter! You probably recall
that.'

'What I remember is you bashing her up, down and sideways.'
'Had to stop her from rousing the whole neighbourhood.'
'Her head hit the marble by the fireplace. She was hanging on
to your foot ...'
'Ah, she was a real pest, that one! She bit my wrist. She
wouldn't shut up. One of them unbreakable ones.'
'All the same, doing her in ...'
'Watch it! That's got nothing to do with me. She run onto
Trocard's revolver and it's gone off by itself ... ripped one of
her tits off, blood everywhere. Only thing to do was finish her
off with a knife.'
'I don't never want nothing like that again,' Wire said sullenly.
'*Of course*,' the gangster answered sarcastically. 'Monsieur is a
thief whose hands are clean.' He picked up his glass and added:
'Once you've opened the safe for us tomorrow, you can leave.'
'All right. I don't suppose I have a choice anyway ...'
'You're right there.' Sniggering, Caracole poured himself
another measure. 'Once you're in the Ourcq gang you're like
one of the fingers on a hand. There's *no turning back*.' He took a
swig from his glass.
Neither man looked at the other. Sounds and scents came
through the shutters from the party in the courtyard: bursts of
laughter, raised voices, the rhythmic sobbing of an accordion.
From time to time a shot sounded in the distance.
'I'd give a lot to know what's going on in the other districts,'
Emile Roussel murmured.

'The barricades are still there and being strengthened. The Line troops have shot Lecomte and old Clément Thomas.'

'Thomas, Thomas ... The one from '48? Fired grapeshot in the rue Sainte-Avoye?'

'That's the old jackal! The reaper of the National Guard up before a drumhead court martial. *Boum-boum-boum*, end of story for the Hercules of the bourgeoisie. It took seventy bullets to finish him off. It seems the more they punctured the old boy's hide the longer he stood up! Holes all over him, enough blood for a vintage, and he's still stood there with his hat in his hand!'

With a broad smile, Caracole took a paper package from his red flannel sash and unfolded it. 'Take a look. We cut the buttons off their uniforms. Seems these go for fifty centimes each.'

Roussel picked one up delicately. Gravely, he turned the small piece of polished brass in his fingers, stroked its surface. The cutting-off of those insignia, those symbols of a strength that had been hanging by a thread, seemed to him to signify that the past had been swept away. Now there really could be no turning back. But he knew that an immense task faced the insurgents – actors and scene-shifters in their own production – before they could establish a secure gangway to the new utopia.

'Not a bad little souvenir for the families, is it?' Caracole grinned. 'Like one for your nephews?'

Wire shook his head and replaced the button in the middle of the crumpled paper on Caracole's palm. 'Who shot them?' he asked.

'The Line and the militia. A few National Guardsmen too.'

Pretty well everyone, Wire thought glumly. He leaned on his work-bench, worried, suddenly sober, as if aware that the shooting of the generals would later serve as an excuse for other summary executions. He gulped reflectively and stood up.

'I'm goin' back. It'll look strange if I don't.'

'Yeah.' Caracole was refolding the packet of buttons. 'And don't forget to tell your protégé about the spot he's in. Try to hang on to his gravy, tell him. I'm as patient as the Lombard, I am ... I'll find him sooner or later. I got a skewer for pugilists of his sort.'

The red-haired hooligan tossed down one more glass. His ill-focused eyes slid about dangerously under their lids. The little locksmith pressed his lips together, silently took possession of his bottle of firewater and replaced it in the old dresser. Behind him, the other was still grinding his teeth about Tarpagnan.

'You know me pretty well, Wire. You know I'm not the sort to stand about looking hard done by.'

'I know what you're capable of all right. Just remember. I wouldn't like anything like that.'

The horse-faced man became violently excited. His front teeth ground together. He did not want Wire, a member of the Ourcq gang – a pal up to a point – to think of him as weak or humiliated in any way, not for a single moment. He fixed the locksmith with an unsteady, bloodshot, intimidating stare.

'Fancy going up against me, do you? Just remember I got bowels, my son! I've stood up to everything: starvation, sodomy, the cat, everything ... your boy friend just now, I could have carved him up with my pocket cutlery.' A long thin razor-sharp blade flickered out of his sleeve like a snake's tongue. The carrot-haired villain was whipping himself into a frenzy.

'Caracole's honour, your parade-ground steward wouldn't have looked so big when he'd been cut a few times. But you seen how I just warned him off. A stare from a man with death in his eyes, by Christ they don't forget that. No argument, the glorious warrior knew he'd be seeing me again later. That one day I'd become his curse, his unlucky star ... And you seen he was scared!' Caracole added with a nervous snigger. 'He just slung his hook. Never come back to give me no more grief.'

That was true enough, anyway. Tarpagnan had been busy elsewhere.

25

The night of
lost objects

Antoine was in a frenzy. Wire's swift escape had turned his attention on the locksmith's friends. Voutard, cornered in an alcove by the ardent Captain, swore by all the gods that he didn't know where the lovely Gabriella Pucci's crib was. Ferrier, hunted down and tumbled backwards into a wash-copper, swore blind that he didn't know either. So did Marceau and the others, their eyes scared, evasive. There were no blabbermouths in rue Lévisse.

'Don't ask the impossible, soldier,' Velvet-Eye warned, scuttling like a cockroach from the darkness of a cellar. 'No one round here's going to stick their nose in Edmond Trocard's private business ...'

'They care about their health, see?' explained Whitewash gravely, emerging from the same trapdoor with two crocks in each hand. 'I'd forget it if I was you, Colonel. Edmond the Goldsmith's untouchable in Montmartre ... all over Paris come to that ... Why not lead another charge on some of this Butte wine?'

The second wine the house-painter offered had the merit of freshness although it was vinegary and rough, and Antoine started pouring it down his throat. His heart was heavy. At the back of the courtyard, Théo was still dancing with a demure-looking girl in a Phrygian bonnet. Soldiers of the 88th were dancing the polka with some ladies of the quarter. Guillaume Tironneau was trying to photograph his mother surrounded by National Guardsmen leaning on their rifles, the lady posing with her terrier on her lap.

Antoine sprawled gloomily on a bench and tried to compensate for the loss of Caf'conc' by drinking everything in sight.

Night had fallen. Gone for ever! Life was black. Tarpagnan had wandered off into the dark alleyways, choosing his route at random. At about ten o'clock Théophile Mirecourt ran him to earth in a low dive in rue Lepic. If he had not been carrying his camera on his shoulder the ex-captain would not have recognised his new friend. He flung his arms wide.

'What ho! Who goes there? 'S the Marseillaise come back again!'

'Ah, Antoine.'

''S my ol' pal Théo! No need f'ra false nose here, you can take it off.'

Mirecourt leaned the imposing tripod in a corner of the low-ceilinged room, dimly lit by a cowled lamp and candles on the tables, and zig-zagged unsteadily to a chair. The Captain had just lighted a one-sou *crapulos* and was wreathed in rank blue smoke.

'How did you end up here? I've been looking for you everywhere.'

'Been burying my youth.' The ex-infantryman lumbered to his feet, stood there swaying and raised his tumbler of hogwash to the health of all rebels. Then he clicked his heels in obedience to some remembered military as-you-were, grasped the unlucky Théo by the sleeve and turned him round so that they were face to face. His eyes were distraught, his tone drunkenly emphatic.

'Comrade! *Irregular* comrade! My whole existence's been turned upside down twice in twenty-four hours!'

Mirecourt looked at him.

'You prob'ly remember I used to be a soldier.'

The photographer nodded. Antoine lurched suddenly sideways, but recovered his balance.

'Straight and narrow. Honour, thass what I followed.' His tone was mournful. ''N' look at me now, a mutineer, about to become a rebel! 'N' the other thing: I used to like chasing half-naked girls 'n' having passing affairs, lots of them. Now all of a sudden I'm a *monogamist*.'

Dissatisfied by the other's blank response, he seized the

photographer by the collar and shook him slowly back and forth, growling as he did so. 'In a single evening I've become faithful as a new bridegroom! Body and soul captured by one love! Attached ... no, what am I saying, *enslaved*! Bewitched, enchanted ... held by the nose! Longing to taste her rose garden, thorns and all! A mass of nerves, a romantic consumptive, a man ready for fainting fits, rope ladders, six-against-one duels ... for the impossible! A man ready for anything, however uncertain. Ripe for disaster. But I can't help it. She's so tall, so dark, so ... so *animated* and, God! So seductive ...'

'D'you mean la Pucci?'

'Gabriella!' the captain breathed caressingly.

'You poor chap. Keep your hands off her.'

'But I love her!'

'She's a man-eater. She'd swallow you whole.'

'A voluptuous swaying Amazon with a spicy laugh and perfect round hips and a beauty so untouchable that nothing – d'you hear me, Théophile? – nothing at all counts any more, 'cept being with her and having the scent of her breath in my mouth.'

'Pooh! You'd better get rid of that reek of sour wine first,' the photographer said, averting his nose.

'Wine, monsieur, satisfies the famine-afflicted body. It revives the mind and gives courage,' Antoine said with owlish solemnity. Théophile looked at him pityingly.

'And where is your lovely fiancée?' he asked. Tarpagnan seemed to think for a moment.

'Seems she belongs to 'nother,' he said. 'One minute my life's all lit up with human feeling. The next minute Venus disappears.'

'Everyone knows where she is.'

'Are you my saviour? Can you really take me to her roost? Come, my friend! Let's go!'

'My poor Antoine! As we speak, your lady-love is in a pink silk dressing gown, drinking champagne. She's cuddled up on a sofa bestowing her laughter and moist lips on a fat man wearing a ribbon and a round-shouldered prince with a goatee and an air of bourgeois rectitude.'

'You're lying!'

'Hardly even embroidering.'

'Let's go! I'll upend the villains!'

'Sit down. We'll go tomorrow. Tonight your back teeth are awash.'

'I did drink a bit, because I was happy,' Tarpagnan admitted. 'Then I drank a lot more because I was sad.'

'What have you done with your bars of rank?'

''Tore 'em off and chucked 'em away. Formal degradation before you go in front of the squad.'

'What about your gloves? Your lanyard?'

'Gave 'em to a feller with one arm . . . only needed one, bit of a waste really!'

'Pistol?'

Antoine waved vaguely towards the bar, behind which an alert proprietor was bustling about. 'Swapped it with that wine chappie for this *makhila* he picked up on the Polish field.' Triumphantly, he waved Grondin's silver-mounted medlar-wood stick.

'Care to tell me what you intend to do with a smuggler's cudgel?'

Antoine frowned slightly, then gave another vague, dismissive wave. 'It's like this, you see, Mirecourt,' he hiccuped. 'I'll be able to read the motto thing, just below the knob here, once I can see straight enough to read my own name.' As if to prove his point he dropped the *makhila* with a clatter.

'Ah, yes, the Polish field!' The tavern-keeper, his hands plunged in a basin of icy water, could stay silent no longer. 'You ought to've been there, M'sieu Théo! You could just pick up all kinds of things off the ground! Night of the lucky finds! You'd've thought everyone was just getting rid of anything what was a nuisance. In the back room there, just from what my kid bring in, I got six kepis, two wallets, three Chassepots, three left shoes, a flag and its staff, a pair of 'andcuffs, a lot of town sergeants' tunics and three ladies' slippers . . . Old man Three-Nails'll be well pleased.'

Antoine, who was having a lucid moment, mumbled something about having enough jagged scrap iron in his head already. The wine-seller, an Auvergnat, gave him a humourless stare.

'Alfred Lerouge if you'd rather,' he said. 'Geezer what turns bits and pieces into gold. Comes by every week with his barrow.'

Théo gave the man a stern look. 'Look here, Saint-Flour. The Captain's revolver: that's theft, you know. You've got to give him his weapon back.'

'Abs'lutely not, citizen. Drunk as a lord, your rabbit there. 'E was going to spray my shelves with bullets just now.'

'Can't *stand* the sight of empty bottles,' Antoine explained. His speech was slurred in the terminal stage of drunkenness. Théophile sighed, poured himself a glass of *ordinaire*, drank it and stood up to settle with the landlord, realising as he did so that he was in fairly poor condition himself.

'I'd better see him back to his barracks,' he muttered to himself.

'Now that's a good idea,' the sharp-eared wine-seller opined. 'Keep him on his feet ... Your sapper needs a walking-stick more than what he does a cannon.'

Antoine guffawed drunkenly in agreement. ''Sright, y'know! French army ought to be disharmed! 'N' I've got this *makhila* too ... look, here it is! Fam'ly treasure, almost. Could be, I mean. Wonder how it got here? ... 'credible coincidence ... astral, sort of thing.'

'Not as astral as all that,' Saint-Flour said. 'I've told you half a dozen times where that bleedin' stick come from.'

'Where?' Théophile asked.

'It's a weighted club what used to belong to a nark ... a enemy of the people if you'd rather. Right bleedin' Chinaman ... big tall bastard, grey eyes'd scare you half to death and the strength of a madman ... Took fourteen people all going at once to crack his nut! But he ain't going to need his truncheon where he is now, believe me.'

''S astral, all the same,' Antoine insisted with the sombre conviction of the reasoning drunkard. Théo scooped the *makhila* up from the floor.

'Let's take a look at this device...' He raised the cudgel to eye-level and slowly rotated its pommel encased in braided leather, deciphering aloud the words engraved on the copper crown. '*Hitzá*. Then ... *Hitz. Hitzá Hitz*! What is this gibberish? Fat lot of use that is.'

'That *gibberish* is a noble tongue, ignoramus! It's Basque!' Antoine had turned as white as a sheet. He seized the skullcracker from Théo's hand and tried to focus on its pommel, murmuring. '*Hitzá Hitz ... My word is my word*! A man with grey eyes ... tall ... Charles Bassicoussé! Charles Bassicoussé, after all these years!' He turned to the others. 'What would a notary have been doing in the Polish field this morning?'

'Notary?' the bar owner said. 'He wasn't no notary, I can tell you that. A copper, more like. A guillotine-stoker.'

'Not possible!'

'That's life, ain't it? Can't help rememberin' what things was like years ago,' the wine-seller philosophised.

Mirecourt did not feel qualified to join this discussion. He surveyed his companion, sprawled on a chair with his uniform in tatters and its insignia and accessories missing. 'Basically, apart from this stick, you have nothing left in the world?'

'Nothing, comrade! I've divested myself of contingent possessions. But I hope my name will one day appear in the archive of social struggle, on the list of deserving altruists.'

'I'm sure it will. Fancy a final goblet?'

'Certainly do.'

'What are you going to do now?'

'I'm rather counting on being shot,' the Gascon replied haughtily.

'Perhaps that can wait until tomorrow.'

'Certainly can.'

They clinked glasses. There was a long silence.

'You used to be a soldier,' Théo said at last, 'and now you aren't. That's the situation. You could become a militant.'

'Certainly could. Can you put me in touch with someone influential?'

'I used to live next door to Jules Vallès. We could have a word with him.'

'Jules Vallès? Really? He's related by marriage to my nephew!'

'What's your nephew's name?'

'Vingtras. Arthur Vingtras.'

'You're having me on. That's a comic-opera name.'

'Exactly! That's it! We're comic-opera cousins, Vallès and I!'

Théo stifled an immense yawn and fell off his chair.

Glass of wine followed glass of wine, from bistro to wineshop to tavern, one drink leading to another in an interminable, wandering, incident-packed course back to the Latin Quarter. An odyssey of clinking glasses. How huge Paris was when you had to stop at every bar to restore your strength! Gutters and kerbstones. A glass to the health of the Commune at every barricade. The parched throats of the National Guard . . . Here you are, my brave fellow, rinse your tonsils with this. The maze of walls and streets.

It took all night for the wreckage to reach the photographer's apartment at 23 rue de Tournon, left him by his mother: six fine rooms connected by an interminable L-shaped corridor whose peace was shattered by an appalling jangle of the doorbell, followed by elephantine footsteps on the creaking parquet and the intemperate growling of a voice with a Franche-Comté accent.

26

Monsieur Courbet,
Chairman of the Arts

Gustave Courbet was a corpulent but still vigorous and active fifty-two. His stentorian voice trumpeted his host's name, echoing through the open doorways and rattling the glass doors of the bookcases.

'Théophile! Théophile! Where are you hiding? In some cupboard crooning over your bromides and gelatines? Come out! Leave your den! Show yourself! Move! A new world is dawning! Drop your reclusive habits! There's life outside! The weather's fine! Paris is taking flight! There's going to be fighting! The chaps in epaulettes are on the run! Monsieur Thiers has scampered off to Versailles! We're in our own home at last! A new force is going to crush poverty! Socialism is a restoring sap for all! Modernity will rescue mankind from its mudbank of immobilism! Open your windows! Let the sunshine in! Look at the streets of the quarter, decked in the unanimous stridency of the red flag! The whole city supports the Revolt! This time it's really happened! Education can eradicate illiteracy! Industrial development can provide jobs for everyone who's up to it, and workers' control of the instruments of labour will lead to redistribution!'

The vociferous native of Ornans penetrated to the centre of the apartment, bawling slogans all the way, and invaded the photographer's studio, a glass-walled space two floors high looking onto the courtyard. On a long haberdasher's counter was piled a jumble of coated papers, rolls of painted canvas, sheets of glass, lamps, tubes, photographic plates, bottles of chemicals, silver nitrate, collodion, retouching inks and colours.

Courbet made his way round an imposing studio apparatus on a wheeled pedestal, a masterpiece of cabinetmaking whose gloriously polished rosewood his hand stroked in passing, and stopped in front of a painting of the Golden Horn in the style of Ziem, propped up on a cloth-draped column. Perched half-sideways on a plaster balustrade, fists on hips, gaze lost in a blazing sunset over the Bosphorus, the painter listened to the deep silence. After a while he thought he heard a furtive movement in the distance.

'Hell's bells! Théophile, my little freedom-lover, is that you? If you can't be seen, at least show your big toe!' Getting no response, he sprang to his feet, hurried past the looking-glass used by citizens to adjust their dress before studio sittings and rushed out into the interminable corridor. At the far end of this, a dark cul-de-sac lined with linen cupboards, the artist stopped outside the door to a small dressing-room and listened for a moment. Gradually his beard parted in a radiant smile.

'Théophile! I've caught up with you! I'm sure you're not answering for reasons of visceral introspection! Knock once for yes, twice for no! You are, are you not, in that low intestinal place where human thought, however fertile it may be – even that of the century's geniuses – is bent in congested obstinacy on the crucial effort of evacuation? Could it be a spasm of the sphincter? Are you shitting bricks, proud photographer? Would you like me to sing a soothing boating-song to facilitate the unblocking of your languid bowelry?'

The door made no reply, and the painter rattled the knob. It was locked from the inside. 'Come out, dear boy! I've got you!' he crowed. 'Come out quickly and listen to the day's news! Here, look! Or rather listen, how respectful I am of your privacy! I'm going away.'

He withdrew a few paces and for a minute or two remained silent except for his breathing and the rustling of his clothes. His alert senses could not detect the slightest sign of life. 'Very well,' he said at last, his patience exhausted. 'Very well. Today, as Chairman of the Arts, I wrote to the painters and sculptors of

Paris. I told them that the School of Fine Arts, patronised and subsidised by the government, was misleading our youth and depriving us of French art in favour especially of Italian art, which is emphatic and religious, therefore contrary to the genius of our nation! All right, d'you think?'

Unbroken silence answered him, and he cleared his throat. 'Very well,' he said again. He crossed his arms and waited, staring into the darkness of a tapestry, his prominent stomach relaxed in its fine sand-coloured waistcoat; then, like a sentry, started to pace the panelled corridor. So anaesthetised was he by the calm, broken only by the ticking of clocks and the rhythmic creaking of his boots (but showing no other sign of life), that he found himself stifling a yawn. He came to rest again in front of the silent door, bursting with outraged vanity, groomed and buttoned into his good clothes, but with the ruffled look of a country cousin whom no one has come to meet at the station.

As if to thrust away some fear of the void, he cleared his throat and resumed his harangue. 'Yesterday, at noon, Victor Hugo buried his son. Just think! Charles so soon after Léopoldine: the suffering! I was there at Père-Lachaise ... There were a lot of people. I saw Millière, looking pale and very moved ... after the gare d'Austerlitz, the cortège had to make its way through the barricades. The national guardsmen at la Roquette reversed their arms and formed a spontaneous guard of honour ... The people cried: "Hats off!" When the great man passed, everything became gothic! Roadblocks were moved aside, piles of cobblestones shoved out of the way ... Drums were beating in the fields! Flags were lowered, soldiers presented arms! Bugles sounded!'

He stopped abruptly, eyes alight, and added: 'And if you were to come out of your sentry-box, I could tell you about Edmond de Goncourt...'

The sound of a door-bolt slipping gently back in its housing answered these words. Courbet bounded forward and with a chubby hand pushed the door wide to reveal Antoine, wearing only a pair of drawers and holding the *makhila* in his hand. The painter's mouth stayed open for several seconds.

'Monsieur...' he muttered at last with embarrassed formality.

'Monsieur.'

The two men examined each other with undisguised curiosity. Courbet found it difficult to take his eyes off the skullcracker. 'You sleep with that as well, no doubt?' he enquired courteously.

'Not necessarily.' Antoine walked past the other man with the stiffness of a sleepwalker and headed for his room, pausing in the doorway to ask: 'Have you seen Théo?'

'I was going to ask you the same thing.'

Without being invited he followed Antoine into the curtained darkness of the room, passed in front of the sunlight-flooded window and made his way through the shadows.

'You know,' he remarked, pretending to examine his toes and then leaning forward slightly to see the cut of his shoes, 'I'd never noticed before that these boots squeak at every step.' He flung his head back and laughed.

He was a man of considerable presence. A magnificent beard surrounded a vigorous and humorous face set on a babyishly white neck. Whenever he moved, even slightly, the muscles rippled on the shoulders under his greatcoat and in his sculpted forearms, giving an impression of force and vital energy wholly in keeping with the rural origin that was both the setting and the source of his genius.

Now he moved some of the ex-Captain's military effects out of the way, sat down on the back of the sofa and looked at Tarpagnan. 'Who are you exactly, monsieur?' he asked. 'I'm Courbet.'

As he pulled on his civilian trousers and knotted his grey silk tie, Antoine Tarpagnan gave his names and identified himself. He emphasised his status as an ex-officer of the Line, and told the painter at what juncture of history he had met Théophile Mirecourt and the manner in which they had become friends. The savour of the words warming his Gascon voice, in phrases punctuated with his distinct mute 'e's, he poured out a torrential account of the previous night's Homeric odyssey of drunken wanderings, starting with the morning of the 18th and ending with their noisy and disreputable dawn arrival at the photographer's apartment, after Théo had managed to persuade him not to spend the remainder of the night on Jules Vallès' doormat on the third-floor landing.

'Vallès? He left this building nearly two years ago.'

'I was too drunk to accept it last night. D'you know Jules Vallès well?'

'I enjoy his company enough to have been in a few escapades with him. We went to Besançon together last year. He was living at 9 rue Aboukir then . . . Said the police were watching him . . .'

'Does he still live there?'

'Alas, no.' Courbet's expression was sombre. 'Since 11th March the editor of le Cri du Peuple has been living at government expense in the Cherche-Midi prison. He got six months.'

'Surely not! Think again! He can't still be there!'

The painter made a face, but said nothing. Antoine seized him by the wrists and gripped them hard.

'Think again, I say! Paris has just shaken the dust of feudalism from its feet . . . Yesterday the people won! No more bastilles! No more imprisonment!'

'You've got a point there, by God . . . That devil Vallès ought to be at work already reconstructing the world!'

'I so want to consult him! Only someone like him can show me what path to follow.'

Courbet blinked, and with some difficulty extracted his wrists from the other's iron grip. 'Why bother?' he cried. 'Why seek noon at two o'clock? Your destiny's already mapped out for you. The Commune's going to need officers.'

'I want to hear Vallès say it.'

'Don't you trust my judgement?'

'I'll only do what Vallès suggests. We're cousins through the Vingtrases.'

Courbet smiled and linked his arm with the ex-Captain's. 'It shows a lot of merit, wanting to reinvent a whole existence,' he said approvingly. 'With the help of people like you, in love with the ideal, the patriots will soon vanquish the mystagogues of the régime, the Versailles tormentors!'

Chatting like old acquaintances, they made their way back into the photographer's studio, a room that amazed and delighted Tarpagnan. He slowly scanned the walls, covered with posters and passepartout-framed photographs, asking questions to satisfy his curiosity. The oval-framed portrait of Augustine Kaiser reminded him of her work *La Plébéienne* to the glory of women at the pavillon de l'Horloge. He passed a photo of Céleste Vénard, whom he knew as Mogador. He stopped in front of the next picture: a portrait of a man in a straw hat under a deluge of white sunshine.

'Who's this with the moustache?'

'That's Jean-Baptiste Clément. Poet and songwriter.'

'I'm with you! "The Chambermaids at Duval's! And being such brave damsels, as Amazons they dress!"'

'And "Cherry Time",' Courbet added. 'Funny thing, a song. Comes alive in people's throats in the damnedest way. Flies along, apparently banal, then discovers an afterthought in some circumstance . . . and becomes political.'

'Who's this young man?'

'Auguste Vermorel, a friend of Théophile. And there, if I'm not mistaken, is Théophile's mother. Pretty woman, by God!'

'Bit imperious, don't you find?'

'I didn't know her well, but I can tell you that she was a great beauty.' Courbet looked more closely at the portrait. 'And then . . . she was carefree and rich, too. Our young prodigy was raised in the scented shadow of her skirts.'

The painter's eye fell on a row of new prints, still weighted down at their corners but now nearly dry. 'Look!' he cried, 'some new stuff! Isn't that the barricade that blocks the rue de Charonne at rue Basfroi? Looks very like it . . .'

Tarpagnan peered over his shoulder. 'Yes. These photographs are from yesterday. I was there when Théo took them . . . he can't have slept at all, developing them.'

Courbet peered at one of the prints through his spectacles, examining the faces of National Guardsmen mingled with civilians.

'I love looking at Parisians!' he exclaimed. 'Look at that baby there in its little white dress . . . and that lady in her best gloves. How happy they are, being photographed arm-in-arm with the heroes of the day! Ah! look at this, it's incredible, this bugler perched on his mountain of cobblestones ... he's playing, too: look at his cheeks!'

Antoine laid the print back on the table. 'Will you introduce me to Jules Vallès?' he demanded.

Courbet took off his pince-nez with a tired look, and shifted about in his creaky boots. 'You're not going to let that drop, are you?' he said. 'Very well. If we can find him, I will. But I warn you, he's probably moved house three times while we've been talking.'

'A bird of passage?'

'He's a pretty funny bird all right, always short of thirty thousand francs in subscriptions to start a journal and six francs thirty to get the landlord off his back ... Ever since I've known him he's feared the end of the month as if it were the day of his execution.'

'But what a pen! What a talent!'

'Depends on your point of view. So far his verve has brought him more fines, duels and jail sentences than recognition.'

'I admire his courage and endurance. They bring him close to the poor.'

'It's true enough that to propagate his fine ideas, friend Jules is capable of subsisting indefinitely on ink in some freezing attic.'

'I love his eloquence. That mordancy that grips you by the throat, the way he brings the streets to life and speaks for people on the margins. The things he says are frighteningly true!'

'I won't argue with that. He knows how to talk about mud and vagabondage, but you must admit there's a tinge of blood and bile in Vallès too.'

'Yes. He's very like Eugène Sue.'

'That's quite intelligent of you. Victor Hugo thinks the same thing, anyway.'

'Which brings us back to the devastated poet.'

'Just so,' the painter murmured. The creator of *L'Origine du monde* and *Sommeil* stared moodily at the shining toes of his boots. 'Do you really admire him that much?' he asked after a while.

'Vallès? Oh yes! I'd like to work alongside him. Be *committed*.'

'He's in luck,' Courbet murmured, hanging his head. 'I myself am not so well-liked.'

Antoine looked at him in some surprise. 'Sorry I was so vehement,' he apologised. Then, as if injured human beings could be glued together as easily as broken porcelain, the Captain flung himself down on the sofa and added kindly: 'I am now ready, Monsieur Courbet, to return to the subject of Hugo . . . to hear the whole story of Père-Lachaise . . .'

The belated attempt at courtesy was lost on Courbet. The unfrocked soldier had been making extreme demands on his own tolerance, and now the damned hobbledehoy wanted to go even further! Devil take it! The most important thing was being ignored: his own narcissism! And he had shown such restraint! Hadn't he just allowed his admiration for Vallès to take first place over his infatuation with himself? Hadn't he taken an interest in Tarpagnan's fate when he usually derived most of his strength from a carefully cultivated self-esteem?

'I'm a Courbettist,' he said abruptly in a peevish voice. Black and brilliant eyes looked at the other man through long silky lashes, the gaze of an antelope. 'I live for my painting!' he added energetically. 'It's the only thing that counts . . . I'm the first and only leader of my time!'

He could not help himself: before starting to talk about Victor Hugo, he had to establish securely that he was the centre of the world, the first painter of France, far more important than Ingres and Géricault. He loved the limelight – great floods of it.

'They'll tell you I'm vain,' he went on. 'Well, it doesn't bother me. I look at myself in mirrors and shop windows as freely and happily as the proudest man on earth. At Père-Lachaise, when I approached the grief-stricken poet between two graves and held out my hand to him, all I could think of to say was: "I'm Courbet." And it was entirely natural! That's how it is when men of genius meet. Their renown serves as their passport! I had exchanged letters with the author of *Les Misérables* many times, but had never met him. I said simply: "I'm Courbet," and he turned to me a face bathed in tears, the face of an old lion at the end of his strength. He gave me a smile of friendship. Tears gathered slowly in the corners of his eyes ... A meeting of giants!'

'Sin of pride, Courbet!' cried a new voice. 'Giants of today, midgets of tomorrow!' The athletic form and laughing face of Théophile Mirecourt were framed in the doorway. He brought good news. 'I've just seen him at the Hôtel de Ville, free as air! Vallès is back, forging the revolution!'

'The last I heard he'd just been given six months by the Council of War,' Courbet said.

'He got out the same day.'

'With Vallès things always happen quickly.'

'He found refuge a stone's throw from the Cherche-Midi ... his friend Henry Bauer. He was holding court in furnished rooms ... that's where they found him.'

Antoine was on his feet. 'What was he doing?'

'Covering paper with marks!'

'Did he know anything?'

'No. Completely in the dark.'

'He'd been brought up to date?'

'He listened to the account of the inevitable killing of the generals.'

'What did he say?'

'Nothing.'

'Not a word?'

'He shivered.'

'Then what?'

'He gathered up his pen and notebook. He said: "Let's get moving, since it's the revolution"!'

27

Gunshot in a clear blue sky

'God damn and blast it to hell! It's really too much! I don't know whether to laugh or cry! It's ... it's *extravagant*! The opposite of what any sane man would have expected!' stormed Commissaire Mespluchet as he fastened his last piece of luggage, a morocco-leather document case stamped with his initials in ornate interlaced letters. The shirtsleeved Commissaire was pale and dishevelled from the effort of filleting fifteen years of police records and concentrating the real treasures in three travelling bags. He stared gloomily along a set of shelves crammed with folio-sized registers.

My precious memories, he sighed to himself, my trinkets, my best things, my favourite books: you're up for pillage now. God, what a blow! What an *insult*! Our soldiers show the white feather to a howling mob of ragged scum and just look at us, scuttling off to Versailles like a bunch of milksops ...

He blew the dust from the gilded edge of one of his precious books and made his way past several heaps of files containing reports, trampling a mass of leaves bearing notes in red ink, security chits scattered all over the floor. He stuffed a last shirt into a leather briefcase that he had decided to take into exile after all, and sat down behind his desk. After a moment he brought the flat of his hand down on the blotter strewn with rubber stamps, seals, assorted fragments of paper and postage stamps, hard enough to make his 'Old Man of Bordeaux' (a porcelain cup inherited from his poor mother) jump into the air.

Yes, it's extravagant, he was thinking. You wouldn't believe it!

Not two days ago Monsieur Thiers's verbose and despotic diatribes were still echoing through the corridors of power. Today, Monday 20th March, the civil service is on its own, getting no directives, under the thumb of the workers!

Eyes blank, moustache bristling with fury, the little Commissaire of Gros-Caillou district allowed himself a soothing pinch of snuff from the back of his hand and blew his nose with a muted-trumpet sound.

I knew I'd have to put up with a lot, he thought as he refolded his large red-chequered cotton handkerchief. It was obvious that the first rifle shot was going to send hordes of brainless petty-bourgeois scattering like starlings out into Seine-et-Oise. But that the example of total collapse should have come from the very top, that really makes me choke! Apoplectic!

Breathing heavily, the policeman smoothed his moustache. His myopic glance probed a shadowy corner of the room where a dark immaterial presence, vaguely outlined inside a shapeless grey shirt, could just be distinguished from the yellowish woodwork.

'Where are you exactly, young Hippolyte?' he rasped aloud, putting on his spectacles to penetrate the gloom enveloping his ectoplasmic drudge.

'Here I am, sir,' Inspector Barthélemy stuttered, 'at your service, guv.'

Guided by the voice, Mespluchet made out the whites of his subaltern's eyes lurking behind the hatstand on which hung, in solitary splendour, the Commissaire's legendary capsule hat. Letting his pince-nez fall to the end of its cord, he asked in a funereal tone:

'D'you know what piss-pot full of shit they're emptying over us now, young Hippolyte? In all the wine-shops, rioters eager to eat the bourgeoisie are calling us bed-wetters, eunuchs and cowards!'

'Too facile by half, that, sir, isn't it?' Inspector Barthélemy said distractedly. His nervous hand had launched itself into space. Like some flying creature it soared through the cone of dusty light thrown by a lamp and came gently to rest, swathed in a mitten, on the Commissaire's forearm. 'We ought to do something with the *agents provocateurs*.' Barthélemy's voice was firm. 'I know them. They're everywhere. Former agents of the Empire, ready and eager!'

'Don't you believe it, Hippolyte! That's simply what any Commune beggar taken at random thinks, and for once those ranters with their hats askew have a point! One reason we showed them our arse was that we'd got it pretty dirty. The problem now is that our generals, our strategists, have left us in the lurch. We've just got to carry it off. Yesterday on the esplanade I saw Lieutenant Desétoiles ... you remember that brilliant officer?'

'Yes, sir.'

'Well, I saw the fine hussar, not looking back, galloping through a big cloud of white smoke towards his new quarters at the Sun King's palace. And all this dirty underwear, dear boy, all these nauseating capitulationist faeces, do you know whom we have to thank for them, *in fine*?'

The inspector had a pretty good idea, but was too prudent to say so. He liked a good diatribe and knew he was about to hear one.

'That whey-faced Adolphe Thiers, of course! You heard, I imagine, that the head of the French executive fled in such haste that he didn't even have time to tell his wife or mistress where to send for his washing. He left on his own. Pissing his pants! Ah, the noble courage of it! Our spiritual guide fleeing like a paunchy rat over the icy roads in a barouche! It's pitiful, and according to my last report deserves a vaudeville sketch ... You can just imagine old man Transnonain invading the residence of the Seine-et-Oise Prefect and taking over the whole first floor of the left wing, while his valet Charles, his wife, his sister-in-law and his three chambermaids search for him everywhere, house to house ... isn't it a theme worthy of Victorien Sardou or Ludovic Halévy? They could play out their exile before packed and appreciative houses! The very thought of being stuck with those Koblenz émigrés[1] makes me want to vomit.'

The Commissaire stopped, visibly upset. Then, cheered by

---

[1] *Translator's note*: London and Koblenz had been the two main refuges of those who felt threatened by the 1789 Revolution.

these ridiculous reports, he managed a grimace resembling a smile. 'Christ's blood! There's something damnably hilarious there, don't you think? Genuine farce!' His eyes veiled, Isidore Mespluchet emitted a strangled croak. 'I'm laughing!' he said. 'Sounding like a cracked calabash, but laughing.'

His shoulders shook briefly in a mirthless guffaw. After a moment the caricature of enjoyment faded from his congested features, and horizontal lines reappeared on his forehead. His face, touched fleetingly by vestiges of the energy of which age and fat had slowly deprived him, resumed its normal scarlet shine, the flat nose and heavy lids expressing profound fatigue. He slid down in his chair and listened to the sounds from the street.

Raising his head after a long moment of silence, Mespluchet saw that his subaltern had taken a chair and was watching him intently. The long-legged pursuit and surveillance specialist was holding a workman's cap in his hand. He was unshaven and wearing a roofer's overall made for a much heavier man. The Commissaire sat up.

'I'm listening, Inspector Barthélemy. Make your report.'

'The streets are pretty calm this morning,' the beanpole replied instantly, drawing his chair forward. 'Most of the exodus seems to be over. There are a lot of people in the railway stations, though, still trying to get to the country. The rue du Havre is jammed with luggage on hand-carts. The omnibuses are no longer running. Now and then you see a stampeding horse with one of the new government's despatch riders clinging to its mane and trying to make it stop . . .'

'All right. Any incidents? Reds distinguished themselves with any new ferocities?'

'Two town sergeants trying to pass for ordinary citizens were unmasked and shot immediately. Some loudmouths are egging on the rabble to liquidate all traitors. Others want to put down the rich along with priests and nuns. A mob invaded the offices of the *Figaro* in rue Rossini. But the editors had scarpered.'

'Anything else? Stock Exchange? Politics?'

'Money's getting scarce. The business of the Commune's being done at the Hôtel de Ville. Every street is guarded by men from the quarter. A lot of villains and ugly customers round the barricades. A few assorted battalions are making for the porte Maillot.'

'Can people still go through the bois de Boulogne?'

'Freely, Monsieur le Commissaire. But private telegraphy has been suspended in Paris. And rail traffic looks as if it may be interrupted.'

'Letters?'

'The Post Office under Rampont is still working normally.'

Mespluchet was listening to an approaching clatter of wheels, which stopped under his window. 'That'll be my barge,' he said, rising to his feet. 'I had to pay through the nose to persuade the coachman to stay behind. Agents Dupart and Rouqueyre are going to drive. Houillé's coming inside with me.' He raised a corner of the curtain. 'Ah! That imbecile cabman! I told him to wait at the back door of the shop . . . oh, good, Houillé's dealing with it . . .'

He turned back to Barthélemy and resumed his seat. 'Madame Mespluchet and her sister took the train from Montparnasse,' he said in a low voice. 'I hope they got through . . . The problem was that my wife insisted on taking her things, a Corot she got from her parents, her silver-gilt service and her Barbédienne bronzes . . . I urged her not to bother, but you know what women are like.'

'D'you know where you'll be staying, sir?'

'With my cousin Léonce, not far from the Viroflay roadblock. The hygiene will be a bit dubious, but we'll get fresh eggs.' Mespluchet felt that he should reciprocate his minion's kindly interest in his well-being. 'What about you, my boy? Where are your quarters?'

'At les Halles, Monsieur le Commissaire, in a cardboard shelter. I sleep with eaters of cabbage stumps.'

Mespluchet's jaw dropped. 'Hell and damnation! You aren't living at your place?'

'I had to give it up. The doorkeeper denounced me as recalcitrant, and Rigault's clodhoppers are lying in wait for me there every night.'

'The devil you say! What do you do for food?'

'I go to soup kitchens run by do-gooding ladies, give you a bit of rather tired hot gruel.'

'This is appalling, my boy, what you're telling me.'

'Can I take the bags, Monsieur le Commissaire?' Houillé, another inspector, had appeared in the doorway. Mespluchet nodded, shrugged his shoulders, took a last look at the ashes of a compromising file smoking in the grate, and stood up on his short legs. He opened his desk drawer, took out a loaded revolver and put it in his pocket.

'Well, *au revoir*, my dear Hippolyte. We will see one another again before long. In the meantime, keep us informed about what you pick up here. Your information will be precious to us.'

'I'll do my best, Monsieur le Commissaire.'

'Don't go risking your life.'

'It is a bit dodgy, sir, to tell the truth. We stand out a bit, as a species. Takes more than dirty nails to give you a poor man's hands.'

'Just so! You really must secure some back-up. I was about to advise you,' the Commissaire added hurriedly, fixing his wavering, myopic gaze on Barthélemy, 'to make contact with the head of the Sûreté. Eh? What d'you think? Why don't you go and ask Monsieur Claude to lend you a hand?'

'I met Monsieur Claude in a lodging-house in rue Neuve-des-Capucines.'

'Well done! He's always been under our feet but he's untouchable. He can help you.'

'Hardly, sir.'

'He made it clear he was going to stay in Paris as long as his position was tenable.'

'It won't be for much longer, sir. Some of his top people have gone into sedition. Bagasse, his own deputy, is parading in front of a platoon of federals, gesticulating like Talma! Monsieur Claude called on "the grace of God" ... He expects his own arrest any minute.'

'Did he have any news of Horace Grondin?'

'None. He gave me the key to Grondin's apartment so that I could go and ferret about. It's in the rue de Corderie. I'm going to try to get in there at night.'

While talking the two men had paced a succession of corridors to a small service door at the rear of the commissariat. It opened onto a quiet street in which a cab was guarded by two armed sentries. Isidore Mespluchet screwed his hat firmly on his head and climbed into the carriage next to Houillé's black-clothed form.

'Hippolyte,' he said as he shut the door, 'do promise me you'll be careful. If the situation persists for more than a month, I'll send someone to relieve you . . . Forget about all routine matters, of course. Exceptional circumstances call for exceptional behaviour. Don't bother with the drowned girl from the pont de l'Alma. There'll be plenty more unexplained deaths in the days to come!'

I don't give up, the long-armed man murmured to himself. His eyes glowing with a pale zealous light, he held up between thumb and finger the number 13 glass eye found on the body. 'I'm not dropping the case!' he said aloud. 'I'm a proper policeman. You'll see, guv! I'll have the whole business settled before you're back.'

'I'm not doubting your talent, lad,' Mespluchet mumbled, gazing at the white expanse of the pavement. He seemed to have recovered from his momentary exposure to feeling. Eager to end this leave-taking, the details of which were beginning to depress him, he reached with sudden inspiration into the pocket of his greatcoat, then stuck his arm through the open carriage window. Seizing in his two square hands the long mittened paw of his subordinate, he thrust into it a wad of banknotes and his handsome pearl-handled revolver.

'Take my Adams, Hippolyte,' he murmured. 'An irreproachable five-shot weapon. I have great pleasure in giving it to you as a token of my confidence.'

The inspector whitened still further. 'Sir! Your Deane, Adams & Deane from London!' he stammered. 'Ah! Sir!' An immense wave of pride rose within him.

Mespluchet maintained a cold expression. Seeing that the great lanky Fleming was overwhelmed by his present and gazing in awe at its jewel-like finish, he rapped on the glass with his stick. 'Get moving!' he called to Rouqueyre and Dupart on the box.

The conveyance lurched forward with a great flexing of springs, hurling the little Commissaire back into his seat. He straightened himself and arranged his clothing. Below his moustache, his mouth relaxed and lost its firm line. He felt Houillé's curious gaze pressing on him. He undid the stud of his stiff collar and untied his black silk tie.

'Don't envy your colleague, you lummox,' he snapped irritably. 'He has abilities, but he's the next thing to a dead man.'

28

Alfred Three-Nails
does some business

Alfred Lerouge was whistling cheerfully through his teeth. He couldn't help it: today was a historic day in the annals of the rag-and-bone trade. Since the day before yesterday, Sunday, the working conditions on the Butte would have satisfied a duke: there weren't any coppers to move you on, not one. Not a single officious nosy bastard. You could mooch about the streets unmolested, cadging and pilfering to your heart's content. You could graft in broad daylight. And no one after you for once!

Usually, you had to earn your crust with the sweat of your brow. You had to scuttle from pavement to pavement, starting at the hour when the rest of Paris was closing its eyes. You had to kick the piles of garbage apart, search with a dark-lantern, probe through the filth with your hook – a 'number seven' in ragpicker slang – and slowly fill your basket before transferring the gleanings to your handcart.

Yes! Since the guns had been taken back from them foul-mouthed riflemen of General Vinoy's, the profession of itinerant merchant had seen a bleeding great change for the better. On that score alone, old man Three-Nails chuckled to himself, it's long live the Revolution, long live the Commune! I'm not proud. I don't hide it from the patriots that this is my best week for a very long time.

He had not been inside his shack at the tail-end of the route de la Révolte for three days, and still his ragpicker's hod was full. At the end of the rue des Pressoirs, he stopped and leaned on a low wall to give his back a rest from its weight. He squinted at the sun and spared a thought for his heliotropes, which seemed to have survived the frost. He began to stuff his pipe with recycled shag, humming the refrain of 'Charlotte la républicaine', a patriotic little number by citizen Noël Mouret in memory of '48:

I'm Charlotte the plebeian,
The people's pride and joy,
Republican rose
Of the district of Montorgueil.

A yellow dog with a curly tail passed, intent on its own afternoon affairs. It sniffed a colleague's turd, dispensed a parsimonious jet of urine at the foot of a well-used bench, trotted across the cobbles to give a street lamp its corrosive ration. The animal scratched for a moment at some discarded food wrappings, then left with the hurried air of one who is on his own territory, far too busy to waste time talking to a crazy old man who is part of the furniture and smells like a drain.

Puffing contentedly under his hat-brim, Three-Nails felt that he possessed the secret of true wisdom. His bowels, long punished by a diet of very heterogeneous rations, gave a tweak, and he lifted a buttock to release a cloud of noxious gas with a prolonged sound of tearing linen. Ah! Another good moment.

Even if he drank a bit more than he should, he had not done too badly in the rag-and-bone trade. Did he not possess a small piece of land in Cow City, with a shed, a donkey named Bugeaud who could count up to ten by scraping the ground with his hoof, and a cart consisting of four planks on two wheels, grandly referred to as his carriage? These, among other things, made him a potentate in the kingdom of planks. A judge, a man of probity, a settler of conflicts, reigning benevolently over the malodorous, the rejected and outcast, people who had got used to living on the margins of society – between city and countryside, at Saint-Ouen, Clichy, around Batignolles and as far as the Ourcq basin – and preferred their proud and impoverished independence to the constraint of bailiffs, families, laws, the everyday and the home-loving, the strict discipline of factories and the boring routines of organised life. Lovers of the open air, bankrupts, fugitive husbands, failures, all sorts of rolling stones, companions in misfortune supported by an *esprit de corps*: a common law, based on experience of the traps and pitfalls of human treachery, that was at least as just as the more formal codes of ordinary social hypocrisy.

Three-Nails knew what clay men are made of. He had been round the world three times, something that also added to his prestige. He had wandered the earth in vessels belonging to his father, a very rich Nantes shipowner, after being given an eldest son's education. In his stormy youth he had haunted the Café Riche and the Maison Dorée: now, after a wandering course through the slums of Tamatave and the brothels of Sumatra, he kept his quarters at the Ragpickers' Casserole, the most celebrated of Clichy's low taverns.

There, this evening, on the straw-covered tiles, he would be feasting with others as ill-clad as himself, back from their own rounds. He would see Greaseball and Bonebag, Short-Boots and Doorkeeper. They would drink grain spirits flavoured with cloves, pepper and a few drops of sulphuric acid, a cheering tipple that made the taste of cabbage-stems acceptable.

Should he feel after the banquet that he had drunk to excess, that the white moon was going to rob him of sleep, he would smoke a little of the 'dreaming herb' which he kept in a small box in his pocket. By general request, he would climb onto a cask where, with tears running down his face, he would recall his travels in far-off places: Aden, Bombay, Calcutta, Foochow; Puerto Delgado, Valparaiso, Vancouver; his travels in the Chinese province of Chekiang. In practised phrases, he would recite for his neighbourhood cronies the catalogue of landlubber's complaints, and would soothe his regrets by telling the story of the princess Pi Chu, a fifteen-year-old beauty, swaying like wheat in her silk dress embroidered with carnations, who long ago had spoken words of love to him through the bluish curtain of her palace window overlooking Lake Tai.

This evening the rag-and-bone men would toast the defeat of Vinoy's troops and raise a welcoming glass to windfall profits. Resolutions would be passed urging the Commune to dismantle the conservative order and bleed the rich. Money would be spent.

While awaiting the feast of hot turnips garnishing a dish of donkey sausages, Three-Nails was sustained by the warming memory of the three shots of twenty-five-year-old brandy that had been poured into his cup of coffee that morning while he did business with the Auvergnat in rue Lepic.

Quite apart from his gleanings of the previous day from courtyards, gardens and alleys on the Butte and all the streets leading off the Polish field, he had left Saint-Flour's establishment in possession of a small fortune in immediately negotiable weaponry. Three Chassepot rifles, two service revolvers, five sword-bayonets and assorted pouches, cartridge-belts and leatherwork, kepis, gendarmes' tunics, and Line-troops' insignia, lanyards, medals and epaulettes filled his bundle. At that rate even a beginner would have managed to make something solid. A brisk circuit of the alleys of Montmartre enabled the old anarchist to shift the bulk of this soldier's hardware, which he held in the most sovereign contempt.

'Long live peace and well-being!' he cried from time to time, as if to give himself courage. 'Long live freedom and a proper binge! Long live anarchy and the boundless ocean!' Every few paces he stopped facing the sun and shifted his burden on his back, grunting with the effort. His gravelly voice went on bawling out his credo for anyone who cared to listen: 'Long live the individual! Free access for ragamuffins!'

He had already sold two of the three rifles and hoped to find a buyer for the third before getting back to his cart. He had left the vehicle behind St Peter's Church in the charge of one Ziquet, a fourteen-year-old on whose chin a few stray hairs drew attention to themselves.

Ziquet was quite a character. He was clever, and might have gone far in the order of enforcers and assassins if Alfred had not taken him under his wing after the death of his mother, a streetwalker who hawked the last of her charms in angles of the city wall. Lerouge had taught the youngster to count, and some rudiments of geography, how to read maps, take a bearing on the stars and sort bones for the refinery. He had taught him that they are classified in three groups according to their suitability for gelatine, glue or bone-black. The boy learned fast. So long as he was given food to assuage his hunger, he followed in the old sailor's wake. He had the whipcord body of an alley cat, boundless energy, exceptional effrontery, and sweetness of nature to spare. He called Alfred by the pet name 'Papa Rust', and helped him push his cart when Bugeaud-the-Pigheaded got stubborn and refused to pull.

For the moment, the youth waited for Three-Nails reclining on an old tombstone in the Merovingian cemetery, hidden in the undergrowth. Bugeaud, at liberty, was peacefully eating grass.

Alfred Lerouge suddenly had a wish to return to his trolley and his donkey, and quickened his pace. Bent under the weight of his ragpicker's bundle, he walked along humming his song to give himself heart, while his mittened hands gently massaged kidneys bruised by the burden. Suddenly Montmartre seemed as steep as the Alps. A frock-coat approached him and he bawled routinely: 'Two francs seventy the Chassepot, complete with its own kitchen knife!'

The man had a hurried air. He signalled to a woman on the other side of the junction and weighed the rifle and bayonet in his hand. 'It's too dear,' he muttered. 'Can't you come down a bit?'

'You're joking, matey!' Three-Nails rasped with theatrical indignation, setting his bundle on the ground. 'I don't bargain over prices. I'm licensed, me!' He displayed a medal on which his names were engraved.

'Show me your clarinet, then. How it works.'

'This is an 1866 model, a very nice rifle that shoots true. Some of my colleagues are asking three francs for one the same. Even three francs is nothing for one of these. A tool like this is going to be scarce before long. These breech-loading jobs'll be fetchin' five francs before the weekend, you can bet your life on it!'

'All right, I'll take it,' the man replied, rummaging in his pocket. 'I'd like a broadcloth tunic too, and a bit of wool braid to sew on my kepi . . .'

'Artillery or Line?'

'Artillery. I'm going to be serving a piece.'

'Talking of pieces, m'sieu, I can't help hearing the music of a pile of the right stuff jingling in the depths of your saddlebags ... if you was to slide a bit more of the ill-gotten in my direction, I'd have the honour and privilege of sending you on your way with a tasty little souvenir ...'

'What kind of souvenir?'

'Something amazing for Madame ...'

'Go on. I'm tempted. What have you got?'

'Your choice: a revolving pistol, or bullets dug out of the the wall in the rue des Rosiers.'

'Rifle bullets? From outside number 6?'

'You've got it, sir. Genuine vintage Lecomte lead! Three francs per projectile! It's philanthropy, that's what it is! In a year's time that'll be worth five times as much as a Suez Canal share!'

'I'll take two.'

Ah, what a day that was for licensed rag-and-bone merchants!

29

A grey-eyed cyclops

His burden thus lightened, the old rag-merchant completed his journey with a longer stride. Reaching the Merovingian cemetery, he sank out of sight among the undergrowth. He passed among tumbled gravestones and wrecked sarcophagi, expecting at any minute to find Ziquet sprawled in the sunshine, polishing and carving bits of bone into umbrella-handles or nail-buffers, as was his habit. But he was nowhere to be seen.

Bugeaud was wandering some distance from the cart and its unsupervised load. His belly was distended from grazing, and on seeing his master he lowered his ears rebelliously. When Alfred approached him he trotted rapidly away.

Three-Nails did not chase him. He put down his hod of plaited osier, and after thinking for a moment headed for the small hidden doorway which led directly into the choir of St Peter's church. His hat still low over his eyes, the old man made his way round the building looking into the the side-chapels in which he and the boy had often dined on one of the altars and urinated against a pillar.

After a moment he distinctly heard a terrible sound: a groan, human in origin, but so shapeless and so involuntary that it froze the old man in his tracks with horror. Another groan followed, wordless, helpless, frightening.

'Christ Almighty!' The old man hurled himself forward like a charging bear. 'Ziquet! Where are you, sonny?' Peering at the floor, he lumbered over a trail of blood, still red, smeared on the tiles. He did not have far to go. He found the urchin behind a pillar, on a raised step, in the shadow of an old tomb.

The boy was on his knees, holding the narrow end of a gourd

to the lips of a motionless man who gurgled and rattled at regular intervals, and muttered disjointed words. A bloodless hand clutched a large crucifix in a white-knuckled grasp.

'I found him outside, in the long grass,' Ziquet whispered. 'Days he must have been there. He'd been dragging hisself along, he'd slept in a crypt, I followed the blood back. He was pukin' his guts up, and I pulled him in here ...'

Three-Nails looked at the man. He was massive and craggy, his face bruised and livid, a frightening mug it was too, tortured and white, the high forehead completely coated in a dark crust of dried blood. Ziquet and Three-Nails looked at each other, appalled. Both knew that they had to do something.

'D'you think he's going to snuff it?' the youth asked.

'Not far off it by the look of him,' Alfred Lerouge replied. He bent over the injured man and said loudly: 'Keep your guard up, m'sieu! We're going to see what we can do for you.' He indicated the man's bald head with his dirty hand. 'Bloody great bash on the nut.'

The wound was very long, running from the top of the forehead to the occiput, gaping in places, but so congealed, especially on the back of the head, by blood-clotted hair, that it was difficult to gauge its real depth. The left eye was totally closed and blackened, the cheek below it and the eye itself grossly swollen, the cheek in addition cut to the bone. The man's shirt was in tatters, revealing other flesh wounds on his body, some bleeding heavily. But the most striking thing about the man was the extraordinary intensity with which his right eye looked upon his rescuers from between two threads of blood under a heavy lid. Illuminated from within by a strange light, that dark slaty iris seemed to concentrate the man's last forces in a bitter struggle against slipping into the void.

'Funny geezer 'e is,' Ziquet said. 'Friend of the devil I shouldn't wonder. A while back, he found enough juice to get hold of me wrist ... he was sweatin' and yellin' fit to start a riot ... I couldn't get away, I thought 'e was going to pull me arm out. His eye rolling about, looking up in the air, red sparks in it, burning like ... He's mumbling, 'e wants the crucifix what's up on the wall! So I get it down and give it him, and he grips the little long-'aired geezer like he's stranglin' 'im. Like he wanted to kill 'im!'

Three-Nails tried without success to prise the injured man's hand from the crucifix. 'Bit unusual, that,' he admitted. 'First time I've seen a bashed-up geezer trying to unscrew Baby Jesus's nut.'

The man's single eye was fixed earnestly on the rag-merchant. He swallowed painfully, and mastered a shiver that ran through his entire body. His features became more distinct in the deepening shadow and with his ashen immobility gave him more than ever the look of a dying man.

'Look!' Ziquet murmured, 'He's trying to say something.'

Alfred Lerouge answered with a blink of his eyes. His gaze had become fixed. His pendulous cheeks hung down on either side of his toothless lower jaw, which looked as if it was about to meet his potato-like nose. The boy was getting worried.

'Papa Rust! Hey, Papa Rust! Can you hear me?'

Three-Nails made no answer. He seemed to be losing consciousness before Ziquet's alarmed eyes. The youth mastered an impulse to flee and shook the old man by the arm. There was still no response, and Ziquet knew that they were already out of their depth in the power of that glacial spectre. It was as if the two ragpickers no longer commanded their own limbs, as if some suffocating force held them motionless in the dark church. They gazed down at the recumbent man's features, his bald scalp under its coating of dried blood, the single eye fixed on them, and knew that the first word he uttered would commit them to an unknown narrow road. The adolescent felt cold in his very bones.

'Let's go,' he whispered. 'The big goat's in this man. The geezer with horns.'

As if to comfort the boy, a sort of jerking began in the bloody phlegm that filled the injured man's throat, a hollow gurgling terrible laugh like a sad and gloomy song of victory. The rag-merchants felt suddenly dizzy.

'Hear that, Papa Rust? 'E's 'avin' a giggle now. Strange geezer, ain't he . . .'

'I hear him. Laughing in his blood! Just now he looked like he was ready to close his umbrella for good. Now he's got Jesus by the gullet, he seems to be getting better.'

The spectre was, in fact, moving a little. The horrible giggle had stopped. Panting for breath from his broken ribs, he seemed to be gathering his last forces. He dropped the crucifix and his freed hand moved slowly into the air.

'God is to blame,' he blasphemed, striking the crucifix on the ground. 'God is a vile invention of abominable suffering! God is corruption! God is nothing but hatred and indifference!' A rictus of pain twisted his mouth and his one grey eye radiated such intense malevolence that it made the two rescuers uncomfortable.

'I don't think the old Geezer upstairs 'as got much to do with your bit of bad luck,' soothed Three-Nails, 'and you're lucky to have come across a couple of cupids like us. Not all that religious, like.'

The injured man's free hand travelled through the air, groped around, fell on the hand of Three-Nails and closed on it like a claw.

'Help me,' the spectre said. 'I'll pay you well.'

The effort of speech seemed to exhaust him. His face turned waxy and his eye closed. He looked ashen, his panting breath had a catch in it. Enclosed in his matrix of pain like a man in a straitjacket, he seemed to struggle fiercely to recover his powers, and pulled at Three-Nails's wrist as if to speak into his ear.

'Gold,' he seemed to mutter. 'I'll give you gold . . .'

'Are you saying you'll slip us some yellowjackets in return for our services?' the old merchant asked in a low voice. 'Is that what you mean?' The recumbent man nodded weakly.

'That'd be a help,' Ziquet said.

'Gold . . . my house . . . a lot of gold,' the injured man panted, his eye still closed. Alfred Lerouge smiled broadly.

'Very glad to hear it, sir!' he cried. 'Of *course* we're going to get you out of this! The young shaver and me, we're going to take you to a bed we know of. My wife'll look after you like a sister! La Chouette knows all about infusions, herbs and remedies. But just so's we know each other, why not just give us your name and the address of your pretty doss-house?'

The spectre's eye reopened. 'My name is Horace Grondin,' he murmured. 'I am Monsieur Claude's deputy.'

The old sailor knew at once that he was looking at the underchief of the Sûreté. 'Hey, Ziquet!' he exclaimed unsteadily, 'we've really caught something this time! Run and get the donkey and cart. This here gent's a big fish. We might even be able to auction him off!'

30

Trout in the rue
Hautefeuille

Tarpagnan walked along between Courbet and Théophile, his face radiant. He was going to meet Vallès! Théo had agreed to pilot him to the Hôtel de Ville and introduce him to the great man. The three friends were devouring the pavement of the boulevard Saint-Germain with confident strides.

Courbet had allowed himself to be persuaded to come with them as far as the rue Hautefeuille, where he lived. Although it was not on their direct route to the Hôtel de Ville, it was not far off it. The air was very fresh and the sky clear, although in the far distance a few furious clouds still suggested grapeshot, enveloping the Suresnes hills and mont Valérien in rainsqualls.

How quiet the streets of Paris were! The sunshine helped infuse the gentle breeze with a scent of triumph. The shops were open as if on a normal day. Cooks and housekeepers were going about their work. After the tumultuous groups of the day before, an occasional disoriented bourgeois could be seen wandering about taking his bearings. One stout citizen was testing the air at the Odéon junction with an interrogatively lifted nose.

Courbet was evidently a prankster. He nudged his companions and darted off on tiptoe, his noisy boots meowing cheerfully at every step. He slunk along a wall and vanished round the corner, only to reappear in a chequerboard of light and shade, approaching the citizen stealthily from behind. After gesticulating for a moment or two behind the man's back, he leaned forward and bawled suddenly into his ear:

'Hey! I bet you're smelling the drains to see if the stench of rabble is as strong as they say!'

The unfortunate citizen jumped a foot in the air, gobbled like a turkey and went pale. He stared straight ahead of him, obviously terrified, and waited for something else to happen. Courbet, elegantly turned out with his yellow kid gloves, walked round him and looked into his face with an amiable smile and sympathy in his large eyes. 'Something wrong?'

'Not at all, not at all.'

'Any news?'

'None. I don't know . . . ah yes! It seems there was something in Montmartre a day or so ago.'

'There was indeed,' the painter confirmed in a funereal voice. 'Just about as grave as could be.' He looked at the man to gauge his reaction and added brokenly: 'Are you not aware, my dear sir, that we are on the very brink of revolution?'

'I don't know! I haven't seen anything.' The poor man was practically out of his senses, his nerves raw. Doubtless he had been pacing his apartment for forty-eight hours like a blind-folded terrier, completely cut off from the events outside. Théo took pity on him and drew closer. 'Consult the posters,' he advised. 'It's all up-to-date stuff . . . At least they'll let you know what sauce you're going to be eaten with!'

'Posters?' the bourgeois stammered, backing away from his tormentors. 'But . . . they're white . . . so they're official . . .'

'Yes, they are.' Tarpagnan was blocking his retreat. 'They attest that Paris has got itself a government even under the red Republic!'

The man approached a paste-spattered wall, dug out his spectacles with a trembling hand and hurriedly read this placard:

French Republic

To the people.
The people has thrown off the yoke that some were attempting to impose on it. Calm and impassive in its strength, it waited without fear, and without provocation, for the shameless madmen who tried to interfere with the Republic.

This time, our brothers in the army would not raise their hands against the sacred ark of our freedoms. Thanks to all; and may Paris and France together establish the foundations of an acclaimed Republic, with all the consequences that follow ...

'Consequences!' quavered the citizen with a moan. Fearing the worst, he moved on hurriedly to the next poster.

French Republic

Liberty, Equality, Fraternity.
The Central Committee of the National Guard,
considering that the constitution of a communal administration for the city of Paris is of the utmost urgency,
Decrees:

1. Elections for the communal Council of the city of Paris will take place on Wednesday 22th March.
2. Voting will be according to the electoral roll and by *arrondissement*.
3. Voting will take place from eight in the morning to six in the evening. Counting will begin immediately afterwards.
4. The municipalities of the twenty *arrondissements* are charged with the execution of this decree in so far as it concerns them.

A later notice will indicate the number of councillors to be elected in each arrondissement.

Hôtel-de-Ville, Paris, 19th March 1871.

Signed, The Central Committee of the National Guard,
Assi, Billioray, Ferrat, Babick, Ed. Moreau, C. Dupont, Varlin, Boursier, Mortier, Gouhier, Lavalette, Fr. Jourde, Rousseau, Ch. Lullier, Blanchet, J. Grollard, Barroud, H. Géresme, Fabre, Pougeret, Bouit, Viard, Ant. Arnaud.

'Who are these people?' asked the tail-coated gent in an astonished voice. The three hooligans could not believe their luck.
'Complete unknowns!'

'Bloodthirsty types!'

'Jacobins. Alcoholics! Communists!'

'This is serious! This is serious!' the bourgeois wailed. 'Last night I heard the *curés* ringing the alarm!'

'Very very serious.'

'One'll have to leave! Go into exile!' The man was in total panic.

'Yes! Get your things together and rush out into the street!' suggested Courbet.

'They want to shoot prosperity!' Tarpagnan put in.

'The editors of the *Figaro* have left the key under the mat,' Théophile added. 'The *Gaulois* isn't going to come out! The press has been routed!'

'This morning the stations were besieged by respectable people trying to save their silverware,' Courbet said, suppressing a mad laugh with great difficulty. 'The ministries have been occupied!'

'When I hear that, I fear for my family,' the gent said, and slunk rapidly away in the direction of Saint-Sulpice.

'To Versailles! Every man for himself!' the photographer bawled after him through cupped hands. The man stopped and turned round. 'I left the oldest of the children on guard, but there are two doors,' he called. 'You can't be too careful!' And he vanished at full speed up the rue des Quatre-Vents.

On the other corner of the crossroads, the three friends seemed to be rooted to the spot. They were leaning on walls, holding their stomachs with their hands, uttering strange little cries and pointing at one another. When they started to laugh in earnest, their eyes were soon blinded with tears and they laughed for a long time. Even passers-by were infected. A man dropped a box of toothpicks in the gutter and started to laugh too, pointing to the spilled toothpicks. A woman who was passing had started with a fine, sensual pout and progressed to showing her teeth in full-throated trilling contralto laughter, setting the three men off again. A lady in a hat with a red flower on it, who was thinking of perhaps crossing the road to avoid the rowdy group, was overcome first by curiosity and then, joyously, by the contagion, infecting in her turn a baker, an underhead of department in town gas supply and a pretty blonde girl delivering some ironing. Through her laughter she asked what was so funny. No one could tell her. On the corner of rue Pente and rue Danton, they continued to fall about, pointing at each other and laughing about something long forgotten. Until they had washed away all traces of pride. Until they had exhausted their forces.

One by one the victims recovered their poise, went through a diminuendo of giggling, straightened up and walked away. They no longer knew one another. Antoine, Théo and Gustave were among the first to leave, their faces cheerful. Soon they turned into rue Hautefeuille. Outside number 32, Courbet blew his nose and held out his hand.

'I'm going to fiddle about with a nude I've begun,' he told them with greedy relish. 'A red-haired woman ... absolutely fascinating skin tones.'

'If you don't go on working too late, come and join us at the café de l'Union,' Théo suggested. 'With Vallès, the evening's sure to wind up in rue Monsieur-le-Prince.'

'Without me, my dears. I'm already in hand for this evening. Champfleury and some other hooligans of the same stripe are coming to dinner. We'll play the horn and sing old songs!'

'You're a horn-player?' Antoine asked delightedly.

'I love popular music! I often burst into song after a few drinks. I've composed one or two ballads I'm rather proud of, actually.'

'It's quite true,' Mirecourt said in response to Tarpagnan's incredulous glance. 'Courbet's a really talented songbird. Hardly anyone sneezes at his music ... apart from the late Berlioz of course.'

'Berlioz! Berlioz!' grumbled the painter. 'May his soul rest in peace, but between you and me he was a sparrow who thought he was an eagle!' He backed into the doorway. 'I'm going. I've said too much!' He turned back immediately and added through cupped hands to Tarpagnan, his newest audience: 'Berlioz quite simply never digested the picture I eventually painted of him ... It was a canvas full of dark browns that showed too accurately the truth of his charred face.'

Soothed by the delivery of this rather caddish footnote,

persuaded that he had made a successful exit, he had got as far as entering the gateway and greeting the black-toqued concierge through the lodge window before he froze and spun round yet again.

'Ah! Théo! I was forgetting why I came to see you! I'm going to need you to photograph some trout for me, on a nice dish or a bed of greenery.'

'Don't you use Nadar or Le Gray any more?'

'Nadar was for portraits. Le Gray was for waves. Reutlinger was for Proudhon. And you're going to be for trout! I only go to the best. So don't be vexed, young photographer!'

'I'm not vexed. But just at the present moment, surely, there's something a bit more alive to paint?'

'What? Barricades?'

'Yes. Or the *people* on the barricades . . .'

'I'm not in the mood just now. And to keep my mind off human beings, I'd like to draw some trout.'

'Oh all right. You shall have your dead fish.'

'Thank you, Théophile. Rest assured that I won't take my eyes off this revolution.'

'I do like that man,' Tarpagnan said, watching his receding figure, 'excesses and all. He's monumental!'

31

An exchange of confidences

After the pont Saint-Michel, the pavements came alive. The road was crowded. A squadron of horsemen clattered up the boulevard du Palais at full gallop. The officers had not had time to decide on their uniform or standardise it, but they were already very noticeable. A lot of red tunics and plumed headgear, kepis at rakish angles, gleaming boots, big epaulettes. Antoine gave an incredulous whistle.

'God's death! Staff College is going to have its hands full! At least there won't be any shortage of people to give orders.'

'It's your own fault officers' pips are going so cheap,' Théo said. 'All you had to do was hang onto the ones you had.'

'I don't miss them!' Tarpagnan assured him. 'I'm not bitter. And I have plans that don't involve the profession of arms.'

'What are you going to fight with?'

'A pen!'

'Journalist?'

'Why not? I'll tell the truth as I see it.'

'Then you'll be welcomed!'

As they approached the Hôtel de Ville they started to see more red scarves and buttonholes. Bourgeois people in party clothes strolled stiffly and self-consciously among the populace. They laughed and went red in the face when the flower-sellers offered them blood-red carnations, but they accepted the purifying flowers readily enough and spat their three sous into the basin of revolt.

'The people's friends have become uncountable!' jeered Théo

as they passed a middle-aged couple apparently thrilled to be out slumming. The two men slowed their pace as they passed the pair. The lady was being winsome. Hanging on her husband's arm, she had just leaned towards him to express acute anxiety for his health, which seemed excellent judging by the line of his waistcoat.

'I don't regret coming out, despite this awful cold,' the husband replied, rummaging in a round box of throat-soothing Nafé creams. 'It's beautifully sunny.'

'Of course you're right, Amédée,' his spouse agreed, snuggling into her cashmere shawl and leaning against him, 'there's such gaiety in the air! Look at all these good people leaning from their balconies! The youngsters climbing up the statues and waving flags! I'm going to tell your father all about our walk just to annoy him! He was in such a grumpy mood after the jakes this morning that he wanted to tear up his share certificates to load his gun!'

'Introduce me to this spendthrift imbecile, quick,' Tarpagnan interjected, taking the lady aback. 'I'll change his coupons for wads and live on his dividends.'

'It's true, dash it,' Théophile said as they walked on. 'You can't have a bean left.'

'I've got just about a hundred francs in my wallet. After that, nothing.'

'Vallès will provide,' Théo said. He thought for a moment. 'No, I'm talking rubbish. Vallès has *never* got any money. He's the original knight of the thin purse!'

Antoine gestured dismissively. 'From him, I only ask advice.'

'Oh yes,' Théophile cried happily, 'and who else can you ask for help?'

'Not you, brother. You've already done more than enough for me.'

'There's no one else. I'm the only family you've got.'

'I've still got Caf'conc'.'

'La Pucci? An attractive slut!'

Tarpagnan chose to pretend that he had not heard this expression. 'She sings at the Glass Eye. She told me that if I was in need, she'd help me.'

Théophile had stopped at the edge of the pavement. 'Pinch me, someone, and wake me up!' he exclaimed. Looking incredulous and angry, he swept an errant lock of hair out of his eye. 'This girl is a tart! A kept woman! Get her out of your mind!'

'I've got to tell you something, Théo. I haven't thought of anything but her for a single second since yesterday. The thought of her has taken me over.'

'Hard to digest.' The photographer's glance was hurt and worried. He had come close to the other and was twisting one of his coat buttons in his fingers, a sign of ownership apparently beyond his control.

'You mustn't leave,' he murmured, sounding a little like a spoilt child. 'My house is your house. That languishing Italian is just there to be had ... she'll lead you on to your downfall.'

'Too late. I see her eyes whenever I close my own.'

A shadow seemed to cross Théophile's face. He had turned pale, and stopped fiddling with Tarpagnan's button. 'I'm not afraid of anything,' he boasted, rolling powerful athlete's shoulders, 'but with you, I feel protected.'

'Protected?' Antoine allowed his astonishment to show. 'Nobody would dream of doing you any harm.'

'I see that you haven't really understood anything,' Théophile answered rather haughtily. He mumbled for a moment, chewing on half-words, then waved his hand in the air like a drowning man. He stared stubbornly down at the ground.

'I've got a bullet here,' he said, thumping his chest. 'I'm completely for freedom and I want to show it and bear witness to it, but I have no social past. I'm one of those children raised in the boudoir! My entire adolescence was spent in the perfumed enchantment of caressing women! At the end of a garden of long grass that was too pleasant, too reassuring! When Vallès was shivering in the light of a taper in a thirty-franc room, I was dining at Ramponneau's! And you can see that even in anticipation of the prospect of blood and shooting that awaits us all, I always want someone to pass me the strawberries and sugar bowl!'

A heart-rending sigh escaped him. He seemed to listen for a moment to the calls and laughter of those about them, then gazed into the grey distance between two buildings. 'I've botched my entry to the world, Antoine,' he said gloomily. He seemed unable to say more, but poked with the toe of his shoe at a twig on the pavement, his face set in a pitiable smile of derision.

'Talk!' Tarpagnan urged. 'So talk, you mule! Open the floodgates! There's no doubt at all that your salvation lies in words.'

'What do you know about it?' Mirecourt growled. Everything seemed to make him sore. He seemed to be making the sort of effort that might be required to scale a high wall. 'The fact is, you're the only person I feel like giving any confidences to,' he admitted at last with an accent of unmistakable sincerity. He looked at his friend with a face filled with humanity, animated by waves of energy that gave it a fleeting beauty. 'Poor Antoine! A burdensome gift indeed!' he joked. He started to talk. As if a dam had given way in some dark corner of his being, the words poured out in a torrent.

'Mamma died five years ago. She was beautiful, lovelier than you can possibly imagine. She had been widowed very young. Her white dresses billowed before her like the bow wave of a graceful vessel. When she made her entrance at a ball or gathering, her high bosom, her fine shoulders, her queenly brow framed in the curtains of her heavy hair, everything about her established new standards; a sort of folly of nature. The sun followed her about like an obedient pet. It caressed the little curls at the nape of her neck, dusted with gold. Suitors sighed with love and desire all around her. Threw themselves at her feet. Men of all ages – paunchy bankers, devastated gentlemen, seducers in cassocks, all sorts of smart people, landowners, artists, doctors – all ready to stoop as low as necessary, to suffer the humiliations and inconveniences that make lovers so absurd, just to win her favour. The buzz of their voices at the other end of the drawing room used to make me mad with jealousy. I was twelve, fourteen, sixteen; I was, wanted to be, the only man in her life. She laughed. She moulded me. She made me read and dream. She took me into her bed, welcomed me against her skin, taught me the scent of her armpits, her foamy whiteness. After midnight, she would retire. She would send the retinue of admirers out into the street. Their bouquets, presents and notes would lie forgotten in vases, in bowls, at the back of desk drawers. That was my time, my triumph. Our happiness shared with no one else. Her silk chemises revealed her whole body. I would kiss her pretty statue's feet. I would rub the snowy back of her own son's lover ... for twenty years she held me in her tender power. The night she died I wanted to kill myself.'

He stopped short, then after a moment launched himself into the void: 'Since that time, I've hidden my problem with men by showing an excess of muscle. I row on the Marne, I fight duels when provoked, I militate for a more just society, but I blush when people stare at me. A fear of being unmasked, no doubt ...'

'You manage pretty well, Théo. I've seen you dancing with girls, and there was plenty of fire there.'

'I smell of stale air,' the young man replied with shy abruptness.

'We've all got monsters lurking in our cellars,' Tarpagnan replied, laying a hand on his friend's shoulder.

Théophile looked up. 'Sorry,' he said. 'I apologise for burdening you with my secret.' He felt washed, like the air after a rainstorm. His dreamy gaze looked up into the Paris sky, which had suddenly turned dark and damp. He turned back to Antoine. 'Do what you like with your affections,' he said impulsively. 'Forget this whole ridiculous episode! Of course, it is I who am being unbearable.'

People passed by without showing interest in their conversation. Groups of them: volunteers in crumpled tunics buckling their belts; federals christening their first boots, Communers' wives carrying baskets of supplies. Théo had recovered his normal air of calm, firm rationality. He was ready to resume their journey, but now Antoine stopped him.

'I, too, made a bad start in life,' he murmured. 'A lot grimmer than yours, let me tell you.' There was a short silence. 'I abandoned the girl I was engaged to,' he began. 'The day of our wedding I ran away after another girl. I was so young! So independent! So very unsuited to the confining routine of marriage! This was ... a good sixteen years ago.'

'*Hitzá Hitz*! Am I right?'

'Yes. The broken word!' He shrugged his shoulders and turned to face Théo. 'I was a cock of the village, you see. A *drolle* who used to plant rosettes on the foreheads of running heifers, and do the perilous double somersault over their horns to soften up the skirts.'

'What was your fiancée called?'

'Jeanne. A wild and nervous girl who would bridle at the slightest caress.'

'Charles Bassicoussé's daughter?'

'No. Jeanne was an orphan. Her mother died in a typhoid fever epidemic and her father, who managed Bassicoussé's property, begged him on his deathbed to become Jeanne's guardian.'

'The fellow with slate-coloured eyes!' Théo cried. 'Our friend Saint-Flour's madman!'

'Yes.' Tarpagnan was sinking into his memories. 'Monsieur Charles was a powerful man. Strong as an oak. A sombre face in the depths of which lived two exceptionally magnetic eyes. He had fists that could fell an ox. When he pinched the cheeks of children he found among his vines it used to put the fear of God into them. It was also rumoured that on stormy nights he took off his gold watch and chain and made his wife hold them, so that she would be the one struck by lightning. And he could enjoy his armagnac in peace.'

'Delightful! How could anyone live with a creature like that?'

'They can't, obviously. They disconnect at the first opportunity! Angèle Bassicoussé passed on after ten years of use. She was dried up like the kernel of a withered nut. She had no pulse. She complained of unknown maladies.'

'What did she die of?'

'Wear. Madness. Uselessness.'

'And he?'

'Strong as a Turk! A rich notary. When giving us permission to marry, he had sworn to ensure the well-being of two poor children and to leave them his fortune. And for a simple shopgirl in Mont-de-Marsan I'd laid waste to all his plans!'

'He can't have been terribly pleased.'

'A typhoon within seconds! He booted me out of paradise. I was destitute in no time, I can tell you! I'd only been a young farmhand on one of his properties. I went on the road in Gers, I did this and that . . . a pedlar at Eauze, a shepherd in Chalosse . . . from time to time I had news of Jeanne. I used to imagine her new life. She'd become housekeeper for a priest at Mont-de-Marsan. It was said that the abbé Ségouret had greatly helped in restoring her natural gaiety. And people hinted that his dominion over her had no frontiers. I myself was making constant and rapid progress elsewhere . . . new horizons were opening up, my curiosity being whetted, burning new desires making their appearance. And then,' he finished in a flat voice, 'and then, seven or eight months later, Jeanne was found murdered on her bed . . . eviscerated, covered with knife wounds. She had been carrying a baby, almost at the end of its term. The baby too had been killed, its skull savagely crushed by the murderer . . .'

'Yours?'

'I never found out. I was afraid. I ran for it, left the country meaning never to return.'

'D'you think the man with grey eyes is still looking for you?'

'I think he's found me.'

'To forgive you?'

'Or make me pay. At the time, he was the one accused of the murder. He was the one who spent twenty years in jail.'

'In your place? Was it you who killed Jeanne?'

'No. For what it's worth, I swear before God that it wasn't me.'

'I believe you,' Mirecourt whispered, repressing a shiver.

The two companions had recognised that the slippery slopes of their solitude and interior turmoil ended in the same precipice. The attempt to soothe the moral wounds of one had exacerbated those of the other. They exchanged a wry and helpless smile.

'There's more,' Tarpagnan said with a hint of defiance. 'Since that soiled purity, that murdered beauty and youth, I've never been able to form an attachment to a decent woman. I only like whores!'

It was astonishing to stand there calmly discussing their fate with this total absence of reserve. The two friends stood face to face on the busy pavement's edge, at a loss for the next word. They might have been floating in the air, away from everything. Théophile was the first to speak.

'Oh, well,' he murmured, 'it's not the first time I've fallen in love with a boy.'

'Oh, well,' the Gascon replied, 'it's not the last time I'll ride a slut!'

They had started to walk again. After a few strides Tarpagnan said: 'I don't judge you. You're no different as far as I'm concerned.'

Mirecourt had recovered his offhand poise and the hunger for the ideal that transfigured his face at important moments.

'So we'll be able to carry on making the same revolution and singing the "Marseillaise" together, won't we?' he said.

They strode along in step.

32

Castles in Spain

Alfred Lerouge, known as Three-Nails, couldn't stop thinking about the treasure the grey-eyed man had promised in return for his help and his discretion. He was turning over different possibilities and plans. But although he found the prospect of wealth exhilarating, having never possessed much more than the sky and cold water, he had to admit that such an unexpected upheaval in his life would cause great mental tumult, a terrible agitation of his whole being.

The old ruffian was no longer feeling his age. For the past half-hour he had been walking with the vigour of a youth alongside the cart pulled by Bugeaud and led by Ziquet. From time to time he checked like a nurse on the progress of his most valuable asset: a pallid wreck of a man whom he had to try to keep alive, and hidden from curious eyes. The famous Grondin of the rozzers was stretched on a bed of rags that covered the creaking, rattling planks. He had been wrapped in windings like a dead Egyptian Pharaoh to make the journey more comfortable. On rough ground, Three-Nails held up Grondin's head to prevent it from bouncing on the tailboard.

For reasons of security, the convoy had delayed its departure from behind St Peter's church until the late afternoon: at the five o'clock whistle, they had set off with maximum discretion. The rag merchants had chosen to descend Montmartre by its least populous slopes. They had rounded the cape of the rue de la Borne without incident, endured a hellish passage of cobbles down the diagonal of the rue Saint-Denis, turned off along the chemin de la Procession and taken a long bridlepath leading to the Poissonniers postern gate.

As they walked along Three-Nails was smiling and giving vent to optimistic fantasies. He had started to believe that he was going to have money to spare. The old junk merchant was repeating: 'All this gold just coming to me . . . I'm lucky, that's what it is, lucky! No one can't explain luck! It's like lightning, it just strikes you. An' it often runs in fam'lies, too!'

Ziquet had tried to make him acknowledge his own role in discovering the grey-eyed cyclops in the first place, but Three-Nails brushed the argument irritably aside. Rumbling into his beard, rolling his eyes like the bogeyman and fiddling with his earring, the old seaman resembled a fierce pirate. To silence the ragamuffin's claims once and for all, he hissed nastily in the accents of the Brotherhood of the Coast: 'Go on and wipe your arse, laddie. It's always the big fish what gets the gravy.' Then, as his satellite continued to whine and lay claim to a share of the windfall, the old man had silenced him by saying: 'He'll be told.' This meant: all right, shut up. And Three-Nails had not said another word for at least a kilometre.

Despite Ziquet's efforts to restore harmony, Three-Nails had his nose high in the air, his head in the clouds, and seemed to hear nothing that was said to him. A true lord of the winds. He had moved his hat to the back of his head and was gazing into the distance. As they turned into the very long rue des Boeufs he had started to hum 'En revenant de Suresnes, j'avais mon pompon.' It was a way of thrusting aside all that was contingent, recriminatory, demanding.

'We're still going to have to watch out for the red-pants,' Ziquet said eventually, scattering the old man's dreams and bringing him back to earth with a bump. The two scarecrow figures had arrived in sight of the Poissonniers postern, where a picquet of National Guardsmen, bivouacked at the foot of the walls, was currently preoccupied with a hotly contested game of corkpenny.

Trying not to think of the volley of hot lead that might possibly greet them if freedom were really out of luck, the ragged pair took swift advantage of the clamour aroused by a particularly controversial throw of the cork to hasten their steps towards the guard-post. At a sign from Alfred Lerouge they had broken into a stampeding run towards the gateway. Bugeaud, rising to the occasion, did as he was told without the ear-splitting bray with which he usually protested when made to trot.

What really saved them was not the dashing cavalry-charge tactic decreed by Three-Nails, but the appearance round a bend in the ring-road of a detachment of fifty infantrymen arriving to relieve the little garrison. Greeted by the shouts of men running from the depths of the entrenchments, the newcomers broke ranks in disorder without waiting for their officers to halt and dismiss them with the regulation orders. Swamping their officers and NCOs, the Commune recruits were fraternising eagerly with their more experienced colleagues, already putting on veteran airs. Old friends were embracing and exchanging news of home and family. In a word, at that moment none of the gate sentries gave much of a damn about the traffic.

Donkey, ragpickers and cargo passed behind the backs of the jubilant sentries. The rattle and creak of their cart, their own hobnailed footsteps and the clatter of Bugeaud's hooves were largely drowned by the clamour of that seething mass of men, waving its shakos in the air to salute being relieved, the arrival of the soup and the broaching of a barrel of wine.

Two hundred metres after their victorious charge, already on the kinder footing of beaten earth, Ziquet and the old man congratulated each other affectionately on their fine escapade. Soon after that Bugeaud, spotting a patch of lush grass, swerved without warning down a side path. By common accord, concealed among bushes, the small troupe stopped to recover its breath and take stock of the situation.

The donkey in his wisdom had found a bed of excellent forage. While he grazed, Ziquet lighted a small bent cigar. Three-Nails refastened the wounded man on the planks. Grondin had started whimpering quietly, as if in protest against the jolting he had endured. Reassured by this sign of life and struggle, the old rag-merchant walked to a corner of the glade to relieve himself. He urinated with pleasurable concentration, his mind lost in fantasies involving geese and golden eggs. *Supposing he got too much money?* It wasn't the sort of thing a reasonable rag-and-bone man gave much thought to in the normal course of events. But he wouldn't have minded a clear and unequivocal answer to this crucial question, because ever since it had been going round and round in his head, the palpable world seemed to have dissolved into a sort of fog. As he stared into nothingness, he would not have known the difference between cotton and silk, or a stone rampart and a hawthorn hedge. The potholed path wandering away into the landscape was just a vague blur. Alfred, his old member in his hand, stared blindly into the purity of an evening signalled by a wash of pink, delicate as watercolour.

Ziquet had taken advantage of his boss's reverie to approach the injured man. He had raised the lid of the uninjured eye with his dirty thumb. Bending over the waxen face, the boy had peered into the single grey iris whose gleam seemed to him unvanquishable. As if to dampen its flame, after a moment he had blown a puff of rank cigar-smoke at the forceful pupil, muttering between his teeth: 'You're going to shut your gob, you great humbug, you bleedin' scum of the old regime, or I'll fetch you such a savate-kick in the arse!' Then he had lifted his thumb and allowed the waxen visage to resume its immobility. He had left the big bastard alone with his internal mumbling.

Ziquet felt scurvy.

Three-Nails had been getting on his nerves, so Grondin had been roughly treated. Such was the young rabbit-skin tycoon, a curious mixture of brutality handed down through the ages and youngster dazzled by the ideal. Suddenly, looking toward the line of fortifications, he started thinking about the revolution. He had recently started to feel old enough to bear arms. A cunning idea had just occurred to him. As soon as they had got hold of the fortune, he, Ziquet, would steal the gold and run away. He had resented being under Three-Nails's thumb for a long time now.

He looked up and stubbed out his cigar. The old man had put his lance away in his tattered trousers and was coming towards him.

They set off again. At the entrance to a market garden, as if the time that had been devoted to travelling and looking at the shoots of grass along the road authorised him to resume his delirium where he had left off, Alfred Lerouge had exclaimed anew: 'Fortune smiles on me, sonny! I'm truly lucky!'

He had scratched his chin thoughtfully and returned to the subject of having a fair wind. He was being downright incoherent, cobbling up delusions and empty visions. He shuffled along on his down-at-heel shoes, talking about the great uses to which he was going to put that money. He was going to build houses for rag-and-bone merchants to live in. He would build a whole suburb, called Heliotrope City. The rents would bring in more income than a building in the rue de Rivoli.

Three-Nails was losing his reason. From time to time he farted in the depths of his ragged breeks. He kept repeating that *he* was the lucky man, so it was the youngster who had to keep the donkey going over the uneven cobbles. They stopped. Started again. Alfred Lerouge walked along the bad and stony road, his shoes letting in water, his brain in the land of dreams.

Ziquet was sulking. He retaliated for the old man's selfishness by giving Bugeaud an easy time. In any case the donkey had eaten so much grass that his belly was distended and he approached his task with extreme reluctance. Under these difficult conditions, with one dragging his feet, the second brooding resentfully and the third building castles in Spain, it took the donkey and the two ragpickers a good three hours to reach Cow City.

33

Professor of revolt

In the square outside the Hôtel de Ville, Tarpagnan and Mirecourt passed squads of National Guardsmen patrolling the crowds. Still chatting, they passed through a barricade that had been opened out for the passage of vehicles.

The two old sergeants in charge of it were kippering the whole area with the smoke from their pipes. One had worn away his front teeth by chewing on his pipestem; the other blew smoke through tight lips. Every now and then these Crimea veterans, sanctified by twenty years in the Zouaves, kept the chill at bay with a can of wine. They commanded a detachment whose function was to filter the entry of vehicles. The guards were giving priority to vehicles laden with food; when a florid-faced idler asked in astonishment why the defences were being relaxed in this way the older sergeant, who didn't miss a thing, said scornfully: 'Born yesterday, was you? Use yer head! Got to let them carts through, or the town might go 'ungry!'

'Yus!' the know-all, who was wearing a Bolivar hat, reasoned smugly. 'But it stands to reason if you're building up reserves of groceries, you're afraid there's going to be war.'

'There ain't going to be no war,' the old sweat growled, 'unless the Versailles lot get up our noses. Then we might have to discourage them, like.'

In fact, the place de l'Hôtel-de-Ville still looked as if it was under siege. Twenty battalions were occupying the esplanade, turn and turn about, in a rancid atmosphere of bivouac and cookhouses. Exhausted men were sleeping on straw. Machine-cannon and field guns covered the approaches from adjoining streets.

There was no one to prevent free access to the big entrance hall of the Hôtel de Ville. The monumental 'Mars staircase' of the formal courtyard, so famous for the receptions held there in Haussmann's day and for its meetings between sovereigns, was covered with sleeping troops curled up in their blankets. Every step was scattered with knapsacks, water-bottles and ammunition pouches; rifles and bayonets leaned against the wall or lay abandoned on the floor.

Soldiers without headgear carried sanitary pails to be emptied in the side courtyards serving as equipment dumps and stables. Despatch riders rushed through the smoky atmosphere, canteen-women handed out rations – chunks of bread and bottles of thin wine – while other guardsmen of all ranks were carrying piles of blankets and bundles of overcoats and tunics on their heads.

People called from window to window. Laughed loud and long. Spat on the floor. Surrounded by odours of unwashed humanity, tobacco, leather, mildew and fermenting wine, the two friends crossed a landing where some militiamen were dividing up a consignment of charcuterie with their bayonets, crossed two more offices, smoke-filled but quieter, and reached the Throne-room whose windows gave onto the corner of the place de l'Hôtel-de-Ville and the river embankment.

This state room, with its crystal chandeliers and cartouches bearing fleurs-de-lys on the ceiling, seemed to be an antechamber to the room in which the Central Committee met. The window embrasures were jammed with standing bundles of rifles topped with gold-fringed red flags. The middle of the room was occupied by tables, covered with green cloth, on which various federals were working on files, reading newspapers or simply eating, knife in hand. Along the walls, whose woodwork included panels painted by Coigniet and Muller, had been placed disintegrating pallets leaking rotten straw, on which guardsmen were sleeping or smoking, some dreamy and distracted, others noisy and excited.

'This is where I met Vallès this morning,' Théo murmured in Antoine's ear. 'Apart from him I don't know a soul.'

Antoine nodded, trying to decipher the disorderly scene. He observed with interest a dozen stout young fellows – some still plainly adolescent – who were standing round an NCO with a beery face hidden by whiskers. The soldier was showing them how to strip and reassemble a bolt-action rifle. The recruits were wearing motley uniforms and looked very scruffy. Most had somehow got hold of second-hand kepis with broken peaks that they thought made them look more like old sweats.

'What a shambles,' Antoine murmured. 'What's going to happen to these jokers if they have to fight?'

Evidently the nearest recruit had acute hearing. His ears turned bright red and he spun round angrily. 'Stand back an' mind yer own business, Eustace! No one gives a toss what you think!' bawled the youth, his still-childish face screwed into a resolute scowl. He had a forehead as round as a brandy-cask, periwinkle-blue eyes and the curled lip of a boy who dreams of overtaking his father.

As he focused on Antoine, however, his threateningly narrowed eyes suddenly became round. The civilian he had addressed in that peremptory fashion was the infantry captain he had carried through Montmartre in triumph the day before. His blush of anger was now one of embarrassment. He raised his kepi from which the hastily applied red braid was already coming loose.

'Beg pardon, Captain!' he said hastily. 'What I meant, Captain, was that if we have to fight we'll have anger in our hearts. It'd be a honour to serve under your orders.'

'Guillaume Tironneau!' said Théo, putting a name to the urchin's face. 'What are you doing in the courts of the great?'

'I heard blood was going to run down the gutters. *Babadoum!* So I applied immediately,' Guillaume cried enthusiastically.

'You'll lose your job.'

'Down with bosses and factories! Down with apprenticeship and chilblains! I signed on this morning. For thirty sous, my mother agreed!'

'Done with photography, then?'

'After the war. We'll see about that after the war . . . first I got to learn how to load a rifle . . .' A door opened and a new hubbub arose, the sound of many footsteps. The realistic words died away as the child of the Butte stood on tiptoe to see what was happening. A group of men had emerged from the meeting room into the antechamber. They looked tired.

Exhausted by the previous day's tumultuous interviews with the elected representatives of Paris, barely refreshed by a snack of sausage eaten on the hoof, but condemned to rebuild a whole world by the tempest they had unleashed, the patriots stood in a motionless group under the glittering crystal chandeliers. Their stiff demeanour revealed to everyone their unfamiliarity with the graces of power. As if dazed, they stopped in the middle of the vast floor of polished, geometric parquet, the eyes of all those present fixed on them. Above the general murmur, voices could still be heard through the double doors into the meeting room, which had been left wide open. A stentorian voice cried:

'We're accused of murdering them in cold blood. The truth has to be established!'

'These calumnies must be stopped! The people and the bourgeoisie were together in this revolution,' said another voice.

'Careful, citizen!' cried a third voice. 'If you dissociate yourself from the people, the people could disavow you.'

'That's Ferré!' Guillaume said, thumping Antoine on the shoulder. 'He's from our part of town, I know him!'

As he spoke, a new voice called out somewhere in the room: 'That's it! That's it! Abandon the people! Keep the bourgeoisie! Let the people pull out, and then you'll see whether or not revolutions are made with the bourgeois!'

'Well put!' applauded the youth from rue Lévisse, who continued to air his own views between comments by his elders, who were troubled by this public debate. He had climbed on a bench and was leaning on people's hats and shoulders, prodding his knobbly knees into the back of a stout moon-faced lady who had dressed her three children as miniature Zouaves.

Some of those present were crowding towards the meeting room. Antoine Tarpagnan and Théophile Mirecourt stayed in the doorway. They tried to discern the personalities of these patriots, now suffering from scruples, these delegates disavowed by the *Official Journal* and accused by the right-wing press of murdering generals. It was easy to read their feelings in their faces, for they had no thought of concealment, pretence or official inscrutability. To the naked eye they seemed nervous about violence and bloodshed.

Thus, on the evening of 19th March, before the eyes of the very people who had willed it into existence, emerged 'nascent, babbling, naïve in its popular exaltation, the young Commune – only two days old, a fragile Oracle still in her short dress – a nymph with four red poppies trembling on her bosom, led to the altar of slaughter by bearded men with gentle eyes, with the bearing of saints, whose only ardours were the Jacobin faith, hatred of war and all servitudes, and belief in the holy grail of socialist rationality which was going to save the workers.

But before achieving their ultimate goal, before they would be able to establish a Republic of friends and unrestricted Liberty, what dangers and vicissitudes would the rebels have to face? How many agonised sighs, how many sacrifices, how many deaths would have to be endured?

The militants of the people's battalions had thought about the scale of the task. They knew what inertias would have to be overcome, and that their bitter enemies would make fierce and determined efforts to bring them down. They knew very well that they were going to have to show red credentials 'under the spitting of guns', to lead the people into danger, to drag it into the theatre of great public tragedies and sluice the cobbles with the blood of 'battlers', before they could dream of resting their tired bodies on a bed of fresh grass, and musing over the golden words of Proudhon and Marx under the pink cherry trees of a people's springtime.

Given this black and violent immediate future it is not hard to understand the disorderly state of their minds, distracted as they were by constant barracking and interruptions, by the abdication or withdrawal of the defeatists, the grandstanding speeches of others trying to occupy centre stage – gesticulating buffoons, comic-opera Dantons – whose writings, whose shoddy know-ingness, often got in the way of the innumerable urgent decisions that were needed to transform a good-natured plebeian victory into a triumphant revolution.

Looking out of place in that monumental and luxurious chamber, there they stood – Antoine Arnaud, Babick, Boursier,

Bergeret – conscious of the crushing responsibility that had rested on their shoulders for two days now; there they were – Lisbonne, Lavalette, Nestor Rousseau, Billioray, Piconel, Prudhomme, Avoine and the rest – buttoned into their threadbare uniforms, wrapped in the folds of their overcoats, faces pale, beards hidden behind cab-drivers' mufflers, hobnails skidding on the polished floor, worker and petty-bourgeois, frock-coats and overalls all mixed up together: inventor of cheap goods, quartermaster-sergeant of the Guard, perfumer, unsuccessful actor, forge and factory workers, metalworkers from Puteaux, all doomed to vanish down the trapdoor of history for having sought to reinvent a free and generous world through decrees and posters.

'Peace or war?'

The question came from the back of the room, filled with swirling masses of blue tobacco smoke. A Paris petty-bourgeois called Bonvalet, mayor of the 3rd *arrondissement*, a wine merchant with three chins and a face as red as the cord of his Légion d'honneur, was afraid that these desperadoes wanted to go even further and march on Versailles. 'Peace or war?' he repeated.

'That depends on you,' a committee member answered. 'And now, my well-covered friend, leave us in peace to search our pockets. We have to find a million for our three hundred thousand federals!'

'Well, all we need to do is break open the safes!'

'So they can accuse us of looting?'

All eyes turned to the upright bookbinder Varlin, who had been detailed to manage the finances. That pillar of the workers' resistance associations said not a word. The man who preached the abolition of armies and the arming of all the citizens instead, the man who campaigned for universal secular education at the nation's expense, who demanded a free press and uncensored bookshops, who thought there should be a progressive tax on wealth, who believed all financial institutions should be appropriated and taken over by the nation, the man who said he belonged to the Workers' International, stood silent and erect, his face thoughtful and severe.

'Necessity makes law,' he said at last. 'If the need arises, we'll force the coffers.'

'This time you've all gone crazy!' interrupted a ringing, stormy voice. 'Eugène, you're mad!'

A thickset, nervous character whose high, square forehead framed in bushy black hair conveyed an impression of savage vitality had emerged from the ranks of delegates and crossed the slippery parquet to confront Varlin at close quarters. Théophile dug his elbow into Tarpagnan's ribs and breathed: 'Jules Vallès! We're seeing him at his best!'

The journalist stopped. He turned to the light a tortured white face forged out of rugged bumps and planes. 'This lock-picking is going to involve the Committee just as much as shooting the generals did!' he said, looking round the room for support. A man of medium height with a powerful jaw, wearing a shabby frock-coat. Slightly bloodshot eyes, rich with sombre fire, seemed to subjugate the audience. 'I won't go along with you,' he added to the Committee.

Without waiting for a reaction he spun round and headed for the exit, pursued by imprecations and cheers. Tarpagnan moved smartly out of his way but the citizen, a sheaf of papers in his hand, slipped on the parquet and ended up lurching into Mirecourt's steadying arms.

'Ah! The little photographer!'

'Ah! The great journalist!'

Jules Vallès ran his fingers through his mane, briefly focused brown eyes of different sizes on Tarpagnan and gave him a vague wave. 'How's the miniature photo apparatus coming on?' he asked the photographer.

'Due any day! I'm just waiting for the cabinetmaker to produce the box I've designed. When's le Cri du Peuple coming out?'

'Due right away! Due tomorrow! As you see, I'm heading for the street to write the leader. Ah, I'm late!'

'You're deserting the Committee?' Tarpagnan asked in astonishment.

Vallès gave him a withering look. 'Bad cess to people who hang about in front of platforms!' he said briskly. 'The

Revolution is under way! I'm part of a movement and resolutely of the moment! I'm going back to the paper to tell them what I think. Here, you might as well be at the Smoking Rabbit! The guards are drunk and most of the delegates are just preening themselves. Too many speeches! Everyone wants to lead, everyone's sewing on three silver stripes ... right up to the brilliant General Cremer who came to offer his services as Commander-in-Chief! I'll come back later. I don't agree with any of this ... Lecomte, Thomas, they shouldn't have ... it's a bad start. Their blood makes us into butchers ... now they want to loot France's coffers, they couldn't do better if they wanted to kill the Commune! I'm off to the paper, I say. The words will call for full speed ahead! May the cries of news-vendors awaken dormant awarenesses!'

'Can we come with you?' Mirecourt asked.

'I'm rushing to the brasserie de Strasbourg to write my article ...'

'Take us along. We'll just watch.'

'Yes,' Tarpagnan added, 'we won't say a word. We won't fidget. We'll just adore you in silence!'

'Who is this gentleman?' Vallès asked, opening a very tall opera hat.

'I'm one of your Vingtras cousins,' Antoine said.

'Indeed, monsieur!' exclaimed Jules Vallès, a shadow of perplexity crossing his face. 'Vingtras, what an odd surname! Like chewing pebbles! Ving-tras! Someone's going to have to explain the connection, though, before we can be family!'

34

Cousin Vingtras

'It's perfectly simple,' Antoine said, sitting down next to Jules Vallès on the upholstered banquette of the café in rue Christine. Théophile took a chair facing them. 'We're cousins,' he went on, 'through the grace, and unfailing virility, of your Uncle Joseph, who left the hills of Farreyrolles and your beloved Velay country for love of a girl from the Bacalan quarter of Bordeaux when you were eleven or twelve.'

Vallès's face brightened. 'Célina Garnier!' he exclaimed. 'You're referring to Célina Garnier! That pretty plum! I remember her as if I'd seen her yesterday.' He stopped and tapped on a saucer to attract the attention of a long-necked waiter who was cruising nearby, looking like a bored swan in his big triangular white apron. 'A *vespetro* for three corpses!' Vallès ordered.

'*Vespetro?*' Antoine murmured to Théo. 'What sort of ignoble gut-twister is that?'

'Brandy and sugar with a bit of angelica. Three *double vespetros*, Gustave!' Théo called after the waiter. 'We need a restorative.'

'*Boum*, gentlemen!' the fellow replied, increasing his pace. He flapped his napkin over the shining surface of his silver-plated tray and called loudly: 'Three *vespetros* for knackered gents!'

'Célina Garnier!' Vallès resumed, his nostrils trembling as if in memory of the scent of new-mown hay, 'she was a tall brunette with black eyes that really burned! When I first caught sight of her, on the edge of a sofa, I was struck completely dumb! Because I had fallen madly in love, she'd stolen my heart, and I was still knee-high to a sparrow, a child of ten! You can imagine the damage! At the time, I begged her not to marry my Uncle Joseph. Later I realised that they really loved each other, and they *were* both fifteen years older than I was ... They got married and went off to Bordeaux, and I lost track of them ...'

'I can give you the rest of the story! Your Uncle Joseph settled in Bruges, and fathered five children.'

'Five, eh? Uncle Joseph was certainly capable of it. He was a famous cabinetmaker!'

'All girls!'

'I'll take your word for that. People can exaggerate!'

'All girls except for the eldest,' Tarpagnan corrected. 'So nothing tonight prevents me from disclosing that my sister – Amélie Tarpagnan, native of the commune of Perchède in Gers – married in due and correct form Arthur Vallez – dealer in cattle feed at Houga-d'Armagnac and future musical artiste at the Grand Théâtre under the stage name Vingtras; who was the son of Célina Garnier, Bordelaise, and Joseph Vallez, native of Saussac-l'Eglise, dutiful husband and artisan of repute. That marriage makes me the brother-in-law of Arthur Vingtras, and consequently your cousin!'

'By God, your case is limpid and the story is tempting!' Jules Vallès agreed, falling in happily with this catalogue of connections. 'If I follow the details of your portable pantheon correctly, my Uncle Joseph, born Vallez, had a son called Arthur, who, when approaching middle age, abandoned the worthy trade of distributing silage in the obscure wastes of Gers for the make-up and paste jewellery of the Bordeaux lyrical stage?'

'That's it!'

'Calling himself Vingtras?'

'Absolutely.'

'Vingtras ...' said Vallès, trying to get the name the right way round in his mouth.

'Yes, Vingtras!' Tarpagnan echoed. 'A stage name borrowed from the surname of my late Great-aunt Séraphine, who was without issue.'

'Yes, yes, I see ...' Vallès said, nodding his head in a knowing way. 'That, of course, by virtue of our cousinage in the

Armagnac sense, would make me a little bit Vingtras myself, and tie us to each other.'

'That's it, exactly!'

'*Bloody* Uncle Joseph! This could only have come from him! With his big stick and long ribbons ... he'd have inspired anyone! He was a hell of a carpenter. Best-known plane for miles around ... I loved him more than anything. I respected him for his strength! After having a drink, when I was a kid, he used to take me by the belt, throw me in the air, catch me and throw me up again and give me drinks of wine! He smelt pleasantly of wood and shavings.'

'He died last year. His fingers had become deformed from arthritis. In the end he worked in pine from the Landes ... easier to work, you see, than oak or chestnut.'

Vallès looked away. His brown eyes rested for a moment on the movement in the smoky room; his expression became fixed, a dreamy expression pervaded his face, and it became apparent that his thoughts had travelled far from Paris and from the people around him. There is no other way to put it: Vallès was away, travelling. Judging by his rapt face, he was gazing at a vast sky with the mountains of his beloved Velay on the horizon.

At last he seemed to come back to earth, focused once again on his companions, a nostalgic smile on lips edged with a fine scar.

'This Arthur,' he asked in a gentle goice, 'was he half-witted? Mad? Or did he have talent?'

'Talent to spare!' Antoine assured him. 'Although looking back, I see that his career was strangely blighted.'

'How so? Vocal cords gave out, did they?'

'Certainly not! Our man was a tenor. His pipes were superb and he knew all the roles for his tone and range.'

'So he was all set for a triumph.'

'Apparently. But Arthur didn't sing for five years. He was dragging his anchor, he was beating his wife, but he wasn't singing!'

'How could that happen?'

'He was signed on as understudy to the celebrities visiting Bordeaux, in case some vocal or health problem prevented them from appearing. For five years all the roles in his repertory paraded past his nose ... The visiting artists were all as fit as racehorses! Not a single cold or sore throat! Not a sausage, not even an occasional walk-on part. The Parisians – every last one of them – sang, strutted, bel-cantoed, postured, collected the plaudits and bouquets ... Arthur stayed on his stool.'

'You're not telling me that he *never* had the chance to try his talent in public?'

'He was on the poster on two occasions. The first time, for the second run of *The Grand Duchess of Gerolstein*, he was so drunk they had to lower the curtain.'

'What was left for him to sing the second time? *La Badinguette*?'

'More Offenbach.'

'And very welcome! Everything ends in song. I love comic opera and Offenbach!'

He leaned back on the *banquette*, shot Tarpargnan a collusive glance and stuck his thumbs in the armholes of a waistcoat shiny with wear. 'I've enjoyed your exercise in fiction,' he said, 'and I can't see any major objection to our being cousins ... apart from the fact the Vingtrases don't exist ... I mean they don't exist on my side. Or rather, *they need me to write about them*! ... you'll admit that dents the tracing of our relationship just a trifle?'

'They don't exist *yet*,' Antoine corrected. He was looking into Vallès's eyes. 'But there's nothing to stop you from remembering our meeting some day in the future. There's nothing to stop you inventing a Jacques or Paul or Arthur Vingtras who will stick closer to your skin than an undervest, some paper being whom you will cause to act like a relation of yours, in a novel worthy of your thought!'

Vallès scratched his beard for a moment. '*Vingtras*!' he murmured. '*Vingtras*! Actually it's a name to rattle the pans. *Vingtras*! Sounds good, wouldn't you say?' he asked, glancing towards Théo.

'It does,' the photographer agreed.

'Life's a strange chessboard and we're pushed about like pawns,' Jules Vallès went on. 'Your friend has the gift of second sight and has no idea of the importance of what he's just revealed to me.' He turned towards Antoine a face on which bile, passion and intelligence had left their unequal traces. 'I think about this novel a lot, you know. My dream is to do an intimate portrayal of naïve emotion, of youthful passion, that would be accessible to everyone and have a social meaning ...'

He seemed to wander further into the dream, placing his hand mechanically on the glass of spirits the waiter had just placed in front of him and stopping there as if paralysed. '*Vingtras* with a V, like Vallez ...' he mused in a low voice. 'I ought to mention this novel idea to Hector Malot ...' He swallowed his drink without noticing it and turned back to Tarpagnan. 'So you think I might have a future as a novelist, do you?' he asked drily.

'Laugh if you like,' Antoine said, 'but I'm persuaded that your literary nature will sooner or later take you away from the uncertainties of journalism.'

'Proper writing takes time. Literature is like the Ganges! The spirit must be at peace ... no debts, no revolution ... no confusion in people's minds, no whiff of violence ... I'd say the time isn't right!'

'The times are pretty topsy-turvy,' the former officer agreed. 'But the streets are going to speak ... They're going to give you a literature of primordial emotion, Mr Vallès! It's up to you to get it on its feet.'

'How is it,' the journalist asked suddenly, 'that you have, so to speak, overtaken me in the appreciation of my own plans? Clearly your sensibility is out of the ordinary. Do you write yourself?'

'No. Although it's my most precious ambition, the course of my life until now hasn't allowed me the leisure for it.'

'Cousin Vingtras would like to start as a journalist on *le Cri du Peuple*,' Théophile interjected. Ignoring Antoine's furious glance, he added: 'I'm not just saying that to tease him.'

'I wouldn't have dared to ask that,' Tarpagnan babbled in confusion. 'I was just going to ask you for some advice about my future ...'

35

Staff writer!

Jules Vallès drained his glass in one and looked at Antoine Tarpagnan with a new kind of suspicion. 'Have you got the right stuff for a journalist?'

'I think I have a fairly curious mind. And I've travelled here and there . . .'

'What's your motor?'

'I try to tell the truth about the apparent events of my life.'

'Have you anything to show us? A text with a bit of oomph to it?'

'I've kept my notebooks, but I lost all my possessions two days ago. I don't even know where I'll be sleeping tonight.'

Vallès gestured irritably. 'That's not very important. You can sleep anywhere without your talent disappearing. But at least tell me something about what you've read . . .'

'I like Dickens more than anything else.'

'Very good! Charles Dickens is an excellent influence. On every page he prises out some secret of life as it is really lived!'

'"One feels with him that one is no longer reading but seeing"!' quoted Antoine. 'Isn't that more or less what you wrote in the *Sunday Post* . . . ?'

'You've read my stuff?'

'*Money* . . . *Rebels* . . . and of course *The Streets* . . . I've gutted more or less the whole of Vallès!'

'D'you hear that, Théophile?' The journalist was blushing with gratification. 'I *am* recognised, by a handful of worthy men! The hour of the plain speaker and the irregular artist has come at last!' He turned to Antoine. 'So, my dear Cousin, it's quite simple: we have hardly any money but we need courageous minds to help free Paris. Would you like to join us?'

'With gratitude! How do I start?'

'By fighting! The writers of *le Cri du Peuple* are at their posts. One at the Hôtel de Ville as a member of the Commune; another in a town hall, as mayor; another is commanding a battalion at the porte Maillot outpost. You should join them. You'll write your pieces with a bayonet!'

'And I'd been expecting to retreat behind the rampart of a nice solid library!'

On the table, Vallès's fist closed. 'Reassure me, my dear fellow,' he said in a grumbling tone, 'that you're not one of these refined *littérateurs*, or backward recluses, who have to dress their stuff up in fragments of Cicero or lines of Virgil?'

'Jesus Christ! You haven't got it at all! Until yesterday I did most of my work with the edge of a sword, not old Roman poems!'

'I'm not all that impressed by the sword,' Valles said. 'It has no talent, the sword. I've seen duels won by the most *staggering* cretins. As for classics professors swollen with learning, I've known some of them to dry up on the job when – because! – they had two hours to fill a page with a surge of finished prose!'

'Do I look like a professor of Greek?' Tarpagnan exclaimed loudly, pulling out his shirt to display a few scars. The two men had faced one another angrily. Théophile separated them.

'Surely you're not going to quarrel over a minor difference of attitude?'

The Gascon was so sincerely shocked that doubt could be cast on his writing or fighting abilities that he had fallen into a sulk. After a moment he rose and walked nervously to the cloakroom. Vallès turned to Mirecourt for an explanation of this petulant behaviour.

'Tarpagnan is a straightforward character,' the photographer said, 'and you've offended him – you, whom he holds in such high esteem! Apart from that, I happen to know there's a skirt on his mind at the moment. He should be allowed to go through with it, left alone to plumb the depths of his folly, even if it breaks his heart.'

Vallès wanted details, and Théophile supplied them. The words tumbled from his mouth. He was so eager to defend Antoine that he made the ex-Captain's military career glitter a bit, described the charge at Puebla and other Mexican feats, ending with their extraordinary first meeting on the Polish field.

'I wasn't expecting all that, Captain,' Vallès apologised on Antoine's return. 'It seems you really have chucked your helmet to adopt a worker's cap and overall . . .'

'You could put it like that.'

'Let's turn it another way: you've changed loopholes so radically that now you're firing alongside a party of ragamuffins!'

'Since elevated people like you are encouraging me to, I'll fight for the Commune!'

Vallès turned a rugged, kindly face towards him and said rather hurriedly: 'As soon as you've settled your affairs of the heart, Cousin, come and see me wherever I am. I'll introduce you to Dombrowski. He'll give you a rank befitting your experience and a barricade to defend.'

'Thank you, monsieur.' The stiff reply was reserved, almost cold, and the Gascon was looking into the distance. He feared, perhaps, that through his uncontrolled behaviour he had ruined any chance he might have had of working on *le Cri du Peuple*.

Jules Vallès by contrast was gnawing his lower lip and frowning into his empty glass. His open hand slapped the table. 'Er, and by the way,' he said as if delivering an unimportant aside, 'since you'd come to ask for my advice, it seems to me that . . . er . . . well, here it is: if this woman you're chasing leaves you any time, don't forget to be a journalist.'

Antoine stared at him, his cheeks reddening. Was this another cruel piece of mockery? He was ready to lose his temper again. But Vallès went on: 'I'll expect your first piece on the defence of Paris in two days. But don't let it keep from the front line or from fighting!'

'D'you mean you're taking me on as a writer at *le Cri du Peuple as well*?' cried the incredulous ex-soldier.

'Good God, yes! It's quite a common arrangement: you give your blood, I take your ink. Tell you what,' Vallès went on, 'why don't we drop this *vous* business?' He stood up, pushing the table aside, and drew Antoine into a sort of bear-hug, with vigorous accolades and much thumping on the shoulders. 'You're family, Tarpagnan,' he said several times. 'You're one of us!'

He called for three more double *vespetros*, flung himself down on the *banquette*, rubbed his face vigorously and blared in his brassy voice: 'Aside from all that, I've got an urgent article to do myself. The *Cri*'s readers are expecting a beefy piece in the relaunch issue, and that's what I'm going to give them!' His square hand swept the table clear. 'Gentlemen, give me ten minutes. I'll speak to the paper and be all yours again in no time.'

From the pockets of his frayed suit he took a small dark blue bottle and a pen. He threw off his overcoat, loosened his detachable collar, and without another word to his companions began darkening his leaves.

A quarter of an hour went by. Tarpagnan and Mirecourt, who had moved to the next table, observed with interest the struggle Vallès was waging with slogans, with words. His face showing absolute concentration, his colour pale, he worked very fast, with a ruthless and decisive way of pulling phrases. Sometimes he would strike out half a line. He seemed to operate as it were by surprise, his shirt clinging to his body, his back soaked in sweat, an athlete of his métier, transforming the act of writing into a compressed and violent effort like a forced march.

Vallès's pen seemed to be taking longer than predicted. After a while the two friends divided one of the day's newspapers between them. One was reading the account of a heavyweight musical evening among the Saxon officers stationed at Chelles, the other a report of a collision betweeen a goods train and a convoy of Prussian wounded at Puteaux, when the scratching of the pen suddenly ceased and a furious hand shuffled a number of sheets roughly together. The journalist seemed to remember the presence of the other two. His face was tired.

'Inspiration isn't coming this evening,' he said as he put his things away. 'I'm too excited. Apart from that, I'm *starving*. D'you think we might go and dine, Mirecourt? While our Gascon cock goes elsewhere and drinks love to the dregs?'

Without bothering to say goodbye, but quite unselfconsciously, his detachable collar in his hand, Vallès like an indefatigable urban greyhound rushed outside and vanished at running speed as if grapeshot were chipping the pavement behind him. Mirecourt dropped two francs into the saucer and set off after him, but as he reached the revolving door he turned, signalled to Antoine and came back.

'Look, where you're going, watch yourself,' he said, placing a revolver on his friend's knee. 'The Ourcq is cut-throat country. And don't forget: you're always welcome in the rue de Tournon!'

Tarpagnan sat there for some time, his mouth set in a half-smile. He felt the revolver which he had slipped into his pocket. He ordered an absinthe.

When he had drunk it, his gaze started drifting into the pearly glow of a mirror in which the movements in the room floated trapped in bevelled light. With a simple snap of his fingers, he caused the swan-necked waiter to bring another absinthe. Antoine watched the sugar dissolve in its perforated spoon. The clamour of the café, the smoke, the bite of the alcohol, dazed him slightly and slowed time down. A pale sort of gaiety appeared on his face.

Suddenly, out of some noise or reflection, la Pucci surged into his mind in a spray of laughter. With her yellow dress, its froth of flounces, her shining black hair, she was lovely as a midsummer flower. As he rushed out into the street to look for her, Antoine Tarpagnan wanted to offer her his whole life, all his time, all his being.

Cheeks on fire, hat rammed on his head, Tarpagnan hurried down the wet pavement looking for a cab. Night was falling.

36

The valley of
renunciation

Standing back off the route de la Révolte, Cow City had the outline of an elaborate house of cards: a village of hovels and shacks, inhabited by ragpickers, scrap-metal dealers and receivers of stolen goods. Even from a distance it stank of stables, rotting meat and the suffocating smoke from smouldering piles of rubbish.

Its streets, or rather alleys, were filthy and sinister places peopled by wandering shadows. They zigzagged through a labyrinth of tumbledown cottages and sheds with tarred roofs, cardboard shelters, hovels, huts and hideouts, lock-up stores, places that never closed – last-chance brothels, drinking dens for old whores with mud on their backs – stores for broken glass, old rags, sheds full of shoes, brushes, corks, dovecotes and chicken-houses, stables and pigsties, dives and dwellings of every sort, whose anarchic tumbledown layout provided anonymity and privacy of the highest order for those who lived and worked there. But there was a price for this obscuring of identity: establishing a niche beside those stagnant waters was not a project for the faint-hearted.

The adventurer taking that decision was choosing to break his stick, in other words lose his civil status. In becoming a ragpicker he accepted the inevitability of disappearance into that lunar landscape of swamps and scrapheaps. He was abandoning ordinary civilisation for clandestine lands. He was taking himself out of the records, he could no longer be summoned for questioning. He was identifying himself as one of the capital's outcasts. Henceforth he could survive only by clothing his malodorous despair in a new dream-outline. In the short term he would only be able to deal with that inferno of wreckage and rough planks by absorbing a damaging quantity of raw spirits.

He would go down. He would tumble, he would sink to the bottom of the very lees. His nose would acquire a tubercular look, he would be pierced by stabbing rheumatic pains. Proud of his freedom, hugging his own secrets, he would make a pact with misery, cold and promiscuity. He would sleep on a pile of rags, huddle with others in a room, feet towards the stove, face to the stars: a companion of the great outdoors.

Three-Nails had found his natural place in Cow City long ago. The time of the oceans was so remote now! Overcome by fatigue and emotion, the old sailor had stopped talking. He rammed his hat down on his square head and ruminated in silence.

I'll buy some teeth, he was thinking. Some new boots. Spectacles to see with. And a new map of the China Sea.

Before reaching the settlement, he had hidden the injured man under the load of tunics and old clothes and tied everything down firmly with ropes. Ignoring the quarrelsome drunkards passed on the way, who were threatening to do things like 'scrape yer parchment' or 'unscrew yer bean' in their momentary fits of rage, he pushed at the back of the cart with perfect serenity.

As they drew closer to his own cottage, which he called his *pagoda*, the future owner of The Heliotropes was singing a rude song, in whose chorus Ziquet joined, clearly not feeling too resentful. Donkey and boy could both smell the stable.

37

La Chouette

The old man called his wife the moment he put down his basket. La Chouette was an extremely tall woman with visionary eyes, wearing colourful clothes, with a big apron hanging from her waist. He showed her Grondin, who looked very close to letting go.

'Get busy on him, you big jade! He mustn't kick the bucket. This man's worth a fortune!'

'Pewter, you mean?'

'Banknotes! A bleedin' gold mine. 'E's got to be able to talk.'

La Chouette stared at the recumbent, deathly-pale figure with wide dilated pupils, and bent over him. Whenever she moved the tinkling of amulets sounded from under her layers of coloured rags. Her dry and graceless face peered closely into the sufferer's. 'Your windfall's in a bad way,' she said. She examined him all over, then gave her reserved prognosis.

'This is a man who's been pretty well emptied,' she murmured. 'He's smashed up everywhere, and what's left of his blood is so cold it won't take a rainy spring to send him over the edge.' Before heading for her pharmacopoeia of herbs and potions, solutions and infusions, she turned to the adolescent who was dogging her footsteps and ululated: 'No foolin' about, Ziquet, this is serious! A big basin of hot water. Stoke up the fires, make it warm. Goin' to take big remedies to get *this* geezer's costume mended!'

She assembled infusions of chinchona, different oily juices, powdered cantharides. She threw into a simmering pot a mixture of valerian, sage, extract of couch-grass and ox bile. On the cold earth floor of the cottage she spread a mass of well-dried male bracken leaves, and over this insulating layer placed an old mattress. She got the men to help her move the patient to this bed.

Ignoring the pain she was causing by such rough handling of his broken body, the sorceress started to chafe one limb after another with a mixture of Marseilles vinegar and German spirits. She went round all the man's limbs three times. His eyes turned up. His mouth lay open.

'He ain't movin' at all,' Three-Nails said worriedly. La Chouette went on rubbing stubbornly.

''E'll be back,' she said. ''E'll be back. Like a sauce what's turned.' She laboured over the helpless body. 'Keep rubbin' him. Got 'er take him back from the cold!'

She lay on top of the dying man to drag him back from the ice. She breathed her execrable breath, smelling of cloves and rotten teeth, into his mouth. La Chouette started again, did everything again. She fought against the creeping stasis. Forced it to withdraw, little by little.

'He's helping me!' she crooned from time to time, lifting her face. 'He's helping me!' Presently she smiled in triumphant recognition of her own power. 'I'm going to carry you! I'm going to carry you!' she said to the man. She was prising him out of the very claws of death.

Her hair had come down. She was blotchy red and ugly. She breathed her stinking life into the former notary's mouth. She lavished on him all that she was deprived of herself by poverty, abjection and decrepitude. She gave him strength and attention. The milk hidden beneath her shift. She talked to the dying man like a bride. She made use of her big carcass, her fallow dugs. Cradled him on her lean belly. She had found the mysterious sources of the act of maternity. She compelled him to live. Passed back to him the lily and the rose.

Their battle with the angel lasted two hours. Then Grondin's nose wrinkled slightly; his nostrils flared and a shiver ran up his back. Instead of the scents of ether and disinfectant, he was breathing the damp and foetid atmosphere of the cottage. His left eyelid started blinking rapidly. Gradually his lips parted, his breathing steadied and became regular. Finally his single eye opened. The fixed gaze wandered through the shadowy space lit by two lanterns, the worm-eaten beams of that infamous hovel, and came to rest on la Chouette.

The ugliest woman in the world feverishly grasped the two hands of the returnee. She felt herself lifted by a troubled happiness she had never known before. Without a word she shook her head so that her hair flew out, heavy with human tenderness. For a brief moment a smile illuminated her face with a strong light, unmasking a secret cavern of her being where Three-Nails had never ventured, a hardly seen shore, fine sand, a bleeding heart, a compassion hardly distinguishable from beauty, from grace.

Words came to la Chouette but they got mixed up. Her voice was strangled by emotion. She gazed with gratitude on the man to whom she had given life, and felt a need for violent speech.

'It was me!' she cried. 'It was me who done it! He's alive!'

The ugliness and wrinkles came back into prominence. Padlocked tightly back in place the broad coarse face, the drooping eyelids, the inveterate boozer's fiery, broken-veined nose.

She disappeared. Grondin had reclosed his single eye.

PART 3

TIME OF THE ASSASSINS

38

Near Pantin

Antoine Tarpagnan found a cruising cab on the corner of the boulevard Saint-Michel, the horse walking slowly along and the driver asleep. The Captain jumped onto the four-wheeler's step, reached forward and shook the man by the sleeve. Raising a heavy eyelid, the automaton begged to be left in peace.

The cabbie was an ugly little man with a flattened skull like a frog's, called Gavin McDavis. He spoke French with the slight rolling of the *r*s permitted in one of Scottish descent. He launched into his life story with an expression of distaste, chewing tobacco the while as if his life depended on it.

He claimed direct descent from an Edinburgh banker, related to John Law, who had moved to Paris in about 1715 and ruined his life with paper money. The little man said that his ancestor had had too much faith in Cousin John's talent as a juggler of bills, and had allowed himself to be tempted into wild speculation. He had eventually gone under in the rue Quincampoix bankruptcy and immediately fled to Australia, leaving wife, children and descendants to clear up the mess and suffer the tribulations of a century and a half of Parisian shit.

It was tacitly understood that this pernicious lineage had left McDavis with a lot of financial catching up to do. He thus cheerfully quoted a small fortune to take the passenger to the Glass Eye tavern, situated, he pointed out, in a remote northeastern suburb known for its bad boys, unscrupulous porters, neighbourhood flirts and numerous stabbings.

He insisted that his client take the same risks as himself by sitting on the box beside him. Then, swaddled in a tartan blanket, he talked throughout the journey about his nine children, when not describing in sepulchral tones the monstrous crimes committed by the former butcher Avinain, nicknamed the Terror of Gonesse. A quid of tobacco stuffed deep in his batrachian cheek, the Scot opened wide an enormous mouth carpeted with black juice to entertain his passenger with minute details of the way the knacker had dismembered his victims with a saw and an axe, before chucking the bits down the drain.

Tarpagnan said not a word in reply or encouragement throughout the journey. From time to time a barricade appeared in front of them in the darkness of a crossroads. Some of these were substantial, defended by a field gun, with trenches and embrasures that gave them the appearance of fortifications. Others looked more casual.

On seeing the cab the National Guardsmen would send for their chief; a sleepy sergeant who had been dozing by the stacked weapons would approach the cab and scrutinise its passengers by the light of a torch. Tarpagnan would identify himself and smilingly name Vallès as a reference. Thickening his Vic-Fezensac accent, he played the provincial Gascon on the way, he claimed, to join his young bride.

On three of these occasions the communers let the cab through. It was after all a quiet night, the men were tired and the orders rather vague. The lilting deep-south accent did the rest. McDavis would put the horse in motion, carelessly spitting jets of tobacco juice, and they would wind through a narrow gut between two ramparts of cobblestones, sandbags and old house timbers, past the recumbent bodies of patriots wrapped in blankets or surrounded by empty bottles.

On one occasion, however, in the faubourg du Temple at the intersection with the boulevard de Belleville, the detachment chief jibbed at the pretext given to justify this nocturnal trip. The sergeant was a bossy giant in Garibaldesque uniform, his shirt open to show thick black hair, his hat importantly decorated with a bunch of moth-eaten feathers. He brushed up his enormous moustache and decreed in a gravelly voice that anyone disobeying orders would be shot. Those orders – clear and utterly sensible because he had given them himself – were that no one was leaving Paris without an identifying document or written order duly signed by a member of the Committee or the military authority.

'I'm a journalist with *le Cri du Peuple*,' Tarpagnan argued, 'and I'm doing a story on the capital's system of defences.'

'Watch it, citizen! That's about the worst thing you could have said, that is!' the NCO replied. Clearly he was from a backward tribe. 'If you go on trying to get round the regulations, I'll have you put up against the wall for spying.'

Two dangerous holes brimming with stupidity looked out of the braggart's face. The travellers had no choice but to go another way, taking outlying alleys to the rue Claude-Vellefaux, cutting through by Grange-aux-Belles, joining the Saint-Martin canal and following its bank for a good kilometre. Tarpagnan pretended that the swaying of the vehicle had sent him into a doze, hoping to stem the driver's obsessional chatter. In reality, the incorrigible lover of women of easy virtue was trying to concentrate on the luscious image, the provocative face, the fleeting scent, of Gabriella Pucci.

Unattainable Pucci, venomous Pucci! Who was she, exactly? A cabaret singer who had fallen into the hands of pimps? A kept courtesan? A ruined woman?

There was no folly of the bedchamber into which the Gascon had not hurled himself at one time or another. Tarpagnan meditated on his inability to govern his love life. What was he doing in this cab? Was falling for a tart an act of the same type as, say, taking a box at the opera? What counterfeit ecstasy, what sullied treasure, could he really expect from the oft-bestowed caresses of a woman of easy virtue? What sort of white rabbit did the magician hope to find in his top hat? Why wasn't he sitting with Vallès and Mirecourt at a decently laden dinner table? Why had he left the company of people dedicated to changing the world? What a task! Things like the future of the Commune or the building of a more just and humane society were enterprises on a completely different scale from petty individual lives or trivial loves.

Tarpagnan despised himself for his frivolity. His butterfly behaviour. But that's the way it is with desire: when you reach one of those rollicking passages, passion robs you of strength and common sense. Neither reason nor the light of experience was going to influence the Gascon now.

His malady was quite simply that he was a man. He was inflamed. He was feverish. He was drawn towards a red and glowing space. When he closed his eyes, he recalled the turmoil awakened within him by the valley of fresh skin between Gabriella's heavy breasts. He envisaged the amber buttons of her nipples, imagined the hot sweetness between her thighs, the promise of grains of fire seething in the furnace of her sex.

All is mystery in the depths of the human soul, and Tarpagnan's, that night, harboured all sorts of inadmissible ideas, the kind of stunning marvel that makes saliva taste of heady wine and the brush of fabric feel like a caress on the skin.

The horse jogged along steadily, passed the quai de la Loire, then the quai de la Marne, then the quai de la Sambre, the driver talking endlessly, Antoine drifting gently in his dream of seduction. With the passage of time and distance, marked by the restful clopping of the horse's hooves, his timid fantasy of possessing the lovely Italian's body grew by imperceptible degrees into a violent, irresistible determination.

They crossed the Ourcq canal.

39

The damsels of
the district

The urban landscape had given place to a motionless plain in which factories alternated with the low houses and gardens of workers. From time to time there were signs of a mysterious and remote life: from a small wood might come the sound of coarse song, the screams of drunken women. Or out of the shadows for a moment would appear a pallid, almost childlike face, blue eyes, a sinuous body belonging to some bawd of no-man's-land.

McDavis had urged the horse into a fast trot. Very young girls in party get-up started to appear, running close to the cab and risking injury from its wheels. Their gaze had a curious wild look of hallucination. Hair loose, soaked to the skin, misleading expressions of candour on their pallid faces, they reached out towards the occupants, mewing a variety of strange calls – a throaty laugh, an obscene phrase – before dropping back into nothingness, swallowed by the night, pariahs of the back of beyond, delivered to a life of serving men's lusts, of beggardom, of utter destitution of body and mind.

To exorcise the appalling spectacle of these most wretched of the people's children, McDavis turned his eyes to heaven and appealed for universal deliverance. Teeth clenched and eyes rolling, he tickled the horse with his whip to remind it to keep going. Then he resumed his bloodthirsty monologue, reciting a rosary, an uninterruped litany, of crapulous murders featuring splashes of blood, stabbings with scissors and mutilated breasts and genitals.

With a final expulsion of eye-wateringly evil breath, the

coachman's black mouth ceased its lugubrious croaking. He pulled on the reins and stopped his horse. They were at the corner of a long brick wall, the perimeter of a disused factory. Before the two men, still shaken by their passage through the human swamps, opened a sordid lane, a dark enigmatic road whose wandering course lost itself somewhere in the fields.

'Here you are, *milord*,' the amphibian grated. 'At the other end of this insalubrious rural alley you'll find the Ourcq canal. If you've got that far in one piece, turn to your right and cross the canal. On the other bank you'll see the Glass Eye. They dance all night there. It's far and away the most dangerous place round here . . .'

Tarpagnan thanked the Scotsman with a surly salute. He paid the agreed price, plus a little bit more, and climbed down from the box. He walked forward, patting the horse's nose as he passed. Then, turning resolutely away from this last contact with a known being, he faded into the night.

40

Journey to the gates of night

One hand holding his hat in place, Antoine hopped from one mudbank to another. He found it very difficult to make his way between the many puddles that pocked the limestone causeway along which he was feeling his way. He was passing a zone of fields interspersed with sheds and market gardens that smelt of manure and wet earth. Deep night covered the countryside with its dark blue veil.

Antoine zigzagged along, hoping he would not fall on a nest of footpads waiting for late passers-by. He closed his hand on the comforting butt of the pistol Mirecourt had lent him. He was determined to give an unpleasant surprise to anyone who seemed aggressive. He splashed along briskly. Although he was spattered to the fetlocks with liquid mud, his heart was singing. He had no thoughts that did not concern la Pucci.

Lifting his head and peering forward, he semed at last to see a cutting with wide banks, bordered with bushes that could well have been alders. As he moved into the open he saw outlined against the dark sky, just as McDavis had predicted, the line of poplars that marked the canal.

As soon as he started to walk along the gravel of the towpath the Gascon heard, between two of his own crunching footsteps, a continuous festive noise coming faintly from the opposite bank: a joyous clamour of voices punctuated by notes of music, by a rumble of cadenced dancing footsteps, cries and laughter. He hurried along, peering across the canal, and almost immediately came to a lock gate whose metal walkway enabled him to cross. His steps boomed for a moment over the murky still water below, in which the moon was reflected, while on the other side of a patch of wasteland a channel choked with rushes exuded a slow mist that writhed to the door of the tavern.

When he had crossed the canal he redoubled his pace, drunk with longing to see again, to press in his arms, a woman who had by now become no more than a gracious shadow engendered by his fevered imagination.

41

At the Glass Eye
tavern

Now Antoine could hear waves of sound: excited voices, violins playing a polka, the thumping clamour of unrestrained dancing. Another thirty paces and he found himself close to a thick wall. In the middle of the façade, a double-sided metal sign cobbled up by a rural blacksmith hung from two rusty chains, squeaking lugubriously in the slightest current of air.

The sign consisted of the effigy of a hooligan in a sailor's cap. The figure's mouth was opened extraordinarily wide, and below its frowning eyebrows the artisan had set an immense glass eye: a glass sphere painted to resemble a pale blue iris and illuminated from within by a candle, giving the impression that the demonic figure was staring into the night.

Pushing open a door in the wall, the Captain found himself in an enclosed garden centred on a rockpool. The space around it followed its rectangular shape, and was itself surrounded by leafy alcoves and bowers. From their shadowy depths came indecent murmurs, stifled laughter and the strained panting of fornicating couples.

Tarpagnan peered through a window into the interior of the building, eyes shaded by his hand, forehead pressed against the uneven yellow glass. He saw a big smoky room illuminated by a number of gas-mantles whose shining brass necks curved over the heads of the customers. Chattering girls in magpie-like attitudes leaned with equivocal intimacy against men out for a good time, bold sturdy fellows yelling at the tops of their voices in the hope of being heard above the clamour.

At the sight of this general licence, the display of pointed gallantry, the faces congested with desire, the laughing women and their exposed, disordered bosoms, the Captain experienced a sort of breakdown of his entire being. In the presence of such pagan sexuality, so frank a celebration of unfettered congress, among such painted girls, hooked noses and fat matrons, morality was banished to the dungeons of nothingness. In this place any good feeling would soon founder.

On the day following the seizure of power by the people of Paris, one might have expected the working classes, tired of their shaming, enslaved condition, to redress the balance by occupying their workplaces, or at the very least to regroup massively behind the barricades to fight those who had grown fat in power. But instead of that the most deprived classes, stupefied by long years of misery, could still think of no better way to disown a quarter of a century of resignation than befuddling themselves with drink. Here at the Glass Eye, everyone was soused to the gills.

From the factories and workshops of Pantin, Saint-Ouen, Clichy, had come the lowest and most dissipated of the workers, the unskilled and the navvies, apparently by agreement, to celebrate the mother and father of all binges. These men were the excluded – the outcasts, really – of the respectable proletariat. They were the underpaid, the badly off, the men who did the very worst jobs: breathers of sawdust, iron filings, ammonia, the damaging fumes of paint and molten lead. They had felt a sudden need to let the pot boil over, to visit another state that would transport them out of their ordinary condition, to forget for one night the ragged brats, perpetually hungry as a nest of fledglings, waiting for the wages in some semi-rural slum. To forget for an evening the reproachful-eyed wife whom (on getting home drunk and enraged) they would end by calling bitch, hag, trash, and treating as a punchbag.

In their way, of course, the labourers were showing that they had had it up to here. Their simmering violence, their rabid yearning to live by a new set of signals, had a significance of their own. You only had to listen to the rumble of their conversation, to the recriminations, the assertions coming from the tipsier individuals. Without realising it, they were whetting their violence for the morrow. They were already sketching the folly, the words and gestures of a future desecration. They were carried away in advance.

And to hear them talk, you would not have thought that the revolution had been an exemplary one with irreproachable aims. You would not have been made aware of its dogmatic cohesion, its idealistic component, its historic purpose, the religious exaltation of the great resplendency that the masses would one day enjoy. The International's promises were as if swallowed up by distance. Contradicted by the rude simplicity of live human beings. Flattened by the brute reality of flesh and guts, muscles and calloused hands, gaunt faces, skins ingrained with dirt: things that were far more eloquent than the glib patter of politicians on the slow-burning, enormous, blind, irresistible anger of the wretched of the earth.

Tarpagnan felt shaken by this apocalyptic angle on the condition of the workers. He thought of Vallès, of Varlin. Of Louise Michel. He thought bitterly of Mirecourt, of the people of rue Lévisse, of all those whose faith in a better world was leading them towards a barely discernible dawn. He had a sudden vision of a bloody evening when the mob of misfits and rejects, guided only by its instincts, would surge out of its pit of ignominy and come down with burning eyes and wolf's jaws, armed with picks and iron bars, on the houses of the rich; to throw them down, burn them with paraffin, pillage them from cellar to attic, level them with the ground so that eventually a new ploughing could replace the brambles of the wasteland with new shoots.

Antoine had moved to the door of the ballroom. He hesitated on the threshold like an innocent passer-by trying to get used to the shameless savagery of some place of perdition. He was looking over the 'talent'.

Just in front of him a red-haired beauty, fine-featured, her hair down, her pale skin set off by magnificent green eyes, was feeding a bald middle-aged man out of the palm of her hand. The man had a stringy figure, a disagreeable beast's snout and red-rimmed grey eyes. Enslaved by the charms of the lovely child, who was ordering him about from the height of her eighteen years, he was pretending to be a cat, on all fours in front of her, lapping some sort of brew – doubtless Jaqueson champagne at two francs a bottle – which she was giving him with an indifferent air.

A tall skinny wastrel, a habitual player to the gallery, came up to them between the seats. With theatrical signals and grimaces he was imploring the girl not to give his presence away. Then, drawing the attention of his public with a broad wink, he gave the drinker a mighty kick in the rump.

'Wallop!' chorused the audience happily. With a second kick the joker sent everyone into hysterics. From the gallery over-looking the floor a group of artistes in a froth of tulip-yellow petticoats was jeering at the victim.

'Right up the arse, Charles Henri!' the damsels shrieked. 'Spot on, that was! Right in the haemorrhoids!'

The unfortunate butt had got to his feet. Red in the face, he vigorously rubbed the affected part while trying to discern which of the hilarious faces behind him was the one responsible for his discomfiture.

'Him!' voices shouted. 'No, not him, *him*!' It was like a parrot cage.

'Not that one!'

'The other one! The other one!'

'The blond geezer! The one what's gone!'

Everyone was laughing fit to bust.

The keenest dancers had launched back into a rowdy *chahut*. On the floor, the girls uttered shouts as they flung up their skirts, then stood hands on hips and shook a leg from the knee. Charles Henri, the lanky practical joker, had rejoined his flock. Nose like an anvil, eyebrows outlined, he was the mascot and the leader of a troupe of yellow petticoats. He shook the *chahut*, gave a shout, lifted a leg to the height of his kiss-curled brow, took a running jump and landed with his long legs separated in a splits. A row of girls in boas did the same, one, two, three. Came down, stood up, wriggled, folded.

The contagion spread among the over-excited dancers. Who would dare to do the jumping splits? A waiter, carried away by the craze, tried it without dropping his tray: *boum* on the floor, *boum* in his black waistcoat and big apron, open like an umbrella. People shouted and laughed, rocked back and forth, got up again. Some were too heavy and fell over on their sides. People went down on one knee. Their pals hauled them to their feet. Some got out of it by coyness or flight.

The piano took up the refrain immediately. Violins called dancers back to the floor. They ran through the prance, the scrape, the gallop, the round, the glide. A cascade of petticoats and pomaded manes whirling to the cadence of hobnailed heels on the floorboards.

Amid the thunder of feet, the cat-feeding redhead had risen from her table and, leaving her former *cavaliere servente* to his discomfiture, walked straight up to Tarpagnan. She came to rest before him, holding her breath.

She was small. Her mouth was painted, her imperious little face already spoiled by a touch of vulgarity. The disturbing glow of her big green eyes ruined by a nasty little gleam of cruelty that showed in them from time to time. Through the shining agates she stared wordlessly at the handsome dark man.

'Well, what are you waiting for?' she asked at length, turning the green gaze away. 'Have I got to beg before you'll ask me?'

'Bloody hell, go on an' dance with 'er! She won't eat yer!' said a teasing voice behind the Gascon's back. His eye fell on two troopers in red trousers, their boots muddy, who were looking at him and sniggering stupidly. The ex-officer placed them in a second: riflemen from the 107th, lost soldiers like him.

'Ah, hello chaps,' he said, surprised. 'What are you doing here?'

'Us, citizen?' asked the one wearing a red scarf, whose puffy face still bore a silly smile. 'Heh heh heh! We was brought to this here madhouse by my cousin, Amélie la Gale. A green-eyed red'ead what doesn't just sing canticles. Allow me to interduce yer!'

The damsel looked sidelong through her hair and dropped a little curtsey. The former Captain inclined his head in response. 'Tarpagnan,' he said. 'Antoine to ladies!'

'Shit! Panic!' the hussy cried, taking a step backwards and

fanning herself rapidly with her hand. She seemed genuinely put out. 'Are you *the* Antoine then? The *famous* Antoine? If it's like that, my precious, you're not for me. Private property, you are. With Caf'conc', I behave proper!' Seeing that Antoine had not understood, she added: 'Try not to look stupid! I don't want a quarrel with Gabriella, she's a pal!'

'Where is she?' he asked immediately.

'Over there,' the girl said, waving vaguely. 'She's been going on about you since yesterday! You've caught her eye good an' proper. I'm off to tell her ... discreetly like,' she added in a vulgar accent. She turned on her heel and vanished, hips rolling, into the crowd.

'Cousin Amélie's a famous bed-warmer,' the trooper enthused, 'and the Glass Eye's a famous brothel!'

'Pity it's such a long way from our quarters!' the corporal added. 'Otherwise we'd be tucked away in here every night!'

'That's true,' Tarpagnan murmured. Suddenly he regretted dismissing McDavis and started wondering how to get back. 'How did you get here from Babylon barracks?' he asked the red-faced soldier.

'Riding a bidet,' the soldier boasted, laughing into his hand. 'We borrowed the second lootenant's gelding and when we got 'ere, fresh as a daisy, we stuck 'im in the stable.'

'What's happened to your officers?'

The soldiers looked at each other with silly smiles. 'Officers?' one asked. 'What officers? Are there still officers in these here times?' He peered into Antoine's face with the exaggerated kindness one reserves for the half-witted. 'P'raps the poor gent's not quite up to date on what's been 'appenin', Benoît,' the taller one joked.

'All the generals fell off of their 'orses, m'sieu, see,' the other informed him.

'Do you know Lieutenant Arnaud Desétoiles?' Antoine persisted.

The old sweats stiffened slightly and withdrew half a pace. Their faces showed a mixture of suspicion and fear. 'For a start,' the one who had been a corporal said, 'how d'you know Desétoiles's name?' His tone had changed.

'He's an old comrade in arms. We were officers together. He used to be in the 88th, then was transferred to the 107th last month and seconded to the Luxembourg palace.'

'Desétoiles has gone over to Versailles,' the corporal said gloomily.

'And we gone Communer the minute we got here from Le Havre,' the other soldier sniggered. 'Makes a bit of a fucking difference, that does.'

The corporal was walking round Tarpagnan inspecting him from all angles. 'And you,' he said, 'er . . . what're you up to, got up like that?'

'A bit like you,' Tarpagnan said. 'It seemed to me that honour had changed sides.'

'Good on yer!' the corporal smiled. 'In that case, don't just stand there in the draught!'

'Not half!' the private said. 'If you stay in the entrance too long you can catch a inflammation of the organs!'

Hugely pleased with this sally, the facetious fellow started giggling behind his hand, but the senior man silenced him with a stern look. 'No need for a lot of details,' he said firmly. 'Let's all go into this fine buttock-boutique, seein' as we're 'ere to salute the ladies.'

'Off yer go then, me old bucko, after you!' the idiot enthused, giving his friend a shove in the back to propel him onto the dance floor. Tarpagnan was in the way and the fellow jostled him a bit. 'There's no officers what counts any more, sir,' he said, 'so I can tread on yer feet now!' A second later the two Normans had melted into the throng of spectators.

Antoine followed them into the smoky room, where a surprise awaited him. On his right he discerned a steep staircase, whose flight of treads led to the gallery overlooking the dance floor and the tables around it.

Leaning on the ornate balustrade was Léon Chauvelot, alias Caracole, dressed in a fresh white shirt and maroon waistcoat, cleaning his fingernails with the point of his knife. Flanked by Jaccal the Zouave and Zinc-Neck, two other swell pimps of the same stripe, the knifeman carried himself confidently, sure of the elegant impression his bright red silk cravat would make on the ladies and keeping an eye on his string of breadwinners. The light playing on his scar suggested a supercilious smile, but the twist of his lips and the black look he threw Tarpagnan were anything but good-humoured. From the ironic salute he addressed to the ex-Captain, it was clear that they would soon be seeing each other again.

Tarpagnan went on, his movements slightly more tense than before and Mirecourt's warnings echoing in his brain. He walked along the edge of the floor. Heads back, kepis on sideways to give them a carnival air, the two soldiers of the 107th were shaking a leg with the best, hurtling back and forth with incredible velocity.

Suddenly, a tired farandole of men and women moving between the gallery and the dancers bumped into Tarpagnan and distracted him from his sombre thoughts. A flight of green, red, mauve and yellow skirts, a mishmash of stripes, floral prints, shadow-prints, moirés and fading dyes alternating with twill jackets, full-sleeved shirts and tight trousers, a festoon, a chain of humanity, an avalanche of throats all howling *Zim-laï-la*! and launching into 'La Gaudriole' before vanishing suddenly to lurch around in the darkness of the bowers.

A nervous, shrill-voiced woman in a canary-yellow bodice moved out of his way, sitting down on a *banquette* and placing her arms round the shoulders of a young fellow with a receding forehead and meagre features. Through the resulting space Tarpagnan could see across the floor for a moment.

Standing at the edge of the floor, among other laughing girls, head erect, arms bare, wearing a long white dress that left her waist and slender legs free, la Pucci was smiling at him! Amélie la Gale pushed her gently in the back to bring her back to earth. From an open window a puff of passably clean air cooled Tarpagnan's temples, caressed his face, turned back the lapels of his coat.

One look from the beauty had washed away his fatigue. The journey had been worthwhile.

42

Lovers are always
alone

Gabriella suddenly felt strong again. Her languor disappeared. She felt with serenity the thumping of her heart in the depths of a bosom heaving with desire. She listened to it enthralled. Then distractedly, trembling, she stuck a graceful foot out of the froth of flounces that seethed at her heels, and walked towards him.

Her forehead burning, her mouth dry, devoured by ardent longing, she cut through the close ranks of the dancers and made her way right up to her captain. She stopped for a moment before reaching him to take in his face, his coal-black eyes, his reassuring calm. She sighed and looked longingly at him with her superb sleepy eyes. Her right hand moved as if to caress his cheek, then settled on his wide shoulder. A white leather bag hung from her left wrist.

She was shaking her head unbelievingly. 'Oh God!' she cried, 'I can't believe you're really here! I've been so hoping you'd come . . . If you only knew!' She stepped forward and buried her face in his chest. Her hands caressed the back of his neck, his hair. She growled quietly in his ear and nibbled the lobe with her teeth. Then she leaned back to look at him. Her eyes darting this way and that. 'I didn't realise what you'd become to me. When I didn't hear from you I couldn't bear it! I wouldn't see anyone. Said I'd got a migraine . . . You'll do me some harm in the end!'

As if she was already his mistress. His woman, so to speak. She stared breathless into his eyes. 'Kiss me, for the love of God! On the mouth! The lips!'

Her voracious lips, her hot breath, the taste of her saliva,

propelled him in turn into a place where he was alone with her.
His heart raced. Each was wholly absorbed in the other's touch.
They radiated a sort of glow. Rich in their bodily fusion. Alone
with each other in golden silence in that clamorous hall. Visible
to all.

A big man was approaching, working his way round the room,
checking everything. He was watching the way the dance-floor
girls were working, the vigilant running of the waiters. He was
counting the short times being stacked up by the house harlots.

When his porcine gaze fell on the couple formed by Antoine
and Gabriella, locked in a passionate embrace, he stopped short
and crossed his massive arms in front of his chest. His was not an
expressive face, but his mouth twisted and blood rose to his
cheeks. Somewhere in the colossus's brain there occurred
something roughly equivalent to the collapse of a gallery in a
coal mine. His little eyes stared fixedly as the dust cleared.

His name was Raoul Biloquet, although most people called
him Marbuche. He was a fairground strongman who chose to
drive the point home by dressing in wrestler's shorts. To the
single shoulder-strap that supported this costume he had pinned
a posy of violets, given to him by that same Gabriella Pucci.

Marbuche yawned. He had something to yawn about! In him
it was a sign of anxiety, of bafflement. He yawned to give himself
time to reflect.

His problem was that he was very fond of the Italian. She
always had a kind word for him when he was going into the ring
to face some terrible district champion. The mastodon hoped he
was dreaming. The boss's woman in the arms of a stranger! And
there she was, at it again, pulling the geezer's face down to hers,
opening her mouth ... bloody hell! There was no mistaking
what was going on there. The geezer was kissing her back. He
swung Gabriella into an ecstatic waltz. The mass of dancers,
intimidated by the perfect couple, parted for them and closed
behind their whirling enlaced bodies.

There they were again. La Pucci's eyes were closed, her head
back, her hair flying, her body surrendered. There was no longer
any possible doubt. Something unforeseen had occurred. In fact
an unprecedented catastrophe was taking place before his very

eyes. Marbuche gave an involuntary groan. He felt as vulnerable and defenceless as a child. He stirred his gigantic carcass and left the floor.

He made his way into another room where customers were playing billiards and affectedly smoking pale three-sou cigars. Nut-sellers and mussel-women were plying their trade through the open windows. Outside, everyone seemed to be singing 'I've got a foot that moves'. A new farandole was forming around him in the doorway as he passed; the workers' binge was becoming more frenetic by the minute, but the red-eyed Marbuche headed straight for the bar, scattering all before him.

Like a charging elephant he arrived in front of Victor the Auxerrois who presided jealously over the dispensing of drinks. An old jailbird with a face crisscrossed with scars, he held a glass up to the light and looked through it with his single eye before pouring a dose of absinthe into it. Then he looked at Marbuche who seemed to have collapsed at the bar, legs like jelly, panting. The fairground athlete burst out: 'Victor! Victor! We should warn the Goldsmith. His woman's gone off the rails!'

The one-eyed man looked through the doorway into the smoky distance. On the dance floor, unaware of the rest of the world, Antoine and Gabriella were waltzing, waltzing. The Auxerrois's glass eye glittered nastily, but he just stood there staring with his mouth open. The Crayfish, his legal wife, came from the end of the bar where she had been wiping glasses. An ex-dealer in gaming rooms, she looked over her man's shoulder and gauged the situation instantly. She whistled.

'Just look at that! I always knew Caf'conc' wasn't worth her keep!'

She was already digging her bully in the ribs to jerk him out of his apathy. 'Well, what are you waiting for? Stoke yer boiler, Auxerrois! Get your pins moving while they're still bleeding at it! Go and tell Edmond she's putting horns on 'im. If he don't see it with his own eyes he's never going to believe us.'

Unthinkable! The most widespread reaction among the habitués of the Glass Eye was incredulity. The gangsters and tarts along the banks of the Ourcq knew what laws ruled the lives of the swell mob, the underworld aristocracy. The ruffians fell silent, the girls put their heads together in groups. They watched Caf'conc' dancing with pity in their eyes. For they knew full well that where the traffic in bodies provides income, any affront to honour is taken with deadly seriousness.

'But with Trocard she had a life made of gold and silk!' sighed a girl from the city wall, Rose by name, twenty years old, with flashing eyes.

'She'd got everything here!' agreed Julie, a streetwalker with thin tow-coloured hair.

'If only she was doing it for money,' whispered a third, Céleste of the round back, sullen voice and ferocious overlapping teeth.

'She's doing it for love,' Amélie la Gale said. 'Love, Céleste. You wouldn't understand! It's not something you plan for ... It's more like getting sunstroke in the belly.'

Julie the streetwalker, two seats away, shrugged her shoulders. 'Love? You do it without even turning round. It's nothing but slime and ruined flesh!'

Rose kept her thoughts to herself. She gave a distracted little smile. Put her hands together. With a fretful air, she began cracking her finger joints.

'If you're lucky,' Céleste went on, 'love means havin' your own furniture. A nest with some old geezer. Domesticity, like.'

Amélie brought her face closer to those of her friends, a face with the pallor of childhood privation. She lowered her eyes to the hillocks of her bosom, buried in lace. 'Love's a battle,' she said. 'It's not just soft feather beds. It's what we're all waiting for. What we long for. And when it comes to call, you'd better let it in! I'm expecting it, meself. Expecting it any day!'

Rose looked at her pityingly from the pinnacle of her two extra years of experience. 'Don't hold yer breath, darlin'. Love ain't comin'. You're just a whore.'

These blunt and cold words stopped everyone's mouth. A shadow of melancholy flickered across the girls' faces. Crushed by the sordid balance-sheets of their lives, eyes lowered in separate solitude, they were lost in silent thought.

The ordinary revellers too were casting sidelong looks. No coarse jokes or mockery came from the ranks of the clients. Even the staff were affected. The waiters grouped opened bottles together on the tables. Their movements slowed. Fatigue seemed suddenly to paralyse their limbs. Napkins draped over their forearms, they leaned exhaustedly against the pillars supporting the gallery. From time to time they wiped their trays with a mechanical movement. They mused vaguely on closing time, after which they would have to sweep out the rooms before finding their mattresses in the attic and laying them on the floor for a few hours of log-like slumber.

Little by little, the clamour subsided. Contagion took the edge off the party, then slowly drained it of enjoyment. Even the dancers, couple by couple, left the floor. The room fell silent. All eyes were on the floor, on the red and white whirl of Caf'conc's dress, the handsome air and well-knit shoulders of her partner, the elegant ease with which he swung the young woman round in a blind and continuous vortex. Their charming naïvety, their provocative boldness, bewitched for a moment even the most hardened of the people present in that depraved place.

Endlessly, Antoine and Gabriella spun out their waltz. Even after the music had stopped, they danced on until their rapture like a dying ember cooled little by little and went out. They found themselves standing face to face alone on the dance floor, feeling raw.

'You have no idea,' Caf'conc' murmured, 'how dreadful it is, what we've just done.' She kept her eyes on him, not daring to face the room. She was pale and stiffening with a fear that left her frozen as if after a sleepless night. 'It's ... it's like we'd signed our death warrant!' she added. She turned at the sound of running feet and saw Amélie la Gale, her pretty eyes filled with tears. Caf'conc' threw her arms round her friend, trying not to sob herself. 'Mélie, oh Mélie, my friend, my sister, what shall I do?' she asked.

'Don't ask me. You're done for.'

Above their heads the heavy running tread of Victor the Auxerrois crossed the gallery. Raised voices followed by Marbuche's thunderous gallop on the stairway.

'They're going to tell the Goldsmith,' Gabriella murmured.

'He's in his office,' Amélie told her. 'They're all up there with him, Wire, Handsome Auguste, Saint-Lago, Greaseball. The whole gang. They're planning a job for tonight.'

'It's Handsome Auguste what's leader tonight,' confirmed Rose.

'And I've got to go and decorate the bed of some sweaty bourgeois again while they're busting his safe,' Amélie added.

Céleste, Julie the streetwalker, all the girls from the birdcage, had drifted up and clustered round. Excitement glowed in the women's eyes. All had advice.

'Leave! Leave at once, while they're still surprised.'

'No! That'd *really* be askin', for it. Much better stay. Stay here and plead yer cause!'

'She's right. The heavies'd catch you for sure, and then you'd waltz all right, the bleedin' punch-up waltz!'

'Or vitriol in yer mug. The latest beauty cream!'

Amélie la Gale grasped her friend by the shoulders, stared into her eyes and shook her. Gabriella had fallen silent. Amélie said in an urgent voice: 'Wake up, Caf'conc'! Pull yourself together, eh? Listen, we're all with you. We'll get in the doorway so them from upstairs won't be able to chase you.'

'Come with us, Mélie,' Gabriella whispered in her ear. 'Give up the street life. Your body belongs to you!'

'Too late!' That was Rose's voice.

'Too late,' Amélie said resignedly. 'Caracole and Jaccal the Zouave are outside already. Waiting for you with their big knives!'

Glancing up at the balcony, Tarpagnan saw that Léon Chauvelot and his henchmen had gone. 'No matter,' he said shortly, trying to draw his beloved away with him. 'I know where there's a horse. We can break out.'

'Stop yer yap, you trollops!' cried a rasping voice. 'That's enough gossip! Get yer arses back to work now!'

'Look sharp, sisters!' Céleste was keeping lookout. 'It's the Ogress coming back! Swimming quick!'

The Crayfish's gaunt old profligate's face was indeed advancing through the human surf. The female underboss was taking enormous, rapid strides, jostling girls out of her way and distributing blows as she came – a slap here, a backhander or box on the ear there – bang! and wallop! with a weighty and malevolent hand, clearing a path like magic to the two lovers. In the general seizure that had gripped people's minds, she ground out deadening words. Her tortured, hate-filled gaze fell on la Pucci like a blow, and from her thin lips issued, one by one, toads and serpents of words that hissed in the girls' ears like maledictions and poisoned any dream of getting away from the pimps. She dripped gall, struck fear into their hearts. What she said was:

'Instead of making things harder for yourself, Italian, run and ask the boss for forgiveness. My advice is, abase yourself. Beg your master. Make your sacrifice. Say you'll work long hours on short times to pay your debt. For ever. Till your thing bleeds! And as for you, monsieur, with your pretty mug and your teeth so neatly lined up: I advise you to evaporate. Disappear into the night, in drops so small that you'll be just like the morning dew. To the back end of the Americas, the jungles of the Orinoco, in a cave so dark and wet that no one has ever gone into it. Otherwise you're dead. Cut to ribbons. Tripes like a colander. Castrated. Stuffed. In fact you're a ghost already!'

'You're wrong there. I'm alive and I can prove it,' Tarpagnan said. He brought his pistol out, seized Gabriella by the hand and walked straight forward, forcing the old witch rudely out of the way. The crowd parted in front of them. But before they had taken two steps Edmond the Goldsmith appeared at the front of the gallery.

43

The man with
gold-sheathed fingers

Edmond Joseph Jules Marie Trocard knew how to assume the air
of importance suitable to a parvenu. His face was lengthened by
a forelock that added, he believed, to his physical charm.

When he appeared at the front of the gallery and his voice
clacked above their heads, the hearts of those present missed a
beat. His appearance among them put them in the same state of
fear that Zeus would have called forth had he stepped down from
the pantheon to restore order among mortals. They gazed up at
him with anxious eyes.

At fifty, the boss, owner, gaffer and guv'nor of the Glass Eye
was untouchable. His nickname came from the many gold rings
that sheathed his fingers. The diamond in his left ear-lobe, the
charm-laden watch-chain, the magnetism of a deacon's voice,
contributed to his reputation as an ogre with women, a purveyor
of easy girls and a great manipulator of souls.

He had passed through every level of the underworld in his
time, but his career as a criminal was behind him. No one would
risk trying to encroach on his territory these days. He carried
himself like a well-fed notable. His suits were cut by an English
tailor. His exceptional vitality, implacable eyes and choice of
lieutenants – criminal aristocrats, no-goods from the upper
reaches of the milieu – contributed to the legend of his influence,
which was said to reach into the fringes of the political world.

So when his voice rang out above their heads it carried a
charge of authority for those in the room. The tarts withdrew
into the shadows under the gallery, the pimps regrouped.

Footpads, enforcers, villains and hooligans held themselves in readiness and flexed their muscles, judging that a free-for-all was going to occur. The blue-collar clientele, suddenly sober, withdrew to the sidelines, anxious not to be involved in any incident concerning a private individual's honour.

'My dear friend,' the potentate said to la Pucci, 'this time you've committed an act of great, of *irreparable* foolishness. All the faults are on your side. You just don't slight a man like Trocard in front of his friends. Irreparable,' he repeated.

His face grim and thoughtful, he rested his bishop's hands on the balustrade of the gallery. He was flanked by two of his lieutenants. One smiled on the ladies under the handle of Handsome Auguste; the other, his face scarred by smallpox, answered to the nickname Saint-Lago, his given Christian name being Lazare. A narrow, coughing, vaguely familiar silhouette joined them: Antoine recognised Wire, the little locksmith from rue Lévisse. Their eyes met for a brief moment. Wire pressed his two hands against his chest as if the atmosphere was stifling him, and with streaming eyes gave a prolonged belch. Trocard raised a hand for silence.

When he spoke his words sounded so sincere, his smooth tone so guileless, that a naïve listener would have been taken in by his bland cheerfulness. He waved a disdainful hand at Tarpagnan, who was still holding the weapon to clear a path to the door.

'Control yourself, monsieur,' he said, 'and rest assured that I wouldn't wish the blood of a hero of the Paris Commune to be shed under my roof.' The Goldsmith stopped for a moment and snapped his fingers. As if by magic, ruffians of every description appeared out of the shadows and formed a menacing circle around Tarpagnan. Back to a pillar, he held them at a respectful distance with a slight movement of the pistol. He heard Caf'conc' gasp. She lifted a hand to her heart.

'As you see, my dear Captain,' the boss of all things went on with a modest laugh, 'my knights of the bidet are so many that even if you were to use your firearm you couldn't get the better of them.'

With a comprehensive sweep of his eye Tarpagnan weighed his chances. To tell the truth they didn't look at all good.

Between him and the door, a good half-dozen determined-looking scallywags with knives. To his rear, watching from the edge of the crowd, other scar-faced killers with muscles like cables were hovering in tense, frozen attitudes, eager to get on with it and open him up with their blades. Slowly, he raised the muzzle of the pistol until it pointed at the Goldsmith.

'I could just shoot you and leave it at that,' he said quietly.

'Come, come, sir,' the other answered with an equally successful affectation of calm, 'we must keep our heads! You're certainly no cold-blooded murderer. Why not just lay that shooter down and come up and talk to me?'

'Don't go,' Gabriella breathed instantly. 'He'll have you knifed in the back.'

'Don't move whatever you do, it's a trap,' echoed Amélie la Gale's tiny voice in the same instant.

Trocard stared down at the lovers. 'We're getting nowhere,' he decided. 'My patience is at an end.'

In the bandit's implacable gaze Antoine could read his own fast-approaching doom. His only clear thought was that he had to find very quickly some means of catching this terrifying man off balance. If he had a weakness it would be vanity. Since his escape route was blocked, the Gascon's courageous character told him to fight honestly, on the ground of his passion. Carry the battle to the enemy. Generous blood rose to his head, as before an engagement.

'I love Gabriella Pucci!' he shouted in his rival's face. 'That at least is something you can't do anything about!'

The nabob had not expected the officer on that terrain. 'You shouldn't make assumptions about my own feelings on the matter,' he said evasively. Then, sure that he could mislead the customers at least, he operated a skilful change of tone. Adopting the manner of an affable, straightforward fellow who, despite his visible position, was willing to discuss his troubles in front of his friends, he affected to be greatly hurt. He gave Caf'conc' a wounded smile and asked in a tremulous voice:

'So you don't love me any more, dear heart?'

Gabriella looked up at him, her big eyes brimming with tears. Her voice was frightened and imploring.

'I beg you, Edmond, drop this pitiful charade. In the name of all that was most precious to us, in the name of our shared days together, accept that I love someone else! Give me my freedom! Open the cage!'

'The cage, my sweet? Is that how you refer to the little breeding-coop I gave you in a mansion in the Marais? Shame on you! It's a bit hard to swallow, my little song-shouter! And aren't you being rather quick to forget my generosity, my dear diamond-scoffer? Ask around, Gabriella! You've made a lot of people envious, you know!' He looked at Tarpagnan as if seeking his support. 'A twelve-room trinket-box, monsieur! A little folly in the 18th at thirty thousand francs a year. Not counting furniture and domestics, of course.'

'Take it all back! I don't ask anything for myself!' Caf'conc' cried. Unable to say any more, she burst into tears and flung herself against Tarpagnan. He looked up at Trocard again and called:

'If you're so attached to her, come and get her. Let's fight decently, and if you're the better man you'll take her back!'

'A duel, monsieur? Rather old-fashioned, surely?'

'I'd let you choose the weapons.'

'Who do you think you are, Gascon? You're in my place here and you don't impose anything on me. In any case, it's you who have, or rather don't have, a choice. *You're* going to put your weapon down, and *I'm* going to decide what to do with you.'

Antoine's blood was up, his restraint gone. 'God damn it!' he cried, 'I'm a bad man to know! To hell with you, you fat shark, I'll just rearrange your beak for you!' He had burned his boats, but could already take comfort from the joy of battle. Detaching himself from Caf'conc's clinging embrace, he sprinted across the floor towards the staircase. A knife whistled past his ear and he fired twice to deter the two nearest ruffians, hitting one in the arm. His way clear, he bounded up the stairs four at a time.

Before he was half way up he had been seized by many hands. His jacket and shirt hung from him in ribbons, he had lost his pistol and his torso was striped with half a dozen cuts. In a storm of blows the mob carried him face-down to the stairs and settled down to kick him from all sides, but the Goldsmith called off his dogs with a gesture and addressed Tarpagnan in a tone of insincere commiseration:

'You can see for yourself where all that has got us, Captain.'

The evening had turned into a nightmare. Amélie la Gale was hiding her face in her hands. A little pimp came up to her: an ugly weasel's mug, close-set eyes, a red scarf and high-heeled shoes. He was known as the Ventriloquist. Immediately, rigid as a boot-tree, he slapped her twice and she fell as if poleaxed. 'That's on account,' the rat told her. 'You can have the rest of your spanking later.' He stopped in front of Céleste who had just muttered something between her teeth. His blank gaze settled on her, and a shining blade rested gently against her cheek. 'You're in luck tonight,' he grated, 'but next time I'll mark you.'

Order had been restored at the Glass Eye. People and things had been intimidated by violence into resuming their proper places. Complying with the wishes of the voice from above.

'Bring the girl up here.'

La Pucci, her arms limp, her face waxy as a doll's, was dragged up the stairs by two ruffians and forced to her knees at the Goldsmith's feet. Tears running down her face, she begged him to spare Tarpagnan. He was being held down by two harsh-voiced, black-browed bullies, their knees pressing on his battered kidneys, his face to the stair-treads and one arm held behind his back. Antoine was grimacing with pain. A stripling of eighteen, a young man with white hands and a kiss-curl, a dance-hall Adonis who had only recently joined the gang, came up and placed his muddy shoe on the recumbent man's cheek. He smirked round at the room, showing that he could stand on Tarpagnan's face if he felt like it.

'Don't hurt him, Squirrel, I beg you!' Gabriella cried. She turned back to Trocard and grovelled: 'I'll do anything you want, Edmond! I'll sell my body! I'll pay for my folly!' She held imploring hands out to him.

The Goldsmith did not respond to this statement of submission. He wrapped himself in a mysterious silence. He was enjoying himself. He smiled. He came to the first step of the staircase and picked up the Captain's revolver. He rotated its cylinder and inspected the chambers.

'There are still three bullets left,' he observed in a bland voice, giving his rival a look of capricious irony but keeping his intentions to himself. 'I'm wondering, Mr Tarpagnan, what form of madness you have,' he went on. 'And why this crazy idea so tickled your fancy that you've laid yourself open.'

With the elegance of a big cat he turned his back and made his way to the slumped form of the young woman, whose spine was racked with sobs. He looked down at la Pucci's disordered mane, and with a sort of tenderness parted the locks with the muzzle of the pistol. He exposed the milky furrow in the nape of her neck, dreamily caressed the downy hair there with the blue steel barrel.

'Beauty,' he said bitterly. 'Perfidious beauty! Ephemeral, cheating beauty!'

Gabriella looked up. She turned her tear-stained face towards her tormentor. Her lips parted in an involuntary twitch. An unnatural light bathed her forehead and illuminated her face with a look of pathos.

'It's no use trying your little repertoire of artifices on me,' Trocard told her. 'I don't like the lines of your pretty face any more, my dear child,' he went on in a sudden access of honesty. 'I loved you passionately, you know. My ardent adoration of you was my only respite from the odious activities of the working day. Trapped in the sordid routine of my role as a leading entrepreneur, I had come to depend utterly on your untamed beauty. I listened to your songs and forgot the dark . . . I gazed at your beauty, your immobile languorous eyes that brooded over my restless sleep. All that blood, all those sins . . . loving you was like a rebirth! I loved your laughter, the cruelty of your teeth! When I look at you now, tonight, all I find is duplicity and all I see is a lie. And since you haven't been able to love me, perhaps we can arrange at least for you to hate me instead.'

He turned on his heel and abruptly became an autocrat, an executive above petty emotions. He looked towards his henchmen and settled the whole affair with three snaps of the fingers. His eyes smouldered as he pronounced the filthy words.

'Saint-Lago! Squirrel! Handsome Auguste! Take her to Saint-Denis, Clichy, Saint-Ouen, wherever you like – I don't want to know the place, ever. Put her in full-time short-time, in the darkroom! Let fifty pricks work over her guts every day and fifty poxes seethe in her vitals! Let her faint under the weight of men! And beat her up every day, when dawn comes!'

'Count on me, boss,' Saint-Lago promised, cosily. 'Every morning at first light, I'll lash her arse for her.'

Edmond the Goldsmith felt his shoulders bow under the weight of the cruelty he had engendered. Coolly, without blinking, he watched the three pimps lay hands on the woman he had loved to distraction.

A wild animal's cry made everyone look round. The pimps stopped, with difficulty holding onto the Italian who was struggling desperately to escape. The Gascon, with a supernatural effort, had managed to throw off the men who had been holding him down on the stairs. He stood up. His bruised cheeks were red as if from fever. He took two steps towards Trocard.

'Show us some more of your great courage, Trocard,' he cried, 'and kill me in front of everyone!' His voice was harsh with fury and pain. His body, strained beyond endurance, jerked with nervous tremors. His teeth ground together, the veins on his neck stood out blue and swollen. His tormentor cocked his own pistol to keep the unarmed ex-Captain at bay. The two men measured one another with menacing hate-filled eyes. 'Do the proper thing, then at least we can have done with it!' Tarpagnan shouted again.

'This is nothing to do with you, Captain or whatever you are!' Trocard bawled back. 'Everything's being put back in order,' he added more quietly. 'Miss Pucci, who used to be a friend of mine, has placed herself under my protection once more. She has acceded to my pressing invitation and entrusted me with her life. I'm accepting it from her in my own fashion, and will retain its usufruct for myself. In return I promise her that no harm will be done to you while you are in this building.'

Saint-Lago and Handsome Auguste were again dragging the half-fainting Gabriella Pucci off to her destiny as a human mattress. She turned her head and threw a devastating backward glance at Trocard. 'Edmond,' she begged with a look towards Tarpagnan, 'do you promise me to protect him?'

A bilious smile illuminated the Goldsmith's face. 'If he can run fast and avoid deep water, he's quite a robust fellow and may well survive. You're at liberty, Mr Communard!'

Tarpagnan couldn't believe his ears. 'I'm to go?' he asked in amazement.

'Back the way you came! I've recovered my goods. You just go back to wherever you came from.'

'I'll be in hell.'

'No worse than you deserve.'

44

Knights of the
bidet

'Straight ahead! You can't go wrong.'

They had just let him go. Thrown him back into the pond of night. Four pairs of hands had sent him sprawling in the middle of the yard among the recumbent drunks.

'Straight ahead!' one of the jackals repeated. 'That's the best way to a quick death!'

'The Squirrel's got a point there,' agreed a specimen holding a knife. 'Zinc-Neck goes straight for the heart. He won't make a mess of it!'

'Pers'nally I'd advise you to turn left,' the third man said in a mocking voice.

'Shut it, Cut-in-Two!' the first man said. 'If 'e goes left, he's a dead man! See, Caracole's dead keen on a bit of the old red, m'sieu! When 'e sees blood he goes *mad*, and there's no knowin' what he'll do next.'

Like an exhausted animal, Tarpagnan lay on the cold ground and listened to these charitable souls discussing his future. He could not forget the expression of terror on Gabriella's face as those vile men dragged her away to her destiny as a public dishrag. He doubted that his own future was going to be much more enviable.

He's got no go left in him,' the Squirrel observed.

'Enough of this pissing about. Give him a swig of something to drink, Chair-Leather, and let him get hisself knifed somewhere else.'

The brute addressed as Chair-Leather without further ado

forced the neck of a flask between Tarpagnan's lips. He drank
deeply, thin sourish red wine that vividly recalled the bottom of
the hogshead and carpeted his throat with grit.

'You've had it, you'ave,' the man said as he restoppered his
bottle. 'Might as well get it over with.'

'Yeah,' Cut-in-Two added, 'there's killers waiting for you
everywhere in the darkness of the night. You can't miss 'em!'

'On yer feet and sling yer'ook!'

They stood him on his feet and shoved him towards the
darkness. Their invective grew louder and louder.

'Yer gonna see how much it 'urts to get stung!'

'Hoooo! Haaah! Drra drra! Gee up!'

The pimps started giving hunting cries.

'View halloo!'

'Stretch out!'

'Strong scent!'

'Tooot tooot!'

The Squirrel drew a pistol from his coat-tail and fired in the air
to start the chase. Tarpagnan started forward abruptly and in a
moment had left the circle of partygoers, still staggering around
emptying their bottles before collapsing in some thicket. He
began to run, expecting to find an assassin behind every bush.
The loudmouths went on shouting after him, baying like smelly
animals, placing joke bets:

'Ten francs on the hare!'

'Fifty on Caracole!'

'Everything I've got on Jaccal!'

Tarpagnan ran straight ahead until he was out of their sight.
They wished him a pleasant death, and a moment later the tavern
door closed on their sniggers. The fugitive stopped in the space
outside the wall. From inside he heard muffled cries, and soon
afterwards music struck up anew. The party was picking up
where it had left off, isolated notes and phrases of violin music in
the distance. No one was near. Tarpagnan stood still and tried to
assess the situation while attuning his senses to the night.

His passionate desire to stay alive was accompanied by a
debilitating pessimism. How could he hope to slip past a gang of
murderers on their own territory? He looked about him,

dismissing the stables as unreachable. He wouldn't be able to get hold of the soldiers' horse. He decided his only hope was to get back across the lock gate and onto the towpath.

I can do it, he told himself. To give himself heart he thought of Paris and the country's destiny being played out there. He thought of his new friends. The regiments of patriots being formed. The revolution that awaited him.

I can do it, he repeated. And as if to draw a line under the sad débâcle of his love life, he told himself that if he managed to get back to Paris safe and sound he would go on the barricades, offer his own valueless life to defend threatened fraternity . . . breathe powder smoke with the communers!

His foot touched the stone edge of the rock-pool. He knelt, plunged his hands in the cold water and was splashing his face when a suppressed cough told him that someone was nearby. He stood up. He heard feet brushing through the grass and felt the same impotent resolve as a cornered fox, unarmed compared to the hounds but determined to defend his life to the last.

A shadow came towards him. A familiar voice hailed him quietly from the darkness:

'Psst! Hey, don't panic! It's me, my son!'

The Gascon relaxed and smiled with relief. He had recognised the inimitable voice of Wire the locksmith. 'Rue Lévisse!' he murmured. 'Advance and be recognised! I was on the point of taking your head off.'

Emile Roussel covered the last few paces. 'Keep your hewing activities for someone else, citizen Captain!' he rasped. Then he lowered his voice conspiratorially. 'Whatever you do stay away from the coachyard,' he murmured. 'That's where most of the pack are waiting for you . . . you'd be best off going along the canal. You take your chances in the mist, and I'll get the attention of the ones who're roaming about, and try to lead them back here . . .'

Without further ado, the little lunger cut loose with cries and shouts that filled Tarpagnan with alarm: he made strangled noises, called for help, squawked with all the power of his gypsum-lined windpipe. He had seen the quarry, he bawled, near the arbours.

'Have you lost your mind?' Antoine hissed.

'Not me, mate, believe me! I've got more than one pin-key in my toolbag.'

He dropped to all fours in front of Tarpagnan. 'Give me one in the nose, Captain!' he ordered. 'Make it bleed! Go on, jump to it! A big swipe on the smeller! Quick! Jesus Christ, what are you waiting for? I've got to be bleeding! Every second counts!'

Tarpagnan was still incredulous. 'Why are you taking this risk?'

'To give you a more honourable idea of mankind,' replied the specialist in breaking and entering. 'In memory of 18th March, if you must know.' He screwed his mouth up under his nose in a characteristic expression and added: 'Because you'll be a lot more use on a barricade than at the bottom of a well. Because you've given me the chance to stop being a criminal and join Louise Michel.' Then, as Tarpagnan still hesitated to hit him, he added hurriedly: 'Get a move on. They aren't going to take centuries to get here. I can hear running feet! Leave quick, so I can say you've done me over and had it away on yer toes into the greenery . . .'

The upper of a solid shoe smashed into the little consumptive's nose. The mucous membrane ruptured, the upper lip split, and a torrent of blood washed around the victim's gums.

'Woooh! *Fuckin'* 'ell! Shit!' groaned the locksmith in all sincerity. 'How'm I going to eat? I've lost two front teeth at least! Thanks a bleedin', bunch, Captain!'

Tarpagnan rushed away into the night, headed for the fence and cleared it in one bound. Behind him he could hear Emile still calling for help and coughing, deep cavernous coughs that sounded as if he was choking.

The Gascon tried to see where he was going, but it was like looking through the bottom of a bottle. He ran forward, stopped, listened, ran forward again, listened to the gloomy silence. He had picked up an iron-shod stick belonging to an unconscious worker, and possession of this improvised weapon made him regret leaving the grey-eyed notary's *makhila* behind in Mirecourt's flat.

Hitzá Hitz!

The fleeting image of the dead Jeanne – tortured, eviscerated, humiliated Jeanne – suddenly crossed his mind. His feverish state brought other images: his disordered imagination gave him the vision of a motionless cohort, an endless file of bare-legged men, men with bad teeth, with sagging bellies, waiting for their six-sou ration of pleasure in Gabriella Pucci's bed. Jeanne dead and Gabriella a whore: two women's bodies, two terrible soilings. He was seized by a violent feeling of disgust. His stomach twisted with nausea, he stopped, salt saliva ran in his mouth and he vomited painfully in the grass, froth and bile.

Leaning forward with his hands on his knees, retching and gasping for breath, he saw the grey eyes of Charles Bassicoussé, heard the curse pronounced behind his back, the same blasphemer's voice condemning him to drown in sewage and filth whenever he approached a state of pure happiness. The same old familiar malediction.

He ran on shakily. As he drew closer to the Ourcq the mist rose around him. Insensible to the pain in his bruised legs as he charged through boggy places, unaware of the blood pounding in his temples, legs pumping like connecting rods, he held his arms before him to brush aside the ghostly forms of bushes and brambles. Hands cut and grazed, clothes tattered, he ran blindly, like one possessed, terribly aware that the first dagger-stroke might come from behind. He ran, panting, out of breath, miraculously missing obstacles, until he heard gravel and felt the proximity of black water. The canal! He mustn't miss the walkway over the lock gate. He peered into a darkness made of milky stuff. His hair was wet with it and with sweat. The mist was thick here. He stopped.

Where were they? When were the murderers going to materialise out of the curtain of obscurity? He heard nothing. In his anxiety he was again prey to the sacrilegious images, the appalling, exaggerated, telescoped fantasy that his guilt and agony generated, of that endless sordid unwashed procession of ugly diseased men, one after another, possessing briefly and brutally the admirable, the graceful body of la Pucci – drooling idiots, filthy drunks, smelly old fools with the ring of a chamber-pot imprinted on their pallid buttocks – six sous a time, full-time short-time, a queue of fifty others with big red hands, filthy nails, waiting their turn. Drooling. Covering her with sweat and slime, slowly obscuring, taking away, bending and corrupting, that vivid beauty for ever ... God!

Tarpagnan gave a deep involuntary groan. I'll kill the bastards, he thought. I'll kill them all. I don't fear death, that's for sure. The way things look just now it would be a relief. His feet crunched on the gravel of the towpath. On a mad impulse he shouted into the mist: 'Here I am! Come and get me!'

They were waiting for him near the lock. As he approached he glimpsed three blurred outlines, the faint glow of a lantern. Three black shadows shading into grey in the hanging mist, fading, unreal, as it were dreamed.

There they were again, hardly ten metres away. They were searching, rooting around, beating the wet grass.

'I heard his voice, I tell you,' one protested.

'Just find the mug, and let me knock him off,' growled another.

The shadows disappeared again. A damp silence. Then Antoine heard a rustling in the reeds, getting closer to him. He stood still and waited. A moment later they were on top of him, well spread out. Good! Action had always suited Tarpagnan. He walked straight at them, without hesitating. Remembering the Squirrel's remark, he headed for Zinc-Neck first, the one who would be most willing with his blade. Get him out of the way at least.

The hero of Puebla charged with a furious yell. He kept his eyes on the hand holding the knife, a big blue-steel chopper sharpened at the point for stabbing. The men were disconcerted by his rush. Without slowing he feinted a swing at Zinc-Neck's head and smashed the stick down with all the strength he could muster on the knife arm. It struck the wrist, breaking the bones, and the man fled the field with a brief cry of pain, dropping his big blade.

The club-wielding warrior knew that the next man would now be coming at him from behind to knife him in the side. He spun instantly, whipping the stick in a terrible whistling half-circle that caught Jaccal across the temple and felled him like an ox.

Tarpagnan turned to face Caracole.

The carrot-haired man with the leering scar was compact and controlled. He worked his way through small arcs of a circle with a knife-fighter's dancing step. Agile on bent legs. Ready to snake forward and sting, or to leap back at any moment.

From time to time he stood up, pretending to drop his guard, trying to tempt the adversary into advancing. Or with a simple bend of the knee the ugly horse-faced villain would make a brief, terrifyingly quick advance. The razor-sharp leather-worker's blade would flick out, whistle past Tarpagnan's face and be gone again as the knifeman stepped back.

The death-dance went on in this way for a long minute. The two men were sizing each other up. Léon Chauvelot came and went ceaselessly, withdrawing only to make a snake-like return. Like a wild animal who liked the darkness of caverns. From time to time he let fall a phrase or fragment designed to distract the adversary.

'Gravy soon, Cap'n Three-braids! After this little polka we'll move on to something a bit more serious...'

He came forward, two skips. He seemed to have relaxed, but took another step forward, very quickly. The point of the long sinuous knife described a hypnotic, complex arabesque through the air and cut Tarpagnan's forearm. His backward leap came too late.

'*Beeootifool*!' cried the former convict, his English returning at the sight of vermilion blood, '*red and beautiful*'. With his free hand he stroked his sparse red side-whiskers. He stepped back, head on one side like an artist, and judiciously examined the effect. An eager expression came into his face.

'Glittering blood,' he said. 'Ah! I want more of that. *Blood*! Red blood!'

With a sure, precise movement he shot the knife into his other hand and lazily reached out again. This time the blade avoided the stick, which swiped at nothing, and cut the Captain's shoulder before withdrawing.

'*Blood again*!' the villain cried. He was savouring his revenge on the man who had humiliated him. He meant to kill him by slow degrees, a little at a time. He circled his prey. Without warning he darted in again, leaving a long cut down Tarpagnan's ribs. Again the Captain's reflexive leap came just too late. The redhead stared at him with dreaming eyes, looked at the thread of blood running down his arm. He adjusted the sailor's cap which had fallen low over his eyes, and giggled. 'I told you I was yer worst nightmare, didn't I? Now here I am, carving you up.'

Throwing caution to the winds, he came in again. But this time Antoine managed to parry the blow, and delivered a counter-swipe that caught the hooligan in the Adam's apple. Now it was Caracole's turn to withdraw into the darkness.

'That wasn't very clever,' his voice said after a few seconds. 'Gettin' a bit ahead of meself, like. It's the sight of blood done that ... it won't happen again.' He sidled back cautiously. Sinuous. Lethal. 'Don't you worry, son. I'm going to cut you to ribbons, you'll see.' He feinted once, twice, went under Tarpagnan's arm like an eel and was gone, leaving another long stinging gash across the ribs. The ex-Captain was beginning to feel faint from tension and loss of blood. This wasn't his sort of combat, he realised, this nibbling at a fellow with a carving knife. At least with a sabre you could see it coming. It occurred to him that he might be about to be killed, but he felt no alarm. What he felt was helpless, undefended.

'Knight of the bidet ... remember that?' Caracole asked, circling slowly, with flushed face and shining eyes. He lunged again, twice, each time catching Tarpagnan off-guard, grunting with satisfaction.

'Huh! Huh! See that? The taste of steel! Just a touch, like this ... Huh! *What do you say?* It's not a garlic-grater, admit it! 'Ere's another for yer ... not yet ... Huh! Huh! *Not bad at all, what do you say?* Two or three more little razor-strokes and you're going down, my glorious soldier!'

The killer's patter stopped abruptly. A look of astonishment crossed his face and his mouth opened, but no word came out of it or ever would again. A huge leaden fist had come down out of the darkness and delivered a piledriver-like vertical blow to the top of Caracole's skull. Eyes blank, legs wobbling, the killer took two short steps to one side. Who knows what he was seeing: perhaps the gates of heaven or some other place; perhaps old friends or enemies long dead and desiccated. His head was at a funny angle. Eyes staring, he fell on his face at Tarpagnan's feet. Behind him a mountainous silhouette had loomed out of the fog.

Tarpagnan's mouth fell open in amazement, for the mountain was Raoul Biloquet: low of forehead, small of eye, still dressed in nothing but wrestler's shorts, with the posy of violets still pinned to their strap. He looked at the officer without speaking, massaging a bruised fist the size of a ham.

'Thank you,' Antoine murmured at last, 'for saving me from certain death.' Biloquet made no answer. He stared at the Gascon with a stunned air, while rubbing with a gigantic paw the sides of his head, as if to restore the circulation there. He did not seem interested in what he had just done, or even aware of Caracole's resulting death. He was remembering something else from the recent past, something that made him sad and rather resentful. He shook a scolding forefinger at Tarpagnan and grated between his teeth:

'All the same, I damn near unscrewed your nut when I seen you kissing Miss Caf'conc' like that! Your conduct wasn't proper, not at all! That's what made me raise the alarm, like a bleeding donkey. Ah! If I'd'a known the consequences ... the boss doing his nut like that, and Handsome Auguste dragging Mademoiselle off to the clap brothels! You might think I wouldn't have forgotten to think, but that's what's happened!' He whacked himself on the top of the skull and wrung his enormous hands, moaning:

'Ah, Marbuche! Marbuche! Miss Caf'conc' always used to tell you that you should stop and think! She used to say Marbuche, log-head!' He looked up at Tarpagnan. 'I'm telling you word for word what she used to say, m'sieu. She used to say that, and a lot of other things I can't recall for the moment ...' He knitted his brows, but the generous ideas he wanted to utter remained imprisoned in the subsoil of his damaged mind. He fell silent. After a tussle with his exasperatingly slow understanding, he lowered his expressionless eyes to Caracole's corpse and gave it a shove with his foot. Its presence was clearly an embarrassment – a reproach even – but he felt no remorse. He tried to explain his murderous act:

'Miss Caf'conc's always been good to Marbuche. She knew how to speak to him gently about happiness. It's a real art, you know, monsieur, to teach a person about happiness what's never had none . . .'

The colossus had had little enough, indeed. A Russian lion-tamer for a father, a drunkard, crippled by his animals; a foster-mother, a Manchurian contortionist, who died on stage; years of drudgery in a circus. A lot of whacks on the head. He had had to earn his bread while coping with the meanness of some people, the brutality of others. Of the creatures he knew Marbuche made the polar bear, that refugee from the far north, his model. Like him, the bear was strong; like him, it bent bars and flattened men; and like him, too, the bear broke its teeth on stale bread.

The giant stroked his posy of violets. An idea was trying to form in the depths of his mind, very slowly. It disppeared before coming to the surface and the fairground athlete, unable to retrieve it, adjusted the diagonal strap of his flesh-coloured costume.

'Miss Caf'conc' used to give him flowers,' he resumed. 'She used to stroke Marbuche's head. She made his headaches better by breathing on his forehead. She used to sing 'A Kiss among the Corn' to him. Sometimes she let him fall asleep with his cheek on her lap. He liked that.' The strongman smiled suddenly, as if the fog had parted before his porcelain eyes to disclose a sunlit footpath.

'You know, monsieur, Miss Gabrielle can stand up to forced lechery, even to venereal sickness! She's got the strength for it! She'll send her body to sleep. Everything bad will just pass her by! She's a strong and clever lady, she is. A brave and beautiful person. We got to go and look for her, everywhere! We got to rescue her!'

With the straightforward movements of a park-keeper tidying up, the colossus lifted Caracole's limp body onto his shoulder, walked stolidly to the canal and tossed the cadaver into the dark water. He came back wiping his hands and stopped in front of Tarpagnan, high and wide as a Manchurian hill. A tear ran down his face.

'Marbuche loved Miss Caf'conc' like a child,' he said. He

thought concentratedly for a while and added: 'The rustle of her dress, monsieur, made a child of Marbuche.'

Then the strongman, without any further explanation, enclosed Antoine's hand in his enormous paw, and indicated in rudimentary but not unfriendly fashion that he should walk at his side. 'Come, Tarpagnan,' he said, dragging the Gascon along as easily as a small child, 'come along, before I forget important things!'

'What's got into you? Where are you going?'

'We're leaving for Paris. We walk straight ahead. We walk till daylight. We're going to my wagon.'

'Where's that?'

'Monmartre fair. A good place to think.'

'Why have I got to come with you?'

'Because Marbuche has decided you're not going to leave him. Because Miss Pucci used to say *we've always got love!*' He looked round at his helpless companion with pathetic earnestness. 'Because Marbuche and Tarpagnan are rich with the same love! Because now they're one and the same person! Because together they're going to find her who sings and who loves us!'

'How are we going to get there?'

'You'll do the thinking. I'll do the rough stuff.'

'Paris is crammed with brothels!'

'We'll look in all of them.'

'Let go of my hand, at least!'

'Cock! You'll run away! Marbuche'll've lost *the person* who's s'posed to do the thinking.'

'Stop squeezing my fingers, anyway!'

But the behemoth crushed them all the harder. He was possessed by the unbearable fear that he might lose his new friend. His new brain. And then he would again be a child alone. 'Then Marbuche might get a headache,' he explained aloud, standing tall and striding forward.

The bullet-headed colossus took long strides. As they walked, he turned just once to Tarpagnan and with infinite gentleness, an almost painful considerateness, said between his teeth:

'I know you're an excellent man, Tarpagnan. So this is the last thing I'll ask of you, and the most sacred . . . the most crucial: *don't force me to do you any harm.*'

PART 4

CRAZY DAWN

45

Delirium, secrets
and storms

A string of dull days had passed since Horace Grondin's arrival
at Three-Nails's pagoda, without its inhabitants having the least
awareness of the alternation of sunny but windy afternoons and
cold and marshy nights punctuated by the croaking of frogs.

Apart from the stove, consuming peat and wood with brutal
greed, the Chinese-style cottage had become as silent as a tomb.
The stove roared constantly in the middle of the shack, giving
out a warmth quickly dispersed by the draught. Its heat hardly
reached the dim, dirt-encrusted windows, but succeeded in
reviving a stifling odour of the mildew that had got into
everything.

La Chouette had lost count of the days since the beginning of
the nightmare, of which every single minute was devoted to the
struggle to keep the stranger alive. But in all that time she had
not once deserted her post, and her whole existence had taken on
the character of a wordless celebration. The slightest gasp, the
smallest murmur from her patient, any sign of discomfort at all,
would make her tremble. A mere blink of his grey eye from the
depths of the shadows constituted a call that brought her
running.

She lavished care on him with the devotion of an emaciated
but faithful animal. Under the touch of his fixed and singular
gaze, she renewed his dressings. She massaged him with fresh
unguents, brewed fever-reducing infusions. To soothe his pain,
she parted his lips with gentleness and skill to coax between his
clenched teeth a little tincture of morphine, stolen from Three-

Nails who used the medicine occasionally when he 'wanted to go to China'.

Although no word was ever uttered, there grew between Grondin and the ugly healer a curious friendship tinged with mystery. La Chouette, all of whose feelings resembled love, but who knew that in this intimate domain she was disqualified by her gargoyle-like hideousness, profited secretly from the sharp, ideal, carnal well-being that the proximity of her cold-skinned protégé brought her, and allowed herself – will I be believed? – guilty pleasures, obscure lapses.

She took every risk whenever she knew she was unobserved. She was ready to attempt the boldest moves, the most inexplicable acts; to transgress rules of behaviour, break her oath of fidelity to her man, just to experience for a brief moment the strange and guilty turmoil of the spirit, the irresistible madness, that ran through her every time she approached the big, muscular, helpless body of the grey-eyed man. At the dark hour when the tiny patterings and rustlings of small creatures on the tarred fabric, and the vague humours rising from damp earth, immersed the shack in the dead water of oblivion, at the turning hour when beings are alone and their awareness fogged, she liked to venture to the bedside of the tall invalid, asleep on his couch.

Unmoving, she would listen to the beating of her heart brimming with tenderness, listen to the haunting wind that precedes the dawn, and gently lift the coverlet. She would slide her forearm under the piece of cretonne that served as a sheet and place her hand between the injured man's thighs. This ceremony for herself alone was celebrated without vice or perfidy; she simply allowed her inert palm to rest for long moments in the hollow. La Chouette's mind would drift, as if wrapped in a thick cloud.

The invalid's eye would suddenly open and its gaze rest on her. Then would begin a frightful, silent struggle. The howling of wolves would pierce the lost thoughts of the immobile woman. Her hand would not move. It was waiting. A dirty hand fissured with a thousand cracks. A hand which would never have its moment of softness and romance. The hand of a slave, a pauper, an outcast. A hand meant for cold water, for filth, for junk.

Every time, the mystery would run its full course: the grey-eyed man would say nothing. His twisted mask of pain would gradually relax. His eyelid would close again. Abandoned on the threshold of sleep. La Chouette would remain, throbbing with her desire to love and horrified by the violence of the words that rose within her.

Illuminated by the glow from the stove, her flat face took on the colour of the flames. Standing in her colourful rags, stunned by what was happening to her and her inability to understand it, she looked down on the flaccid sex of the man she had at her mercy. She knew every inch of his shipwrecked body: did she not bathe him as one would a baby? In her impassioned determination to serve the invalid she would move her hand with a calm and deep tenderness, happy to stroke his forehead, to hold her fingers out to feel the touch of his breath.

One morning at about six, after the frogs had fallen silent, she closed her hand on the man's sex.

46

Shipwreck dreams and field-stripping bolt assembly

Alfred Lerouge usually kept out of the way during those obscure and instinctive days. He hoped earnestly that Grondin would not die, that he would not dance the stiff's jig before disclosing the whereabouts of his gold. He expected la Chouette to prevent his departure to a better world, and hoped that the tall harpy's healing skills would set him on his feet.

In the expectation of better things to come, all commercial activities – ragpicking and the collection, evaluation and resale of junk – were suspended, and all domestic activity was pivoted on the 'banker's' well-being. Unable to assemble two coherent ideas, to take any interest in the outside world, even to meet his friends at the Ragpicker's Casserole, the old scarecrow stayed slumped at the rickety table that encumbered the entrance to the main room. He sat there boozing, smoking and farting, sleeping too, head resting on folded arms, intelligence scattered by the fumes of alcohol.

When laid low by the hooch he would become a sailor again. He would go back to sea, sign on for a bit of privateering. He would invariably wander back into dreams of piracy, of surprise boardings, of leaks causing a list to port. He launched longboats; his brig ran aground on hidden reefs; he cruised off unknown islands.

In his Caribbean haunts, deep in sandy palm-fringed coves, he handled doubloons and pearls as commonly as you would wash your hands, tippled old rum like nobody's business, cavorted through the night with wenches in loincloths.

A few feet away, Grondin struggled grimly against the circle of suffering. From time to time he would seek a more comfortable position on his pallet. The smelly mattress under his bruised and wounded body accommodated the shape of his back well enough to soothe some of the pain of his broken ribs.

In lucid moments he estimated that it would take a good month to restore the use of all his faculties. His worst injury was in the side of the abdomen, where he had been stabbed. But the woman looking after him said that he had been very lucky: the blade had been deflected by the pelvic bone and missed his liver. There were three more superficial wounds: one in the flesh of his left shoulder, one in the chest and one in the forearm he had used as a shield when the communers set on him.

When he was sure that he was alone, that la Chouette was busy with her routine chores, the invalid opened wide his single eye. He moved his head about inspecting his tiny environment. Of his immediate surroundings he could distinguish only a plank of wood on which a line of cigar butts and cigarette-ends had been placed to dry by the master of the house. The corner opposite seemed to be devoted to the very rare ablutions of the occupants of this pigsty reeking of spices and camphor. A glass served as a soapdish, an old tin as a dressing table, and there was a coloured print of a three-master going down in a storm. A water-butt slumbered in an alcove.

Nearby stood the statue of a woman, an exotic casting, the central piece in Three-Nails's museum: a bare-breasted Balinese dancer, with long extended eyelids like rainbow trout and greenish cheeks with a flaky patina, frozen in the sacred attitude of some striking *mudra*.

But if he tried to move any further to explore more of his surroundings, the injured man often ended by grimacing with sudden pain. Then it would take him a quarter of an hour to restore the precarious balance of his bony armature and find a more comfortable position on the greasy mattress. To reduce the stabbing pains that ran through his chest at every breath and deliver his body from piercing neuralgic sensations, the former convict concentrated his mental forces. In the penal colony, chained every night to a timber partition, he had learned to ignore the sufferings of a body ravaged by forced labour and malaria by withdrawing into a dark corner of his mind where the steady passion for vengeance occluded the mere torments of the human envelope. Grondin's experience of this game had left him with the ingrained habit of referring to his permanent obsessions when he wanted to ignore physical pain. He only had to think of Tarpagnan to forget all about his fleshly sufferings. He only had to imagine the man going about town, free in his movements, wandering at will through streets crowded with people, for a new anger to form within him. He would retrieve intact his vocation as a bringer of justice, determined to recover his strength as quickly as possible, and then to investigate and unravel the crime of le Houga, albeit fifteen years late.

Shaken by feverish trembling, he vowed that his undying hatred would take him once more across the path of the man he believed to be his ward's murderer. He would ponder thus through the bitterest hours of the night, a tireless bloodhound casting about stubbornly for the lost scent.

Ziquet, meanwhile, continued with his ordinary business. He spent a lot of his time sitting in the dust, spidery legs stuck out on either side, in the shed where he usually slept. The tadpole had the job of separating the rags intended for resale from those destined for pulping. He generally ended this sorting work on the most delicate stuffs. He handled the bottle-shards skilfully, passing them through a grinding mill and delivering the resulting powder in small bags to the man who used it for making sandpaper and match-strikers.

Once he had wiped his fingers (their nails in permanent semi-mourning), the boy would be able to smoke a *crapulos*. He would sit in the doorway of the barn puffing his bad cigar like a veteran, surveying the other ragpickers as they set off on their rounds. He himself would not be going out with his basket. He was busy with other business.

He glanced over at Papa Rust's pagoda. All was quiet under the planks. From time to time la Chouette would lift the jute sacking that served as a door and emerge with a vessel in her hand. She would throw red-tinged water away in the mud and rush back into the shack. Greasy hair hung down around her moon face.

Ziquet spat out his dog-end, retrieved it immediately and stored it in a small tin. He glanced once again at the shack with its overlapping roofs, built around a dead tree with twisted branches. Silhouetted against the bars of his cage under the porch he could see the hunched form of Bosco, Alfred Lerouge's cockatoo, an ugly little creature good for swearing at and little else. With a vigorous kick he got rid of an umbrella-skeleton that had entangled itself in his legs, and turned his back on the flue-pipe belching black into the grey sky.

The youngster was telling himself that there hadn't been much progress 'across the way' in the old sailor's affairs; that they were not about to come into sudden wealth, and that to escape from poverty it was a better plan to count on the riches of the known world than to believe promises of Peruvian gold from a geezer who'd bled to death, almost.

There *was* no Peru, or anyway it only existed in the ramblings of Alfred Lerouge. What did exist was the revolution. That was what Ziquet believed in.

Once or twice he had wormed his way into meetings. On one occasion he had got into the Motherland in Danger Club. He had listened to a speech by a woman worker in a blue apron. Her head wrapped in a chequered kerchief, she had asked whether the Commune was going to do anything about 'the people dying of hunger even when they had work'. Afterwards the organ had struck up the 'Marseillaise' as if it were a new sort of hymn. The men and women had stood up to sing it, and then everyone present had embraced as comrades.

Another time, Ziquet had left Cow City at the end of the day and crossed fields and wasteland to hear speakers from the International. Under a dirty drizzle he had crossed land scattered with small branchless trees protected by nail-studded palings. As he zigzagged between bramble thickets, knackers' yards and stinking factories belching industrial smoke and gases, he wondered if he would ever reach the place where the Batignolles branch of the International Workers' Association held its meetings.

He had returned to his barn from that expedition with his head buzzing with crazy resolutions. He would get educated! He would become a tribune, with a mouthful of promises! He cobbled up a red flag from a suitable bit of material and, using Bugeaud the donkey as a practice audience, repeatedly uttered the stirring words: 'I am a revolutionary socialist! I am a revolutionary socialist! Emancipation of the workers must come from the workers themselves!'

He so longed to learn how to make speeches like Varlin, or fight like Garibaldi.

For various reasons, and because Three-Nails had kicked his arse to make him stop telling everyone that God had come to the end of his useful life, Ziquet had ended by muzzling his more strident emancipatory demands. But the libertarian seed had germinated under his scurvy and unbrushed scalp. He went about saying that the industrial feudal bourgeoisie had been around for quite long enough. That the exploiters were going to bite the dust.

Ziquet was going to be a proletarian soldier.

He knew he had all the necessary guts and more. Cuffs and invective from the old man – who had a heavy hand when in his cups – changed nothing. The tadpole already saw himself winning his corporal's stripes on a barricade at the porte d'Asnières. Less officially (so to speak) he was also nurturing plans for looting and burglary, and discreetly but cheerfully imagined himself spending his leisure hours digging silverware and valuables out of buildings in the boulevard de Courcelles deserted in panic by the big bourgeoisie.

Against the possibility of his recruitment to the armies of the people, Ziquet had set aside a Chassepot for himself: a well-polished weapon complete with its sword-bayonet and a handful of cartridges. He had kept it secret, meaning when the time was ripe to abandon the junk trade for patriotism. He kept the rifle under a pile of rabbit skins, and from time to time took it out and greased it.

He also owned a book he had rescued from a dustbin, *The Militiaman's Theoretical Manual*, published in Limoges by Ardant & Thibaut. Every night he would use this to swot up on the handling and maintenance of the Chassepot or bolt-action rifle. He had reached the chapter on 'Shouldering weapon (right shoulder).'

Eyes half-closed, he tidied his clothing and recited:

'One movement in three stages!'

He stood to attention and bawled: 'Here, sar'major! At your orders, sar'major!' He stuck his skinny chest out, hollowed his stomach, drew in his chin and snapped firmly: 'First stage!'

Then, without drawing breath, he went on: 'Article 187: *Raise* weapon with right hand vertically facing shoulder, cleaning-rod to the fore, *grasp* with left hand above lower band; at the same time *place* right hand under stock with its toe between the first two fingers, the others placed under butt-plate.'

He opened his eyes and snapped in the instructor's voice: 'Second stage?'

Screwing up his eyes and springing back to attention, he recited his lesson: '188! *Raise* weapon with right hand into position on right shoulder with bolt-handle upward.'

'Third ditto?'

'189, sar'major! *Bring* left hand down *smartly* into position alongside trouser seam!'

Sometimes he would drill at night, or take aim at the moon.

47

Strolling players

Since his fate had become linked to that of Raoul Biloquet, alias Marbuche, Tarpagnan had seen some pretty strange days. He had fetched up in one of those riddled zones of wasteland at the end of the roof of the world, on the very fringes of society. He was breathing the air of monsters. He had slipped under the table, disappeared from the surface of the known world.

His new environment was an encampment of itinerant booths and attractions to which crowds of idlers, people who refused to bow to pressure from Versailles, came in party mood to watch on plank platforms, under cheap chandeliers, spectacles providing a noisy and meretricious form of enjoyment.

At the invitation of barkers – broken clowns, buffoons and strongmen with drooping braces – the johns and punters would gather in a circle. Bloated mugs and pretty little faces all paying attention, the air vibrant with bellowed exaggerations. Roll up, roll up! Bamboo hut! Great prizefight! Lethal drinks! Graeco-Roman wrestling! Educated fleas! Love spells, guaranteed! This way, this way! It'll take your breath away! Patriots and federals! Citizens and citizenesses! Gape at the balance of the tightrope-walking juggler, the sound-quality of the musical acrobats! Hear the high-speed petomane! The man with the inflatable belly! Miss Eve in porcelain! Magnified view! Gorgeous vapour of illusion! Behead Monsieur Thiers! Run Galliffet through for only two sous! Have you seen the bearded woman? The dislocated ventriloquist? The one-legged albino? Would you like to wrestle with the greased snake or make free with the Venus of Carcassonne? It's all plain! It's all fixed! Treat yourself to the corridor of fun! Enter the tunnel of greenery! Watch out for the

mineral cold! For the spider's caress! For the costume-remover!
Commit adultery but keep your veil on! The ladies will laugh up
their sleeves! The gentlemen will touch that awful hairy thing
that wakes the children!

Antoine would long remember his first arrival on the
fairground of Montmartre. As Marbuche dragged him up by the
hand, the troupe of showmen parading on the trestles facing
the snake-man's booth came to an untidy halt in a cacophony
of trombones and drums. Madame Tambour, under her feathered
hat, interrupted her patter. Palmyre, the pretty weight-lifting
midget in gipsy satin, stopped with her arms above her head.
Tsé-Tsé the human fly, who was walking on the ceiling of his
stall, came to a halt, head down, wings folded and brow
furrowed. Trombine, the hydrocephalic, removed the beret from
the swollen water-skin of his poor noddle, and with loose lips
gave the captain a sunny, slobbering smile.

'How handsome he is!' pretty Palmyre exclaimed. 'How
intelligent he looks!' She had allowed her dumb-bells to fall to
the ground.

Immediately, from the ill-stopped holes of the bassoon, there
arose a string of blackguardly notes, the drum following on a
parallel trail: *zim boom boom*. The cymbal came in with a
shattering sound; with his zinc bow the clown in the tight blue
jacket wrung a cry from the musical saw; and the trombone slid
in with a cheerful blare.

Marbuche, walking tall, saluted his friends in passing by
raising his free arm high in the air. His shaven head nodding in
time to the music, he walked to his caravan and disappeared
inside, dragging the handsome stranger behind him.

Soon after nightfall that evening, the wagon's two windows
filled with faces and heads, angry red noses and pearly cheeks.
Framed in hands that wiped the mist from the glass to see better,
twenty-five conks pressed against the panes. Twenty-five pairs of
eyes avid with tenderness, watching Tarpagnan undress.

After a while Madame Tambour unwisely let out an 'Oh!', and
Tarpagnan hastily extinguished the lamp.

'God's *death*!' he cried, causing all the heads to vanish. 'Is it always going to be like this?' He had wrapped a towel round his waist. Marbuche, yawning, tried to reassure him.

'No. Go on, go to sleep. It's just the first night.' Then the giant, cudgelling his overburdened brain for an explanation that would sound convincing, added: 'They're intrigued because you've got all your arms and legs. Because your ears don't wiggle and you haven't got a trunk.'

Hounds of hell, have mercy on us!

That night, on the threshold of uneasy sleep, Tarpagnan realised that he was going to have to fit into a grotesque and fantastic underworld. That he was going to have to get used to rubbing shoulders with breathless monsters, beautiful equestriennes with breasts like moonlight, lion-tamers with curled moustaches, one-armed women with luxuriant beards, trapeze artists in diadems, blue-eyed midgets, ogre-voiced giantesses, monkey-children, the prawn-sisters and their Siamese fathers with four waistcoats, six fingers and an eye set in the belly.

The next morning Madame Tambour knocked at the door of the wagon. She opened it slightly and poked her head and one enormous breast through the gap.

'Good morning,' she said to Tarpagnan with a virginal smile. 'Is there anything you need?'

'No, thank you.'

'Nothing we can do for you?'

'I don't think so.'

She slipped inside, simpering.

'We're worried about your health.'

'No need. As you see, I was about to shave . . .'

'*Very* worried,' Palmyre said. The pretty midget had got into the caravan too. She perched unceremoniously on Antoine's knee, kicked out her legs to show off her fine slippers set with carbuncles and added, pulling at her skirt: 'I told all my friends, I'm going to love that man. I know it. I feel it.'

'Thank you madame.'

'*Mademoiselle*,' the midget corrected. 'My first name is Palmyre.'

Tarpagnan could feel that she was trembling slightly. A fly

that had come in behind her crossed the wagon and began to beat itself blindly against the lamp-glass.

'You'd think it wanted to die,' Palmyre observed, 'poor little creature!'

'I know something about that,' Trombine said as he too came in. 'Sometimes I dream about smashing my head against the wall!' The hydrocephalic sat on the bunk beside Marbuche, put his trunk to one side and waited.

Tarpagnan no longer dared to move. The midget stroked his hand.

'I'm sure what's wrong with you is inside your body,' Madame Tambour said, showing yellow teeth. She fluffed out her coarse red hair, started powdering her face again despite the lateness of the hour, and added: 'I'm very sorry for you, monsieur, if instead of being apparent, as is the case with most of us, your infirmity is hidden away in the depths of your being.'

'Yes, I'm sincerely sorry for you, too,' said Soupir the clown, entering in his turn. 'I used to know a fellow who could hear a ticking noise inside him.'

'Might you not have swallowed a clock?' Palmyre asked ingenuously, giving Antoine's hand a delicate kiss. By now almost everyone had crowded into the caravan: Clé-de-Fa, Mi-Bémol, Crépon, Tsé-Tsé, even the prawn-sisters. All, despite their rough skins, badly stopped holes and blistered flesh, were eager to be his friends.

'No,' Tarpagnan replied to the room at large, 'no, I haven't swallowed a clock ... but you could say without any risk of error that the sickness gnawing at me is certainly internal.'

'Tell us about it,' they urged. They were so vibrant, so sensitive. They had spoken virtually with one voice.

'Yes ... what is it?' repeated pretty Palmyre.

'It's the sound of a woman,' said the giant Marbuche, addressing his audience with the elegance of a dignitary. 'What Tarpagnan has under his skin, and making his heart pound as if he had thick blood, is the sound of a woman!'

'It's a gigantic tumult,' Antoine confirmed. 'It's the disease of love.' And he told them about Caf'conc'.

48

The great bivouac
of the revolution

Paris by contrast had seen some days of true splendour. Out with politicians in false noses! Down the drain with the ghosts of tyrants and bounders! The bourgeoisie's bloodlettings, lancets and prescriptions had miscarried!

The people had voted on 26th March. The Parisians put the triumph of their ideas into practice by expressing through the polls a wish for changes suffused with light. The Commune was a solid reality now! It would fly the colours of liberty, it would flourish in mutual respect with the most deprived classes. Eventually it would speak through the mouth of a working class that was now acceding to adulthood. And since everything would have to be relearned, it would create a new form of citizen: one resistant to tyranny, a judge, a partner, an actor with his own resources. Welcome, then, to those elected to sit in the grave and silent house of the sovereign people!

The new assembly – a third of whose members were workers – had an average age of thirty-eight. The youngest representative, at twenty-five, was Raoul Rigault; the doyen at seventy-six was Beslay, who had been a deputy many years earlier during the July monarchy.

These representatives were not organised into parties. Although they accepted each other – united as they were in a common desire to reform society – the Blanquists, Jacobins, romantics, independents, socialists and representatives of the International did not all speak with one voice. But what did that matter? And what did it matter that the range of their convictions, the diversity of their dogmas, the reasons for their commitment were often shifting or contradictory? For the time being – at a moment of solemn triumph spilling over into a vermilion celebration of fraternity, a transcendence of the self – the important thing was that a surge of collective anger had given these representatives of the people the energy to rise to the level of their aspirations. For the time being, disparities were forgotten. For the time being, the members set aside their rancours and hatreds, their vengeful passions, their ambitions to be adventurers in power.

The inauguration of the 26th March Commune did not conform to the starchy, ceremonial model of how to celebrate a new regime. It was beggarly. It was jaunty. It was spontaneous. It was spicy as a happy laugh. Its hair was all over the place. It didn't have much of an overcoat. Nor a centre parting. It wasn't a meeting of fine gentlemen in white ties. It was a mob of unknowns let out into the street. A red soup. An assembly of the deprived: victims of speculation, exploited factory hands, inhabitants of working-class quarters, all the great underground reservoirs of the poor. The shadowy and divergent destinies of that crowd on the move were masked by the fraternity of the moment.

And how impossible it was not to be moved by the sight of a hundred thousand people flowing and babbling through the streets towards the Hôtel de Ville, like blood flowing back to the heart! How marvellous to see turners from la Bièvre, dockers from the quai d'Ivry, students from la Huchette, outcasts from the slum alleys, ragamuffins from the Wolf-Hole, cabinetmakers from Picpus and all these people from the Petit Charonne, finding themselves side by side and astonished by their weight of numbers! It was dizzying, dizzying! And how powerful history is, to propel the citizens towards a new dawn just as they are about to fall asleep from discouragement!

On Tuesday 28th March 1871 the rain and snow had disappeared as if by magic. The blue sky blessed the Communards like a poster for spring.

Early in the afternoon woolly spaced-out clouds like a peaceful herd of ruminants moved slowly across the azure pasture of the sky. The fat white clouds floated idly over the celebrating crowd, growing and changing shape. The brass of musical instruments glittered. People greeted each other joyously. Wind musicians blew fit to burst their cheeks, drummers threatened to split their skins. The great festival of Thermidor could begin!

Early that morning the people of Montmartre, of the rue Lévisse, the ones who had voted for Ferré, for Theisz, for Vermorel or Dereure, had gathered to march to the centre of Paris. By group and natural affinity, they were connected with those who had voted for the workman Hubert, for the boilermaker Chardon, for the metalworkers Duval, Assi, Avrial, Chalain and Langevin, for the shoemakers Serraillier, Trinquet and Léopold Clément, for Eudes the proofreader, for the bookbinders Varlin and Adolphe Clémence, for the joiner Pindy or the hatter Amouroux.

'The blood of our ancestors is in us once more!' Jeanne Couerbe, Louise Michel's friend, had cried to the other tenants of her building. 'At times like this it surges in our hearts!'

'The woman's right!' answered the people of rue Lévisse. 'Jeanne's right!'

Jeanne of 7, rue Lèvisse . . . you could as well say all women! Women prepared to fight to the last drop of their blood. Women in quest of eternal justice. Today is their festival too.

Citizen women. Women of the suburbs and the market. Women from the factories and slum areas of east Paris. Women of the barricades. The wives of national guardsmen paid seventy centimes a day subsistence. Nurses, waitresses, workers in kitchens and hospitals, red Amazons. Women with their hair down, in spotted camisoles, in grey dresses with black flounces. Women in shawls, with their hair pulled back at the temples, in a flattened knot at the back of the neck, women with pinchbeck crosses round their white necks. Warlike women with drums, with pistols. Soldiers in skirts, little hats down over their eyes, mutinous, lisping, in red sashes, with children's voices; furies naked under their working jackets, cursing like alley-cats, running to defend the barricades, drunk on rum and ready to die in the riot.

The woman's right! Blood surges! It surges right up, in a trice. What a fine bellow it is, that famous people's cry! An immense rhythmic rumble in a thousand chests.

'Long live the Commune! Long live the Social State!'

Jeanne led the procession from the 18th *arrondissement*. She had made herself a Phrygian bonnet and put on a red coat. National Guardsmen around her stuck their kepis on the ends of their long bayonets and waved them over their heads. Jeanne turned and called out to those behind her.

'Louder, you useless animals! They've got to be able to hear us from Versailles!'

They heard and they complied. Their voices grew raucous.

Oho! It'll go! It'll go! It'll go!
String 'em up, every last aristo . . .

They were all there: Wire, missing a few teeth from Tarpagnan's famous kick; Velvet-Eye, who had turned his hump and gone over to the cause; Abel Rochon the loudmouth housepainter, hand-in-hand with his pretty mealticket Adelaïde Fontieu, wearing a cockade in her hair for the occasion. They were singing, yelling, barracking: coming back to life.

The girls from the rue Girardon were there too, the boarders of the Abbesses walking behind them with colour in their cheeks. They looked smart surrounded by handsome sailors in blue collars, wearing glazed leather caps that the girls snatched with laughing boldness. They gave the cries of wild things set free. They walked arm in arm, they covered their ears when passing in front of the baying brass and roaring helicons.

Behind these streetwise women came Léonce and her daughter Marion, quieter and more respectably turned out. And Marceau. And Ferrier and Voutard. And Blanche whose breasts were lovelier than hills in the morning, Blanche who worked with Jeanne Couerbe in the dressmaker's workshop.

The 'Marseillaise' broke out again and again. Even when heard often, how compelling is that vengeful anthem when sung in chorus by thousands of determined voices! What a marvellous resource for men doomed to misery, men who are humiliated, divided, broken to the core, that ability they have to pick themselves up again! To reconquer the streets with a universal voice, just as they were about to capitulate to discouragement!

They were all there, two hundred thousand of them at least, in front of the platform on which the Central Committee had just handed power over to the elected assembly. From their throats arose a single cry, tender and powerful:

'*Vive la Commune!*'

All classes intermingled, telescoped ranks pressed together in disorder, they filled their lungs and shouted in an unforgettable spirit of communion. They were still arriving, they were nearly all there but new arrivals kept on coming. They believed in the advent of the people. They were proletarians with clear eyes, black fingernails, radiant faces. Still flowing in, arriving, milling about.

They filled the space, people from the districts, from the factories, clusters of humanity, girls clinging to sculptures, children up lampposts, sitting on the heads of statues and clinging to roofs, swarms of people of all ages and conditions – cripples, bohemians, old men, urchins, workers in blue blouses, petty-bourgeois in frock-coats – while the imminent arrival of the military procession was announced by the thunder of cannon firing blank charges into the great clear sky.

There they were, the yelling crowd, craning and jostling to get a better view of the bearers of their hopes.

'The one with the beard there, the young one . . . it's Rigault, I tell you!'

'D'you see the third one, then? He's got a beard too . . . the one who's writing . . . surely you can see him?'

'Yes.'

'Don't you know who he is?'

'No.'

'Well, that's Jules Vallès. *Le Cri du Peuple*'s chap. Elected in the 15th. And the one at the side there: that's Varlin. Elected three times, in the 12th, the 6th and the 17th!'

'What about him, the one in the chair?'

'That's Assi, for Christ's sake. On yer feet, Assi!'

They roared with laughter, pointing to the centre of the platform where the mechanic–fitter–manager of the Hôtel de Ville was sitting on a grand gilded throne upholstered in red velvet.

Assi stood up. This commonplace act was greeted with such a prolonged cheer that his remarks could not be heard. Ranvier, a major on the Central Committee, stepped forward next, wearing the red sash, but was too deeply moved to make a speech. Jules Vallès would write later that his livid face seemed to have lost all its blood. 'Even his hair hung down like the tangled hair of one undergoing torture. His lips were white.' He stammered his speech 'with a child's smile, and a voice roughened by consumption murmured in his scorched throat'. Boursier was next to speak. He read out a list of those elected to the Commune, but his voice too was drowned by the hurricane of applause.

Wire and Velvet-Eye were standing on tiptoe to see, beyond the living hedge of tricolour banners and revolutionary red crepe, the Guard battalions due to take part in the review. Between them and the platform several Montigny machine-cannon were set up as a symbolic defence against any attempt at violence. Their crews of veterans were sitting on the ground smoking contentedly.

A young federal of about fifteen, a child-volunteer whose kepi was too big for him and rested on his ears, was keeping people away from the Guard.

'See him, there? Ain't that the Tironneau kid?'

'Yes, that's Guillaume all right. Hey, Guillaume! Yer ma's with us somewhere! She's looking for you to give yer a kiss!'

The boy gave them the dismissive glance of an experienced veteran. Lost inside a vast greatcoat, rifle on his shoulder, he went on marching back and forth as regularly as a pendulum, doing a smart about-turn at each end of his beat.

A photographer came up and took a picture of him. Of course it was Théophile Mirecourt, photographer of the barricades. Hunter of faces, recorder of expressions. Captor of historic moments. For him it was a far from ordinary day. He was christening his first portable camera: a much-lightened, very compact bellows device that weighed under four pounds and could be used without a tripod. After months of experiment, Théo had succeeded in eliminating the constraints of collodion, with its delicate handling requirements. He was the very first photographer to use gelatino-bromide plates, although fifteen years later, in 1886, the invention would be credited to a British citizen, one Charles Harper Bennett. But that dazzling late-March day in 1871 saw the triumph of a man whose deserved fame was swallowed up in the dark fate of the Commune.

'For the parade: Battalions ... march!'

General Brunel bellowed the order on the stroke of four, raising the glittering blade of his sword high in the air. Relayed from mouth to sword to sword by artillery officers, the order was echoed almost immediately by the guns on the Seine embankment, spitting big gobs of black smoke into the sky.

''Talions: quick ... march!' The colonels had taken over. Immediately, an ill-coordinated tramping hammered the cobbles and stirred the public soul.

In a vibrant clamour of marching bands, alternately playing the 'Marseillaise' and the 'Chant du départ', the first companies appeared under a forest of bayonets and banners in the national colours. Side by side, under flapping flags whose staffs were surmounted by a Phrygian bonnet, symbolising restored independence and freedom, units from the working-class quarters and bourgeois volunteers paraded past for several hours.

'We've taken Paris back!'

'*Now* we're in our own house!'

'A new world sweeping the old one away!'

People had their own slogans, their own emotions. The bursts of cheering were like gunfire. As the battalions passed the tribune they dipped their colours. The officers saluted with unsheathed sabres. The troops had their tunics buttoned, and marched in straight ranks. From the paved river embankments, artillery salutes periodically drowned out the trumpets and bugles; when it was their turn, these cut loose with cascades of bright notes that covered the cheers of the audience.

Little by little, as the shadows moved, the military parade gave way to a more civic celebration. The 'Marseillaise' started to flag, and as the crowd ran through its own favourite tunes the strains of Offenbach and Auber became predominant. A sort of gigantic cross between a *carmagnole* and a torchlight tattoo was substituted for the official programme more or less everywhere. Fashionable tunes and songs, like the one about 'Le Sire de Fiche-Ton-Kan' (and his big 'before behind-way-round' sabre), 'The Bearded Woman' and 'The Firemen of Nanterre' combined in a barbarically energetic fusion with fragments of Henri Rochefort's, 'La Badinguette' and some songs from 1792, along with a few echoes of Rouget de Lisle.

On the podium, in a disorderly shambles of chairs, the representatives – tired of saluting the battalions and the crowd hour after hour – got to their feet as the last brassy arias of the review died away in the distance. Stretching their legs and rubbing their thighs to restore the circulation, these gentlemen tumbled down the steps from the podium and mingled with the crowds of noisy enthusiasts who surrounded them to congratulate them on their election.

Théo wormed his way through the forest of elbows and buttocks.

'Press! Press! Let the press work, please!'

The magic word attracted the attention of Jules Vallès, who was chatting with Lefrançais and two or three other people wearing diagonal red sashes. Théo snapped them at a fifteenth of a second. Vallès laughed with pleasure and asked:

'Is that it, then? You can take photographs at last without having to use a scaffolding?'

Théo nodded happily. With one hand he waved the camera, with a sweeping wave of the other he designated the colourful multitude. 'Don't you think the present time favours lightness?' he exclaimed. 'It seems to me today that everything's being debourgeoisified! So long live freedom without bounds or brakes!'

Vallès held out his hand for the photographic apparatus. 'Let's have a look at your rosewood box . . .' He hefted the device and peered at the flawless blue shine of its lens. 'Crikey, that's a nice machine! You'll be able to magnify the moment with it and make a note of today's sky!' Turning to his colleagues, he added:

'Here, gentlemen, is the thing that's going to relegate the Greeks to the dictionary once and for all!'

As he gave the camera back to Théophile he murmured: 'Actually, Mirecourt, I've been wondering what's become of my journalist.'

'Tarpagnan?'

'That's right. Where's Cousin Vingtras got to?'

'Haven't seen him since the other day . . .'

'I've been waiting for his piece.'

'Well, he hasn't come back.'

'God Almighty, photographer! D'you think your pal might have snuffed it?'

Théophile resettled the shoulder-bag containing his precious plates and holders, and shrugged fatalistically. 'How do I know? I just hope the hoodlums on the banks of the Ourcq haven't made mincemeat of him.'

'Fuck! You'd better get over there. That would be most upsetting for Cousin Vingtras!'

'It would certainly be a pity,' Théo retorted energetically, 'if Antoine had got himself killed for the love of a tart!'

He instantly regretted this bitter piece of misogyny, even before noticing the faint, indulgent smile on Vallès's mouth with its thin scar. The sun had vanished from the sky. The two men looked at each other in silence, thinking of corpses in the canal, drowned in the tide of shadows, caressed by the reeds, cradled between the two dark banks.

'That Velaunian by marriage had greedy eyes,' the journalist said eventually, in a sober voice. 'I liked him a lot. A young fellow crammed with life.'

'I miss him too,' Théophile murmured. A look of sadness, dry-eyed but terrible, crossed their faces. Then Vallès snorted, hating the idea that anyone might think for a single moment that he felt sorry for himself, or had given up hope of seeing the Captain again. He seized Théo by the shoulders and shook him roughly.

'Tchah! Imbecile! Put away that onion!' he scolded. 'A man of Tarpagnan's calibre doesn't die over some woman's rump! Mark my words, young photographer . . . Cousin Vingtras'll be showing his mug again in a day or two ... when he's finished shaking the hedge-warbler's nest! So forget about corpses, to the devil with them! Fuck it! End of session! If you see your protégé, just tell him my offer's still good and I need writers who are on target. Meanwhile, since he hasn't shown up, I've got an article to think about for tomorrow.'

'So you're not going to attend the first sitting of the Council?'

Vallès made a dismissive sign and his face darkened with exasperation. 'I'm told they haven't got a room ready for us yet!' he said. 'Only the Central Committee's got one so far.' He rubbed his hand the wrong way through his beard, making it bristle, and added: 'Anyway, don't you feel after a day like this one that politics seem ... a bit much? I'll be far more useful at the paper. What interests me today is Paris. Citizens' town! Free city!' Distracted, absent, he let his gaze wander through the dying glow of twilight.

Warmed by laughter, by songs and impudence, long lines of young people arm-in-arm were dispersing into the corners of the square. Grey outlines quickly swallowed up into the halo of ill-lit alleys, fine clusters of blouses, helmets of yellow hair, strapping fellows with mahogany side-whiskers, hands clamped round the waists of their tall, aproned gawks, were carrying the embers of the party to a new setting in a last clatter of footsteps.

'God Almighty! What an evening!' the journalist cried. 'Even if we're reconquered and have to die tomorrow, my generation will have been consoled! I'm going to write – while the ideas are still hot – a new chapter in the history of the achievement of the great dream! then later ... I'll go and eat like a starving wolf in some place where they'll serve me ... Yes! I've still got my slate at Laveur's ... Will you come and join me there?'

'I don't think so,' Théo said apologetically, raising his cap. 'Since the time for rolling in the blood of patriots is still before us, permit me, Mr People's Councillor, to follow the example of our dear Tarpagnan and have an evening to myself!'

'It's all yours! I yield it to you!' cried the new representative of Grenelle. He saluted his young friend with a pompous wave of his vertiginous silk hat. 'Goodnight, Mr Modern Reporter!' He set off at his usual breakneck pace, then half-turned and called over his shoulder with malicious glee: 'Great pleasure, Monsieur Mirecourt! I'll keep praying that the young men of the low districts don't distract you too much from the duty you owe the people of the barricades!'

49

A rippling of flags

Théo was left alone, a smile of friendship engraved on his lips. The windows overlooking the square and esplanade were empty now.

A few officers were still exercising their heavy boots, a few guardsmen still stood with their hands behind their backs, but most of the tumult had drained away into the neighbouring streets. Gradually, as the murmur of the revolution withdrew towards other districts, municipal employees started folding up the awnings that had been placed over the platform and rolling up the banners.

A last belated group crossed the empty square at a run. In the distance, black dots were hastening towards a row of carriages. A nervous horse, well reined-in by its rider, passed with a rapid clatter of shoes skidding on cobbles. Lamplighters were using long lances to ignite the five-branched gaslights on the embankment. Théo left.

He vanished into the shadows. There was little or no illumination in the smaller streets. Supplies of the coal from which gas was made were running low. A lot of shops were closed. Business people, the shopkeeping small bourgeoisie, had deserted the Paris of the poor and outcast to set up shop in Versailles, where the money was currently lurking.

Théophile was on his way to Montmartre, an hour's walk away. He had ample time to think about change, how every day was taking him further from his languid youth. He was proud of being one of the million-odd Parisians who had chosen to live out a new social order. He chuckled at the thought of all those fat exiled property-owners in their cramped lodgings in Seine-et-Oise, shivering with fear for their possessions, their luxurious houses and apartments in the smart quarters left at the mercy of the adventurers of the Commune. He smiled at the memory of his own personal anger, the drive behind his iconoclastic wish to lay waste the privileged caste to which he had been fitted by his sheltered upbringing.

He crossed a square in which the worn face of an old stone lion endlessly vomited clear water from its gaping maw into a basin. At certain moments the faint light gave a ferocious look to his handsome face, modified by a new beard and moustache. Was it his fault if he felt a lot happier as an insurgent than in the camp of the frock-coated classes? Was it a blemish, a further proof of his difference, if the desire for fraternity attracted him more to the sound of chopping-machines, the hot breath of forges, the stench of tanneries, than to the glitter of chandeliers?

He hurried on. Gentlemanly under his ordinary clothing, he slouched along in the style of a man in the street, taking on the manner of what he wanted to become, and entered another square in which children were playing marbles with spent bullets. He longed to enter body and soul into the envelope of a proletarian, to become the equal and the brother of the humblest, to be esteemed for his courage alone and become one with the people who, when the time came, would unhesitatingly face canister-shot rather than accept the yoke of the fine gentlemen of finance.

Passing the grey building of a women's enrolment office in the rue de Turbigo, he came to a sudden halt just before the sentry-box guarding the front steps. The sentry, a gamey amazon with the red cheeks of a laundress, had propped her light carbine against the wall behind her, and with the ample swing of an experienced housewife was on the point of flinging a pail of water across the pavement. Dressed in trousers, a woollen tunic and a black hooded cape, the distinctive uniform of her battalion of volunteers whose duties were to defend the barricades and render the male combatants *every domestic and fraternal service compatible with moral order and military discipline*', the patriot, whose looks alone more or less guaranteed her unsullied virtue, bestowed an appalling gap-toothed smile on the young passer-by. With a jerk of the head towards her Enfield carbine and a wave of the dishcloth in her free hand, she trumpeted:

'That's what work is, citizen! Me chores as a 'ousewife *plus* the duties of a soldier!'

'I can see that!' He stood back to let her finish what she was doing. The dirty water sluiced across the pavement and down the gutter, and the matron resumed her sentry duty. Théo skipped over the gleaming cobbles and crossed the road, whistling. He passed a line of shop-fronts with closed shutters, windows criss-crossed with tape for fear of breakages: echoes of battle. Further on, the clamour of hand-carts. He passed a one-man band somewhat the worse for drink, *zim-booming* a meandering path. Then, emerging into the Boulevard where the usual cries of the local fauna of 'dolls' and 'sissies' were tonight drowned in the flood-tide of the people, he plunged into the happy crowd where there slumbered an odour of bouquets.

As he walked on, he became aware that the joy of the entire city, repainted in innocent colours, was being reproduced without much fanfare in every corner of working-class Paris. Under pressure from the multitudes, clinging to their moments of exalted joy with the indescribable intensity of the poor, for whom the white bread of happiness constitutes a promise of cake, the Communards were granting themselves a night's grace before waking to confront their destiny. The people, elated and dressed up, all intermingled with rallied line troops, Turcos in glittering uniforms, Garibaldists in red cloaks, barmaids carrying small barrels on their hips like infants, were launching into another celebration.

New tunes, the rumble of voices, the sounds of life echoed through deep shadows in avenues still warm from the day's sunshine. Unrehearsed song rattled the café terraces and filled the squares and great road junctions, where platforms had been set up. In the districts, at the top of the Montmartre Butte, they were playing skittles and drinking strong wine. The Dead Rat, the Café du Théâtre and the Brasserie des Martyrs were all displaying 'full up' notices. People fraternised under the surviving plane trees, poured food and drink down their throats, guffawed. That was the life all right, and none too soon neither!

It was in that state of mind that Théophile was going to join the people of rue Lévisse. He would spend the evening with young Guillaume Tironneau. No doubt it was their destiny.

They laughed, drank together, wondered about the fate of Captain Tarpagnan. Guillaume, pointing to the sky, spoke of his hunger for heroism. Théophile burned with strange joy. With the crazed enthusiasm of children in love, they remade the world. Wove together the kindling of their internal revolt.

They spoke with distaste of the reality of poverty, revolted by the hunger and cold that are the iniquitous lot of the poor and suffering. The corset-maker's son from Montmartre betrothed to the rebel son of a rich lady from the Senate district chose the language of a street-corner hero to express his determination to conquer or perish. Linked by subtle bonds of word and glance, they were walking side by side at that grave time when the clocks are striking midnight. They turned and looked at one another, petrified by the depth of their understanding. Théo took Guillaume by the hand.

Both listening to the echo of the streets and distant strains of music, they sat gazing out over the murk-wrapped vastness of Paris. Paris seen from Montmartre, Paris of two sorts sprawled at their feet: Paris of velvet and diamonds, and indigent Paris with nothing to wear but work-clothes. They thought of those who would stay up all night on the ramparts, at Issy, Montrouge, Vanves or Asnières. The lookouts, the brave fellows who would only get three hours' sleep, hollow-eyed, open-mouthed, head back, pillowed on a sandbag, pale-faced as men half dead. They had stopped speaking, seized without knowing it by a Victor Hugo-like vertigo in the presence of the history of Paris 'in which everything is abridged and exaggerated at the same time'.

Straightforwardly, aware of the enemies of the Commune lurking in the foggy loops of the Seine, smiling, astonished by their own gentleness in the face of a world bulging with imminent violence, they looked at each other and learned each other.

'When d'you rejoin your battalion?'

'At dawn. We'll be moving off immediately. We're going to lend a hand to them on the ramparts . . .'

'Dawn?' Théo looked worriedly into the sky. 'Dawn is now, dear boy . . . hardly two hours . . . we're in God's hands.'

But the intrepid child did not share the adult's anxiety, and reverted to his warlike ardour. 'We'll be stiffening the defences at the pont de Neuilly. Bergeret's in command! With him there we won't be afraid of nothing.' Peering through the mist, he waved in the direction of Versailles. 'They're out there,' he said without putting a name to them, 'lots of them.'

Théo lowered his head. His wide shoulders slumped as if an invisible weight had pressed on the back of his neck.

'There are a lot of them, yes,' he agreed in a muffled voice. 'And they'll be pitiless . . . Seven generals lined up in their boots! One day they're going to come, with swords between their teeth . . . In a few weeks . . . the day after tomorrow. What I'm saying is soon . . . they're champing at the bit. They're clumping up and down the rue des Réservoirs, snarling. Vinoy wants to get straight to it. See that glow over there on the horizon? Those reddish lights – those campfires? The fort at mont Valérien with its electric lights? They mean to scour the Commune to the bone!'

When Guillaume asked point-blank the question that nagged at his mind – 'D'yer think many of us're goin' to get it, then?' – his mouth twisted childishly, but he did his very best to hide his fear with a gruff delivery. Only a heart of stone would not have been moved by such youthful bravery. Théo took the boy in his arms and answered without hesitation:

'Guillotined or shot, same difference: it's our only choice!'

The kid emerged instantly from the dark thicket of his fear, crying in tones of heartbreaking sincerity: ''*Zackly* what I told my mother! If we get shot, it'll mean we been lucky!'

50

Cockaigne!

On the sixth day following that orgy of emotions, just before sunrise, Alfred Lerouge was drifting with his shipwrecked companions on a stormy ocean and urging them, from a mouth thick with the previous night's cane spirit, to consider eating the cabin boy, when an event occurred of such importance that he slipped into the icy water and immediately woke up.

Very briefly, these were the events that caused Three-Nails to be awakened so rudely:

La Chouette, despite the early hour, had decided to straighten and plump up the litter of bracken on which their lodger's pallet was spread. Grondin, disturbed in his sleep, had moaned slightly in protest at the inhabitual upset.

Once tidied up and tucked in again, after his nurse had made him swallow her infusions of sage, her murky potions, and dressed his wounds with rare herbs, spirit liniments and plasters, Grondin was trying to go back to sleep. The witch, however, seized by her usual fantasies, had put her hand between her half-dead patient's thighs, and was just starting to wander down the road of inadmissible thoughts and blushing dreams when the invalid's penis suddenly stood up like a mast. The sight of this large and incontrovertible erection told la Chouette immediately that the survivor from the Polish field had started to recover. The recovery of this faculty meant he would soon be on the road to convalescence. It brought Grondin back from the land of delirium, restored him to the status of a conscious being, and took la Chouette's tall love-object out of reach of the stolen intimacies she so treasured. The raw-boned, owl-eyed healer was faced with the bitter thought that she had just lost the free use of her motionless lover.

She stood wiping her hands mechanically on her big apron, her face stricken, biting her lip, unable to tear her eyes from that unprecedented tumescence. She looked afraid. Suddenly, she hid her hands behind her back. The next moment, blinded by black sorrow, surrendering to the sick knowledge that her life was going to be ugly again, she replaced the cover with a rapid sweep of the arm and withdrew into the shadows, where she uttered a single unrestrained cry of distress, followed by a dry sob.

That strident signal of despair set in train a new, irreversible sequence of events, a new vortex of energy. Alfred Lerouge emerged suddenly from his ocean torpor with the sound of a chair being overturned. Eyes red and crazed, nose flat and fiery, forehead still sweaty from the sinking liferaft nightmare, he pattered unsteadily across the room in rabbit-skin slippers, confident as a bargain-basement emperor, and slumped down at the patient's bedside. He clapped his hands briefly for attention. The time had come to claim his due.

'I've given up my bed for you, m'sieu,' he said without preamble, 'but you know what they say: you get what you pay for!' With a sweeping gesture he indicated his wife in the shadows, the roaring stove and the smelly mattress, and added in a formal tone: 'I can't extend no more hospitality without some guarantee of yer solvency.'

The tall one-eyed invalid smiled weakly and uttered a few unintelligible words. Then the humanity faded from his wasted, craggy face and his lips became thin and severe. He signed to them to come closer and indicated that he could only whisper.

'Where d'you live?' Lerouge asked. 'That's the main thing.'

Grondin made no difficulty about letting Alfred have his address. He was genuinely grateful to the rag-and-bone man and his wife. It seemed quite natural to him to allow his benefactors to go and open his lodging, get in with the key from 'under the seventh tread of the third-floor staircase' and get into the attic where, he explained, 'after the fifth chestnut beam, between tenon and mortice' they would find 'a newspaper package containing brand-new large banknotes'.

Alfred Lerouge was again dreaming of the goose with golden eggs. His wife gazed at him with her big staring eyes. He didn't move. 'If it don't sound too ungrateful, m'sieu,' he persisted, bringing his potato-like nose close to the patient's face, 'haven't you got anything else to offer us? Pr'aps a few saved small coins, bit of gold, a medallion, something like that? It's for my son, almost, that I'm asking this favour ... my little Ziquet, a kid who's always been hungry, and bloody unlucky in his mum!'

The one-time convict fixed his grey eye on Alfred Lerouge's glassy stare as if trying to gauge the man's intentions. The junk-dealer responded with the sweetest and gummiest of smiles. Three-Nails knew how to oil the wheels.

'You'll find a biscuit box,' the spectre panted, 'in the bottom of the grandfather clock ... and that's the last of what I've got to give ...'

'Are those the whole of your savings, m'sieu?' rasped the ugly old scarecrow. 'You wouldn't have a proper strong-box hidden in the cellar, would you? It wouldn't be p'lite to hold stuff back ...'

But the single grey eye had closed again. He's told us everything, Three-Nails thought to himself. 'He's shot his bolt,' he said to his companion. 'This here's a citizen who smells of pine already. Prob'ly won't last the week.'

'Don't you believe it, Alfred,' la Chouette murmured, not without a touch of malice. 'I reckon 'e's quite a bit stronger than he looks, your client there.' The sorceress knew a bit about it, after all.

In fact, Grondin had simulated loss of consciousness, turning up his eye and sinking into a coma. He wanted to be left in peace. To him it was simply elementary caution: given his weakened state, the former convict was afraid the ragpickers would tickle the soles of his feet with hot embers to make him admit that there were other disposable goods hidden in his house. He had moaned to drive them away, pretended to be feverish.

You don't teach an old dog new tricks. Nor is it a simple matter to induce a former notary, chain-gang foreman and undercover police and security agent to disgorge all his secrets. He kept his eye closed. He was smiling faintly.

No two ways about it, he was thinking, I won't be crossing the big river this time around. You're going to get back on your feet, 2017! You're going to get there! Grondin had not forgotten his fieldcraft. He was already taking care to appear as weak as possible, to conceal the extent of his recovery. He exercised his muscles discreetly when he could. You never knew what would happen.

He was ready, ready as possible. Chain-gang experience, convict reflexes. Furtively, he felt between the mattress and litter with his right hand to make sure that the pruning knife he had taken from the nail where it hung, a long arm's reach from his bed, was still where he had left it.

51

Gold rush

Three-Nails had dropped everything and set out from his home ground in Clichy, Ziquet close on his heels. In his shoulder-bag he carried a good quantity of rotgut for the road, and he shared a chunk of bread and an onion with the boy as they walked. The two ragpickers had made good time from the rue de la Révolte, taking the shortest route across wasteland illuminated by braziers, then turning along the railway track from le Havre, which would take them directly to the station at les Batignolles.

At the corner of rue Legendre, Three-Nails hailed a carriage that was drifting through the night without lights, believing it to be a cruising cab. The vehicle, covered with dark cloth and pulled by an elderly, limping nag about the size of a deer wearing silver-rimmed blinkers, changed direction immediately. Within a second or two the old man and the boy realised that they had hailed a hearse.

Slumped on the driver's seat was a grumpy, loutish streak of piss wearing a narrow-brimmed hat of the type called a *morillo*. This rigid-necked postillion of funeral cortèges was so monumentally drunk that in the darkness he was unable to distinguish a rag-and-bone man from a national guard or an adolescent from a waitress.

'Wotcher, Blunderbuss! Mornin', Adelaïde!' hiccuped the swaying coachman, trying to focus on them from his perch. 'Where's our wounded got to then?'

'Er . . . haven't got any wounded,' Alfred Lerouge mumbled. 'But we were looking for a lift to the Saint-Martin side . . .'

''S the whole trouble with Parisians!' the undertaker lectured them. 'The honour a' the revolution's under threat, and what're they doing inna Boulevards? Goin' about their business, thass what!' He made another effort to focus on them in the darkness. 'You wouldn't believe it! The same day that I unload the mortal remains of more 'n a hundred brave souls on the blood-soaked straw at Beaujon, the Gymnase *would* have to be showing *M. Perrichon's Journey*, and I *would* have to come across a coupl'a birds who don't care for nothing but their own pleasure!'

'We're not going to the theatre,' Alfred Lerouge assured him hastily. But it was too late. The corpse-bather was in full flood, pursuing his patriotic sermon with bitter relish.

'I'd *just* like to point *out* that a workers' hearse transformed into a ambulance by the Paris Commune can't jus' be diverted from its sacred mission like as if it was some sort of donkey-trap! I'm under *orders*, I am, citizen! I'm givin' assistance to the servants of the people, the ones what're ripped with such big ugly wounds they've got to be evacuated urgently to get *heavy surgery*!'

'There's been fighting, then?'

'Ignoramus! Vile, unclean ignoramus! The first of our dead are rotting in the clay of the battlefields and he asks me if there's been fighting! People's tripes are being ripped out at the gates of Paris, monsieur! They're being spitted at Courbevoie, dying proudly on their feet at Clamart, Val-Fleury, Bas-Meudon!'

'I didn't know. I got my reasons why.'

'You can't have,' croaked the buzzard in a husky, funereal voice. 'Yesterday, the federal noose seemed about to close on Versailles. Today, 3 April, Bergeret's beaten . . . and despite his courage, young General Flourens was surrounded between Rueil and Chatou and killed, run through by a gendarmerie captain . . .'

'We'll walk,' Three-Nails decided, cheered by the thought that he had played no part in all this heroism. 'We can perfectly well do it on foot.' He took Ziquet by the sleeve and set off.

'Wait a minute!' the undertaker hissed after them. They stopped. The black vulture put his jade in motion and caught them up. 'Since we've all got to die tomorrow,' he said in a calmer voice, 'we might as well lend each other a hand . . . Where was it you were going?'

'Between Temple and Château-d'Eau. Rue de la Corderie.'

'It's not really on my way.' The man gave them a sidelong look, then risked revealing a dark, corpse-washer's beggarliness. 'You wouldn't have a little change for anyone that could help?'

'It's conceivable,' Three-Nails admitted unwisely. The undertaker instantly advanced an exorbitant figure.

'*Ten francs?*' huffed the ragpicker. 'You must take me for a greenhorn, my friend! You've got the wrong person!' He moved forward into a patch of light and displayed the tatters of his scarecrow's raiment. 'I'm no swell, see? No stiff collar, no decoration in the buttonhole!'

The corpse-undresser's experienced eye scrutinised his patched frock-coat. 'Ten francs to you, old hook. Take it or leave it.'

''S about what you'd get for your old screw at the knacker's!'

'Fifteen francs if you insult my bay mare, citizen! Cécile's got thoroughbreds in her bloodline!'

Fifteen francs! Alfred Lerouge walked round in a circle, took off his visored cap and mopped his brow. A fine rain had started to fall. He replaced his headgear and returned to the fray.

'Come, come, my friend!' he began grandly, forgetting his unwashed and verminous state and reverting to the manner and vocabulary of his worldly youth, 'I can expect you to be reasonable, surely?'

'You disparaged my mare,' the driver said stubbornly, 'and I resent it.'

'I observed dispassionately that your yellow horse was wheezy and I'd willingly pay seven francs for her effort.'

The undertaker shook his head in refusal. Melancholy was engraved on his long emaciated face. 'Cécile didn't survive human hippophagy all through the siege of Paris just to listen to reproaches about her asthma,' he said gravely.

Badly though it had begun, the conversation might still have subsided into an ordinary transaction, but instead took a quarrelsome turn, an uncompromising tone attributable in equal measure to the corpse-driver's cupidity and a sudden loss of temper on Three-Nails's part.

'Oh come *on*, my good fellow,' he exploded suddenly, 'admit this nail of yours is a midget ... it's a doe wearing horseshoes!'

'She's a mare, whoever you are, related to the tsar through cavalry horses!'

'It's a sunken-backed pony!'

'At Topol in the Crimea, her father – a colonel's stallion – shoved the French army back with his chest!'

'It scuffs its toes! Its legs shake! Even in a carriage the trip would barely be worth eight francs!'

'It's worth twelve since you see fit to gripe, you old shitbag! More than that! You smell worse than a cadaver! You deserve to be charged for your shitty arse and stinking breath!'

Things weren't getting any better. Ziquet tugged at his sleeve, but the old man was examining the nag's yellowish fangs to see if it was of canonical age.

'Alive before Voltaire was born!' he crowed triumphantly. 'You should demand a rebate!'

'Fuck off out from under my wheels!' burped the coachman. He lifted his whip as a warning that the rabble were about to be driven off.

'Oh all right, nine francs then,' the old sailor said resignedly, rummaging in his pocket.

'Twelve, I said! Or you can do the whole trip on your little trotters.'

'Ten.'

'Twelve!'

'Twelve bullets? You must be barmy!' Ziquet put in. 'That's a no! Bleedin' wineskin.'

'Thirteen, because of your kid here,' the corpse-coachman escalated. 'I never even noticed you were lugging a snotnose around.'

'All right,' Three-Nails capitulated. 'Twelve and that's it.'

He only agreed to this extravagant expenditure in order to shorten the tingling impatience that possessed his entire being. The sooner he got there the sooner he would be rich. He covered Ziquet's mouth with his hand, for the boy was not expecting the undertaker to get off so lightly. Stifling a flood of disobliging remarks in his gullet, he propelled the boy onto the bloody straw in the back of the hearse. He himself put a foot on the step before climbing onto the box next to the vulture. But the driver was tough and suspicious. He wanted to know with whom he was dealing.

'The Negus of all the Ethiopias! The last king of Aksum!' boomed Three-Nails, hoping to suffocate the ugly driver in the eiderdown of his colonial culture. 'The heir to King Solomon's mines!'

'You could make a bit more effort about the stink, citizen,' the coachman said, holding his nose. 'Thirteen francs dead, payable in advance,' he added. 'You really do punish the beak.'

Three-Nails capitulated completely and unbuttoned the front of his patched-together waistcoat. Disarmed by the sight of a medium-sized fortune in his client's possession, the driver pocketed the sum and argued no more. 'Embrace me, comrade!' he cried, falling on the old ragpicker's neck. 'You really stink but your money smells of lilies!'

He lashed his nag into motion. Cécile, stung on the crupper, lurched into a jolting, plodding motion. The effort it cost her to move her stiffened shoulders, her knock-kneed legs, was painfully obvious. By the end of the street, encouraged by the exercise, she had lumbered into a gait resembling a trot. From time to time, when the slope went upward, she would slow to a walk. Her lungs wheezed as if there were an air-leak somewhere. She coughed frequently. Head down, sides heaving, mouth working, she would drag her load stubbornly over the shining cobbles, one rear leg splayed to the side. When the ground flattened out again the coachman would whip the exhausted beast, give her her head, call out to her encouragingly.

'We're nearly there,' Three-Nails said suddenly. 'I reckernise the area!'

52

Horace Grondin's den

To avoid attracting attention with a clattering arrival in this peaceful part of the 3rd *arrondissement*, the rag-and-bone man made the driver set them down at the edge of a windy road junction. It was past midnight by the old man's timepiece, and the area was deserted. The gaslamps dimly illuminated leprous housefronts, silent, dark and gloomy under the thin rain.

Alfred slid his behind off the carriage-box. The springs creaked under his weight and the step flexed as he climbed down.

'There's an east wind,' he grumbled as he reached the ground. 'My sciatica's playing up and my heart's out of breath.' He stood for a moment at the edge of the pavement listening to the irregular pumping of his blood in his arteries. He felt tired. He helped Ziquet jump to the ground and returned to the front of the hearse holding the small of his back.

The driver grinned balefully down at them as they passed.

'No offence meant,' he said in his sour, slovenly voice.

'None taken,' the old sailor replied. 'Don't expect a tip.' Turning his back with ostentatious finality, he waddled away across the wet, empty square bounded by four rows of houses, the boy at his heels.

The undertaker watched them go, rubbing his chin in pensive silence. His horse, well used to interminable waits, was standing with one foot off the ground, dropping dung.

Alfred Lerouge, fifty metres away, had stopped facing the houses at the other end of the square and was looking up at them, hands on hips. He had scanned the attic floors, inhabited by the poor, and his observant eyes were moving downward.

They stopped on Grondin's third-floor dwelling and examined the curtained windows minutely.

'That's where the goodies are,' he murmured. 'Nice new notes in a newspaper folder ... a fortune in a way, within reach!'

But he didn't seem to want to try the narrow door of number 6.

'What are we waiting for?' whispered Ziquet, who had been observing the old man closely.

'No point in taking any risks. Better to take our time than run into a jumpy concierge or a night patrol after looters ...' Three-Nails stepped back to widen his field of view. Again he scanned the tightly shuttered shops at pavement level, then carefully and repeatedly stared into the adjoining courtyards and alleys.

'I can't seem to get a proper grip on this business,' he declared suddenly with a shiver.

'The concierge's asleep, the curtain's drawn,' said Ziquet who had eased the door open and was looking inside.

'I can hear voices upstairs,' Three-Nails said. 'There are lights on the second floor.'

How could there not have been? For behind the shabby damp of that narrow house in the place de la Corderie, on benches in a room as bare as a college classroom, the revolution was at work despite the late hour. The impassioned voices of Benoît Malon, of Camélinat and the cream of the trade union Federations – Antoine Demay, Louis Pindy, Aminthe Dupont, Antoine Arnaud – were discussing the disastrous military expedition against the Versailles forces that had been decided by the Central Committee. As the bourgeois legitimists of the rue des Reservoirs danced round their unfortunate prisoners uttering vile and filthy words of triumph, from the Commune there arose angry voices calling for retaliation. In the heat of the moment many workers wanted to answer General de Galliffet's summary shootings by taking the head of a Parisian Bonapartist, Orleanist or legitmist for every patriot's life taken by Versailles. Others, more interested in symbols than blood-feuds, said that priests ought to be arrested.

The turmoil going on in front of the building may well have been far more trivial, but reflected nevertheless another aspect of the ant-like concerns of the human species, and showed in its small way that the great upheavals of history are often intermingled with the tumult of small lives.

'I don't like this place,' Three-Nails said, as he entered the damp, narrow cutting that led to the staircase. 'This dark passage is like a noose ...'

That is how it is with the atmosphere of places. Fifty years earlier a man from the provinces, visiting a mistress who lodged in the building, had been brutally garotted in that shadowy passage by a footpad who had followed him there to steal his purse ... but of course it can always be argued that Paris is a town tormented by memories. That there is no street, no alleyway, no staircase – or column of smoke rising straight into the sky – that does not recall the sufferings or ecstasies of earlier times; no bank, no tree, that does not speak of tender kisses, odious denials or violent deaths.

All the same, forewarned is forearmed. By striking fear into Three-Nails's heart, the dilapidated and insalubrious passageway of 6 rue de la Corderie had at least succeeded in making our friend realise the blindness of his enterprise. Might not the old ragpicker have bitten off more than he could chew? Had the lure of money drawn him into a hazardous expedition? What was he letting himself in for? Was he not betraying the libertarian principles of a life based on indifference to material goods, free from custom and inheritance alike, one lived without bargaining except to secure daily bread and a share of the sun and rain? Could he be about to make an irreparable mistake by violating the secret lair of a police heavyweight?

The spectre of Grondin rose before his eyes. Horace Grondin, the grey-eyed man missing since 18th March ... a man of prestigious calibre! Was it conceivable that he was not being sought by his friends and colleagues?

Even if the people's seizure of power had chased Monsieur Thiers's spies out of their gilded ministries, such people of course were a race of rats, able to keep afloat deep in the drains and lose themselves in the mass of urban flotsam. Nothing, not even Monsieur Claude's arrest and the recent installation of Rigault as prefect of police, was sufficient reason to assume that these informers would not still be installed in good vantage points, keeping their eyes open and awaiting their return, papering the walls with their grey shadows and grey eyes, a legion of hardened men ready to re-emerge at any opportunity.

The old sailor's heated imagination was starting to generate abominable images of himself being bled like a porker by the secret police. 'What if it was a trap?' Three-Nails wondered in a weak whisper.

'You've always said you believed in Grondin,' Ziquet said reproachfully. 'That's a good one, that is! Just blather, was it?'

'No, it's true,' the old man tried to reassure himself. 'A man on the point of death wouldn't get tricky with his benefactors . . .'

They were just passing the lodge when a voice from nowhere made them both start. They looked at each other, and with one accord tiptoed rapidly back to the doorway. Looking out, they saw their erstwhile coachman running towards them. Head down, arms pumping, the beanpole was running fast close under the fronts of the buildings. He skidded to a halt in front of them like a pale, unkempt sapling and shot the two ragpickers a sidelong look.

'I'm sure you two crooks're up to a bit of breakin' an' enterin'!' he panted with a rather surprising leer.

Three-Nails stared. Ziquet tensed. The undertaker smiled ingratiatingly, stuck out his vulture's neck and said: 'I just had a thought . . . In case you might need to get out of the neighbourhood a bit quicker than you come . . . would you like me to wait for you, my *gentlemans*?'

'Not worth your while,' Alfred said woodenly. 'We live here, third floor.'

'Yes,' the boy confirmed, 'my mum's up there. She's waiting up for us. We blow out the light, lie down and sleep till morning.'

'My eye! Alphonse Pouffard wasn't born yesterday.'

'Here's your tip, my friend,' Three-Nails said, putting his hand into his lining again. 'Here. I wish you goodnight!'

'You paying me off?' the driver demanded with a hint of angry threat.

'Best for everyone,' Alfred Lerouge advised him.

'I'm not convinced,' the undertaker said, leaving reluctantly at last.

When he was out of earshot Ziquet looked up at the old man and whispered: 'Another five francs for the crow, what you playin' at, Alfred?'

'It's just that I don't want any complications.' The rag-and-bone man's forehead furrowed with the effort of calculation. 'You're right, though,' he groaned bitterly, 'eighteen francs all told! In other words, the good money the Chassepots brought in's all gone on this expedition!'

'Pr'aps it was just a investment, like,' the youth said consolingly.

'Perhaps. He doesn't look like a poor man.' Three-Nails shook himself. He could hear hobnailed footsteps approaching. 'Let's not stay out here in the street. The Guard might take us for looters ... even court-martial us!'

'Even though we're only heirs of Ethiopia being rewarded for our merit!' the youth protested proudly. Head high, nose twitching like a ferret's, he slipped his hand into the old man's as they both vanished into the building again. 'Keep your eyes open, Papa Rust,' he whispered as they hurried past the porter's lodge. 'Three more floors to endure, and then the money of valour will fill our pockets!'

Young Ziquet was starting to take this treasure yarn seriously.

53

At which point the Commissaire's dog reappears

Hippolyte Barthélemy, lurking in Grondin's apartment where he had been living undercover for almost a fortnight, cocked an ear. A cotton cap jammed on his head, sprawled in the armchair where he had fallen asleep over a book, the ex-inspector of Gros-Caillou district stared with wide eyes. His mouth hung open, for he had just recognised the furtive sound of a key turning in the lock of the front door.

'God Almighty!' muttered the policemen through clenched teeth. 'Could this be Grondin returning to the fold?'

Without further delay he gathered his spindly legs under him, took off the dressing gown which he had been borrowing every night from the master of the house, and stood up in a simple shirt. As he put on his jacket he heard the key rattle in the lock again. He went out into the entry passage feeling that it would be polite to greet the owner of the apartment in person.

Just as he was about to open the front door, however, Barthélemy peering worriedly at the lock mechanism noticed that the key was rattling against the tumblers without turning the lock. Was it possible that the master of the house did not have the right key?

Barthélemy retreated into the room in which he had been camping primitively. Senses alert, he retreated to the angle of the fireplace, in which three logs still smouldered, leaned against the marble mantel and kept quiet. After a pause, the key had been withdrawn from the lock. There followed an exchange of whispers outside the door, the jingle of a bunch of keys. The policeman gulped. He heard another key being tried, a hurried scraping and back-and-forth rattling in the throat of the lock.

This put another complexion on things. Grondin would not have taken so long to get into his own dwelling; nor would he have needed to do so with such caution. Now persuaded that this persistent scraping of metal was the harbinger of serious trouble, and that it would soon give place to the hobnailed clamour of a police raid to search the dwelling of a former underchief of the Sûreté, Barthélemy prepared to receive Mr Rigault's heavies with the dignity and courage that became his lofty idea of the duties of an ex-official of the old régime. He tiptoed to the door of the room and closed it, blew out the nightlight and waited tensely.

The doorlock had yielded at last. A loud creak from the hinges, then the click of the door being carefully closed, were followed by a quiet trampling in the corridor and the urgent whispering of what sounded like a consultation.

How many were there? Perhaps three, even four. Barthélemy had a lot of experience of house visits. He had no difficulty imagining the commissaire who was leading the operation, and assumed he had been mandated by the Commune to look through Grondin's secret files, and if possible take him by surprise and arrest him. First Monsieur Claude, now his deputy: the purge was well under way! They broke into people's houses at night to surprise them in their sleep. Yes, really, what danger, what courage! These characters feared, no doubt, that the grey-eyed man would be holed up behind a large piece of furniture and would resist them fiercely. Obviously they hoped to prevent anything of the sort by invading his lair with this pitiful attempt at stealth!

Crouched behind an armchair, the skinny beanpole of the old police awaited his colleagues' entry. He expected at any second a thunder of boots, a violent invasion of the room and and a barking clamour of voices. Instead of which he heard clothes rubbing against walls, someone's throat being cleared, a long cautious silence and laboured breathing outside the door.

Barthélemy scratched at the centre parting in his black hair. The tension had become unbearable, but a new theory had made its appearance among the storm of contradictory thoughts that besieged his mind. You were wrong, 'Polyte, dammit! he scolded suddenly. His eyes darted madly hither and thither as he sorted through the flood of words washing rapidly about in his skull. Your comfy armchair's really messing you up, he told himself. You're going soft in front of the fire, flatfoot! Losing your finesse and your flair! All right then, forget the communers. They've got nothing to do with this. These jokers outside the door are a different type altogether!

He looked round, then rose from his hiding place and withdrew rapidly and silently behind a heavy double curtain of velvet. In two seconds he was breathing dust, hidden from sight in the folds. Thieves! Amateur burglars, nothing more! Opportunist looters visiting deserted dwellings!

Why on earth didn't I think of that sooner? wondered Commissaire Mespluchet's dog. In a crimefighter's reflex, he stuck his hand in his pocket and gripped the pearl butt of the Adams revolver. So the rascals wanted a nice surprise, did they? Bit of trouble, perhaps? Well, they were going to get it!

The long tall pale copper almost chuckled at the thought of the song he was going to sing the bad boys. He was ready to fall on them and give them a drubbing as soon as they entered the room. Barthélemy, remember, was thirty-six and had been raised in the streets of the city. More than once, when dealing with petty criminals, he had had to resort to fisticuffs to nail the villains down. He was pretty hard in a ruck and toerags of every description were his natural enemies.

Let them come!

54

The time is nigh

They came. There were two of them. One said in an undertone:
'I still don't feel right, Ziquet ... I'm all out of breath from climbing the stairs and this strange expedition doesn't seem to make sense ...'

'We aren't going back though, Papa Rust,' the other replied. 'You'll be able to buy yourself some teeth ... an eyeglass for your sight ... dreaming herb ... we're half-rich already!'

Their outlines showed against the light from the corridor. One was corpulent and clumsy, the other a thin, spiky adolescent figure.

'What's happening to me?' the older man cried. He staggered, and clutched at the door-jamb for support. 'You see? I nearly passed out again. My heart's seizing up! Can't get my breath ... legs don't work proper.' From his hiding place Barthélemy could hear the man's laboured, wheezing breath.

'I'd say it was more a matter of being scared of yer own shadow on the way up here!' the one called Ziquet said irritably. 'On the second-floor landing, where they was all shouting against Versailles, I seen you lookin' proper nervous!'

'I really don't feel well,' the older man insisted. 'And don't forget you owe me respect, you little weevil!'

The youngster did not pay much attention to this remark. He was carrying a lighted bedroom candlestick, evidently found in the entry passage, and now used it to light the six candles in the candalabras on the chimney. Their light revealed the visitors' faces: a verminous-looking potato-nosed sixty-year-old in a visored hat, and his son or grandson – a shock-headed urchin of fourteen or fifteen – already opening drawers like a thieving magpie.

The very sight of these sweepings from the no-man's-land between districts, these animated dregs, made the policemen lurking behind the velvet feel more cheerful. He felt he would have no trouble at all nabbing the two thieves, although he wondered where he would be able to put them. Then he remembered that the rear of the building housed a spiral service staircase whose stone steps plunged into a deep cellar. He thought he could probably lock these two characters down there until Grondin came back to deal with them.

The chimney clock was striking three, and Hippolyte Barthélemy was getting ready to put these muscular measures into effect, when the conversation between his visitors took a new turn that gave him pause.

'No need to untidy the drawers, Ziquet!' growled the fat man in the ripped frock-coat. '*Nor* to mess with the papers in the desk. Grondin told me where his lovely money is and I mean to respect his other property, 'cause the payment he's giving us ought to be enough to make us happy ...'

Grondin! Barthélemy started in his hiding place. Yes, he had really heard the name. These two scruffy Lascars know Grondin! They could even have been sent here by the man with slate-coloured eyes!

'D'you mean we ain't going to help ourselves to anything what catches our eye while we're here?' the youth asked indignantly.

'That's right, lad. We'll just take what's due to us. An honest man is one who's content with what God's given him.'

'The trouble with you, Alfred, is that you used to be a toff,' the youth replied. 'All old hat and proper behaviour ... you'll never change!'

Barthélemy's mind was racing. But, he thought, but, holy pudenda! If these two know the whereabouts and present situation of Monsieur Claude's chief spy ... they'll be able to take you to him ... This is an important development! *Ergo*, you've fallen on your feet, Hippolyte my boy! You've found the one you've been seeking in vain! Your blood brother! The ace of aces, the very best, your tutor in a sense, your shadow master!

The yellow-faced sleuth was beside himself with joy. On the verge of ending his long fortnight's isolation, sprawled stiffly in front of the fireplace, he turned his head to listen to the visored ragamuffin, whose voice had risen a pitch to lecture the youngster.

'We'll only take what we've got a right to, son,' he repeated. 'And if I was in better health tonight, I'd teach you a lesson!'

'By tannin' me hide as usual?'

'Giving you the spanking you deserve! From time to time, Ziquet, you need setting straight.'

'Hypocrite, Three-Nails!' the shock-headed youth said. 'You just want all the brass for yourself and your old woman ... child-exploiters, that's what you are!'

'How can you say that, you miserable imp? I saved you when your mother died in the street! I raised you under my roof. I taught you to read and count!'

'And haven't I paid you back and more, you old spectacle?'

'You've learned from me the rudiments of the noble calling of junk-dealer,' the old ragpicker pleaded.

'Bilge, Alfred! You've tanned my hide with your belt! I've ground bottles and bones, I've scraped skins! I've sorted through rubbish for you for seven years! Now I want to live my own life!'

'That's wrong talk, sailor, and you're upsetting me a lot,' the old man panted, distressed by a hard glint he had never seen before in his protégé's eye. His face was suddenly grey. He seemed to be thinking very hard about something. His hand went to his chest in surprise. He was struggling with a stabbing pain. Stunned dread in his eyes. 'Ah,' he sighed with a kind of regret, 'how disagreeable it is, that black mark in front of my eyes ...'

He took off his visored hat. His bald head, splashed with a port-wine stain and haloed with grey hair, was that of a worn-out man. He sighed and slumped into the hollow of the armchair. He fought for breath, his clenched knuckles gleaming white.

Ziquet shrugged impatiently. 'On yer feet, Alfred! The stuff's waitin'! This ain't the moment to get scared!'

'I've told you several times ... tonight,' the old ragpicker gasped, 'there's like a heavy weight on my breathing ... I got no air in my lungs. And I don't feel well. Not well at all.'

'Bit of a problem with yer liver if you ask me!' the youngster jeered. 'The great Caribbean adventurer, the scourge of the China Seas, is really a milksop drownin' in the sweat of his fear!'

Alfred Lerouge said nothing. From a deep well of discouragement, the wanderer of wastelands and dreamer of exotic shores raised defeated eyes to the insolent little cockerel who had chosen this moment to mutiny and thus revealed his stony heart. Sorrow printed small deep ravines across the ragpicker's face.

'It's true, Ziquet,' he said in a broken voice, 'all through my useless life, I've been cowardly. Cowardly, drunken and grasping. And now that it seems I'm about to close my umbrella, I ought really to confess something to you ...'

'Go on then, spit it out and have done with it!'

The old man turned his drawn face away and spoke with genuine humility.

'Well, laddie ... I'm not going to see tomorrow morning, so here's what you need to know, here's your last lesson ... I've never been round the world. I've never been a captain. My father wasn't a shipowner: just a simple sailor on coasters in the Seine estuary. Nothing but a deckhand on barges. And me too, when I was a young sailor on coasters, anything beyond Caudebec-en-Caux, outside the tidal bore, made me seasick ... made me throw up, and want to do my travelling in my head ...'

The youth was interested now, but he didn't seem really to understand what was happening. Behind the folds of curtain, Hippolyte Barthélemy found the scene moving. He could see the old man's waxen face through a slit in the velvet. He did not think he had the right to interrupt at such a moment, when a man about to report to the officer at heaven's gate was tying up the loose ends of his life. He kept quiet, waited and listened.

'What about the China Sea then?' the spotty adolescent asked. He frowned resentfully, his shrewd eyes staring closely into the tear-stained face of his tutor.

'China Sea?' Three-Nails smiled bitterly. 'Simple long-range dreams over the atlas ...'

'The brothels of Tamatave?'

'Suburban drinking dens ...'

'Princess Pi Chu?' the kid insisted. One by one the castles of his own fantasy world were crashing about his ears.

'An old flame, over Chatou way ... a white shadow with eyes like the moon ...'

'But Foochow at least? Valparaiso? Chekiang province?' the ugly little caterpillar almost begged.

'No. None of it,' the old man said, taking away the ladder.

'Nothing to be saved?'

'Nothing of nothing, I tell you! If I go, you're going to have to be on your own and courageous.' Three-Nails closed his eyes. In death as in life. He saw himself going out with a thin smile.

Seeing his lips turning white, his cheeks hollowing, his awareness slipping away, the signs of impending departure, the boy Ziquet was suddenly filled with anxiety for his own immediate interests. The thought that the old man might be about to be so selfish as to turn in his hod without warning made him panic. Roughly, he pinched the dying man's nose.

'Impossible,' he muttered, 'impossible!' With all his force he was thrusting away a thought that enraged him. 'Hey, you big lump!' He shook the old ragpicker violently by the shirt. 'Hey! Hey! Don't go droppin' off! At least tell me where the treasure is before you pass out!'

Alfred Lerouge's eyes opened. 'I've seen you coming for a long time, son,' he said bitterly. 'The old tree's not even properly down before you're hacking at the branches ... Ziquet ... my son almost ... when are you going to understand that we're nothing but flies, beating ourselves senseless against a window with unattainable freedom on the other side of it?'

'Unattainable freedom? Never mind that, tell me where the stuff is!'

Three-Nails closed his eyes. 'A bit at a time, I'm leaving,' he stated simply. 'I'm on me way. Ugly, it is.'

His imminent departure was like a thunderbolt falling at Ziquet's feet. It left the acquisitive youth prey to a dreadful anxiety that drove all veneration from his heart and revealed the true nature of his wounded soul in an immediate outpouring of violence. His voice cracked and squeaky with rage, the boy cackled:

'For years, you old bag of guts, you been pourin' booze down yer hole without giving me nothing, and now I ask you you *still* won't give me nothing!' Losing all restraint, the miserable boy gripped his benefactor by the collar and shook him back and forth like a plum tree.

'Four hairs on your chin and you want to prevail by force,' the old man panted, signing weakly to the boy to stop. But the adolescent had lost control completely. He was sobbing hoarsely. He took a small bronze casting, the bust of a philosopher, from the desk and raised it menacingly over the dying man.

Three-Nails looked at the boy calmly with glassy eyes. 'I've had it,' he sighed. One hand twisted in the clothing over his heart. 'Don't do what you can't undo, son.'

'He's on the point of leaving us,' Barthélemy's grave voice said at Ziquet's shoulder. 'Don't become a murderer.' He nudged Ziquet gently with the muzzle of the revolver and took the bronze out of his hand. The boy offered no resistance. He started to tremble violently in every limb, returning from his brief fit of insanity with a stricken cry, as if awakening from a nightmare. He recognised his fault, the horrible stinking abyss into which he had so nearly fallen. He turned to Barthélemy the face of a young boy whose eyes were fogged with tears. The policeman lowered his pistol.

Dishevelled, flushed, pouring with sweat, Ziquet flung himself on his knees beside Three-Nails's slumped body. His fingers stroked the forehead sticky with the sweat of death, deciphered the braille of its filth-clogged wrinkles with a longing to relearn one last time exactly what sort of hero had been this adventurer in miniature, whose true nature he hadn't been able to discern through the mask of smelliness.

At racing speed (What a seething there is in human consciousness! How mysterious is the secret way that leads to reflection!), that adolescent, about to become a man, travelled again the roads of his apprenticeship. He retraced his steps as one pays one's debts. O wondrous time of earliest youth! His pilgrimage took him to those magical evenings when, as a child of four or five, perched on the knee of Alfred Lerouge and enveloped in his stench of sardines and rum, he had had the happy impression that he could levitate, that his body was free of material weight and he could become a white bird able to cross infinite spaces.

He recalled shadowy and rumbling stormy evenings under the lamp of the pagoda, with Three-Nails describing his adventurous landings on the atolls of the Austral Shelf. He saw clearly in his mind's eye the marine charts spread on the rickety table in the route de la Révolte. The captain's compass gleaming in the old ragpicker's hand as he set a course for the Pearl Islands. Ziquet heard the slow booming of surf on distant shores like the labouring of a fading heart, the rustling of wreckage washing back and forth on a reef, the grave moaning of native trumpets; vomited seawater, was washed up broken-bodied on the shore, fought off fever while dusky girls with necklaces of blossom and gingerbread breasts soothed his troubled sleep, and the ocean, sated after wrecking the ship, hissed quietly among inky rocks as night fell.

That was the heritage, the whole hidden treasure! A few diamonds gathered from a man's chest! Sobbing, Ziquet stroked the face of Alfred Lerouge, sculpted by poverty and rotgut. He smoothed the scars engraved there by privation and disappointment. Gently, he comforted the passing of one who would be travelling alone.

Gradually, as he made his final preparations, the dying man's brow cleared. Ziquet as in the days of dreams recounted gazed under a white sun across the boundless pasture of unmoving ocean to its distant junction with a pure sky. Reflected in this double mirror he followed the twin trace of a flock of white-gleaming seabirds. But as the birds converged on that mental horizon he cried out, and cast about floundering for a shore. He knew that he was losing Three-Nails, the only being who had ever tried to guide him in the nightmare of life. Beating himself wildly on the chest, haggard-eyed, spine racked with nervous shivers, inexplicably cold, he wailed openly and begged the old man's forgiveness. His despair was unimaginable, a sucking undertow of his entire soul far greater than any normal human suffering. His mouth twisted fantastically.

'Papa Rust!' Ziquet cried. 'I've understood! I swear I've understood!'

As the breath rattled in his throat, the old man seemed to stir in response. Anyway, Ziquet felt him move, and that was the important thing. A moment later Alfred Lerouge had stepped aboard and pushed off.

As he had arrived, so he left. He had packed his baggage and set a course for the mystery of the great light, set sail across the endless pasture of fish, among Sargasso oceans, flying squadrons, the thousand tempests of which he had dreamed so much; and was gliding over the billows at the helm of a fantastic white boat, smiling. His last act in this world.

Ziquet flung himself weeping on the body and crowned the old man's career as a father, almost, by repenting, by expressing love and gratitude, by begging forgiveness, by saying and repeating that he would join the federals' army, and that Three-Nails would be proud of him.

PART 5

HOPE DESTROYED

55

Route de la Révolte

Bosco the cockatoo, who served as ornament and sign outside the extravagant pagoda Alfred Lerouge had built on the edge of Cow City, gave a loud shriek inside his green cage and puffed up his feathers indignantly. Crest raised, breast inflated, the bird beat its wings in protest as a large dog came sniffing around the yard outside its master's house.

The animal toured the yard as confidently as a postman. 'What are yer, yer cow?' Bosco screamed, but he might have saved his breath, for the verminous cur paid him no attention whatever. Now, tail at half-mast, it was sniffing, absorbed, all around the plank base of the building.

'Repel boarders!' the bird squawked. 'All hands on deck!'

The short-haired visitor continued with its minutely detailed inspection of every nook and cranny, sniffing at the walls of earth-filled sardine tins. Bypassing the caulkings of tarred fabric, the dog came to a halt in front of a pile of cups and saucers decorated with gold leaf, awaiting the chemical treatment with which Three-Nails intended one day to extract the bullion.

'Bloody hell! Fuckery!' the parrot swore. 'Stop thief! Stop thief!'

With extraordinary delicacy, the mongrel had in fact taken a cup in its mouth, and with its canine teeth hooked through the porcelain handle was about to walk off with its booty when a stifled noise from nearby made it put the cup down and cock its ear. After a long moment, reassured by the ensuing silence, it inserted its snout between the folds of a sack that served as a curtain and poked its head inside the building.

Once inside, seeing a human form stretched out under

bedcovers, the dog sat down to think. It beat its tail against the ground in a friendly way and gave two or three sociable little whines, but getting no reaction decided to investigate more closely. The shrewd mongrel examined the pale, wasted face of Mr Grondin by the light of a candle in a bottle on a stool nearby.

Reassured by his immobility, the animal ran its tongue over its chops and started ferreting around the shack. Sniffing hither and thither, it quickly laid its nose on a bloodied dressing that la Chouette had accidentally dropped between the bed and the wall after a treatment. Abandoning all caution, the canine intruder had just snapped this up in its maw when a sledgehammer-like fist slipped out from under the carpet that served as a bedcover and descended on the dog's head with great force and accuracy. The brute gave a yelp of pain and made a scrabbling getaway without staying to argue. When it reached the rickety table, however, it lifted a hasty rear leg and pissed on its nearest leg. Then, ignoring the gilded cup that had originally attracted it, but hanging onto its ignoble piece of lint, it left the Chinese shanty as busily as it had arrived.

Bosco the parrot, surprised by the vagabond's unexpected departure, squawked a stream of fucks! shits! and cows! after it. He sidled along his perch puffing himself up at the cur with the outraged air of a concierge when a tenant in rent arrears passes the lodge.

In his alcove, Horace Grondin came to life. His eye lively, he turned towards the rag-curtained doorway and looked through the gap the dog had left. He could see in the main room the greasy table, a sheaf of straw and a pile of rags. In the opening of the entrance door, on the other side of the room, he could see the outline of a man in multicoloured rags and the back of a woman dressed in black, gesticulating vigorously. He could hardly hear what they were saying, and it was only from the matron's shrill voice that he was able to recognise la Chouette.

The nasty piece of work who was sniffing round Three-Nails's woman with a nice smile and making her shout was called Greaseball. He was soft-looking, with gleaming skin. His remarks and intonations oozed affectation and falsity. He had just complimented la Chouette on her neck-scarf, and added a suggestion to the old jade that they might 'go and lie down for a minute' together and 'get the old hide working' on a nice soft bed.

'An ugly old thing like me?' la Chouette bridled disgustedly.

'I'll warm your arse good and proper,' Greaseball said. 'I'm sure that in bed you're a real goer! Three-Nails won't know nothing.'

The sneak-thief brought his shining nose close to the healer's large bosom. He spoke gently, as enterprising and determined as if her rags had covered the pearly and palpitating flesh of a maiden in bud, rather than an ageless monster perched on two unappetising rear hams.

'I like a nice handful,' he was saying. 'Come on! We'll slip Villejuif into Pontoise . . .'

La Chouette loosed an appalling squawk. 'Back off, slimy! If I was to go behind my man's back it wouldn't be with a thing like you!'

But the tiresome oil-spot wouldn't go away. He had decided to come to the point, and was now using con-artist's wiles to worm out of her the identity of the mysterious lodger that she and her husband had been sheltering for at least three weeks in their tarred pagoda.

'Nobody in our place,' the old woman said. She was scowling fiercely. Her big round sepia-ringed eyes, her pinched nose in a flat face, vividly recalled the screech-owl that had given her its name.

'That's not what the neighbours say,' Greaseball said knowingly. 'Three-Nails came home at dusk on 21st March. A man was carried, I been told.'

The lady of the house shook her head so firmly that her hair came undone. She shook all her feathers. All her amulets. Strings of cat claws, a crucifix, brass curtain rings, an assortment of wooden beads, a compass that Alfred had given her.

But Greaseball wouldn't leave her in peace. Rustling in his theatrical rags tied on with string, the villain kept filling the air around her with seductive words. Smiling like a whole gang of confidence tricksters. Now he was suggesting that he and the old woman go and drink a couple of belts at the Casserole, for he knew her tendency to fray at the edges after drinking too much.

'Just a little crock or so, Chouette! A cup of frien'ship t'keep out the cold and the loneliness . . .'

'I don't want a drink! All I want is for you to leave me alone,' la Chouette was saying. For the fact was that Greaseball's reputation was not all that good in ragpicker society. Although he did collect junk and make his rounds with a hook, in Clichy and Saint-Ouen they knew where his true interests lay: he was closer to the criminals along the Ourcq than to the brotherhood of the hook and hod. The tall harpy wasn't going to be taken in by his blandishments. She launched a counterattack.

''Oo's took the trouble to send you here?'

'No one, Chouette! I'm just asking out of general curiosity . . .'

'Oh yes? Save yer breath you old lump of gob. And save yourself the trouble of walking yer fat hand across me privates. You'll get nothing from me. I ain't stupid! It's Trocard the Goldsmith what's sent you sniffin' around down here.'

'He did ask everyone who was getting round Pantruche[1] to fish around in the lodging-houses,' the fellow admitted. 'The Goldsmith's lost sight of one of his richest customers . . . ain't seen him since 18th March would you believe . . . and here it is mid-April! He was last seen on the Butte. Since then, not a trace! Vanished! A geezer what owes him a fortune! And the boss don't like to be out of pocket . . . he's worrying.'

'There's no one like that in this house,' la Chouette repeated. She flapped her apron three times to counter the bad luck that had been raging since the tall grey-eyed gipsy had arrived in her house, then had a panicky thought for Three-Nails who had been away for three nights now. Without any kind of farewell, she turned her back on her interlocutor and rushed into the pagoda.

'Be seein' you!' Greaseball called after her.

He walked a few paces through the rubbish in the road outside, paused thoughtfully, stuck two fingers in his mouth and

---

[1] *Translator's note*: Paris.

whistled. At the signal a big yellowish pelt heaved itself out of the dusty floor of a rabbit-skin shed and emerged into the daylight. The big verminous mongrel arrived at full speed and fawned crouching before its master, tail clamped between its legs. Greaseball scratched the top of the beast's head and it gazed meltingly up at him.

'Well, Gobseck, you old dishcloth, what news?' he asked. 'What did you find in the shithole? Little bit o' gold? Silver-gilt spoon p'raps? A secret maybe? Tell yer dad! Show me what yer got. Open up, yer bastard! Got something stuffed in yer cheek? Come on! Show Greaseball what you got stashed in yer stinkin' mug!'

He wedged the submissive animal's jaws open and felt about in its throat. A moment later he was flattening out an unattractive wisp of cloth. 'Old dressings ... with blood! Mazette, you beautiful hound you! You're better at this than getting truffles! You've found the first prize in the bran-tub. He's there, ain't he, the feller with grey eyes? And you've seen him, my fine huntin' dog! He's right there, we've got him! And Mr Trocard won't be tight neither! 'E'll pay up, open-handed!'

56

Miss Palmyre's afternoons

April breezes flapped the canvas on the Montmartre fairground. Entwined couples were enjoying the hot breath of the new season. Drunk on the warmth of a Communard sun, the Parisians were still filled with the party spirit. Indeed as the final tragedy swept relentlessly down on them, an extraordinary sort of exultation shone from their eyes.

Swarming and talkative crowds roamed the dusty alleys in their Sunday best. The fairground swings sailed high in the sky; roundabouts squeaked, stallholders offered samples of gingerbread. Children flew flocks of small paper kites.

Despite the competition from profiteers charging ten centimes for a look through a telescope at the theatre of military operations outside the city gates, the itinerant showfolk kept up their patter.

Madame Tambour's harangue streamed forth as usual. Palmyre, in gipsy satin, lifted her dumb-bells. Tsé-Tsé, the human fly, sipped nectar from big paper flowers. Soupir, Mi-Bémol and Clé-de-Fa played music offstage, putting the strollers in the mood. Pifastre and Crépon went round with the hat, or passed the plate below the stage. Trombine, the hydrocephalic, awaited customers at the back of his booth, seated in the lotus position on a gold-fringed plinth. Other show people nearby were exhibiting their own trunks and missing parts. Their twistings and cripplings. Their humps and deformities.

The people of the Butte were queuing to see awfulnesses amid real life. The war was on the skyline. Seven generals lined up in their boots ... their names were Maud'huy, Susbielle, Bruat, Grenier, Montaudon, Pellé and Vergé. Everyone knew they were eager, that their divisions were at the walls of the forts to the south and west, already riddled by Versailles shells. But the sword-swallower continued to enjoy great public success, and the human cannonball was still volunteering himself as a projectile for use against the rue des Réservoirs.

Accompanied – indeed closely supervised – by the giant Marbuche, Antoine Tarpagnan was still living in his caravan in the middle of the fairground. He was counting the days, spelling out the life of a recluse. He was virtually the wrestler's prisoner, unable to leave the fairground except in his company. If he ever looked like drifting out of the village of tents and wagons, the strongman would invariably descend on him, offer him every kindness, and beg him not to try to flee: for that would oblige Marbuche to strike him dead.

The hot-headed captain was not much enjoying this miserable adventure, which was depriving him of military glory and blinding him to the revolutionary events going on around him. He had only decided to submit to it in the hope of finding Gabriella quickly and rescuing the woman he loved from Saint-Lago's brutality. Longing fantasies about grinding his boot-heel in that infamous pimp's pockmarked face made his generous heart beat irregularly.

A strange smile stitched on his face, fists clenched, jaw set, Antoine Tarpagnan watched through the small wagon window as the daylight faded into evening. He looked forward to the coming night as a deliverance.

Ritually, through dark, gutter-like streets, along footpaths between allotments, the two men made their nightly pilgrimage to the most ill-famed districts of the capital. They combed the short-time houses, the Belleville stamping-mills, the pox-farms of Clichy, pursuing their endless quest for news of the unhappy Pucci from one bordello to the next, on and on. No buttock-boutique or clap-ridden whore stable, not a single up-against-the-wall soldier's bargain-priced two-minute sex-canteen, was omitted from their survey.

Sometimes the slits and ponces laughed in their faces. In the end they were known from the rue Saint-Vincent to la Chapelle and from Bastille to Rochechouart as the ones who came to look over the ladies in the salon but never got round to doing anything. Some called them the Two Oglers, others the Sisters of Charity, while still others assumed they were homosexual and called them Buck and Nanny, the knights of the arsehole.

Tarpagnan paid little attention to the insults, mockery and nicknames. The Gascon accepted the affronts to himself quite cheerfully, taking the philosophic view that they were a necessary expiation, an inadequate counterweight to the intolerable, tooth-grinding ordeal being undergone by Gabriella Pucci. He likened her sufferings, the defilement to which she was being subjected, to those once endured by the murdered Jeanne, and his longing to be reunited with his great love was vastly accentuated as a result. In his view it was akin to saving human life.

He and Marbuche returned as usual in the early morning. Exhausted by their night's travels, the two companions climbed back into the big travelling caravan the Manchurian had taken over from his father, the one-time lion-tamer. The giant yawned. He took off his flat zebra-skin slippers, loosened the single strap of his wrestler's costume revealing the massive white musculature of his shoulders and back, and rubbed his eyes, an invariable sign that he was contemplating sleep.

He stretched out on his bed and heaved a soul-ravaging sigh. Then he rose and took down from a brass clothes-peg the splendid dress that Gabriella Pucci had given him as a gage of her affection.

He lay down once more clutching his treasure in his hand, buried his nose in the fabric and inhaled deeply. He wallowed in its perfume, then began rubbing it in his hands. And when Tarpagnan, irritated by the silky rustling, asked him what, Jesus Christ! he was fiddling with under his covers, the colossus replied as he always did:

'I'm making a dress noise, my friend. I'm breathing Mademoiselle so that I won't forget her. I'm doing the things she taught Marbuche. Marbuche is doing what he must to become a child again . . .'

His eyelids were closing. His head starting to droop sideways. Almost immersed in the liqueur of sleep, he awoke with a start.

He saw Tarpagnan's eyes on him and remembered that if he fell asleep there was every chance his partner would try to leave. Rising once more, he walked to the door, leaned outside and called: 'Palmyre! Can you come over?'

The lilliputian always arrived straight away. She always dressed herself up first thing in the morning. Every day she tied a fresh pink bow in her hair. She lived and dreamed Tarpagnan. She blushed when he spoke to her.

Beautiful moments extracted from the unstoppable flow of time! More surely than an unthinking, untroubled happiness, intimacy with the most deprived beings often leads those who dare to risk it into a new sort of enlightenment. It is a whole school of love. It gives substance to invisible things and reveals what one was hitherto incapable of seeing.

Tarpagnan had found some very endearing defects in his new friends. While it is true that loving yourself in another is sometimes tiresome, the Gascon's contact with unfamiliar depths of gracelessness and abjection, his daily familiarity with extreme hideousness, was at least teaching him as the days passed to discern beauty and grace even in the darkest caverns of murdered flesh. To spot the glint of humour in the rheumiest eye; to ignore the attached nubs and stumps in the fraternal glow of a face nuzzling suddenly against him. He was beginning to realise what passion he inspired in the midget.

Sometimes, with Palmyre, he was invaded by the sweet intimacy into which women can lead you. Despite her small size the lilliputian had finely drawn features, and was buoyed up by a laughing attitude to life. She had a gift for making him calmer. If she felt that he was tense, she would climb on the bed without hesitation and ruffle with worried tenderness the dark and bushy locks that sprang from above his obstinate brow.

He would relax. He liked listening to her stories which sang of travelling wheels. She would tell him the news and gossip, or offer to play music to him. One day she had turned up with a violin in her hand.

'Can you read music?'

'I learned to play by ear.'

She played wonderfully. When she was there she was always

doing something peaceable. She would make tea. She would pour it. There reigned between them a calm and tranquil harmony. But when he thought he had said enough he would fall silent, very silent. And waste a good minute or two thinking about Caf'conc'.

He would imagine the young woman's distress, the air thick with men's panting. The state of moral and physical dilapidation into which she must be falling. Her closed face frozen with distaste, the shiver between her shoulders each time she had to endure the loathed pumping of the dominator of the moment between her glistening thighs, in the ultimate privacy of her subservient sex.

Antoine was haunted by the fear that he would arrive too late at the bedside of his beauty. By finding intact the lively glow of her flesh and the prettiness of her face, he hoped to repair in some sense the scattered breakages of his own youth. He could not forgive himself for having been the cause of such a cruel shipwreck.

The thought of that stifling air, those odours of arousal, the human sweat, the congested faces, the daily roughnesses and affronts she had to endure, made Tarpagnan stop feeling his own flesh, lose contact with his own body and command of his muscles. Or to be more exact he did his level best to forget them. He had come to detest even the ardent surge of his own virility, and angrily dispelled the clouds of erotic longing whenever he felt himself starting to dwell on the memory of one he had known in the magic of her absolute beauty.

Beside him in the cool shadows, Palmyre would slip her little hand into his and leave him to his thoughts. When she dared to speak at last, she would toss a handful of shingle into the pond of his secret thoughts.

'You're thinking about *her*, aren't you?'

'Yes . . .' He lifted his head. If someone had asked him at such a moment if he was in love with the Queen of Spades, he would have given the same answer. If Palmyre had added, 'Shall we go to bed together?' he would have said yes again. It would have been an automatic response. He would not have known what he was saying. And of course the tiny woman knew this very well. So all she did was to whisper:

'You often leave me in your thoughts. I know it, your mind wanders. I've noticed it. I talk to you but you aren't with me. You're with her.'

'Yes. I am with her.'

'You think I'm too small. That I'm just a fragment.'

'No. It's just that I love her too much.'

'You can't love someone too much. It's a big thing.'

'Yes, a big thing,' Antoine agreed. His mind was already wandering again.

Palmyre said no more. She had learned to forget herself so long ago.

57

The blue Besillon
mountains

At the same despairing time that Tarpagnan was learning to carry on living despite everything and to find his bearings in the limbo of a sub-world of acrobats, contortionists, snake-men, bearded women and midgets, Gabriella Pucci was having to endure the feverish heat of other people's pleasure, the distasteful demands of the gutter clients who came to slake their gross lusts, sexual frustrations and cretinous fantasies in her body.

In the small area around rue Girardon and the Abbesses, the secret word had spread that Saint-Lago, the pimp with the pockmarked face, had in his stable a marvel of marvels: a girl of great beauty, a soft and passive doll whose cold and disdainful air could not be disturbed by any love technique, from whom no embrace or caress could extract the slightest whimper, momentary glance or faltering word. A painfully shivering woman, a courtesan who was compliant despite everything (Saint-Lago beat her every morning in accordance with Trocard's orders); a lover with the eyes of a dreamy child, whose transports looked like death, whose queenly manners challenged vulgarity, whose wounded animal detachment enabled her to withhold her pleasure instead of sharing it, in short a prostitute of an entirely new sort for a modest establishment like Venus's Staircase.

The truth of the matter is that Gabriella Pucci's universe consisted of four dirty walls. After her morning thrashing, she breakfasted on a slice of bread soaked in milk. For a quarter of an hour she could look outside, through a barred window from which a well could be seen at the bottom of the garden. She would open the casement, shake the bars with impotent hands, breathe the cool air flavoured with fog and listen for the rumble of artillery. Sometimes it seemed very close, as if shells were falling inside Paris.

Then she would turn away with the movements of a sleepwalker. Two chairs, a table, a candle. She would use a pot of water to maintain a semblance of hygiene.

She would listen to the sounds of the awakening house and tidy up her bed. Her face slightly hollowed, the flesh as if collapsed around the bridge of her nose, sunken eye-sockets and cheeks, she would pass some dull hours tending a few flowers in pots or reading an old newspaper. In it was mentioned a decree issued by the Commune on 12th April proposing the demolition of the column of the Grande Armée in the place Vendôme, that 'symbol of Bonapartism and monument to hatred'. It also reported a deliberation on the proposed outright closure of all brothels, which the authorities held to be incompatible with the 'dignity of emancipated woman'.

Gabriella Pucci shrugged her shoulders. She wore a fixed smile that spoke of her constant struggle against sighing. God knows, the landscape of her days was grim and dreary enough. God knows too that the frightful Saint-Lago laid into her with a heavy hand. Utterly vile was the gusto with which he cuffed her each morning. Hit her. Beat her. Humiliated her.

With the passage of time a private sensation of impurity had slowly invaded her, and the constant defeat of her body took her further away from Tarpagnan every day. Feeling that their flouted love was now unattainable, she had ended by forbidding herself even to think of her handsome sweetheart. She had effaced totally the memory of his rumbling voice, his vivacious eye, the elastic spring of his stride; and as little by little she became used to the squalid licence of her condition as a public woman, even the need to weep subsided in her. She breathed just enough to stay alive.

Her limp hand let the paper fall. She was thinking of her home village: her mind travelled to Barjols, a hamlet of tanners perched on the flank of the Besillon mountains. She imagined the streets flooded with sunshine, the little squares framed in gold and reflections. She heard the song of crickets and the buzzing of insects. She entered the small house of her parents, Italian émigrés washed up in the countryside of inland Provence in search of a second country. She followed her father to the factory gate, saw him when he was not too far gone in wine, singing in Piedmontese the praises of the village of thirty-two springs that had welcomed him.

In the fastness of her mind the prisoner strode free, her lips parted. Her wandering spirit lingered for a while in her mother's garden.

There were more bitter days when she measured the failure, the emptiness, of her life. On those mornings she would be a hair's breadth from giving up the struggle, launching herself down the slope that would take her irrevocably beyond the limits of reason. Merciful God! Why not just get it over? Find rest under a plot of earth in a faint odour of leafmould. Goodbye now and for ever.

She thought of the admirable women she had encountered. Louise Michel and her followers in rue Lévisse. And she always ended by writing a letter to Edmond Trocard, one more letter, telling her tormentor that she had paid sufficient tribute to his vengeance, begging him to release her to enrol in a corps of nurses. She knew that the next day, when she gave this supplication to Saint-Lago, he would give her a smack with the back of his hand, that she would get six extra swipes with the belt. She knew the letter would never reach Trocard. But she persevered: stubborn, ill-looking, pathetic in her determination.

Around three in the afternoon, however her time had been spent, the poor entombed girl would start on hearing the first ring of the doorbell. She would hear the jingling of the female underboss's keys in the corridor outside, and a key would be inserted in the lock to unfasten the snib that kept her prisoner outside working hours. Cascades of icy shivers would run down her spine.

Her hand would go to her mouth when she heard the clatter of footsteps on the tiles, the laughter and loud voices of regular customers arriving. She would breathe steadily to give herself the courage to face another day of short-time. When she felt especially miserable she would close her eyes and conjure up a mountain with two humps, like the Besillon. She would breathe steadily. She would leave for the mountain. But what did it really mean in her case, leave? Nothing, of course. Unless we accept deep down that life has a hidden meaning and that the designs of the All-Highest are sometimes even more unfathomable than the void that contains them.

58

Ziquet goes off
to war

With narrowed, watering eyes, one hand trying to shade them from the sun, the other in the front pocket of her apron, la Chouette stood beside the road, trying to identify the strange vehicle that had just turned off the route de la Révoke and was approaching in a cloud of dust, a dot on the bright horizon.

In these times of military priority and requisitioning, horses were sufficiently rare for her to be surprised by the presence of one near a village of shacks and hovels like Cow City. Keeping her back to the pagoda with the overlapping roofs, she withdrew into the yard, ran across to the building's only window and rapped on the glass.

'M'sieu Horace!' she called to the man hidden inside. 'We've got visitors!'

Then she ran to the front door which stood open to let the sunshine in, a door her husband had painted a fine shade of Chinese red with gold jambs. She closed and double-locked it. She liked to take her precautions and place a barrier in front of visitors, even if the planks were worm-eaten, even if the whole shack was just a tottering pile of cardboard.

She tossed the key into Bosco's cage, shut up you filthy brute, bleeding macaw, they'll never think of looking for it under your claws! Christ in heaven! That bloody American parrot swore worse than an old navy man. Shut up, I said, dirty animal, hold your beak! The old woman made cabbalistic signs, her amulets and fetishes jingling on the necklace of claws about her scraggy neck, swaying rapidly along in her full skirt. She was very anxious.

She was acting from a strong intuition of danger. She would not have been able to explain her behaviour but she could taste salt in her mouth. That was the taste that always came to her tongue and made her thirsty when misfortune was prowling nearby.

She left the yard again and ran back to the road. Yes, the carriage was coming this way, no doubt of it, bounding over the potholes, the horse shooting its feet out in all directions as it snaked among evil-smelling bonfires. It took a short cut through the rubbish field.

The tall harpy kept a cool head. Behind her back she gripped a ragpicker's billhook, a number seven. She wasn't going to just stand by if things turned nasty. If the intruders turned out to be henchmen of the Goldsmith, Ourcq thugs sent by Greaseball. Some bunch of wrong 'uns here to cause grief to her *gent with the grey eyes*, Mr Horace, as she called Grondin these days. She thought she had some say where he was concerned. He was her work in a way, her product. Hadn't she got him back on his feet, that big vulture from rozzer central?

He had been looking a lot better the last two or three days. His cheeks had a little warmth in them. His left eye had opened. The blood-blister had gone down, leaving a white scar. He had asked for water, he had wanted to steep himself in soap. I mean fancy! He only bleedin' wanted white soap: that was all! White soap in Cow City! As if! La Chouette had bustled about, and brought him a *necessary* in the pockets of her skirt: a towel, a razor with a fine edge, a splinter of mirror to see himself in. All squalid and whiskery, he had shaved. She had even helped him at first. He was thin and weak and could hardly hold himself up. She held him tightly round the waist and helped him relearn how to walk. It didn't take long. He had given her a smile, a real one. 'Call me Horace.' She had bitten her lip with happiness, promised to get him some clothes. He had asked for a pipe and a bit of tobacco. She had found him a short and porous clay thing, a marseillaise.

For the moment, though, the maker of ointments, potions and

infusions, the healer of humours and sores, had something more pressing on her mind. Her night-hunter's eyes travelled through space. They fell once more on the cartload coming, outlined against the low fuzzy sun.

'Oo could these bleeders be, then? Bravoes with long knives? Communers from up by the revolution? Unless it *should be*, thought la Chouette – and why shouldn't it? – that old wreck Alfred, with a wagonload of other drunks of the same stripe. Eh? ... unless. Unless, like I say, it's the old hook coming home to his quarters and residence? Bloody old junkman, with his hod and basket! Christ Almighty! la Chouette thought suddenly. So ... could Lerouge have got hold of the loot? Invested in a horse? Five nights he'd been away, Three-Nails had! He had to've been takin' his time in the pubs, boozi his face off with hard stuff, bloody old pig! Swilling with that wine-seller Saint-Flour! Pouring his gold down his throat in great gobfuls, the old camel! Sternly, la Chouette folded her arms.

The ramshackle vehicle was almost there. In the glory of the setting sun its black body in a halo of golden dust had only to maintain for another fifty metres the dishevelled downhill trot of a horse flinging what looked like seven or eight legs in all directions, although its overall speed was sedate.

'Christ! A stiffs' omnibus! A cadavers' carriage!' exclaimed la Chouette, crossing herself three times as she recognised a hearse decorated with red flags and pulled by a small spavined nag still dressed in a mourning blanket. Her heart was in her throat. She felt a strong impulse to vomit in the road as in a great clattering of axles and shafts, a rascally coachman leaning backwards on rigid legs and hauling on the reins with all his strength halted the demented tap-dancing of his little yellow mare.

'Alphonse Pouffard, undertaker and Commune ambulance-driver, at your service,' greeted the red-eyed vulture, raising his *morillo* hat to the old witch. 'Got to really want to see yer, my good lady, to come all the way down here!'

'Where's my husband?' La Chouette asked.

'Ah, don't you worry, little lady! We ain't in a hurry,' the driver replied. He stank of winewash. 'You wouldn't have a bit of clean water for my Cécile to drink, would you? My mare's knackered. She comes before everyone else.'

'Where's Alfred Lerouge?' the healer repeated. The salt taste flooded her mouth again. 'Where's my old hook gone?' Her piercing eyes were fixed on the other side of the box where, next to the driver, a tall, knobbly-kneed, pallid workman with a cap on his head was preparing to step down.

'Your husband dropped his guard,' this man said as he placed a foot on the step.

'What did you say?' The old woman suddenly felt as if she had been abandoned alone in the middle of a desert.

Hippolyte Bathélemy – for of course it was he – stepped onto the ground, removed his cap and swept the crone a grave formal bow. 'On Tuesday night, Lerouge Alfred, age sixty-seven, licensed ragpicker and retired deep-sea captain, took the high jump,' he repeated. He held out Three-Nails's tortoiseshell snuffbox and pocket chronometer. 'Here's his baccy and his watch.'

'It's beyond belief,' la Chouette muttered. The hand holding the watch and tortoiseshell box disappeared into the folds of her long, full skirt. She stared at the messenger with huge inscrutable eyes. Interpreting this as a sign of suffering, Barthélemy felt obliged to add a few comforting words of hope.

'Your husband, that fine sailor, suffered a major cerebral stroke that laid him so low that he chose to put out the light ... Even on the point of going down, however, he sailed his vessel with the greatest dignity ... It's in acknowledgement of his irreparable loss that we offer you, madam, our sad and heartfelt condolences.'

The tall flat-faced harpy gave him an unblinking stare. 'Don't give me no flannel, citizen,' she said quietly. 'What I mean is, tell me straight, m'sieu. What happened to him?'

The copper tried a different formula. 'His heart killed him. There was nothing we could do.'

'We?'

'The lad and me,' Hippolyte Barthélemy explained. He indicated Ziquet whose dishevelled poll had just slunk into view from behind the hearse. 'This young chap's very upset ... step forward, young Ziquet ...'

La Chouette turned on the apprentice. 'There you are, yer little toad,' she said in an unfriendly tone. 'What was you hiding for? Why d'you let others speak in yer place? Speak up! Got nothing to say, is it?' She placed the snuffbox and watch in her apron pocket, whacked her hook into a nearby stump and ran across to him. She seized his hands in hers, which were rough and cold. Ziquet had grown and their eyes were almost on a level. They stared at each other without speaking.

'Well?' she grated at last without batting an eyelid. 'Spit it out, yer dirty little beast!'

'It was the thirst for gold killed him, Mama Rust,' the boy murmured, lowering his head, 'like what M'sieu Barthélemy said, the excitement suffocated him. And he was wore out already ...'

'Worn out?' La Chouette's jaw dropped incredulously.

'Well, yes ... Papa Rust give his health when he was young, on them long voyages ...'

'Forget the fairy stories, son, for Gawd's sake! Let's have the truth!' the ugly harpy cried. 'Three-Nails worked hardest at the bar, first and last! 'E drank like a bleedin' sponge.'

'The ocean!' Ziquet pleaded. 'The adventures ... Borneo. Shipwrecks, risks of the sea, that wears a man out, that does.' He was trying to sanctify the rag-and-bone man's memory with pious untruths.

'Tchah! You're confused. Three-Nails was poor, that's all. I've always known it.'

Ziquet repossessed his hands. 'Three-Nails was the only father I had,' he said with dignity. 'Now he's gone, and I haven't got anyone.'

La Chouette didn't demur. She and the snotnose had never really been close. Perhaps he reminded her that she had not been able to have children of her own. She glanced at the tall man. 'What about the money? The gold? Did you find the savings?'

'All we found was a small sheaf of notes hidden in the roofbeams,' Barthélemy told her. He came closer and handed her a folded newspaper. 'Here's what's left of it. The rest, at least three-quarters, has gone into Mr Pouffard's pocket . . .'

The black vulture, who had managed to find a bucket of water for his jade and a bottle of wine for himself, looked round at the mention of his name.

'Come here, Pouffard, and say your piece,' Barthélemy said, adding to the widow: 'If he's not too soaked yet, he should be able to explain the scandalous way he made us cough up . . .'

The coachman bowed to her with his hand on his heart, and passed in front of Barthélemy as if he didn't exist. There was obvious antipathy between him and the former policeman.

'When these gentlemen approached me to arrange the obsequies,' the corpse-washer began, 'it was the middle of the night and I was asleep in the straw in my ambulance. From their alarmed expressions, from their whispered exhortations to be discreet, I immediately realised we were dealing with a specific case . . . I therefore followed them where they asked me to go and . . . when we got to this house in the 3rd *arrondissement* where the drama had taken place, I knew immediately that the evacuation of the deceased was going to cost my clients a lot of money provided they had some . . .'

'Pouffard robbed us,' Ziquet explained.

'What ingratitude, lad!' the villain cried with affected hurt. 'I only helped you to arrange a decent burial for the unfortunate Mr Lerouge . . .'

'What have you done with my Alfred?' yelped la Chouette. The sorceress was looking quite frightening. Barthélemy tried to explain:

'The presence of his body was an embarrassment to us . . .'

'Why not just admit you couldn't do without Alphonse Pouffard!' the undertaker rasped. 'I could tell straight off, come on! Your situation was too shady. The ragamuffins was having a bit of a burgle, and you, beanpole, you was of the general type of cunts on the run . . . Plain as the nose on your face, I could see you didn't want to run across the federals!' He sidled up to the tall policeman, gave him a knowing wink and added: 'I could've, I just as well could've, denounced you to the authorities, my long heron! A spy for reaction, a kicker-down of doors, I

could've said anything! Rigault and Théophile Ferré would've
been only too pleased to ask you a few questions. Give you the
treatment.'

'You chose to line your pockets instead, leech that you are,'
the former policeman snorted.

'Because money drives men mad. Because I'm always thirsty,'
Pouffard added, taking a quick swig out of his bottle. 'And *also*
because you had a revolver.'

'We had to wait two whole days for him to sober up,' Ziquet
explained to the old woman,' and another whole day before he
came by with a load of bodies for the Commune.'

'You chucked my Alfred on a pile of bodies? Buried him in a
mass grave with a collection of topers and tarts?' gasped the lady
of the house.

'Hey! You old dishcloth! Don't you dare talk about patriots
like that!' bawled Pouffard, pointing at la Chouette with a
furious finger. She flapped her blue apron in his face. They were
about to come to blows. The coachman, increasingly affected by
alcohol, was nearly out of control. Waving his bottle, his
moustache soaked in a froth of winewash, he had launched into a
lecture.

'Those dead'uns you're insulting was *heroes*, citizeness! A
battalion of National Guardsmen what'd died bayonet in hand in
a 'uge great infantry action . . .' Out of his senses, the coachman
of final journeys had gone close enough to touch the woman's
hideous face. 'Listen to the story, you old mare!' he belched.
'The remains of your old geezer was lyin' in state for twenty-
four hours in a room at Beaujon hospital bein' filed past
respectful by the people of Paris! Seems to me you couldn't
hardly do more honour to an old ragamuffin of his sort what
never lifted a finger, let alone a weapon, in defence of freedom! A
bag of guts what smelt worse when he was alive than what he did
dead! And getting that old wastrel laid to rest among heroes
what was picked off under the walls of Vanves in the crossfire of
Versailles's machine-cannons: I *think* I can say that justified me
in, er, empocketating a fistful of the old . . . er . . .'

He fell silent. He felt there was something wrong with
empocketating. With a fresh half-litre of wine washing about in

his stomach, his ears had turned from their usual grey to a bright shade of red. He lurched about gathering up his reins.

'Having said my piece, I'm off,' he said. 'I hope you've had a nice rest, Cécile. Oi, shrimp! If you want to come with me, hurry up and get your stuff. I'm not going to moulder much longer in this rubbish-dump.'

'Just got to get my Chassepot to go to war!' Ziquet cried. 'I'll be right back! My bag's already packed!' The adolescent bounded across the road, glanced over his shoulder and vanished into the rabbit-skin store. 'Coming, M'sieu Pouffard!' his voice called. 'Long live the Commune!' He reappeared almost at once waving his rifle, a shako over one ear and a greatcoat on his arm. He was slightly out of breath. He heaved his belongings into the hearse, then hesitated, turned and went up to la Chouette.

'Goodbye,' he said, wiping his lips where the sour odour of his sweat mingled with his panting breath. 'I don't think we owe each other anything.'

'Nothing,' the old woman replied. 'Off with you, Ziquet. And don't show your face here again till you've changed the world.'

'I'm going to try,' the youth said earnestly. 'First with the gun. Then later, with ideas ... I'll study! Be a schoolmaster! Three-Nails used to say the future's in books ...'

The mop-haired boy suddenly stroked the old woman's cheek, an act of tenderness that made her go rigid on her big hams. She looked away from the affectionate expression on his face.

'Three-Nails taught me to read,' he told her. 'Something I'll never, ever forget.'

Touched despite herself, amid the smoking ruins of her life which was now without prospects, la Chouette glanced wildly about through reddened bloodshot eyes in which two big tears were trying to form. She tried to dash them away.

'Here,' she said. 'Take it, go on. In his memory ...' She slipped her husband's watch into the boy's palm. He leaned towards her.

'Ah! Go on with yer!' she gasped in a strangled voice, flapping her hand to prevent him from embracing her. 'Shove off, Ziquet! Let me be! All this waterworks ... it's just, I was used to him. It'll dry up in no time.' She shut her eyes.

She heard the dry cough of the whip, the sounds of the vehicle lurching into motion, the rumble of its wheels diminishing in the distance. A chapter of her life was over, a part of daily living had gone away from her.

When her eyes reopened, dust was settling in the field of bonfires. She wiped away the biggest of her tears with hardened hands. She buried her face in her handkerchief and started back to the house.

As she crossed the yard she saw Horace Grondin leaning out of the window. The spectre was dressed in a white shirt and opening his arms wide to embrace Barthélemy.

'La Chouette!' he called when he saw her, 'unlock the door! This is a friend of mine!'

She had never seen him laughing before. There was something rather frightening about it.

59

The hundred faces of
Horace Grondin

Inspector Barthélemy's height forced him to stoop as he entered the Chinese shack, the vertical furrow of a frown between his brows. In response to the curiosity that showed in his visitor's face, and to give him time to get used to the shadows, the destitute appearance of the shack, the stink of dirty rags and the sight of the rotten straw scattered on the floor, Horace Grondin stood, silent and reserved, in the middle of the only room.

He had resumed an air of perfect normality, something that was disturbing in itself. Here, suddenly, was a man with a changeable personality, one whose face could encompass the most bizarre contrasts. At the moment it was cold, calm and serious.

La Chouette had followed the visitor into the hovel and made her way across to him, walking fast. They looked into each other's eyes.

'My old man's kicked the bucket,' she told him. 'Dead and buried. I'm alone in the world.' Grondin said nothing. The tall harpy stood in front of him for a moment, her eyes washed-out and red. She did not expect any compassion. She flapped her apron, and was seized by an urge to keep moving. She turned on her heel and walked away as fast as she had arrived, shut the door which she had left ajar and took off her clogs, staring at the mildewed cardboard wall and muttering a jumble of inaudible words.

She raised her head, rattled her amulets. A sort of brutality pervaded her flat face set like marble. Without looking at Grondin she said all in one breath:

'I'm pretty sure you're going to leave, well go then! But if you need me at all I've resolved to follow you. I'll keep your house for you. I'll sleep on the floor. I won't want anything from you. No more than an animal.'

Grondin's face remained inscrutable. He stepped back a pace through the stuffy and malodorous air of the room as if to widen his field of vision. His terrible gaze rested on the two lowly creatures destiny had placed in his hands to serve as the instruments of his resurrection. He directed a pale smile at la Chouette and instantly, without a word having been said, she ran to place three bowls on the rickety table and stoke up the fire under the cooking pot.

Grondin's penetrating eyes drifted onto Barthélemy and examined his worker's get-up. In an undertone, he praised him for his skill at disguise. He placed a familiar arm round the inspector's shoulder and led him to the table, urging him to sit on the worm-eaten bench. The long tall heron held his hat respectfully in his hands and wouldn't sit down until the former underchief of the Sûreté had seated himself.

From the eager haste of the one and the subservience of the other, the man with the gimlet eyes knew he had not lost any of his ability to rule and manipulate, to gauge the dark turns of the spirit and the infinitely varied adaptability of human character.

Presently, over the split-pea soup, he asked la Chouette to get him some worker's clothes so that he could move about Paris in safety. As soon as the meal was finished the sorceress left without a murmur of protest to make the round of her contacts.

Totally won over to the service of that shadowy man who was capable of gaining ascendancy over anyone just by looking at them, she had gone clip-clopping off on a path cut through the rubbish-tips to make the shortest route to a clique of old-clothes experts who lived in the next shanty town. The people she had in mind were professionally incurious fences and refurbishers, some of whom were indebted to the late Three-Nails in one way or another. She decided in advance to buy no more than one garment in each place, for fear of arousing curiosity.

After la Chouette's departure Grondin had started to fill his pipe. With the first drifts of blue smoke a distinctively police type of dialogue set in between the two men. Grondin said in a commanding tone:

'Make your report, Hippolyte. What's been happening outside? I haven't seen or heard a thing since I've been buried here ... To start with, how did you find me?'

'Not without a lot of twists and turns, sir!' cried the sleuth, and embarked on a discourse so meandering and sprinkled with digressions that Grondin knew he was in for a long and painful narrative.

In fact the heron omitted nothing. Speaking in a tone that varied between contemptuous bitterness and nervous urgency, he gave a chronological account of Commissaire Mespluchet's departure to Versailles, his visit to Monsieur Claude, the latter's arrest by the Communards and incarceration in the Santé prison, and how finally, tired of risking his life at every crossroads, of hanging about in public rest-rooms and licking the bowls in soup kitchens, he, Hippolyte Barthélemy, had gone to ground in the flat in the rue de la Corderie, taking refuge there for two long weeks until the utterly unexpected arrival of Three-Nails and his shock-headed tadpole.

Grondin looked at his young colleague and in a strangely honeyed voice thanked him for having tracked him down to pull him out of the bad spot he was in.

'Honestly,' Barthélemy demurred, 'it's not through any merit of mine ... So many slopes led me down to you, sir! Firstly of course our police business. But also, in a roundabout sort of way, something more intriguing that I don't really understand ... an instinct, a curiosity, a *current* of some kind that draws me towards the dark. It's like there was some hidden energy circulating between us and conspiring to bring us together ... it feels a bit as if, when I left the straight path where ordinary decent people walk to look for you, I entered profane country – your country – and started learning to hold red-hot embers in my bare hands ... and with much more zeal and satisfaction than I'd ever have expected ...'

At these words, pronounced with a dissociated air, a distracted rigidity that somehow suggested a hypnotic trance, Grondin took his silver fox's eyes off those of his companion. He rose to his feet with a surprising bound, a strange smile still fastened on his mouth. With the rapid lope of a wild animal he gained the other end of the room. He turned and stood lost in shadow.

'The vertigo of Evil,' he grated. His frightening mask vanished for a second. 'Evil, Hippolyte! I'm accursed, and you've discerned it. I smell of sulphur. And you've a good nose!'

Barthélemy seemed to have come back to reality. He struggled for a moment, then let his shoulders slump. Controlled without knowing it by a will stronger than his own, the wary policeman fixed his eyes on his master.

To his amazement Grondin's mask had changed once again, becoming the face of a man in the grip of painful emotion.

'Forgive me, sir,' Barthélemy stammered, 'if I've disturbed some sensitive element that touches on your personal configuration ... I ... er ... I wouldn't want to have upset you, knowing only too well as I do that each of us buttresses his conscience behind a certain appearance of things ... that under a mountain of regrets, in the shadow of our secret corridors, there roam unfinished works ... botched efforts ... betrayed friendships ... unopened doors ...'

'Barthélemy! Barthélemy, my dear, dear friend, you touch the very spot! Sixteen years now I've been quarrelling with God!' Grondin murmured in a voice of profound suffering. 'Sixteen years I've been trampling His perfect clarity! Sixteen years I've been rooting Him out, and He's still in me!'

He was painful to see. He was unrecognisable. Waves of irrepressible energy undulated along his fleshless backbone in shuddering cascades.

'Sixteen years I've been wicked, inhabited by ferocious hatred! Sixteen years I've been driven by malevolence!' he groaned. He pounded his head with his fist, wandered round in a small circle and disappeared like a grey ghost into the alcove where his squalid pallet lay. Barthélemy could hear his teeth chattering in there.

'Is there anything I can do for you, sir?' he ventured at last, peering in and trying to see through the gloom. But the other man, cornered in his den, was as alarming as a wounded bear. His harsh, deformed voice growled:

'God's death! To each his own hell fire! Don't come near me, Barthélemy! I don't need anyone. I'm shivering, that's all. I've got a fever.' After a few heavy sighs, he fell silent.

A few minutes later Grondin reappeared looking as if nothing had happened. The light gleamed on the grey of his eyes which had retained a secret and dreamy expression. He paced up and down for a moment and then, standing firmly to show the policeman that he had recovered, cried in a disdainful and jeering tone:

'Conformisms! Customs! The unbearable whiteness of virtue! You shall see, young Hippolyte, how quickly one learns to navigate the margins of Evil! Evil guides us towards a very pure despair!' The smile reappeared, effacing the terrible distaste he seemed to feel for himself and his tormented life. He approached his subordinate and said in a tone so light-hearted that it changed the atmosphere entirely: 'Anyway, never mind that, my friend. On a more down-to-earth level, I'd been meaning to mention your stay at rue de la Corderie . . .'

'Sir?'

'Of course you're more than welcome to use my place. But . . . just an owner's reflex . . . I suppose you must have damaged the locks a bit?'

'But no, not at all!' Barthélemy defended himself. 'Believe me, I got into your house properly, I mean by opening the lock.' To add substance to his words, the stork-like policeman fished out a bunch of lockpicks from under his shirt and jingled them in the air. 'Permit me to introduce my daughters,' he added smugly.

'Oh *aren't* they sweet!' the former convict said appreciatively, fingering the collection of sleeves, splines, hooks and skeletons. 'A charming little kit! So, er . . . who taught you the skill of lockpicking?'

Barthélemy didn't answer. Now that the public was showing a bit of interest he suddenly felt like being coy and mysterious.

'Well?' Grondin persisted. 'Where did you get your knowledge?'

'From a master-thief,' bragged the heron. 'A really first-rate safecracker that I chained up with the rest after a sweep, and agreed to release if he'd teach me.'

'Turning a man round ... The method is excellent, my dear fellow,' Grondin murmured admiringly.

'Bit by bit – because that's how I work best – I managed to instil the idea of being turned round in my housebreaker's own mind,' Barthélemy said with a rather conceited smile. 'I'm just about to slip the cuffs on, when my client starts to suffocate, doesn't he? Goes red, carries his hand to his throat. "Holy shit!" he cries, "I'm having a fit!" He doubles up, choking, going black in the face, he coughs, he spits, he pukes a bit! He's panting like someone whose lungs can't take going upstairs ... by this time I'm holding his head. Between one spasm and another, all seized up, half purple, midway between stifling and a convulsion, I hear him saying: "I'm a lunger ... last stages! I'll never survive the damp in the stone-quarries ... take the bracelets off an' I'll do anything you want." Imagine, I took him at his word. And the next moment the rascal was better!'

'Has this superb tragedian got a name?'

'Wire.'

'Wire,' Grondin repeated, giving no hint that the name was more than familiar to him.

'Yes. He's a Montmartre locksmith who's keen on the new ideas. He's a good friend of this Louise Michel who's so much in the papers since she promised to leave Paris without firing a shot and reach the rue des Réservoirs without being recognised ...'

'What a skirt, eh! Did she do it?'

'The legend in the camps is that she hid in a fruit-barrow to get through the lines and passed right under the noses of the Versaillais ...'

Grondin smiled. He had a fleeting memory of the skinny Louise on 18 March, her pulled-back hair, her evangelistic air, her fierce will. The smile broadened. Barthélemy was puzzled by the gleam of light in the slaty eyes, and wanted to know more. He opened his mouth to speak.

'Wire, you say?' interrupted Grondin before he could do so, with drooping eyelids and an air of indifference.

'Yes. Emile Roussel. He lives at 7, rue Lévisse,' the copper said eagerly, happy to impress the Sûreté potentate with detailed local knowledge.

'Damnation! That's useful information,' Grondin mumbled appreciatively, chewing his pipe. He leaned across the table to pour himself a small glass of the proof spirit la Chouette had got out in honour of the occasion. He tossed back the illegal hooch, smacked his lips and admitted that it was the real hard stuff. He poured a dose into Barthélemy's glass, relighted his marseillaise which had gone out and changed the subject, his voice serene. It was his way of getting into other people's heads. Walking about in the minds he rifled without their owners' knowledge.

'What sort of state are the Parisians in?' he demanded suddenly.

'Paris has changed a good deal, sir...'

'Details, please! Living stuff,' Grondin probed, pouring himself another glass of spirit and knocking it back in one.

'The guillotine's been smashed up. It went up in smoke in front of the statue of Voltaire. And the people danced round the flames!'

Grondin drew on the rank pipe. No trace of weakness was apparent on his emaciated, scarred, battered, unreadable face.

'And what other news, my friend?' he persisted. 'Just what's significant! Sketch in the big picture. I want to witness the whole period through your eyes! I want to understand it as if I'd been there myself!'

'Paris is fighting, sir. The cannon are firing over the heads of the infantry. The buildings on the Neuilly side are being destroyed. The communers are willing to die for the love of freedom. They're pretty determined, it seems.'

'But where's the battle going on?'

'In front of the forts. Around them. At night, in the dark. Without a plan, without strategy. Bullets fly like hail. The Versaillais engage; then they suddenly withdraw. There are snipers firing from the houses. Soldiers from both sides skewer each other, yelling. The morning rain washes everything away.'

'I want to know more. How's the population managing?'

'People are still going out. Guignol has closed down at the Palais-Royal but the cafés are packed! Theatres are open. The boulevards are crowded with people heading for the Champs-Elysées to watch the battle. The same flow of partygoers at night! You can hear the spree going on behind closed shutters.'

'But how are people *managing*? Ordinary people, the ones who fall flat on the ground when they hear a shell whistling, what are they doing?'

'They're learning to live with danger.'

'They're resigned?'

'Anything but, monsieur! They're enraged! Even the non-combatants are climbing on the ramparts to follow the fighting. The bourgeois have their spyglasses. The smartest kids climb up the railway signals. Every now and again the place de l'Etoile gets a dose of canister. Or, *bang*! a shell explodes in the road. Women scream. Ambulances arrive. The wounds are pretty nasty. Professors from the medical faculty are in the front line, stethoscopes round their necks, forceps in their pockets. Students help them operate on the spot.'

'You seem impressed by their courage.'

'Shall I come clean, sir? I've been surprised everywhere by the revolutionary solidarity of the Parisians ... A lot of the wounded die. The dead are buried in groups, with great military pomp. Guardsmen with their weapons reversed, muzzle down, escort the carriages draped in red flags. The corteges go along the main Boulevards, their approach announced by bugles and the Vengeurs de Paris.'

'Tell me about the living.'

'They're doing everything they can to send "the Pope's soldiers" packing! Even guttersnipes are helping! And a law's just appeared in the *Official* saying that "every man, married or unmarried, between the ages of nineteen and fifty-five, is shortly to be enrolled and required to march against the Versaillais".'

'What are their defences like?'

'Put up in a hurry. But with such heart! You should see how they work, men and women at four francs a day, putting up barricades and ramparts out of earth, planks, railings and cobblestones ...'

'And the bourgeoisie, you were saying ...?'

'They've been requisitioned! They're digging latrines and shoring up redoubts here and there.'

'And are they, er, wielding the pick and shovel with a will?'

'Some grumble very quietly, sir. But there are others – less docile or more vengeful – who do their best to spread all the rumours put out by Versailles.'

'The Commune's perfectly right to grind their faces a bit, wouldn't you say, Hippolyte?'

'Well, as for that, sir, some of those stock-market sharks had plenty of fat to spare . . . and to be quite honest with you I don't have the slightest sympathy for them.'

Grondin smiled. There was a perverse glint in his eye. 'Basically,' he insinuated, slipping collusively into the familiar *tu*, 'you're even wondering whether the authorities shouldn't just put the rich up against the wall by the dozen in the usual way, aren't you? Eh? What d'you think?'

'That's a *calumny!*' protested Barthélemy with a sheepish upward look. 'I never said anything of the sort, sir!'

'No need to overstate the anger, my fine knave! I heard it between the lines. You detest the propertied class, that's clear!'

'Whatever you think, don't go believing I'm in favour of insubordination! Or that I class myself as one of the insurgents!'

'For the last quarter of an hour or more, haven't you been chanting that the proletariat is an immense, a beautiful, an inexhaustible reservoir of virtues?'

'You asked me to give the feeling in the streets!'

'But how *well* you did it, my dear fellow!'

Grondin seemed to be greatly enjoying the confused feelings playing across his bag-carrier's gormless face. 'Ah!' he cried with extraordinary animation, 'who would ever have expected *you* to turn your coat, my dear Hippolyte? Is Mespluchet behind you in this attempt to sort out the fine street people?' He continued in a more coldly ironic tone: 'Tell me, what did he ever do for you when you were risking denunciation every day? Wasn't it a bit easy for him, warming his feet in slippers in a cousin's house in Seine-et-Oise while you were slinking about in dangerous alleys?'

'I don't know . . . Not any more . . . I mean . . .'

Barthélemy was more and more confused. His eyes swivelled wildly about. Wringing his hands, drawing blood from one of them with the nails of the other, he tried desperately to understand where Grondin was leading him. Was the old devil just setting a trap to test him, or was he deadly serious? Unsure, the lout tried to restore his façade of professional virtue.

'Of course I'm only a humble uniformed policeman,' he said, 'but I take my duty as a public servant very seriously.'

Grondin's terrible eyes settled on him, and Barthélemy looked down to avoid meeting the disturbing gaze of that extraordinary man. Anxieties from the distant past were returning at a gallop. Who was Horace Grondin exactly? A former convict as rumour suggested? An unusually talented bloodhound? A cynic? A visionary? A henchman of the Emperor? A sharp-toothed Marat eager to share the trough with a slavering populace? A Communist carried away by Marx's subversive ideas?

'I want you to know,' the policeman said vehemently, 'that I was ordered to stay in Paris, to keep my superiors informed of any cracks or weaknesses in the front presented by the new masters.'

'Working as a nark,' Grondin murmured, resting his pitiless gaze on the other. 'Hard luck!'

'All I did was report to Commissaire Mespluchet on the deeds and utterances of the Commune whenever I could get a message through to him. Was there anything so wrong in that, sir?' the informer asked uneasily. He was now struggling in a morass of doubt. The man with slate-coloured eyes did not reply, being occupied with the rekindling of his pipe.

'Look here, sir! *Have* we turned our coats?' the beanpole burst out again, fixing his superior with worried saucer eyes.

Grondin unmasked his frightening laugh. Anyone who had known convict 2017 would have recognised him at that moment. The ex-prisoner's eyes were watering slits, his smile was wide and beatific and he held his sides. God knew his broken ribs still hurt!

'Hippolyte, only donkeys never change their minds.'

'No doubt, sir ... You're probably right, sir ...'

'Well, stop being careful if you want me to have any faith in you at all,' Grondin snapped abruptly, returning to the formal *vous*. He looked away to conceal his opinion of his companion's moral rigour, and added: 'Let's take a turn outside. After being laid up all this time I really need to walk a bit in the fresh air.'

60

The sunshine of revolt

A moment later, inscrutable behind his metallic mask, Horace Grondin was walking up and down the dirt road in front of the pagoda, a hundred paces out, a hundred paces back, gauging and testing his strength. The starved-looking Inspector Barthélemy trotted naturally at his heels, with the look of a dog greatly relieved to have found a master again – even a peculiar one who went walking in his shirt – after a long period without one.

Lost in his thoughts, the ex-underchief of the Sûreté cast an occasional mechanical glance at his companion over his shoulder. That cringing jackal, who had a sort of blind and profound faith in him, was a new source of strength. Without knowing exactly how, Grondin felt intuitively that he would be able to make use of his services to get back on Tarpagnan's track as quickly as possible.

'Here,' he said after a minute, 'give me your arm, Hippolyte! I think I'm going to lean on you to walk more easily.' An iron hand closed on the policeman's forearm. 'Come on,' Grondin said, striding out vigorously.

Grinding his teeth, standing tall and white, with the raging determination of a character who wanted to force his body to obey him and to extirpate from his mind one of the less glittering episodes of his life, he began to describe in a muffled voice the way the people had lambasted his carcass and left him for dead on the Polish field.

'I did a lot of thinking on my sickbed,' he ended as they passed the pagoda for the third time. 'Here, down this dark hole stinking of disease, I was cared for and warmed back to life by poor people. They were outcasts. In earlier times I wouldn't even

have noticed them . . . A ragpicker . . . a woman so hideous it'd
make you cry . . . that degraded species with nothing to offer but
the open palms of their cracked and bleeding hands . . . only
these people had a unique form of riches, the sort of riches you
only see clearly from the threshold of the great divide. What they
had, d'you see, was the power to give me back my life or let it go
. . . they possessed nothing, but they had what was important. La
Chouette's breath lingering at the bottom of my lungs to warm
the soul back into me will always be worth far more to me than
any nostalgia for the scents of the Spice Isles!'

Breathless from the rapid pace he had maintained, looking
suddenly like an old man, he stopped abruptly at the side of the
road and let his gaze wander over the surrounding jumble of
shacks.

'You're very pale, sir,' Barthélemy said worriedly.

Grondin made no reply. He was elsewhere. The shirt-clad
spectre of the one-time notary offered to the pallid light the ugly
hatchet of his mask, crossed by a lurid new slash. The stooping
way he gripped his companion's shoulder accentuated the image
of a body ruined by malnutrition and inactivity. He gave the
impression that his thin legs were so reduced by lack of exercise
that they were barely able to carry his exhausted body.

'I have realised,' he continued, resuming his walk, 'that we
can't drive indigents out of any human society with blows or
indifference. On the contrary, by using the broom to humiliate
them or the cudgel to make them go further away, our prefects
of police have condemned them to shameful misery . . . a state of
frightening destitution. What they have done is to accumulate
nurseries of resentment at the gates of the city.'

He paused, then burst out suddenly: 'Are we blind or half-
witted? Must we wait for the poor to become so poor that they
can only revolt? One day a ragged garment hanging on a nail will
become the standard of hatred, for sure! Our leaders forget that
the heart of France beats in the breasts of the desperate, too!
That people who smell of sweat are worth just as much as people
who smell of cologne! And never mind that drunkenness, decline
and brutality are widespread in the mass: all those who have

wielded the broom, all who have beaten the poor and trans-
ported those who are ragged through poverty, deserve death! In
circumstances like these, when it's a matter of revolt, what a
disgraceful profession is ours! When I set foot on the Polish field
on 18th March I was nothing but an informer myself! I looked
it! I was wearing the uniform! In every respect, I stood out like a
bluebottle in a bowl of cream, and I can hardly blame the
insurgent people for wanting to tear strips out of my hide and
give the corpse a going-over!'

He had stopped again beside the road. The wind blew across
his bald head and stirred the halo of grey hair. 'Excellent tears!'
he said, wiping two glistening streaks from his emaciated face.
'You're assuring me I still possess a heart! And reminding me
that among all the ordeals I've suffered, even as I advanced
deeper into this suffocating fire of vengeance that's driven me for
the last sixteen years of my wandering life, the gaze of the Lord
whom I have so often denied has never been withdrawn from
me! And you remind me too that in sacrificing my nature, my
reputation, my very appearance, to the devouring ogress Vengeance, I became by imperceptible degrees an awful man, without
attachments, meditating nothing but evil day and night...'

He fell silent. Body limp, eyes fixed on the distant sky, he
watched the ravens of his reawakened nightmares flying away.
Their beaks laden with meat. He stood quietly with tears
running down the furrows of his motionless face.

'Ah, Barthélemy!' he murmured after a deep sigh. 'Does
wanting your own justice make it possible to walk on red-hot
coals without burning your feet?'

Vengeance? Sixteen years of struggle, of rage in the heart! A
life thrown away! A man who had looked into the abyss!

The things Grondin was saying fascinated Barthélemy.
Although they did not yet make much sense – for the narrative
was coming out in disordered fragments – the despair expressed
in them awakened his bloodhound's instincts. Aware that part of
the screen veiling the mystery of the former underchief of the
Sûreté was about to disintegrate before his eyes, terrified that
even the sound of his voice might break the flow of confidences,
he hung back and tried to make himself invisible.

Grondin stood alone in his shirt-tails beside the road, crushed by the light. He looked into the sky, in the general direction of the Almighty, his scarred face radiating a sort of supernatural savagery that seemed to place him outside all ordinary existence. Barthélemy saw him shake an angry fist at the sun; then the fingers straightened one by one, and the hand very slowly opened. Watching the former big fish of the secret police locked in battle with invisible forces moved him deeply in unexpected ways. He saw the man's wide-open grey eyes staring into the reddening furnace above the horizon, his opalescent irises fixed on that which cannot be gazed upon. Defying the bite of that incandescent star. Facing down the energy of the universe with the same patient firmness he brought to all tasks. Steadily the sun shot out its piercing rays.

Grondin's eyes looked as if they were bleeding. They were filled with a vast emptiness and his knees gave way, instinctively. The sun's harpoon was piercing the centre of his hatred. But Barthélemy, a little way away, felt that no fire, no glitter or radiation, was fierce enough to blind that madman. It was he, the watcher, who from staring too long at the majestic violet blaze of the sun found his vision briefly blocked by its white image imprinted on his retinas.

He heard the deep, unconscious murmur of Grondin's voice raised in furious denunciation of the immorality of God Himself, the undeflectable challenge of a man not held to the observance of absolute rules, whose anathemas spread in a tidal wave far across that plain of rubbish dumps, demanding recompense for his suffering from the Ruler of all things. A familiar rumbling in rhythm with an oppression in the breath. A grinding in the belly that had nothing to do with normal human ways of revering the name of God. Something that opened a direct path from heaven to the route de la Révolte and went something like this:

'Hey, You, decoy, pitfall of life, all out of balance! You who create beauty! Who have so very little to say on the depths and the miseries of this world! God of servitude and God of hatred! God of blindness and God of meekness! Hear me, hear me, I who sometimes spurn you and sometimes beseech you! Let me catch the one I'm pursuing! Cast your light on my path! Guide me to him! Permit me to chastise the criminal who defiled purity and murdered an infant! Let me commit the crime of justice! After that, take me! Do what you like! Chop my miserable envelope in pieces! All within me is already disfigured: the soul, the face. Ah! Tears, back again? No peace, my God, no peace for the wicked!'

His arms fell back to his sides and the storm of words stopped suddenly. His head hung as if exhausted, his breath came in dry sobs. He turned and muttered: 'Take me inside, Barthélemy. The fresh air's made me light-headed. I've been alone for quite long enough.'

As he spoke a mounting clamour caused the two men to turn. Bearing down on them at speed, already so close that they had to step back into the undergrowth to avoid being run down, was a blue vehicle pulled by a lathered, wild-eyed black horse. With cries from the driver and a tremendous clattering of hooves, wheels and running gear, an elegant cabriolet was violently sawed and braked to a stop a little beyond them. They stood amid a settling cloud of grey dust while the carriage door opened and three men got out.

One of them was Edmond Trocard.

61

The short and stuttering life of
Agricol Pégourier, market gardener

Smiling with quietly arrogant self-satisfaction, the boss of the Ourcq gang approached with measured steps. Gravel crunched under the leather soles of his fine English shoes.

He was wearing a hand-made suit of exquisite blue-and-white herringbone tweed, whose fine tailoring and Norfolk cut, in the style currently fashionable among English 'sportsmen', identified him immediately as one of those untouchable men whose hands have long remained unsoiled by low economic activity.

Flanked by Greaseball, gnawing on a sausage, and the Squirrel, smoothing down a kiss-curl, he advanced towards Grondin with a stately tread. The fingers of one hand in his waistcoat pocket, face blotchy as that of a well-fed alderman, he was playing with his fine gold watch. Yes, his demeanour seemed to be saying, people may be killed, murdered, chopped up all around me, but make no mistake, I live a peaceful life, detached from all that crime and everyday blackness, concerned only with the big, the strategic picture.

He stopped in front of the former secret policeman, touched his hat-brim with a forefinger in salute, and looked the other man up and down, measuring his gaunt and weakened state.

'Someone's done you over good and proper, Horace,' he observed. 'You could do with a bit of Aroud tonic wine to build you up, looks like.'

'I'm getting a lot better,' Grondin replied in a firm voice. 'I've been wondering when you were going to turn up, Goldsmith.'

The villain's teeth showed in an agreeable smile; the sort that is kept for old friends. 'Well, here I am, old cellmate! Of course I knew that with a man of your kidney any delay would have an explanation, and outstanding liabilities would be settled in no time.'

With the air of importance that goes with the status of successful scoundrel, he allowed his bland gaze to drift across the worried eyes of Barthélemy, who stood resolutely at Grondin's elbow. The elegant Edmond lifted one eyebrow and the corner of his mouth twitched: what, he seemed to be wondering, was the role of this tall grey-faced beanpole in a visored cap? In fact, of course, the bejewelled gangster had identified him by type, if not name, more or less instantly.

'I know you'll say it's absurd,' he murmured, all amiable helplessness, 'but I don't seem to remember your name, m'sieu!'

'Perhaps b-b-ber, because you haven't *heard* it,' stammered the inspector, who felt that playing the fool was probably the best policy.

'That must be it!' the caïd exclaimed with a droll air of seriousness. 'So, er, how should I go about it, addressing you I mean?'

Barthélemy sniggered foolishly, but identified himself readily enough. 'Mermy name's Agricol Perper. Perper. Pégourier,' he said. 'I'm a mermer. I'm a mermer. A mermer*market* gardener on Ecouen perperplain.'

Trocard appeared unable to contain his merriment. 'Excellent, my friend, *excellent*!' he cried. 'And to what exactly do we owe your opportune presence among us here in rabbit-skin country? Passing through on the way to the agricultural show, perhaps?'

Barthélemy jerked his chin towards Grondin. 'When you saw me with this gerger. With this gent berber. Beside the road here,' he said unblinkingly, 'I was on the way to Paris to jerjer. To jerjerjer. Join the ferferfederals, and I was asking him if there was a short cut across the ferferfer. The fields.'

'Ah! That's it!' Trocard cried happily, allowing a genuine guffaw to escape him. 'All clear now! No mystery!' He wiped away a tear, turned to his henchmen and added: 'No, but look, boys! We've found a patriot!' He went on chuckling and repeating: 'A patriot! A patriot!' for some time. His long experience of crime and blackguardry identified the man before him as a disguised member of a noxious race: a damned dog who reeked of copper and obviously represented the Big Boutique.

'But in all seriousness, my friend,' he purred like a big cat, 'your colour's not at all good, for an open-air man. I recommend a course of philodermic milk, plus aromatic baths, to give your skin back the spring sunshine it so signally lacks!'

Mechanically, he touched the diamond in his left earlobe, a signal known to all the Ourcq thugs, to warn the Squirrel and Greaseball to stay alert. Then he held out a charitable hand to the the convalescent to help him back across the ditch he had leapt to avoid being run over.

'Come over here where it's dry, 2017,' he urged cheerfully. 'Give me your arm, Iron-Fist!' Of course there was nothing innocent in this use of the old convict's number and prison nickname. He was getting his own back for the false stutter. Putting this perfect copper to the test. He passed in front of him, noticing the look of suspicion that had crossed the copper's bilious face and delightedly aware of the man's eyes on his back as he led Grondin towards the pagoda. Without turning round, he trumpeted:

'Right, on your way! To Chaillot, gardener! Paris is straight in front of your nose, my good fellow. The rest of us can settle our accounts, old stick!'

At this point in Trocard's comedy Barthélemy, whose brain was working furiously, suddenly decided to become himself again. He escaped the vigilance of Greaseball and the Squirrel and in four spidery strides had caught the two men. His long face under the visor of his cap was imprinted with dark severity. Walking backwards in front of the Goldsmith and Grondin, looking insistently into the latter's face, he had the air of a faithful dog ready to die on the spot if necessary.

'Would you like me to come along, sir, to help settle this matter in your best interests?' he asked, ignoring the two bodyguards who had again drawn near.

'No, Agricol, old chap ... thanks all the same,' Grondin said quietly. 'It's too late, don't try anything.'

The Goldsmith bent a look tinged with irony on the ex-underchief of the Sûreté. At the same time Barthélemy noticed that the bandit's gold-encrusted hand held a small Chaîneux-type pinfire revolver whose muzzle was jammed between Grondin's ribs. He was working out what to do as Trocard, still with an air of affected calm, snapped the fingers of his free hand, and an instant later the Squirrel had twisted the inspector's arm behind his back.

While Barthélemy grimaced with pain, Grondin's metallic gaze settled for a moment on the half-closed eyes of Greaseball standing in his theatrical rags. The fat blackguard had produced a knife with blinding rapidity from the recesses of his strung-together clothes of a thousand pieces. Its long blade, razor-sharp on both edges, pointed slightly upwards at the inspector's fleshless abdomen.

'Goodness me, Agricol!' cried that irrepressible joker Edmond Trocard, 'I'm forgetting my manners! I haven't introduced my pals!' Smilingly, he made a signal to the Squirrel, who twisted harder and forced Barthélemy to put a knee on the ground. In his finest stage voice, the landlord of the Glass Eye made the introductions: 'On the *twisted arm* side, that Adonis of tarts, the Squirrel! Pretty as a girl, nasty as a man! Full-time pimp who likes taking it up the arse!' He pointed at Greaseball and went on: 'Don't take any chances with that evil fellow there: he's dangerous. The king of windpipe-slitters. Card-sharper with a kitchen knife, known as Greaseball! Cures hearts with the balm of steel!'

The Ourcq potentate's good humour and fluency suddenly seemed to run out. He took his fat gold watch from his waistcoat pocket and consulted it. Then, face sombre with unspoken plans, he waved a hand at Barthélemy.

'All right, boys! Enough blather! Take that dummy there into the barn and ask him firmly whether he's ever grown any vegetables!'

'If he ain't a gardener?' Greaseball enquired.

'Leave your glass eye in his hand,' Edmond Trocard ordered. 'Give him an enema with that chopper of yours. I'll expect him to be dead in fifteen minutes, number 14.'

'Party!' rejoiced the Squirrel, wrenching Barthélemy back to his feet. 'Come on, capstan of all my desires,' he breathed in his ear, 'let's go in the barn and see if you can dance without violins . . .'

As far as the boss of the Ourcq was concerned the fate of the witness was sealed, and he turned back to Grondin with a strange smile.

'Not going to be any tiresome activity between us, Horace, is there? Tell you what, I'll put my spring-crucifix away and we'll stroll over to the Chinese palace like pals, eh?'

The man in the shirt shot him a stone-coloured glance and nodded sombrely in assent. They moved towards the shack. The Goldsmith's weapon had vanished.

'If there's any fucking about,' he warned, 'I'll shoot you through my pocket. Nine-millimetre sweeties, made in Liège, guaranteed tummy-ache.'

A moment later, with Grondin walking ahead, they had entered the yard and passed in front of Bosco the parrot's cage. The bird awoke with a start and squawked: 'Halt! *Fuckin'* 'ell! 'Oo d'yer think you are, sailor?' before replacing its head beneath its multicoloured wing.

62

In which the Goldsmith
swallows his tongue

The first thing Trocard did on entering the shack was to bolt the door.

Faint, gloomy daylight penetrated the dilapidated room, festooned with thick cobwebs. With a calculating sweep of his eye he evaluated the low den, randomly assembled out of planks to an irregular plan. He walked to the centre of the insalubrious, muddy hovel and smiled despite himself as he examined the crazed construction which, to achieve its ambition of creating an oriental pagoda, gambled on the stability of a roof assembled out of anything to hand, its frame a mixture of twisted acacia posts and wormy laths, ascending in five steep layers to a Chinese-looking peak covered with greenish tiles.

Edmond Trocard's smile gradually faded.

'It's been a good six weeks since you vanished off the face of the earth, 2017,' he said at last in a reproachful tone.

'But only three days since your buzzard was scratching about outside the door,' Grondin replied, remembering the visit by Greaseball and his four-legged spy. 'I knew you'd be along yourself sooner or later, Goldsmith.'

'Driven by my anxiety to find you alive, Horace,' the villain bridled.

He stared ironically down at the floor of beaten earth strewn with rotting straw, paced the length of the soggy, blackish cardboard inner walls, walked past the rickety table and glanced suspiciously into the dark hollow of Grondin's sleeping alcove.

'I'd had no news of you at all,' he said, circling through the unexplored part of the room. 'And appearances were against you, old fruit ... It looked as if once you'd dealt with the quarry you were after, you'd slung your hook straight off, without remembering my little fee.'

'Fuck! D'you think I was in a fit state to parade my arse about the place?' Grondin asked angrily, knotting his fists. 'I was at death's door! Unconscious half the time, delirious, feverish, eight days on the edge of the night without end ... and when that was over, weeks of staring at the wall.'

'How was I to know that, Horace? You told Caracole you were going to honour your debt a day or so after your meeting at St Peter's church ... And even though we knew that under that guillotine-steward's greatcoat there beat the honest heart of an old colleague from the Islands, you've got to admit your disappearance looked suspicious.'

As he spoke, the Goldsmith lifted the patchwork curtain that hung across the entrance to the alcove, sniffed the mildewy darkness, stuck his head into the den and came back into the room dusting the lapels of his fine 'sportsman's' suit.

'Not a bad joke to be found,' he admitted, 'but you can't be too careful. Especially with a slippery character like you!'

'Backstabbing's never been part of my religion.'

'Your time in the copper-shop could easily have changed your principles.'

'Don't go too far, Trocard!' the tall spectre said. 'There are insults I won't stomach.' His voice had become icily calm and the scars showed on his face. He stared at the gangster with angry eyes. 'I'll pay you the forty thousand francs I promised as soon as I get back to Paris. You have my word on it.'

His drowned man's pallor told the Goldsmith that he had indeed gone too far. Affable once more, he hunted around for – as they say – a patch of grass with singing birds.

'Oh, go on, old thing!' he purred cheerfully, thumping Grondin on the shoulder, 'you're not going to pout, surely?'

Grondin did not reply. He threw himself down on the bench, elbows on the table, head in his hands, face closed, in an attitude of utter fatigue. His temples were covered with a network of veins that the Goldsmith had never noticed before.

'Horace, Horace!' the villain cried in a pleading voice, 'Don't let's have any bad feeling between us! It's not my fault you were done over!'

'Why don't you just tell me what you want? You can't have come here just to tickle me and make me laugh.'

The Ourcq boss pirouetted on his English shoes, walked back and forth around Grondin's lean outline, swathed in his long cotton shirt, and sighed:

'As you and I know only too well, my dear Horace, life's a bit of a seesaw: up today, lying in the shit tomorrow. Now I wouldn't be so unkind as to make fun of a man when he's down . . .'

'Could we dispense with the flim-flam?' the former secret policeman interrupted drily. 'Cut to the chase?'

Trocard gave him a sad and serious stare. He hesitated a moment, then seemed to take the plunge. 'Well, to go straight to the point, it's that forty thousand in gold, notary, that I've got on my mind.'

'You mean you're sulking about the amount? You think I'm not bunging you enough?'

'Not at all! No, what's making me look a bit *askance*, Horace, is the strength of your, er, irrationality,' the blackguard replied. 'What I can't help noticing is how very keen you are to nab the man you're after . . . The *nasty* way you want to get your teeth in his throat. 'Cause that isn't the attitude of a normal policeman, if you see what I mean . . .'

'It's a matter of personal justice. Damnation! Stick your nose in your own business!'

'See? Getting angry, showing your teeth! Unusual, you'll admit? This folly of yours seems to have taken over from everything else. It's clouding your whole way of looking at the world.'

'Mind your own business, I said!'

'No need to shout. We're just having a quiet chat. My instinct tells me that you would have put your last drop of blood into the effort to catch that fellow! That if I'd asked for a hundred thousand francs, you'd have paid it . . .'

'Yes, I would. I'd have paid anything to get him. And I still would, even if it ruined me. I'd give everything I own to get back on his trail.'

'D'you mean you've lost him?'

Grondin looked down. 'Yes. I was just going to grab the louse when the crowd set about me.'

At these words the master of the Ourcq felt that the situation was well in hand. He strolled round the table in his fine suit and perched an elegantly-clad hip on the rickety edge.

'Let's talk straight,' he said, exerting the full resonant force of his baritone voice. 'Last time we met, you were dining at the high table. You were a bigwig in the world of coppers, and you had a hold over the, er, underworld, that you don't have any longer. You're just a man of straw now! You should get used to your fallen state, Horace.'

'Is that what I'm in?' Grondin asked, looking up with a sad smile.

'You're nothing but a common-or-garden old-regime nark on the run these days,' the Goldsmith said, leaning across the table.

'When I get to Paris I won't be entirely alone.'

'I don't think you understand how precarious your situation is.'

'I'm still at large.'

'The Commune's looking for you.'

'I have my hideouts.'

'So you're not expecting raids?'

'I know where to go, I tell you. I've got my perches. My little birds.'

'I wouldn't set too much store by the network of old aviary hands if I were you,' the Goldsmith murmured sarcastically. He preened himself in silence for a moment. 'Let me try to make you understand: we're in a period of emergency and the streets belong to the populace. Someone like you can't even show his nose out of doors! Your lowliest plainclothes constable would stand out like a sore thumb. Like your clown, just now ... he *reeked* of rozzer!'

'I don't know the man!' Grondin cried. He looked at the villain with an open expression and added nastily between his teeth: 'I don't give a damn what happens to that commissariat snooper! I'm not paid to protect him.'

'Quite right!' Trocard said, watching Grondin's face closely. 'You reassure me, 2017! 'Cause just about now I imagine the stupid tart's having rather a nasty time of it.' The killers' boss took his watch from the fob pocket of his flowered waistcoat. 'Quarter-to,' he stated, like a stationmaster pointing to the smoke of an approaching train. 'The Squirrel and Greaseball will have just about finished roasting his feet by now. The poor bastard's about to get the final cut, I should think.'

As if in answer, two muffled but clearly audible shots sounded nearby in rapid succession.

'All done, *ite missa est*,' Trocard said smugly, putting his watch away.

'Two shots, though,' Grondin commented. 'I thought you said Greaseball preferred the discretion of cold steel to the vulgar clamour of firearms.'

'Ah, no doubt the Squirrel's enthusiasm got the better of him as well,' Trocard sniggered. 'He's a jumpy little pouf who just *loves* the sight of blood. He can't stand being left out!'

Grondin maintained an inscrutable mask. His instinct told him to play for time and explore the terrain, and he deliberately gave the impression that only his own well-being was of any interest to him.

'When I get to Paris,' he resumed, 'I'll find cover and change my identity.'

'Might not be much use.'

'What d'you mean?'

'These are confused times. Anyone being sought is at the mercy of the first pointed finger. Concierges are making the law behind their curtains! There's a storm of denunciations raging. Even priests are being arrested.'

'So I'll melt into the mass! Howl with the wolves! Wave the red flag!'

'You'd still be completely vulnerable if a musician of my sort were to denounce you to the Committee ... they'd shoot you out of hand.'

'You wouldn't do that, Goldsmith . . . Not you! You wouldn't blab on an old pal from the Island . . .'

Edmond Trocard stroked his forelock and left his audience in suspense for a moment, then flashed his charming smile.

'No, of course not, not me. I was teasing you! Playing war games to see how you took it . . . But really, you know how I feel about morality. And apropos . . .' He walked thoughtfully up and down the hovel for a moment. '. . . Apropos . . . every time I think about it, I realise that you and I are sort of *fated* to be associates in this business.'

'What d'you mean?'

'I have just as much reason for wanting to smash that bastard Tarpagnan's head in as you do.'

'You remember his name, then?'

'Who can forget the name or the grinning mug of the son of a bitch who's got them jilted? Your handsome sabre-waver walked off with the heart of the woman I loved! How could I forgive the creeping seducer who'd done that to me?'

Trocard had changed registers so suddenly that he seemed almost a different man. Colour rose in his cheeks. He stopped pacing up and down and startled Grondin by seizing his hand, then gazed into his face with a tortured smile and eyes swimming with tears.

'I can't get through a night without sobbing like some stupid sissy,' he said earnestly. 'D'you understand? Listen. I had a mistress – a lover – called Gabriella Pucci. You can't imagine how stuck I was on her! Sunstroke, like never before! The velvet of her bosom, the crystal of her laughter, her hands from the centre of the universe touching my body, her white hips, her dewy moistness, gave me back at night the purity my crimes had taken from me during the day . . . And what I did, accursed fool that I am, what I did in my jealousy and wounded pride . . . may God strike me down for it! What I did in the blindness of my anger was to snuff out the light of her life as she had cast darkness over mine. To punish her for her treachery I chucked her in a brothel. Condemned her to clap, to the pox, to fifty men a day!'

He released Grondin's hand and slowly straightened his

shoulders. 'All because of that knave of hearts, you see,' he said, gazing haggardly into the distance. He took out a handkerchief and noisily blew his nose. 'Ah, the human reality behind each one of us!' he cried derisively. 'I was wounded, inconsolable. I started drinking. In my room in the evening, I open one, I reel about, I'm awash! I end up with my face on the tiles ... you do believe me, don't you? Look at my colour, my grog-blossom nose, my congested, blotchy skin ... you can see the effects of drink there, can't you? Of course I try to keep up a normal front to hide my sorrows ...'

The dandy inflated his chest under his waistcoat and started to crack the joints of his gold-encrusted fingers. He pulled his belly in and attempted to mask his distress with a great display of dignity, straightening his clothes and pulling at his sleeves.

'Well, there it is,' he said. 'Life treats us badly enough already. No point in making it worse! D'you know, when the luck of the game sends mugs across my path these days I can hardly be bothered to have them skinned and trussed ... In other words, I'm letting go the reins. I've felt my grip loosening ever since that Gascon made a fool of me. The young pimps, the girls, even the low-grade old tarts are talking behind my back! Making fun of me, laughing, not taking me seriously! People have been questioning my orders ever since that madman Tarpagnan turned up. Since, actually, he messed up my two most reliable enforcers and knocked off my best lieutenant in passing!'

'Are you telling me Léon Chauvelot's, er ... signed off?'

The Goldsmith sadly inclined his head. 'Caracole's a goner and I'm in the shit!'

There was a moment of silence. It was absurd, these two men mourning – although that is not really the word – the same person, for such different reasons.

'A hundred thousand francs if you tell me where I can find my ward's killer,' Grondin rumbled suddenly. 'I'll give you a hundred thousand, d'you understand? And settle your grudge and my own at a single stroke.'

Trocard made no reply, but started pacing again, head down, hands behind his back, meditative as a priest saying his breviary in the garden. Once or twice he caught Grondin's furtive glance in passing. Suddenly he stopped in front of the tall savage and faced him with a sort of shaky determination. His lips were trembling.

From outside came a vague sound of voices and stifled noises. The parrot Bosco let out a *Goddamn* and a *fuck* or two, but neither man paid any attention to the disturbance. The Goldsmith managed at last to say in a bland voice:

'Whatever you may want to do at first, Horace, what I'm going to say to you is in your interest alone.'

The ex-convict's eyes smouldered feverishly, their irises like the steel of scissors or medical probes searching the face of the other man. His ears were scarlet. The words choked in his throat.

'You know where he is, don't you?'

'Yes.'

'Let me have him! I'll make you a rich man.'

'I'll go straight to the point, notary. I want to retire from business and leave Paris. There's nothing to keep me here . . .'

'How much?'

'The lot!'

'I'll empty my money-box.'

'Not enough!'

'What are you saying?'

'That that isn't enough,' the gangster repeated, resuming his to-and-fro pacing. 'Just think a bit!'

'So?'

The villain stopped again, facing Grondin. 'I want Perchède.'

'Out of the question!'

'I want la Tasterre and its woodlands. I want Mormès and its vines. And I want les Arousettes!'

'It's my skin you want.'

'That's the price of your vengeance, notary!'

'It's my soul thrown on the fire!'

'All your Gers properties, Charles Bassicoussé! Then I'll deliver your man with a nice bit of string round his wrists.' Grondin stared dully as Trocard produced a sheaf of documents from his briefcase. 'Sign, notary.'

'You're talking about the cornerstone of my life, Trocard. That part isn't negotiable.'

'It's an emergency! I'm taking you to your own furthest extreme! Putting your vengeance in reach!'

'You want to bleed me dry!'

'I want to help you reach the end of the journey you've been on for so long ... Pestilence, sin, unknown lands, order, sufferings: when you get to the end of the road you'll have got the better of everything! You'll never have seen anything half so fine!'

Grondin struggled on for a while. The air he was breathing seemed to be burning him in an extraordinary way. He felt terrible pains in his temples. Only the thought of the land enabled him to resist. He thought of his native Gers, the sweetness of summer evenings in the rye fields, the fawn carpet of magnolia leaves under boughs laden with white blossom. He saw the double grove of cedars lining the gravel drive to the tall gateposts of his estate. He smiled at the shadows dancing on the walls of the house, and struggled with all his strength against what was happening.

'Your smile misled me,' he said loudly. 'Your friendliness is a pose, Trocard. You're set on one thing.'

'Oh, stop worrying about nothing! I'm giving you entry to the lost garden!'

'What I smell certainly isn't flowers. You're dragging me into some evil-smelling undergrowth, Goldsmith!'

'You haven't understood anything, Horace. It's something that takes your breath away! You and I are both here *for love*! Think of Jeanne eviscerated! Dry Gabriella's tears for me!'

'Very well,' Grondin capitulated suddenly. His eyes were mad. 'I agree.' His head hurt like hot iron. 'It's all yours,' he said hoarsely. 'I'll strip myself naked. I'd sign my soul to the devil to lay hands on that man.'

'Don't sign anything, sir!' called Barthélemy's voice from outside. Glancing to his right, Grondin saw the policeman's morose face pressed against the window. Another shadow, more indistinct, was moving about behind him.

'The door's bolted on the inside!' squawked a female voice which Grondin recognised as la Chouette's.

'So that's it!' Trocard yelled. 'One of your traps, eh?' The resonant, modulated voice had roughened and sharpened. The bandit's hands closed round Grondin's emaciated throat. Taken by surprise in his weakened state, he struggled fiercely to break the choking grip on his windpipe, and the two men fell to the floor.

The door gave way under a tremendous barge from Barthélemy's shoulder. His impetus carried him into the room where he tripped over the struggling men and overturned the table. Behind him came la Chouette. She raised her ragpicker's billhook, her joined hands grasping its iron handle, and brought it down with all her force on the back of the person who'd got her Monsieur Horace by the gullet and was trying to squeeze the life out of him.

Three times, four times, she raised her number seven high in the air and whacked it into the wicked beast's back. Her eyes were shut and she was shaking. She had the taste of blood in her mouth. She chopped down one more time, like a woodcutter. The beast relaxed his grip and slumped with all his weight on the poor gentleman with the grey eyes. He wasn't moving, but that didn't stop La Chouette. She kept making holes in him, made sure he got his full ration. Huh! Take that, bastard! Huh! Sharp, ain't it? Huh! Had enough? Twenty times, twenty-five. No one was counting.

Hippolyte put the Adams revolver back in his pocket. It wasn't going to be needed again. The old woman eventually stopped battering at the bloodstained remains. She opened her wide, visionary eyes. With a movement of her hand she readjusted the bonnet that had slipped to the back of her head. Her cheeks were slightly hollowed.

With the melancholy of a waning moon, she sniffed the smell of old bedding and gaminess that clung about the hovel. She stretched out her neck and sniffed at the room as if aware for the first time of its abject stench. Her blue-veined hand opened and allowed the billhook to fall to the floor. She looked down at the man with gold-encrusted hands and said: 'There's no better bed than a deserved death.' She looked at Grondin who was getting shakily to his feet, exhausted by the violence of his nightmares. Giggling like an ogress, she added: 'This time, gaffer, if I'm thinking straight, you can't go back . . . and now I've bashed *that* thing's mug in for him, you really got to take me with you . . .'

She made a strange noise with her mouth. She even made a sort of curtsey. In her armour of rags, she said cheerfully:

'Here I am, so to say, like yer housekeeper! An' Bosco, he can be yer parrot!'

'And I'll be your Michel Morin, sir!' Barthélemy added, unfolding himself like a telescope. 'Because I've killed those other two blackguards, and I'm not leaving you alone again.'

63

Commissaire Mespluchet's dog
hangs onto his bone

So saying, the ex-detective of Gros-Caillou district dusted himself down and slowly massaged the small of his back, which had been bruised against the table. He smiled wanly at Grondin, one of his reddened eyelids twitching with the nervous stress of the last half-hour, and rummaged at length in the depths of his shirt.

A moment later he opened a bony hand to display three small porcelain spheres. Grondin recognised them at once.

'Here's a funny thing,' Barthélemy said. 'Just as they were about to finish me off, those two bacon-slicers started arguing about which of them would have the right to put one of these marbles in my hand.'

'It's clear enough, surely? They both wanted to claim your neck.'

'What's the difference? A bullet from one or a blade from the other ... if I hadn't fired first, those ugly dogs would have done for me.'

'They were arguing over the rule.'

'The rule?'

'In the closed hand of a corpse, the glass eye is a signature. In the open palm of a living person, it's a sign of friendship.'

'You seem to know what you're talking about, sir. I suppose you couldn't spell it out a bit further for me?'

The former secret policeman's reply was to bend over the Goldsmith's corpse. He turned it over on its back and closed the glassy eyes. Then after rummaging in the pockets of the fine sportsman's suit he straightened and displayed yet another marble-like object between thumb and forefinger.

'Show a bit of respect, you great numbskull!' he said, dropping it into Barthélemy's hand. 'That's glass eye number one: the boss's emblem.' He looked down thoughtfully at the body and added a short obituary:

'Here lies an example of genuine big game: master of the Ourcq, extra-large size, first among the wicked! A killer all his life, generally for profit, without ever getting caught. Impeccable front and nerves of steel. Before he ever had his lawyers and placemen on the payroll, he moved through every stage of gambling with crime.'

'*Gambling* with it? What for, I mean!'

'An absurd game with death . . . a monstrous project that the Goldsmith managed to impose on his people. A sort of pact with immorality, you could put it like that . . .' Grondin paused and glanced at Barthélemy over his shoulder. The inspector's narrowed eyes, tight lips and air of animal cunning revealed how very interested he was in his superior's revelations. He was doing his best to look encouraging, his jaundiced face set in what was intended to be an engaging grin. 'Give me some more of this Sûreté stuff, guvnor,' he begged, 'I'm dying of curiosity!'

Grondin turned and faced him. He looked ill, his back rounded, shoulders slumped forward in the bloodstained shirt. His merciless eyes stared into the detective's face. 'You really want to hear it all?' he asked sombrely. 'You want to stir up the mud?'

Barthélemy did. In two spidery strides he was staring straight into Grondin's face. 'Tell me,' he said. 'I want to know everything.'

'Then listen carefully to the unspeakable,' Monsieur Claude's former deputy said. 'These are very murky waters. On entry to the Ourcq brotherhood, each probationer – each new member of the gang – is given three glass eyes bearing his number. It's up to him to get rid of them . . . to sign his crimes with them. It's up to him to toughen himself. After three killings, provided the next number is free, he's promoted to it. So by following the path of blood, the enforcer rises in the gang hierarchy. Every time he *does one*, the apprentice cut-throat rises in the estimation of his peers. And every time, of course, he draws a little further away from any principles he may have had, any feelings ... and the villain becomes a little more familiar with the abominable. And as he drinks ever more deeply from the chalice of evil, so his share of the take gets steadily fatter!'

'Good God, sir!' Barthélemy was genuinely horrified. 'That's just about the lowest thing I ever heard. It sets your teeth on edge!'

'You haven't heard the worst of it yet, my lad. There could be a bit of an upsurge soon. Because when the news spreads that the Goldsmith's kicked the bucket, the villains' scoreboard's going to explode! It's going to be a war of succession, every big blade for himself. The numbers'll go up by the day.'

'I get it now,' Barthélemy said, gazing in fascination at the three marbles on his palm. 'The Squirrel still had two number 17 glass eyes in his waistcoat pocket ... Greaseball only had one number 14 left!'

'And the number 13 slot was empty,' Grondin said in a curiously sorrowful murmur.

Barthélemy looked up at that with an intense stare. 'The number 13 eye, sir, is of great personal interest to me,' he said, 'in connection with the case of the drowned girl at the pont de l'Alma, which I promised to investigate for Commissaire Mespluchet.' The hunter quickly gave a detailed account of the macabre discovery of the dead woman on 17th March. He pointed out in particular that the 'cadaver brought ashore at la Bourdonnais', since identified as the Baroness de Runuzan, had a glass eye bearing the number 13 clenched in one fist. 'I'm still nineteen sous short of a franc, sir,' he ended in a suggestive tone,' ... but I've got a sort of idea you know the identity of the criminal. If so, you ought to let me have it.'

Grondin made no reply, but went into the alcove and opened the iron box la Chouette had given him to keep his few remaining valuables in. He returned with the blue-irised glass eye that had been given him by Caracole, his old comrade-in-irons, at St Peter's church, and held it out to Barthélemy.

'Here,' he said tiredly. 'It comes from your culprit, may he now rest in peace.'

'Come on sir, please. Cough up. I want his name.'

'What does it matter?'

'Get at the truth, sir. Close the file.'

Grondin looked down thoughtfully. His mind wandered a bit. His eye fell on the bloody mess around the Goldsmith's corpse. There wasn't much to be discreet about now, he thought.

'Léon Chauvelot was his name,' he said quietly. 'For some, a villain ready for any murderous enterprise . . . a real cut-throat. For others, a cheerful cricket ready to share his warmth, his money and his bread . . . Personally I'll always remember him. When I'm asleep I'll see his red hair . . .'

'You talk as if he'd been a friend . . .'

'I talk as if he'd been an old stick who said friendship wasn't a vain word in his book, and everything else was just wind.' With a brusque movement he tried to erase his memories, cut them short. He turned on his heel. Going up to la Chouette, he asked her to hide the two dead men in the barn under piles of rabbit skins. He was taking control of the house once more. They would leave later that night, he said, after setting the whole shack on fire. He was heading for the alcove when the tall detective with the yellow face stopped him with a hand on his forearm.

'Justice will be pleased with the work its servants have done even in these dark days in the history of Paris,' he said. 'And I thank my lucky stars for having met you.'

'Well, faith! if the dwarf in gold-rimmed spectacles comes back into office, *your* future's pretty well guaranteed. You'll be a principal commissaire!'

Barthélemy waved one arm like a wing, a movement that showed how tent-like the overall was on his thin frame. 'One more word,' he murmured. A nasty little smile played at the corner of his lips exposing bloodless gums. He had become a bloodhound again, an ugly tracking dog with its belly to the ground and an air of mean docility, but nevertheless capable of following its infallible nose to the end of any trail. Now he asked the one question that could bridge the frightening abyss Grondin had always tried to put between himself and others.

'Forgive me for speaking so crudely, sir, but how did you come to know those villains so, er, *intimately*, without being one of them?'

Seeing the great irritation that overcame the man with grey eyes at these words, the stony face and uncertain eyes, Barthélemy knew that one day, sooner or later, the former notary was going to have to settle his account with the truth.

He awarded him a yellow grin and sidled away.

64

Marbuche has an idea

Tarpagnan's thoughts became ever blacker with the passage of the cruel days. The less likely it became that he would rescue his beloved in time, the more repulsive he found the thought of finding her buried in a house of pleasure as a battered, degraded, sullied woman, half dead with shame. So haunted was he by the certainty of failure that his own strength, the surge of his health, started to desert him. He stopped shaving. Neglected his appearance. Gave up washing his hands.

Eventually he spent most of his time lying prostrate on his bed at the back of the caravan, drinking vinegary, acrid wine and going over the past, rummaging endlessly through the journeys he had made in former times.

Over the days he had made friends with a family of travellers and performers got up in red noses, spangles, stage-paint and sham. He had learned to live with the distress of freaks, hermaphrodites, midgets, the two-headed, weird and sinister aquarium creatures. Little by little, in a strange, shared convulsion of feelings, he had come to feel sympathy for his new friends. It became usual, after nightfall, to see the former Captain coming and going like a family dog, sniffing round the backdrops of the show-booths and lifting a corner to look or listen into caves and pools of dark water that contained, on the very outermost edges of human appearance, sad-eyed, rejected beings who lived (if you could call it living), anyway breathed, in a state of reclusion and extreme filth.

Once, at the end of a sleepless night, one of those black, ashy nights when everything seemed unattainable, Antoine had got up and slipped outside without awakening Marbuche. He had wandered among the tents of the camp, listening to the magnetic woman's snores and the silence outside the caravan shared by Palmyre and Madame Tambour. Wandering further, he had found himself in the alley beside an isolated tent, and lifting its flap had found himself face to face with a ghoul with seaweed-coloured hair and elongated eyes, a grossly deformed child of great gentleness. That burning gaze, coming from the surface of a bluish fluid in which the devastating dog-woman had to float her head, which was far too heavy to lift, made it impossible to speak.

For a long moment, she and he had looked into each other's eyes. Time seemed to have stopped in the near-darkness. Looking across an abyss, his mind empty, his guts twisted with nausea, Antoine had kept perfectly still. Then the creature's eyes, dull with separateness, with loneliness, had half-closed. She was going back to sleep, leaving Tarpagnan with an urgent need to find new reasons for living. He emerged into the night, an icy calm pervading his whole being.

For a human being (that miserable little tangle of secrets), the spectacle of suffering is sometimes reminiscent of one of those tiring journeys where nothing turns out as expected, and damage to the soul or the sharpest pain, even if only slightly tamed by the heart's intelligence, at the bottom of the abyss can become one of the dimensions of life.

That night Antoine tried to remember the peaceful fireside in a house, he tried to remember Gabriella Pucci's smile, but he could not. He allowed his gaze to wander over the changing canvas of the approaching day, launching his imagination over the wagon roofs into the sweep of indigo sky. In the clouds he saw the hallucinated image of his beloved. He discerned behind the cloud six times her eyes and six times the same fear engraved on her face. Unfastened linen undulated behind her white legs. He saw her run towards a dark square and throw herself into it with a distant splash to escape from a forest of hands.

Bitterness invaded him. He looked towards Paris, and was just deciding to start walking there when the hulking form of Marbuche appeared from the shadows and his gigantic hand seized Tarpagnan's.

'Where are you going, my friend?' he rumbled.

'I'm going towards my dream. I'm going to jump down a well too.'

'Well? Dream? Jump?' The giant was upset. He gripped Tarpagnan's wrist with the force of a vice. 'You're making fun of Marbuche,' he said, shaking his head.

'No. I swear I had a vision of a house where Caf'conc' was being held. A hovel at the end of a cul-de-sac, with a felled tree. A cherry. A flowering cherry ... can't understand why such a nice tree should have been cut down.'

'Nonsense! Confetti! You can't fool me!'

'I saw Caf'conc' from behind. She was naked. They were chasing her. She was running towards the bottom of the garden. She turned towards me and threw herself into the well.'

'You're mad! Your ideas are all fogged up! You want to worry Marbuche! Drag him into some dream! You just want to run off and leave him!' He scowled and raised a terrible fist as if to strike Antoine. 'You're not my friend,' he growled. 'Mademoiselle isn't dead! Mademoiselle can't die!'

He was on the point of smashing Tarpagnan's head in as casually as he had Caracole's, but abruptly changed his mind, turned his anger on himself and fetched his poor noddle, filled with inadequacies and errant fragments, a mighty clout. The blow, which might easily have killed an ox, seemed to let some light into the attic of his intelligence.

'You're not a bad man, Tarpagnan,' he said in a friendlier voice. 'It's just that you're feeling discouraged. Today was another failure, but perhaps tomorrow will at last take us to where Miss Pucci is!'

'I don't think so, Marbuche. You know as well as I do we've been trying everything, for week after week. All we can do now is admit we've failed.'

'Abandon our search? You can't be thinking of it! Marbuche never will!' The obtuse colossus pointed to the lights of Paris in the distance. 'It's extraordinary!' he grumbled. 'Miss Pucci is certainly somewhere out there! She's there, all alone with nothing but our love! Shut away in a house, crying! Marbuche can hear her cries. He's got a headache! She's struggling! She's weeping! She's alive!'

'I dream of nothing but finding her,' murmured Tarpagnan. A mournful silence enveloped them.

'Marbuche'll take you back home,' the mastodon mumbled gloomily. He took Antoine by the hand, then with a certain gentleness pulled him along in his wake in the usual way. Tired and depressed, the athlete in his purple costume walked heavily. He seemed plunged in deep thought. Then suddenly, in the middle of the fairground, he stopped short and whacked himself on the forehead. His face was a picture.

'Stop! All four hooves!' he said, acting accordingly. 'I've got an idea! A wonderful idea!' The Manchu giant's little eyes, in the depths of their cavities, glowed with sudden inspiration. 'I can hear angels! The sound of their trumpets!' he cried delightedly. 'Their advice is formal: instead of going home to bed, we go and try your vision on Professor Chocnosophe!' His face, scarlet with effort, had become deeply agitated.

'The professor's a seer, a clairvoyant,' he cried. 'Tarot readings, love spells ... he lives in the Queen of Hearts in the playing-card Palace, it's just a step away! Extra-lucid work! Great concentration!' And as if he was offering Tarpagnan an undreamed-of-springboard to hope, Marbuche added: 'I'll ask him to read our future in his Egyptian crystal. He'll search the map of Paris with his pendulum! He'll question the winds! I'll be damned if he won't unearth your famous whore-house!'

Exhausted by this tirade which had temporarily dried up his brain, the wrestler frowned at the scepticism in his companion's face. 'Well, what?' he roared furiously. 'You find that perplexing?'

Tarpagnan shrugged helplessly. He felt suddenly that he had lived all his life in the presence of incurable injuries. 'My poor Marbuche,' he said, 'of course we'll go and see your Chocnosophe, but d'you really think he'll be able to help us?'

'Marbuche isn't sure of anything any more,' the giant murmured, lowering his head. 'His luck's running out.'

His energy was gradually fading. A trough had formed in his

understanding. His nervous tension diminished little by little. Eventually the bird-brained giant was himself once more.

'If Chocno doesn't find anything,' he mumbled, 'we'll go to see Palmyre. She'll keep an eye on you. Then I'll be able to get some sleep.'

Having returned to the simple configuration of a mass of blind force, the giant seized the captain with one unarguable fist and drew him towards the Card Palace, towards new zones between becoming and nothingness.

And Marbuche, that obscure instrument of destiny, by plunging Tarpagnan into ever closer intimacy with fairground freaks and monsters, by making him familiar with the bottom of the heap, letting him feel the cold wind of misery and the abandonment of certainties, was preparing the Gascon without knowing it for the infernal aftermath of his beautiful devastated love.

65

Venus's Staircase

Only when it seemed that her enslaved condition could become no worse, when it was more painful than it had ever been before, was Caf'conc' at last awarded a tiny chink of faint light that resembled some sort of hope. And it was to her dishonourable renown as a frigid and exciting whore that she owed that first glimpse of clear blue sky.

Usually she was approached by men of a brutal type fascinated by the captivating depth of her gaze, people who simply appropriated her mouth and played the game of trying to lead her to the higher stages of pleasure. One afternoon, though, in Saint-Lago's absence, it happened that Venus's Staircase was visited by a cheerful group of guardsmen on leave from the outposts along the Sceaux railway, determined to taste the warmth of the lovely hetaira's body.

Led by a quartermaster-sergeant, these boisterous youths and young family men on the spree, who had seen some action and wanted, as they said, to 'clean their crockery', invaded the big parlour where the girls were waiting for them.

These damsels were gossiping nineteen to the dozen, trotting about the room in a clattering of little boots and all talking at once in a way that suggested unusual excitement. It should be said at the outset, however, that their parakeet-like chatter punctuated by sudden bursts of laughter and equally sudden worried silences was caused not by the unexpected arrival of the impertinent-handed, jolly-faced federals but by the persistent presence of a rumour which, if it turned out to be true, had the potential to turn their tarts' microcosm upside down.

Yes, this was a major event, no mistake. That very morning, at the speed of a powder-train, starting no one knew where, the rumour had flashed through the alcoves of Venus's Staircase that the boss of the Ourcq, Edmond Trocard himself, had been found dead on wasteland, riddled with holes like a sieve, stabbed repeatedly between the shoulder-blades by some group of back-street, low-road cut-throats who had of course taken his gold watch, his rings and even his fine earring.

A hundred metres away the bodies of two of his henchmen lay half-immersed in a hole full of muddy water, their eye-sockets emptied by the crows of the Saint-Denis plain. Handsome Auguste, sent to the spot, had no difficulty identifying the two gangsters, the Squirrel by his rodent's teeth and Greaseball by his multicoloured garment.

What a thunderclap in the universe of bullies, bravoes and hoodlums! What an unexpected affront! Who could have dared this crime of lese-majesty against the potentate of the Ourcq? An untouchable man who had notaries on his payroll, placemen in the Stock Exchange, his own land agents and estate managers; and whose art – whose great art – it was to turn a blind eye to the doings of the lower criminal strata, to project the image of a thoroughly nice fellow of simple manners, who despite dazzling success would mix with ordinary people at the bar, and who was known sometimes to help indigent families with money so that, for example, the eldest son could continue his education. Was it a rival or an enemy? Who wanted to kill the man with gold-cased fingers? Who stood to gain? There didn't seem to be any clues. Everything had gone: gold and wallets, watches and papers. Even the superb grey cabriolet and big black horse of which the nabob had been so proud seemed to have evaporated. The wheel tracks, carefully analysed, seemed to suggest that after the presumed ambush, the coach had been turned and driven back towards Paris.

In every corner of Venus's Staircase, tongues wagged furiously. After a while, with natural exaggeration and elision playing their usual parts, it was being whispered that Saint-Lago had been identified by the Glass Eye Brotherhood as a likely candidate for the big boss's murder, and had sensibly enlarged the gap between himself and those who suspected him of manoeuvring for the Goldsmith's succession. Such at any rate was the commonly accepted explanation for the pock-marked ponce's hurried departure.

He had risen early, flung his clothes on and left at a dead run, even forgetting in his haste to give the recluse 'down the corridor' her morning beating. He had entrusted the management of the house to his longest-serving girl (and occasional mistress), the sprightly Coraline Eugénie Beaupré, forty-three years old, swearing her to secrecy and discretion and forbidding her to mention the Goldsmith's death to his former lover. Cora Beaupré can be assumed to have fallen short of perfection on the first promise, but she had certainly fully respected the second. For she herself was anxious to keep la Pucci in darkness and silence.

From the time of the unfortunate young woman's arrival, Coraline – or Cora the Knowledge, as la Beaupré was called – had been a strict jailer. She did not have to force herself, for she was jealous as a tigress, terrified that Caf'conc' might supplant her in Saint-Lago's affections and relegate her, Coraline, to the rank of ordinary girl in the chicken-run. She assured anyone who would listen that the new girl's sickly-sweet 'respectable' manners were winning the clients away from her more honest colleagues, girls who tried to obey the rules of the house and exercise their profession in a conscientious way.

On this particular afternoon, then, as the soldiers fresh from the front crowded into the parlour demanding attention, Cora the Knowledge, draped in her cashmere shawl, promoted to chief pimp in Saint-Lago's absence, greeted those miraculous survivors of a decimated company in friendly fashion. She asked the heroes of the ramparts to leave their swords and bayonets in the cloakroom, then spread out on the big red sofa the argument of her own charms, including the beauty-spot on one hip that suggested something even prettier for anyone who cared to search for it.

When the men trooped back into the parlour in their socks, Cora was ready for them. 'Make yourselves at home, pretty troopers,' she cooed, fluttering her eyelashes like anything. Then, removing the cigarette that hung sluttishly from the corner of her mouth, she followed house practice by offering, with refreshments included, the modestly priced services of Henriette the Blonde, Clara the Redhead, Adèle with the Birthmark and Rosine the Schoolgirl. At the mention of her name each young woman, doubtless to give a better idea of her charms, would each in her own graceful way remove or unfasten one of her garments; then, one with a half-open bodice, another whirling a cheeky pair of knickers on her finger, they would salute the troops of the Commune with a charming twitch of the bottom or a smouldering, sidelong pout.

But even during the parade of physical charms, even under the salvoes of underwear tossed so generously into the cauldron of desire by those conscientious damsels, the happy expressions on the soldiers' faces started to fade, and eventually their lack of enthusiasm became positively insulting.

'What kind of start is this, soldiers?' the madam asked in surprise as the clucking in her chicken-run died away. 'Is it possible that my nymphs aren't well-formed enough for you?'

The quartermaster-sergeant – shepherding his men to the brothel more or less exactly as he would have taken them to the cookhouse for soup – sank his head between his shoulders, inspected the troopers' faces and mumbled to himself:

'Mmer, naah, bugger that, the lads ain't keen . . . They ain't keen . . .'

In fact the soldiers were eyeing the tarts in a hangdog sort of way, without real enthusiasm. They chewed and trampled where they stood, sniggering bashfully, a right herd of smelly cattle, but not one of them seemed interested in the prodigious accomplishments of any of the ladies present. Time passed slowly under Cora the Knowledge's big brown eyes. She had absinthe served, which gave her the social advantage of protection against mockery.

'Well, young fellows, what shall we do?' she asked eventually. 'Are we just here to pass the time and let pleasure go to waste? Is there a problem about rates? Do we need to repeat ourselves on the warm welcome extended to all true patriots?'

'Naah, cit'zeness, it ain't that,' said the sergeant whose silver bars seemed to give him the right to make all the decisions, 'I'll tell you what the problem is.' And without further ado the decorated warrior demanded for his valorous troop the privilege of making 'the springs creak' with the famous Caf'conc'.

Cora the Knowledge reddened slightly at the affront. She objected that 'the sugary one' was already working. She remarked drily that all her pleasure girls (most of whom, incidentally, between you and me, were cleaner and more experienced than the hussy in question) deserved their share of the feast.

Nevertheless, she had to admit that as there were six gentlemen, and the girls here present were only five, someone would inevitably have to end up with that stuck-up cow. She added that as far as having 'a nice afternoon' was concerned, she didn't especially envy that soldier. For although the odalisque 'down the corridor' certainly appealed to some people, and could even be said to have quite pretty shoulders, she was a long way from being really attractive, know what I mean?

The NCO adopted a bored expression to maintain face in front of his men. He twirled the points of his moustache and said in an authoritative voice:

'We been told . . .'

'Fiddlesticks! You've had the wool pulled over your eyes,' said the pleasure-dealer, drawing on her Egyptian cigarette. With a wriggle of her shoulder she advanced a well-filled, low-cut bodice towards the NCO, giving him a good look at its contents. She exhaled a plume of blue smoke through her nose and added with great energy 'To the devil with flim-flam! That Caf'conc' is a *wax doll*, sergeant – do you understand me? – who has no idea how to play the clarinet and jibs at taking it from behind!'

Then, determined to persuade the troopers that only her girls had the slightest idea how to behave, she added in one of those sour-sweet accents kept for connoisseurs: 'Don't go there, soldiers! Believe me! That girl's *affected*! A timewaster who doesn't even know how to fuck except on her back! About as lazy as they come. The sort of smooth-as-silk prodigy that just lies there and does it without a word . . .' She looked round at her girls for support. 'Sod that! Is that the way to behave? Not even saying hello to the gent?'

A unanimous cry of disapproval went up from the damsels' throats. Influenced by this stream of negative sales talk and the girls' apparent agreement, the soldiers went into a huddle. Cora the Knowledge thereupon suggested they draw lots to see who would 'have to go down the corridor when the place is free'. A noisy game of cork-penny was immediately organised in the corridor, the final loser (or winner) turning out to be a young National Guardsman who was hardly sixteen and only there to lose his virginity.

'That's it, boys!' the sergeant decreed. 'It's Guillaume who gets to do it. It may be a trial run, laddie, but do your best to make it a bleedin' masterpiece. If you make the lady miaow I'll stand you a bottle of Veuve Clicquot.'

''Ave a nice charver, Tironneau!' his pals called after him. And it was in this unexpected way that Guillaume Tironneau, of the rue Lévisse, at last opened the spyhole of his curiosity concerning the secrets of the female body.

66

The little recruit's
virginity

He pushed the door ajar and stuck his head inside. A languid voice said:

'Come in. Put your trousers on the chair. There's water in the crock . . . wash your little bits and pieces.'

In the gloom he could see a form stretched out on the white pallet. He wondered if he ought to say who he was. Identify himself to Miss Pucci, a person who seemed to have gone to the dogs a bit since he had heard her singing 'La Canaille' on the Polish field. In the end he said nothing, so apprehensive was he about the initiation that awaited him. Heart racing, he closed the door behind him and did as he had been told. Guillaume undressed.

Another client. Stretched waiting on her couch, Caf'conc' could hear the stubborn machinery of her will murmuring in her ear. An interior voice whispered to her to stand fast. Another day. Just another day.

The newcomer had stopped moving once he was naked. Slowly she descended from her mountain. 'Come on,' she said.

The trembling Guillaume slipped under the cover. It was too dark for La Pucci to see his face properly. But she could feel his tension, his body rigid against hers. Expecting the usual assault of an overheated male, she was surprised to feel the gentle touch of a cold, hesitant hand caressing her breast. These clumsy moves told her that the boy in her bed was violently excited.

'Do what you've come to do,' she urged. 'You're not supposed to take hours!' With a wriggle of the hips she helped him climb onto her belly. The body in her arms was slender, brittle almost. His arms trembled under her fingers like ropes stretched taut. This tense person weighed little more than a child. His voice whispered:

'You'll have to help me, m'dame. It's my first time. I've come to lose my virginity.'

She helped him to enter. Found maternal gestures to guide him in the deployment of his energy. He was skittish as a horse and started to pant loudly. She stopped him.

'Gently, young stallion,' she murmured. 'You'll wear it out like that.'

But he was carried away and didn't even hear her. Within a very short time she felt the spasms of his long orgasm.

'Is that it?' he panted, out of breath as after a long sprint. 'Is it over already?'

'Well, yes. It's over.' She smiled in the darkness. 'Twenty seconds of forgetfulness!' she teased gently. 'You must be really young to be satisfied with a garden as short as that!'

As he recovered his breath, however, he felt that he would soon want to know more. 'You're right, m'dame,' he said. 'But I'm sure I can do better than that. I'm ready to start again.'

'You're not entitled to any more,' she said, drawing away to the side to emphasise the point.

'Go on, give us a chance, M'dame Pucci! I just want to learn how to give pleasure, that's all, honest!'

'You know my name?'

'Don't I just!' the boy said, sticking his head out from under the sheet. 'Mine's Guillaume. Guillaume Tironneau from number 7, rue Lévisse.'

This was so unusual that at first she did not appreciate what advantage she could draw from the situation. Nothing of the sort had happened before.

'You're in the National Guards, aren't you?'

'Yes, m'dame! I'm down there, Sceaux way. A volunteer scout. We got it pretty hot, too!'

She had taken his hand, but now let it go and was mechanically feeling his skinny arms. She did not speak, and he respected her silence. After a while she asked:

'But ... er ... I suppose from time to time you still see your people from rue Lévisse?'

'Whenever I get leave I go home to give my mother a hug. We split my thirty sous. She really needs it!'

'Well then ... d'you ever see Emile Roussel, the locksmith?'

'Wire? I'll say! Although he's hardly ever in the shop these days ... he helps man the outposts with Louise Michel's geezers.'

She thought for a while. Delayed the question she longed to ask. That burned her lips.

'You haven't seen Captain Tarpagnan again, I suppose?'

'Your mutineer, m'dame? No one's seen him! Seems he's dead or missing. That's what Wire says.'

She closed her eyes. They were dry from too much weeping. Not a single tear came.

'I see M'sieu Théo, though,' Guillaume went on. 'You know Théo, the photographer? He's been down to see me at the front. He says he really likes me. That's another reason why I'm here. To see if I'm a man!'

She smiled mysteriously. 'Come on, Guillaume,' she said suddenly. 'I'm going to show you who you are. So that you'll have an answer for Monsieur Théo.'

'Honest? Will you really? What made you change your mind, m'dame?'

Instead of answering, she turned to him and accepted him inside her. Accepted him while bending him to the majestic slowness of a woman vanquishing savage force. Gently, she showed him the way. In the darkness, in this refuge where time was suspended, Gabriella had just arrested the pendulum of her scruples. One thought assailed her, invigorating as the caress of sunshine. God, she was thinking, despite everything I've endured, at the age of thirty I still nurture hope! She could see a fragment of life for herself, in the distance, at the end of a long tunnel. At first the thought frightened her. With Tarpagnan dead, would she still have enough appetite for life to try to recover her freedom? The answer seemed to be yes! A thousand times yes! Use the beauty that the Lord gave you! Be a serpent, my girl! Get your freedom!'

She moved delicately, slowly. She took the young man with her. Carefully piled fuel into the brazier. 'Come on,' she said suddenly. 'Harder! Again! More! That's it!' Unstoppable iridescent waves of perfect warmth flooded her own belly and she uttered a long, shaky cry.

They lay motionless for a moment, silenced by their reciprocal astonishment. '*Thank* you, M'dame Pucci!' the boy panted. 'That was ... that was ...'

She stroked his hair. She knew what she was going to do. 'Guillaume,' she heard herself whisper, 'one good turn deserves another. I'm going to give you a letter for Wire. Don't say a word to anyone, not a word. Just get it to him. Whatever it costs you.'

'It's already done, m'dame, I swear it! Anything you want, anything!'

While she was writing it he put his clothes back on. He lifted a corner of the curtain and looked out into the garden. A flowering cherry tree stood beside the well.

'Ah,' he cried, 'How good it feels to be a man!'

Outside, it was indeed spring.

67

The butterflies of death

But at any season the trees seem bare when one is sad. Tarpagnan resisted the advent of spring. He shuffled his feet like a sleepwalker. Blinded by tears, he followed Marbuche about, his hand trapped in the giant's colossal paw. They went out every day, kept up the hunt. They went where their informants suggested they might look.

Professor Chocnosophe's crystal ball had clearly established that the house at the end of a cul-de-sac, with a well and a fallen cherry tree, existed in reality as well as in Tarpagnan's nightmare. The troupe of show-people and Madame Tambour's orchestra had volunteered spontaneously to help cover the city, and thus speed up the search.

The professor had supplied a plan that conformed to Tarpagnan's idea of the place. The tumblers and musicians worked wonders. They combed the streets. They listened. They questioned the girls. They spied on pimps, looking for one with a poxy face. Sitting on the steps of his wagon, the wrestler in the mauve costume, with his eternal posy of faded violets, awaited their return.

He would watch the tired procession of his trufflehound friends returning from the town. Leading the procession would be Marjolin, giggling behind his hands like a half-wit, the living skeleton with his knobby knees and shrivelled look, behind him Soupir the trombone, ridiculously deformed with a double hump, and Professor Chocnosophe who cast horoscopes and read the tarot.

The others trailed in behind them, hobbling up the slope: one-armed men, broken-down clowns, sword-swallowers, chewers of glass and machinery, all limping back under the sails of the windmills. Madame Tambour raised her hand: music! Clé-de-Fa blew assembly call as they all trooped into the fairground. Trombine inevitably came last, slowed by his big wobbling head. He sniffed the terrain with his trunk-like nose, his tiny eyes – that had shed such floods of tears in '70, when the militia had killed the elephant in the Jardin des Plantes for food – rolling in their sockets.

Marbuche scowled with the effort of getting his brain moving. From the platform at his wagon door he would ask: 'What's new, friends?'

Heads bowed with the weight of fatigue.

'Nothing. We haven't found anything.'

'Nothing.'

'Nothing in Belleville.'

'Or Bastille.'

People looked down and stirred the dust with their toes. Shoulders slumped. Sometimes they couldn't even say anything.

Marbuche looked down too. He made a sign of dismissal and the troupe scattered to rest for a while before the evening parade.

The giant went back into the wagon with its curtained windows. In the dim light he rejoined Tarpagnan, who now refused to see the dawn and stayed in bed. After lurching massively about, the strongman with the rolling muscles leaned over the recluse and looked into his gaunt face, bearded, muddy-looking, staring-eyed. Marbuche growled over and over again: 'Monsieur Byron! Oh we *are* important, aren't we! Wake up! Deign to notice us!'

He stood up again, filled the space between the beds with his size, walked up and down with enormously heavy tread, his anger rising as he did so. The caravan rocked on its worn springs, Marbuche's storm imprinting itself on them.

'In the end you're managing to get on my nerves with this field marshal act!' the colossus rumbled at Tarpagnan. 'All bloody day in bed! The rest of the time being led about like a child! I've had more'n enough of your superior flannel, Mr Clever Dick.' He ran up to the bed and bawled: 'I've got a mind to give you a thrashing! Get it done! I'm going to fetch you one!'

He looked as if he was on the verge of doing it. He was snorting like a buffalo and waving a clenched fist the size of a largish ham. He held it in the air for a moment or two.

'Stop looking at me,' he said to Tarpagnan at last. 'When you look at me like that, I feel like I'm covered with hair all over and an animal's trying to hide inside me.'

To clear the chaos boiling in his head, he gave himself an enormous thump on the stomach, the only method he had come up with for preventing himself from taking Tarpagnan apart. That was how it was with the giant Marbuche. He could hardly reason as well as a grizzly bear. He could have drowned a litter of fifteen kittens without even thinking about it, but the frank, handsome face of his friend, its energetic honesty, always brought him up short. He never struck him.

Better still, after these quarrelsome sessions the big fellow would feel so ashamed of his threats of violence that, as a plea for forgiveness, he would brown some onions and bring the captain a dish of boiled vegetables, serve him a meal as gracefully as a girl.

'The Chocnos have come back empty-handed,' he grumbled. The giant stretched out a leg before him and sat with his head in his hands. 'One day I'll end up forgetting what we were looking for.'

'We were looking for grace and beauty,' Tarpagnan reminded him, pushing his plate away.

'Aren't you hungry?'

'No.'

They sat in silence, their hearts low. 'We were looking for grace and beauty,' Tarpagnan repeated, 'but if and when we track down the person who embodied them, she may be so different from the infallible woman you remember that you won't even recognise her.' He thought for a moment and added: 'We've changed, too.'

Marbuche shook his head incredulously. 'Bloody thunder and lightning! That's a bit strong what you're saying there, shrimp!'

His eyes were like two empty slots as he peered with residual suspicion into the face of the miserable unshaven creature before him. Ideas washed about in his poor skull, renewals of purpose, obstinate necessities. But he had to accept that the essence of his plan had seeped out of his memory.

One morning he walked right up to Antoine's bedside. His face and hair were dripping as he had just dunked his head in the horse trough. His pale blue eyes looked as clean as orbs of porcelain.

'You can leave if you want,' he said. 'Marbuche won't keep you any longer.' So saying, the Manchu wrestler had taken his stage cloak down from its peg and left the caravan, his shoulders bowed.

Tarpagnan had not reacted immediately. In total silence, he had plumped up his pillows. One hand planted in his matted hair, he had sunk down into his bed. He seemed to be considering what action to take.

More than fifteen minutes passed without any purposeful gesture on his part. The entire world seemed to have escaped his awareness. From time to time, however, the caravan windows rattled to the continuous series of dull detonations in the far distance, reminding anyone who cared to listen that the Versailles guns were stepping up the shelling of federal positions. Antoine had only to lift the curtain to see the great smudge of sooty smoke low in the sky over Asnières. The explosions followed each other in rolling sequence. No doubt the ground over there was liberally strewn with corpses.

Behind his mask of indifference the former infantryman had a very good idea of what was going on over there across the hills. His neck stiffened as he thought of the men downing a last belt of raw spirits before going into action. He could hear NCOs yelling through the black smoke just as if he was there himself. He heard bayonets being snapped into position, hastening medics. He saw the men surge, shouting, from cover. The front ranks rebounding from the wall of bullets, arms flung wide as if in the attempt to fly over it.

Blossoms of smoke and flame. Generous swathes of turned-up earth. Greyish salvoes and volleys covering the poppy fields with their tragic movement. Always the same music! Hot-muzzled machine cannon barking raucously as they traced their roadway of evil light. Men half out of their minds on brandy and fear running for their lives.

It was awful! Awful! Antoine had been through it on other battlefields. Charge. Regroup. Withdraw. Align. The troopers who went straight to heaven without striking a blow. Another killed, and another. Another corpse! Another boy! Another lost child wailing for his mother in the storm of shrapnel!

Tarpagnan watched the butterflies of death passing. He had no need to lift the curtain. He could smell the butchery going on under a strangely pure sky. Turcos, Defenders, Avengers, hit in the hip, tripping suddenly over their rifles, shot through the chest, rolling over and over, swords unsheathed, eyes veiled with road dust, he watched them fall. He watched them fall and kept his eyes closed. Until a tiny mouse-like sound made him open them with a start.

68

Love can't live
on almost

The caravan door had opened to admit Palmyre. The pretty midget was paler than usual, and on her curly head was a Phrygian bonnet in place of the usual pink bow. His eyes focused on her.

'Issy?' he asked in a blank voice.

'Heavy firing,' she answered instantly.

'Clamart?'

'No losses.'

'Montrouge?'

'Long-range shelling. The corner bastion took down an enemy battery. Forty men were surrounded by two companies of Versailles cavalry. Four of the Guardsmen lowered their weapons when about to be overrun, and were shot out of hand on a sign from an officer.'

'Porte Maillot?'

'Several wounded. Pietri's constables are shooting prisoners. They cut the throats of the wounded and fire on ambulances.'

'Asnières?'

'You heard the noise just now, I imagine? An ammunition dump went up. Dombrowski's counterattacking.'

She fell silent and looked searchingly at him. He was ashamed of the irresponsible posture in which she had caught him. 'I was just going to get up,' he said.

The tiny woman shrugged.

Palmyre had become Tarpagnan's main link with the outside world. Every day she brought him the latest news. She was proud of her ability to read and count. That morning she looked charmingly serious in her stage makeup. She fixed Antoine with her clear eyes and said with great gravity: 'Tarpagnan, listen to me.'

She jumped onto his lap. That was her place now. She said: 'Out there everything's going faster and faster.' She said it several times, insistently. She wanted him to understand.

She said: 'The Versaillais are going to come. The fire will go up everywhere.'

She said: 'Our lives are doomed. Paris is going to have to fight.'

Mechanically, she touched her cheeks made up in light vermilion. She breathed: 'Thiers isn't going to wait much longer. He's sprinting already, like a squirrel in a treadmill.'

And she sighed: 'Spies are swarming everywhere. Galliffet is pitiless with prisoners. He insults the women. He shoots the men, even children. The Parisians aren't the same any more. They can feel the blizzard coming. They're tasting their first defeats, the bitterness of withdrawal. They know that the wide glow illuminating the clouds on the horizon will soon be above their heads, and that the walls of their town will be crumbling on the pavements.'

Then she said: 'I don't like men who stand by while others do the fighting. And instead of crying over this woman who doesn't exist, you ought to go and join the friends of the people and take up arms at their side.'

He gave her a sombre look. 'D'you think I'm a coward?'

'I'm looking for your flame, Antoine! Some men are alive. They stand up! Others are dead to humanity. Some are real. Others are imaginary. What sort are you?'

A strange awkwardness had arisen between them. She was looking at him sharply. He smiled suddenly at her pretty little face under the bonnet.

'Well,' he said roguishly, 'whoever would have expected my little rosebud to turn Jacobin!'

'Stop wasting time! As your friend Vallès says: fewer statues, more men! Live in the present! Get up! The Commune needs all its children!' She added in a murmur: 'Even the small ones. In a while I'm leaving for the barricades. I'm more than strong enough to shift cobblestones.'

She laughed and grew serious again. She said: 'Even if the wisdom to keep quiet is the first necessity for a girl like me who has no future, I've got something to ask you before we never see each other again ... would you refuse to love me just once for half a minute?'

Without asking leave, the lilliputian flowed against him. Her little hand caressed his pectorals. She looked into his eyes with a lover's authority. 'Each new flag has to have its baptism of fire,' she said. And without another word she flung herself hungrily on his neck, her lips pressed to his. She lifted her head, gazed tenderly into his black eyes and breathed: 'I'm leading the women's revolution!'

Palmyre had wriggled into the bed. Her hand stroked his hot belly. She sought his skin, squirmed against him with strange force. She was the size of a child. She pressed herself against him. Climbed onto his belly, close, close. Opened herself. 'Let me,' she said. 'I'm nothing.' She moved delicately. Took charge. Murmured. After a while Antoine's breath quickened. 'See?' she murmured. 'Is that better, like that? I'm nothing.' She hardly weighed anything. 'We're nothing,' she said. He let her be. Helped her find the way to a happy place. Encouraged her to stay there. She cried: 'Until the end of time!'

She became quiet. No remorse, no regrets. And no additions either. She got up, left his couch, went to wash her very white thighs over the porcelain of the basin. She sat on the edge of the bed. They smiled at one another.

Palmyre cocked an ear. New explosions were rumbling in the distance.

'Weather's getting nasty!' she observed.

He stroked her painted cheek and said: 'You did well to do that.'

She looked deep into his eyes. Twined her arms round his neck.

'You've taught me that life's full of surprises,' Tarpagnan told her, 'and that the beauty of human beings is eternally mysterious.'

She breathed peacefully in his ear. 'I got everything I wanted,' she murmured. 'My little volcano's covered in snow but the cherry trees are in blossom.'

Tarpagnan thought of the tree in his nightmare. The tree by the well. He thought of Gabriella Pucci. He said nothing.

'It's time to part,' the small woman said, passing her nose across his mouth, sniffing his lips. She added in an apparently offhand voice: 'Oh yes, I meant to tell you: there are some friends of yours waiting outside ... three fellows who turned up just now ...'

Tarpagnan's mouth hung open. 'Friends?' he spluttered. 'Did you say friends of mine?'

'So they kept claiming,' Palmyre answered.

'Who are they? How did they get here? Where have my trousers got to?'

Palmyre didn't know. They hunted the garment side by side. As they felt about under the bunk, she turned to him and said:

'One's athletic, blond hair, fiery eye, strong arms, civilian clothes but a revolver in his belt, quite a handsome face; the second's calmer, an old Avenger type with a red-chequered scarf round his neck ... blood in his beard, nasty cough, beaten-up kepi and half-boots ... and as for the third, well, a blind person'd know him, impossible to go near him without noticing him ...'

'There they are, found my breeks! The third chap, you were saying ... ?'

Pretty Palmyre laughed. 'Monsieur Vallès in person bringing up the rear!'

'Good God! Are you serious? Jules Vallès here?'

'You can tell it's him by his gold-edged red Commune rosette.'

The Gascon went scarlet in the face. 'Jesus Christ Almighty! And you didn't even *tell* me?'

Palmyre saw how angry he was. She skipped off the end of his bed and scuttled down the middle of the caravan looking over her shoulder like a fleeing chicken-thief. Tarpagnan, standing on one leg, in his haste and fury entangled the other foot in the lining of his breeches, swayed for a moment and fell clumsily on his side. The midget turned and looked down at him with her hands on her hips and her head on one side. She giggled behind her hand. Laughed at his ferocious anger.

'As for that, m'sieu, sorry, but too bad if it's annoyed you. I was just thinking of myself for once! I'd planned it long enough.'

'Are they still here?' Antoine, suddenly anxious, hopped to the window and lifted the curtain. He saw Jules Vallès moving among the clowns and tumblers distributing smiles and handshakes to the show-folk as if he had known them all his life, easy with giants, pally with albinos, trotting among the wagons to come to rest in front of a fat lady with one arm, a single finger and no legs, set on top of a drum. He kissed her on both cheeks.

'That's Césarine, our *Pointing Venus*,' whispered the small woman, who had come back and was looking over his shoulder. 'She's going to read his fortune with the *Rhotomago*. They shouldn't be interrupted.'

'Rhotomago?'

'The *Thomas* if you'd rather! I've already told you about it!' said the lilliputian irritably. 'It's a sort of jar with a wooden baby in it ... with the end of her one finger, Césarine'll push the manikin under ... And every time the ugly fellow comes back to the surface of the liquid, he reveals the future ...'

Antoine did not reply. Bored with the bobbings of the wooden swimmer, his gaze drifted to the other side of the dusty path. There, on the other side of a merry-go-round, he spotted Théophile Mirecourt in shirtsleeves, busy taking a photograph of Wire, standing on the edge of the roundabout, leaning against the giant Marbuche. Emile Roussel, in bright sunlight, was giving a wide, toothless grin. His skinny flanks leaned against the Manchu's massive torso. The giant was screwing up his eyes against the light, and the locksmith had one arm round his neck and the other proudly displaying a red flag.

Antoine couldn't hear what Wire was saying but as soon as the shot was taken, he climbed onto the nearest thing to a platform, one of the roundabout horses. His arms rose, his mouth opened and closed, he was obviously letting himself go, showering his listeners with slogans and saliva. It wasn't hard to imagine the sort of things the locksmith from rue Lévisse was saying as he preached in support of his beloved Commune.

'What an excellent picture of life!' Tarpagnan exclaimed.

Suddenly he was in a tremendous hurry. His heart hurting with joy. He was dying to join his friends then and there and with them suck the juice of this fine spring of adventure. Instinct took over and he felt a great urgency to be outside. He forgot all about Palmyre.

He leapt to his feet. He dunked his shaving brush in soap-suds. He laughed and hummed. He turned round suddenly. Palmyre was standing on the bed waiting for him to look at her. She looked deep into his eyes. Unbroken. Undamaged.

'Your energy's twice what it was,' she said simply. 'Your friends are here. You don't need me any more.'

He licked dry lips and hung his head.

'I know,' she said. 'I understand. There's no sense in it any more. You and me, that was ages ago.' She added: 'Long life, Tarpagnan. Don't waste any more time. Don't forget we're already on the way to the void.'

She jumped off the bed, ran lightly to the door of the caravan and – careful not to attract any attention – slipped out of his life without once looking back.

69

Among friends again

A dozen strokes of the razor swept the undergrowth from his cheeks, leaving only the moustache, and he had become Tarpagnan the Gascon again. When he appeared outside the caravan door he had already recovered his bold glance and sparkling eyes. His friends greeted him warmly, although reproaches were not far from the lips of some.

Théophile Mirecourt handed his *makhila* over with a scowl, and said in a complaining tone: 'You've been gone a century! I really thought you'd taken the Commune a bit more to heart than that.'

As he slipped Gabriella's letter into his hand, Wire took a different line, pleading for tolerance in his Butte sparrow's muffled twitter. 'You can't blame a geezer for followin' his flesh ... He fell in love! Who can make a fuss about that?'

Jules Vallès added in his hurried way: 'Quite, quite, Antoine's an honest gallant with gifts in the boudoir ... A hot-blooded Gascon, a great omelette-beater no doubt ... but that doesn't make him a coward.' He looked round at his companions and added in declamatory tones: 'Don't forget, my friends! In the present grave situation, we should do our best to resemble a united family rather than a bunch of people who've gathered to wash dirty linen ... Surely we should be concentrating on other matters ... more interesting ones, at that! And listen, I'm taking bets: when the time for bayonets arrives, Cousin Vingtras will be in the front rank! The lucky dog'll work wonders ... die without a hat on ... on the barricades!'

'Does he really have to die a violent death just to get forgiven for his absence?' Mirecourt demanded indignantly, changing sides and redirecting his resentment.

'Oh, come on! Don't put words in my mouth, dear portable Nadar! I'm not predicting Tarpagnan's death any more than I am yours! Or mine, come to that. But the word from Césarine and the Rhotomago is quite clear: we all die tomorrow! That's our fate.' Suddenly possessed by the wild vitality of the Vellay region, Vallès blinked, ran his hand through his forest of wiry hair, turned a tortured face to his companions and cried:

'Yet another reason to go and eat a bite at this little wine-merchant's on the corner of rue des Petits-Champs and the place des Victoires. Eh? What d'you say? I'm in good odour there ... With Pierre Denis and Casimir Bouis, we can gargle down a chicken-claw soup assiduously enough, don't you think? God, I do pride myself on having taught my writers the art of putting wine in the soup without splashing their shoes!'

Neglecting to consult anyone to see whether this suggestion had their votes, the ebullient boss of *le Cri du Peuple* gave the signal for departure. He galloped three lumbering paces before skidding to a halt, thumping his knobbly forehead and announcing a new inspiration.

'Or rather, *no*, my dears! Better idea! Since today's a celebration, let's go to the place Vendôme! Protot'll certainly find us some corner on the ministry balcony ... Perhaps we'll see Courbet there in his nice blue overcoat! A chance to clip him round the ear with his Vendôme column! Guaranteed spectacle! With the right sort of prodding our Caravaggio-about-town will be climbing the walls and chewing the carpets in no time!'

70

At Protot's

Two hours later they were seated joyously round a table sharing a frugal repast with members of the Justice Delegation. Protot, minister and restaurateur, presided. Around him, in no particular order of precedence, were sitting Léon Sornet, who as well as being an attaché at the delegate's office was manager of the newly relaunched revolutionary journal *Père Duchêne*; Charles Da Costa, brother of the deputy to the Commune's procurator; and two or three officers with three silver bars, waxed moustaches, common accents and the stony faces of exhausted warriors, who were passing the wine back and forth and murmuring among themselves about supplies of boots for the guard battalions at Issy fort.

Alongside this handful of regime crocodiles sat Vermersch and Vuillaume, the *Père Duchêne*'s two most activist journalists, arguing about the fall of the Moulin-Saquet redoubt at the southeastern end of the Villejuif plateau.

Protot said that the upper classes over in Versailles were shouting themselves hoarse with triumph over this feat of arms, which they saw as a vindication of General Lacretelle's tactical intelligence and the gallantry of his troops. At that, Vermersch made a nose-blowing gesture into his plate, and muttered that repeating and amplifying what was after all only an ordinary setback of war would contribute to the deployment of a machinery whose purpose was to discredit the federal command. He added that Rossel was being undermined through attacks on his officers because he was the only man with any rigour and represented the last vestiges of discipline. Vuillaume amplified this remark by saying that anyone criticising Rossel was attacking the *Père Duchêne*. Colonel Rossel was a friend of the paper and an all-round excellent chap.

Da Costa commented that 'that pitiful skirmish' had nevertheless cost the Commune two hundred casualties plus three hundred prisoners from the 55th, 20th and 177th battalions. And ten guns as well. His piercing voice had something of the effect of a bucket of cold water thrown over the party, especially when he pointed out that a whiff of treason seemed to have been present at every juncture of that deplorable business.

'Treason allied to weak leadership!' escalated one of the captains, wiping his moustache. 'The enemy was allowed to mutilate our soldiers' bodies. It's an outrage!'

Vuillaume boiled over instantly. Like a bolting horse, he pushed his plate away and growled that if National Guardsmen getting sozzled in the village of Vitry hadn't blabbed the password to a captain of the 74th infantry, the idea of surprising the garrison at night by cutting the sentries' throats would not have occurred to the strategists on the other side.

'But actually, that's a piece of negligence that *can* be blamed on Colonel Rossel,' Protot interrupted.

'Careful what you say, citizen!' Vermersch snapped angrily. 'The fact of the matter is that Rossel wants the soldiers not to drink at all! He wants them to obey and not argue. Accusing him like that makes *you* look suspect!'

'Oh, *do* stop pretending to be Hébert!'

'Well, you stop trying to be Camille Desmoulins!'

'Gentlemen, gentlemen!' soothed Léon Sornet.

'Anyway, that's a doubt that bedevils the people's house,' Da Costa put in. 'Worse than that: it's a suspicion that poisons the trust the Central Committee of the National Guard had in the authority of the delegate for war!'

'The Commune will sort it out,' Vallès said. 'Rossel's summoned for tomorrow.'

'The harm's already done!' Vermersch answered. 'There's talk of a letter to *The Times* from Rossel, in which he supposedly defends himself for having asked Monsieur Thiers for a commission. It's a calumny!'

'More like a deliberate plant,' Mirecourt said. 'Old man

Transnonain's playing with our nerves. He's privy to everything that happens in Paris. His spies – and his rumour-mongers and *agents provocateurs* – throng the boulevards unmolested.'

Tarpagnan was sitting between Mirecourt and Vallès. He listened in horror as Vallès described the climate of disloyalty that reigned even at headquarters in the Ecole Militaire. He listened to his sardonic account of the way Thiers's spies and the agents of Versailles were operating: how people like himself, Vermorel and Lefrançais had received visits from a squad of sidewalk Venuses calculated to gain entry more or less anywhere in short order: a shower of very pretty and agreeable persons, sprightly and communicative, always laughing to show their white teeth and dressed to emphasise the valley between their breasts: a regiment of ostensibly shy working girls, charming and talkative, with confidential information to impart – very interesting revelations! – who in mid-interview proposed a further meeting at a later hour, hinting broadly that in more private and discreet circumstances there might easily be a slide into, er, a bit of boomps-a-daisy.

'It's the Versaillais idea of a joke,' he ended. 'They think they'll catch us out one day. And just imagine how they'd love to catch us in bed with tarts! Besmirch us for ever in the eyes of the virtuous provinces!'

The diners guffawed noisily, but there was a feeling of forced enjoyment in the air, crossed with bitter disarray. Suddenly in the grand salon of the ministry the weak and the strong alike shared a feeling that the time was nigh. That the assailant was going to be pitiless. That Paris had made the sleeves too short in its overcoat of reconquered liberty.

The giant Marbuche was one of the few who showed no fear or apprehension. His blunt instrument of a head was struggling with a fixed idea. He mumbled:

'Will Marbuche find a tunic to fit him if he goes to fight? Is there still a rifle for Marbuche?'

But nobody answered. He wasn't important enough. He rose from the table, taking a chicken leg with him, and went to the end of the room where he joined a group of greying lions, four or five veterans in torn and dusty uniforms to whom the cooks had given the leavings, as if to retired servants at a banquet. Wire was eating with them. They were sitting on the floor.

Marbuche smiled. He knew he wasn't very bright but that his mountainous presence was impressive. The small group of rampart troopers stared up at him with round eyes as he held out the chicken-leg to the oldest of the federals. The old boy stared attentively at him for a moment from under thick eyebrows, then accepted the Manchu's offering with a grateful nod.

'Set yer hams down,' this man said. 'Can't get yer arse no lower.' He resettled the kepi that had been on his head for weeks. The giant squatted down beside him.

'Marbuche,' he introduced himself.

'Léon Voutard,' the trooper mumbled through a mouthful of chicken. 'From rue Lévisse.'

'And these here,' Wire croaked in his gypsum voice, 'are two more of my pals, Marceau and Ferrier. Fellows who know how to keep the cold out. Who knock it back proper. Sonny-jims of the Commune.'

Marbuche wrung their hands. He was never going to leave them again. They were going to share fleas and cold. Heat and bullets. Chaos and death.

Their conversations resumed. They were licking their plates clean and discussing the latest news. It seemed that Thiers had installed a monster battery at Montretout, a device that could rain hot steel down in the very centre of Paris.

'It's going to be really terrible before long,' somebody murmured. The vision of buildings set on fire by incendiary shells lowered people's spirits. Cartloads of corpses paraded by in their mind's eye.

'S'long as we're 'ere,' Marceau said, 'I think I'll jus' write a little letter to the missus. Remind 'er to tell me boss to keep me job open till arter the war.' His eye wandered involuntarily over the eternal row of stacked rifles surmounted by the gold-fringed red flag. Gently, he took his ink-pot out of his cartridge-pouch and unscrewed the lid, adding. 'What with these here American machine guns and the Freemasons on our side, it could all be over in a coupla weeks . . .'

'Gammon, carpenter!' Ferrier said. 'It ain't going to stop till arter there's been a big 'uge bleedin' slaughter'ouse of chopped meat, mate. I wouldn't count on coming back with both yer 'ands if I was you.'

'Knock it off, you bunch of bleedin' lance-recruits ... If you want to spare your children the sufferin's and miseries you've had, you're going to have ter fight like the people did in '89. Capture your own Bastilles ... march on Versailles. And beyond, if need be!'

Wire's neighbour, a down-at-heel character, shrugged his shoulders while gloomily inspecting the pitiable state of his feet. 'That's all stuff what's wrote in offices, Wire,' he groused. 'It's just Philosophy, aint it? Just a while back I was listenin' to the rep'sent'ive for foodstuffs and subsistence ... 'E was sayin' that as long as we 'ad iron and bread we could go to China if we wanted. Only – *fuckin*' Grouchy – 'e never says a bleedin' *word* about givin' us no shoes!'

A ruminative silence fell. Marbuche joined his new pals in mopping up the remains of a casserole. The comrades had promised to find him a tunic and introduce him to the CO of the free corps. In a dark corner of Raoul Biloquet's uncultivated brain, a fraternal wish to share the common danger was slowly growing. Marbuche felt as if he had just emerged from a void. He no longer had anything to fear, for he was no longer alone. He would be dressed just like the others. He would be defending the same ideas. No need to tire himself out wrestling with his own any longer, for now he could share those of his colleagues.

Open-mouthed, he listened with delight as Emile Roussel told him about the army of bare-handed proletarians and Léon Voutard spoke of an intrepid café-owner called Jeanne Couerbe. A woman as brave as a man. Who would rush out among bullets and shell-bursts, give brandy to the wounded without fearing the shrapnel, who kept her hottest kisses for those who were going to die.

Wire drained his tumbler of *ordinaire* and squinted down the room towards the bigwigs' table. Coffee was over and it was time for the collection: the official in charge of the till was passing the plate and every diner was paying his two francs: all except Tarpagnan, 'exempted by reason of unexpected return', who had withdrawn to a quiet corner where he was reading la Pucci's letter for the third time.

Wire struck a match on the wall and lit an *infectados* that crackled like a bush fire as he drew on it. Through the rank blue smoke he gazed intently at the former captain's face. The little locksmith knew every word of that damned letter. He could have recited it by heart. Caf'conc' had written it in front of him, you might say on his advice.

My handsome friend,

Thanks to Wire I have just come back into the light.

I know already that my road from now on will be without shelter, without a man, without love. My tread is heavy. My eyes are cold. The old me exists no longer. Never again will I know the pleasure of loving.

For a long time I wanted to get rid of my body. But eventually a sort of will to live came back to me. Not like before, of course. But by shutting out the past (because I don't want to see it) and the future (which I cannot envisage), I can be content with a continuing present. So I'm not going anywhere further than today's road can take me.

No hopes. No regrets. No tears.

I pray that the madness of the fighting, the cries of the dying, the fragility of the moment at a time when every new detonation can extinguish everything, will bring the beginning of a logical answer to the question I will no longer be asking.

If you ever loved me, do not try to see me again.
Gabriella

Wire sighed as he watched the blue thread of his smoke rise through a beam of light. He was remembering his last meeting with Caf'conc'. Three days earlier he had gone with her to La Presse ambulance service in rue Oudinot, and accompanied her into the enrolment office for the nursing corps. That was what she had chosen to do. He had watched her walk out of sight down an interminable corridor where wounded men lay on stretchers waiting for attention.

Unless something irresistibly magical happened, she would never be seen again. She was finished, that little woman there. You didn't have to be an expert in human flesh to see the damage. The wear. The sparkle in her eyes veiled by a sort of dullness. She no longer felt brambles or thorns. She had become dead to the world.

Antoine, over there, was resting his forehead on a window pane. There were tears in his eyes. Suddenly he crumpled the letter, marched over to a fireplace and threw the ball of paper onto the unlit fuel that had been laid there. He rejoined the diners. Some were buckling their belts and leaving for the outposts. Others were deciding to smoke a cigar on the balcony.

Tarpagnan was chatting with Vuillaume and Vallès. The two journalists had lit Havana cigars given them by Protot in a gesture of appeasement. They leaned on the balustrade drawing on their bankers' cigars with relish.

Outside it was the hot time of day, the hour of post-prandial torpor. The place Vendôme was as still as a photograph. Sitting with their backs to the heaps of cobbles barricading the rue de la Paix and the rue Castiglione, federal pickets were snoring the sleep of the just with their kepis over one ear.

Antoine inhaled the rich odour of tobacco. His hands warmed slightly by the ironwork of the railing, he felt strangely new and available.

At that very moment, on that balcony, he had the feeling that a miraculous spirit had taken possession of him. That where life led him, there he was made to go. And that pushing towards a more equitable world would fully justify him in continuing to breathe. In the course of a human existence, he decided, taking refuge in the fringe of his innermost thoughts, everything is written in advance. And I'm supposed to be the one who's only complete after a gruelling journey!

He smiled at his friend Théo. He turned to Vallès and said: 'I want to fight. I'm ready.'

'I'm dealing with it,' Vallès replied. He pointed to the rue de Castiglione exit from the square. 'That's the way Dombrowski

will come when he arrives. I've got a meeting with him round the
corner, at staff headquarters. To talk about you, Cousin Vingtras.'

'Thank you,' Tarpagnan said. He stopped short as Vuillaume
nudged him and pointed to the right with a jerk of his chin.

'Poor Gustave!' breathed Vallès. 'If he has to wait much
longer his robust sanity will be at risk.'

At the end of the balcony Antoine saw the heavy outline of a
solitary man. Only something familiar in the posture told him
that it was Courbet. An unlit, wide-bowled pipe between his
teeth, the painter was sitting on a folding chair and gazing across
the sunlit vastness of the place Vendôme. His posture was that of
a patient angler on the bank of a lake. The great artist sat
motionless, his back soaked in sweat, staring at the bronze spike
of the Vendôme column with inexhaustible patience. He watched
it with the single-minded fascination of an angler watching his
float bobbing on some piece of water patrolled by unsuspecting
carp. He was waiting.

At his feet, Paris sprawled on its back in the shade with its
mouth open, overcome with torpor. It was that heavy and silent
hour when insects cruise over the somnolent glare of the city.
Everywhere a contented lassitude reigned. The very sentries were
dreaming.

But Courbet sat tense on his uncomfortable chair, alone at the
end of the balcony, listening down into the music of silence that
accompanied the languid hour. When Tarpagnan approached to
greet him, he showed a fisherman's grumpy anxiety and did not
turn round.

Only then did Tarpagnan imagine he understood. From the
base of the column, a faint scraping noise broke the monotonous
quiet. The sound was made by a long loggers' double-handed
crosscut saw being hauled slowly – very slowly – to and fro by
two workmen squatting on either side of the pedestal supporting
the famous answer to Trajan's column.

'They're turning on Caesar,' Antoine murmured. 'It's a
historic moment.'

'Yes, but you see the imposture, Tarpagnan, don't you?'
answered Courbet without even glancing over his shoulder. 'I
mean, the way we've been led to believe for decades that they

melted down twelve hundred cannon captured at Austerlitz to make that thingummy, when the truth of the matter is that their bronze pipe is no thicker than a fingernail!'

As if to show what he meant, a tiny puff of white dust came out of the bronze pillar as the workmen sawed painfully away. Forty years later Vuillaume would write in his 'red notebooks': *'By watching closely, it was possible to see how this small cloud was formed: the men sawing through the very soft stone, of which the gigantic tube is made, covered with a thin sheet of bronze as a stick of fairground candy is enclosed in its gold paper wrapper.'*

'Their *phallus*!' Courbet snarled, looking round. His eye fell on Maxime Vuillaume and Jules Vallès who had also drawn near.

'Hey! Dismantler!' trumpeted the co-director of *Père Duchêne*, 'contemplating your work of destruction, are you?'

These words had an immediate effect on the petitioner, who on 14th September the previous year had expressed the wish to see no more of the column, which he had described as 'badly placed and decorated with grotesque figures': he went crimson, his eyes rolled and he waved a furious fist at his tormentor. Almost handsome, the bullnecked artist bawled with a half-smile on his face:

'Dismantler! Oh, *very* funny! What should we call you – Red Terror? What I said, of course, was that we should take that ridiculous pipe apart! *Take it apart*, Maxine, d'you understand me? I wanted to take that bloody turd of a column apart *aesthetically*, not chop the fucking thing down!'

Hunching his shoulders, he dismissed them all out of hand and returned to his patient contemplation. After a while he sighed:

'All the same, twelve hundred cannon to produce a single lousy leaf of metal . . . it does make you want to stay a socialist.'

A few days later, on Tuesday 16th May, at 5.35 in the afternoon, in front of a large crowd that had been softened up by bands interpreting patriotic tunes, the capstan was given one last turn. The Vendôme column leaned slightly and then, breaking into three as it fell, thumped down into a bed of stable-litter. Caesar's head came off.

Those who witnessed the event said that the Parisian ground hardly shook.

PART 6

DISINTEGRATION

71

The hot breath of May

In greatcoats with two rows of buttons or in overalls, dressed as Amazons or as Flourens's Avengers, as Zouaves of the Republic or under the Communard flag of the Lost Children, the Parisians put their revolutionary zeal into practice with a fraternal determination breathed into them by the ferocious tone deployed in *Père Duchêne* by people like Vermersch and Vuillaume.

They spent whole nights listening into the threatening darkness. During the burning days, dressed in the uniform of the National Guard, belted, booted, swords at their side, they went forward into the firing line. They did their duty with the lyrical intuition instilled in them by the proud, inflamed prose of Jules Vallès in the *People's Cry*: '*The white flag versus the red flag! The old world versus the new!*'

To erase the unchanging past, to put an end (as they thought) to the misery and exploitation of the poorest classes, the workers – men, women and urchins of Paris – mounted guard on the ramparts. They manned the outposts in the avenue des Champs-Elysées, churned up into sinister furrows by fire from the batteries at mont Valérien and Courbevoie. They dug trenches with pick and shovel, they endured their share of awfulness from the shelling, they worked in the hospitals where the first evacuees from outlying areas were already arriving. They manned the barricades.

Their calm was admirable. Women and adolescents served as stretcher-bearers at the forward casualty sations, sprinting, doubled up, along the chipped facades of buildings as shells ricocheted from their cornices. They helped evacuate elderly residents.

With a faith and courage to confound the slavering hacks of the Versaillais press, those rabid spewers of anti-Commune tracts whose job was to encourage the literal murder of 'those crazed halfwits' at the Hôtel de Ville, work continued in the factories. Paris, free city, Paris, rebel city, Paris, a long way from bowing to artillery, to intimidation by the lackeys of calumny, to the underhand pressure of the manipulators and other scum who were doing their best to spread false information. Paris kept a cool head.

Of course, the general call to arms sounded from time to time. Of course, from time to time some tiresome blockhead would call for all the sewers to be blown up, or for priests and nuns to be executed *en masse*. Of course, the fort at Issy had been evacuated under a storm of fire, its garrison shot to pieces, the bodies of its brave defenders piled two metres high, La Cécilia wounded. Of course, it was whispered that the National Guard had lost the will to fight. Of course, it was reported that as a disciplinary measure, and to expose them to public disapprobation, the uniforms of those who fled under fire, especially officers, had had a sleeve cut off. Of course, Colonel Lisbonne had fallen back before the advance of the Versaillais killers, and the tricolour was now flying at the very gates of the capital.

Needless to say there was talk of plots, and of mysterious explosive charges ready to send Notre-Dame sky-high. But although the atmosphere in the capital became quite feverish as day followed day, the Parisians continued undeterred to live in the streets. A radiant sun in the colours of renewal seemed to be colluding in their dreams of deliverance.

In a fine surge of sap, the rose bushes in the public gardens broke into cheerful smiles, their scented gaiety making the Tuileries resplendent. Blouses and bodices weighed less heavily on the bosoms of the citizenesses. Harvests of flowers were piled on the stalls of Les Halles. On the other sides of squares, at nearby road junctions, there danced undulating forests of bayonets. Red flag at the head, in a rhythmic tramp of synchronised footsteps, the people's battalions were leaving for the front. Revolution eddied back and forth on the cobbles, clamorous in the warm night, borne on the strains of old vengeful songs revived to push back the fear of tomorrow.

In the *People's Cry*, Vallès trumpeted: '*Paris has survived! The sun shines on the Rebellion! Dauntless Liberty stands erect, unsteady, but supported by its host of red flags and defying all the murderous spectres of Berlin and Versailles!*' Purple prose that anyone would find excusable, praiseworthy even. But how badly the party was going in reality!

Having sacked Rossel, the Commune had now put its own Committee for Public Welfare on trial. Chunks of governmental debris were already littering the cobbles. Joins – scars – had become visible. Buried animosities were rising to the surface, factions digging in. How difficult it is to set hatreds aside, even when it is the only hope of saving a country! At that crucial moment, with doubt starting to infiltrate many minds, the defence of Paris rested almost solely on the People.

Horace Grondin was about to take his first unaccompanied steps. His strength, while not yet normal, had been greatly restored by the stern regime of Hippolyte Barthélemy, a professor emeritus of *savate* and baton, who had attached himself to Grondin as to a living God and was lodging in his house: he had been exercising muscles and joints and building up his suppleness for two hours a day.

Soon these exercises became too little to channel the burgeoning energy of the man with grey eyes. Having healed the bruises and stiffnesses in his body, Horace Grondin was walking briskly about between the armchairs and the table. The dwelling seemed to him too small for three people. He said he found it hard to breathe. He complained that the hangings smelt rancid, and when la Chouette – the only one who could leave the house without risk – came back from shopping in the market, he would rush to meet her for the scent of fresh outside air that clung to her clothing.

'News, news!' he would clamour. He would overwhelm the old woman with his hasty and demanding behaviour, drive her mad by rooting in her shopping bag for the daily gazette. Feverishly, he would unfold the sacred newspaper. He felt as crazy as a rattlesnake.

The day he learned that Delescluze – the unassailable, incompetent civil delegate Charles Delescluze – had taken over the conduct of the war in Rossel's place, Grondin started to pace round the apartment like a caged tiger. During such times of restlessness the others hardly dared speak to him. Usually he would come to rest after a while in front of Bosco the parrot's cage.

He would look at the cockatoo through his bars, tease him into uttering a few *shits* and *fucks*, then say that he was hungry. His wishes had the status of orders. La Chouette would get busy serving the neighbourhood monarch.

'They've decided to pull down Thiers's house in the place Georges,' she announced that evening, as she refilled his soup plate. His face expressionless, the former resident of the penal colony ate his way through the three further dishes the tall harpy had cooked. After the rice pudding he got up from the table, wiped his lips and said:

'You won't see me shedding any tears over that little Tamerlane in gold specs. They can flatten Monsieur Thiers's house for all I care. I don't give a damn.' Half an hour later, outlined against the daylight, the scarred man's silhouette filled a window on the street side. Like a ghost or wooden carving, forehead resting on the glass, he watched the people passing, and sent his thoughts soaring far beyond the darkening sky.

'Don't show yerself so much in the winders, Monsieur Horace,' begged la Chouette. 'The neighbours round here're proper nosy! They don't trust us, neither. They're on the lookout for anythin' what's at all out of the ordinary, and they see spies on every roof and down every alley!'

Grondin shrugged slightly. He thoughtfully rolled a piece of paper into a spill and lit his pipe, then returned to his vantage point. He loved above all things the wavering undefined period that precedes nightfall.

At about eight o'clock, brushing aside his housekeeper's pleas and Barthélemy's warnings, he left the apartment in the rue de la Corderie, muttering over his shoulder as he left:

'I don't want you trampling on my heels, Barthélemy, d'you understand? I need air! I really need to be on my own!'

72

Tipsy Paris

Outside there was life, life to make you dizzy. He had been so long shut away from what he liked most: inhaling the street, its scents, leafing through its open book! There was such deep pleasure in treading the Paris cobbles once again.

Grondin allowed himself to wander at random: to turn this way and that, to slip back into the crowd. As he felt his strength returning he lengthened his pace and ranged further afield. Beyond the Temple, he slipped through a foul-smelling passage between two decrepit buildings whose attics were filled with poor families, then drifted through a maze of alleys to the fringes of the faubourg Saint-Antoine.

So long as he was sheltered by the mass of dark buildings, the clamour of the city, weakened by distance and filtered through the maze of winding alleys, reached the wanderer like a tracing of distant tumult, more relaxing even than total silence.

But he wanted more. He clenched his cold fists and emerged into the open, ignoring the risk of recognition.

At the entrance to the faubourg, a rampart of cobbles. Further back, another barricade showed the muzzles of three artillery pieces. He passed a detachment of sentries, too busy discussing the desertions at Vanves and Montrouge to take any notice of him, and continued on his way.

Around Richard-Lenoir, rue Sédaine, rue Bréguet and rue des Taillandiers, the district was as animated as ever. The cafés were well-lit and thronged with local working-class customers. A clientèle that wore caps or went bareheaded, the men in ducks, the women wearing shawls over their shoulders and skirts worn from long use, sharp-eyed, sharp-tongued and quick-tempered.

Children played in doorways, their imitative spirit making them adopt the style of old sweats. One was blowing a tin bugle bought from a toy-pedlar. Another, with an oversized Phrygian bonnet down over his eyes, carried a real sabre with an air of extreme gravity.

Outside a pharmacy groups of citizenesses, some with slung rifles, lingered in interminable women's chatter. Two local concierges were telling anyone who would listen that they had seen some suspicious characters about. Funny-looking geezers accompanied by gallows-birds with long beards, wearing unknown uniforms, listing supplies of sulphur and powder and tracking down depots of mineral oil and phosphorus.

Busy housewives moved about, their nippers under their feet. Clusters of idlers strolled in the open spaces whose trees had been sawn down, a curious ants' nest that constantly dissolved and regrouped around any apparent point of interest.

One rabid she-wolf, a canteen-keeper called Papavoine, wearing a headband made from a violet ribbon and a skirt so short in front that you could see her shins, was saying that in the rue de Varenne on the Left Bank – number 78 to be exact – they were taking on all the unemployed embroiderers and folders they could get for some mysterious purpose. Another woman with her hair in a flat bun on her neck was saying that if it came to a battle of Paris *fire would be thrown from the houses*. The cellars would be stacked with bottles of paraffin, people would be afraid of nothing and, if all else failed, 'the women would be unleashed on the Versaillais!'

'What, us again?' protested a canteen-keeper in a dress striped in red and black. 'Them *bloody* men!'

'To do what? Flutter our eyelashes?' piped the child-like voice of a presser who liked to play the rebel.

'No, to shake them by the hand.'

'Fat lot of good that'll do!'

'No, listen, you pretend you want to make friends. You hold out your pretty hand, palming a rubber bulb armed with a short, hollow gold pin, squirting prussic acid. Death will be instantaneous!'

'Well, let's have one of those and we'll see,' said the little presser through her heart-shaped mouth. 'I might shake a lot of hands!'

'You'll get one soon. Parisel's ordered three hundred. The acid's being supplied by Assi.'

The rumours were crazy. The compass wasn't working, people's judgement had gone, but Grondin knew that here beat the real pulse of the revolutionary movement. He passed a cohort of wives, walking behind a red flag to join the 'conquerors of Versailles'. He watched them recede, trying to interpret the meaning of their violent shouts, demands for the head of some traitor. He gave up trying to decipher the name they were yelling and resumed his walk.

But when a convoy of ambulances passed with its load of wounded, he read hatred in the faces of the crowd. Hatred and fear, the unease that comes from a glimpse of the reality of danger. Its truth. Its proximity.

The convoy was from the village of Issy where furious fighting was still going on. Names unknown, bodies jolting, faces livid and bruised, piles of bloodstained cripples, the survivors of a devastated company were making their last exit from the grand slaughterhouse towards a forward casualty station. An escort of scruffy soldiers, a gang of unknowns in armbands, half civilian and half military, wearing kepis without insignia, ran ahead of the exhausted and frightened horses. The crowd opened ahead of them and closed immediately after they had passed. People gazed reflectively after the sinister procession.

Cries arose as the wounded clattered past. Women trotted alongside the cartloads of defeat, their faces pale and stunned. Hair flying, haggard-faced, they ran doggedly along as if held up by springs. Talking to one another.

'Butchery! Butchery!'

'D'you see the driver? His shoes are red with blood!'

'This really ought to be stopped!'

'There's at least one passing every fifteen minutes!'

'It's going badly at le Bourget. Champigny, too.'

'They're at it with bayonets, pistols, rifle-butts!'

Unaffected by fatigue or emotion, Grondin could not make up his mind to go back home. That skilled meteorologist of popular weather continued to press through the multitude, to float through the simmering murmur. The fact was, though, that the district was not very safe for a bird of his feather. The whole landscape belonged to the poor and ill-dressed. Prudence would have sent him straight back home to hide in the cellar before the street got annoyed and started looking askance at anyone out of place.

Attracted by loud shouts and jostling, by a trampling surge in the crowd, Grondin came up behind a forest of backs. Among a cacophony of bugle calls and drums he heard cries of 'Death!'

A squad of guardsmen passed on the other side of the crowd escorting half a dozen priests and three women with shaven heads. He was being jostled at the time and did not get a good view. He wondered what was happening. A red-faced, bad-tempered-looking officer obliged him by bawling over the heads of the crowd: 'Who're they for Christ's sake?'

The answer came from a tall pug-nosed devil in red trousers with a mop of hair under a soft Lost Children's hat: 'Don't you know? Them's the hostages being taken to la Roquette! Six sky-pilots and three nun-farts, going to be shot in the ditch!'

Among the accompanying crowd were children in arms and women carrying rifles. One of these matrons, a rather frail and sweet-looking brunette with a cockade in her hair and a revolver stuck through her sash, had suddenly appeared beside Grondin, about whom she had divined some false note.

'Smells a bit flyblown round here,' she said, turning a muddy combatant's face towards him and fixing him with stern periwinkle eyes. Grondin was taken aback, for he was not wearing a suit or tall hat. He was dressed inconspicuously in black trousers, an overcoat and cap. But either because there still clung about him some impalpable odour of officialdom, or simply because his physique was so striking that people always gave him a second glance, there rose about them an instant babble of voices that reminded him, most disagreeably, of 18th March.

'I seen you before somewhere,' the little woman insisted. Her inquisitive gaze sought Grondin's evasive one. 'Oh, you can look innocent all you like,' she went on with patient confidence, 'I'll remember where I've seen you, see if I don't.'

Anyone but Grondin would have been on the point of losing his footing, but the grey spectre dealt with the danger merely by consulting the archives he had amassed as an outside agent of the political police. Buxom, rowdy little person ... who was she, who was she ... Damnation! Her name, her name! Yes, Fontieu, Adelaïde Fontieu! The painter Rochon's meal-ticket! And him ... a cowardly type, an informer ... alcoholic too, 7 rue Lévisse. The underchief of the Sûreté had stood next to him at the bar, on three occasions. That's it, three. With Wire. Rochon, a wreck of a man. Couldn't stop talking. A loudmouth.

'You couldn't be someone from the copper-shop, still on the run?' Adelaïde wondered.

Grondin had been leafing swiftly through the drunkard's confidences on the various ways in which his woman supplied the needs of the household.

'Listen, citizeness, d'you mind?' he cried with unblushing amiability. 'You're thinking of someone else there! Don't you remember me? I'm a mattress-maker at Crépin & Mercier's. And last time I saw you you were making the johns' ting-a-lings sneeze at a *certain address* in rue Girardon!'

'So why didn't you say? Why make me play guessing games? Only too likely the last time I seen you was on a kip, cit'zen!' Hands on hips, the pretty nymph turned to the ring of faces around them and explained with a radiant smile: 'Crépin-Mercier used to look after the bedding at "14 rue Girardon", and as it 'appens I used to bung the staff a free one now and again if I fancied one of 'em ...' She leered sidelong at the grey-eyed man and added: 'I done well to take advantage of *your* mattress, comrade ... yet another charver the Prussians didn't get!'

Everyone within earshot exploded into laughter, as if those present had been awaiting the chance to be carried away by an enormous roar of mirth. For joy had become rather a scarce commodity. When people had the good luck to find some they savoured it to the full. So the bystanders let themselves go, slapped their thighs and laughed till their ribs hurt.

Grondin, after aping the general hilarity by displaying his

teeth, faded away and made himself scarce as soon as possible.
Fortunately for him the crowd had other things on its mind. A
drum-roll of growing speed and intensity had captured the
attention of Adelaïde and the nearest dozen or so bystanders. A
new hubbub had broken out at the end of the boulevard. Heads
moved rapidly about in the distance.

'Ain't that a bit of a barney over there? Looks like they're
fighting.'

'Come on, quick! Give us yer arm, colleague! Hear the
shindy?'

Red sashes. Pushing and jostling. Rifles brandished overhead.
Posies on bayonets. There was something to see wherever you
looked.

'Let's get over there!' cried Adelaïde. She looked over her
shoulder for a moment and waved to Grondin. 'Farewell, old
body-warmer! Come and show me your operation again one of
these evenings! 17 rue du Télégraphe. I've left my Rochon!
Shelved my Othello!'

She was already some distance away, running lightly along.
The sound of a small-arms volley rolled overhead signalling
another round of executions. What a mess! What confusion!

To find his way back to the 'faubourg Antoine' (as it was then
familiarly called) he entered the maze of passages that opened off
both sides of the road. In these insalubrious backstreet islets
everyday work was being pursued in a semi-composed manner.
From factories and workshops came the sounds of human
endeavour: the hissing of a plane, mallet and hammer blows, the
fleeting snort of a machine, the regular buzz of saws. It was as if
in these crannies of a busy hive the refuge of unremitting labour
was more essential to human dignity than all that warlike
posturing. So long as (Grondin thought to himself) the voice –
the great voice – of the tribunes has not yet penetrated to their
cold beds in the ill-swept hovels and garrets that redouble the
burden of being poor.

At the corner of a leprous wall he entered a small shop with
the simple intention of getting one of his shoes repaired. Despite
the late hour the cobbler, a short man with a bald head, was still

bent over his last. Without looking up to see who had come in, the artisan remarked:

'I'm working for a garrison of ragamuffins over at Vannes, where things are getting a bit hot for us!'

He frowned in concentration and gave several more taps with the hammer, then looked up allowing the light to fall on a face full of grief and exhaustion.

'A few revolvers and rifles and a couple of Bengal lights against the batteries of Châtillon, the Tour-des-Anglais and the Stone-Mill . . . what are they supposed to do?' He looked down and delivered another volley of hammer-blows. 'It's impossible down the dugouts . . . Mud up to here. The cold, the hunger! And I've still got three more pairs of these to get to them before the counter-attack t'morrer mornin' . . .'

The man looked exhausted. Grondin would willingly have sat down with him. He would happily have conversed with this citizen cobbler, he would have liked to cheer him up, talk to him straightforwardly about the prevailing atmosphere, the threats of destruction looming over Paris. But he was not invited to do so. While continuing to smooth a boot-upper over the form to soften it, the cobbler now shot him a sharp and suspicious glance.

'You poor man, don't you ever get any rest?' Grondin asked with a slight, amiable smile. The man returned to work, beating his soles with a will, then stopped suddenly and mumbled angrily:

'Get any *rest*?' His tight lips held a row of small nails. His hammer was raised. Seeing that the would-be customer was holding his left shoe in his hand he added: 'Go on, show us yer canoe . . .'

The cobbler inspected the back of a shoe where the stitching had given way, evaluated the softness of the fine leather. Almost at once he abandoned the idea of repairing a shoe whose origin seemed suspect, and his manner became openly irritable. He made a vague but annoyed gesture towards Grondin, as if unable to work out that what bothered him was his upright posture, so unusual in a son of the people.

'I don't much like the look of you, citizen!' he declared. 'And

you've come at a bad moment. Yesterday my nineteen-year-old
son got a bayonet through his belly and several pistol bullets
through the chest. Another kid his age lost both eyes. His pal
had his head separated from his body. They brought 'em here
this morning. They're here now, above our heads ... in the
bedroom. The missus and her friend from next door're up there
now keepin' vigil with 'em.'

The shoemaker stood up in his leather apron. 'We're gettin'
ourselves killed by other Frenchmen like bleedin' savages in
Africa! I want you to understand that I don't know you!' He
hustled the intruder towards the pavement, hurling his shoe past
him into the middle of the road.

'I don't know you from Adam, m'sieur!' he repeated in a voice
of profound suffering. 'Go and get your footwear sewn by
someone a bit less partic'lar than me!'

Grondin picked up the shoe, put it on and walked away with
long strides. From time to time he cast a tense, discreet look over
his shoulder. He changed course abruptly on more than one
occasion when approaching some group that looked threatening.

Back in his own Temple district, as he passed through the
entrance of his building it seemed to him, although he couldn't
be absolutely sure, that he had spotted a man's face in a dark
corner of the archway, that a grey shadow followed him in little
silent jumps as far as the staircase, that (to cut a long story short)
he had been followed by Mr Casimir Cabrichon, the new
concierge appointed by the neighbourhood committee, whose
predecessor, the father of three children, had perished on the
field of honour.

73

Alcoholic confidences

When Horace Grondin hurried back into his lair he found Barthélemy sprawled in an armchair, cleaning and oiling his Adams revolver by the light of a wax taper. La Chouette had lighted a fire in the grate not so much for warmth, the weather being clement, as for the agreeable impression given by the flames dancing in the chimney.

The duenna from no-man's-land was wearing a black dress cut, sewn, trimmed and embroidered to fit her, and was putting on the airs of a lady-in-waiting. A kerchief neatly tied at the front contained the wavy undergrowth of her grey hair which she had rolled into a bun. A black velvet ribbon tied round her neck slightly smoothed the blue-veined skin. She was wearing the silver brooch Grondin had given her as a sign of gratitude. That same morning, to mark (as it were) the advent of a new, city-dwelling era and further deepen her relations with her protector, she had told him her real name: Augustine Hortense Juliette Raboiseau, the widow Lerouge.

As one would expect, the tall woman presided over the household of the two gentlemen with fierce devotion. She ironed their underwear and linen, she wore herself out folding the table napkins in three equal parts, 'the way Mr Horace liked them'. Her lips were pursed from the incessant concentration. 'Careful!' she would repeat in an inaudible mumble. 'Get the folds right, and be sure to get the embroidered monogram the right way up and on the visible side of napkins, pillowcases and bath towels.'

That evening at 6, rue de la Corderie, all three of the inhabitants were absorbed in the mute but sincere enjoyment of a delicious plum brandy, a potent and fragrant spirit from

Lorraine that the master of the house had taken from one of the cupboards whose keys he kept about his person. Horace had ceremoniously wiped and set on a tray three handsome round glasses and then, offering the tray to his companions in turn, had provided each with a brimming glass and taken one for himself.

Barthélemy's spidery form was heaped into the chair nearest the fireplace. His drink in his hand, he furtively raised his yellow eyes, but said not a word. When la Chouette took her glass from the tray she breathed her thanks as if in church, a sigh rather than a murmur. Each had concluded that his treating them in this way meant that Monsieur Horace had a great secret that he wanted to impart. Indeed, the man with slate-coloured eyes ensured no fewer than three times that his guests were not running short of those delicate plum fragrances.

By midnight the atmosphere ᵕ become quite relaxed. The mood between the three was friendly, with vague smiles on each face although they were still not talking. With the third glass, la Chouette's face had become very red. The clock ticked steadily, the fire crackled and hissed about a log. Grondin had taken the second armchair and was leafing through his newspaper.

Nobody seemed to feel sleepy. It was as if by delaying their bedtime, each hoped on this unusually harmonious occasion to exchange the rather frugal conversation of normal evenings for an outpouring from the heart, that essential precondition for all reconciliations and all admissions.

Grondin folded his paper. To get the conversation going and encourage the others, he pretended to have been convinced by a recent plan to construct an airship with a carbonic acid motor and propellers. Without seeming to be interested, therefore, he had started to discuss the sort of tactics the insurgents could use, advancing the idea that dirigible airships would make it possible to drop explosive bombs on the Versaillais lines and loosen Thiers's stranglehold on the capital.

Of course in raising this subject he was still very far from the heartfelt sincerity that enables people to expel the lurking demons, but it was a start. They had started talking, and that, surely, was the important thing. They were certainly on the way towards something better. Something more intimate.

Barthélemy had laid down his revolver and replaced the swabs and cleaning-rod in their box. At Grondin's invitation he held out his glass for another refill. La Chouette gave a strange throaty little giggle and said slyly:

'You're *pouring* rum down us, M'sieu Horace! It reminds me of my husband when 'e'd a mind to, er ... get us together.'

While working her way through some mending and darning, she started recounting in a subdued voice the imaginary journeys she had shared with Three-Nails, that 'Cupid of great lost shores'.

'We done some travelling on hard spirits in that blamed pagoda, di'n't we just!' she said. 'I seen every reef there was, every landfall, every twelve-metre sea ... *an'* I been ashore as well!'

And with burlesqued belly-dancer's sinuosity the frightful old witch of the wastelands, enlivened by the bite of the mirabelle plum, gave a brief demonstration in her petticoats of the way Balinese girls shook their hips. Overcome by the fruity fumes, constantly searching for the right exotic words, she described the way her old freshwater sailor had drawn her through the magic of his stories into his swashbuckling adventures in the warm oceans.

'The old liar!' she said fondly. ''E used to talk about the Sunda Isles when where 'e'd really been was Chatou and Conflans!'

She moistened a thread, raised the eye of the needle to the level of her own staring orbs to thread it. She laughed a little, and wiped away a tear or two. Then she returned to her mending, concentrating hard enough to damage her eyesight.

Grondin smiled. As the old woman heaved a deep sigh, Hippolyte Barthélemy had climbed onto his spidery legs. The crow's black eyes gleamed with excitement and something about his attitude suggested that he was thinking of taking over the podium.

At first he looked at his hearers without speaking, giving the impression that he just wanted to take his turn and had nothing much to say. Then, at the cost of a change of mood in which the foolishness of the drunk became entangled with the old way of life, he had started to talk while swaying rather dangerously on his pins. He held out his collection of glass eyes on his right palm, rolling the blue irises about with the pleased air of a miner inspecting a nice cluster of agates.

'I'm most grateful to you, Mr Underchief of the Sûreté,' he began carefully, 'for helping me resolve the business of the drowned woman at the pont de l'Alma ... But I realise that I've got a great deal more to learn from you. That you're my master and guide in the byways of crime ... and I'm also indebted to you for giving me shelter in these uncertain times ...'

He paused for a moment to recover his balance, which was still less than perfect, and suppressed a belch of the brandy whose sourness had blocked his oesophagus. Then he frowned as if trying to remember what he had been saying. But after catching Grondin's eye Barthélemy raised one finger, which was his way of indicating an intention of taking centre stage. He became firmer on his feet, his words disentangled themselves, and that foxy individual, recovering at a stroke the investigator's instinct that his feeble and homely aspect concealed so effectively, launched himself with a famished smile into a voluble tirade as suddenly as if a trapdoor had been opened.

'Apart from our police business as such,' he began in a rush, 'I want to use the opportunity offered me tonight to mention once again the strange and intriguing force that seems to draw me towards you, monsieur ... that leaning, that curiosity, that buried energy that impels me to stay with you in the hope of knowing you better and exploring the swamp where your real personality is hidden ...'

'Are these the beginnings of an inquiry you're thinking of launching on my case, scorpion of the ramparts?' Grondin's tone was almost playful. He had risen briskly to his feet, a sign that he was on his guard.

'Certainly not!' the spindleshanks cried. 'It's just that this evening I felt in the mood to have a chat with you.'

'Admit you wouldn't mind coming up with a juicy bit of dirt on me while you're about it!'

'Really, sir! You shock me!'

'You're unmasked, you long Fleming!' replied Grondin with

ferocious amusement. 'I know your game! You think Mespluchet and his clique are coming back. You want to hand me over to your new masters. Get some advancement!'

An expression of deep vexation on his gloomy face, Barthélemy remained standing on tiptoe. To avoid upsetting the superb temporary balance he seemed to have found, he gravely inclined his head.

'I'm merely fascinated by the truth,' he murmured.

'What a beautiful soul, Hippolyte! Have you already forgotten our walk outside the pagoda?'

''Course not, sir!'

'So you must remember that truth is like the sun: it blacks out your eyes and won't allow itself to be looked at.'

The inspector seemed to have sobered up. He thought for a moment.

'I just want to try to understand why when I'm with you I can happily and eagerly handle red-hot embers that in other company would scorch my hands ... For example, can you explain how I managed to end two lives without feeling the slightest remorse?'

'Surely that's already been dealt with?' Grondin exclaimed, coming close and speaking directly into the other's face. 'Seems to me we've discussed it more than enough! If you hadn't done for those two blackguards while they were busy warming your feet, they'd have done for you!'

'You could put it like that,' the heron answered gravely, 'but I prefer to think that the One who sees everything wanted to spare me.'

'God?' Grondin asked loudly, his face black with anger. 'Let Him sneeze in the dust of his Tabernacle! I know better than anyone the alluring extent of His dyspeptic influence! And I have a large number of personal reasons for detesting the side of the angels towards which He's always shoving me!'

The violence of these remarks told Barthélemy that he had touched on a sore point.

'Sir,' he said after a moment's hesitation, 'I don't want to upset you, but my modest experience inclines me to think that it's the urgent needs of society that prevent you from living in ignorance of good, not hatred of God.'

'Balderdash! Or do you just want to send me completely round the bend?'

'Of course not, sir! I'm trying to think logically. You used to be a policeman ... so the demands of your job kept bringing you back to the foundations of virtue ...'

'Rubbish, I tell you! Imbecile! I've never thought for a single moment that the functions that the state glorifies and rewards so highly have any connection with principles, rectitude or honour.'

Grondin's grey eyes, gleaming with rage, stared for a moment at the flames in the hearth. He turned a furrowed brow towards this copper who was bothering him against his will and added:

'I've come across the most despicable villains in the corridors of power, you know, more times than I care to remember ... investigated fat smirking bastards who owed the great ease of their lives to scummy arrangements reeking of respectable blackguardry. Frankly speaking, I find it hard to see the rich as important repositories of the essential virtues!'

'Why should the badness of the rich be worse than anyone else's?' insinuated the cunning vulture. 'Logically speaking, you'd expect someone well off to want to look after his property ... *ergo*, he must be on the side of virtue!'

'Oh, for God's sake, Barthélemy!'

'No, really! The bourgeois who knows the value of money must inevitably have some morality.'

'He's a tight-arse! An egotist! A small-bore slave-driver! And apart from that – why not admit it? – I've come across individuals of great worth in the most unlikely places, one-eyed establishments, thieves' kitchens ... I understood long ago that the criminal underworld had more exemplary lessons in morality, much more terrible punishments for evil, than those brightly lit salons where "virtue" preens itself in a smug glitter of trumpery!'

Barthélemy smiled. Here we are at last! he thought, almost choking with pride. The great master on his knees! I've brought him to the threshold of confessing! The die is cast, and the door to the mystery will soon be wide open! 'You yourself have had your share of sunshine,' he remarked in an offhand tone. 'Weren't you a notary?'

'I really must ask you to hold your tongue absolutely where that is concerned,' rumbled Grondin, who could now see the light of provocation in the other's eye. 'You don't know where I come from. You don't know the awful secret that orders my whole existence!'

'I know how heavy it is, sir. And actually your familiarity with Trocard confirmed some other intelligence I'd gathered on you . . .'

'I thought so! You were needling me on purpose!'

The two men looked at each other, smiling vaguely. They felt a little like two people one of whom had caught the other after a long chase. Now each was hanging back waiting for the other. Violent dislike hovered in the wings.

'What d'you want?' Grondin asked bluntly after a while. 'What d'you want me to admit?'

Barthélemy paused for a second and then poured out a flood of discourse in machine-gun-like bursts. 'I want you to admit, monsieur, that your game has taken you through the penal colony! That you were once known as Charles Bassicoussé, alias Ironfist! That by judgement and decree passed at Pau assizes, you were sentenced to twenty years' penal servitude for murder and infanticide and deported to the Iles du Salut on 17th February 1856! That you were once a convict doing hard labour, bearing the number 2017! And that as a first-class convict, after twelve years' *hard*, you were pardoned and released for good conduct!'

La Chouette, who had been nodding over her mending, sat up with a start. Through sleepy eyes she saw Grondin's tall outline against the candelabras. He looked like a man stunned by cold and weakness who was managing with great effort to suppress a shudder of his whole spine.

'Bloody 'ell, Mr Horace!' she whispered. 'Are them fairy stories true what that big skellington's tellin'?'

'They are, my good Chouette,' the spectre said, giving her that curious look both humble and haughty. 'I'm afraid my net was trawling some very muddy waters for quite some time ... But only because that was the way events ordained it.'

'From what you say it's you what's the adventurer,' the tall harpy exclaimed, coming fully awake. 'Not that old fraud Three-Nails with 'is barrèr and 'is any-old-iron!' At a stroke Augustine Raboiseau, the widow Lerouge, had recovered the full force of her love for a man who had known dungeons, irons, the ill-treatment of turnkeys, vermin, the knout. She leaned forward distractedly. Grey locks had escaped from under her headscarf. She joined her hands over her stomach and begged:

''Ere, *please*! Say something! *Anything*! You got ter tell us about it! All me life till this moment, I've always 'ad the feelin' I was lookin' f'r a fam'ly of me own ... It was so *cold* bein' by meself! I looked and looked, I knew it was there somewhere ... well, now I've found it! A sign at last! It's *you*, M'sieu Horace! I'll be yer old fiancée in misfortune! Tell us first how you got yerself enrescued out o' the island! I bet you done it by swimmin'!'

'You're closer to the truth than you think, sorceress!' Grondin murmured as the memories stirred in his brain. 'I was a class-one convict and had been granted the right to cultivate a little snippet of land beside the Maroni estuary. One day I saved the director's daughter from drowning in the muddy whirlpools. This exceptional circumstance enabled me to get my sentence reviewed.'

'So the law had doubts about your conviction?' Barthélemy asked.

'Over thirteen years of forced labour I never stopped protesting my innocence!'

'They discharged you?'

'They repatriated me. My sentence was commuted, they gave me the benefit of the doubt. I became a work-gang chargehand in Marseilles jail, then they put me in charge of the whole work detail.'

'And straight from there to bein' an 'igh-up in the rozzers?' squawked the old woman. 'Oh, right then. Bleedin' conjuring trick, like. What d'you take us for? Chuckin' sand in me eyes. Come clean! How did you do it, M'sieu Horace? Don't give us no flannel, do us that favour at least.'

'She's right,' Barthélemy pressed. 'Who exactly *is* Horace Grondin, sir, besides being an underchief in the security police?'

'A creature concocted in his entirety by the prefect Ernest Cresson. An ingenious shell fashioned by the authorities of the time to slip in an old convict, a genuine big fish from the colony, who could bring with him an unparallelled mass of intelligence on top villains.'

'A true heir of François Vidocq!'

'A simple ghost, to start with. A manipulated prisoner who to recover his freedom had agreed to melt into an eternal night of shadows.'

'A subversive! A *provocateur*!'

'An enraged man who had declared war on the society that unjustly condemned him! A rebel against God and the rich! A survivor of fever and foulness impelled through some strange immorality to submit to the authorities, the better to circumvent them ...'

Sick with rage, and in the hope of hiding the tears that had sprung to his eyes, Grondin had taken his powerful frame to the other end of the room where he stood with his head in his hands. He opened red-rimmed eyes and said with great energy:

'I swear, though, that on the way through the black labyrinth through which the criminal justice system dragged me, I never wanted to ignore humanity! I often felt compassion for the reprobates I met. I liked their swagger. Their comradeship. I bowed to outcast law, down in the dungeons. Tasted vermin on the planks, in leg-irons. Listened to the true confessions of men who had escaped the executioner's neck-snipper. I pitied the unfortunate. Perhaps that's the reason why both of you are here. My stray cats!'

'Steady on, gaffer!' la Chouette protested. 'No need to go namecallin'! I might've done Trocard in, but it was only to save you! An, as for pilferin' stuff off of the rich, me an' my old guzzler when we was workin', it was just for a livin' and a hot meal!'

'People are what fate makes them. I'm not judging you, la Chouette. Or you, Barthélemy. Even though I know you'll be my Judas one day. Inform on me when the moment comes.'

'Why would I do that, sir? I have nothing but admiration for you!'

'It's your nature.' Horace Grondin's grey eyes had recovered their implacable glitter.

Barthélemy's by contrast veered slightly off to the side. Of course he was a humbug of the first water. He hung his head, bridled and pouted like an unjustly punished schoolboy, cast a hangdog glance at la Chouette and lapsed into offended silence. It was good to know the strings.

The clock had just struck one. The widow Lerouge was absorbed in her mending, and perhaps wondering at the same time why her Mr Horace had been so rough on that poor Hippolyte. Grondin was reading his paper again, after refilling everyone's glass by way of a truce.

The sly and inventive Barthélemy had again sunk into the depths of his chair, legs folded under him, warming his glass in the hollow of his fleshless hand. Casually, as if it were the most natural thing in the world, he had relaunched the conversation from the place where it had run aground. Face turned to the wall, without trying to catch anyone's eye, he murmured with unfeigned curiosity: 'But ... before Horace Grondin existed, who was Charles Bassicoussé? Even assuming that he's just a faded memory, we know nothing about him except that he was a rich notary ...'

The hypocrite sank his head between his shoulders, expressionless as a stone gargoyle trying to pass unnoticed on some high cornice. He waited in a state of sombre private excitement as the words sank in, and a few moments later felt a wave of demoniacal pleasure as Grondin's harsh and poignant voice answered:

'Charles Bassicoussé was an unhappy man. A man torn between his sense of duty and the strength of his own feelings.'

As he spoke the former scrivener stepped back from the table in front of him. Perched on his long legs he had the air of a man peering into the bottom of his life's well. Hardly a new story! A man always recoils a little when about to warm over his past and examine the upsetting enigma of his existence. So it was with Horace Grondin. In the black shadows between the golden patches of light cast by the candles in that room there was something frightening, even to that man of dark madness and destruction.

'I want to try and tell you the pitiful story of Charles Bassicoussé,' he said at last in a low voice. Calmly and deliberately he detached the stem from his pipe, blew through it as if to clear it and put the marseillaise down on the table. 'I'd like to try to do it in a detached way, as if it had nothing to do with me. I want to explain how the devil dragged the notary across the frontier of reason. I want to tell you about a family at peace under the cedars, beautiful starry nights, and the terrible murder of an infant still growing in his mother's warm belly and believing the world owed him a life!

'In other words, I'm about to confront you with a crime so horrible that you'll lose your sense of moderation. And I hope that the bitter disgust caused by this narrative will eventually give rise to a tide of compassion...'

74

The notary of
le Houga-d'Armagnac

Charles Bassicoussé took a step forward, looked his audience up
and down and said clearly:

'I owned a hundred and ten hectares of vines, slightly less than
half under picardan; two hundred hectares of deciduous wood-
land; six let smallholdings, and three viable farms. My friend
Joseph Roumazeille, who was the manager of the estate, died
suddenly of pneumonia contracted from a chill when he was
trying to save our maize and rye from being beaten down by a
terrible storm one night.

'Joseph was a widower. He was a man of irreproachable
virtue, without ancestry or relations. So when he was about to
face the officer of heaven, it was I whom he naturally asked to
care for his most precious possession: his only daughter Jeanne, a
charming child of twelve, whom I swore, at his request, that I
would treat as my own daughter.

'Legally, then, I became the girl's guardian; and when, five
years later, the death of my own poor wife left me in solitude, I
transferred all my affection to that pretty young creature, who
adorned my house at Perchède and grew daily in beauty and
grace.

'Having no children of my own, I made her my heiress. I
watched over her progress with jealous care, pressing forward
her education while striving to maintain her in the purity of
childhood. I brought her up to be God-fearing and had
ambitions for her future which I kept to myself. As the years
passed I was moved by my pretty nymph's transformation into a

lovely young woman. I loved having her under my roof, where she brightened our evenings with her laughter and enchanted our passing guests with her talent as a pianist.'

Standing in the shadows, the man who had just opened the book of his life at these pages unknown to almost everyone passed a tired hand across his forehead. Gently he murmured her name: Jeanne, Jeanne. His grey eyes, filled with yearning for a tender world, lingered on the candle flames. His mouth too dry for speech, he turned away to keep his eyes hidden from his companions. After a moment's fierce internal struggle he resumed:

'We shouldn't be grudging with the colour of the past . . . My house was big – twenty-eight windows in the main façade – and Jeanne was its sun! She was the scent of sweetness, the sound of laughter! I was a hundred leagues from imagining that our glowing life could ever come to an end when, one terribly hot day – one of those afternoons of light and shadow that you never forget – as I cut through some fallow land on the way home to la Perchède, I saw her emerge from a spinney and jump over a ditch with a graceful leap. The moment she saw me her cheeks blushed scarlet with emotion in a way that emphasised the shine of her eyes. She had just turned seventeen, and she confessed to me her love for the son of one of my tenants, a boy of her own age whose name was Antoine . . .'

His gaze veiled by inexpressible sadness, the former notary listened for a moment to the interminable echoes of his narrative. Then with characteristic briskness he emptied out the bag of his fascinating past in front of the old woman and the policeman. He hated to hear his voice waver but it did not always obey him. And when he came to lay out all the circumstances of the abominable crime of the Houga he was unable to contain his tears. From time to time he would stop and look over his shoulder to make sure that his listeners were following the terrible story before continuing.

From time to time Barthélemy or la Chouette would ask a question. The housekeeper did not miss a single word of what was said. Her staring eyes filled now with horror, now with sympathy, she sometimes gripped the arms of her chair and sometimes slumped back into it.

'Christ Almighty!' she burst out eventually, 'I don't believe what I'm hearing. A young girlie gutted ... cut up ... a baby crushed, that's just butchery! 'S the work of a right wrong'un, that is!'

'Not so much a butcher's crime, more the act of someone who's completely round the bend,' Barthélemy said. 'The miserable brute who did that wasn't in control of himself.'

Charles Bassicoussé had covered his face with his hands, unable to say another word on that scene of carnage burned into his memory, and was peering at the policeman and the ex-ragpicker between his fingers. Devastated by the rebirth of his despair and the howling permanence of those ineffaceable images, he turned a livid, distant, stunned face to them and said:

'Accursed! I deserve to be accursed! I've just told you, my friends! After a murderous madness like that one's eyes close of their own accord! I could no longer look myself in the face. Wouldn't you call that true guilt? For I surely had my share of responsibility for Jeanne's misfortune. I cleared the poor little thing's way for her but I didn't watch over her fledgling flight carefully enough. I hadn't noticed that she was ready to leave the nest! I was blind! Accursed notary! Male pride! Always trying to accumulate wealth so that she'd be richly provided for! Money! The lure of profit! Crime before the event!'

When he came to accuse Tarpagnan of the terrible crime of infanticide and ritual murder a sort of irrepressible violence made the man who had once again become Horace Grondin clench his fists and fixed his face in a wild animal's snarl. His bony features, the frightening scar across his left eye-socket, his ashen rage, said more than any words about his hatred of his ward's killer.

'Let me say that from the day of that abominable crime, no part of my inner being has been charitable!' he cried. 'I've been too revolted, too obsessed, too hardened! I've got used to the sound of sobbing, the sound of crying. I became a policeman the better to track down the perpetrator of that crime. To catch the only murderer I've really wanted to arrest throughout my career! One man! One single man! And on his trail, avid for his traces, I was like a snake that lives on dust ... I came to an arrangement with the underworld. I was willing to do anything at all to get at my quarry the sooner ...'

'This man you say is a mad criminal and infanticide had the appearance of an upright young man,' Barthélemy interrupted. 'You've described him to us yourself as lively and rather amusing. I find it a bit difficult to see the skirt-chaser you've described as a killer of young women.'

'On the contrary, that's him through and through! *Hitzá Hitz*! The given word ... the broken word! I've told you the story of the *makhila*! I gave him my trust. He could always mislead people!'

'You admit yourself you had no real proof of his guilt.'

'I said I didn't catch him in the act! But when I arrived at the scene of the murders, I'm certain I saw a shadow slip outside from behind the curtains ...'

'It wasn't necessarily his.'

'It couldn't have been anyone else!'

Barthélemy's face frowned slightly. The cable-like muscles stiffened in his arms. 'Well then,' he asked, 'what was it that caused you to be suspected?'

'I was present at the scene of the crime. I discovered it. I was maddened with grief. Under pressure from the gendarmes I admitted my guilty love for my ward. That was considered a motive! I was accused of all the vices, and I knew then that I was lost.'

'So you loved her?'

'How could I not be moved by the music of her body? Her slender torso seemed so ... so *fragile*! Her presence always brought fresh air with it! Admit it was a wonderful stroke of magic that had happened before my eyes! A sudden flood of illumination! What an extraordinary change in the steady uneventful life of a provincial notable whose existence until that moment had been exclusively concerned with the sale of property and the composition and witnessing of legal documents!'

The former notary fell silent. Augustine Lerouge in mechanical fashion raked together the dying embers in the grate. The candles had burned low. In its winding-sheet of deepening shadow, Horace Grondin's terrible secret had closed all three faces and cast a pall of melancholy over the room. Grondin fell into an armchair and swallowed with a dry and aching gullet. Hippolyte Barthélemy looked up at him with round but weaselly eyes, and awarded him a yellow grin.

'I'm, er, flattered, I mean . . . we're *honoured* to've been made the recipients of such a terrible confidence,' he said. 'But I'd like you to give us one or two further clarifications.'

'What d'you mean? Still suspect me, do you, you nasty fellow?'

'Never fear, gaffer,' cried la Chouette, 'I believe you, heart and soul!'

'Yes, but all the same,' teased the tall hop-pole, 'I heard what you said, you were eyeing your protégée, you old rogue!'

'Don't be disgusting. She was eighteen when misfortune befell us. I was already forty!'

'Her beauty bothered you, you said.'

'I never showed my feelings. On one occasion only, I took her in my arms. But I couldn't declare myself. The duty I owed her was too sacred! She was virtually my daughter. When she told me she loved Tarpagnan, I did the only thing that wisdom seemed to suggest: I decided then and there that they should marry. And later . . . when the gallant had fled rather than keep his promise to marry Jeanne, I entrusted the sweet dove to the care of a priest to avoid being tempted to offer her my shoulder to lean on, as I should have been if she had come to live under my roof after being jilted.'

Grondin had become aware of the bad thought that was lurking somewhere behind la Chouette's eyes. 'Speak plainly, Augustine,' he said.

'What was 'e called, yer black crow?' The tall harpy was no friend of the clergy.

'Abbé Ségouret. He was Dean of the parish. A very holy man, believe me! He kept an eye on Jeanne and comforted her, had her to stay in the presbytery until the frightful day of her murder.'

'D'you mean she was murdered at Abbé Ségouret's house?' cried Barthélemy.

'No. At mine. One of mine, anyway . . . on my Mormès property. A shooting lodge.'

'What was the girl doing there?'

'On a whim, she'd run away from the presbytery and found shelter in that house in the forest. She knew the place well and often stopped there when she was out riding. She must have had a rendezvous with the murderer.'

'Tarpagnan.'

'Who else? The miserable brute had come back to the area not long before.'

'I reckon it were the crow what done it!' la Chouette squawked suddenly.

'How can you be so blasphemous, you great wheelbarrow!'

'Them tonsure-stands is capable of *anything*!' the old woman said. 'And the proof, my good sir, is that the people are shootin' 'em in job lots!'

Grondin shrugged dismissively. 'Abbé Ségouret was a holy man and a brilliant young ecclesiastic! He was certainly noticed by the hierarchy from an early date. He was senior priest for a while at Mont-de-Marsan and then got promotion. For nearly three years now he's been with Archbishop Darboy as one of his assistants.'

'He's in Paris?'

'I've just told you. He's on the Archbishop's staff . . .'

75

Augustine goes the
way of all flesh

At this point in their conversation they were interrupted by a thunderous triple knock on the apartment door. They looked at each other in alarm.

'A search,' Barthélemy whispered.

'What, at this time?' la Chouette said doubtfully. 'It ain't the right time of night for coppers!'

As if to silence her, the front door shook to a storm of blows delivered from the landing outside, a drumming of calloused fists and hobnailed feet delivered by what sounded like several bad-tempered persons. A clamour of wine-soaked voices followed. Grondin was the first to stand.

'Is the door bolted?' he asked.

'Bolted, barred, double-locked, all tight,' assured the former dame of the hook. She padded silently along the wall in her slippers, picked up the poker and hefted it experimentally to gauge its qualities as a weapon.

'I can pepper them a bit if there aren't too many of them,' Barthélemy breathed. He had slipped his hand into his pocket and was holding the reassuring weight of the Adams.

'I can help you hold them off, but I don't think it's the right thing to do,' Grondin said. He nevertheless opened a drawer in the sideboard and took out a Lefaucheux revolver of useful calibre.

The banging on the front door had stopped. The call of a bugle erupted suddenly, but the blower's wind gave out almost at once, causing the sound to trail away into a lamentable tuneless sigh.

After a short silence, a voice thickened apparently by several litres of wine called indistinctly:

'Open up! No one lorabidin's got nothin' to worry about! 'S yer porter, cit'zen Cabrichon, come up to *entertain* yer!'

Stifled giggles greeted this boozy sally. Another silence followed outside the door, ending in a loud fart and another storm of drunken giggling.

'That stinkin' bugger of a doorkeeper's narked us up,' La Chouette muttered.

'Open up for the people's avengers!' the voice sniggered. 'It's spring cleanin' time for people like you!'

'Hurry up and open!' another voice said. 'Station chief from rue des Francs-Bourgeois speaking! We're armed, and we'll put the door in if you don't open up.'

'Give yerselves up, yer bunch of bastards, we know you're in there!'

'*Lovely* bouquet for the firing squad, you're going to be!'

These jovial warnings and predictions ended in another rain of blows on the door.

'We're fucked,' Barthélemy said coolly.

'I don't think so,' Horace Grondin replied. A few rapid strides took him to the tall bookcases at one end of the room. Removing a few books from one of the shelves, he selected a small key from his bunch and inserted his arm through the space, reaching into an obscure angle of the shelving. There was a tiny click. A moment later, operating an almost hidden catch with his thumb, he swung a section of shelving about a central axis, revealing a low arch into a dark, cramped roofspace beyond.

'Quick,' Barthélemy said, 'they're bashing the lock in with rifle-butts!'

Grondin turned to la Chouette. 'Augustine,' he ordered with frosty calm, 'as soon as we're hidden, go and open the door. You'll be looking sleepy ... put a dressing gown on.'

'Bloody hell, M'sieu Horace, now you're calling me *tu*!' la Chouette exclaimed, ignoring the urgency of the situation. 'And that's twice now you've called me by my Christian name!'

'You've earned it with your devotion,' Grondin said earnestly. 'Come on now, chatterbox! This is hard! I'm depending on you, on your brain too. What you say is that we're not here any longer. That we left at the beginning of the evening. You're my housekeeper and you only know me as Monsieur Julien.'

'And if they know perfectly well who you are, what do I do then?'

'Stare at them wide-eyed and play the bonehead! You don't understand any of it. You're a bit deaf. I hired you in the street. You can't even read or write . . .'

'That's not far off the truth!' the old woman cried. 'I can reckermise the name of Mr Victor Hugo on the newspaper, but beyond that . . .'

'Good! Let's leave it at that. Go ahead and confuse these people for me . . .'

'Aren't you sending this woman to a certain death?' Barthé-lemy interrupted with a rebellious scowl.

'They won't harm her.'

La Chouette overheard this exchange. 'I'm doin' it with me eyes open!' she put in. 'I'll take care of them wineskins for you, M'sieu Horace, never fear. I'll give 'em the speech, the false beard and the parade! They won't 'ave you, not's long as I'm alive!'

In a moment the matron had flung off her dress and petticoat, revealing herself for a moment in graceless nudity, her wrinkled belly, her arms covered in sailors' tattoos. Flinging on a dressing gown she was already running down the passage to the front door, shouting through it to the visitors:

'For Gawd's sake! You're draggin' me out of me bedstraw! Here we are! Here we are! Comin'! At yer bleedin' service, never mind the time! Stop that racket!'

'Open in God's . . . er . . . Noisy old biddy! Open in the name of the Commune!'

''Ere I am, I told yer! 'Old yer noise, bunch of bleedin' drunks!'

During this exchange the fugitives had entered the roofspace, the bookcase closing behind them with a clicking of locks and plunging them into darkness. Grondin struck a mechanical lighter that he kept always about his person and lighted a small lamp, which he placed at the back of their refuge. Inspector

Barthélemy's gaunt face swam into its light. 'You foresaw everything,' he noted, peering about to take the measure of the room. He discovered an elongated wedge-shaped space under the roof, extended by a similar but somewhat bigger space in the roof of the next-door building. Stooping, Barthélemy discerned a camp bed, tinned food and the like, two seats and a hanging-space containing various clothes for use as disguises.

Grondin did not want to listen to any comment, and made a sign for silence. He was much more interested in events on the other side of the bookcase. La Chouette's squawks of protest were interspersed with the sound of rifle-butts hitting wood, marble and brick, and sounds of breaking glass.

'They're turning the place upside down,' Barthélemy breathed.

Through the wall they could hear a voice sharper than the others, that of Casimir Cabrichon, saying: 'Talk, you old toad, or I'll cut your tongue out!'

There followed a discovery that caused general approval. 'Hey! Booze on the table! Make mine a double.'

'The old bat's been drinkin' out of three glasses, look. So she's lyin'!'

Rifle-butts pounded the walls. An unsheathed sword probed hangings, prodded among the books, poked hard into the wood of the shelving and showed its point to the two fugitives. Both had quietly cocked their revolvers and were holding their breath. The drunkard on the other side was panting and struggling to retrieve his blade, swearing like a carter the while.

'Suffering Christ of a son of a whore!' he puffed, 'this wood's got to be wormy! It don't want to give me back me trimmer!' He would have been surprised to know that his cutlass had very nearly blooded the very man he was looking for. There were renewed giggles, and a drunken clinking of glasses. From their hiding place the two men heard a vague cry: '*Vive la Commune!*'

Then a voice ordered: 'Take the old hag. She don't look too tasty but at least we can shoot her. Write down, clerk, that she spat on my big nose! Bring her along. She's sentenced!'

Heavy footsteps trampled the parquet for a moment. Drunken cries died away in the distance. A door slammed. Silence returned.

Grondin gently lowered the hammer of his revolver and stuck the weapon in his belt. Barthélemy was opening and shutting his mouth like a drowning fish, gasping in the mildewy air of the roofspace. He rubbed the back of his neck as if from great fatigue and turned towards his master a jackal-like yellow grin in which reproach was plainly apparent.

'You've sacrificed the old woman,' he said. 'She knew too much about you.'

'Don't try to be clever, Hippolyte,' Grondin said wearily. 'Every one of us is moving towards his fate. La Chouette has a thick skin. She may get out of it.'

Almost immediately the sound of a volley nearby seemed to contradict him. Barthélemy's accusing gaze weighed down on his slumped shoulders. Grondin had turned his back. The secret policeman's dark grey irises glowed in the dark with an extreme coldness. He did not need a mirror to see what was going on behind him.

'You hate me, Hippolyte, don't you?' he said. 'But the things that happen aren't entirely under our control. Storms of anger and killing are coming that are going to sweep everything away ... Our ambitions, our torments of soul, our backs hardly scarred by flogging, all of that is as nothing compared to the abyss of blood and hellish fire we're going to see soon! And it won't be long before it all starts to happen.'

'I'm aware of that, sir. And I would add that even if you and me now have a better idea of the true nature of our relations ... we're still chained together. I've got nothing left but you. And you've got nothing left but me.'

'On the basis of hatred,' Grondin agreed, 'our association is both fragile and indissoluble ... And I've one last thing to ask you, Barthélemy: that you accompany me until I find what I'm seeking.'

'No danger of my leaving you,' the hop-pole assured him. 'I want to go all the way myself!'

'You want to know whether I'm guilty?'

'I want to unmask the real murderer.'

'You have vice in your bones, Barthélemy.'

'I'm a true policeman, sir.'

'I myself remain an unhappy man. Apart from tracking down Tarpagnan, I'm not interested in anything.'

'What's your plan?'

'At dawn,' the grey-eyed man said, moving into the next compartment, 'we shall leave this hole by the staircase that starts behind the hanging cupboard. It's a spiral stair in the thickness of the wall, and it leads to the back courtyard of the house next door. You, Barthélemy, are to go and find the locksmith whom you so brilliantly turned.'

'Emile Roussel?'

'Yes. He used to be a member of the Ourcq gang. And since Tarpagnan's amorous pranks took him right into the Gold-smith's lair, it's a good bet that Wire can give you some idea of what happened to him.'

'He'll just tell me to go to hell!'

'In exchange for any information, tell him that when the regulars are back in charge in Paris you'll forget he carried the number 7 glass eye and that he was a stalwart Commune supporter.'

'Dunno ... what about our consumptive's patriotism? He'd *never* sing the name of a comrade in the struggle to one of Monsieur Thiers's lousy coppers.'

The former senior secret policeman shrugged, made his way to the other end of the roofspace, felt behind a beam between the rafters and battens and brought out a small heavy package which he slapped into the other's hand. 'Here's some cough syrup for your client,' he said laconically.

'And you, sir, where will you be while I'm making these enquiries?'

'It's all arranged. I'll wait for you at another lodging I've got, over by Saint-Julien-le-Pauvre. Abbé Ségouret's got the keys. I left them with him so they'd be in trustworthy hands. All I need to do is get them from the Bishop's Palace.'

'The address of this haven of peace?'

'Number 4, rue des Grands-Degrés. At the end of the garden.'

'I'll be there.'

76

Dombrowski's black Sunday

They were coming. There they were: red trousers. The Line.

Through his binoculars, Tarpagnan watched the red trousers advancing. The Vergé Division.

A column had marched into the place du Trocadéro. A thousand federals, entrenched behind barricades of a sort, but too ill-led and unblooded to defend themselves, had surrendered there.

The soldiers of the Line were pushing on, along the boulevard Murat, along Suchet. Twinkling red trousers advancing in sudden rushes through the ruins. Sometimes an officer's sword reflected a gleam of sunlight.

'Forward!'

The regular troops surged out from behind cover. With the loose, practised unison of a flock of migrating starlings, they gained the cover of a white stone wall and vanished once again. They were closer now. Reappearing all along the front of la Pépinière barracks.

Troopers poured down the sloping lawns. Bugles calling the charge. Shouts. Running. There they were!

General Blot had just taken the porte de Passy.

On the previous day, Dombrowski had been wounded in the chest by a shell splinter. Then he had asked for reinforcements and been given none. In the evening he had gone to the Hôtel de Ville. He had arrived, handsome and erect, on his fine little black horse.

The members of the Committee of Public Safety – Eudes, Arnault, Billioray, Gambon and Ranvier – were sitting round a table smoking. They had thought he was dead. He told them there was pestilence in his heart, and gave them the news, the very bad news.

He told them his battalions had given battle fiercely in front of Auteuil church.

He said his troops had fallen back on the château of la Muette where they were well dug in and well deployed. They were trying to make a stand there under Major Tarpagnan, an excellent professional officer.

He was pale.

He said Tarpagnan wouldn't be able to hold out for long if his troops went on deserting and fleeing back to their home districts in disorder. He said his officers were doing their best to regroup these angry deserters, but the men were insulting them openly and going home to fight on their local barricades.

He said that Tarpagnan had barely five hundred usable troops left with which to resist the advance of Mac-Mahon's columns. He warned the Committee that Paris would awaken the next day, 22nd May, under the jackboot of Versailles.

Then he left to fight alongside his own.

There they were, closer than ever, the red trousers of the Line.

At la Muette the firing was intense. Everywhere else was wide open. Seventy thousand men were pouring into Paris.

Chassepots barked in the gloom. Bullets knocked chunks out of doors and joists, zigzagged about in caterwauling ricochets like nasty hot insects.

Next to Tarpagnan lay a man with open eyes, open mouth, open hands, his throat too opened into a smile by one such leaden hornet.

How sorely everyone was needed – the whole nation, all the people, women and children too – to complete an organised resistance! People's courage needed stiffening, more hands were needed, more rifles, to resist, to hold them off for a few hours longer!

They were advancing. To the right, to the left too. On all sides, nearly. They were shouting. Tarpagnan stared into the night, indifferent to bullets, probing the shadows. He was trying to evaluate the level of resistance that could be offered by his meagre unit, at that moment pinned down by fire from a machine-cannon.

The officer was submerged by a feverish churning of the entrails, a racing clock counting the entire summary of an eventful life. His eyes glowed with a strange light. Rage in his heart, he raised his arm.

'Sergeant,' he cried, 'they're surrounding us! Sound the retreat!'

The stretcher-bearers were doing what they could to look after the wounded. They piled straw into the wagons and carried hand-stretchers.

The other side kept advancing.

Now the sides were only thirty metres apart. Men shooting each other point-blank. And at closer quarters still, skewering each other. Looking into each other's eyes and killing each other at arm's length. Eyeball to eyeball. In a frenzy. Burning each other down with pistol shots, cutting each other with sabres, eviscerating each other with bayonets.

The Line troops were here. They had taken everything.

The last federals were fleeing under a hail of bullets. The most resistant turning to face it, thumbs through the slings of their rifles, muzzle-flashes spitting at them from all sides. Insulting their killers from frothing mouths. Defying the death that howled past their ears. Hatred, evil bloody-minded rage, bodies that did not care whether they died now or in a few days' time, gave them a last hiccup of resistance. Shell fragments showered from the sky. Projectiles whistled and zipped. Strange things showed in eyes feverish with fear and defiance.

They would sink suddenly to one knee, take aim once more. Load and fire, load and fire. From the slight cover of a fallen tree, a collapsed sentry. Many making the last voyage of a human being at the end of his destiny. Of these furious warriors with gritted teeth and shoulders black with powder, many were boys – children aged between twelve and fifteen. Canteen-keepers threw lime branches, torn in haste from the trees nearby, over the corpses that had to be abandoned.

And when at last the crackling blaze had consumed everything and passed on, the early morning sun rose on the remains of spent courage.

Knapsacks. Ammunition pouches and shoes. Dislocated legs, bodies drawing their last rattling breaths, feasting insects. Kepis balanced on their edges, and dented water-bottles. In a hole, strips of minced flesh. Gnawed shirts, lacerated greatcoats. Against an iron grille, white-lipped corpses. Lying in a sloping street, burst bellies and ashen faces.

All carrion. Or soon to be carrion.

What a bitter thing is a rout!

77

Last kiss

That same Monday 22nd May, at number 19 rue Oudinot, at the grey hour when the temples of the wounded are pouring cold sweat, that icy moment when the grim reaper surveys the dying to make them spit out their souls, when the white form of the nurse bent over the dying man is confounded with the limbo to which he is about to return for ever, a young soldier, mortally wounded in one of those famous bayonet assaults, uttered his mother's name and, before going at last into the blinding brightness of purity, tensed his body for a last bound forward and received on lips already cold a farewell kiss from the young woman watching over his last moments.

That act of solace in the last extremity of life, that ultimate courtesy of human compassion, that kiss bestowed on the casualty about to take up permanent residence elsewhere, was intended to let the dying man know that his sacrifice inspired respect. It had been dispensed by a pale-faced ambulancewoman of perfect beauty, her face grave under its helmet of dark hair.

It brought the savour of life close to the horror of war. The pious ceremony of that last flower of love offered to the soldier entering the starry rainstorm of the beyond had been standard practice in the La Presse ambulancewomen's service since a nurse called Jeanne Couerbe had first practised it on the battlefield.

Gabriella Pucci – for she it was – had just bestowed 'the kiss of death' for the first time. She knew that from now on she would be granting it to the dying just like all the other women – housewives and women of easy virtue, scowling viragos and gay little faces, big fat matrons and slim waists, pressers and workers, charitable ladies and schoolmarms – who, like her, were sacrificing their own lives in butchery's outposts to heal and succour those who needed their help.

Caf'conc' closed the young soldier's eyes – he had been almost a child – and gradually straightened herself on the low chair where she had spent the last several hours. Looking at Guillaume Tironneau's smooth boy's face, she was suddenly overwhelmed by the sorrow of seeing one whom she had initiated into manhood's estate deprived for ever of the colour and taste of life, and managed only with great effort to suppress a convulsive sob. She stayed there motionless for some time, gazing into the distance with her forearms clasped across her belly. She swayed a little as the images moved across the screen of her inner eye. There was little sign of her inner turmoil.

Dry-eyed, without making a sound, she gazed for a moment at the translucent veil of curtain moving lightly before a window open on the imminence of dawn. Gradually the sounds in the building – a banging door, footsteps on a distant tiled floor – brought her attention back to reality. She breathed deeply to restore herself. Across the beds where the night's casualties lay restless, she saw coming towards her the other member of her team: the coachman with whom she would now have to go and collect the dead.

The fellow stank of winewash despite the early hour. He lifted his *morillo* hat briefly from a skull shaped like a white knee, and his blotchy, broken-veined cheeks wrinkled into what was meant to be an engaging smile.

'Alphonse Pouffard, undertaker and ambulanceman to the Commune, at your service, princess,' he announced. 'Cecile and me've had two full hours of sleep and we was wondering if you was coming to the Champs-Elysées with us for the first round?'

'Champs-Elysées?'

'Well, yes. It's all caving in there, proper nightmare. Shells falling in the Concorde!' said the Vicar of Death hoarsely. 'I'm not having you on, they need us. Scrape up the meat and guts.'

Caf'conc' didn't move. Her lips twitched and an urge to vomit threatened to get a hold on her stomach.

'I c'n quite understand yer eagerness to get started,' the ugly charioteer grated. His eye fell on the still and waxen Guillaume

Tironneau and he added: 'Ah, another one gone! My poor princess, you've lost yer nice little volunteer! Look at that, eh? A kid what was still on the nipple ... It's a bastard of a time, ain't it! Hellish bleedin' dirty, and we're just carried along. I get the feeling,' he ended in a different tone, 'that this one's affectin' you a bit ... friend of yours, eh?'

'You could say he was my last child,' Caf'conc' replied, sitting up straight. She mastered a slight trembling of the lips and added: 'Go ahead, citizen Pouffard. I'll catch you up outside in a minute.'

She stayed with the body of the dead youth for a minute or two longer, crossed herself as she covered the waxen face with the sheet, then moved just far enough not to be in the way, standing with her back to the chalk-white wall as two porters lifted the body onto a stretcher and took it away to the morgue.

From her rapid breath, blind gaze, clenched fists and heavy, wordless posture as the phantom of youth was carried from the ward, an observer might have concluded that Caf'conc' was weeping without shedding tears.

78

The Commune or death

At the same time that young Guillaume Tironneau's bier was leaving the rue Oudinot, to be laid on the cold ground in the Chapel of Rest at the nearby Incurables' hospice to await an uncertain burial in company with a hundred and twenty-seven other mutilated corpses, Horace Grondin and Hippolyte Barthélemy, taking advantage of an undecided condition mid-way between dew and mist, slipped into the fresh air through the postern of a low gate giving onto rue Dupetit-Thouars and, without turning to see if anyone was following them, rapidly distanced themselves from the rue de la Corderie of sinister memory.

Hands in their pockets, two grey shadows on the pavement of the boulevard du Temple, the two men walked towards Château-d'Eau at a good pace. The streets were unlighted or virtually so. The unbearable stale stench of the drinking shops that were especially numerous in the area, and the hordes of armed drunks they stumbled over everywhere, added to the feeling of insecurity around them.

They had arranged to part at the corner of boulevard du Prince-Eugène. From there, one would climb the slopes of Montmartre to try to find Emile Roussel, who had perhaps slept at home in 7, rue Lévisse, while the other would hurry to the Left Bank and find Father Ségouret, living in the Archbishop's palace where he now worked.

The fugitives had both chosen new costumes to blend in with the crowd and pass unnoticed. The finery they had taken from Horace Grondin's wardrobe made them unrecognisable. Barthélemy was wearing an old, torn frock-coat, carpenter's trousers

and a sheepskin waistcoat, topped with a round brown hat of
new and relatively well-brushed aspect, a get-up so disparate,
with its hints of Landes shepherd and foreman joiner, that he
could easily be taken for a corpse-robber. Grondin was miserably clothed in a threadbare and faded blue greatcoat, a collarless
shirt and grey trousers tucked into his boots. He was hoping to
pass as a soldier in retreat, with a battered kepi on his white hair,
a slung Chassepot, a water-bottle, knapsack and assorted kit
jingling on his back and giving him an outline commonplace at
that moment. The dreadful scar across his gaunt cheek, stubbled
and dirty, and pronounced features, completed the image of a
veteran whose big checkered neck-scarf had long served as a
snuff-cloth, boot-buffer and heat pad for taking the coffee billy
out of the campfire.

As they approached the place du Château-d'Eau the two men
slowed their pace, surprised to find an unusual amount of
activity. Officers were attempting to regroup disorganised bodies
of troops by exhorting them and appealing to their civic sense.
They were haranguing guardsmen who had the upper hand.
Their horses were prancing a bit from being held on a tight rein
by shouting individuals. Battalions that had almost reformed
would dissolve into groups and then disintegrate completely, as
if every bit of bad news or contradictory order caused a sort of
wavering in their consciousness making it impossible for them to
behave in a disciplined consistent manner. There was at all times
a margin of excited men doing the wrong thing. The ranks would
collapse as if struck with sudden madness, or in response to the
yells of an NCO would start to reform in regular lines. The
soldiers were shouting angrily that they had been betrayed.
Drums were beating in nearby streets.

'The situation's getting steadily worse,' Grondin muttered.

'It's the creaking before the beam gives way,' the starveling
Barthélemy replied sarcastically, craning his neck to see better.
Church bells were ringing the alarm with all their might. Seven
women – three pulling, two pushing and two others turning the
wheels by hand – came past them trundling a machine-cannon.
They were greeted with cheers from the next street corner where
an improvised barricade was going up.

Grondin and Barthélemy were going to have to pass through a mass of bystanders. While being jostled and hemmed in by the movements of the crowd, they glanced at each other and agreed without speaking not to separate until they had taken further stock of the situation.

They were soon up to date on the previous night's events: the sudden intrusion of the Versaillais into Paris, and their lightning advance. The rumour was that in Auteuil and Passy the streets and parks were cluttered with piles of corpses, and that in the Javel district the human flood of Line troops, accompanied by battalions of gendarmes – hand-picked town sergeants, in fact – had quickly submerged everything. There had been summary shootings, charnel-houses of the executed. Hundreds of federal corpses proved the savage ferocity of Monsieur Thiers's butchers.

Jules Vallès, who had been present at the rout in the Champ-de-Mars, and who had been barracked and jostled by the fleeing crowd, blind 'as a herd of buffalo in its cloud of dust', had run up the stairs at the Ministry of War four at a time to describe the rout but had found 'nobody' there.

Lord! Where were things going? What general could take charge?

The answer seemed to come from the anxious voices of those describing the latest alarmist measures taken by Delescluze. It was said that in the Hôtel de Ville the disorganisation had reached such a point that all hierarchy and all idea of discipline had collapsed.

'Brunel's organising the defence at the Concorde!' shouted a well-informed passer-by who carried two rifles and did not seem to be exaggeratedly dashing.

'His legion's deployed in a skirmishing line on the terrace of the Tuileries!' confirmed a recruit of barely fifteen wearing a dirty, bloodstained band round his forehead.

'Three fours, a twelve and two sevens!' shouted his woman neighbour, as excitedly as if half a dozen small field guns could turn the tide. 'We're sure to win the war!'

There was a crush everywhere, with people standing on each

other's feet in their eagerness for news. The fact that it was still too dark to see your hand in front of your face made little difference. People were breathing in each other's faces. Grondin and Barthélemy were jostled by waves of anxious people.

On the walls smeared with still-drying paste was a new generation of posters. The neighbourhood concierges jostled with groups of excited hussies and women in silk dresses, trying to decipher the proclamations that had been hurriedly written during the night. A big fellow in overalls with a prominent nose over a thick moustache read out the text of one in a stentorian voice:

> *TO THE PEOPLE OF PARIS!*
> *To the National Guard!*
> *Citizens!*
> *'No more militarism!'*

A nervous little man with a face like a dog barked the gist of what he had read to others behind him:

> *'Citizens!*
> *'No more militarism! No more general staff with gold braid on every surface!*
> *'Make way for the people! For the bare-handed combatants!'*

'Hey! That's us!' cried a carrot-haired servant-girl, keen to respond. 'Cloves with bare hands, that's what we are! Girls what don't get nothing and what provides most of the elbow-grease!'

A hundred throats shouted their agreement. The workers were of course giving vent to their frustration in their own way. And that raw violence, that furious rage to live without chains, paid at a stroke the whole price of the Commune.

The bass voice of the man in the overall rose from the front of the crowd reading further down the poster:

> *'To arms! Citizens, to arms!*
> *The hour has struck for revolutionary war!'*

The little fellow with eyes like a basset-hound and a repetitive nervous shrug added immediately in a falsetto yap:

'If you do not want the generous blood that has been flowing like water for the past six weeks to go to waste, if you want to live in freedom in a free and egalitarian France ... march on the enemy! And may your revolutionary energy show that Paris can perhaps be sold, but can never be surrendered or vanquished!'

To follow up these inflamed slogans, these promises of almost immediate artillery fire, the carrot-topped enthusiast had climbed onto a marker-stone. Her dress tucked up into her belt, one hand on her hip and the other holding the staff of a red flag bearing the words 'The Commune or Death', she instructed those around her as follows:

'Sound the castrator! Beat the general call to arms! To the barricades! I give you my personal guarantee, citizens: if we set up fire-traps in front of every house, the Bismarcks and aristos from the Petit Clamart won't get by!'

All around, as if in agreement with these irrational assertions, there was a constant coming and going of armed civilians, women without bonnets or hats, others with red cockades in their hair, running from one house to another, talking excitedly in the courtyards and gathering in the the entrances to buildings. Those witnessing this scene of agitation had a strange confused impression, as if somehow the only defence envisaged by the authorities had been the deployment of a delirious mass of verbiage and a naïve belief in the efficacy of revolutionary energy.

'God! How idealistic the people are!' Barthélemy sighed.

'They believe in revolution,' Grondin corrected. The former meteorologist of popular convulsions watched the seething of the crowd for a moment in the slowly lifting darkness, cocking an ear to a rumble of artillery that sounded frighteningly close. 'What's tomorrow got in store for us?' he wondered.

'Hard to say, sir,' replied Barthélemy, who was sticking close beside him. 'The horse has bolted good and proper. Even hauling on the reins of history won't stop it now!'

'It won't be any easier to lay hands on Tarpagnan if Paris collapses into chaos!' the spectre said with sudden anxiety. The obsession with vengeance, the law of the thunderbolt, the fanatical pursuit of justice, could all be read anew in the outlines of his pitiless face.

'I have to get that man, Barthélemy,' he murmured. 'Wherever he is, I have to get him, d'you hear? I want to administer justice for myself.'

'No need to say another word, sir,' the policeman grated. 'I haven't forgotten my promise. And I'll keep it by giving you your man.'

'Well, off you go then! Fade into the scenery! Bring him to me!' Grondin murmured, gripped by an awful change of mood. 'And forgive me for putting you in danger.'

Lost in the tattered folds of his black frock-coat, the crane-like inspector displayed his eternal yellowish grin. 'Come on, monsieur, none of that between us, please! You know very well I've got my own reasons for doing this.'

'What? Still want to see me on my knees?'

'I just need the obvious truth, Mr Underchief of the Security Police, *sir*!'

Grondin looked down, frowning. 'The devil's not always the one we think he is,' he said in a muffled voice. Then he touched the brim of his old, colourless, torn, stained kepi in salute to the vulture he was sending after his prey. 'Tomorrow in the rue des Grands-Degrés, or in hell!' he added with his usual brisk authority.

A moment later, stoop-shouldered and blank-faced, he had become a tired old man, weighed down by the burdens of his rifle and knapsack. Watching him, Barthélemy could see only an ordinary man melting rapidly with long strides into the swirling crowd.

79

Hôtel du Châtelet

Crossing the Seine by way of the pont Notre-Dame and the Petit Pont, Grondin became aware that he was perspiring under his greatcoat and that the misty dawn was rapidly giving way to a warm and sunny day. He had decided to get to the rue de Grenelle by the shortest route through the side streets, but although he took care to avoid open spaces whenever he could, he was obliged several times to lend a hand to citizens strengthening a barricade or improvising a two-storey redoubt, who were mobilising all passers-by. Much delayed in his journey, dragged into helping against his will, he found himself with a pick in his hands, busy prising up cobblestones in the rue Saint-André-des-Arts.

Constructions were rising at almost every crossroads in the 7th *arrondissement*. Pickaxes were digging up the road surface in the rue du Regard, the rue du Four, at the Red Cross junction. The last trees were being felled. Brigades of children were trundling barrowloads of earth. Chains of men and women, some of them in rags, were passing from hand to hand blocks of stone, beams, mattresses and sandbags. Everyone was helping with the civic works: shop-assistants and shop-owners, children and the elderly, even the passers-by. The shops were shut tight. New posters had appeared everywhere, exhorting people to resist. The latest ones read:

Arise, good citizens!
   Parisians! The struggle now under way must not be abandoned by anyone, for it is the struggle of the future against the past, of freedom against despotism, of equality against monopoly, of fraternity against

servitude, of the solidarity of peoples against the selfishness of oppressors. To arms!

To arms, then!

All over the town people were displaying goodwill. The work was being done without orders or directives from above. Rebellious Paris, Paris shouting its pride and defiance, the Paris of the crazed, the just, the proletarian, seemed to be breathing in unison with the tumultuous rhythm of popular improvisation. Everything was giving way. Nothing was going right. The street was superb, generous. It would be unvanquishable.

The chapel rotunda of the reformed Cistercian nuns of Pentémont was striking eleven when Grondin finally reached the rue de Grenelle. Cautiously, he moved up the street against a clattering stream of wagons loaded down with furniture and ministry files, escorted by a scrum of mounted guardsmen. Once past this difficult passage, where couriers were rushing hither and thither with notes and orders, he went on, hugging the walls to pass unnoticed. He had to take shelter again to avoid being run over by a last squadron of dragoons, a great clattering of sabres and horseshoes across the whole width of the street. A drunk officer, lying on the mane of his chestnut, was making vigorous uncontrolled gestures and bawling to his men that Clinchant's army corps was threatening Saint-Lazare. The cavalrymen, also loud with alcohol, were bending low with the effort to stay on their stampeding mounts, heads down, giggling to each other in a cloud of dust. Sparks showered from the horses' hooves. They were heading for disaster, horrible and bloody butchery, unbelievably ferocious. Grondin watched them up the street until they turned the corner and the ringing of hooves and sabres died away.

His way clear at last, he headed at a brisk pace for the Hôtel du Châtelet where, at number 127, was the palace of the Archbishop of Paris, which at one time had been the house of the Emperor, then of the king.

He entered the courtyard of the sumptuous building by the Tuscan main entrance. His gaze was immediately drawn to the building's portico, with four Corinthian columns of such colossal proportions that he had the impression of being crushed and flattened by grandeur. After crossing this giant's antechamber, in which his footsteps echoed, he reached the front wall of the palace, somewhat less formal with its garlanded windows, and entered by pushing open the tall and heavy glass entrance-door.

Inside there was no doorkeeper, no priests, nobody at all, not even a minor monsignor in cassock and dog-collar. He moved forward with a shorter stride. Still without finding a living soul, he crossed the hall, floored with black marble and overlooked by a gallery that traversed its whole width. Skirting the monumental staircase that led to the audience and reception rooms, the Archbishop's offices and Monseigneur Darboy's private apartments, he reached at the back of the entrance hall a narrow flight of stairs descending into a sort of mysterious well.

Grondin entered a long, straight, empty corridor and walked to the far end, stopping finally in front of a small door painted in *trompe-l'oeil* fashion to resemble wooden netting. For a moment, as if the intuition of a malign force was making him hesitate, he stood in front of it, examining the brass plate that identified it as the lair of the Vicar-General, listening at length to the gloomy and total silence within.

Lifting his hand to knock, he paused again to glance slowly to left and right and probe the shadowy corners for movement. Only when he was sure of being unobserved did his gaunt, bony hand seize the brass knocker and bring it down several times on its base, causing its heavy metallic voice to echo through the abbé Segouret's apartment.

There was no reply at first.

Grondin had withdrawn into a shadowy alcove. Listening hard, he heard a distant pattering of many sandals, drawing rapidly closer. From his vantage point he saw a troupe of young priests come into sight at the other end of the corridor. The seminary blackbirds were moving with a terrified alacrity very different from the weighty and dignified comportment of most groups of priests. Their flying cassocks and anxious faces suggested that they were being pursued, and when peace had descended once more on the ancient walls, Grondin took good care to remain in hiding. He waited.

His face drawn, he peered and listened into the distance for any pursuer who might catch him in the corridor. After a while he heard a door slam in the distance, perhaps closed by a draught. Someone, an old person, was coughing at length some distance away. Then came the sound of someone's nose being blown. Silence fell once more.

Grondin emerged from the niche where he had been standing behind a big walnut carving of St Antony, stepped over to the door and knocked again several times. This time there was a rustle of furtive movement behind the door, and a cautious woman's voice asked:

'Who's there?'

No sooner had he identified himself as the notary Charles Bassicoussé than the door opened on a dark hallway. As he stepped inside, trying to accustom his eyes to the gloom, a being of indeterminate size and twisted shape with ropy limbs, scuttled out from behind the woman who had opened the door, passed in front of Grondin trailing an odour both rancid and sulphurous, and shot out of the door leaving him with a disagreeable, strangely poisonous sensation like a spider's touch.

'Come in,' the woman said. 'I had another visit before yours.'

80

The housekeeper

Madame Ursule Capdebosc was of indeterminate age. She might have been seventy, she might have been ten years younger. She had white hair, pulled into a bun under a headdress. Despite years in Paris she had preserved the aspect of an incurable country-woman. That way of standing solidly on her legs. A look of cleanliness, a skin white and smooth, high cheekbones with a red spot on each, a clear and well-outlined forehead, very deep-set blue eyes and miraculously swollen eyelids like the ones on Fra Lippo Lippi's paintings of the Virgin in the churches of Siena.

She had lost none of her vivacity, nor of her rolling southwestern accent, nor of her old presbytery-maid's memory. At a single glance she recognised the man who had just knocked at her door.

'God in heaven! Gers!' she cried, as if at the sight of a good ghost that frightened her a little but also reminded her of a past, and a region, that she should never have left. 'Good heavens above! It's beyond belief!' repeated Ursule Capdebosc with her hands joined in front of her mouth. 'The Houga notary! Monsieur Charles! It's really you! At a time like this! With all these not very nice things going on!' Suddenly she noticed her visitor's clothes, his gallows-bird air, his frightening stubble, the slung rifle, the kepi in his hand, and added in a tone of simple alarm: 'Are you one of them? You too, Monsieur Charles, are you eating priest? Scoffing curate?'

'Don't get yourself into a state, my good Ursule!' Grondin replied instantly as he laid down his burdens. 'This disguise is as distasteful to me as it is to you. I'm just wearing it so that I can move about in streets that aren't under control.'

'Well, that's a relief!' the old housekeeper cried. 'I was getting so worried! After all that's happened to us – enough to make you bang your head against the walls it is – you can't help expecting the worst.'

'What's happened that's so terrible?' Grondin asked. He felt a sudden sense of foreboding. 'Where's Abbé Ségouret?'

The housekeeper looked at him with a pathetic face in front of which she shook her joined hands. 'Ah, my poor gentleman!' she said, her forehead ridged with an alarming expression. 'Misfortune has come down on us, I can tell you that!'

'So where's Abbé Ségouret?' repeated the man with grey eyes.

But Ursule Capdebosc had dropped her imploring madonna's attitude, and was hurrying in her black stockings into the depths of the apartment, signing to the ex-notary to follow her. She led him to a low-ceilinged, rather dark dining room giving onto an arcaded garden. At the door she warned him not to slip on the polished floor, then invited him to sit down.

'Are you hungry?' she enquired when he had seated himself. 'Would you like to break bread?'

He made a negative sign. She seemed vexed, and he realised that he was going to be there for some time yet.

Ursule had always done things in a way that was all her own. The notary knew her too well to try to change the liturgical order she was going to impose on the conversation. The account of the misfortunes that had befallen the house and its inhabitants was not going to come until after the usual civilities had been completed.

In any case, the old servant went instinctively through the motions of Gascon hospitality. Ever since her birth, where she came from, a proper welcome for visitors had had the force of law. That's the way things had been done at Houga, and these little attentions had always worked with decent people. There would be a spot of armagnac before anything else. That was the way things had been done in the *curé*'s house in the past, and people could perfectly well do them that way now, however burning their curiosity might be to hear of recent events.

Ursule accordingly brushed her hand across the table to remove imaginary crumbs, murmuring Monsieur Charles's name two or three times as she did so, then bustled to the sideboard and very quickly, in haste, placed before her guest a plate of sugared sweetmeats and a small glass of very old armagnac.

'It's from Mormès,' she specified. 'From '31. Some *real stuff* you gave Abbé Ségouret for Christmas in '54 . . . as a thank-you for the care he took to protect Jeanne from the difficulties of life. That was . . . it was just after she was jilted by that skirt-chaser Tarpagnan. Just a year before the *awful thing* happened.'

Grondin rested his penetrating gaze on her. 'I've come to get the keys of my little hideout in the rue des Grands-Degrés,' he said bluntly.

'I'll get them for you, they'll still be in Father Ségouret's room. I haven't touched anything,' said Madame Capdebosc, scurrying off across the gleaming and fragrant tiles. 'I'll be back in two minutes.'

When she came back with the keys she was crying and Grondin saw that she was almost ready to talk. 'Well, here's a fine flood!' he said. 'That's twice the Adour has overflowed its banks!'

'Ah, old crybaby! I'm ashamed of myself! Sorry, Monsieur Charles!' cried Ursule Capdebosc, looking at him through red-rimmed eyes. 'I seem to be blubbering all the time now!' She wrung her hands. 'I've been like this a fortnight or more, a proper Madame Cerfeuil!'

'Perhaps if you *explained* a little, Ursule . . . I won't be able to make head or tail of it otherwise.'

'Explain?' she said in a tired voice, slumping into the chair facing the notary. 'Lord, Lord! There's no savour in anything for me now. I mean it, none! Everything's going to pot! Ever since Monseigneur Darboy got arrested, this house has been going nowhere.'

'The Bishop's been *arrested*?' Grondin asked in genuine astonishment.

'Two months ago. Didn't you know?' asked the good woman.

'I haven't always been able to move about freely,' he replied evasively. 'Where did they take him?'

'To Mazas. But he's just been moved to la Roquette. With his priests . . . With the *curé* of la Madeleine, President Bonjean and the banker Jecker. A holy man like him! Of his rank! You wouldn't even imagine something like that. A great gentleman like that! Sleeping on straw and eating ration bread!' Ursule crossed herself rapidly, but she hadn't finished yet. 'There's worse to come! More sinister than that! Even thinking about it takes my voice away . . . listen to this: our Abbé Ségouret left us two weeks ago! He'd just been made Vicar-General in place of Abbé Lagarde, who'd already been arrested along with the Monseigneur . . .'

Her voice rising an octave, she added tearfully: 'The Communers *molested* him! Ignoramuses! Shouting the place down, you should have seen them, the nasty ragamuffins, shirts open, bellies all hairy! Draped in red like scarecrows! They came for him at the crack of dawn. They beat him on the pretext he'd been saying unkind things about their revolution . . .'

'Where is he?'

'At la Roquette with the others,' Ursule said unhappily. 'His face was bashed in by a nasty blow from a rifle-butt. And two suppurating sores are making him weaker by the day.'

'How did you find all this out?'

'From one of his warders. I slipped him a little *foie gras* to make friends, and keep him sweet with a bit of money.' She lowered her eyes and added: 'That was him, Monsieur Charles, that you passed in the doorway. A real toad, ugly as they come, but I force myself to talk to him.'

Grondin walked round the table and laid a sympathetic hand on the faithful servant's shoulder.

'Dry your tears, my good Ursule,' he said. 'It's all going to be over in a few more days.'

'Until then, we ought to be ready for anything,' the old lady said, allowing her mind to wander obsessively over thoughts of death. 'I can smell the taste of blood already.' She brushed a sleeve across her fine eyes.

'Well, now,' she scolded herself, placing her slim, dry hand on the notary's, 'as we say at home: dogs piss, women cry! I'm ashamed of myself for being so weak.'

She smiled through the remains of her tears, and started to talk.

81

The prisoners at
la Roquette

In their cells the captives obeyed three different rhythms: the rhythm of sleep, the agitated restless slumber that would overtake them on their dusty pallets; the rhythm of fear that seized them at all hours, fear of being called out and marched to the ground floor for summary execution; and the rhythm of prayer that threw them on their knees on the crumbling floors of their cells beside their worm-eaten beds, faces buried in their hands, souls famished for images of compassion, entreating God to grant them the courage to face whatever ordeals awaited them.

To these priests abandoned by the light of heaven, to these men shut into gloomy eight-by-four-foot stone coffins, the slightest sound – a muffled volley in the courtyard, a dull shudder through the floor, shouts attenuated by distance – represented the possible imminence of a violent death. The sound of a rifle-butt scraping a stone wall, the scuffle of a nailed boot on a corridor floor, made these unfortunates start, wide-eyed with the onset of terror, arms instinctively clasping their gaunt bellies, the muscles in their flanks jumping convulsively. In three strides each would have his ear straining close to the heavily bolted door of his cage. They tried hard to be ready for the ignoble, the unbearable walk downstairs from the first-floor corridor where they were kept to the edge of the perimeter path where, like others before them, they would be struck down by executioners' bullets.

Archbishop Darboy's cell bore the number 23. The Archbishop was in the last-but-one cell on the right, at the end of the corridor. He had the privilege of an iron bedstead. When he was not stretched out on it he was walking tirelessly up and down his cage, head bent, face sombre, indignant and bearing the tired expression of one whose belief in human decency had been gradually invaded by doubt. It was rather as if the slow poison of solitude and helplessness were preventing that good and pious man from retrieving his own inner calm by constantly facing him with the dark prospect of his approaching death.

Monseigneur Darboy was a deeply afflicted man. The lack of response to the many letters he had written to Monsieur Thiers, and his consequent sense of failure, had something to do with the indefinable air of sadness that hung about him. In his last message to the executive head of government the holy prelate, far from showing hostility to the Commune, had been so naïve and well-meaning as to propose exchanging a number of people detained by the Commune for Auguste Blanqui, who had been interned since 17th March. But the little shit with the polished chestnut head had answered with a brusque and categorical refusal.

So Monseigneur Darboy was being scorned by the dwarf in office, as well as unjustly maltreated by the Commune. What hope could he have, when even representations by the papal nuncio had had no effect whatsoever on the attitudes of that inflexible homunculus?

One cannot help wondering why such ferocious hostility should have been shown to a Church dignitary so signally lacking in influence, an archbishop whose voice was gentle (except on certain specific questions concerning the doctrine of papal infallibility). One cannot help wondering why there was so much perverse malevolence towards a man of the cloth who bothered no one apart from a few Vatican ideologues. And to pursue this line of reasoning, one cannot help wondering, either, what sort of rabid lunatic would have wanted to kill the Archbishop of Paris; who the devil *could* have wanted to commit the foul act of his execution, when everyone, from the politely astonished to the frankly indifferent, even the most intransigent fanatics, really favoured leaving the poor man alone.

Historians would tell us we weren't looking through the right side of the magnifying glass. Well, sorry! We abase ourselves! Obviously we should have looked closer, down in the dirt, instead of thinking in terms of everyday savagery! We should have seen that the truth of Monsieur Thiers's plans, carefully hidden behind a feigned apathy, was far more sordid and deeply calculated than his offhand attitude suggested.

The fact was that the respectable 'little man' *needed a corpse*. He needed a martyr, an important symbolic sacrificial victim. His well-being required the Commune to cut off a head of some importance. The populace must commit an iconoclastic, irreparable act that would place it once and for all in the butchers' camp, making everyone connected with the revolt subject to the vindictive legalist vengeance of triumphant respectability.

In a word, Monseigneur Darboy dead was worth more than Monseigneur Darboy living. His death would justify any repression, however cruel. The stunted executioner was opening the road to a landscape of bloodshed with cold, heartless logic.

While awaiting the great flurry of violence that was being prepared, let us return quietly to a few more details of the way the hostages of la Roquette were living in the greatest deprivation by following Ursule Capdebosc's narrative to Charles Bassicoussé.

Apart from the one occupied by the Archbishop of Paris, all the cells were double. They opened onto the same corridor. One was occupied by Deguerry, the *curé* of la Madeleine, sharing with Bonjean, the former President of the Supreme Court of Appeal; another by Fr Clerc and Fr Ducoudray, arrested at the Jesuits' house in rue Lhomond; a third by Fr Allard, chaplain of the ambulance service, sharing with Vicar-General Lagarde, imprisoned on 5th April.

The last cell in the hostages' area was occupied by Vicar-General Ségouret. It was the only cell without a number on the door. The Vicar-General was sharing his captivity with no one.

82

Abbé Ségouret's 'sin'

In the faint bluish light thrown by three widely spaced lamps, the weighty tread of a warder was approaching these rat-cages. He was pushing a trolley on which a basin of thin gruel steamed: wine-harvester's soup. It always contained cabbage. Cabbage, or a few bits of turnip.

Here in the drying-room (as it was familiarly called) the diet did not vary much. Of course the prison breviary never got tired of repeating that curates are *meant* to fast. That sky-pilots, monklets, black crows – call them what you will – think paradise is synonymous with famine. Might as well give them what they want. And the same rations for the archpointyhat of Notre-Dame and his attendant cassocks! It wouldn't do the bish and his deacons any harm to shit small turds. There was a sort of justice after all in their having to clash their teeth and lose a bit of weight. It would help reduce the bellies they had built up carousing over the years in their handsome palaces and well-appointed presbyteries! So it was no surprise that that sturdy pot-emptier, the cook at la Roquette, was starting them off on the road to heaven already.

With every turn of its wheels the trolley bearing the frugal evening meal gave a plaintive and discordant squeak, but the warder pushing its handles paid no attention as he clumped heavily along.

His outline was low and massive, his tread deliberate, his eye sunken and covetous, his jaw hollow and missing a row of teeth. He had heavy eyelids, a low forehead, a flattened skull. But of all these features, each more unattractive than the last, the most unforgettable was a pair of amphibian's eyes.

As he approached the cells, more, probably, from habit than from any special wish to be unkind, this hideous turnkey would invariably open a wide mouth, eject a stream of vile black tobacco-juice and call to the prisoners in a yapping voice:

'On yer feet in there, baldies! Time to feed the corpse!'

But before we accompany this fellow into the first of these cages to smell the acrid stench of mildew and damp, to see the state of physical dilapidation into which the detainees have fallen, to witness at last the size and aspect of the abbé Ségouret, to give some account of the course of his life and mention the torments of that servant of God, torn by the sufferings of a soul washed again and again but still tolerably unclean, I must ask to be allowed, in a process favoured by my illustrious forebears – revered Alexandre Dumas! Eugène Sue my brother almost! Beloved Victor Hugo! All who were not pale midgets or navel-gazers but workers with the pen, prolific renderers of feverish lines, frank recorders of life on its full scale – to interrupt the book, suspend time for a minute, open the gates of the future and draw your attention to the fact that the Eternal is always lurking in the furrows of the everyday.

So take a longer look at this repulsive turnkey. Come closer to this man who moves with the deliberate tread of an ox. Examine him closely, for although you have already come across him, he was perhaps insufficiently supplied with drama or mystery to have stayed in your memory. Look again, for this man whose earlier role was episodic – a small walk-on part – is soon to be given the much more gratifying and noteworthy task of messenger of destiny.

I invite you to recognise his features under the uniform of a prison warder, to identify this frog-like mask as the same distant descendant of the illustrious Scotsman John Law who had driven Antoine Tarpagnan, one foggy night not long ago, to the banks of the Ourcq.

In the space of a mere two months Gavin McDavis – of course you remember him now – had allowed himself to sink into alcoholic intemperance and general loathing of humankind. By now he detested the entire world. The requisition of his cab-horse for military uses, the desertion of his old camel of a wife after nine pregnancies to the braid-decked arms of a loafer whose yellow boots trotted up and down the boulevards, had turned the former cabbie into an utter wreck and brought him to his present sewer-like employment as a junior jailer.

He had become the nastiest piece of work you could possibly imagine. A listener to fear. An expert on cowardice. An eater of *curés*. He lurched on his ropy legs when he walked. He was taciturn and hated the law. His eyes were savage, his neck scarlet. He abhorred women. He was permanently caressing a vast anger against the human species. He was more fascinated than ever by violent death.

Here he comes, with the views ar i attitudes just described, a hideous ambassador of evil, pr￼ ￼t of apocalypse, preacher of threats. Here he comes. Stopping before each door, banging on the wood with a knotty fist: connoisseur of other people's afflictions, bird of ill omen.

He filled the bowls. Distributed bread. And to each captive, as usual, he handed out their ration of bad luck.

To Lagarde and Allard, he grated: 'The reactionaries bin givin' 'em a right goin' over all day long! They've took the National Guards by surprise on the Champ-de-Mars, shoved Dombrow-ski 'ere and there and fetched up at the town 'all of the 15th. They'll be arrivin' at Montparnasse any minute ... Not so good for you, that ain't. People're goin' to want to wring your necks!'

He spat out a black stream of tobacco juice and banged the door shut. The two Jesuits got a different refrain. 'Your mates ain't goin' to catch us bendin', don't you worry! They're forgettin' the people of Paris! My nine children's all at the barricades! *And* the workers ... they're buildin', pilin' up stones ... barrows everywhere ... earth, sandbags ... Walls are goin' up! Six-metre towers! Priests' blood's goin' to flow like water, mark my words ...'

As he ladled out the gruel for Bonjean and Deguerry, the warder let fly with some real, growling rage. 'The Chassepots're bangin' away! Machine guns spittin'! Cannons bustin' people's eardrums! Rue de Rivoli pourin' black smoke! But the red flag's still flyin'! The females is there an' all! Demolishin' the banks! *School*teachers're there instead of old church dames an' nuns! Worth every bit as much, too! Wenches made to straddle men! Rabid 'ores, like me missus! Them Versaillais won't get past without getting their stummicks scraped!'

By the time he reached Archbishop Darboy he had become calmer. He said confidingly: 'Your Monsieur Thiers keeps talkin' about justice, order and 'umanity but 'e's nowhere near lettin' yer out, Bish! From what I've 'eard, 'e's ready to let Paris burn if 'e 'as to! An' *another* thing they're sayin' is that for every one Communard that's shot, *three* bleedin' clerics can say ta-ta! *Startin' with bishops*!'

Monseigneur Darboy inclined his head sadly. He held his pastoral cross out to the grimacing warder and murmured in a calm resigned tone: 'Then I'll die, like Monseigneur Affre. And I'll die with his crucifix on my chest...'

On went the ignoble turnkey. Soon he would be clattering the enormous bolts of the ironbound door behind which was incarcerated the former parish priest of le Houga-d'Armagnac. He would give the prisoner his ration of black bread – a random hunk of brutal institutional stuff – along with his ladle of gruel and his crock of clear water for the night. Then, following the directives of Mr François, the governor of la Roquette, he would prod the verminous pallet with the point of his bayonet to make sure there were no shards of glass hidden there. And he would search the abbé down to the skin and take away the belt of his cassock to prevent him from hanging himself from the window bars – something he had threatened to do more than once – in one of the fits of insanity to which he was subject.

The heavy door was ready to creak open on its hinges. But as we know, that beastly screw liked to stretch the pleasure out and make it last. He liked to tease his customers a bit. He knew the intense hunger and thirst that gnawed at the vitals of those unfortunates, and tried to wring small coins out of them for the ladle of soup he was about to give them. 'On yer feet, Ségouret!' he cried. 'It's St Blow-Out's night tonight! I've saved yer a leaf of cabbage, mate. Like a bit, would yer?'

The horrible McDavis paused, sniggering, his hand on the

bolt. Do you recall now the cabbie's obsessive interest in crime and all its details, his pathological logorrhoea on the subject? His fascination with the behaviour of famous murderers? The way his unstoppable monologue had eventually caused the genial Tarpagnan to turn his back on the fellow?

Do not suppose – far from it – that the substitution of a warder's uniform for his cab-driver's blanket had reduced in any way our man's – our *sick* man's – devouring passion for the ghastly details of murder. The change from round hat to shako, from whip-handle to bayonet-hilt, had not reduced his deviant obsession in the slightest.

Drunk, cuckolded, nasty and lonely, he had become a shameless gatherer of blood-soaked stories, an expert on unusual eviscerations, a collector of perfect crimes. Simply to hear a first-hand account of the deeds of someone like the ignoble Tropp-man, or Hurledieu the Ripper, made him feel that life was worthwhile after all. He associated with a group of particularly ferocious and depraved drunks, firing-squad volunteers willing to shoot anyone and tumble them into a common grave for half a cup of coffee laced with brandy. Long untroubled by any hint of morality, he breathed deep of the world's misery and in his present job could fill out his enjoyment of ordinary murder with a morbid interest in the confessions of those about to die.

For he knew that on the threshold of the high jump men confess their sins; that the wish to die purified or the fear of divine retribution can make them admit things they have kept hidden for a lifetime.

McDavis's special interest in the door without a number dated from a very unusual scene that had occurred in great secrecy some time earlier, two days after the abbé Ségouret's arrest. The events had taken place during the night of 5th May, during a storm of exceptional violence whose imminence, and then its savagery, had set everyone's nerves on edge.

From out of the walls of the prison, from the dripping void of its stones, there had seeped gradually a sort of rumour, an uncertain feeling finding its way through the staircases, corridors and dungeons, at first impalpable rustlings like small natural tremors, the fluttering of frightened birds, the slither of wild animals in the dark. These almost soundless vibrations had slowly formed into panting breath and remote despairing cries, the long muffled moans of a broken voice in the distance: the despair of a man facing the tumult of a final loss of hope.

Of course the repellent turnkey's sensitive ear picked up the distant muffled concussions and uncommon groans as he made his nightly round of the damp and weeping entrails of the prison. They were so promising that at the end of his round McDavis had made his way to the cell from which they came: that of the recent prisoner. He had opened the door and entered.

The priest lay delirious with fever, his livid face illuminated by shuddering lightning-flashes. The Commune's Zouaves had maltreated him severely during his arrest, beating him about the face and genitals with rifle-butts. At least two of his facial bones were fractured. This frightening physiognomy seemed to float in an undulating fountain of light flashing from the open heavens. The *curé* lay delirious on his pallet with his one usable hand lifted imploringly, gripped by a sort of supernatural agitation. The storm was on his skin: his forehead was burning, his temples running with sweat.

Usually the sight of a dying person is touching in various ways, but on the night in question the abbé Ségouret's crazed condition, his bruised face and infected wounds, his bent, thin, sharp nose, his long crooked teeth and stunned, sleepless, bloodshot eyes would have aroused only the most invincible disgust in any normal person.

But these things – the newcomer's downfall, his wild state and the painful vibrations of his psychic despair – had almost the opposite effect on McDavis. The Scot's sparse brows knitted together. He felt not the slightest feeling of revulsion. Nor did he feel any compassion, or any desire to comfort the afflicted man by offering him water or binding his wounds. The impulse was more like curiosity. Not exactly sympathy, but a sort of attraction. He drew closer.

Standing over the couch of that unhappy madman whose gaunt arm flailed at the air, the abominable turnkey remained utterly motionless. McDavis was rooted to the spot with selfish happiness. He was in the right place at the right time for once in his life. For the first time in countless years, a smile slowly appeared on his face.

A smile! A breach in his ugliness, a rainbow blessing him in his disgrace! The way the lips peeled back from that wide and bottomless maw: that would have stopped your breath.

How strange are such unclean pleasures! Yet is is true that some individuals feel at home, or know that they are in the right place, only when plunging into foetid swamps or skirting infernal precipices. The former cabman quickly decided that he had been sent to the abbé Ségouret's bedside at a particular moment. That he had been mandated in some way by a supernatural entity to bear final witness, to receive the last confidences of a man burned out by remorse. That his destiny had been fixed long in advance, and he would not have been able to avoid this rendezvous with the flaming hoop of the last judgement.

The ugly creature stepped forward, gripped by the certainty that he had a pious duty to accomplish, and knelt at the raving cleric's bedside.

Outside, the storm continued to howl and sizzle, but McDavis hardly noticed it. He couldn't believe his luck: the Evil One, right before his eyes, twisted with pain!

The collector of assassins drank in the words of the afflicted priest. And as he deciphered and recomposed the disconnected phrases, the shreds of narrative, that fell from the delirious man's lips, the sombre Scot began to recognise the thread of tormented thought that visited and revisited old paths and old times, witnessing with terror and abomination the scene of a crime that had never stopped being relived by its author. He was, he really was, at the bedside of a murderer faced with the imminence of death and anxiously confessing his mortal sin to God.

He listened for hours in fascination, hypnotised by the terror-filled life of an assassin who sixteen years after his crime could still see the beseeching eyes of his victim as vividly as if it had occurred just the day before. He listened to every snippet of random delirium, absorbed the mad distracted words all intercut with exalted prayers. He imprisoned in his calloused hands the sufferer's fleshless wrists to stop him from clawing his cheeks and flinging his lousy and bleeding body about in hallucinated horror. With successive psychic jerks, McDavis shook the sufferer's word-bag empty and inhaled the odour of his fear. He registered from beginning to end a river of words that expressed heart-wringing terror and begged for forgiveness.

It was abominable to see, abominable to smell and to hear.

From time to time the priest crammed the filthy blanket into his scummy mouth to stifle his sobs. And eventually McDavis could see so clearly that the battle was unequal, that the white-winged angel really couldn't lose, that the Evil One would be vanquished unexpectedly this time, that that ignoble frequenter of zones of fear and anguish experienced a surge of supernatural joy.

Gavin McDavis started to tremble in all his limbs. Tears of happiness flowed unnoticed down cheeks furrowed by the injustices of life. His great ugliness cried out with sorrow and repentance, and that callous reptilian creature felt a terrifying wrench in the core of his being. Words jammed motionless in his throat, and in the silence of an immense struggle he understood at last the reason why his own obsession with crime had been made. He understood that the warp of destiny had accustomed him to the darkness because the confession he would one day be required to hear from the lips of a vicar of Christ would be too much for the strength of an ordinary man. He would have to be the repository of the most abominable thing there could possibly be on earth. Hyenas went chuckling by and he heard the hissing of squirming knots of snakes. He had to accept the weight of this uncommon confession because no man of God could cope with it, not even an archbishop. Because the sin was too serious. Because only Satan can forgive the murder of a child, the evisceration of a mother, the breakage of an oath to God!

Until the chalky dawn McDavis stayed at the sufferer's bedside, staring, until the words ran out, at the white flattened lips, silent now and gummed together, of that palpitating criminal who by tomorrow night would be burning in the eternal fires along with the putrid miasmas of his body and the vermin of his soul.

He had helped him at last to rest. To find a sort of comfort.

And when, with the first rays of the sun, the priest, having miraculously escaped death, slowly recovered consciousness, opened with astonishment blinking, reddened eyelids in a pale, pinched face collapsed with exhaustion and illness, and recognised that he was still alive from the presence of the grimacing turnkey, he gave a long, stricken cry and let his head fall back on the mattress.

Thus did Louis Désiré Charles Marie Ségouret, one-time *curé* of le Houga-d'Armagnac and murderer of Jeanne Roumazeille, timid white dove, and of his own son, come to understand that in a state of semi-consciousness he had just placed a soul damned in advance in the hands of Satan himself.

That same day he started to write his confession.

I have asked very little of you, reader, except that you believe me. I am a writer, after all. And although I recount the abbé Ségouret's confession to you without much feeling, I ask you now, above all, to have pity and compassion for McDavis, a poor creature on the margin of humanity, unloved, twisted of limb and ideas, who despite his passion for the sheen of dead flesh and the runny noses of murderers remains, behind the carrion-eater's plumage, a child of God sent to confront the full rigour of duty.

He approached the abbé, a man who continued daily to shed bitter tears of regret. His extreme ugliness deserved sympathy. He pushed open the cell door and raised the lantern to the level of his wrinkled forehead to illuminate the hole where the abbé Ségouret was sobbing on his knees in front of the window with its five herringbone-spiked iron bars.

The priest turned his face towards the jailer. He had small deep-set eyes, thick brows, a tangled thatch of greying hair. Cheeks hollow with insomnia. He spoke.

'Brother McDavis, did I speak last night?'

'Yes, Ségouret. Just like every night! Bleatin' as usual, Abbé!'

'Then be so good as to beat me.'

'How many?'

'Twelve. That's the very least. And don't give me any bread this evening.' Humbly, the priest removed his shirt and turned a back striped with lash-marks towards the Scotsman. 'Let us do penance,' he said.

McDavis beat him. Not with cruelty. Not with any pleasure or anger. But also without pity.

'That's all,' he said when he had finished. 'You owe me a bit more money.'

'Go and see Madame Capdebosc. Tell her you did something for me. I'll give you a signed chit.'

'Anything else?'

'Please. Did you see Madame Capdebosc yesterday?'

'I seen her. I give 'er your news. At her place I seen a geezer with grey eyes what go right through yer. He was lookin' for yer an' all.'

The abbé Ségouret started. 'Charles Bassicoussé!' he murmured. 'At last! Thank you, Lord, for hearing my prayer!'

'That's him, is it?' the turnkey asked.

'That is indeed he. Whom earthly justice condemned in my place.'

'D'you want me to talk to him?'

'No need,' the priest said, taking a letter from the rickety table. 'I've written to him. Just give him this on the evening of my death.'

83

Théophile Mirecourt's
last photo

The picks bashed away, and up came the cobbles. Paris had another exhausting night.

Under a threat-laden sky, the weapons had fallen silent for the moment. The Versaillais had interrupted their advance. No doubt their leaders were afraid of seeing the whole town going up in flames under their feet, quarter by quarter!

The insurgents laboured on by gaslight. As they worked through seven hours of silence each was brought face to face with the imminent prospect of a nightmare far worse than the bawling of artillery and the deluge of shells they had known so far. Not a single combatant was unaware that the next time would be the real thing, the final ordeal. That they were going to have to confront men directly and at close quarters. Hand-to-hand, the fiercest sort of fighting. Insurgents, athirst for the ideal, against other Frenchmen: sturdy Line troops, little riflemen bronzed by the Algerian sun.

Eyeball to eyeball. Using the rifle as a skewer. Straight in the guts! Victory or death.

The people had come at last to the tragic rendezvous.

Those who answered 'present!' at the roll-call were people who were tired of being hungry, and who knew that the cause of freedom had to be defended today. They possessed the courage of despair.

They were a crowd of exhausted and starving people. Flooding into the trenches and fixing bayonets, humble proletarians with hands deformed by labour. They had come to fight. They had been working until the last minute in their workshops and factories. They were a ragged and rough-looking lot.

But what good would it have done them to deck themselves out in Garibaldist cock-feather plumes and handsome leather accoutrements? Without the salary of a ministry pen-pusher you couldn't afford the luxury of poncing about all toffed up!

Anyway, when it came to turning the soldiery upside down, popinjay's trousers were worth just about as much as a dandy's detachable collar!

They all came. Cobblers, urchins, porters, pedlars, metal-workers, tinkers, fitters, cabinetmakers. They came from their gloomy homes, their four-sou apartments. Telling themselves that it was better to tremble before something truly terrible than to be cowardly and slavish.

One against ten. They were going to fight. From their lips fell words that were straight and just. They were accompanied by their wives and brats. Babies were legion among the ragged. Still sucking their mother's nipples. In the bottom of a trench, a hundred communers sat and lay chattering, living their lives and peering vigilantly into the darkness. A hundred metres away a group of children knelt around the eviscerated body of a horse, slicing off big chunks of meat.

An almost full battalion, weapons on right shoulders, billy-cans on their backs, bread on the ends of their bayonets, hurried towards the Church of the Trinity. Among these troops was Ziquet. He was wearing a bloodstained greatcoat the skirts of which had been hurriedly shortened with scissors. A thin smile appeared on his face. Yesterday, at Passy, he had fired his rifle point-blank into the head of a big devil of an officer coming at him with a sabre.

He was no longer playing at war. He was defending his life. Nothing remained of his childhood.

It was a long night. Everyone nervous, afraid. What was going on? Who was that advancing in the dark? A shadow only had to appear from a gateway for a worried-looking young girl holding a Chassepot, with a cartridge belt round her hips, to call down from the barricade: 'Halt, citizen! No one passes here!' Here in place Blanche a hundred and twenty Amazons were watching over Paris.

A night of meditation. Moments of hope cemented together by hatred. Exhausting periods of lookout spent trying to see what the enemy was up to. Just now, among the outposts at Batignolles, a sentry had been kidnapped by a Versaillais reconnaissance patrol.

'Vive la Commune!' the man cried. His comrades snatched up their weapons, but a moment later a volley sounded. They knew their friend lay dead at the foot of a wall.

Waiting. Senses tensed to breaking point. Intolerable stress that loosens the bowels and stiffens the legs. That makes people wonder whether they are really in that much of a hurry to sink their teeth into the dust.

People fidgeted. Cracked their fingers. The odour of earth and rot. A decomposing corpse? A drain? An eviscerated horse? There's nothing so gloomy as sniffing the shadows where death lies hidden.

Voices challenged:

'Who goes there?'

'Keep your distance!'

People searched for each other in the darkness. Counted each other.

Which way would they come? How many would they be? Clinchant's men. Ladmiraux's. Cissey's as well? A hundred and thirty thousand, they say.

We won't be more than ten thousand ourselves.

As the sky began to lighten just before dawn, all knew that they were going to march a bloody road. People took refuge for a time in their own thoughts. Charnel-house dreams, battle mincemeat, burned-out half-slumber. Sometimes at the hour of danger men instinctively turn in on themselves, journey in thought to their origins and birth, contemplating them once again with the wide eyes of a child. For many, this opportunity is a singularly beautiful, fresh and unusual experience.

One man lights a clay pipe. Another consults an old letter from his mother. A third, thinking of his home village, gazes into the distance while bandaging his feet. Someone else is sewing a button back on.

The youngest distinctly hears sobbing. The most self-possessed raises his eyes to an open window in which a girl's face can be seen. A husband unfolds a cloth on a table of cobblestones, and spoons up the soup that his wife has just brought him.

A worried individual counts and recounts the barricade contingent. There will be thirty-seven of them to stop the tidal wave of Line troops. Thirty-seven, including two boys of thirteen and fifteen.

People were steeling themselves, resigning themselves. They had the courage of self-respect. Bent over the soil, still digging up a few cobbles and sinking trenches a little deeper. The promise of the imminent attack made even the bravest nervous.

Who was the idiot who had just claimed he'd heard a linnet singing in a copse?

The entire street population had been navvying. The last trees were on their sides. With pickaxes, sledgehammers, crowbars, spades, mattocks, everything had been turned over. Workmen, mugs, fine gents in suits, women in rags, local spinsters, had dug ditches for the shells to fall into. Mattresses thrown from top-floor windows were woven into defences bristling with iron bedsteads, desks, hastily laid stones and overturned wagons.

Palmyre, the pretty midget, had been working without respite on the barricades at Batignolles. Her hands were bleeding. She looked at her palms and licked them gently. She turned to her neighbour, a long tall fellow with a wrinkled face who had been bricklaying for four hours, and said:

'Bung us a swig of plonk, citizen.'

While she took a rest and a drink her spirit flew to Tarpagnan's side. Where was her hero now? Where was her handsome dullard? Had he again become the dashing officer he should never have stopped being? What storm of smoke and shrapnel was he advancing into? At whose chest was he pointing his sword? It was said that battle had been joined over by the Panthéon.

O God, she murmured to herself, how I want him to survive! The awful thing with me is that I still love him!

The faces all around her were long. There wasn't a single four-bar officer to command the redoubt.

The place Pigalle was occupied by women. Valiant little sisters, soldiers in skirts, full of martial ardour! How beautiful they were in their pride and anger!

They posed for a photographer. Formed up in a group and smiled at Théophile Mirecourt's lens. Through the beautiful ground-glass viewplate of his marvellous portable apparatus he focused on them: the Photo Gent, the first photojournalist. A man ahead of his time.

Another cheery group of women combatants camped in the rue des Carrières. They wore Phrygian bonnets. Stood in front of the barricade. One had a child on her hip, a rifle on her shoulder. A noisy comedienne with a revolver in her belt was wearing a waitress's skirt and a soldier's tunic. The other matrons, ugly or comely, wolfish or sly, were all armed with Enfield carbines.

Behind them, twenty guardsmen watched from the top of the barricade.

The sound of running footsteps made everyone turn. A troop of fleeing combatants had appeared at the entrance to a courtyard. Their faces were blackened with powder, some had lost their ammunition pouches, at least two had slight wounds.

They were greeted with cries by the insurgents. They came up to the barricade.

'Where've you come from, my fine fellows?' asked a woman wearing trousers. She walked rapidly across and gave the wounded men first aid. Her face showed great determination.

'We've been jumping over walls! We were firing, now we've fallen back.'

'They're advancing!'

'I come from round here,' said a young fellow with a head-band over one eye.

'Where're the rest of you from?'

'All over the place! The factories! Montmartre!'

'Clinchant's coming! He's advancing through Batignolles. Malon won't be able to hold out for long.'

'So that's it then, is it?' an old man said. 'We're going to get it good and proper, eh?'

'Yer. They're coming from every direction! Thirty thousand on the north side. Seems they're just swamping the ramparts! They're taking all the gates and going round the Butte.'

'Well, we're going to be ready for them!'

A little way off, the insatiable photographer eyed the strengthening light with approval. A last shot before making war! He started getting the apparatus ready. He had spent the previous evening with Tarpagnan. This evening the two friends were going to meet at Laveur's in the rue des Poitevins to dine with Jules Vallès.

Théo – too-handsome Théo – was sharing his last laughing thoughts with a young mother cradling her child. He joked politely that he too had had a mother and had loved her very much. Théophile laughed happily. Under his photographer's cloth he felt as happy and secure as under his own mother's skirts. He could inspect the beauty of the world in all its forms. Maternal love.

The young woman leaned over the wicker basket in which her baby was whimpering. She brought her pretty eighteen-year-old's face close to the child and gave him a plaything, a brass rattle. The nipper started to shout. He was letting it be known that his stomach felt hollow. The little creature puffed out his cheeks, waved his small wrinkled fingers and demanded a bite to eat. A fat lot he cared for impending battles or whistling bullets!

A child of the poor is hungry every day. Even behind a barricade. The saucy beauty took out her breast and picked up the child. She helped the baby with her hand. Milk ran.

Exposure ten seconds ... the sky was clean and blue. The subject centred. The photographer adjusted the focus. How beautiful life would be after the war! A whole song of words rolled around inside Mirecourt's head. Although he didn't know it, he was breathing his last oxygen. He brushed a rebellious strand of hair off his forehead. The tongue in his mouth was shaping its last syllables.

He placed his thumb and forefinger on the brass lens-cap, prepared to let the light into his dark box to fix the blessed moment of ephemeral grace. The radiantly pretty young mother gave the nipple to her son. She did it unceremoniously.

Ninon. Or Justine. Or Léonie or Seraphine. Théo would never know the little darling's name.

(Just a minute there, please, gunners! Life's just about to be smashed, so wait a few seconds so that it can be made eternal!)

From the barricade the rough-faced guardsmen smiled in their beards. They were enjoying the spectacle of harmony. They smiled at the baby, that pink scrap of flesh drinking with such appetite. At the bead of milk at the corner of his gluttonous lips. At the young mother caressing the perfect roundness of the little skull so new and soft. And of course they were moved by the velvety living globe of Ninon's breast – or Seraphine's, or Julie's.

Three seconds more! Three seconds, and Théophile would have captured the mystery of beauty! Two seconds! One more second, one last and infinitesimal division of eternity, and he'd have that precious image graven on the sensitive plate ...

Alas! Things don't always work out the way we want them to. The way anyone would want them to, even – if they knew what was going to happen – the crew of the gun not far from there, its elevation set to three hundred metres. The breech slammed shut. The gunner sergeant grasped the lanyard.

Fire! In the blink of an eye all is redrawn. A shell ripped whistling through the air and exploded gouging a deep crater. Earth rose effortlessly high, fell back to the ground, and it was all over. Drops of blood.

Théophile lay on his back, eyes open, staring at the sky. Earth on his eyeballs. His apparatus, his magnificent invention for looking at people, smashed to pieces.

The little mama, ah! the little mama, dead. Still smiling. Her eyes still gentle under the fringe of lashes but showing small glints of something colder and sterner.

The baby was still breathing.

A moment later Clinchant's men came charging up the avenue de Clichy. The twenty guardsmen defended themselves, fired until their rifle barrels were hot. Their tears dried up by rage.

Red-eyed, they were going to keep firing. They would fire on the Versaillais until the stench of powder in their nostrils made them sick. In their blind rage they would remember that men had been made to work a seventeen-hour day laying track for the Northern railway, that meat cost three francs sixty a kilo and that in their youth their fiancées' breasts had been as sweet and proud as Marion's, new-flowered like roses in May.

A clamour to put the wind up anyone, bullets slapping and zipping, ricocheting around and knocking chunks out of the mattresses. One hit a barrel of powder. In a vast slow white flash across the whole front of a building it went up bringing down a wall.

Everyone was going mad. Some in a clatter of hobnailed boots vaulted the parapet and ran straight at the enemy with animal yells. They wanted to use cold steel. More ferocious than you could imagine. Machine cannon stuttered in the background, their storms of bullets sending grey chips flying.

The rest of the defenders clung to their entrenchments. Ladmirault's troops had come round the other side of Montmartre cemetery and they were now caught between two lines of fire. The women and the surviving guards would not surrender.

The Versaillais shot them down without pity.

When it was all over, the victors crossed the road without speaking. Stepped over the bodies. The baby cried a bit and then fell silent. With a loud cracking sound a soldier stepped on a photographic plate.

In the wine shop on the corner, the soldiers sent to restore order stood drinking at the bar with a strange feeling that they were in a dream. A young child stood near them trying to light a pipe.

In the distance, a bugle sounded another charge.

84

Dirty hands and
clean hearts

The barricade in place Blanche had just been taken. Most of the Amazons had been massacred. Louise Michel backed by Elisabeth Dmitrieff had led the resistance there until the very end. Exhausted from fighting, the 'Red Virgin' had collapsed half senseless into a trench on the Clignancourt road, and had been left there for dead.

Her captured companions were being insulted and slandered by the cruel, cowardly, ignoble and fickle crowd. The children were particularly vicious, hurling stones at them.

Adelaïde Fontieu was taken prisoner. She walked along in the exhausted troupe of woman combatants, her little Amazon's hat down over her eyes. She looked into the distance, caught no one's eye. But in the rue Girardon a concierge recognised her. The porteress came out of her lodge, crossed the road and approached, full of sick and malevolent curiosity. She tore Adelaïde's hat from her head and squawked:

'Slut! Whore! Shoot her! Shoot her! Bloody tart!'

Poor Adelaïde was shoved forward with a thump in the kidneys from a rifle-butt.

The survivors from the place Blanche tried to regroup and resist at the entrance to the boulevard Magenta. Winkled out once more by the Line, not a single woman survived this time. Jeanne Couerbe died with a bullet through the forehead. Léonce and her daughter Marion died alongside her, weapons in their hands. So did Blanche the glove-maker. And so did Guillaume Tironneau's mother, still wearing her apron.

Palmyre, sole survivor of the butchery at Batignolles, was grinding her teeth. Shame showed in her face. She was crouching in a sort of kennel made of piled-up cobblestones, where a soldier had confined her as a joke, and thinking of Tarpagnan. She was trying to remove the dog's collar that the old sweat had fastened round her neck, and wiping other people's spit off her face. What can you call love, when you are so small?

The Versaillais climbed the Butte by rue Lepic. At noon one of them raised the tricolour on the Solférino tower. The guns of 18th March, the hundreds of artillery pieces on the Polish field, had been useless. For lack of crews, and for lack of ammunition, they had stayed silent.

At one o'clock La Cécilia, still skirmishing with a hundred men from behind the fragile protection of earth banks being worn away by enemy fire, had the retreat sounded.

Montmartre town hall was occupied. And with the Versaillais staff HQ established on the Butte, the large-scale massacres could begin.

The first victims were shot for nothing, shot on their knees: forty-three men, three women and four children. Shot at number 6, rue des Rosiers, at the bottom of the garden. Shot in memory of General Lecomte. In his honour. May his soul rest in peace!

Then the Communards, then their sympathisers, then those suspected of being sympathisers. Anyone with black hands, anyone slow to disclose his identity: up against the nearest wall. People who believed Blanqui, who believed in fables about freedom, equality of opportunity, decent wages.

People who were hungry. People who wore cockades. People who had cartridges in their pockets. Riddled, all of them, women, brats, loonies, drunks – anyone – riddled with bullets in Montmartre cemetery. In the parc Monceau. At Château-Rouge.

To the abattoir! To heel!

And after that, reds! Socialists! The International! Deserters ... tally-ho! Everywhere the scum who volunteer for firing squads did their filthy work.

The stripped victims lay everywhere asprawl on pavements, in the road, in workshops. Shot the defenders of Batignolles, shot someone who just happened to be there, shot Adelaïde Fontieu, the pretty mealticket with the blue eyes.

Her little hand mutilated by a sabre cut. Holes poked in her dead body with the sharp ferrules of umbrellas and walking sticks. Her skirts raised by salacious old women, her belly ransacked by crazed concierges.

A strange thing, the human heart. Very strange sometimes.

PART 7

A TIME OF BLOOD

85

The Pole

Up in flames! Off the rails! Left Bank, Right Bank: red
everywhere. The sky shook to artillery fire. Skulls stove in by
the *coup de grâce*. Stray bullets forced wavering passages through
the hot air posing a constant random threat, whirring alarmingly
overhead or without warning stamping the star of death on
someone's forehead.

Tarpagnan had not slept for two days. Since the withdrawal of
21st May he had stayed with Dombrowski, who still had no
command. Through the twists and turns of a desperate situation
he had followed the General in company with a handful of other
survivors from Passy, who believed as he did in the courage of
that exceptional leader of men.

When the Gascon had requested the honour of working
directly under his orders the Pole had fixed him with a piercing
blue gaze, and a thin smile had lifted one corner of the delicate
mouth in the icy white face. He stroked his wispy little pointed
beard and said:

'Are you aware, Major, that my aides-de-camp last just three
days on average?'

'I think I can do better, General,' Antoine said smilingly.

'Well then, jump on your horse! Young Berthier who had the
job last died not half an hour ago from a row of machine-gun
bullets right through the heart. Don't hestitate!'

'You mean you're taking me on as aide-de-camp, sir?'

'I mean you're getting on my nerves standing around gawping
in front of the sacristy door, comrade!'

'Where shall I go, General?'

'Start with the rue des Dames. I want a report on the situation of that barricade. After that we'll jump over to Condamine, they're having rather a bad time there ... I've been asked for reinforcements by Jaclard ... there are more stretchers there than people to carry them!'

The whole town was under a giant whirlwind, a hurricane. Yawning craters, black smoke! The drama of it, the horror!

Paris was ablaze. The Luxembourg powder magazine had blown up. The Tuileries, the Palais-Royal, the Ministry of Finance were all in flames. The landmarks had vanished and the compass didn't work properly. For two days now they had been navigating by dead reckoning and line of sight through the storm that was carrying the revolution away. Tossed back and forth across Paris, devoted to a lost cause, they continued to act with the fervour of men going to their death without hatred for their killers, just with regret for the beautiful, the luminous face of the freedom that had been defiled, repossessed, humiliated, trampled, defamed and finally, betrayed.

From one hot spot to another, answerable to no one and belonging to no formally constituted group, they galloped madly about – a dozen men, lying along their horses' necks – restoring spirits here, regrouping the men there, doing everything they could to help the federals, surging out of grey smoke and shrapnel to hold the line in desperate situations, always ready to contribute the boldness or unexpectedness of their charge to the shifting fortunes of an improvised battle, always ready to cover the retreat of insurgents fleeing in disorder.

This game kept our Gascon friend pretty happy. He quickly became, as Jules Vallès had predicted, a hard-core rebel. The very sight of troops scattering, or of an undefended barricade, made him feel that he had been forged for the task of maintaining honour. He thus found Dombrowski's exceptional stature very much to his taste. Since he himself had nothing more to lose, the General's example of bravura and insane courage was a model that suited him very well.

Sometimes, in the middle of fighting, the Gascon would hear a cry of rage – one so raw that it gave you gooseflesh to hear it. He knew that it came from the Pole, and his heart would thump madly. The next moment he would see him galloping past on his black stallion, lying forward along the animal's neck, sabre extended before him, racing ahead into the thick of the hand-to-hand fighting. He would lose sight of him for a moment, then come across him again, his horse rearing amid the smoke of burning ruins, the shadow of a desperate hero.

Then it would be Tarpagnan's turn to put spurs to his horse. He would skim close across the battlefield, reinventing its contours, passing through shrapnel and ashy fragments still marked with red. He would place himself at Dombrowski's side. Then together, with identical dash, coming at the enemy gun crews from behind, ignoring their own rank, placing themselves at physical risk like young conscripts, taking sentries by surprise, unhorsing officers, crossing swords with exaggerated vigour, cutting throats, stabbing chests, proving to all that the temper of steel is only tested in a furnace.

So did Tarpagnan live, a man awaiting death, the shadow of his model.

And so lived Dombrowski, a general without an army, who kept charging in defiance of reason, who went among storms of bullets with some thought in the back of his mind of exposing himself to them. As if, revolted and reduced to despair by the charge of treason that had earlier been levelled against him, the man who rode a black stallion, who dressed in black tunic and trousers, was trying to reach the star of his last dwelling. As if he was seeking death in the fire of action.

His eyes were alive. His heart beat strongly. But the soul was broken within him.

86

Brief encounter

That morning, after a reconnaissance to try to gauge Ladmir-ault's positions, and just as if there were still some hope of restoring the military situation in the north of the capital, Dombrowski had decided to obey Delescluze's last order to him to 'do what he could' by taking his little troop of a hundred men and attempting to join Vermorel, who was taking heavy fire from all directions on the barricades in rue des Poissonniers and rue Myrrha.

Tarpagnan left at a flat-out gallop to scout the intervening terrain.

Paris presented a nightmare spectacle: streets cratered and dug up, houses severely damaged by artillery, façades chipped and pockmarked by bullets. The pavements were strewn with objects thrown from windows during the night by owners suddenly afraid of being executed: uniforms, cartridges, ammo-pouches, even rifles. There were bodies in the streets too.

From time to time, the frightened face of a civilian would look out from a gateway opening. Doors would close hastily as the officer passed at a gallop. Civilians, cowards, Thiers supporters, whole families complete with dogs, nurses and money-boxes, had gone to earth in their cellars. They were lying low and awaiting the defeat of the Commune.

At a crossing of two avenues the horse jinked and stumbled, two of its shoes skidding on the wood-block road surface, the others in a shower of sparks catching the kerbstone as the animal fell, sending its rider heavily into the dust.

Before he could get up, Tarpagnan heard a bullet pass very close to his head. It ricocheted yowling off the pavement and then a nearby wall. Antoine spotted the shooter: a citizen peering from behind his third-floor shutters. Doubtless the fellow deemed it safe now to go over to the enemy, and hoped to curry favour by shooting a Communard in the back from his window.

Tarpagnan turned away in contempt and gathered up the reins of his mount, which had got back on its feet. As so often in very risky situations, when one's life hangs on the hazard of the passing moment, he had become light-headed, with a kind of indifference to death. He jumped back on the horse.

Mitat Cyrano, mitat d'Artagnan. The Gascon *gouyat* coming alive within him, Antoine put his spurs to the animal and leaned along its neck on the side away from the citizen sniper. As he galloped round the corner another bullet zipped past like an angry wasp. He reined in, jumped to the ground and drew his revolver, dropping to one knee.

Close beside him was the body of an elderly man with a white beard, dressed in a federal's tunic. The man lay in a pool of blood but otherwise appeared to have fallen asleep, his pipe still in his mouth. He was one of the veterans Tarpagnan had seen in the place de l'Hôtel-de-Ville two months earlier, but the Major did not even try to identify him. He had spotted the guardsman's Chassepot lying a few paces away on the pavement.

He crawled to the corner of the building and reached out a cautious hand for the rifle. The third-floor sniper sent him yet another ball.

At that moment in a clopping of hooves and creaking of wheels there appeared down the deserted avenue an old screw of a horse hauling a strange vehicle.

The nag moved slowly along in a sort of general flailing of limbs, hooves shooting out in all directions as if walking on polished ice or attempting to learn a complicated dance step. The animal's belly was sucked in with effort, and at every step its labouring lungs wheezed out a curious sound, somewhere between coach-horn and bagpipes, a gasping so unusual that Tarpagnan turned his head to see what was causing it.

He caught the nag's crazed eye and perceived that the asthmatic beast was hauling a van full of coffins, on top of which were piled fresher bodies stacked, for lack of boxes, head to toe:

dislocated, cut, sprawling, open-eyed, their hands swinging, joined together only by the sluggish streams of their blood.

The jalopy's roof was covered by a black canopy with silver teardrops. On either side was fixed a white cloth bearing a red cross, showing that this funeral chariot, once again performing its primary function, had at one time been turned into an ambulance. This morning, bearing four red flags draped with black crepe, it was serving as the tumbril of the Commune's damned, loaded with more than twenty corpses and rolling towards the Lariboisière cemetery amid a vast and hideous stench.

When the vehicle reached the officer its driver, a black raven dressed as an undertaker, hauled on the bit of his old mare and brought the mobile cemetery to a halt. From the box he raised his hat, greeted Tarpagnan in ceremonious style and grated out in a strange gargling voice:

'My respects, officer! I'm responsible for clearing up the fallen, and with your permission we'd like – the princess and me that is – to relieve you of your neighbour there, who don't look too fresh and must whiff a bit severe.'

'I'm grateful, my good fellow, but I'd prefer it if you'd pass me that Chassepot on the pavement there, and help me deal with the so-and-so who's shooting at me from his window.'

The dead men's chauffeur looked up. He showed not the slightest alarm, but waved an ape-like arm in the direction of the house-fronts and stifled an immense yawn. 'Ah, Christ Almighty!' he cried, 'not another one taking potshots! Since the red-pants got here the ugly lard-arses of reaction's been growin' braver by the minute!'

The man turned towards the figure seated beside him, swathed from head to foot in a black shawl and apparently asleep. He dug an unceremonious elbow into the figure's stomach. 'Hey, princess!' he scolded, 'get yer tits moving, we got work to do! Here's another wants to poke us in the eye! Forgive us for being so knackered,' he added to Tarpagnan, rubbing red-rimmed eyes, 'but since yesterday my assistant Miss Pucci here, my mare Cécile you see there, and meself – Alphonse Pouffard, at your service – we've collected up so many corpses, dead'uns and stiffs that we don't hardly know if we're alive or dead ourselves...'

On hearing the name of the woman he had loved so much, Tarpagnan climbed to his feet. Gabriella had recognised her handsome friend from 18th March, and now lifted the shawl from her face. Two magnificent sepia-ringed eyes directed a warm and shadowy flash at the Gascon, a look without passion or regret, from an inscrutable sun-tanned face.

Antoine struggled with a suffocating sensation. How could it have been otherwise? If he had had to describe his mental state, he would have said that it was dominated by the drunkenness of a waking dream.

Caf'conc' was looking down and waiting for her interior calm to return. Her heart beat wildly. She took slow, deep breaths. After a moment or two she folded her arms firmly across her stomach, and discovered a capacity for glacial cold within herself. She was amazed and saddened by this unexpected encounter, by the way it confirmed how impossible it was to resume ... what had once been. She knew she was a different person now, that she belonged to another world.

Tarpagnan meanwhile was reading the new face of his beloved. What he saw there was a sort of feverish energy. A remoteness of the mind and spirit. Adieu, insouciance! Withered, the lightness of loving. Gone for ever, smiling lips.

'Hello, Gabriella,' he said in a neutral voice. He realised as he spoke that he was no longer governed by her.

'Hello, Antoine,' she replied, repressing deep within her what was after all merely the illusion of a weak chemical pleasure.

Unaware of what was going on, Alphonse Pouffard climbed down from the box and with his foot shoved the rifle towards the officer. A few more seconds passed, further widening the gap between the lovers. Antoine knew that time cannot be bought.

'I was still waiting for you, in a way. I knew you'd come,' he said, in the manner of one repeating an old refrain.

Gabriella trembled, her mouth dry. 'It's much too late,' she replied. 'You know that as well as I do.'

'I searched for you everywhere,' he murmured.

'Don't say a single word to me about love,' she gasped, choking back a sob.

''Ere, cit'zen officer!' Pouffard exploded suddenly, having registered the nature of their dialogue. ''Scuse *me* if I cork yer bagpipes for yer, but it seems to me yer insinueratin' some pretty funny wordage in me princess's ears!'

Antoine's fists clenched. He looked the undertaker up and down, smelt the winewash reek of his breath. 'Is the citizeness your woman?' he demanded icily through gritted teeth. He didn't even dare to look at Gabriella any more. Pouffard smiled with justifiable pride.

'Woman and dogsbody both!' he boasted. 'The princess is all that and more! When you start down that road under heaven, you got to go all the way! We're fastened to each other by the dead. Only a bullet through the head can separate us!'

Tarpagnan inclined his head sadly. So stifled was he by pain. He looked up. The lovers looked into each other's eyes for the last time. The distance between them had grown so great that a vertiginous pit seemed to have opened at their feet. Tarpagnan picked up the rifle.

Gabriella's eyes were misted over with tears. She seemed to struggle for a moment with her inability to speak. Then without a word to either of the men she stuck an emaciated forearm out from under her black cloak, seized the reins and gave the mare several sharp cuts with the whip to force her into a trot.

Cécile, who was unused to such treatment, let out an indignant whinny and clattered lopsidedly away towards the middle of the junction.

Alphonse Pouffard's eyes opened wide with incredulity. For a moment he watched the vanload of corpses drawing rapidly away. Then he set off in frantic, ill-coordinated pursuit of the vehicle, in which the lifeless bodies were now dancing and waving their limbs. As Pouffard reached the middle of the place a shutter on the third floor opened, and a shot rang out. The undertaker's course wavered, and he stopped. He put a hand to his stomach. He swayed and turned, grimacing, towards Tarpagnan. 'Did you know her?' he called.

'Better than that. I loved her!'

'Love?'

Pouffard looked confused. His eyes were veiled by something that made it very difficult to see. Frowning, he fell to the ground.

At the same moment Tarpagnan got the bourgeois nicely lined up in his sights. Dressed in a waistcoat, the man was leaning over his balcony, calling to his family and laughing. His wife hung back, but three handsome children had already joined their father outside the window when Antoine's rifle bullet caught him full in the forehead.

87

A clear gaze extinguished,
a fist raised

On the stroke of midday Tarpagnan reached the barricade at the junction of the rue Myrrha with the Poissonniers. Things were critical there. He told the defenders that General Dombrowski would be there soon. They laughed in his face.

He went to the forward post of the barricade and re-raised the red flag which had just been carried away by shot.

A young boy surged up beside him. An angelic freckled face, a kid of about twelve, a charming urchin, still growing up inside a man's tunic. Firing without a pause, his rifle burning his hands. While reloading his weapon the cheeky sparrow kept talking, as if to show that no one could put anything past him.

'*Vive la Commune!*' he yelped. 'Come an' get us, yer bunch of no-goods! We'll sting yer good an' proper!' Bullets or boastful words, the barefoot magazine contains all the munitions ... Nothing is wasted.

The boy came up to the parapet, hair tousled into a wild mop, the picture of heroism. From time to time he turned to scold a line of civilians, sons of Prudhomme, scurvy fellows in waist-coats who were hanging about the foot of the barricade, tired and discouraged.

'Come on up 'ere, yer bunch of slackers! *If* it ain't too much bleedin', trouble! They're stokin' up their machines again!'

In fact the machine cannon were sending up puffs of dust scattered with golden points of fire. You had to keep your head well down.

The courageous youth fed a new cartridge into the chamber of his rifle. He was becoming enraged, uttering carter's oaths that sounded incongruous in his still-childish voice. Comic enormities emerged as he yelled insults at the enemy officers. When he had finished insulting them he called them out in the manner of one calling poultry to be fed, whistled through a rolled-up tongue, and also yelled: 'Ow! Aieee! Shit!' having burned his fingers on the barrel of the weapon.

He slapped his forehead with his fingers, weighed his ammo-pouch in his hand. His gestures were vivid. He was enraged, ferocious amid the rough-and-tumble of war.

Tarpagnan held him down under cover from the next burst.

'What's your name?' he yelled over the din.

'Alexis Ramier,' the kid replied. 'Ward of the Commune! And I know what I'm doing!' He extracted himself from Tarpagnan's grasp and added proudly: 'My pals have made me a captain!'

He fired. The butt of the weapon thumped into his small bruised shoulder, and he landed bouncing in a seated position. He climbed back on his feet and was enveloped in a cloud of wood splinters.

'Brothel shit! Bunch of bastard idiots! 'Ere's another one for yer!'

He fired again.

Suddenly the boy seemed to have St Vitus's dance. There was a hole in his chest. He weaved jerking for a moment under his feathered hat, a Dervish with a look of astonishment on his face, and fell on his side, dead.

An old fellow with a bare head moved his body out of the way. He didn't say a word, but replaced the boy at the loophole. He looked across at Tarpagnan, who was taking aim at the enemy, and said simply:

'I'm an old soldier of the Universal Republic. I fought in '48 and now it seems I'm dying in '71. There's hardly any time left for politics, don't you think, citizen?'

He fired. The old federal was fighting. There were several others too, a handful, still there shoulder-to-shoulder.

When Dombrowski arrived at half-past midday he was accompanied by Vermorel, just back from boulevard d'Ornano where he had been setting up small field artillery. A middle-aged woman called Marie-Eugénie Rousseau, who was busy cooling Chassepots by dipping them in a horse trough, ran forward when she saw them to get close to the General, whose horse was prancing among the flying bullets. She brought him to the attention of a group of combatants who were retreating in disorder, and made sure that he was cheered. So encouraging was his presence that these defeated people, who came from the quarries of Montmartre, from Château-Rouge and the Clignancourt road, rallied their spirits and helped defend the barricade.

Marie-Eugénie Rousseau was a hairdresser. She had been mobilising the local inhabitants all morning. She had gone out under fire at least three times to collect rifles belonging to the dead. Now, indifferent to the zipping bullets, she walked towards Dombrowski – a fine sitting target on his black horse – and called out to him: 'Get down, General! You're goin' to get yerself topped!'

In fact Dombrowski's horse had already been hit several times. Without undue haste he dismounted, and the animal collapsed on its knees. With long, measured strides he crossed the rue Myrrha towards Tarpagnan. Bullets and shrapnel lashed down all around him.

'What's the position?' he asked his aide-de-camp.

From his vantage point Antoine again surveyed the movements of the Versaillais. A battery of six guns was almost in position on the Clignancourt road and would soon be able to pour enfilade fire down the street.

'They're getting ready to charge. It won't be long now.'

He saw the contempt for death in Dombrowski's eyes as he turned to go back across the road. Suddenly, the Pole stopped and dropped to one knee. A little blood reddened his lips. He turned to Tarpagnan and said in a controlled voice: 'You should hold out as long as you can. As long as your energy lasts. I'm counting on you.' Then he vomited onto the ground. Between two heaves he uttered his last words:

'They actually said I *betrayed* them!'

The bystanders rushed to help the wounded man, and carried him hastily into a nearby pharmacy. Dombrowski's head hanging backwards, his colour chalky, one hand trailing along the ground: that was Tarpagnan's last sight of a man he had thought somehow proof against bullets.

Blood on white lips! The immense murmur of voices! The images of misfortune are too vivid to be erased!

Antoine was left alone, face to face with himself. Now that the time had come, he felt calm. He suited his role. In the face of his share of peril, everything bedded down cleanly. Everything moved at the correct tempo. The blood pounded in his temples. One thing leading to another! And all going so fast! Well, go on then! he thought. Why be concerned with the gravity of steps taken long ago?

Only the present makes the future of the world.

Major Tarpagnan turned towards the defenders of the bastion and cried: 'Dombrowski asked us to stay and fight. How many are we?'

They all replied that they were there. They moved up to the barricade, naturally. They were going to make the 45th line regiment come at them with bayonets. The Social State wasn't going to retreat. This was their quarter and they were defending it. They knew that some of them only had a few more minutes in which to go through the motions of life.

They massed behind a metre-high wall of cobblestones and bedsteads. Let them come! Let them come here! We'll cut the Line to ribbons! Sting into the thick of them!

They started firing.

Fire and flame! The artillery answered with a torrent of roaring concussions. Man chutney! Carnage on display! Eviscerated mattresses spat kapok into the air. Bullets smacked into the flesh of dead horses. Horror upon horror! The spine-chilling screams of the wounded intercut with cries of rage from the living. Unbelievably loud, the yapping and ringing of metal.

Another five long minutes, and the running Versailles soldiery were bearing down on the last defenders of the redoubt. Now they were going to be in it, right in it up to here. Bleeding mincemeat. Boots slipping in man-juice.

An infantryman raised his bayonet at Tarpagnan who had run out of ammunition. Death stared him in the face. He parried the blow with his *makhila*. Yes! The cudgel held good. But it wasn't over. The soldier raised his rifle and fixed bayonet high above his head once more to skewer the man sprawling in front of him.

This was going to be it: no more light, nothing but smoking bowels. Come on then! Get it over with! Tarpagnan filled his lungs with life one last time, awaiting the blow and death. He loosed a yell.

Suddenly he felt himself jerked backwards, rolling like a rag-doll. A big devil surged out of a squall of black smoke, snatched him away from the promised bayoneting, lifted him as easily as if he had been a kitten, lumbered rapidly away through the forest of bayonets carrying Tarpagnan helpless under one arm, and after a bruising gallop put him down safe and sound at the corner of a ruin some distance away: breathless, panting, humiliated to find himself still alive, and without a scratch.

For some time, sitting on a stone half-furious and half-grateful, Antoine was too out of breath to speak. He looked at the man who had just set him down and who was now regarding him with mountainous calm, creamy sweetness and bear-like affection.

Memories flooded back. Tarpagnan thumped the colossus affectionately in the stomach and said at last: 'Thank you, my dear Marbuche, with all my heart!'

He leapt to his feet. Skipped a little. Gazed up at the light, patted the giant's bald skull and exclaimed: 'The trouble with me is that I come back to life so quickly! Come with me, please, comrade! If there's a single restaurant left open in Paris, I know which one it'll be! And I'll buy you a decent meal!'

A hundred metres away a volley sounded. The Versaillais were finishing off the survivors. The officer commanding the firing squad was an up-and-coming captain, still christening his new bars.

His name was Arnaud Desétoiles.

88

Freeze frame

Let us return to the Left Bank where we left Horace Grondin.
How resolute and sure of himself he seemed on that evening of
23 May! With a confident tread he emerged from the maze of
small streets beside the church of St Julian the Poor – rue
Fouarre, rue Galante – alleyways with a glittering scholarly past,
filled with one-time students' eating-houses and lodgings, leading out of the rue de la Bûcherie and the rue des Grands-Degrés
where he had just left his lodging. He was almost hurrying.

His lips bore a smile that spoke volumes on his state of mind.
His eyes were filled with lively clarity; his face carried an excited
expression; and his whole bearing conveyed a perfect absence of
care, despite the threatening situation in the streets where battle
was imminent.

At the risk of displeasing you, we will now leave him. Or
rather – using an expedient of the cinema which in 1871, of
course, had yet to be invented – we will freeze him in mid-stride,
one foot raised above the gutter, the other on the cobbles of the
dark street, his greatcoat flapping behind him. We will learn soon
enough where he is going, radiant under his terrifying scowl, lost
in the world of his own obsessions and galvanised by a strange
plenitude of feeling.

Of course it would not put us out much to give the reasons for
his evening expedition straight away, nor would it spoil the
narrative to start this chapter off by explaining why the old
convict could hear the birds singing. But I am not in a hurry.
That's my nature. It is part of a writer's vocation to push time
back, to lengthen and shorten it at whim. And apart from that, is
it a good idea to travel flat out all the time? It seems to me that

the time in which we now live is so permanently trembling with haste that we sometimes aspire to nothing beyond being alive . . . So many people run without knowing where they are going and end by jumping into a big black hole!

Horace Grondin was no exception to this rule. He too was hurrying towards his destiny. For my part I am doing everything I can to delay the narrative of his impact with the inevitable, being persuaded that the real adventure of a book lies in its capacity to whet the curiosity of the reader (generally an impatient traveller eager to rush straight into the action) and at the same time reflect the dark, sluggish rhythms of life's underlying arcana.

So before the last paroxysms of extreme brutality, before we travel the field of corpses unseamed by sabres, we will limit ourselves for the time being to saying that Horace Grondin was between rue Saint-Jacques and boulevard Saint-Michel. That he had bypassed several barricades whose defenders were getting ready for the final tragedy. That he was indifferent to the threat of the rifles that stirred as he passed.

That he was on his way somewhere. Almost hurrying.

That he seemed a completely different being from the cornered and disoriented man we accompanied, only twenty-four hours ago, into the entrails of the Archbishop's Palace, and left in animated conversation with the abbé Ségouret's housekeeper.

Perhaps we should take a look at the recent past, if we can do it without giving too much away.

89

In which Ursule Capdebosc
sings the *péronnelle*

What had happened on 22nd May?

Of course you remember the warm and respectful welcome
extended by Ursule Capdebosc to the one-time notary of le
Houga. And you will not have forgotten that excellent housekeeper's indignant tone when describing the degrading brutality
with which the soldiers had treated the abbé Ségouret at the time
of his arrest, battering the unfortunate cleric severely with
truncheons and rifle-butts and leaving him half-delirious on a
mattress crawling with vermin.

You will have noticed that Ursule Capdebosc had an easy and
orotund way with words. The Gers matron had told the notary
that she obtained news of the abbé through an intermediary who
had the grim job of turnkey at la Roquette. She had asserted her
shuddering revulsion from that strikingly hideous gnome:
although she recognised of course that he was her brother in
Jesus Christ, she couldn't help noticing that he trailed a pretty
impressive stench of goat, a fat and greasy odour with a sulphur-
and-metal aftertaste that made you gasp and took away your
appetite.

She had crossed herself and laughed. She had poured her guest
another thimbleful of Armagnac. She had expanded on the
hideous prison warder, his frog's head, the knottiness of his
disproportionately long and hairy arms, his fur-covered chest
and thick neck: all the outward signs, she felt, of some sort of
kinship with Lucifer. She had admitted to Charles Bassicoussé
that she did not dare approach the ugly human gargoyle except

from the other side of the grille in the choir at St Margaret's
Church where the fellow usually arranged to meet her. She said
she always remembered beforehand to ask for the protection of
the Blessed Virgin Mary, and to touch her forehead with holy
water.

Without seeming to do so, Horace Grondin had extracted
from her the exact time of their next meeting which was set for
the 24th, at the old St Bernard's cemetery not far from la
Roquette. The brave Ursule was already quaking at the thought
of it, and showed no reluctance when her visitor offered to go in
her stead. Given the rate at which the Versaillais troops were
now advancing, the rue de Grenelle would be in their hands in a
few hours; and it was far from certain that Madame Capdebosc
would be able to get to the mysterious Chapel of the Souls in
Purgatory behind which that very ugly and smelly person would
be awaiting her. Anyway, brrr! What sort of a place was it, a
draughty passageway between rows of graves ... gave her
gooseflesh just to think of it!

Thus launched, Ursule Capdebosc had plenty more to say. She
was one of those people who are afraid of silence.

And she was so afraid of being afraid! She was voluble and
unstoppable. Grondin had needed all his patience, all his self-
control, to listen without quailing to the organ voluntary of her
torrent of words.

Ursule had started with the chapter on half-cooked *foie-gras*
and pie pastry. She had gone into some detail on the Gers way of
bringing up young girls, then, in full flood and transfigured by
the happiness of giving away all those recipes, she had begun
with a gentle heart to describe the radiant light that religion shed
on her life.

This subject was received by the notary with a cold glint in his
grey eye. The evident absence of relish on the part of her
interlocutor, a grinding of the teeth not far short of reproof, had
ended the housekeeper's yearning for unattainable snowy peaks
and brought her back to earth. The *curé*'s maid fell silent. The
squadron of angels landed and folded their wings.

'These are difficult times,' Ursule had babbled. 'I have a strong feeling, that, let's face it, Monsieur Charles, you've not had an easy life at all. And I'll pray for you.'

When Grondin still remained silent, Madame Capdebosc's distaste for the void had begun to verge on naked fear. She had started again by repeating that she prayed morning and evening for the abbé Ségouret's safety, and this led on to her criticisms of the people. She had decreed that the proletariat ought to drink less, then wished once more for the return of her good employer, whom she already saw in a bishop's mitre and firmly believed to be swathed in the odour of sanctity. From time to time she refilled her visitor's small glass. She hopped from branch to branch, embarked on new subjects, shrieked like a jay. She went on and on and on, ingeniously embroidered each anecdote, wove new narratives out of old ones, remembered every pig and every goose liver, gave more importance to her silk than to the convulsions at the Hôtel de Ville. She sang her empty birdsong and chattered her country patois.

Tired out and stunned by the flood of hollow talk, Grondin had started to nod. She continued to chatter in all directions, exorcising her anxieties and her great fear of bloody revolution. To avoid seeing the blue lips of wounds or the destitute going barefoot, she kissed the ground in front of the poor, wrung her hands, mixed everything up. In the end, to avoid falling silent under the notary's cold eye, she had come to roost on the month of May which this year, 1871, always had an early sun.

Eventually Grondin had stopped the flow by clapping his hands and announcing his departure. He had pocketed the bunch of keys of his small house in the Saint-Séverin district and allowed the housekeeper to put an assortment of preserves and terrines in his haversack.

Then for good or ill, rifle on his shoulder, with the exhausted air of an old sweat hobbling to catch a couple of hours of much-needed sleep, he had walked to his house at number 4, rue des Grands-Degrés, without mishap. His veteran's disguise ensured perfect safety.

He had a good night's rest in his quiet house at the back of a courtyard, and spent the whole of the next day waiting for Hippolyte Barthélemy.

90

Dark designs

To pass the time, and to shut out the clamour – howling charges, storms of firing – that punctuated the cries of rage and supplication from the swamped, surrounded, beleaguered insurgents still fighting for their lives between the place Vendôme and the rue du Bac, Horace Grondin had sunk into a wing armchair in the depths of his room, lighted his pipe and tried to force himself to read a book.

He had dropped the book almost immediately. Listening thoughtfully to the thump and rumble of artillery, which seemed to be getting closer, he had started to wonder just how long it was going to take Mac-Mahon's troops to swallow the city and liquidate its defenders.

Gazing into the distance, arms crossed, he had sunk into a sort of grave, reasoned meditation that sometimes made a frown cross his face. He was thinking of his quarry, Tarpagnan; planning to catch him, to bring him back to the rue des Grands-Degrés by whatever means were necessary and shut him in the cellar.

As he pondered these sombre designs night crept up to the window. By furtive stages the velvet of evening had softened the outlines of the furniture, hidden the clock, buried the tapestries in shadow. Grondin lighted a candle.

He fell back into the wing chair. The orange flame of the taper accentuated the angles of his fierce face. He could see Tarpagnan as clearly as if the man were actually standing before him.

His pipe had gone out. Behind a distracted, veiled gaze, his internal monologue continued. From time to time he would raise his two fleshless hands as if gesticulating in answer to the arguments of an invisible interlocutor. As indeed he was. For he was engaged in a ferocious struggle with a different, bothersome self. Little by little, the idea of imprisoning the criminal in his cellar was fading from the hunter's mind. His gaze had acquired a mad glint from the wasting away of his soul.

I'll devise something worse, he thought. I'll be on his heels day and night.

How are you going to manage that, you poor mug? scolded his other self. *The army's at every road junction! You won't be able to get anywhere near him! We're in the middle of a civil war! The events have just swamped everything else!*

He'll have to rest. To eat. Look at the sky, breathe the air of springtime! I'll approach him to start with. I'll let him see me. He'll catch my eye. I'll let him know I want to arrest him for Jeanne's murder. I'll stick to him like his shadow. I'll talk to him about the past. I'll tax him with it. I won't leave him alone. I'll spoil the sweetness of the present. I'll lay waste all his loves, his friendships, his ambitions.

Ambitions, indeed! Amid all this carnage? The whole world's naked, you poor lunatic! There are no plans! There are no loves, not any more! The dance-hall's deserted! Freedom is entirely dependent on the continuation of life! And life itself can only be bought at bayonet point now!

I'll go wherever he is.

He'll be on the barricades.

Then that's where I'll go! Freedom will lose its charm for him! He'll grow more and more uneasy. He'll be gripped, throttled, by mortal fear. That's how I'll corner him into confessing! He'll volunteer to be swallowed by me. He'll tell me everything, just to make me stop. He'll admit his degrading crime. And I'll strangle him with my bare hands!

Grondin was breathing with great difficulty. His bald head had fallen forward, his chin on his chest, face livid, haggard eyes staring fascinated into an abyss. From time to time his gaze would wander in stunned fashion over the shadowy outlines of objects in the room. Then the fixed look would return. He hardly moved. He tried without success to resume contact with reality.

His forehead was damp with cold sweat, his eyes filled with a sort of sacred horror. He had been sitting staring like that for two hours or more, and still he could not bestir himself to think of other things. God, how sad the human soul becomes when it is falling into crime!

91

He can bite too

At about seven o'clock on the evening of the 23rd, while the notary was still trapped in his murderous fantasies, struggling vainly to stifle the conflagration in his brain, the tiny sound of a pick skilfully withdrawing the bolts of the entry-door lock interrupted his internal tumult and broke the circle of his sinister intentions.

Stiff and spectral as one rising from the grave, Grondin got to his feet. At the other end of the corridor, he heard clearly the small sound of a cautious footstep. He reached across and pinched out the candle with his fingers.

A tall man carrying a lantern masked with a perforated shutter had slipped into the house, and his daddy-long-legs profile was standing in the shadows of the entry hall. This man, unaware of the threat hanging over him, was none other than Hippolyte Barthélemy. Surprised by the apparent absence of anyone to welcome him, he had just replaced his bunch of lock-picks in his back pocket and was rummaging in his nose with an index finger as an aid to reflection.

Hippolyte's conscience was clear. His intrusion into the house was natural: he had an appointment, didn't he? So he was coming in. Of course he knocked twice at the door first, using the coded knock arranged in advance with Grondin. Twice the signal had gone unanswered. Anyone but that particular black crow would probably have been alarmed.

He waited a moment, leaning on the wall close beside a hatstand laden with well-worn clothes; then Hippolyte started to move, the light from a hole in his dark-lantern illuminating his face from below, giving it an abominable ogre-like grimace.

Horace Grondin meanwhile had quietly opened a drawer, taken out his revolver and silently cocked the hammer. He turned the weapon's muzzle towards the door ready to send the intruder to kingdom come if necessary.

Barthélemy too had his Adams in his hand. The house was as silent as a tomb. Extending the English five-shooter's nickel-plated barrel before him, he tiptoed cautiously forward.

The sudden, muffled, melancholy vibration of a bell caused both men to start: nine o'clock striking at Saint-Julien-le-Pauvre. Grondin listened. Barthélemy gave way first.

'Sir! Er ... sir!' he ventured at last in a stage whisper, stretching his neck out from the depths of the corridor. He moved stiffly forward a pace or two before his shin came into unexpected contact with a chair that the old convict had placed across the tiles with just such impromptu visits in mind. This time the tall police vulture let out a loud curse or two in an inimitable croaking voice that Grondin recognised immediately. It told him that Commissaire Mespluchet's long tall flunkey had come back to him.

'Hippolyte!' he cried, bounding to the door. 'You silly fellow! Step forward! I almost blew your brains out!'

'Me too, sir. I was so scared that I was on the point of shooting holes through all the doors!'

A moment later the two men were exchanging greetings, genuinely pleased to see one another and linked by something strange and powerful that had esteem in it as well as contempt, curiosity as well as duplicity, and as much friendship as mistrust.

'Out with it! Don't give me any nonsense. Have you seen the little burglar?'

'Yes. It's all going well, sir. Give or take a few hitches. And I'm quite proud of having managed to drag my carcass through all the shrapnel.'

'What about Tarpagnan? Quick! Spit it out!'

Barthélemy yawned cavernously. ''Scuse me, guv. I haven't slept or had a meal for two whole days . . . You're going to have to wait.' From the savage look in his eye the copper could see that Grondin was not in the best of moods. 'It's all the same to me! Smash my face in with your fist if you like, sir,' he added stubbornly, 'but till I've had something proper to eat, my lips are sealed.'

He bore at that moment an absurd resemblance to a gangling calf defying a tiger, but after a long moment the tiger relaxed. 'All right then, companion! Eat up! We can devour each other later.' Grondin was almost affable. He knew the other had not come empty-handed. He moved about lighting lamps.

Five minutes later, sitting at the table, the former convict, whose only thought was an urgent wish to know Tarpagnan's location, watched the policeman hurl himself on his food. The Commissaire's dog was famished. Voracious as any wild beast, he stuffed his face with both hands and the upward, sidelong look of one who has been deprived of everything for ages. Grondin had to let him eat his fill.

When the beanpole had mopped up the assortment of pâtés and conserves washed down with Madeira wine that his host had placed before him, he blinked for a moment. Red-eyed, features drawn with fatigue, looking more jaundiced than ever, he thanked Grondin with a grateful look, pushed his plate away and without further ado launched into his report.

To cut a long story short, Inspector Barthélemy said as a preamble that he had drawn a blank in rue Lévisse: the bird had flown and Emile Roussel seemed to have shut up shop. The shutters were up in front of his workshop. He had hunted high and low, kicked up a row in the courtyard and knocked in vain on several doors.

Just as he was leaving the building, apparently deserted by all its tenants, an ugly cobbler called Velvet-Eye had surged most unexpectedly from the bowels of the earth, asking who was making the clamour in the yard. This strange troglodyte – a hunchback whose eyes were so shaded by long lashes that they looked made-up, like the eyes of a rajah – had emerged from his cellar where he had gone to knock back a few bottles of château bleedin' 'undred per cent before returning to the battlefront. Skilfully handled by Barthélemy who muttered surlily that he was 'from the Ourcq mob' and flashed his number 14 glass eye, the shoemaker concluded that he was one of Wire's associates, and gave news of him without having to be questioned much.

Apparently the little burglar had been fighting in the front line alongside Louise Michel, who had just been routed along with her people at the barricades in the place Blanche, and had been left for dead this very morning in a trench on the Clignancourt road.

Barthélemy said that he himself had been in the fighting in rue Lepic and had fallen back with La Cécilia after fighting through every house, floor by floor. He had, of course, to swathe himself in a little bit of glory to find the effrontery to enquire delicately into Wire's fate after the battle.

The ugly gnome had shrugged lopsidedly and seated himself on a horizontal kerbstone in the yard that served as a sort of bench. He had leaned back slightly and poured half a bottle of château 'undred down his throat without drawing breath. He had wiped his mouth with the back of his hand and said with an air of ponderous mystery:

'Find the *lady* and p'raps she'll tell yer.'

'What woman you talkin' about?'

The toper had given him a wavering sidelong look. 'I ain't so sure about you after all,' he had hiccuped suspiciously. 'If you're one of the Ourcq geezers it's a bleedin' certainty you know Amélie la Gale!'

'Oh, *her*!' cried the skinny impostor. "*Course* I know Amélie, nice pair of legs she got an' all!' When it came to feeling his way rapidly in the dark, Barthélemy had long been a distinguished performer.

'*Right* little darlin'!' the other had said with lascivious enthusiasm. 'Hardly sixteen! Tasty little cunt what Wire bought off of the Ventriloquist. 'Er ponce, as was.'

'Where can I find her?'

The man was too busy to reply, peacefully pouring down the other half of the bottle. 'It's really crazy,' he had sighed when it was empty, 'but being scared gives me a thirst you wouldn't believe!' And he had reached for another bottle. It had taken yet another before the rotgut had its full effect, but once the cobbler was full he had talked willingly enough.

When she wasn't fighting with a battalion of women from Montmartre, Amélie la Gale was with the locksmith. She was his elixir of youth. She was living with Emile Roussel in a nice three-room apartment in the Enclos Saint-Laurent that her new protector had provided for her.

Amélie was a partridge who had been around. She knew how to talk to men. She had bewitched the little lunger utterly. She enjoyed his quick wit and libertarian thoughts, and was considering marrying him, having divined that the burglar (who maintained an effective veil of discretion) probably owned more property than an honest artisan would have done.

The industrious Wire knew that his gypsum cough meant a relatively short life and early death. His attitude to life was serene and straightforward. In the daytime he would go to the barricades to defend his ideas, and at night he would sleep in the apartment, where Amélie sapped his remaining strength under a handsome grey eiderdown.

'Bullet or embolism,' Wire would say, 'the reaper's going to be anticipated one way or another. I don't give a fuck which.'

He was crazy about la Gale.

Hippolyte had made his way to the rue de l'Aqueduc, in the 10th *arrondissement*, where the turtledoves had their love-nest. The building was neat. You went through a porch, then came out into the light again. At the other end of a little rose garden he had knocked at the door of a sort of doll's house, expecting to be greeted by the smiling face of a pretty mistress. But the door had opened on a heartbroken mask of grief. Amélie had been a widow for two hours.

The comrades had brought her Wiry back home with the lower half of his face blown off by a Chassepot bullet. Amélie had almost forced her visitor upstairs to see the remains. Wire was laid out stiff on a bed covered with a crocheted counterpane. Something childlike, a sort of bantering purity, showed in the dead man's bruised face. His chin was tied in place with a bloody handkerchief. On the open palm of one hand lay a glass eye bearing the number 7.

'He wasn't a ponce, he was a *man*!' the girl had murmured brokenly. 'He was my own Arthur ... I still can't believe how he got to me!'

She couldn't take her big beautiful peepers off the cunning waxen face she had so loved. She didn't even dare kiss him. She was wearing a white dress that gave her back her innocence. She stood erect and immobile looking into a darkness so impenetrable that her mouth and eyes stayed wide open in permanent astonishment at the sudden disappearance of the universe she had glimpsed. Her world had fallen down a hole.

'Are you one of his comrades, citizen?' she had asked with tears in her eyes. How could he possibly have said he wasn't? The shameless copper gave her an acquiescent look.

With the heartfelt tenderness that arrives on the heels of grand passion, the beauty had then told him the story in a flood of soft words.

The Versaillais had taken the Butte. Emile and his friends – Marceau, Ferrier, Voutard – had been involved in the hand-to-hand fighting. When overwhelmed they had finally retreated into the galleries of the gypsum quarries, which they knew well, to hold out longer. The infantry had stormed the quarries throwing smoke bombs in through every opening. Of course Wire with his gypsum cough couldn't endure much of that.

Then he had had *the idea*. He and his friends had decided to kill each other rather than surrender. The fellow-insurgents had looked at each other for the last time, cocked their rifles and shot each other simultaneously: one, two, three, *boom!* They had blown the safe one more time. *Vive la Commune!*

Barthélemy fell silent. After a short pause filled with vague thoughts, one of the lamps had suddenly dimmed. Both men were struck by the little locksmith's surge of heroism, so much so indeed that for a long strange moment, their faces in shadow, each mentally saluted these martyrs of the revolution, shot through the head among spirals of turbulent smoke.

After a while Grondin made a noise by moving his chair. His eyes were like caverns. 'Such bravery,' he murmured with unaffected sympathy. 'So much killing.' Then, returning to his obsession, he added in a different voice: 'Did little Amélie give you any clues about the one I'm after?'

Barthélemy fluttered his eyelashes. He maintained his position for a moment, crouched cunningly in his corner like a rat, inventive and underhand. He let Grondin stew for a while. At last, the latter exploded:

'Are you going to say anything, you wall-scorpion?'

'I was just thinking. No, it's gone. No matter!'

He couldn't remember how the subject of Tarpagnan had come up between the girl and him. Ah yes! The pretty nymph had cried: 'Antoine? He's a fine officer! D'you know him? He's with Dombrowski. When they make a sortie, he's always in the lead.' And she had added: 'I saw him yesterday. He was talking to his photographer friend, the handsome fellow with the bullneck. They even arranged to meet for supper at Laveur's on the 23rd. Number 23 on the 23rd! They were laughing about it.'

Grondin was beside himself with excitement.

'Are you sure that's what she said?'

'Of course I'm sure. She even said sadly: "Making plans! What madness!" She sobbed on my shoulder for ages about it. "Going out to dinner! Madness, don't you think? Plans, at a time like this! You can't make any." That's what she said.

'She was devastated. I was eyeing the strap of her bodice slipping down her charming shoulder. She was so ravishing! Then all of a sudden she took hold of herself. Her face went hot. She was carried away. She said: "I see it more clearly now! Since General Ladmirault's skinned me of my Emile, I'm going to send everything up in fucking flames."

'And let me tell you, you wouldn't have wanted to tumble her on a bed any more! She'd become ferocious. Like the plague! All of a sudden under that fragile exterior there appeared a fantastic reservoir of energy! A superhuman impulse drove the girl towards the houses ... I followed her a little way on her peregrinations ... She was running off to burn down the smart quarters, with a flask of paraffin in her hand ... She wasn't thinking of her death, more of her deliverance!'

Barthélemy had fallen silent again. He could read clearly in Grondin's eyes that nothing more that he might say would be of the slightest interest. 'Well,' the beanpole ended, scratching a pallid cheek with black fingernails, 'it's eight o'clock and this is the 23rd. You can nab your man not three hundred metres from here, sir, and I've kept my promise.'

Grondin had already put his coat on, and was checking the charges in his revolver. His eyes looked white as he peered into the shadows around Barthélemy. 'By God, you're right, it's time!' he said. 'We won't be seeing each other again, my dear Hippolyte.'

'No. Goodbye, Mr Grondin.'

It all sounded straightforward enough, but their nerves had been severely tested. Grondin contemplated the debris of their friendship: that unlikely fraternal association shot through with ambivalences.

'No need to look so down in the mouth,' he said with an attempt at joviality. 'You really ought to be rejoicing, my boy! The people in your camp are winning. Commissaire Mespluchet will soon be back. You've solved the mystery of the Ourcq case. You'll be able to turn in a first-rate report on me. You're going to be fêted for your red, white and blue civic zeal.'

'It's true, sir,' Barthélemy admitted, stammering a little. 'I owe you a great deal.' He exhibited on the palm of his right hand his collection of glass eyes, rolling the blue irises about with the ingenuous air of a man who didn't want to push himself forward. 'I'm very grateful to you, really, Mr, er, Underchief of the Sûreté,' he repeated. 'And I've learned a lot as a result of knowing you.'

He lowered his head as if it were difficult for him to struggle against a character dyed in the wool, but also as if he accepted with a sort of private enjoyment his destiny as a dedicated soul.

'I think they'll probably make me a commissaire,' he added. 'But one doesn't turn into a hero overnight because of something like that. I'll soon become what I've always been.'

'An informer by vocation?'

'A man who can't really be trusted where my friendship for you is concerned, sir. A zealous official. But,' he went on, looking up with eyes filled with shameful, fantastic and pitiable enquiry, 'if you end up murdering an innocent man to satisfy your obsession with vengeance, what else can I do but denounce you, since I owe my superiors the truth on your activities?'

'What are you insinuating, you gloomy rogue? That Tarpagnan's innocent?'

'You didn't let me finish just now, sir. I was going to tell you that I'd followed your suspect a bit, and that even if he's a

Communard from head to toe he's a *very* brave man. Valiant! A really exemplary officer. I simply can't see him as a murderer of young girls.'

'You ugly dog,' Grondin growled, 'malevolence has been spurring me on these sixteen years now. You're not going to break my spring! Farewell, Barthélemy,' he said in a different tone, turning away. 'I leave you the keys and indeed the whole shack. I don't expect ever to come back here. In any case, this part of Paris is going to be Versaillais in two hours' time. My future's on the other side.'

'You'll be taken for one of them!'

'What must befall us is already written in the Book.' Grondin stuck his battered kepi on his head, slung his haversack over his bent back and went out into the corridor. At the door he turned back. 'Ah yes, I was forgetting . . . one more thing, Hippolyte. If by chance I kill an innocent person while attempting to enforce justice, have me locked up by your constables! I won't even hold it against you.'

'Thank you, sir!' the policeman said, brightening. 'It's what I would have expected of you!' He felt suddenly that he was entrusted with a responsibility that lifted his soul and filled his mind with a good odour of confidence, a sort of pallid joy that illuminated his entire being like a full moon.

He double-locked the door behind Grondin, thinking that he would have time for a nap before reporting to the military authorities and identifying himself as a loyal servant of the régime.

Now Grondin knew where he was going. Now he was almost walking fast. Now he was where we left him frozen in mid-stride, stepping briskly onto a pavement at the edge of the place Saint-André-des-Arts.

A slightly mad smile illuminated his predator's face. Something about his deadly concentration suggested a barn owl at dusk, emerging from the darkness of some granary and swooping off through rising mist in swift silent murderous ground-skimming flight toward the night's banquet.

92

Last dinner on
a tablecloth

That Tuesday 23rd May, with Paris in flames and the entire Left
Bank from Vavin to the Panthéon locked in fierce combat, the
regulars at Laveur's pension seemed to have agreed among
themselves to share one last meal on the little red-chequered
tablecloths in the rue des Poitevins.

Hardly a stone's throw from the fighting, determined to drink
a 'stirrup cup' before the pincers of Versaillais barbarism closed
on the Latin Quarter for good, they were dreaming one last time
of a life of perfect harmony, their secret thoughts escaping
through labyrinths of pearly desire into caverns filled with
crazed fugitive visions where the women they had loved
sometimes featured.

Others were talking about their day, a day of rubble and
barricades. Showing hands black with powder. Saying that defeat
was certain.

Quite a few well-known faces were unfolding their napkins.
Several friends of Vallès: Langevin, Longuet, Colonel Maxime
Lisbonne. A lot of other combatants including two or three
random Turcos and a few Lost Children. A Garibaldist with his
broken feathers and singed plumes. And some who were really
exhausted: characters who had been under fire for eight days or
more, dodging bullets, frayed by shrapnel, waiting to be diced
amid perpetual uproar.

They were hungry, very hungry. Salivating and impatient. You
would have thought that war had sharpened their teeth. That
familiarity with death had not diminished their wish to live. And

you would have *known* that no one was willing to miss the *fricandeau à l'oseille*, a wonderful larded veal with sorrel, promised by the solidly built Madame Laveur, a lady who (despite her sex) was almost worshipped by her guests, for she could ring the big bells at the bottom of her cooking pots with the dash and authority of a master-bellringer pedalling out 'Josquin des Prés' on a belfry foot-keyboard.

The room, clamorous with loud voices and tobacco smoke, was gradually falling into a monastic silence. All of a sudden it was like being in church.

Not a sound! For Madame Laveur, in all the roundness of her voluptuous flesh, had just appeared with her red napkin folded over her forearm. Majestically, she heaved herself onto the pedestal beside the till. Without looking she reached out and found her stool, and on it rested her imposing buttocks.

Wonderfully relieved of the weight of her body, she smiled. She had thick hair above a square forehead and rings on every finger. She sat enthroned, large-bosomed and wobbling, between the service hatch and the swing doors into the dining room: an unchallenged autocrat poised petween Olympus and earthly vulgarity.

She surveyed her customers as they battled with the last strings of the leek soup that always began the menu of the day, then clapped her hands imperiously. With a stern glance and a click of the tongue she stopped a tall magpie of a waiter, in black waistcoat and white apron, who was gliding rapidly across the room towards a table. Frozen in mid-stride by the bronze of her unfailing authority, the lackey, holding a steaming dish, paused gracefully with a vague smile on his face, balanced on one leg without even swaying.

By snorting Jupiter! What a saliva pump! When she had her audience's attention, citizeness Ernestine Laveur's powerful voice announced that there would be a general amnesty for all current slates. She added that tonight's meal would be free 'to all patriots'. She immersed herself happily in the answering thunder of applause, opened her arms wide to all these fine fellows who were chanting her name – Ernestine! Ernestine! – and in an atmosphere resembling the final scene of an opera, confirmed that today's main course would be 'Home-made larded veal with my own special sauce', a dish so tasty that ordinarily it only featured in the Saturday menu.

The prospect of such succulence breathed warmth into the minds and bellies of the diners.

'Hey, Jesus, what generosity!' exclaimed a young corporal amid the general ovation. 'Why d'you suppose she's being so maternal all of a sudden?'

'It's calculated,' an older man replied. 'All is lost! The flag's bleeding! It's her way of telling us we've all had it!' Their faces were gloomy amid the general happiness.

'I love you!' Ernestine Laveur cried to all her men, blowing kisses in all directions. 'Go on,' she added briskly after a moment, 'eat up, darlings, then go back and fight! The veal juice mustn't be allowed to get cold.'

Released, the frozen waiter placed his hanging foot on the ground and continued on his way. The rest of the staff poured into the room in a cohort and started serving the main course. The room was waiting impatiently. Everyone was dying of hunger!

They set about the meal with a deafening clatter of cutlery. They lined their gullets with fine slices of braised veal. They moved on to the larded joint, succumbed to the effects of that divine fillet, the marrowy succulence of the meat juices reduced in a patient stewing process, mopped up the sauce with bits of bread held in their fingers and left nothing on their plates except for a little smear of sorrel – an impalpable greenish trace – which they stared at for a long time with vague, grateful eyes.

Of course there were second helpings. The last to be served had hardly started before the first were envying them. The diners' jaws snapped rather than chewed. They pulverised, tore, gnawed, sopped up the juice.

You could hear the sound of forks and mouths. Sucking noises. Gulps of wine going down. Murmurs of satisfaction. Sighs of repletion. Creaks from the furniture as one diner after another pushed back his plate and distanced his chair from a table that suddenly seemed too close.

It was a dinner to stuff your guts. A sauce-guzzler's confer-
ence. A throat-warming last sacrament. A last-chance braised
joint.

Tarpagnan had ordered à la carte. He had just that moment
finished the Cod Mithridates that followed the leek soup when a
waiter put before him a plate of the succulent braised veal.
Antoine pushed it away.

'Not for me, my friend. This would be too much.'

'It's *compulsory*, monsieur. It's all got to be eaten! That's how
Madame Laveur wants it.'

The man had already rushed off towards other diners, six
plates balanced along his arm.

Antoine with a loving eye watched the giant Marbuche
reaching for his portion and starting without a word on his
second vast helping of red cabbage with bacon and sorrel. Over
the Manchu wrestler's large shoulder he saw the door at the end
of the dining room opening, and craned his neck to see who was
arriving.

He was expecting Vallès or Mirecourt, but the person who
charged with an air of haste out of the revolving door was just
some gent with brown hair.

93

A last-minute guest

Vertiginous hat in hand, the newcomer advanced a few paces across the parquet.

He was visibly peering about the room for someone. His gaze explored the other end of the restaurant. Suddenly his eyes focused on Tarpagnan, who had the impression the stranger was signalling to him as if he knew him. He looked down immediately.

When he raised his eyes again the man had moved. He seemed to know the place well, for he had already greeted Madame Laveur and placed his long walking stick in the elephant's-foot umbrella stand at the entrance, where Antoine himself had left his *makhila*. Loping rapidly onward, he next stopped at a table at which Régère and Francis Jourde were stuffing their faces, and treated them to two or three vehement remarks. He had a pale complexion, close-shaven cheeks, a bumpy and obstinate fore-head. He possessed very fine, deepset eyes that sparkled with intelligence although reddened with fatigue.

Antoine felt strangely embarrassed. Although the man's white face did not seem unfamiliar to him, he was still wholly incapable of putting a name to it. In another few steps the fellow would be upon him!

Rolling his strong shoulders in a good but slightly torn tail-coat, the man was zigzagging between the rows of tables on a pair of solid, fast-moving legs. He stopped in front of Antoine with the words: 'Sorry I'm late, Cousin Vingtras!'

Without introducing himself he fell into one of the two remaining chairs. He greeted Marbuche and then, while asking in rapid-fire sentences after the clown Kantalabutt, the Pointing

Venus and her *Rhotomago*, coolly and without being invited poured himself a tumbler of red wine, then started to drink it in large gulps.

As he did so the voluble and impertinent fellow turned back to Tarpagnan. His dark eyes were fixed upon him, coal-black eyes that could only have been those of the distinguished representative of the 15th *arrondissement*, had it not been for the melancholy clearly visible in them, giving the pallid countenance a haunting look of pathetic despair that could never have belonged to the ferocious, inexhaustibly energetic Jules Vallès, a man always nimbly and cheerfully one jump ahead of the devil.

Tarpagnan was more and more perplexed. He didn't really want to offend the fellow, but the best he could manage was a bland, polite silence. The other was informing him in machine-gun bursts that today had been a very difficult one for him, he had dashed from one barricade to another, that he had had to sign for the burning of two houses in rue Vavin, and that the news he brought was not good.

Tarpagnan inclined his head with a bland smile. Seeing that the Gascon was hesitating to greet him, that in fact he was looking very reserved, Jules Vallès – for of course that is who it was – cried:

'Really! Today nobody wants me without my face-fungus! All right, a beard's just wrapping! Well, listen to this: just now in the place du Panthéon they were going to shove me up against the wall! The crowd was demanding Vallès ... and I – poor idiot – arrive with my actual real physiognomy! Those lunatics started asking where their great man had gone. I told them that I was he. That I know myself well, I can tell them authoritatively who I am! That there aren't all that many of us wearing red sashes! The people chanted: "Weapons! Bread!" as if I was an itinerant baker and gunsmith. I told them I didn't have any or know where they could find it. They took that badly. A loudmouth got angry. No one was on my side. He started bawling that I was an impostor, an informer! That the real Vallès wears a beard like a beaver. Fuck! They jostled round me. Shoved me about. Wanted, actually, to do me harm. My coat tore a couple of times! If it hadn't been for an excellent Alsatian called Wurth, I can guarantee that the idol of the district would've had a rather difficult fifteen minutes.'

He stopped. He ate two or three crumbs off the tablecloth, and looked at Antoine who had still said nothing.

Vallès went on: 'Well? Nothing to say? Angry with me? Sorry I'm late! I've got plenty of excuses. I've just been trying to calm people down. They're going mad with pain! They want to burn down the Sainte-Geneviève library! *Someone* had to explain what an absurd gesture it would be. Elsewhere there are people who want to set everything on fire. Some are even doing it – a flaming bottle in the basement is all it takes, usually! On my way here I saw women fleeing, pulling their nippers along by the hand. Carrying their things in a handkerchief. I tried to use my red sash to stay their panic, but it doesn't mean anything any more ... The people are saying bitterly that the Defence Committees – fine gentlemen in sashes – didn't foresee the need to fight, and made no preparations for it ...'

He stopped and looked at his friend, discouraged, then went on:

'We're jiggered, cousin! But we ought to stay. Stay behind with those who are shooting and going to be shot. Fulfil our role. The strategy of despair must be rejected.'

Antoine remained silent, and Vallès went pale. He looked down at the floor, abashed, and tears gathered in his eyes. He leaned close to Tarpagnan, patted him fraternally on the cheek and murmured sympathetically through powerful clenched jaws:

'Oh, you poor old chap! What an idiot I am! I've just realised what it is that's muzzled you like this! By God! You must be as upset as I am! Believe me, I bawled like a calf!'

'What are you talking about?'

'The ghastly event that's deprived us for ever of our dear Théo!'

'I hadn't heard,' Tarpagnan said in an emotionless voice. 'Mirecourt? What happened?'

'Just off the rue des Carrières. Killed outright by a shell! I don't want anyone to sit in his chair tonight.'

The two comrades stared at each other for some time. The loud voices around them receded until they sounded like chirping insects. After a while Antoine, his face miserable with sorrow, described how Dombrowski had been killed before his eyes.

His words, as he was aware, rang like a death-knell recalling the poignant insecurity of their lives, the haggard advance into danger that faced all decent people dragged like him and like Vallès into the torment of those bloody days. The grim fate of some people was surely there to remind them that the raft to which they were clinging was drifting ceaselessly towards the dark core of the storm, that the cries of today's dead and dying would be theirs tomorrow, or in an hour's time.

Tarpagnan had never before realised so clearly that every event is a turning in the road. That the horizons of life change, pile up one on top of another, are obscured and eventually forgotten, the fantastic lightning of storms or cruel windswept clouds. That the erasure of faces can be succeeded by the clarities of happiness.

Incredible! He caught himself smiling through his tears. Abruptly, without knowing himself how he got there, he wiped his cheeks and smiled at Vallès. With a sort of instinct that was stronger than fear, he dragged himself out of the great black void. He remembered the cheerful excess of his drinking sessions with Mirecourt, the beauty of the man's photographs; crazy laughter in Courbet's company; one berserk charge after another alongside the Pole.

His eye became fierce again. Brusquely, he stretched his forearm across the table and placed his hand over Vallès's. 'You must eat,' he told him. 'It's what Théo would have wanted. It's what we've all done.'

'You're right, comrade. Life carries the day! Stronger than anything! I want to dine royally before going back to fight! And I want some of that braised veal I can see on all the plates and in people's mouths! Quick! A bottle of burgundy! Afterwards I'll have a too-sweet frangipane and a coffee-plus!'

And that is what he did. He *devoured*. He managed to accomplish a sort of physical regeneration. He held down and cut up his meat with the earnestness of a starving man. He assuaged his hunger for life without false shame, and when he finished his scalding coffee, reinvigorated by good cheer and

Irancy wine, he was scintillating with new energy and holding forth on the unfavourable turn of events.

More rebellious than ever, still driven by a passion for generous ideas and devastated by the defeat of an unselfish and heroic cause, he brought a square hand heavily down on the table. Vehemently, but having to force himself to say it, he grated: 'It's all going belly-up. The Paris Commune's going to founder, even though the idea's invincible! The *idea*, Tarpagnan! That's the revolutionary symbol we've got to preserve! Its tremulous but resolute purity! Its moral and ... exemplary ... meaning!'

Antoine looked at the other man across his glass of wine with a sort of indulgent tenderness.

'Bravo!' he said. 'You're saying the sun's shining in the middle of the night!'

'The sun? You're laughing at me because you think I'm whistling in the dark?'

'Only because I see you and father Hugo agreeing with each other.'

'Absolutely! All the way!' exclaimed Vallès with a booming laugh. 'The revolutionary instinct is a moral one ... That's why the populace can do more than just riot. To make a revolution you have to have the people ... And it's at times like that, Tarpagnan – like this! – that we can really see the people's virtue!'

'Poor people, shoved this way and that by the ideas of every Tom, Dick and Harry!'

'Unconquerable people! Generous with its blood! Loyal to those who work for it!'

The strange sombre words resounded. Words lost for ever. A hundred untamed stars shed in the midst of the tumult, the roar of conversation, the immense post-prandial clamour.

The two men fell silent. For a while Vallès seemed to give way to the torments that preyed on him. With veiled eyes he seemed to have departed by secret ways to the frontier of his doubts. His gaze was vague and distant.

Tarpagnan gazed benevolently at the giant Marbuche whose small spirit had taken the peaceful road to the light and who, in the constant simplicity of his unadorned mind, was content with the taste of the passing moment. How could one not envy the simpleton, so stunned by the sheer abundance of food that he had switched without transition from ox-like vigour to vegetable passivity? Sprawled on his chair with a thumb in his mouth he looked very like a huge baby in the grip of a contented lethargy that nothing, short of a medium-sized field gun being fired close to his ear, would be capable of disturbing.

Antoine turned back to Jules Vallès and asked: 'How many more days d'you think we can hold out?'

'As long as a single brave person remains,' the journalist replied, emerging instantly from his distracted state.

'We're beaten, aren't we?'

'God Almighty! Not for lack of warning!'

'But,' Antoine persisted, 'if the revolution's faltering, isn't it because the great voice of the tribunes hasn't yet reached into the cold beds, the ill-swept hovels, the attics where the fate of being poor is felt most?'

'It's because,' Jules Vallès said irritably, 'philosophers and artists confuse their dreams, their cigar-smoke and the range of their spectacles with the hopes of hands distorted by toil!' The conversation seemed to have brought him back to life. He became heated, displaying an intact capacity for rebellion. 'The very *idea* that after the sufferings and empty stomachs of the fathers, the sons are going to benefit at last from a change of heart! That they're going to get better working conditions from the bosses! What *utopia*! What fuckery! What a swindle! And what injustices to come, before human misery is at last put down! How poisoned it is, the road to progress! And as for the undertow . . .'

'Are you worried about people going too far?'

'I'm afraid of this madness, sowing the seed of murder! People are killing prisoners on both sides. People are just going to finish off the wounded. Settle their accounts.'

He thrust his chair back from the table. 'Tomorrow the whole of Paris will be murderous!' he cried. He stood up and wiped his mouth. 'I'm going back, anyway,' he said, folding his napkin as if he was just going out for a short stroll round the neighbourhood.

'Got to encourage the people who'll be taken apart tomorrow!' He turned away and started to leave, but returned. Looked into Tarpagnan's face and grasped his shoulders.

'Long life, Cousin Vingtras,' he said, embracing him.

'I promise you, I'll stay on the people's side,' Tarpagnan murmured.

'Farewell, Antoine. I knew the moment I set eyes on you that the music of your heart was immense. Don't forget you're a soldier of the revolutionary idea. Duty calls!'

He released Tarpagnan, fleetingly patted the head of the giant Marbuche and left the pension Laveur with his characteristic hurried stride.

94

Man of ice

As the human whirlwind surged outside onto the pavement he cannoned into the massive bony form of a man standing in the shadows, for the street lighting was turned off in the neighbourhood. The figure was bending over slightly to peer into the pension Laveur through a window. With a grunt of distaste Vallès tapped the spy on the shoulder.

'What are you up to, citizen? If your soul's reasonably white, why not go inside? You'll be fed for nothing! And if you're up to no good, clear off! We're already splattered from head to foot in the mud of denunciations.'

The stranger stayed where he was, shrouded in a strange calm. 'You can see what I'm doing,' he said. 'I'm listening to time melting while spying on the light, and I'm getting ready to surprise a man I want to harm.'

Deciding the man was mad, Vallès, who had been about to rush away, stayed and tried to catch a glimpse of his eyes. After a moment he succeeded. It was like going out into the cold.

He saw a grinning face, deeply lined and the colour of ivory. In an instant he had discerned the hypnotic depth of the snake's eyes.

'People eat well here, I see!' the apparition breathed, resuming his motionless observation. 'They give you a pretty solid blowout. And I see people are taking advantage. Doing themselves well.'

Vallès did not reply. He shuddered despite himself.

The spectre fixed him with slate-grey penetrating eyes. 'I don't mind people laughing,' he said, surprising Vallès again with his raucous and inharmonious voice, 'because this evening, you see,

I'm happy too! I'm celebrating myself! Because with a single glance I've assuaged my hunger for vengeance. The dish that's best eaten cold, you know? I've just made up for sixteen lost, wasted years!'

The metallic stridency of his speech conveyed an indelible depth of hatred. Vallès had never heard a sound like it. He could have sworn the damned ghost was speaking to him from the back of an ice cavern. Suddenly the street itself seemed to be frozen.

The man straightened. His gaze was unbearable. He was wearing a long greatcoat.

He raised a hand with long thin fingers and cold nails in front of his grey face, and his body turned gently in the gentle night wind. His tall stooped form started to move. He removed his veteran's headgear and revealed a bald scalp haloed with frost-white hair. He entered the restaurant. As he passed through the doorway, Vallès had time to spot a long whitish scar that crossed the leathery scalp from end to end.

'Monsieur!' he called, hoping to stay this strange person. But he might as well have been trying to control a nightmare. Haunted by sinister thoughts, he watched the turning reflections of the door for a long moment. Then he chased the unreal memory of the apparition from his brain, encumbered with thoughts of death.

Hands deep in his pockets, Jules Vallès set off into the darkness. Almost immediately he was back in the tremulous sweetness of May, its fresh and tender greenery on three chestnut trees that somehow had escaped the axe.

He turned the corner of rue Hautefeuille and hastened his pace. As he walked along the boulevard he heard small-arms fire not far away. He walked close along the fronts of the buildings on his way to spend the night at the rue Soufflot barricade.

There he stretched out on a simple blanket to await the baleful dawn of a new day of bloodshed. He thought of Mirecourt for a while, then fell into a restless slumber. Nearby lay another dead man with a smashed skull.

95

The ghost of
Laveur's restaurant

After Vallès had left Laveur's pension, Tarpagnan tried to shake himself out of a mood of apathy caused by the burgundy. He pulled himself together and scribbled a note to Marbuche, deeply asleep in his chair, telling him that he could find Gabriella Pucci working for the Lariboisière 'corpse depot'. He added that he himself could be found at the rue du Pot-de-Fer barricade, where he was spending the night, and left the message prominently displayed on the tablecloth.

While he was returning the pen, ink and blotter to the waiter who had brought them, his mind wandered a little as he gazed blankly at the restaurant's wallpaper: a faded pink design with indigo highlights in a pattern of circus performers. Antoine's eye was naturally attracted to a caravan on whose steps, which were about her size, he saw Palmyre.

Palmyre was standing on tiptoe. She had a magnificent pink bow in her hair. She signalled to him. The pretty midget said: 'Outside, everything's going faster and faster.'

She said it to him. She repeated it insistently.

She said: 'The flames are rising everywhere.'

And she said: 'Our lives are doomed.' Mechanically, she touched her cheeks lightly tinged with vermilion, blew a stream of soap bubbles and vanished.

Tarpagnan had risen from the table. His eyesight dimmed. There was a singing in his ears, like a train letting off steam. His mouth was fixed in a half-smile. Was the clock of the world about to strike here? Was he dreaming?

His gaze had frozen, fixed on a tall figure at the other end of the room who was staring at him with terrible eyes. His past had just appeared in front of him and was blocking his path!

The man's grey stare transfixed him down the length of the room. It was extraordinary how, without moving or approaching, he still managed to be menacing. It was him all right, no doubt of it! Under the scowling mask of the spectre standing inside the street door was the face of Charles Bassicoussé! The face of a convict who had spent nearly fifteen years wearing a leg-iron, shut in a cage like a wild beast, rejected, reviled, doomed to oblivion by the verdict of the courts; and who had come back into the daylight after all those seasons of isolation, of maltreatment, dysentery, fever and humiliation, looking, in fact, as if he had caught rabies. As if he had come to demand explanations. And to render the justice of the thunderbolt.

Antoine strove to master his feelings. Emotion made a hard lump in his throat. His fate had caught up with him. He had always, always feared this moment but he had also longed for it. How often he had wondered when the grey-eyed man would appear again on his path! Suddenly he realised that he had been awaiting this turning-point in his life. Perhaps wishing for a clearing of the air, an explanation that would deliver him from remorse.

What's still to be done? he thought. I've waited a hundred years for this! Let's get it over with! Although apprehensive, Tarpagnan was buoyed by the thought of his own innocence.

He stepped forward. The singing in his ears drowned everything! His eardrums were disconnected and his heart bucked like a mad stallion. He walked steadily down the room toward the main ghost in his life.

As he approached, the former notary's slate-grey irises slowly filled with a dangerous glow. Malevolent joy dawned in the face with its disfiguring recent cut. Tarpagnan saw the former convict lunge suddenly towards the elephant's-foot umbrella stand, seize the *makhila* in both hands and, raising it to the level of his waxen face with a frightful smile, bring it down hard on his raised knee, snapping it in two.

At the same time he uttered a fierce, almost superhuman cry, a dreadful challenging shout that stopped the breath of everyone in the room, although only Antoine knew what it meant. '*Hitzá hitz! Hitzá hitz!*'

A second later, while most of the startled diners were still turning to see what was going on and Madame Laveur felt her blood freeze, Horace Grondin had vanished again through the turning reflections of the revolving door and fled into the night, shoulders heaving with a dreadful laugh, face in a grinning rictus that exposed his long teeth in terrifying fashion.

As the former convict's cry rang out, Tarpagnan bounded forward, brushing aside a tall waiter in his path so violently that the man fell over a table in a crash of breaking crockery. He rushed through the door and stopped outside, peering into the darkness.

'Notary!' he cried, 'Come back!'

As he stood there he felt the wind of a bullet passing close by his cheek and heard the report of a weapon. He fell instinctively to one knee and tried to locate the person firing. There was another shot, and this time he saw the stab of flame as the bullet flicked past his head and ricocheted from a metal shutter.

He stood up and stepped towards the person shooting. A frightening laugh answered this act of courage.

'Another time!' his invisible tormentor promised. 'Right between the eyes! No respite! No more rest! No more truce!'

Tarpagnan walked briskly towards the voice. He saw the notary's shadow melt away into the darkness at the corner of the street. He heard the whinny of laughter again.

He howled like a wolf and set off running in pursuit.

96

The incendiary of
boulevard Saint-Michel

Now Tarpagnan had become the crazed pursuer. Running with a long elastic stride, he turned the corner into place Saint-Michel. On the esplanade of Davioud's fountain he discovered a world gone mad, a world of shadows dashing about in all directions.

At the corners of adjoining streets, overwhelmed federals were sniping at the next road junctions, occupied by Versaillais troops who were returning heavy fire. When Tarpagnan passed near these sentries they stirred uneasily, and many uttered cries of 'Who goes there?', 'Halt!' or 'Stand back!' Warnings became more frequent, as did unexpected meetings. Gradually he started to hear more stricken cries. Through the thick dust raised by thousands of feet in perpetual scurrying movement, snarling faces marked with powder or blood surged past and vanished again.

Judging by the eddies of smoke, the cases of cartridges broken open on the pavement for combatants to refill their pouches, and the terrifying number and proximity of burning buildings, there was fighting less than two hundred metres away. Everyone was extremely agitated. The enemy was approaching and the defence appeared disorganised and crumbling.

Antoine saw people moving, running away, coming together and scattering. Some were afraid. Others were frightening. They would fight with their heads high. They were heading for the firing line, shouting: 'We're not scared to die!' Others called back: 'They've got through the barricades!'

Volleys of musketry and stuttering bursts from revolving

machine guns filled the night with smoke and flashes. A hundred shots in a second or two. The street corners, the façades at junctions, were as if gnawed, hundreds of small light-coloured craters peppering the stone, each having belched a small cloud of stone-dust. Anonymous cadavers lay about the streets. An almost naked woman's body sprawled over a drain cover.

Tarpagnan kept running. He had not lost sight of Grondin.

He heard a woman shouting, somewhere ahead: 'They're in my house – before it was federals, now it's the Line!' She appeared in front of him, extending hands bound with rope, and asked: 'Untie me! They tied me up. I escaped. My husband's dead! They're taking my daughter to Montparnasse cemetery!'

He cut through the cord with his dirk and rushed on, obsessed by the pursuit. He searched the hallucinatory darkness brightened by muzzle-flashes. The inconceivable was occurring continuously all around him. He spotted Bassicoussé a hundred metres ahead of him, outlined in spectral clarity.

'Notary, stop!' he cried, running even faster. 'I swear I'm innocent!'

Who could have heard him at such a moment? The drama was reaching its climax on all levels, resolving itself in all its stark horror. Paris was ablaze. It's the Tuileries, people were saying. It's the Palais-Royal. The Ministry of Finance.

He could still see the tall outline of Grondin moving away in front of him. He could just make out the line of his shoulders above the mass of heads. He could hardly hear, an urchin having fired a pistol close to his ear and temporarily deafened him. He shouldered people aside. He was catching up. 'Notary!' he cried. 'Notary!'

Ideas crowded Antoine's head. He threw caution to the winds. Everything was so black!

'Notary! Stop!'

Lord! Amid the horrific tumult of the street he had room for only one thought: how to persuade the notary that the crime was not his, that he had loved Jeanne but had been a mad dog. How could he convince him of his innocence after all these years?

The running Tarpagnan had forgotten his officer's uniform, which designated him clearly as an insurgent. He drew his sword when he came across half a dozen cavalry in blue coats with white frogging who were hacking and slicing at twenty cornered federals, dusty and bloody, squeezed up against one another. He unhorsed one of the enemy, split his head open, ran on.

Further on he came across a group of fleeing women. One was carrying a baby on her back, slung in a shawl. Another had her arm in a sling. A third had bloodstains on her jacket.

'Don't go down there,' this last called out. 'It's a right mess! You'll run slap into the gendarmes! They've took the geezers at Saint-André-des-Arts prisoner. They come at them from the rear! They're going to shoot them!'

At that moment Tarpagnan did not much fear being taken prisoner. He ran faster. His lungs were on fire, his fists pumping like connecting-rods. His sword scabbard slapped his legs.

The man was only ten metres ahead now. They ran into another obstacle, fleeing soldiers, their weapons slung upside down. Another group in headlong rout, panting like him but running in the opposite direction.

He forced himself to maintain his pace. His brain was working at lightning speed. He had worked out what to say, prepared his words. It's true, he admitted, that I failed in my duty by not coming forward to give evidence at his trial. It's true that my single day of cowardice sealed the fate of that man who wanted to make me and Jeanne happy. But I'm not the murderer! That's what I'm going to tell him, even if he won't believe me. I must proclaim my innocence! As he once proclaimed his own. Even if I know I'll never find the courage to admit that it was indeed me he saw fleeing the scene of the crime in the early morning. That I had an assignation with Jeanne and had just discovered the murder. That I was too afraid of being accused of the vile massacre to come forward!'

Only two metres! And more obstacles, civilians loaded with bundles and suitcases, pathetic faces lost in shadow.

Tarpagnan reached out his hand, grasped the other's shoulder, turned him round. 'It wasn't me!' he cried. 'I had nothing to do with it!'

The words stopped abruptly. The face looking at him was nothing like Bassicoussé's. It belonged to a tall devil covered in sweat, with a bent nose and rags for clothes: an incendiary, holding in hands fashioned by some rough job in ironfounding or metalwork two bottles with lighted wicks. Their dancing light showed the rictus of fatigue on his face, his worker's leanness, his drawn features and irrepressible energy.

'What d'you want from me?' the man asked. He waved his incendiary devices. 'After one of these, are yer?'

'Yes.'

Why the devil had he said that?

'Grab hold, then. Follow me! Close to the walls. They're everywhere! You meet 'em sometimes! Run straight through 'em! They don't hardly get time to recognise you! They only fire a shot or two, they're afraid of killin' each other. Come on! Move yer pins! Don't hang about! Got to do it proper! Further on, this way. Get in the mugs' and toffs' houses! Toss a bit of fire their way!'

They ran on together. Soon they saw a line of prisoners escorted by a platoon of riflemen.

'They're takin' 'em down the cells. P'r'aps to the slaughter 'ouse!'

A cart carried prisoners who had tried to escape. Some had gaping wounds in the backs of their heads. A woman nursed a sword-cut hand missing several fingers.

They sidled along behind an ignoble throng of *decent folk* howling: 'Kill them!' and booing the captives, whose only remaining defences were pride and contempt.

The firebug stopped suddenly outside a fine house of knapped stone. 'This suit yer? What d'yer think? It's top drawer all right!' He slipped into the paved courtyard, Antoine on his heels, and eyed the lodge. 'The concierge ain't in. Gotter be a p'lice informer!'

They crossed the courtyard and waited immobile in the shadows to the right of the entry staircase. The windows blazed with light. Behind a curtain they saw for a moment the outline of a young woman. Her neck was long, her waist small. Her bare arms reached up in a charming gesture to adjust her hair-comb.

The incendiary murmured: 'Funny to think there's arses what fart in silk, ain't it!'

He stepped back a few paces from the front of the building and looked up. The tricolour flew from a staff. The cellar windows were level with the pavement round the building. The man tossed his bottle neatly in through an air-vent and giggled, showing all his bad teeth.

'See that, did yer? There's a knack! Your turn, mate!'

Tarpagnan thought of Vallès. His companion took his hesitation for inexperience.

'What you 'angin' onto the goods for, orf'cer? Scared? Stingy? Give it 'ere, double quick!' The man took the bottle of paraffin from his hands and tossed it into the depths.

'Thing to do now is *not* bugger it up by hangin' about round here! Leg it for all yer worth! Back home!'

They started to retrace their route. Suddenly the sound of tramping footsteps sounded not far off. The moon faintly illuminated a patrol of seven or eight troops clearing the street ahead.

'A patrol! Dangerous!' The arsonist jinked, glancing swiftly about for a better hiding-place than a simple doorway. A hundred metres back down the street, he dragged Tarpagnan under the entrance porch of a dark building. They were swallowed up in the cavities of the night. They felt their way carefully along a wall and went to ground in a recess. The yard they were in – a square of disused dilapidated workshops – had an uninhabited air. Grass was growing between a pile of tree-stumps and a stack of cast-iron pipes.

It was extremely quiet. No street sounds, no garden rustlings. Time passed. Antoine smelt the sweetish, almost carrion odour of his companion's breath and heard his raucous whisper: 'Before leaving, piss on yer hands! Straight on them, I'm tellin' you, and wash 'em well. 'Cause when you touch them bottles you get covered with it, the stink of paraffin. And if they catch you and smell it you're for the high jump!'

Antoine heard the sounds of his companion following this advice. There was a short silence, a rustling of clothes. Then the incendiary's voice again: 'I'll go first. Every man for hisself! Goodbye!'

'Goodbye!'

Tarpagnan peered into the night from his hiding place.
Running silhouettes passed the street gateway. He heard hobnailed footsteps. He heard cries of terror. Dull hammering
noises. He was seized by something worse than terror, worse
than a sound. Somehow he was aware of the indescribable end of
a man. Agony under the vault of the sky.

Not long afterwards he was on his way again. Three doors
down the street he found the body of the arsonist who had just
left him. Antoine's knees wobbled despite himself. Cold sweat
flowed down his back. What planet was he in, what human
cesspit?

The dead man's face was a shapeless mask, his smashed skull
running blood and brains. He had been nailed to a house door.

97

Paris is a garden
of fire

Not far behind Antoine, the Versaillais were advancing, filled with anger. Cissey's men were demolishing property and arresting people. They had become instruments of the informers' hatred. Guided by porters and concierges, led by mean fellows in striped waistcoats who pointed out Commune sympathisers, they were in a sort of feeding frenzy. Rifling the houses and courtyards, pillaging silverware, wrecking rooms and emptying them of valuables, chucking children down stairwells.

To hasten the work they were shooting people out of hand. They were not sparing women. They were sticking their bayonets in people's eyes. Crushing the truth of the poor. The night had taken on a mad and sinister air.

Passing in front of blazing houses, red and roaring from cellar to attic, running down the middle of streets filled with bright light, bending low under storms of ashes and sparks, having to give a wide berth to shops vomiting flame through their broken shutters, Tarpagnan made his way towards the Seine.

When he reached the river it was difficult to cross, for the bridge was packed with an indescribable tumult, dominated by the screaming of women. Cries of pain, cries of hatred. Unbearable stridencies, shrieking modulations thrown up involuntarily in the outrage and fury of having lost everything.

He stopped for a moment, and felt strongly that the man with grey eyes was on his heels once again. He spotted him almost at once, leaning on the handrail of the bridge. He was in a well-lighted spot as if to be sure of being noticed.

Eyes sparkling, affecting an air of indifference to his scapegoat, he was contemplating the unexpected grandeur of the surrounding spectacle with a gloomy and singular sort of joy. Antoine himself was overcome by the wild energy of the fire now ravaging the town like a furious animal. He could not tear his eyes from the contained ditch of the Seine, its waters gripped by a roaring arch of fire, the dark stretches still clear of fire on its banks like islands in the sea of flame, while the oily water reflected the blinding heat and light with the effect of lava.

So the nightmare of shadows and chimeras had begun. Once across the river, back in the Paris of embankments, towers, courtyards, walls and crossroads, Tarpagnan found himself looking over his shoulder to see if he was being followed. The obsession had already started for him, the hallucinatory fear of seeing the notary's face appear at his side or on his heels, that pitiless mask of old hardwood inhabited by a ferocious and grinning dementia that no exhortation, no reasoning, could divert from its dedication to misplaced vengeance.

The smoke was like thick fog in the streets. It made the tracker's task easier. When Tarpagnan looked back, a hundred moving shadows flickered behind him. Which blackish cut-out was the outline of his follower, his assassin? Antoine slunk along close to the walls and peered anxiously into the shadows of porches. He felt rather than heard the steady hissing of the other's breath labouring in his wake. Sometimes over his shoulder he saw grey eyes like the gleam of a distant lake.

From time to time Tarpagnan would stop, his stomach knotted with anger. Service revolver in his hand, he felt ready to demand an explanation.

'Hey! You! Come nearer!'

But the other would also stop. He would stand there among the hundreds of faces painted red by the glow of fires and torches, staring fixedly at Tarpagnan and grinning. Whenever Tarpagnan tried to approach him, the spectre would avoid confrontation by melting away, impalpable form in the constantly shifting crowd, leaving in the air behind him a few cutting and mocking words, a tuneless disjointed stream of unintelligible maledictions whose litany echoed in nightmare fashion against the sinister background sounds and was lost among the bobbing heads and shoulders of fleeing people.

So Tarpagnan would continue on his way.

But now he kept thinking about that sardonic and triumphant laugh. Now the nagging fear of a bullet in the back made his temples pound; now he had to try to forget the death-threat carried by the other's snatches of laughter as he pursued through that great lumber-room of defeat and fear his wandering and hesitant quest for other resolute faces.

In that dark succession of streets Antoine saw Paris with new eyes. So the city of happy days was reduced to ashes ... Looking at the blackened carcasses of its ruined masterpieces, he apologised for suffering so much. After that, mad as a snake, Christ, he felt capable of anything.

Paris was blanketed in thick eddies of black smoke. Everywhere it pulsated with red glows. Paris had been distempered with paraffin oil. Paris lay gulping under a black snow. Paris had been transformed into a simmering kettle of catarrh and abomination.

Where – in which spout of flames, in which fusillade, on the corner of which boulevard – was the giant Marbuche? In what chaos of wheelbarrows was Palmyre scampering? Among what legions of gutted dead and wounded, through what stinking charnel-houses and what blood-filled gutters was Caf'conc' walking as the fresh face of that pale dawn with its stinking breath became visible above the rooftops? In what situations of blind fury, pointless courage, energetic resistance, unjust reproach, insulting menace or enormous loss was friend Vallès struggling?

The Pot-de-Fer barricade was unreachable. The Panthéon, people said, was still standing up against the assaults of an entire regiment. Tarpagnan was trembling with rage. The grey-eyed man still after him.

Antoine looked at him, then deliberately turned his back. He felt him keeping pace on the pavement opposite, but resisted the temptation to look round.

He heard that mad laugh again. All right! Let him laugh.

But then a bullet made its puff of stone-dust hardly a foot from his head. He dropped instinctively to the ground.

'The colour of a farewell to life!' the spectre's voice cried.

Antoine spun round, revolver drawn, a spark of rage in his dilated pupils. His eyesight was excellent. He saw between two charred beams the diagonal line of the grey greatcoat whipping behind a half-collapsed wall. Gone again, the icy beast! The darkness had closed on the ghost like a conjurer's box.

Tarpagnan rubbed his eye with the back of his hand. The thunder of artillery fired from Montmartre rolled through the air. Perhaps he was dreaming. Facing the red-outlined silhouette of the Tuileries, the black towers of Notre-Dame rose like hieratic mandrakes of stone lace.

He resumed his hurried course through the unbreathable air of the blazing night. He heard a cry of barbaric fury behind him, and broke into a run. His back ran with sweat, his gaze was worried. The yellow and sulphurous smoke burned his eyes. Charred debris exploded and crashed down around him as he ran.

He felt continuously on his heels the presence of the other man – as if attached to him by an invisible thread – driven by a diabolical energy, foaming at the mouth, following his scent, relishing his discomfort and awaiting the moment when he would be lying at the roadside, glassy-eyed and open-mouthed like fresh-killed game already going stiff.

He ran through small dark streets dazzled by the occasional gas-lamp. An artillery duel sizzled and bellowed overhead, knocking holes in the fronts of buildings. To give himself heart he hummed a song Wire had taught him in better days, two or three verses he had got from Louise Michel. A *ritornello* that combat had inspired in the Red Virgin. Tarpagnan remembered it went something like:

Friends, it's raining shrapnel.
Forward, everyone! Take wing!
The thunder of battle rumbles
Over us ... all together, now: sing!

Suddenly, a line of lightning ran along the gable of a building whose roof, along with a big slab of the front wall, collapsed across the street in front of him. He didn't stop. He ran through the smoke, vaulted the fallen beams and debris, deployed his entire body. He ran on through the howling and bellowing of shells.

Fire! Flames! Ash! Dust! Dead meat! The stench of burning buildings seized him by the throat. He no longer thought the impalpable presence of the notary on his heels of much importance. But he was still there, like an old plot, a throwback, an inexorable trap set by time.

So he ran on. The life instinct versus the death instinct. Tarpagnan stopped, searched the darkness for the great night-bird following him and called out:

'You want to chase me, God-damned son of a whore? Go on then, follow me, tire yourself out! Faster! Run after me, death's head! Panting! Look at the clock. In half an hour the sun will be up. The daily horror will be starting again! Fever and exaltation! What an explosion of youth in my legs! Run, spectre! Forward! The dawning day is sending its password. The final battle will be fought in the middle of Paris. I mean to be there! I'll be part of it! I've chosen my own exit door!'

When he came within sight of les Halles it was five o'clock in the morning. As he approached Saint-Eustache a great menagerie of shadows had started to move once again. Bullets were again zipping and whining; cries, curses, guttural groans and hundreds of stabbing muzzle-flashes told him that he was approaching the fighting, that he was back among people of valour.

98

Horace Grondin's crime

The present arrived all at once, suddenly, with the new day. Asserting itself. There would be sunshine. Gold dust, soothing light, let it come, let it assuage people's pain! Revive their courage!

But alas! That caressing light, the emblem of life, only made the pain worse for the children of the Commune. For when it emerged shining and new from the claws of night and dispelled the obscurity, the sun showed them that today, Wednesday 24th May, would be remembered as a day of great carnage.

Burned paper fluttered in the sky like a plague of black crows. Oil smoke spiralled up in fabulous skeins of soot. The new day was going to see a resumption of the violence. The blood-vintners started up their man-presses.

And here came the bloodthirsty dogs of the Ladmirault Division!

Tarpagnan surveyed the position in the square. He skirted the walls of the church. Propped up between the buttresses were stretchers holding bloodstained wounded men who wanted to carry on fighting.

He presented himself at the front line and was cheered by the sixty or so ragged combatants jammed elbow to elbow behind a rampart of cobblestones, casks, sacks of rubble, old mattresses and two overturned omnibuses between which there projected the barrel of a small field-artillery piece. He took command of these stalwarts, whose officer, an engineer captain, had just been killed by a bullet through the neck.

Scoundrels from the slums and loose women. Butchers and porters from les Halles. They were all there. Communards. Reds.

Those truly, rabidly attached to life. The People. Workers or shopkeepers. Fighting as in happier times they had worked. Conscientiously. Scrupulously.

For them, today was the day to stake their all on the Great Future. They were fighting so that their children would not have to work fifteen hours a day starting at the age of eight.

In a galloping of troops, a booming of guns and crepitation of shrapnel, the struggle for control of the belly of the town was beginning. It was going to be grim, grim. It would mean the utter destruction of the defences and the defenders.

The workers fired, dived into the unknown of an absurd battle. The women fired too, and reloaded rifles. Under the Amazons' jackets, the dry misery of bodies hardened by toil and privation. In the heads of the proletarians, the boiling rage of men cheated of love.

A hundred metres from their position, a fiery captain recently assigned to the 45th Line regiment was just completing with his sergeants a plan of attack to deal with the 'obstacle of St Eustace's Church'.

His name was Arnaud Desétoiles. He was a brilliant officer, admirably attuned to the 'odious necessities' of war. When necessary, and without pity, he would have people shot.

We have recently seen him doing so at the rue Myrrha barricades. And we met him at the beginning of the book, when he was a courier working for the prefect Valentin, the arrogant young man sent to see Commissaire Mespluchet on 17th March. He was a typical product of his caste: a very tough nut of good family, whose grandfather had been a peer of France. An ambitious character who had got his course mapped out. A steadfast defender of the values of the family, the Church, progress, merit and education. He and Tarpagnan had been trained together.

In less than ten minutes' time he would order the assault. Now he was ordering his troops to lay down heavy preliminary small-arms fire.

Behind a pile of market barrows, Tarpagnan darted about amid the shrapnel and projectiles. He passed continually from life to death, moving about from one part of the defences to

another, encouraging people, stiffening their resolve. A word
here and a word there. Telling the men to lay the gun more
intelligently, to raise its muzzle so that the shells would reach the
enemy lines instead of falling short.

All around him people were dying, and the wounded were
begging for a drop of water. Some were unrecognisable from
sword-wounds. One man's cheek had been torn off by a bullet.
Another was plugging a hole in his own belly with strips torn
from a red flag.

Antoine was foggily lucid. He felt no fear for himself. Looking
over his shoulder he saw the notary coming towards him.

He indicated the barricade and its party of ferocious combatants, men like wolves who wanted to go all the way. He called
out to him. He signed to him to come and play his part in the
fighting and death. With an untroubled forehead he smiled slyly
at Bassicoussé and turned away to the front line.

He knew that in every man there is a corner of inextirpable
danger. He knew that the work of art that is the body is only
blood and matter, and understood that where he was now would
certainly be the place of his death. He knew that it would be
honourable provided he chose it himself.

He knew that at last he was among his own.

Horace Grondin crouched in the imperfect shelter of a pile of
bodies, listening to bullets whacking into his shield of dead
federals' meat with a flat, disheartening slapping noise. Just to his
left, an overturned greengrocer's cart had vomited bundles of
asparagus, whose morbid whiteness seemed to him unbearable.

He was fascinated by Antoine's prodigiously courageous
behaviour. He watched the proud Gascon fight with the
obstinacy of some general of popular legend: heaving a body out
of the way to take its place, raising the flag of revolution over the
fighting.

As fire crackled everywhere, as people were shot in the nearby
streets while others carried on sniping, as the low and muffled
drum sounded the retreat, as men fought hand-to-hand and
chopped at each other with swords house by house, Horace
Grondin watched in a kind of stupefaction as the stalwart people
died around him, and concluded that once again the least

favoured were not going to win. Once again the cobblestones of the insurrection, the honest fury of the survivors, the titanic grace of those dispossessed of happiness, the violated rights of the massacred people, opened a breach in the former notary's certitudes.

His shoulders slumped. Some combatants fled past him. 'Fall back on the church!' a thunderous voice cried. 'Regroup in the porches!'

Most of the survivors holed up in the church.

They had been five hundred at the beginning of the engagement. Now there were just a handful of invincibles around Tarpagnan. Perhaps a couple of dozen still grouped under the red flag; perhaps not that many. A roaring volley had just laid three more dead on the cobbles.

Grondin could not take his eyes off the man who had been his prey. Antoine was fighting like an injured tiger. His shoulder was bleeding. He was the pinnacle of a swarming pyramid of ragged insurgents, exhausted with drink, fatigue and vain anger, held together by spilled blood. The notary lifted his head above the jumble of bodies behind which he was pinned down by heavy small-arms fire.

Nobody could possibly measure how he felt at that moment. He was losing his footing, running painfully aground. He could feel his righteous determination to kill that man who was almost a son – a plan forged over sixteen years – beginning to slip away from him. For the greatness of Tarpagnan's exploits, his intrepidity, his self-denial, the way he constantly restored the courage of his companions, risking death repeatedly as he moved about to shore up their valour, forced him to stay his hand. Antoine's noble generosity with his life and strength, his unfailing coolness, suddenly relegated to oblivion all Grondin's demons of rancour, all the torments inflicted by his obsession with vengeance.

The grey eyes of the former convict suddenly stopped watching the barricade. He was thinking.

Ravaged by the contradictions in his heart, illuminated despite himself by a love for the other that he tried to reject but that stifled him, saturated with a jumble of emotions, Grondin struggled fiercely to work out what to do. His judgement was suddenly unsound. The relative nature of human justice seemed overwhelmingly apparent. His savage scowl reflected his interior turmoil. He kicked, he dug his heels in, he bucked. A shadow crossed his face.

He cursed God for insinuating the idea of clemency into a mind deranged by desolation. With a yell of rage he surged out of the cavern in the pile of corpses and hurled himself towards the barricade.

Now they were side by side. A sergeant had tossed Grondin a rifle. They were firing side by side. Together they were getting ready to enter the grave. The Line troops were gathering nearby, preparing for the final rush that would submerge them. Tarpagnan turned and shouted:

'I'm not the one you want! I didn't kill Jeanne, I swear it! Would I lie at a moment like this?'

Hundreds of soldiers galloped howling towards them, and they started firing. This time the charge was unsuccessful, but three more of their companions had fallen. Tarpagnan mouthed:

'There's no sense in it, notary! Here we both are, heating up our rifles, killing the same men . . . aiming at the same targets . . . look! The officer there, the one who's just stood up . . . raising his sword . . . sending the charge at us: let's both kill him, because if we don't he's certainly going to kill us. Fire! Got him! We both hit him in the chest and we hate each other!'

This time they were overrun. All red with blood, splashing and dripping. The Line rolled over them. They were knocked off their feet, struggled up again. Tarpagnan hurled himself blindly forward, ready and willing to plunge into sooty blackness. Slashing and stabbing, he sabred a bloody path into the forest of bayonets.

In that slowed-down instant Grondin saw that Tarpagnan was about to escape him for ever. Madness possessed him like a sort of premature mourning. His eyes glowed hard and blank like steel balls. His own truth, the necessary murder, glittered in his mind with crystalline clarity.

He raised his rifle, closed his gashed eye and sent a single bullet through the spinal column of the man who had been about to die a hero's death.

Then, appalled by what he had done, he took a deep breath, dropped his scowl into the brine next to the mutilated face of a white-lipped cadaver, and played dead.

After quite a short time he heard the soft sound of boots on bodies as two NCOs trod the vintage of the fallen, clambering over the heaps of dead. From time to time one of them would shoot a wounded man behind the ear with a revolver. The other, more economical with ammunition, used a bayonet in the guts or a rifle-butt in the back of the head.

Grondin got the rifle-butt. His skull smashed, he toppled into the void and was gone for ever in a great drift of stars.

The whole area reeked of spoiled meat. Big groups of Versaillais soldiers fanned out through the adjacent streets. Three hundred prisoners were massacred on the spot.

99

The devil's messenger

The dial was broken and time took a leap. It ran away, stampeded off the rails, everything out of control and going to hell!

The tocsin stuttered. Sounds yapped. The drums fell silent. The ground was soaked in blood. The flames rolled up their anger.

Shot, young and old; shot the insurgents, the foot-soldiers of the invincible idea! Forty federals caught with weapons in rue Saint-Jacques: shot in the back. Raoul Rigault, attorney-general of the Commune: shot without trial in rue Gay-Lussac. Any woman who was badly dressed or with disordered clothing: shot. Work-boots and rags: shot!

Firing squads rolled out their volleys in the Luxembourg Gardens, at the Cherche-Midi prison, in place Saint-Sulpice. Irregulars were killed in rue Soufflot, in the Jardin des Plantes, at the Montagne-Sainte-Geneviève; they were liquidated in the parc Monceau. The brazenness of it! Every little helps! The great headsman's sword of that fervent Catholic Marie Edme Maurice Patrice de Mac-Mahon, Duke of Magenta and Marshal of France, carried its work into the very hospitals: eighty wounded murdered in their beds along with their doctor. It takes your breath away!

Livid faces. Bloated bellies. Burst organs. Chests smashed in. Scalps torn off. The whole day started to reek under the bright sun.

Has it always been properly understood that the dead call to the dead?

At la Roquette, sinister reprisals were taking shape. The

combatants murdered out of hand at the barricades, the people shot at Caumartin, the widows of the latest men to be executed called for redress. Throats were raw with anger.

The Archbishop of Paris and six of his companions began the gloomy descent of the narrow and vaulted spiral stair that led to the ground floor of the prison. The sinister procession was led by the turnkey McDavis. He carried very high, above his leering amphibian's head, a lantern whose feeble yellowish light made shadows dance on the livid faces of the men who had been chosen to pay the price of Versaillais cruelty in their blood. The names of the sacrificial lambs to accompany the Archbishop were Deguerry, Bonjean, Allard, Clerc, Ducoudray and Ségouret.

Ségouret's name had been added to the list as an extra. This is how it happened: François, the governor of la Roquette, asked to be given the names of those to be executed. The Blanquiste Genton, who along with Fortin was in charge of the business, replied:

'There are supposed to be six. That's what my chit says.'

'What about the Archbishop?' someone asked. 'He's the heavyweight. He's the one they really want to see dancing!'

Thirty or so people were involved in the discussion. Feelings were running high. A number of women had got into the meeting. People were longing to be given some *curé* to eat.

'No orders about him.'

People grumbled and griped revealing blind directionless force. Eventually Fortin raised his hand and called for silence.

'All right!' he said. 'The Archbishop goes too.' That would calm them down.

'Yer, but then there'll be *seven* of 'em,' McDavis pointed out. 'P'r'aps I'd better put this one 'ere back in 'is cupboard ... 'e ain't a very big wheel ...' With his lantern, he illuminated the abbé Ségouret's white face.

Fortin stood on a bench and cleared his throat. Again he calmed his audience, which was in the grip of lynch fever. The situation was uncertain.

'Quiet, citizens!' he cried. 'Seeing as we're here to snuff the Archbishop's candle, what does it matter how many others we put on the cake? Ségouret goes to the party! Right,' he added to change the subject, 'who'll volunteer?'

'I will,' a fireman replied immediately, stepping forward. His eyes were red. 'My brother was shot this morning.'

They set off down the stairs.

They found thirty or so volunteers, loudmouths armed for the most part from the prison weapon racks. Four of them walked ahead of the prisoners. The rest of the escort consisted of a straggling procession of variegated uniforms formed in anger and malice by a handful of excitable types, and included a number of deranged women who wanted to see some daughter-impregnating sky-pilots take the high jump.

They passed through a barred gate into the outside perimeter path, whose surrounding wall ran along the rue de la Vacquerie.

The first of the hostages to enter the yard, roughly surfaced in big pebbles and limestone flux, was Archbishop Darboy. He had a long white beard which gave him a saintly appearance. His head was bent in suffering. He was holding his pastoral cross and undoubtedly praying.

The others followed, the abbé Ségouret last of all. His health seemed to have collapsed alarmingly. He was extremely thin, hollow-cheeked, pallid, with purulent sores. Only eyes lighted from the inside by an unnatural fire revealed the tumult in his soul and his unhinged brain.

At the barred door, followed by a flight of four steps down into the yard, McDavis stopped, raising his lantern, and allowed the sinister cortege to pass him. He fell in with the abbé Ségouret for a few paces, placing a hand on his arm and staring into the criminal's eyes with his captivating and cold-blooded gaze. From the depths of his ugliness the Scot croaked:

'The soil's parched where you're going, padre! May Satan forgive you! You're goin' ter burn in red-'ot cinders!'

The drowning vicar, sweating with fear at the imminence of those infernal chasms, bared his long fangs and in an imploring tone uttered the hurried words:

'When it's over, I beg of you, wash my body! Wash my body!'

'It'll be done.'

'Get my letter to the notary.'

'It'll be done. It'll be done.'

'I'll repent until the end of time!'

McDavis let go of his arm. His usual mask of ferocity was back in place and his smile peeled back enormously wide lips in a disheartening way.

'Don't be discouraged, Ségouret, by all the emptiness in front of you! All that blackness! All that nothingness, nothingness, nothingness!'

The abbé walked on, frightened by the idea of punishment without form or dimensions: without limits. No one had paid any attention to their conversation. McDavis scuttled back to his place at the front of the procession.

The men designated for the firing squad formed up in three ranks. The condemned stood with their backs to a stone wall. The rifle muzzles were quite close to their faces. A raised sword came down smartly.

'Fire!'

The weapons spat long red flames. Ségouret was blasted by an axe of light through the forehead. The Archbishop remained standing for a moment, then crumpled slowly after a second bullet through the heart.

'He's armour-plated, that one!' murmured a voice in the ensuing silence. Two guardsmen gave him the *coup de grâce*. The horde of executioners dispersed. The prison clock struck eight. The night was closing in.

In a short time McDavis was alone there. He extracted the abbé Ségouret's inert body from under the pile, dragged it a few metres away and went to get clean water from the well. Returning with a brimming pail he murmured gently into the corpse's ear:

'I'll give yer a proper rinsin' down, comrade, see if I don't, just you watch me!'

He started to wash the dead man.

Hardly an hour later he walked down rue Mercoeur, cut through rue Guibert, crossed Charonne and slipped into St Margaret's Church. After a short gallop down the nave, the stinking flat-headed hairy-limbed gnome swerved into the left-hand side-chapel, opened the door into St Bernard's cemetery and stuck his nose into the fresh night air scented with fading flowers.

His busy outline scuttling on ropy legs, athlete's shoulders swaying, the ugly wall-toad trotted among the graves of the Temple quarter's dead inhabitants. Just on the left, against the Chapel of the Souls in Purgatory, he stopped in front of a small tomb marked with a stone cross. On this was engraved:

L ... XVII (1787–1795)

And a little lower down:

Attendite et videte si est dolor sicut dolor meus

The ugly gnome sniffed the breeze flowing between the graves. He looked at the decrepit garden of rest. He rested his ugly arse on the kerbstone round the vault in which the child-king lay, and listened into the darkness for Ursule Capdebosc's hurried footstep.

Did he mean to associate tonight's meeting-place in lugubrious fashion with mad murders from the past? What baleful thought, what perverse strategy, what impish humour had moved the ghastly turnkey to choose the last resting place of Louis XVI's son to hand over to human justice the confession of an infanticide priest? Could it have been to play on the old housekeeper's much-vaunted timidity, and drag the old chatter-box to the lowest and most infernal regions at the same time as her master, or did the hideous batrachian really possess the occult powers of a devil's messenger, and know already that neither Ursule Capdebosc nor Charles Bassicoussé would be turning up to the meeting, but the person who was now coming down the path?

A long swarthy shadow approached under the trees and emerged very cautiously from the shadows, feeling the terrain carefully with the point of a toe and stopping motionless in mid-stride to sense the surroundings. Aerial, prudent as a vulture, of the race that chops up other people's food and regurgitates it later.

He had the aspect of a gravedigger. He carried a lantern in one hand and a pick and a mattock in the other. His complexion was yellow and he appeared to be walking on stilts. He saluted. Constructed a grimace resembling a smile. Darted the turnkey a sidelong glance from worried eyes, and murmured with a coy air:

'Is there something we have to do together?'

'Depends,' McDavis replied.

'All clear,' the gravedigger said, relaxing strangely. 'I'm the beadle of Saint-Sulpice. I'm here on behalf of Madame Capdebosc, and I've brought you a little pot of butter from her, and other tokens of gratitude.'

He put his lantern on the tomb and his tools on the ground, heaved the shoulder-bag round on his skinny back and rummaged in it, presenting the prison screw in succession with a purse of gold and four earthenware pots of *foie gras*. McDavis received this largesse with every sign of satisfaction. He hefted the purse in a pleased way and put it in the inside pocket of his tunic.

The vulture leaned forward uncomfortably, his mouth open, musing. After a while he said: 'Getting here from the rue de Grenelle wasn't all that easy, but once I got used to the tempo of the artillery, and of the charges and counter-charges of the two sides, I can boast that I became quite good at making myself very thin and managed to nip across between the lines . . .' He added with slightly bullying distinctness: 'So I wonder if you'd be so very kind as to give us some news of our good priest?'

McDavis gazed at him with the eyes of a contented frog. He didn't hum and haw, but he did sneer a little.

'Well, it's upsettin', to relate, and that, like, but citizen Ségouret's kicked the, er, bucket.'

'I don't get you,' the tall pelican stammered.

'You don't *want* ter get me,' the turnkey corrected, 'but I'm going to tell you anyway. Your Ségouret's gone back to his maker without going to paradise. Twelve bullets in his hide! He got his lot at the same time as the Bishop of Paris and five more of the same kind.'

Hippolyte Barthélemy (for it can only have been he) was flabbergasted. His mouth hung open and he made gobbling noises. 'But, but ... shot? Shot? What an incongruous death for a soldier of Christ!'

He looked up at the moon, the stars, all that shines and is unattainable. He sighed. He had the air of one recovering from serious illness. He slowly moved his hands to the small of his back, and stretched.

'*Dead* dead?' he asked just make sure.

'Belly-up for ever. He asked me to settle his affairs for him.' The turnkey rummaged in his pocket and gave the priest's letter to the policeman. Barthélemy stared at it.

'A testament?'

'Call it a gobbing of the soul,' the Scot said without lowering his voice. He whirled his long hairy arms about giving off mephitic armpit odours and added with a grimace:

'All his life your limb of hell there was pissing in the holy water stoop. When you've read that, citizen, p'r'aps you won't think he's quite such a saint in 'eaven!'

While the other man was putting the letter away McDavis retreated several paces, hopped off the ground like a toad, turning round as he did so, and vanished into the night leaving an evil-smelling fart hanging in the air.

100

Commissaire Mespluchet returns

'God damn and blast it to hell! It's really too much! You wouldn't know whether to laugh or cry! It's . . . it's *extravagant*! The absolute opposite of what any reasonable person would expect!' grated Isidore Mespluchet, dropping his pince-nez to the end of its cord. The Commissaire of Gros-Caillou had just closed the folder containing the two hundred and fifty-four pages of his subordinate's report.

He was still gazing at the handwritten label on the cardboard cover of the fascinating file, an expression of astonished repugnance in his eyes, when there came three discreet – indeed furtive – taps on the door, which opened timidly a few inches.

'Come in, Barthélemy, if that's you! Don't *sidle* like that, dammit, step inside like a man! I've just read your report and I've got plenty to say to you!'

His myopic stare peered about trying to find the author of the explosive document, and rested for a moment on the walnut panelling. The Commissaire knitted his bushy eyebrows as his eye probed a dark corner of the room, a window embrasure containing a hatstand on which coats were hung. Eventually he thought he had discerned a distant profile: a rumpled form, vaguely outlined in a rigid, toweringly tall black overcoat.

'God's blood, Hippolyte!' he swore through clenched teeth, 'is it you? Is it really you?' After glancing through his pince-nez to confirm that it was, he continued: 'My poor beanpole! My dear young fellow! If you only knew how delectably juicy I've been finding your product here! My *hat*, what material! And what *technique* you've acquired in the last two months! The spirit of observation is omnipresent. But there's a certain . . . *causticity* as well! I congratulate you on that: it's the sign of a man who knows what he's looking at. Reading your stuff, everything comes to life! One gets an admirable feel for the ups and downs and the underlying causes of that plebeian revolt! And the rest, too ... *respectable* Paris, limpid as a mountain stream! And Paris in its street-arab misery, described like a bestiary! A blind man would get the picture! All these poor and indigent people, these patched-together lives, what a portrait you give of them! I mean! Having to run away, keeping watch on someone, the reverses of fortune, the no-man's-land of marginal people, the time of guesswork and the time of pursuit ... it's ... it's *fabulous*! Worthy of the highest praise!'

Panting slightly, Mespluchet looked up and saw that his former maid-of-all-work was now standing in front of his desk. He resumed:

'And then again, look, it's the most damnable bombshell! What *dynamite* you've buried in your famous report! Goodness! It makes everything so easy! Those undersides and hideouts, all those loaded guns, the hurricane of lives, all the big gangsters you point out! All those top-drawer criminals, embezzlers, gold-diggers and female thieves, extortionists, jewel-swallowers; all those brothel-keepers and shady entrepreneurs, old hooks, those pimps and bullies, the tarts and the rest, cut-throats, street-women, Commune fire-raisers, etcetera ... My God, how proud I feel when I read your stuff! A plainclothes man I left behind me! A policeman I trained personally!'

'All I did was carry out the mission you assigned to me before you left for Versailles,' said the yellow-faced beanpole.

'Oh, fiddlesticks, Hippolyte! It's me you're talking to! Bravo, my boy! You did your duty splendidly!'

'Enough of that, sir, please! It's events that make men, after all.'

'To hell with that. You've got the right stuff!'

Hippolyte Barthélemy swallowed. Something was undoubtedly happening in his inner depths. He was standing imperceptibly straighter. It was unbelievable. He had stopped being a flatterer. He moved forward a pace.

'I'm a proper policeman,' he said. 'An informed observer of the customs and morals of the street.'

He had spoken in an assured voice, his dull black gaze fixed on the desk where the file slumbered. Mespluchet had not expected this quiet self-confidence and found himself considerably at a loss.

'Ah! Ah! Certainly!' he blustered. 'Certainly, Hippolyte! A proper policeman! That's what you are.' He tittered and then, aware that he ought to erase the memory of that insincere enthusiasm, threw himself on the file once again and opened it in the middle. Leafed through the pages, smoothed his moustache, and panted in some extra oxygen while dreamily running his thumb over the annotated pages. 'All the same,' he added, 'the more I think about it, the crazier this story seems to be.'

He had abruptly recovered his authoritative air of jargonising superiority. He went straight to the real point of what he had to say, so far unsaid for lack of favourable circumstances.

'Hell and damnation, Hippolyte!' he exclaimed. 'The hardest thing to swallow is what you say at the beginning of your memorandum. I mean, a man of Grondin's stature! A policeman high-up who turns out to be an old *lag*, no less! A penal-colony veteran, unjustly sentenced! A provincial notable who was first rejected by society, then chosen to shield it! A hard nut, a leader of men, a man who was half-executioner, half-victim of his own unending rage! A fabulous police animal who – not to put too fine a point on it – murdered an innocent man in the belief that he was repairing the errors of human justice! No, I mean! What a balls-up! What an eternal misunderstanding! And what a loss, incidentally, to that great service, the security police!'

'We must be fair to the late Horace Grondin,' Hippolyte Barthélelmy interrupted, advancing his starveling face into a shaft of bright sunlight. Without warning his long and nervous hand had fluttered back and forth several times like a bat in the space in front of the astonished Commissaire's face, and the humble oaf again found the courage to exclaim:

'How terrible it must have been, sir, to live the way that man lived! Grondin was a soul in torment. A dark creature maddened by his own thoughts. But the thing that most struck me about him was that he was a character built on a remarkable scale. He *invented* people, took them under his wing and then set about changing them to suit him! And I must confess that I myself was . . . affected. But it's through his implacable eyes that I've learned to read the machinations of the powerful, to see the naïvety of the street world and decipher the arcana of the swell mob.'

'Obviously that's why you describe these things so well,' Mespluchet said with simulated enthusiasm, somewhat disconcerted by the turn the conversation was taking. To buy time he gave himself a pinch of snuff, took his big handkerchief from his pocket and cleared the twin bores of his nose with a muted trumpeting sound.

Then, after a long moment of vague sadness, he pushed his chair briskly back from his desk, stood up on his short legs, joined his hands behind his back and started walking up and down the large room, whose shelves had been emptied of their files.

'Monsieur Claude's been released,' he said suddenly. 'Our Sûreté director's going to resume his functions. Detention hasn't dampened his firm attitudes. His department'll have to be reorganised, of course. He'll need an assistant . . . someone who's up to the job.'

Mespluchet stopped walking up and down, put his pince-nez on again and looked at Barthélemy. Yes, he reflected, the one-time oaf-of-all-work had definitely become more assured. For one thing, he had come beyond the centre of the room and was now leaning on the back of the solitary chair placed in front of the desk. His body seemed to have lost its rigidity. Become flexible, so to speak . . . the word Mespluchet really wanted was *free*.

Barthélemy gazed fixedly at the Commissaire's hat, lying on that same chair. He seemed to be considering carefully what answer to give.

'I'm getting a clearer and clearer idea of what a modern police force ought to be like,' he said at last.

'Ah yes?' Mespluchet said before he could stop himself. Suddenly it was as if he had never been away from his office. He looked flat-nosed, heavy-lidded and disoriented. Not even the smallest things were going smoothly today. He puffed out his thick cheeks and tried to blow away a fly that was fluttering persistently between the end of his nose and the breasts of a statuette representing the Republic, and whose presence threatened to capsize his dignity as well as sabotaging the tune that – on orders from the Préfecture – he still had to play.

'Fuck it!' he began, taking the plunge. 'Without going on and on about the impressive future advancement that I predict for you, my dear Barthélemy, what a damned *odyssey* you've had! How I envy you! What an adventure, what a fine and noble journey through insurgent Paris! How precious your notes are. Your *intelligence*. And without pretension, what a great talent you've shown for sniffing out crime! Distinguishing between true and false. Tracking down vice ...actually unmasking someone who, posing as a servant of God ...committed the worst homicide imaginable by snuffing out two innocents on the threshold of their lives!'

Lowering his voice, he added in an intense but somehow confiding tone: 'At least we were lucky on that count. The murderer had the decency not to leave us with the obligation to prosecute him.'

'*Lucky*, sir?'

'Certainly lucky! I believe I'm right in thinking that the abbé Ségouret's dead?'

'He is, monsieur.'

'Strangled, in a word, by the hideousness, the enormity, of his own crime!'

The Commissaire here resorted to a bit of theatre. He punched one fist into the other palm, cast his eyes heavenwards and dropped his pince-nez to the end of its cord. 'A *priest*!' he exclaimed disgustedly. 'A priest, for God's sake! You understand, of course ... this is something that's liable to discredit still further the image – the beautiful, the *necessary* image! – of our holy mother the Church.'

'A murderer's a murderer, sir, the way I see it.'

'The Big Boutique doesn't agree with you, though, my dear fellow. At a time like this, when morale and civic fibre need to be

restored, criminals simply aren't *allowed* to be unearthed among
the senior officers of the state or the servants of the Church.'

'Only dirty bastards have dirty hands,' Hippolyte muttered
subversively.

'*What* did you say?' Mespluchet leaned forward on his desk, a
hand placed open behind his ear to hear better. He was not
absolutely sure that he had heard correctly, and stared at the oaf
with suspicious eyes. The response was a radiant yellow smile.

'Nothing, sir.'

'I should jolly well hope so, Hippolyte!'

The beanpole appeared nonplussed. He had again taken on the
downcast look of a beaten dog.

'Don't be disappointed, Hippolyte,' Mespluchet puffed.
'You've got plenty of other strings to your bow. Haven't you
brought the Ourcq gang to its knees?'

'I've pretty well mapped its machinery, sir, as you can see
from my report.'

'Well, it's at our mercy, then! As soon as Paris is completely
liberated we'll mount an expedition to the banks of the canal and
mop up those riff-raff!'

'Of course, sir.'

'Ah, how happy I am! How pleased we all are with you!
Don't you note somewhere that the new boss of the cut-throats
is called Saint-Lago?'

'That's right, sir.'

'He's finished! We'll set an ambush for him. Come down on
him like a ton of bricks! As for your future ... I'm going to pass
your report on to Monsieur Claude, with a little note of
recommendation. Something should come of it.'

'Thank you, monsieur! It's what I'd have expected of you,'
replied the long tall Fleming, unable to suppress a pleased smile.

'There's certainly a promotion coming your way, you lucky
dog!' grunted the Commissaire, scribbling furiously across the
title page of the dossier. 'Perhaps even a red ribbon!' He
underlined several phrases in red ink, using a metal ruler. 'There!
Perfect! Good work!' The official applied the blotter, re-read
what he had written and looked up, pen poised in mid-air, trying
to compose a conclusion.

'Really, Hippolyte, what a marvellous contribution to the understanding of the passions and the vices it is, your meritorious survey of the Paris Commune!' he perorated. 'While we, at the same time ... poor us! Stuck in Versailles like that with nothing to boast about, not even our valour! Your distinguished colleagues, for example, Houillé, Dupart and Rouqueyre: no promotion for any of *them*! Viroflay is such a *dreary* place! It was a ghastly grind, I can tell you. We were like logs! Turned into priests of the holy Hope! Peering at the battlefield through telescopes! And just to add insult to injury, *short of food*! Exorbitant prices! We were just tapping our feet! Isolated by the upper classes and the nobility: just unemployed officials! My cousin Léonce: a harpy, sour as a crow! And Madame Mespluchet, a young woman, hardly thirty years old, who could think of nothing but her Barbédienne bronzes, leaning her forehead on the window of our tiny apartment gazing at the smoke in the distance! She was so grumpy! Stiff as a nun's wimple! It was the end of everything!'

'Er ... quite. Madame Mespluchet, I was going to ask after her ...'

'I'm expecting her any minute! She didn't want to stay in beastly Seine-et-Oise a moment longer than she had to! She's in a hurry to return to her old ways, her old friends. At least our house is still standing, or so the concierge says. That's the important thing. Madame Mespluchet has become agreeable and pretty again. It's a miracle! She's absolutely determined to have a special dress made to wear at the Archbishop of Paris's funeral. There'll be a considerable turn-out there. The diplomatic corps. Our magnificent generals! You'll see, young Hippolyte, everyone'll soon be back! Paris will be cleaned of all its little corpses. The paraffin will be wiped up. The dead will be cleared away. And universal progress will be relaunched!'

'But, monsieur ... don't you think that's rushing things a bit? It's not over yet. They're still fighting in the east of Paris! Hundreds are dying even now. People who believed in their convictions. Who thought they could renew the world.'

'Piffle!' grunted Isidore Mespluchet, signing and dating the

recommendation he had written for his protégé. 'You're confus-
ing the operatic heroism of a handful of yellow-booted boulevard loafers with the spirit of achievement and duty that
animates *our* leaders! I don't mind telling you I see Mac-Mahon
as a future commander of our enlightened Republic!' He closed
the folder with a cheerful slap. 'And now it's all over, you great
lummox! The revolution's dealt with, swept away! With Monsieur Thiers and Marshal Mac-Mahon we're in good hands. And
I won't hide my opinion, my dear fellow, that with people of
their calibre we're at the dawn of an almost perfect world!'

As he looked up, he saw that his great lout of a subordinate
with unprecedented shamelessness had taken the chair facing him
and, without being invited, had flung himself down on it with all
his weight. Turning the page on this incivility, more than willing
to subscribe to the emergence of a new order, he said with an
amused look that he felt showed him in a particularly good light:

'No formalities, please! I was just going to ask you to sit
down, Monsieur the Commissaire-to-be! My dear colleague!'

As he pronounced the last of these playful words, however,
Mespluchet went pale and sprang to his feet, his moustache
bristling furiously.

'Hell and damnation! My capsule hat!' he bellowed. 'You've
just squashed it!'

Hippolyte Barthélemy had been dreaming of this moment for
more than six years. Unhurried, unabashed, the yellow-eyed
boor smiled with an air of peaceful contentment.

Epilogue

The testament of the ruins

O God! God of violence and injustice, God of oppression, why this cruel ordeal?

The Commune, vanquished. The people of the streets, crushed. The regiment of pale-faced ragamuffins, liquidated. The idea of the Social Republic, vilified. The proud martyrs of the cobbles, condemned out of hand. Freedom, still warm from the oven, blasted to smithereens. Chained women, insulted and tortured. Children caught in possession of weapons, shot, battered, silenced. The wounded, finished off in the streets. Everywhere, butchers strutting in their bloody aprons! Everywhere, insurgents hounded down and exterminated!

Palmyre impaled! A ball of flesh tossed to and fro by Clinchant's riflemen on the points of their bayonets.

Ziquet asked the officer commanding the firing squad to return his watch, inherited from Three-Nails, to his adoptive mother, known as la Chouette, in the route de la Révolte. He was jeered before dying bravely.

Louise Michel, Caf'conc', Amélie la Gale imprisoned, humiliated and exiled: after Arras prison, the military jails of Satory and the cruel ritual of mock executions in the dead of night, they were deported to the Ducos peninsula in New Caledonia.

Hundreds of others – the Marions, Célestines, Léonces and Blanches – were imprisoned, massacred, violated and insulted. Driven by guards and gendarmes with blows from rifle-butts. A resigned herd, tottering with fatigue, dressed in rags, some of them wounded, they were taken to the prisons of Versailles.

Proud Amazons crippled in combat, young girls captured in raids, widows with black armbands, all pleaded in vain. Young mothers clung to the feet of their torturers, but their new-born children were still dragged from their arms. They hid their fear of the growing crowd that followed on their heels heaping insults on them, those humble women covered with dust, a baby at the breast, an aged mother to look after. And so many had died with such unforgettable courage!

On Sunday 28th May, at about one o'clock in the afternoon, the great heart of the Commune stopped beating in rue Ramponneau. A sky veiled with opaque clouds shadowed the roofs of the buildings and echoed the sorrow of beaten men.

'Every man for himself!'

Sick at heart, the companions scattered staggering through the nearby streets, looking for a place to hide. An invisible process began. Life in the popular quarters became furtive, the beat of the black drums muffled. The shutters closed. The macabre machinery of death in place. Lord, cure us of our fear of the dark!

Common graves, horrible great ditches at the square of Tour-Saint-Jacques, at Père Lachaise, black winding-sheets, stacks of coffins, roomfuls of bullet-riddled corpses, cartloads of cadavers, fields heaped with the massacred! Beneath walls, along gutters, in front of hospitals, the murdered fraternity lay resting.

The minutes crawled lopsidedly past. Morality had shrivelled and living bodies had grown used to it. All over the capital the visible horror mounted.

At seven in the evening, over cobbles slippery with blood, there rolled a lurching carriage pulled by a half-dead, hollow-chested, spavined old screw of a mare. Her name was Cécile. So broken-winded and panting was she, so indeterminate had she become in form and colour, that most people mistook the poor beast for an elderly mule. She wheezed and droned like a set of Breton bagpipes.

Cécile had new masters. On the box of the former hearse two men were sitting. They seemed to be dozing and were not talking to each other.

One was a simple driver, slumped stolidly in his narrow and

limited destiny. The other was dressed in a torn overcoat and an ambulance-medic's kepi, with an armband bearing the red cross of Geneva. His clean-shaven face was as pallid as those of the corpses in the back of the vehicle, and he wore blue-tinted spectacles that gave him a gloomy air.

The two ambulancemen were numb with fatigue. They swayed perilously in time to the lurching progress imposed by the nag's busy but ineffective gait.

For seven solid hours they had been sloshing ankle-deep in brine, wandering from one heap of carrion to the next and heaving cadavers about on their backs as they collected up the dead. Their gaiters were heavy with clotted blood, their bodies seemed to be held up by long aprons stiff with congealing intestinal juices, faeces and brain matter.

Time and again, they had to deflect the vigilance of patrolling marines, throw dust in the eyes of those showing too much interest, silence the more insistent NCOs by showing their *laissez-passer*: a crumpled chit bearing the scribbled words:

Received from Dr Jolyen seven cadavers.

'Dr Jolyen' was an identity acquired by chance, picked up as it were in passing. It was the sole remaining rampart between Jules Vallès and death.

Vallès with his big nose and square forehead, his pale but brutal complexion, had inherited a hearse! Now he and his carriage were in crazy zigzag flight through insecure streets among all this fierce, sculpted nastiness. At any moment he could slip on the vast polished parquet of denunciation. Swing into the mazurka of intense and prolonged suffering.

Vallès lashed his unshod jade to keep her moving. But which way should he go? What should he do? In whom could he trust? There wasn't the smallest hole in the cross-grained future to see through. Nor a single friendly face. Nothing but blood and more blood, colour invariably red.

On the way out of the square another ugly heap: eviscerated ones, three more clients to load. Vallès climbed back onto the box like a sleepwalker. Sometimes his eyelids drooped behind the blue glasses. Hugging his stubborn dream of freedom. The carriage started to move.

He clicked his tongue. Gee up, baggage! Faster! Shift your carcass! The hearse turned a corner between ruined edifices, Cécile coughing and wheezing in the last of the smoke, the wagon rocking over smashed rifles between devastated trees, ruptured tree-grilles, stiff-legged recumbent horses swathed in droning clouds of flies.

Keep going! Vallès cracked his whip to wring a last effort from his nag and take his last cartload of blue-faced murdered corpses to their destination, the hospital of la Pitié.

That Sunday 28th May, the executioners thought they had seen Vallès here, there and everywhere. He had been killed three or four times that day according to the newspapers! First in the rue des Prêtres-Saint-Germain-l'Auxerrois, where he had died a coward's death, dragged along screaming by the feet, silenced with rifle-butts and finished off with bayonets. Then in the rue Saint-Louis, where his stand-in was a man called Alexandre Martin who had made the mistake of eating at Laveur's. Lastly at the Corn Exchange, where he took twelve bullets in his hide. They made sure of the beardie that time! Done in by Chassepot! Shot at the stake! Along with Ferré, to make it seem even more convincing. The whole thing witnessed and attested by passers-by.

Vallès listened. Looked over his shoulder. Kept thinking he was going to be recognised, that people were looking at him askance. He took the 'mule' by the bridle and walked. Bent under the weight of the rumours flying from mouth to mouth.

The doughty Courbet was also said to have been riddled with bullets, at the Admiralty, in a *cupboard* for God's sake! And plenty of others: Vaillant, Cluzeret, Billioray, all shot, shot in the street.

Jules Vallès kept moving. Beardless on his veering cartload of corpses, wrapped in his blood-stiffened apron, with plenty more carrion clamouring for attention, the real Jules Vallès passed through it all.

After a stop at la Pitié he set off again alone.

The empty hearse rocked through rue des Ecoles, rue

Monsieur-le-Prince, lurched over the black ground. He was nowhere, his fists clenched on the reins, Cécile walking agonisingly slowly ... suddenly, in the sweetness of the night, the past awakened and touched him with vivid sorrow. A single sentence hurt him more than anything that had happened so far, all the blows he had suffered. A woman yelled from her window:

'They've done Varlin in! Lynched him, one of his eyes hanging out! Dead!'

Vallès had the sensation of one entering a dark fissure. His mind overwhelmed by limitless disorder, he took temporary refuge in memories of his childhood. He allowed the nag to halt at the entrance to an alley, tied her to a railing and with a lurching gait walked into the darkness of the passage.

Devastated, shattered, defeated for now, he sat down against the mouth of a drainpipe and stared at the red and unbearable present in the gutter. His wide forehead furrowed with uncertainty. He took off his spectacles and allowed free rein to suffering contained for too long. He sobbed and thought of his companions. Of Tarpagnan, Larochette, Camélinat, Jourde, Langevin, Mirecourt and Courbet. Then, his heart swollen with affection, filled with an uncontrollable, feverish wish to throw himself, just once more, into the arms of people who wanted to forge a more just and equitable world, he rose to his feet.

He walked past Cécile without stopping and set off through the desolate streets, bursting with hope that he would live long enough to write the famously dangerous and political book that 'Cousin Vingtras' had prophesied for him.

Some time later, in London, people walking past Veglio in Euston Road, or clients of the Café Royal in Regent Street, would see at chocolate or coffee time a man sitting at a table and laughing in his beard. With the pen wedged in his square and nervous hand, the lumpy forehead, the mobile mouth, he would be busy covering a dishevelled sheaf of yellow pages with spontaneous and enraged handwriting.

Once in a while this furious scribbler would lift his pen from the paper and pause. Then his mind, defying the bitter truth and the follies of human behaviour, would take flight to France. He would pass through the walls of the Saint-Pélagie prison and catch Gustave Courbet in his cell, busy painting apples. Then he would smile. Come back down to earth. And resume writing at feverish speed, for he was convinced that artists exist to redeem the ugliness and the sins of the world.

Jules Vallès by this time had greying hair and, in the words of Gounod with whom he was on friendly terms, the air of 'a stone saint in a Cathedral niche'.

The tenant of 38 Berners Street mentioned his enterprise one day in a letter to another friend, Hector Malot. He wrote that he was in the process of composing a book, '*the story of this Vingtras, whom I resemble so strongly*'.

This was the first appearance of his hero's surname in the register of the literary civil state. Vallès never gave any explanation of its origin.

His very biographers confess themselves baffled as to the source of this name *Vingtras*, a name which to this day remains enigmatic and mysterious: to those, at least, who have not read the book you are now holding in your hands.